I0830786

Gulchekhra-Begim Makhmudova

FLASK
OF THE CRYSTAL
HOOKAH – II

OR ADVENTURES
OF THE RUBY OF TEMUR

London 2025

Published by Hertfordshire Press Ltd © 2025
e-mail: publisher@hertfordshirepress.com
www.hertfordshirepress.com

FLASK OF CRYSTAL HOOKAH-II
or ADVENTURES OF THE RUBY OF TEMUR

by Gulchekhra–Begim Makhmudova ©

English

Translated by Yelden Sarybay
Edited by Daniel Akhmed
Design by Alexandra Rey

---

*British Library Catalogue in Publication Data
A catalogue record for this book is available from the British Library
Library of Congress in Publication Data
A catalogue record for this book has been requested*

ISBN: 978-1-913356-93-4

The second novel in the *Flask of the Crystal Hookah* series by Uzbek author Gulchekhra-Begim Makhmudova is filled with captivating adventures and romantic tales, enriched with elements of Eastern mysticism and fantasy. It seamlessly weaves together the past and present, intertwining the lives of modern characters with the distant era of an empire ruled by the descendants of Amir Timur, the Great Mughals.

The novel is intended for a wide audience.

Dear Reader

Through the haze of the Crystal Hookah, the now quite elderly Firuz-begim recounts the bond between modern and ancient generations, their destinies, and their karmic influences... Yet the greatest and truest essence is that the world is ruled by love...

Love is that marvelous, wondrous feeling that has always existed and remains immortal. As we walk the pages of history, we discover numerous fascinating examples of this.

All Seven Wonders of the World, at their core, are dedications and vows of eternal love. The legendary Hanging Gardens of Babylon (7th century BCE) were built by King Nebuchadnezzar II for his beloved wife, Amytis of Assyria...

The Taj Mahal (17th century) was constructed by Shah Jahan—a descendant of the great Amir Temur—in honour of his undying love for his wife, Arjumand-begim...

Love and kindness, honour and justice, faith and hope have ruled the world since time immemorial... They stand in opposition to evil and hatred, treachery and greed, the thirst for gain and envy...

Love... It is ever-living—yesterday, today, tomorrow... It is the Eternal Feeling... leading to PROSPERITY, WELL-BEING, and ABUNDANCE!

I sincerely believe and hope that this book will help us all once again to touch upon this great feeling and dwell in it forever...

Gulchekhra-Begim Makhmudova

1

Tashkent, 2007.

Evening was drawing in… The house was quiet. A pleasant spring breeze drifted through a half-open window. Firuz-begim sat on the ayvan of her room, slowly counted her old prayer beads, and softly sang a verse by her favorite poet, Saadi:

Yesterday—gone from our sight,
Tomorrow—not yet ours to claim.
Only this present hour is real—
And that is enough.

A thin curl of smoke rose from the ancient Crystal Hookah—the constant companion of the wise Firuz-begim—and floated leisurely towards the window. As always, a delicate white scarf covered the silvery head of this elder, a witness to great eras…

Malika, Firuz-begim's young great-great-granddaughter, was reluctantly mopping the old woman's room at the request of her mother, Sitora—an everyday task to keep the dust at bay after the steady stream of journalists and reporters who came ten times a day to interview the long-lived Uzbek matriarch. Catching sight of her great-great-grandmother's hookah once more, Malika wrinkled her nose in displeasure and muttered something under her breath.

"What's wrong, my girl?" asked the old woman, surprised, looking at Malika with kind, wise, and—despite her advanced years—still beautiful eyes. "Why the gloomy face? Has something happened?"

"Nothing happened, Grandma," Malika answered tersely, a hint of annoyance in her voice. "I just really don't like it when people smoke… Smoking is very bad; that's what they taught us at school. They even held a special lesson on it! And it's harmful for my lungs to breathe in that smoke.

Firuz-begim smiled:

"Very well, my little girl, my sunshine, I'll stop now. Truly, my hookah is unlike any other—I don't even inhale the smoke. There is nothing harmful or bad in it for me; only soothing fragrant herbs are brewed, giving off a special aroma… Please, come sit beside me!"

Without much enthusiasm, Malika settled on the couch, which was covered with warm kurpachas, traditional felted mattresses. Embracing her, Firuz-begim spoke gently:

"Malikakhon, my angel, you are a good, wonderful girl—a joy to me and to your parents—and I know you have a kind heart. But I want to give you one important lesson in life. Listen, my dear, and remember it well. If you don't learn this lesson now, others may tell it to you sharply or rudely, or—God forbid—life itself could punish you for not knowing the truth! I wouldn't want that to happen… Do you want to be happy and successful?"

Malika hadn't expected such a question. Happy and successful? Who doesn't want that! Ever since she started attending music school on top of her regular studies, she had almost immediately begun dreaming of growing up to become a star on stage, performing before huge audiences, who would applaud her and find joy in her talent! Naturally, she very much wanted to be both happy and successful… But why was her great-great-grandmother asking her this? Did Firuz-begim somehow discover Malika's secret—that the secret longing in her young heart was no secret at all? How had she figured it out?! Malika was so astonished that she stood there, mouth agape.

Firuz-begim, noticing her granddaughter's genuine astonishment, smiled again.

"I'm going to share a few important secrets with you," she continued. "Knowing and understanding them will pave your way to both happiness and success."

Malika held her breath and listened in silence.

"The first secret: learn to respect every person."

At that, Malika felt another surge of surprise and was about to interrupt her grandmother—after all, she thought, I do respect people, don't I?

Firuz-begim raised her hand, gently signaling Malika to wait and hear her out.

"People in both East and West often only appear to respect someone. They use polite words—which, of course, isn't bad in itself—they bow or curtsey, they give up their seat for older folks, and do many other things that win them approval, because it aligns with widely accepted moral values and rules of conduct. But too often, while creating this outward show of respect, people forget to check what's happening in their hearts and minds—to ask whether they're being honest with others and with themselves…"

Listening to her grandmother, Malika furrowed her brow slightly once again: oh, these grown-ups! They keep lecturing her about everything! She's not a little child anymore; she already understands so much herself! Still, she decided to keep listening.

"Perhaps," continued Firuz-begim, "someone bows to a ruler or their boss, smiles and politely converses with a friend, while inwardly hating and despising them. Worse still, they might speak ill of them or slander them… And that's wrong—this is hypocrisy, and like any lie, it will sooner or later come to light… bringing inevitable punishment. What's truly precious, my dear, is genuine, heartfelt respect for every person you encounter—whether or not you see them as worthy. You can learn something from anyone, and every person is beautiful in their own way, for each is created by the Creator in His image and likeness.

If you teach yourself to truly, sincerely respect other people, it will become easier for you to love them, to understand them, and not to judge them for their weaknesses or wrongdoings… The greatest poverty is the poverty of the heart. And let your love for others be as natural to you as breathing. Demand nothing from anyone—no one owes you anything… If God grants you something, be grateful for it all. And let everyone who comes to you depart as a better and happier person!"

Firuz-begim paused for a moment, then once more drew in the fragrant, bubbling infusion from the hookah. The room again filled with its aroma, and softly humming, she recited her favorite rubaiyat by Omar Khayyam:

> *One may fail to sense the fragrance of a rose;*
> *Another from bitter herbs extracts sweet honey.*
> *Give someone a coin, and they may remember you forever;*
> *Give your very life to another, and they may never understand.*

"And now, the second secret, closely linked to the first: in any situation, try to put yourself in the other person's place—your interlocutor's—and try to understand them. Only then, if you must, judge… It's easy to judge people, my dear, for we are all imperfect.

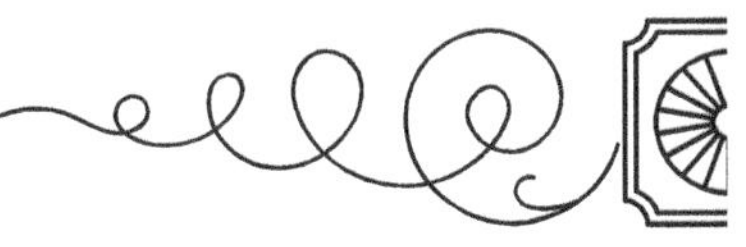

But to understand them—when you condemn others, you have no time or strength left to love them. Not everyone can strive to truly understand another and show them kindness and respect. Yet anyone who masters this will rise to great heights; they will converse with kings and rulers, because even they will esteem and honor such a person… Unfortunately, children and young people today are so brash, rebellious, and disobedient. Things were never like that in my youth…"

"But Grandma," Malika couldn't hold back, "can someone really be meek, humble, obedient—and still achieve great success?! Humility is a road to oblivion… What about strength of character and will?"

"Indeed they can!" the old woman nodded. "'Three things never come back once gone,' wrote Omar Khayyam. 'Time, Words, Opportunity…' So never waste time, choose your words wisely, don't miss your chance! That is where true strength of character lies."

"I'll remember…"

"Now, there are other secrets and four specific rules for young women, handed down from Scheherazade's mother, remember The Thousand and One Nights? I'll share them with you later, right before you marry…"

"Oh, Granny dear, I've already read them and know them by heart," Malika said with a sly smile. "Listen up, and don't say you've never heard them before. So…

First rule: You must accept a man's 'rules of the game,' yet be so gentle that he adopts your rules as though they were his own… The hard can never truly harm the soft.

Second rule: As long as this 'game' continues, I will always remain intriguing to my man…

Third rule: No matter how foul a man's mood may be, warm

him like the sun, so that, in your warmth, he relaxes and finds joy and peace…

Fourth rule: Every day, let your man go out with a mysterious gaze full of self-assurance—and he'll hurry back to me with the desire to solve all my riddles and secrets…"

Firuz-begim, astonished by her great-great-granddaughter's sudden outburst, rolled her eyes toward the heavens and exclaimed with pride:

"Well now, my dear, I'm sure you'll be able to make your man happy… May God's mercy be with you! You've taken it all in perfectly—Scheherazade's four rules each represent a different state for a woman: to begin the game as the 'girl,' to inspire a man to continue as the 'lover,' to fill a weary and angry man with renewed energy as the 'mistress of the house'… And the last rule awakens the 'queen,' who knows how to let her man go forth to accomplish great deeds and gather trophies, which he will lay at her feet! And for him, it will forever remain a mystery that the game is played by her rules, on her terms!"

"Hurray, women rule the world!" Malika cried out, clapping her hands. "Grandma, you're my best friend… I love you so much!"

"Oh, I love you very much, too! And would you like to hear a story about a remarkable woman who lived by these very rules her whole life? Her name was Arjumand-begim, for whom our ancestor, the great Mughal Emperor Shah Jahan, built India's 'Seventh Wonder of the World,' the famous Taj Mahal mausoleum…?

"Look here, you mentioned my Crystal Hookah. Do you know that I inherited it from my mother-in-law—the mother of Alimkhan, the Emir of Bukhara? She trusted me to kindle the fire and fill the hookah with herbs. This hookah was an important member of the Emir of Bukhara's family, and from the stories told by Alimkhan's mother, I came to understand the immense value of this marvelous ancient vessel… After all, it was passed down to my mother-in-law—across countries and generations—directly from the wife of the ruler of India, Shah Jahan, the beautiful Arjumand-begim. She once owned it. Arjumand-begim was extraordinary… And this hookah guards the secret of her undying love and great devotion to her husband…"

"Grandma, please tell me the story of Arjumand-begim!" Malika asked, her eyes shining with open curiosity. "The internet has so little information about her life…"

"Are you really that interested?" Firuz-begim teased, winking at Malika. She chuckled through her few remaining teeth, stained yellow by age and the hookah. She noticed that her granddaughter had completely forgotten about both her cleaning duties and her earlier complaints, and was now comfortably perched on the kurpachas, eager to hear a long and likely extraordinary tale—a story straight out of Scheherazade's world…

"Well then, listen. It all happened a very long time ago, back in the Middle Ages… Believe it or not, in those days, the East was home to the descendants of the mighty Amir Temur, whose realm once stretched across half of Europe and reached into India, as well as the descendants of Babur, the founder of the Mughal Empire… Four hundred years ago, India was ruled by Emperor Shah Jahangir…"

2

**1607, the ancient capital of India—Agra.
The principal governmental residence of the Great Mughals:
the Akbarabad Palace.**

"Mirza Giyas ad-din Muhammad-khan!" a servant announced, opening the doors to the padishah's chambers.

Into the spacious, lavishly furnished hall stepped Giyas Beg with a respectful bow—a tall, imposing man of about fifty, with a dignified face and striking gray eyes. Though he was not Uzbek by birth but a Persian aristocrat of noble Sayyid lineage, he was a loyal subject of the current ruler of the Mughal Empire, thirty-seven-year-old Shah Jahangir, who had ascended the throne not long ago.

It was Shah Akbar, Jahangir's father, who had employed Giyas Beg back when he arrived in Hindustan from Persia, nearly destitute—naked and barefoot. Through his talents and tremendous effort, Giyas achieved considerable success at court and won the favor of the former padishah. However, in one unfortunate moment, enticed by the prospect of easy gain, he committed certain financial indiscretions and deceptions, leading to the loss of his honored position in the palace. When Jahangir came to the throne, Giyas Beg strove mightily to regain royal favor and secure a new appointment. In the end, he succeeded: Shah Jahangir, aware of Giyas Beg's exceptional abilities, brought him into his inner circle. A short while later, he even bestowed upon him the esteemed title

I'timad-ud-Daula, meaning "Pillar of the State."

"What news, my friend?" asked Shah Abul-Fath Nur-ud-din Muhammad Jahangir, in an upbeat tone—thanks to a bright, sunny morning that had put him in high spirits—when his chief adviser, the "Pillar of the State," entered. "Look how splendid the day is! Why so glum? Is our situation so dire? Speak—who wishes us harm this time?"

"Oh, who would dare, Your Majesty? After all, you are the descendant of the great Amir Temur, Babur, and Genghis Khan. Your power is boundless across the earth!"

Skilled at pleasing the ruler's ear, the adviser spoke with practiced flattery. But contrary to his expectations, Shah Jahangir's mood began to sour immediately upon hearing those words, apparently due to a sudden flood of unpleasant memories.

"Then why tell me—why did Sultan Khusrau-Mirza, my own son and firstborn, dare raise a hand against me, his own father, the padishah of the empire—wanted to kill me?! How could you let it happen? How could you fail to see that my son was plotting against me, seeking to rob me of both throne and life? You deserve to be executed for this, Giyas Beg!"

"Forgive me, Your Majesty. Believe me, I would have stamped out any rebellion against the state and against you—no matter who led it. But as you know, Prince Khusrau-Mirza has no fondness for me; he never confided in me. Consequently, I had no way of knowing that behind his mask of submission and filial devotion lay the malice of an enemy. Had I known, or even suspected, I would have told you at once. Yet I could not raise my hand against the padishah's son without your sanction. But why bring it up now? It's been over a year since that mutiny!"

"Since I trust you as my chief aide," Jahangir continued, "you should exercise great intuition, anticipate all possibilities, foresee everything! And yet you are not perceptive enough for my adviser. Perhaps I should replace you with someone else?"

The I'timad-ud-Daula turned red, growing agitated, but quickly managed to collect himself.

"My padishah, I assure you, all is peaceful now. You wielded your sacred authority to abolish many of Shah Akbar's policies—particularly those concerning tolerance toward followers of the Hindu faith. This led to discontent among the Hindu commanders and Amar Singh I, the Subahdar of Bengal. It provided Prince Khusrau-Mirza the pretext for his rebellion! But now, Your Majesty, no such pretext exists."

"Do my people know," the padishah asked, "that Prince Khusrau-Mirza was imprisoned at my command—and blinded?"

"How could they not, Your Majesty...?" Giyas Beg replied, somewhat uneasily. "As you ordered, I had the sightless prince seated on an elephant and paraded him down the street lined with stakes—where his supporters perished in agony... Yet all your subjects know that you, in your magnanimity, spared your son's life!"

"Perhaps that was unwise—he deserves merciless punishment. It would serve as a lesson to discourage anyone from raising a hand against their padishah! But on the other hand, perhaps you are right. And so Khusrau-Mirza shall remain at court forever, chained to a soldier. I commanded him to be blinded so those same envious eyes would no longer look upon my throne. But I do not want the foundation of my throne to be shaken, nor his blood on my hands, nor do I want my subjects to think me a tyrant!"

"Everyone knows how kindhearted and generous you are, my lord," said Giyas Beg. Though his words sounded much like flattery, he truly felt respect and fondness for the ruler who had elevated him to such a high position.

"I loathe conspiracies so much," Jahangir grumbled. "How can one go against one's own fath—…" He stopped short, recalling that not so long ago, he had done precisely that against his own father, Shah Akbar. On the road from the Deccan to Delhi, he had arranged for the murder of Akbar's closest adviser, Vizier Abu'l-Fazl Allami, who advocated for strengthening Akbar's autocratic rule. Akbar had sent Allami to the future Shah Jahangir—then Prince Salim—to negotiate peace with his son, but Salim-Jahangir hated the vizier's mission. Hoping to rid himself of Abu'l-Fazl, he conspired with the rebellious Rajput ruler, Raja Singh Bundela, and ambushed Abu'l-Fazl, leading to his death.

Subsequently, the prince forced his father to halt the war in the Deccan and return to Agra, where—right in front of Akbar—he proclaimed himself padishah, taking the name Shah Jahangir. Akbar even cursed him for that—cursed his own son…

Jahangir disliked feeling guilty about overthrowing his father, and—seeking to justify himself—he took another sip of his tart wine and tasted the fruit from the golden platter, then continued:

"True, it's hardly praiseworthy to judge one's own father, especially since I made peace with him, and it's been nearly two years since he departed this life… Still, I can't help wondering: how can one in a country governed by Muslim law, in defiance of our clergy's will, be so tolerant of Hindu temples and that alien religion of theirs?! 'Only that faith is true, which reason approves'… What nonsense! To abolish a centuries-old tax on nonbelievers for visiting their temples, and even to appoint Hindu feudal lords to the highest posts in the state! How foolish…"

"Would the great padishah not care to march against the unbelievers and become the second mighty conqueror after your ancestor, Temur?" Giyas Beg broke in on Jahangir's musings.

"No, I would not," the padishah replied at once. "We will wage war some other time, perhaps. And make sure that the crown prince, Prince Khurram—our future Shah Jahan—continues his military training and prepares for campaigns. As for me—you know I prefer peace and comfort in my palace over battles! Besides, I must strictly follow my ceremonial daily schedule, and leading the army would only interfere with that. I have made a temporary truce with Raja Amar Singh of Mewar... Now, Giyas, you still haven't told me—what troubles you?"

"My eldest granddaughter, my lord," the chief adviser sighed heavily, "the daughter of my son Asaf Khan..."

"What happened to her? Is she ill?"

"Praise be to the Almighty, she is healthy, Your Majesty. My sorrow lies elsewhere. She's already twelve years old! According to our laws, she should be married by now—but we still have not found a suitable groom."

"What's the problem? Is she... perhaps unpleasant to look at—your granddaughter?"

"Oh no, my padishah! On the contrary—she is as lovely as a crescent moon, like an angel!"

"I forget—what did you say her name was?"

"Arjumand Banu Qadsiya-begim, my lord. For you—simply Arjumand-begim."

"Ah yes, Arjumand-begim. I recall that all women descended from our Prophet Muhammad bear that proud name—'Begim.'... You should have brought her here, let me see her! I'm sure I could have found a way to help."

"Thank you, my lord, but she is not yet worthy to appear before Your radiant gaze!" The adviser gently countered right away, already fearful for his girl, knowing full well the padishah's passionate and unbridled interest in women.

"Very well, do as you wish. I think someday she'll find the very best husband—don't worry about that! But still, it's a pity, such pity, that you won't bring her here…"

Taking the wine cup in his hand once more, the ruler raised it and took a deep swallow.

3

Tashkent, 2014.

As usual, Mukhitdin was waiting for Malika in the city park. They often strolled along the park's pathways, ate ice cream, or sat on a bench chatting casually about music. She enjoyed spending time with Mukhitdin; she felt happy and good with him…

Malika, of course, sensed how much this lanky, slightly pimply, not-too-handsome but smart enough guy liked her, and how he admired her secretly. But she pretended not to notice and tried to maintain only a friendly relationship, never giving him any false hopes.

Above all, music brought them together. They had met a few years earlier at music school, where she studied piano, and Mukhitdin studied violin.

After his lessons, Mukhitdin usually waited for Malika so he could walk her home, considering it his duty to accompany "his girl," as he half-whispered to his few friends—and believed in his own heart. It stung him a bit when, after three years of friendship, Malika introduced him to her friends simply as, "Mukhitdin, my pal." He was upset: just "pal" and nothing more? He had hoped Malika would say to them all: "He's my boyfriend!" But she never said that…

On this particular day, Malika was very upset about something.

"What happened? Come on now, out with it!" Mukhitdin demanded, already starting to imagine himself in the role of her husband.

Malika was a bit surprised by his tone but didn't show it—she took it as a clumsy joke. Still, she was in no mood for jokes.

"It's my dad…" Malika was on the verge of tears.

"What about your dad? Is something wrong with him?"

"No, thank God, he's fine. It's just that he won't let me apply to the conservatory! And you know I can't live without music!"

"That's all?" Mukhitdin smiled. "Well, keep loving it to your heart's content—who's going to stop you?"

"How can you not understand? You're a musician, just like me! What would you do if you were forbidden to play your violin?"

"I'd go crazy!" Mukhitdin's voice dripped with irony. Then, in a calmer, somewhat gentler tone, he added, "But listen, life doesn't end there—especially for a girl. You'll get married, have a bunch of kids…"

"So in your opinion, a woman is meant only to be someone's wife and mother, nothing else? What about vocation, purpose, a main mission in life?"

"You're talking about these lofty matters so grandly! Be more down-to-earth. All that is just fancy talk: 'vocation,' 'purpose,' and now 'mission'!… 'Mission: Impossible,'" he quipped again, automatically recalling the Tom Cruise movie title and linking it to Malika's worries. "You make it sound like you're someone extraordinary, super talented, dead-set on fulfilling your 'mission.' There are thousands, even millions of musicians like you and me in this world. Worst case, you can keep playing at home—for yourself, for your friends and family…"

"But that's not what I want—don't you get it?!" Malika suddenly protested vehemently. "I can't even describe how upset I am, especially because my own dear father doesn't understand me. He tells me, 'Daughter, you need to get a serious profession, so you have

to become an economist, a lawyer, or better yet—a doctor like me.'
But I don't want to be a lawyer or a doctor—do you understand? I
respect those fields, but they're just not me."

"I understand," Mukhitdin said.

"You know, ever since I was a child—after this incredible conversation I had with my great-great-grandmother, Firuz-begim,
about success and happiness—I began dreaming of a big stage…
of how I'd perform in a huge concert hall or stadium, bringing joy
to thousands or, through television, maybe millions of listeners and
viewers. Yet the fame, the fanfare, the trumpets—that's really not
what matters most to me."

"Well, you really do play and sing quite well," Mukhitdin said
unexpectedly, surprising even himself with such praise.

"You think so? Thanks, it's nice to hear. But I still have so much
to learn… I need to develop my abilities, and both of us need to
grow creatively. And I believe the best way is in this profession—in
music. That's why I so, so badly want to apply to the conservatory!
It feels like if I don't get in, my whole life will collapse—it'll all go
sideways."

"Don't say that. Come on, let's think something up!"

"What could we possibly do, Mukhitdin? I don't have a single
good idea. But one thing I know for sure: I will not submit my
documents anywhere else—no way!"

"Then don't. Know what? I'll help you. Want me to talk to your
father? I'll convince him to let you become a professional musician."

"I'm afraid that's pointless. My dad won't listen to you; to him,
you and I are nobodies. And my mom, though she's always on
my side, probably won't go against his wishes in something this
important. I know my grandma Shahlo would totally back me—
she always understands me! But right now, she's living in Europe

full-time with her fashion house and all the runway shows… Her friends might have ideas, but Aunt Lola works at Lazarev's clinic in Moscow, and Aunt Zarina and her husband have long been at the OPEC mission in Vienna…"

"Then there's only one way: you apply to the conservatory, but tell your father you applied to the Tashkent Medical Academy!"

"What are you saying? That I have to lie to him?! But how can I—?"

"What else can you do? Of course you'll have to! Lies always come from fear. You're afraid your father won't let you spend your whole life doing what you love. But look at it this way: those who get lied to are partly at fault for causing that fear—because it means you can't openly lay all your cards on the table, be completely honest, and trust they'll understand without punishing you. Understand: yes, making others happy is good, but first you have to love yourself and, most importantly, become happy in your own life and achieve your own dreams. So, on August first, you'll stride confidently into… the State Conservatory of Uzbekistan to take your exams! Trust me, everything will turn out fine. I'll go in with you, and I'm hoping I'll get accepted too. Come on, my little martyr—start getting your documents ready!"

* * *

"Good evening, dear, I'm home!" Having taken off his shoes at the door, Said Yahyaevich entered the large living room and sank heavily into a comfortable armchair. "Sitora, my wife!"

"I'm coming, I'm coming, dear!" came her clear voice from the kitchen. "Larisa prepared dinner and left. Go wash your hands and come to the table."

"And where's Malika? Aren't we going to wait for her?"

"She's at the library today. She'll be home later and can reheat her meal herself."

As they started eating, Said Yahyaevich said thoughtfully:

"Sitora, do you know if Malika has any friends?"

"Of course," Sitora nodded. "There's Nilufar, Galya…"

"That's not what I meant. Does she have any boy friends?"

"Well, yes! There's Mukhitdin. As for anyone else, I'm not sure."

"Who's Mukhitdin? Someone from a good family?"

"Why, do you need a helper around the house with strong hands?"

"No, not at all. I think Larisa manages everything just fine. By the way, tomorrow, let her know dinner was excellent today… She really is a big help with cooking and cleaning, considering how busy you are with the Fashion House, plus all the household chores…"

"Are you suggesting I wouldn't manage on my own?" Sitora teased him by pretending to be offended.

"No, that's not what I mean! You're amazing… Anyway, you didn't answer me: who is this Mukhitdin?"

"He's a friend of Malika's—a good, humble young man who plays the violin and also wants to apply to the conservatory."

"Ah, I see! The conservatory as well? That must be where the wind is blowing from—he wants to lure our daughter into that breezy bohemian life!"

"Not really, Said. As far as music goes, it's been Malika's own dream since she was a child—you know that."

"Yes, yes, I know. Firuz-begim told me about our daughter's dream to get into that particular institution. Apparently, Malika trusts her great-great-grandmother more than us, her own par-

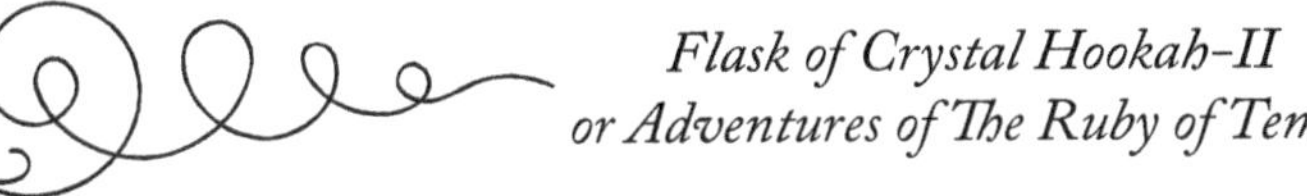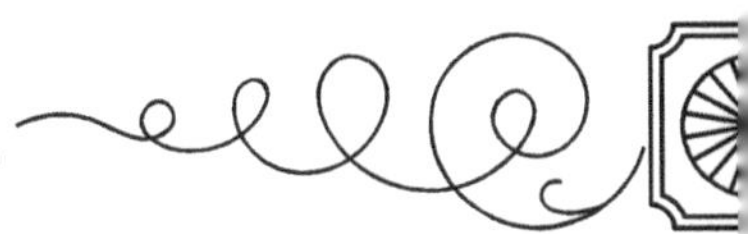

ents; she shares all her secrets with her! It was Firuz-begim who convinced me to give our daughter permission to become a professional musician."

"What, Said?!" Sitora's face lit up. "So you actually agreed?"

"I'm not an enemy to my own daughter. If she truly wants it that badly—fine, let her become a pianist, or even a guitarist if she likes. I already spoke to Malika about it. And I said I have one condition: she must be admitted on her first try, study with top marks, and graduate with honors! Otherwise…I simply won't respect her."

Said Yahyaevich, pleased with himself, smiled. Sitora rose from the table and, overcome with emotion, kissed her husband warmly.

"Just how did our granny manage to change your mind? It's a miracle!"

"Firuz-begim reminded me of how, back before you and I got married, she spoke with my parents herself and convinced them that I had every right to pursue the work I loved above all else, the path I chose for myself."

"Grandma is remarkable, may God grant her a long life—so kind and wise! You know, I really think our girl does have talent."

"Sitora, I asked about her friends for a reason. Studies are one thing, but Malika is already at a marrying age—eighteen. We need to think about this seriously. That Mukhitdin—what sort of family does he come from, how was he raised?"

"It's hard for me to say precisely…"

"He's probably not very ambitious; otherwise he wouldn't want to be a simple violinist. And I doubt he's a Paganini in the making. He doesn't have a real profession yet, so he's not exactly standing on firm ground. What to do? Our Malika should have only the most suitable fiancé! Honestly, part of me hates the thought of our daughter living in another home, away from you and me. But on the other hand, I can't allow her to remain a 'spinster,' you understand?"

"Of course, I've thought about that as well. Malika really is at a marriageable age. She's still young, so in principle there is time. But she doesn't pay attention to any young men. What can we do about that? She's like most kids these days—doesn't listen to anyone about such things; she wants to make all her own decisions. But what if she makes a mistake, or chooses the wrong person, someone who won't love her for her entire life? That's what worries me!"

"I feel the same way. I absolutely don't want just anyone for our son-in-law. It has to be a good, dependable young man, from a distinguished family."

"I agree."

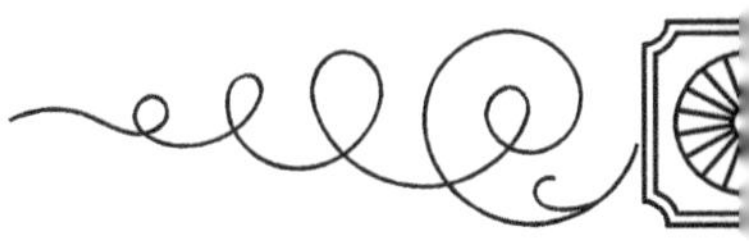

4

Agra, 1608.

Shahzade Shihab ad-Din Muhammad Khurram Bakht Baha-dur-Mirza, the future Shah Jahan, fell asleep and had an extraordinary dream. In it, a girl appeared before him, more beautiful and graceful than anyone he had ever seen. Her face was like that of a peri; her figure as slender as a Cypress tree; and her eyes shone like stars in the night sky. He could hardly tear his gaze away from her long, delicate eyelashes.

The moment the sleeping prince beheld the young woman, he felt a sudden, fervent love for her; his heart brimmed with both a searing, painful longing and a sweet, intoxicating rapture. She looked at him and smiled tenderly.

Next, Shah Jahan saw himself walking in a dream along a wide, magical road strewn with flowers. Towering forests stood around, with paradisical birds singing, while the sky was a blend of yellow, pink, and crimson, like it sometimes appears at sunset.

He walked for a long while. Then he heard wondrous music and angelic singing, coming from a small house off to the side of the road. People were gathered around the house, a crowd reminiscent of a colourful, bustling eastern bazaar, complete with stalls offering all kinds of goods—food, utensils, dishes. There was so much on display, one could choose anything.

"How did all these people get here to such a quiet and deserted place?" Shah Jahan wondered, amazed.

Still, the heavenly music went on inside the house, along with a girl's singing, her voice like that of a nightingale. The music, it seemed, flowed from an instrument called the "ghijak of Babur."

"You wouldn't happen to know who plays the ghijak so exquisitely and sings so beautifully?" Shah Jahan asked one of the merchants.

"Of course I know! That's the daughter of Asaf Khan—the lovely Arjumand-begim!"

The prince felt an irresistible urge to see her, no matter what. But he didn't dare enter the house uninvited. Instead, he circled around the enchanted little dwelling, thinking, "How can I meet this songstress? I wonder if she's truly as beautiful as everyone says…" And with those thoughts, Shah Jahan woke up.

"What was that? What a strange dream!" the prince mused in bewilderment.

* * *

The annual Mina Bazaar was a game and a diversion for court ladies, who were usually stuck at home bored… They would bring out various knickknacks and household wares, decorating their stalls to attract the men who came to this playful spectacle, ready to spend symbolic sums for entertainment and amusement. Music played everywhere; dancers and actors performed respectful scenes from the Mahabharata, while street magicians and snake charmers wove among the stalls.

"Persian clothing and carpets for sale! Come by, take a look, don't pass us by!" called out Mehrun-Nissa, smiling coquettishly at the padishah. She was a woman of extraordinary, almost sorcerous charm. At this magical Mina Bazaar near the palace in Delhi, ac-

cording to long tradition, she played the role of a humble vendor. Her stall was at the most prominent and bustling spot, right next to a fountain.

Shah Jahangir, accompanied by Giyas Beg and a couple of other courtiers, walked on a special carpeted path laid out for him. The shah was dressed in a showy and lavish outfit, sparkling with precious stones: rubies, pearls, and diamonds. At his waist hung Humayun's sword on the left, and on the right curved a dagger inlaid with rubies.

Jahangir recognized the woman, just as he knew almost all the participants in this playful show, mostly made up of court ladies. But Mehrun-Nissa, with her graceful figure, gray eyes, and long black lashes, stood out even from this vibrant crowd, despite being past thirty by then—an age no small matter for a seductress! He had first noticed her some years before in the harem of Ruqaiya Begim, the childless widow of his father Akbar, and the padishah remembered her name forever: Mehrun-Nissa.

But how he wanted to call her something else—Nur, meaning "light," for her radiant face shone like the sun. She was worthy of becoming Nur Jahan—"Light of the World"—for everyone.

Moreover, as the padishah had heard, she sewed those fabrics, fashionable dresses, and carpets herself. And one glance at her keen eyes was enough to see that she was no ordinary person. People at court said she wrote verses with ease and could shoot tigers from a closed pavilion on the back of an elephant. Allegedly, she once needed only six bullets to kill four tigers. Perhaps this was only a rumour, but repeated so persistently that it could not be dismissed.

And how could Shah Jahangir fail to recognise her? Mehrun-Nissa had been in the harem of his stepmother for several years. Some time ago, when he first saw her there, Jahangir—half in jest (a padishah could afford such diversions)—asked her to become his wife. But the unapproachable Mehrun-Nissa refused.

Now, at this enchanting bazaar invented by the palace amusements, upon seeing her again, he was utterly robbed of peace and sleep! Oh, how he longed to possess her!

But the padishah already had a first wife, and Mehrun-Nissa had a husband too—Sher Afkun, a valiant military commander with whom she had a daughter, Ladilli. She had no grounds to divorce him. Even if she stood before the Emperor of the Great Mughals himself, she was much too proud to become just another concubine, or even his second or third wife! And she knew perfectly well the mighty power she held over the padishah's heart...

* * *

"Muhammad, today you and I shall visit the Mina Bazaar," Shah Jahan informed his devoted ward. "I want to indulge my concubines by choosing the finest ornaments for them."

"As you wish, my lord," replied Muhammad, ever obedient to his lord. "You know I am ready to accompany you anywhere and everywhere."

Shah Jahan loved going to the Mina Bazaar. There was always a lively, festive bustle there, with several thousand women present.

Together with his servant, he strolled past all the rows of stalls, delighting in the wonderful wares, until finally they arrived at a solitary and rather modest tent, set somewhat apart from the others. Standing next to this small tent stall was a petite, slender young woman, delicate as a cypress sapling. At her feet lay a piece of cotton cloth, and she was moving a few silver adornments from one spot on the fabric to another, all the while holding in her hands...

a pair of very simple wooden beads. It was evident she felt ill at ease in this marketplace, not knowing what to do with herself. But every woman in India knew the Mina Bazaar was the best chance to meet a suitable groom, so they all tried to appear there, to display themselves before the world!

The proprietresses of the nearby stalls called out to the heir apparent, loudly and flirtatiously coaxing him to come look at their goods. Indeed, there was so much of interest, beauty, and necessity here, even for a prince. But Shah Jahan did not approach every stall. On the contrary, for some reason, he lingered as though transfixed at the modest little tent and its young mistress.

"How may I help you, honourable sir?" the girl asked politely yet with dignity. "I would be happy if my humble necklaces and beads could adorn your life in some small way, and if you would carry them back with you to your land."

"Do you not recognise me, child?" he laughed. "I am the crown prince to this realm—Shah Jahan!"

The girl blushed, her velvet cheeks turning rose-pink.

When the prince looked fully upon her, he was struck speechless by his astonishment and awe! Right before him stood the very same peri he had seen only recently in his dream—a maiden with enchanting gray eyes, a magical smile, and a graceful figure.

"What is your name, wondrous being?" asked the padishah's son, having forgotten entirely why he had come, so shaken was he by her beauty.

"Arjumand-begim, my lord," the beauty replied softly, bowing her head.

"Arjumand-begim? That cannot be!" The prince nearly lost his power of speech in his joy. "Surely you are that same Arjumand, the daughter of Asaf Khan?"

"Yes, that is so, my prince. But how do you know of me?" The girl was alarmed, and she too felt a surge of astonishment.

"Oh, I know all about you. But do you know, Arjumand, that you are destined to be mine? I am Shah Jahan, and I have searched for you everywhere, having first met you in a dream. And it turns out you actually live here in Agra?"

"Yes, honored shahzade. I live here with my father, mother, aunt, and grandfather."

The prince was about to ask the girl, who had set the wooden beads down on the ground, what such a simple adornment was doing in the midst of all this bazaar's vivid and splendid wares—sparkling jewelry, fabrics, trinkets both useful and purely decorative. Suddenly, he had the uncanny feeling that these wooden beads in the girl's hands were gleaming, as though made of diamond as pure as a tear. Shah Jahan was amazed at what he saw.

"I shall buy from you… yes, these wooden beads. How much do you want for them?"

"Please take them as a gift, my dear prince!"

"No, I will not accept them for nothing. I implore you to accept these ten thousand rupees for them—it will be my gift to you, and let every woman in Hindustan envy you!"

"But that is far too much, shahzade!"

"I am not poor. I would give you anything in the world if I could—even my very life!"

"Thank you. My lord is most kind and generous toward me…"

Only now did Shah Jahan notice that near the girl, on the ground wrapped in an old scrap of cloth, lay a musical instrument—a ghijak! He could hardly believe that of all the details in his dream, this too was appearing before him in reality!

Still, the prince asked the young beauty, "Tell me, why do you have a ghijak here? Who plays it?"

"My lord, I do—your humble servant."

"A marvel! Could you play it for me now?"

"Yes, if it pleases you."

The girl picked up the instrument, and from it poured such enchanting sounds that a crowd immediately gathered around the stall to hear her magical performance. And when Arjumand-begim began to sing, Prince Shah Jahan felt as though an arrow had pierced his heart right through—an arrow of fiery love for this maiden. Having seen her in person but once, he understood that never again, for all the treasures in the world, would he be able to forget her. One day, he would make her Padshah Begum, the chief consort of the ruler, and shower her with every jewel possessed by himself and by the entire empire!

As soon as the girl stopped singing and playing, the prince said:

"Oh, lovely Arjumand, light of my eyes, my moon and my star—you are forever my fate and my happiness! I ask you to become my wife. At our palace, marriages out of love are uncommon. Still, I swear—were I not the son of the padishah—ah, my joy, I would take you to wife for the sake of this great love! Will you consent? Am I dear to you as well?"

Tears filled Arjumand's eyes.

"Yes, my prince!" Her heart pounded like the hooves of a swift-footed gazelle. Never before had she known such a powerful passion. But the prince was so handsome, his eyes so intelligent, so deep and clear, that Arjumand had not the slightest doubt: she loved him passionately as well… She paid no heed to the envious stares or spiteful whispers around them.

Just then, the padishah, Shah Jahan's father, summoned him

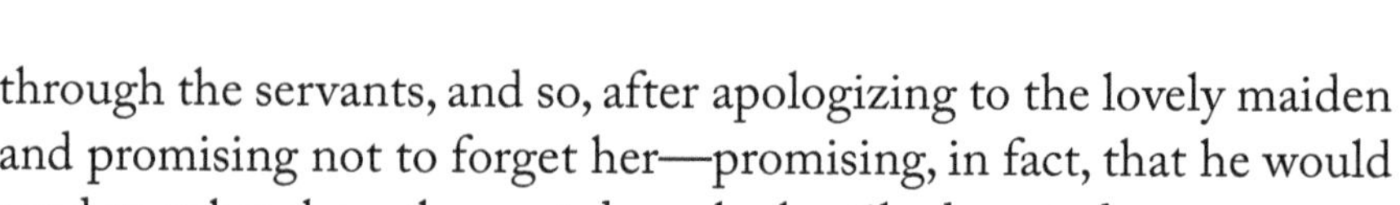

through the servants, and so, after apologizing to the lovely maiden and promising not to forget her—promising, in fact, that he would send matchmakers the next day—he hastily departed.

Enchanted by the prince and agitated by this marvelous, wondrous, and astonishing encounter with him, Arjumand could not sleep all night.

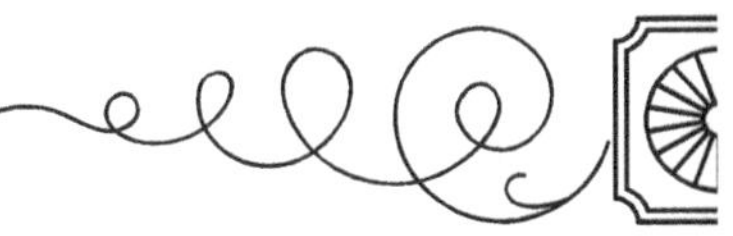

5

Tashkent, 2014

Malika was riding back from the conservatory, where she had just submitted her application, thinking about Mukhitdin.

"What am I being so picky about? Why am I hesitating? After all, Mukhitdin clearly cares about me. He's thoughtful, attentive, and tries to cheer me up however he can… What more could I want? A prince on a white horse?!" She smiled, recalling a joke Mukhitdin had told her recently—where the prince writes to everyone waiting for him, "My white horse died… I'm walking on foot… which is why I'm late…" Yes, let's hope he doesn't dawdle for too long. After all, I'm already nineteen. Maybe it's time to think about starting my own family. And why not Mukhitdin? He's also a musician, a violinist, so we'll always understand each other and share common interests. That means we'll never be bored together, and that's already something."

Malika noticed that the minibus driver kept glancing her way. She pretended not to notice. By now, she was used to this kind of attention. She had never considered herself a great beauty, but she had heard compliments many times. People told her, both directly and through others (her mother would repeat them to her), that Malika was lovely, sweet, and, most importantly, possessed a special inner beauty that shone from within.

She was grateful for those words. But Malika wanted to truly fall in love with someone herself. She dreamed of the most wonderful man in the world, and she wanted with all her heart to be loved by him with undying devotion.

"Is Mukhitdin the right person for that role..? It seems not. Sure, he likes me, he appreciates me. He doesn't just pay compliments or admire me— which makes me feel embarrassed—he also tries to do good things for me, helps me, supports me, and rushes to fulfill my every wish! Any woman would want that kind of husband, wouldn't she?... But… there it is, that uncomfortable and awkward 'but.' Where does it come from? And why does it appear on the path of my life, giving my thoughts and heart no rest? But – I just don't love that person… That's all there is to it."

When Malika arrived home, her phone rang again—it was Mukhitdin. From his voice, even over the phone, she could tell he was anxious and agitated.

"What's going on?" Malika asked. "By the way, why didn't you come today to submit your application? You said you would. Is everything all right?"

"Yes, yes, everything's fine," his voice trembled slightly. "I still have time to bring in my documents. It's just… you see, Malika…"

"Well? What is it?"

"I wanted to… there's something… I need to talk to you about one very important matter… that is, it's important to me. For both of us…" he trailed off.

"Then go ahead, of course. I'm listening!" Malika smiled. She was always very kind to him, trying not to hurt his feelings and to be gentle.

"No, well… it's not something I can talk about on the phone… We need to meet in person. It's an important matter… I mean a serious talk…"

"You already said that. I understand!" Malika laughed. She

didn't mean to be rude or dismissive, but a wave of laughter suddenly overcame her.

"So will you come on our da… I mean to our meeting, the usual spot in our park?" Mukhitdin grew even more nervous. "I need to show you something… we'll go somewhere. All right? You see, there's something I need to say to you…"

Suddenly, Malika felt as if she'd been struck by lightning. Only then did she guess what he wanted to talk about and confess to her.

"Great, here we go," she thought in alarm. "How can I refuse to meet him? I don't want to push him away or reject him entirely—he's a good and loyal friend. But I'm not at all ready for declarations of love or marriage proposals that might come afterward."

"You know, Mukhitdin, I'm so sorry. I'm really exhausted today. I just got home, and I've got a splitting headache. Let's not do it today. Maybe another time, all right? Besides, both of us need to spend a lot of time studying now if we want to get accepted into the place we've both dreamed of for so long, right?"

There was a tense silence on the line. He was probably trying to process her polite refusal—or at least a postponement.

Finally, he answered, "Well… all right… so you really can't right now, right? Then… I'll wait a week, or two at most… Just please, you must come… Just… please promise me that afterwards we'll find a time and you'll come to our usual spot!"

Malika reluctantly, without much enthusiasm, agreed. She couldn't argue with her friend, especially when he was so anxious and emotional. After all, there was still time. She could think everything over and decide what to do.

* * *

Amin Fattakhov was unlucky in his first marriage. His wife turned out to be spoiled, had a moody character, and what's more she didn't wish to have children. When she accidentally became pregnant by Amin, she secretly had an abortion at an early stage without telling him. Madina was so skillful at hiding everything that her husband never suspected a thing. He only found out later, by chance, from one of her friends.

Amin was deeply hurt and distressed by this betrayal and deception on the part of his wife! For a while, he tried to maintain a normal marital relationship with Madina because he still loved her, but when he realized that she had little genuine feelings for him and was unwilling to set aside her own selfishness for his sake, he couldn't bear it any longer. In the end, he left her, and shortly afterward they divorced. However, as a man of honour, he gave his ex-wife a sizable sum of money to support her until she remarried someone else.

But he kept the centrally located apartment, which his father, businessman Abdulla-aka, had given them as a wedding present. In truth, Amin could already afford to buy his own place, given that he worked actively and conscientiously alongside his father at the family firm distributing imported perfumes and cosmetics, and their business was doing quite well. Still, he had no intention of refusing his father's heartfelt gift to him, the eldest son; and the young man didn't want to hurt his father's feelings.

Amin worked a lot, partly because he felt somewhat lonely. The only people who occasionally eased his loneliness were his parents (though they often had generational differences in their outlooks on life), and his younger siblings, a sister and a brother. Despite

Rano being a wonderful, kind, and extraordinarily caring sister, he was already a grown man (Amin was already thirty-three), while, in his eyes, she was just a "little girl" who had just turned twenty-two. He couldn't imagine spending all his free time outside of work with his sister, even if she was dear to him. He wanted something else, something more.

As for his relationship with his younger brother, Bahadir, it was always complex and ambiguous. Both brothers had strong, inflexible personalities and the desire to be leaders. Each wanted to be the best, the most successful and accomplished, both in business and in the eyes of their parents, sister, and everyone else. What's more, Bahadir, even though he cared about his brother in his own way, sensed that their father loved and valued Amin more, viewing him as more talented and promising. This bothered Bahadir a bit.

Amin, idealistic and a perfectionist by nature, very much wanted to reach great career heights. It wouldn't be right to call him a ruthless careerist, because he wasn't after success at any cost; he wanted to achieve it through his own hard work and intelligence. He also wanted everyone in the family to get along in perfect peace and harmony. For now, though, that wasn't happening.

Rano worried deeply about both of her brothers, noticing how their relationship had become increasingly "tense" now that they were both adults.

Being more romantic and gentler by temperament, Amin did not want to upset his parents or, above all, his sister by clashing with his twenty-year-old brother. Yet he often felt powerless to make things better.

He began withdrawing more, spending his evenings either alone in his empty, newly "bachelor" apartment or with his few friends. He had neither the time nor the desire for a large circle of friends, believing that one can't have too many real friends anyway.

Sometimes, to pass the time in the evenings, Amin would go to the Chelsea Pub near his home, where they aired international matches via satellite channels. For him, this was the best way to relax and distract himself from sad thoughts and life's problems.

One evening, a few months before the events described earlier, while watching a match at the pub, Amin met three teenagers around sixteen or seventeen. Normally, the serious and fully grown Fattakhov wasn't looking for conversation or new acquaintances, especially not with "kids." But his compassionate and generous nature led to a dialogue with these boys, which later almost turned into a kind of friendship.

It happened like this:

One time, Amin stopped by the pub to watch an Arsenal vs. Manchester United match. He ordered a mug of beer and some snacks. Of course, he was focused on the screen, especially because it was an exciting game, but being sensitive to others, he couldn't help noticing that three boys at the next table kept glancing at him—more accurately, "watching his every move."

At first, Amin felt a bit uncomfortable, but then he quickly realized what was going on. These young guys were only drinking mineral water. From the looks of it, they couldn't afford any extras like beer or snacks. Immediately, Amin offered them food and drinks from his table, and it turned out they were all big football fans just like him.

They were glad to meet him. One of them was Mukhitdin, the second was Gosha, and the third Roma. They'd all been classmates at the same school, though they had recently finished different colleges.

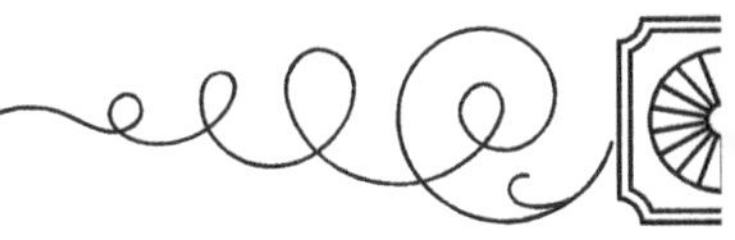

After the match, they exchanged phone numbers, and from then on, Amin began helping these young men financially now and then. They looked up to him almost like a mentor and benefactor, listening closely to everything he had to say—his ideas and life views. They still "hung on his every word," though no longer out of hunger, because he often treated them to snacks in cafés and bars. They simply listened attentively to whatever he had to share.

The young businessman couldn't say that he found their company particularly interesting. In fact, something about these boys, especially Gosha and Mukhitdin, left him slightly uneasy. However, he enjoyed and felt flattered by their respect for him—like students toward a teacher.

Time went by, and these acquaintances continued to see one another and stay in touch.

***

One evening, Mukhitdin called Amin late at night.

"Amin, hello! I have something to ask you. Can you help me?"

"Did something happen, Mukhitdin?"

"No, not exactly… It's just… you live alone in your apartment, right? The one Gosha and I came to once?"

"Yes, I live there alone. Why?.. I'm listening, go on!"

"Well… so… would you be able to give me the keys for one evening? Don't worry, I'm not a thief; I won't steal anything from you! You know I'm a musician…"

"I trust you, my friend, and I know you're a musician, which means you can't be a bad person—after all, you're not Salieri. But still, please understand me: I live here and am responsible for everything that goes on. Besides, this apartment was given to me by my father. God forbid he finds out strangers are coming here; he wouldn't like that!"

"So you still see me as 'a stranger,' huh, brother? Understood."

Amin realized he'd spoken harshly without thinking, and he felt embarrassed before his friend.

"No, wait, please, don't hang up! That's not what I meant… Forgive me. Of course, you, Gosha, and Roma haven't been complete strangers for these couple of weeks we've been friends. But still, you've got to understand that two weeks isn't all that long, and we haven't really tested or proven ourselves to each other in different circumstances…"

"Understood."

"No, you don't understand anything! You're still offended… But really, I'm ready to help you!"

"I do get it, Amin. Don't worry. It's just that… I wanted to invite my girlfriend there, to your apartment, for a date. You understand?"

"Your girlfriend? Why in the evening? Why not invite her during the day, maybe to a café or restaurant? If you like, I can help you out financially."

"No, I want to set up a romantic dinner for her… but in private, so there won't be anyone around to bother us. You get me?"

Amin thought for a moment.

"Yeah, I see… Sure, I understand. But forgive me if this seems blunt—and don't think I'm being stingy—but how come you can't do this at your own place? Would your parents refuse to let you do that?"

"Oh, no, Amin! I wouldn't dare tell my parents I've fallen in love with a girl…"

Amin let out a soft, melodious whistle.

"Wow! So you're in love, huh? Good for you."

"Well… yeah, I really like her, and I have for a while. But my parents keep telling me I need to study, work, 'get on my feet,' that it's too early for me to marry. They believe I'm not ready… And my father doesn't even give me any pocket money!"

Mukhitdin nearly broke down crying on the phone. From his voice, Amin could tell how deeply the subject of money pained him. Feeling his despair even over the distance, Amin hurried to reassure him:

"Hey, don't worry about that, my friend! If you need help, of course I'll help. I'll give you money for the date. We're friends, after all, even if you are—"

"I know, I know—still really young."

"Yes. Well then… So that's it. All right, it's been settled. I'll stay at my parents' for one night—my mother hardly ever sees me and misses me anyway."

"Just please don't say anything to your parents about me, okay?"

"Of course I won't. Honestly, I wouldn't want them to know I let someone else stay here in my absence—especially for an evening and overnight. So this will be our secret. Tomorrow, come see me at work, and I'll give you my spare keys to the apartment and some money. But I'll keep one set of keys with me… just in case."

6

Dr. Said Mumtazov drove his Nexia toward Abdulla Fattakhov's company. Near the entrance to the firm's office, he spotted his friend's older son, Amin. Amin was talking to a skinny, younger fellow with a pimpled face and, at first glance, slightly shifty eyes. It looked like Amin was handing the young man something—it appeared to be money and something resembling a set of keys.

Said Yahyaevich was a bit puzzled by the keys, but immediately told himself it was none of his business.

Amin, ostensibly unaware of his father's friend approaching, continued to speak with the young man. Then, as Said Yahyaevich drew closer, Amin said to the youth, "All right, Mukhitdin, but be careful there, agreed? And please, don't lose the keys! Remember, I'm trusting you. Alright, see you."

"Mukhitdin?" Dr. Mumtazov thought, somewhat surprised. "I feel like I've heard that name somewhere recently… But anyway, what am I thinking? There must be countless Mukhitdins in the world!"

The skinny, pimpled fellow nodded quickly at Amin and went on his way. At this moment, Amin noticed Said Yahyaevich, who had already come quite close.

"Good afternoon," he greeted him warmly. "What brings you here? You decided to stop by our firm to see dad?"

"Yes, Amin, salom! How are you, son? I need to speak with your father. He invited me to his office about something he said was important. So here I am."

They went into the office of the head of "Fattaxov PC."

"Ah, Said Yahyaevich!" The elder Fattakhov stood up from his chair to greet his friend. "Greeings, our dear doctor! How are you? All is well at home—your wife, your beautiful daughter? Everyone healthy?"

"Yes, praise be to God, everything's good, Abdulla Rustamovich. And how are you yourself? Blooming I assume?" Said gestured with his eyes at the luxurious, Euro-renovated office.

"We're doing fine, blossoming and flourishing, little by little," the businessman smiled.

"And your health? And how is your wonderful wife, Mukhabbat? Nobody complaining of eye problems? If anything comes up, you know where and to whom you should turn, first and foremost, right?"

"Of course! After all, I have a close, reliable friend—an ophthalmologist of worldwide renown, plus the owner of his own clinic!" the perfume distributor said seriously.

"Thank you, thank you," Said Yahyaevich beamed. "I just saw Amin. He's a fine young man, really grown up. It's a pity things went poorly with his wife…"

"Well, let's not dwell on sad matters…"

"Yes, of course, forgive me."

"He's doing well now, and as his father, I'm very proud of him. He does an excellent job, helps me a lot, and profits are even up. He's a real go-getter in business…"

"Yes, your Amin really is a clever guy, and in general a positive one. And as I know, all three of your children are hardworking and help you with the business!"

"Said, let me share something with you as a friend: I'm at ease about Amin and my daughter Rano; I'm sure both will go far. But

I still worry about my youngest, Bahadir… He's still too 'green,' not too serious yet. When will he finally come around?.. That's precisely what I wanted to talk about… Here's the thing… You have a wonderful daughter, Malika, and I, as you know, have unmarried sons. Perhaps you would be willing to give your precious daughter to one of them?"

"Well, that's a bit unexpected for me, but… it's a pleasant and flattering proposal. I suppose you had Bahadir in mind, first and foremost, right? Even though you say you're worried about him, I know he's a promising, kind, and well-mannered young man. Bahadir and Malika do know each other superficially—they've seen each other when we visited you and vice versa—but they've never really talked one-on-one. I think we should give them the chance to get to know each other better… Don't you agree? After all, you're my best friend, and honestly, I wouldn't hesitate to entrust my daughter to your family, so to speak, under your and your wife's wing. And we, her parents, would still be able to see Malika often…"

"Thank you, my friend, that's music to my ears. But we do need to think it through. Bahadir was sick a lot as a kid, and his mother spoiled him out of love. He's used to living large, denying himself nothing. Yes, he's good-looking, and the girls swarm around him, and though he's kind and generous, he doesn't have a real goal in life. He wants everything for free, doesn't like to earn it himself. That part of him didn't come from me or his mother… In my opinion, my elder son, Amin, is a much better candidate for marriage. Besides, I need to find another wife for my older boy first, then worry about my younger one's future."

"Amin is definitely wonderful, Abdulla," Said agreed, "but there's a big age difference between him and Malika. He's over thirty, and my daughter isn't even twenty…"

"Well, thirty-three isn't sixty-three! That's no age at all for a man. On the contrary, it's better if he has some experience and a firm footing. Besides, Amin once casually mentioned that he has a lot of respect for Malika and is fond of her."

"That's good to hear. But still, I think Amin might need a slightly older woman. Please don't misunderstand, Abdulla, and no offense: I'd like to give my only daughter to a man who's never been married and who will always love only her—my Malika, you see?.. If you're offering one of your sons, let it be Bahadir who marries my daughter. And I'm certain that once he's married, he'll immediately become more serious and mature. You'll see for yourself!"

Abdulla Rustamovich thought for a moment. Then he said,

"I won't deny it, my friend, your Malika would be the perfect wife for my son. I never even dared to dream of such a daughter-in-law. But right now, Bahadir has both his studies and work, and he still needs to learn to be a reliable mainstay for his future family, to be able to provide for them!"

"And that's where we come in, dear Abdulla. If, God willing, your Bahadir and my Malika like each other, and if we marry them, then for the first while after the wedding, we'll both help and support them. After that, they'll find their own footing."

Abdulla Rustamovich fell silent in thought again.

"Well, actually… maybe you're right, Said. Such a sweet, intelligent, and kind girl as Malika could likely have a wonderful influence on my younger son. With her help, he might grow into a truly worthy person in every respect."

Abdulla Rustamovich then called his older son by the internal phone.

"Amin," he said, "Said and I have just decided to introduce our children, Bahadir and Malika. If they like each other from the first meeting, we'll marry them. What do you think about that, son? I want your opinion!"

Amin seemed to blush slightly and was a bit thrown by the sudden subject.

"Father… well, what can I say… I suppose… Yes, it's a good idea. Malika is, in my opinion, a wonderful girl, and I've never met anyone like her. A lot of men would consider themselves lucky to have a wife like that—if fortune smiled on them! As for our Bahadir…"

"What?" asked Abdulla Rustamovich. "You have doubts about your brother?"

"No, no, Father. Of course I don't doubt him. God grants that Said Yakhyaevich's daughter will like him . And I have no doubt that he'll find her very much to his liking."

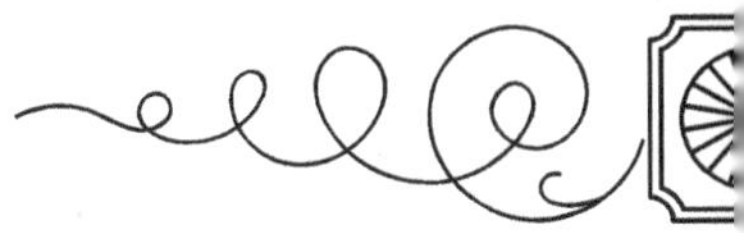

7

Malika hardly slept all night. Finally, after almost two weeks, she had agreed to meet with Mukhitdin. She had felt awkward about flatly refusing his request to meet and have to talk about "that" topic. But she already knew for certain that she would turn down his proposal of marriage. She just had no idea how to do it without hurting Mukhitdin's feelings, and she hoped they could stay friends.

She wanted to meet him in the daytime, but Mukhitdin asked Malika to come to the address he gave her in the evening.

"What kind of place is it?" she asked him over the phone, sounding surprised. For some reason, it made her uneasy and nervous, though she couldn't figure out why.

"You'll see when you get here," Mukhitdin said gently.

"Still, tell me up front," Malika persisted.

"It's an apartment. I'm inviting you to my place for dinner," he said, telling a small lie. Malika thought his voice sounded either impatient or slightly irritated, which surprised her. She had never known this side of him before.

"So, your parents are inviting me? Is that okay? And you'll finally introduce me to them, like I asked you to do a while ago, and you promised?"

There was a brief pause.

"Yes," came the voice on the other end. "It's fine. What's with the questions?"

At these words, Malika felt a weight lift from her heart. She wondered why she had been so worried in the first place.

"Parents…" Mukhitdin hesitated somewhat. "Well, they…"

"They will be there, right?" she asked, feeling slightly embarrassed by her own suspicions and meticulousness, but wanting to be sure.

"Yes, of course… my mother will be," he lied outright.

"Great, I'll definitely come, and then you'll walk me home, right? So my parents don't worry. I told them to put them at ease since you'd be with me."

"You told them about me? Why?.. Well, all right… Don't worry, everything will be fine!" Mukhitdin reassured her. "It's just dinner, that's all. Oh, and of course, meeting… my parents… or rather, my mother…"

No one but him knew just how far from the truth that really was.

8

Agra, 1608

Shah Jahan did not send his envoys, nor did he come himself to see Arjumand—neither the next day, as he had promised, nor a day later, nor even a week later. Many weeks and months passed, and he did not appear, while Arjumand continued to wait for him. Perhaps, for any other man, she would have quickly moved on, but not for that splendid youth! Even if he had been not a prince but a poor commoner, her heart would still have wholly belonged to him!

Rumors reached her that the prince, heir to the Mughal throne, was indeed in love with her! And of course, those around her—especially the women who loved to gossip—had not failed to notice that the prince had bestowed upon Arjumand an incredibly generous gift, buying a pair of trifling wooden beads from her for the staggering sum of ten thousand rupees! Such extravagance was unheard of, even for a person of his rank. She became the object of envy. And where envy exists, genuine goodwill for another's happiness does not. Who among them would want the heir apparent to set his eyes not on them or their daughters or sisters, but on some other girl—even if she was, by all accounts, gentle, sweet, and genuinely beautiful?

Nevertheless, people whispered everywhere, unable to hide the truth: Shah Jahan had lost all peace of mind. He wandered the palace like a shadow, finding neither solace nor relief in anything, thinking only of one person in all the world—Asaf Khan's daughter,

Arjumand. The beloved son of the padishah was head over heels in love. Clearly, something—or someone—was preventing him from meeting with her, much less marrying her...

"Will I ever see him again, even just once?" Arjumand wondered in despair. "If only he would send some word, give me some sign to show I matter to him!"

But time passed, and there were no letters from Shah Jahan, no invitations to meet.

***

General Mahabat Khan had been teaching the future ruler, Shah Jahan, the art of war. For several years now, he also served as an advisor on difficult matters.

"Forgive me, Your Highness," he said, "but as your teacher, I must point out that you have become very distracted. Is something troubling you? Are you weighed down by some heavy thoughts?"

The prince sighed.

"You are very perceptive, Mahabat. Forgive me—I was just lost in thought."

"You must understand, my prince, that such inattention would be wholly unacceptable in battle. Were this a real war, your enemies would already have defeated you and taken your arms. Besides, in war, the padishah is the soul of the army; he is the center of every skirmish, and all look to him. If a general lets his mind wander or falls into daydreams, he will be killed, and defeat for the entire force is inevitable... Now, who is she?.."

"There's no hiding anything from you, General!" Shah Jahan replied. "You're right—it's about someone named Arjumand."

"So you're smitten with her, yes? You did not guard your heart from worries and turmoil?"

"My heart? She is my heart!"

"Oh, things have gone quite far, then," the seasoned warrior said with a shake of his head. "Princes and rulers are not meant to drift into dreams and torment themselves with passion."

"And what if it isn't mere passion or some passing bodily desire, but real love?" Shah Jahan said excitedly. "I'll share this with you: with great difficulty, I managed to speak privately with my father about it. I told him I love only Arjumand, that she is truly wonderful, that she must be my first and principal wife! I asked for his consent to our wedding."

"And what did our padishah say about your choice?" Mahabat Khan asked politely, trying only to show some support, although he could guess the answer.

"My father forbids me even to think of her... and he goes on swearing I am his favorite son! I fear, Mahabat, that a ruler can never truly have a 'favorite grown son,' because sooner or later he begins to see him as a rival—jealous either over women or, more likely, the throne, the power itself! He also told me that what I feel for Arjumand is not love but mere lust that will soon pass and dissipate like smoke."

"Perhaps your father is correct, Your Highness?"

"No, no, and no! I know—know it for certain, Mahabat—that my feelings for Arjumand are different from anything I've ever felt for other women who can gratify me physically only. She alone can make me truly happy! How can he not understand me, when he is in love himself? That Mehrun-Nissa seems to have bewitched him..."

"Tss!" The general pressed a finger to his lips. "That is a secret, my prince, one that must not be spoken of. But if it remains strictly between the two of us: perhaps because your father is not very happy in his own love—after all, he is not married to the woman he desires—he wishes to deny you, his heir, the same rapturous luxury."

"So he's jealous of me in his heart? Jealous that I can openly talk about my love for Arjumand! He told me he has already chosen a 'suitable' bride for me. Imagine! Without ever asking whether I want to marry someone I don't know and don't love! Oh, woe unto me, Mahabat! If only anyone knew how miserable I am. But what makes it worse is the thought that she—my beloved, to whom I gave my word yet failed to keep it—she, as I hear, is still waiting for me, suffering, just as I am, still hoping… Will these hopes ever come true? What do you think?"

"I fear you must forget her, prince," the general said gravely.

"If you only knew how hard it is to hear that, and from you of all people… And the padishah also told me that as a prince, I must not serve my personal interests but concern myself only with the interests of the entire empire! He made it clear that marriage to Arjumand offers no benefit to the state—no increase in wealth, no added power or strength, no new useful diplomatic alliances, no territorial expansion. 'Marry first for the good of the empire,' my father concluded, 'and then, if by that time you still haven't lost your passion, take her as your second or third wife. I'll allow it. But never as your first—I will never grant consent to that! You are still young, my son, and you will soon forget this longing. Enjoy the women the eunuchs bring to you at night. And stop brooding over this girl, this Arjumand!'"

"And what have you decided, my prince?" Mahabat Khan asked. "Will you heed your father?"

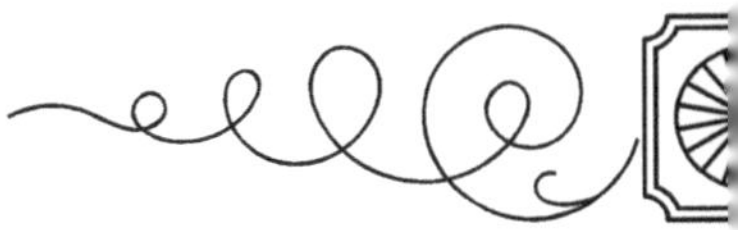

"Never, not for anything," Shah Jahan answered resolutely. "There is no power in the world that can force me to cease loving my Arjumand or make me renounce her!"

* * *

On the other side of Giyas Beg's house, shouts and angry voices broke out. Hearing them, Arjumand stepped into the hallway to see what was happening.

"I refuse to go so far away, to Bengal!" Mehrun-Nissa was shrieking at her husband. "Couldn't you find some excuse to turn down this awful appointment?"

"But it's an honor for me, my dear," Sher Afkun tried to argue. "It's a high post. I'm now the Divan—overseeing all the country's storehouses and workshops!"

"Yes, yes, the ruler has shown you an 'unheard-of kindness' by banishing our family to the ends of the earth!" she retorted, clearly enraged. "It would be completely different if he'd given you a position here in Agra, at the palace itself or at least in government…"

A brave commander on the battlefield, Sher Afkun now sat before her meek as a rabbit cornered by a python. He was at a loss for words in the face of his wife's wrath.

At last, she softened a little.

"All right, it's not your fault. And nothing can be changed now. Of course, dear husband, I'm happy for you and I congratulate you on this respectable post! I'll go pack our things, and the servants will help me. Clearly, we are going to Bengal!"

The day before Sher Afkun, Mehrun-Nissa, and Ladilli were to leave, the house of Giyas Beg—father of Mehrun-Nissa and Asaf Khan—received a visit from none other than the padishah himself.

Shah Jahangir was in the habit of occasionally visiting the homes of his subjects. During these visits, the masters of the house were obliged to present their ruler with expensive, lavish gifts in order to avoid his wrath and win his favor. For those hosting such a high guest, it was a heavy burden, as some were forced to offer up their last valuables, while for the already wealthy padishah it was largely an amusement. He might, by whim, reject many of the gifts and take only some bauble for remembrance—or, on the contrary, ruin officials who had incurred his displeasure.

All the women in the household, where Arjumand also lived, laid out on the carpet their necklaces, beads, earrings, rings, and bracelets. Stripped of their customary adornments (taken off to be presented to the padishah), they resembled plucked hens. Beside them on the floor stood golden and silver vases, cups, and bowls. As for Giyas Beg, knowing better than most in the entire country the tastes and preferences of the padishah, he had prepared a gift for him that was not costly per se, but was genuinely valuable and practical: a copper spyglass brought from distant lands.

The clamour outside—produced by musicians, soldiers driving back onlookers, and the padishah's guard—announced that the padishah was already at the door. Running ahead of the procession were palace servants and elegantly attired attendants who rolled out sumptuous carpets at Jahangir's feet and scattered rose petals upon them.

All the residents of the house, belonging to Arjumand's grandfather Giyas Beg, went out to greet the honoured guest and the officials accompanying him. When the padishah emerged from his palanquin, both men and women bowed low before him.

Right away, everyone noticed that the padishah regarded the household with favour. He warmly embraced and kissed Giyas

Beg, as though an old friend, then gave Sher Afkun a hearty pat on the back. Jahangir pretended to show the most interest in the gifts prepared for him, so he immediately examined them. Showing his benevolence to this family, he refrained from stripping them of all their possessions, taking only one item for himself: Giyas Beg's fascinating spyglass. Holding it to his right eye and aiming it at a window in the distance, where the domes of buildings and treetops were just barely visible, the padishah smiled, very pleased.

"What is this called?" he asked.

"It's a spyglass, my lord," Giyas Beg replied. "I wanted so much to gladden you, to give you pleasure…"

"And you have succeeded, my friend!" the padishah responded enthusiastically. "From now on, I can observe the habits of birds and beasts, and even gaze at the stars at night. More than that—I can discreetly keep watch from afar on my subjects and guess what they say and think! So this is truly an excellent present."

Jahangir turned his attention to the women. Each had a veil covering her head. Suddenly, at Mehrun-Nissa's feet, he noticed a small box inlaid with mother-of-pearl. The padishah motioned to a servant to hand him the box. Jahangir took it, opened it, and… glancing at Sher Afkun's wife, whose face was partly hidden by the thinnest of veils, closed the box again, letting out a quiet gasp of admiration.

"This is for me?" he asked, to be sure, although she was the only woman in the house who looked at him without fear or submissive bows, as if his equal despite the fact he was the ruler of the great Mughal Empire.

"Yes, of course, it's for you, my lord," Mehrun-Nissa replied softly and politely, yet without any sign of flattery or servility.

Giyas Beg also wanted very much to see what was inside that

mysterious box belonging to his daughter. But Shah Jahangir gave him no chance to do so.

"There's nothing special in here, my friend," he lied to his chief advisor, swiftly hiding the box inside his robe. "Just a little puzzle of the sort I enjoy. But if you don't mind, I'd like to solve it on my own."

"Certainly, my padishah," said Giyas Beg, bowing. "As you wish."

"You may remove your veil," the padishah addressed Mehrun-Nissa, "I give you permission."

He would sometimes do this in public so that he himself could admire a woman's beauty, and so the men in his retinue could do the same.

Arjumand could see plainly that this was exactly what he had been waiting for, that he had come to the house specifically to see Mehrun-Nissa again, his secret, passionate love! Mehrun-Nissa did not obey the command at once, but took her time—seemingly wanting the effect of her revealed beauty to be as striking as possible. When at last she pulled off the veil, it looked as if the padishah nearly wept with joy.

Only Arjumand in the entire house knew exactly what was hidden in that box, because she had once seen it opened in her aunt's room. Inside the box was a skillfully painted miniature portrait of Mehrun-Nissa herself! And in that likeness, she was enchanting.

"Could it be that my aunt is seriously plotting to capture the padishah's heart?" Arjumand wondered. "Yet I know her all too well. She doesn't truly know how to love, and she never does anything without a hidden motive! Does she want to become the ruler of all Hindustan?.. And if she doesn't love Jahangir, does that mean her aims can only be pride and self-interest?... No, I could never do such a thing!"

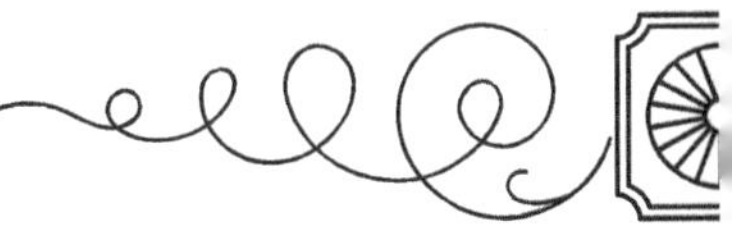

9

Tashkent, 2014

Amin had told his parents he would spend that evening and night with them. His mother, Mukhabbat, was overjoyed. While his father, brother, and sister saw their eldest son and brother at work every weekday. Mukhabbat sometimes went months without seeing him, speaking with him only over phone.

To celebrate her son's visit, Mukhabbat decided to make her "signature" plov and bake a delicious pie for tea.

When Amin arrived, his mother surrounded him with all kinds of affection and care. Later, Rano came home and happily helped her mother look after her beloved brother. Amin, for his part, also did not come empty-handed: he brought all sorts of sweets for the family and a big bouquet of peonies—his mother's favorite flowers.

"Amin, how wonderful you are, my lovely boy!" said Mukhabbat to her firstborn, when he sat down beside her and Rano in the kitchen.

"Mama, come on now, I'm not a 'boy,'" Amin grumbled good-naturedly, giving in a little to his mother's tenderness. "I'm a grown man."

"Yes, grown," Mukhabbat sighed. "But to me, you will always be my child… and the best one… That Madina of yours missed out on a great happiness."

"Mama, she is not 'mine'…"

"I know, I know—she's not yours. But you're no saint either:

you shouldn't have spoiled your wife that much. Love her—yes, absolutely—but you shouldn't let her walk all over you. 'Grown man'? You still haven't understood much about life or about women."

"Mooom!" Amin groaned.

"Son, understand me: I only want you to be happy. It's what I want most for all three of you. I was fortunate with your father—I'm happy with him in every way. But how can I sleep peacefully, knowing that none of my children are settled yet, that none of you have built your own 'nest'?.. As for you, my boy, you need to marry again. Have you thought about that?"

Suddenly, Amin recalled the discussion at their office with his father and Said Yahyaevich about the latter's daughter, Malika, and for some reason he felt sad. Why had he let such a wonderful girl slip away?.. Now it was too late—she would probably be given to Bahadir, that flighty Don Juan who takes every woman lightly! Yet Amin believed that he himself would have been far more deserving of a wife like her! And why was it that in relationships with the opposite sex, he often turned out to be so weak, shy, and indecisive?..

This thought suddenly triggered a shooting pain in his head. He cried out.

Mukhabbat and Rano grew alarmed, rushing to his side.

"What's wrong, my son?" his mother asked anxiously.

"Nothing, Mama. My head really hurts. Seems like that migraine again."

"It's my fault, dear, forgive me," his mother fretted. "I made you nervous. Look how many years have passed since you were in the army and had that bad fall. You got a serious injury, and these pains still haven't gone away completely."

"Mama, maybe we should call an ambulance?" Rano said, equally worried about her brother's condition.

"No, no need for an ambulance," Amin protested. "I promise I'll see my neurologist in the very near future."

"You must do that, son! You can't 'play around' with your health. In the meantime, take a painkiller. And please, don't put off getting proper treatment—go to the clinic tomorrow morning, straight from here, to see your doctor."

"Well, actually, I have a lot of work tomorrow…"

"It's all right, I'll help out at work," Rano reassured him. "It's not going anywhere."

"Then tomorrow I'll definitely go, Mama," Amin said through the splitting pain. Then he remembered something. "Oh, and I have some paperwork left…"

"Where?" both women asked in unison.

"At home… Listen, Mama, Sis, I need to go right now, urgently…

"Go somewhere? In such a state? We won't let you!"

"To my place. Not for long, just to get those forms and the latest test results… I'll just go and come back… I don't want to be delayed tomorrow because of it."

* * *

Malika called her friend Galya to share what was on her mind.

"So you're meeting his parents?" Galina asked in a spirited tone. "That's great! I wish someone would invite me on a date like that—I wouldn't know how to contain my excitement!"

"Come on," Malika disagreed. "When you love someone, it's different—the two of you meeting is always a joy. But if you don't have feelings for him, what's so great? It's like torture."

"Still, I'm jealous," Galina sighed. "But in a good way. You're lucky, being so beautiful that everyone loves you—just like your grandma Firuz-begim always says, you're a 'true lady of noble blood.' And even though you're an aristocrat, and your name means 'Princess,' you still have to be polite. Buy them a cake or a box of chocolates."

"Thanks for the tip—I already did that. Any other advice?"

"Nope. Off you go, lucky girl…"

* * *

Mukhitdin was waiting for Malika at the agreed spot, not far from Amin's apartment.

Before leaving home, she wanted to stop by Firuz-begim's room and, just in case, share her doubts. But her elderly grandmother was, unfortunately, asleep.

Peeking into the old woman's room, Malika was astonished to see, on the small table by the mirror, an incredibly beautiful ruby and diamond necklace.

"I wonder where such gorgeous, luxurious jewelry came from, and whose it is…" she thought.

Malika had to make the decision herself about whether to go on the date or not… In the end, she decided to take the risk, hoping God would guide her. Let whatever would happen, happen.

On the way, she thought that even if her heart wasn't soaring with true love, it was still a pleasant feeling to be courted by someone, to feel needed, to be liked, to know she brought someone delight simply by her presence. The thought boosted her mood.

Approaching the building, for some reason she pictured Mukhitdin looking elegant, very well-dressed, and, most obviously, holding flowers. And most likely it would be her favorite white roses! After all, this was an important moment, at least for him: introducing a girl to his parents surely called for something special, right?..

Spotting her friend from a distance, Malika was slightly taken aback. He wasn't carrying any flowers. In fact, he had nothing with him at all. And he was dressed completely ordinarily.

When she came close and greeted him, she caught the smell of alcohol on him.

For a few seconds, Malika hesitated. Her first impulse was to silently turn around and leave at once. Only the thought that his parents were expecting her—a meeting presumably arranged with them in advance—held her back. It would have been awkward not to show up. What would they think of her? That she was snubbing them?

But so much for Mukhitdin! Malika was upset and offended by how he looked, and especially by the fact that he'd come to this important meeting inebriated. How could he act so disrespectfully toward her?.. Still… maybe he was just jittery? Perhaps that was why he had to drink a little?

"Mukhitdin, is something going on?" she asked him very seriously.

"What could be going on?" the young man responded unexpectedly cheerfully. "What's up, Malika—my friend? Everything's great!!! Mother is waiting for us…"

Those last words were what stopped Malika, who was already on the verge of heading back home. Pulling herself together, she followed Mukhitdin into the right entrance and went with him up to the third floor.

Mukhitdin fiddled with a key at the door to Amin's apartment. It took a while, but finally the lock gave way.

"Mukhitdin, why didn't your parents open the door for us?" Malika asked in surprise. "… Where are they? Where's your mother?.. You said she'd be here!"

"Don't worry, everything's fine," he replied, just as cheerful and buoyant as before. "As for my mother… well, she'll be here soon… I mean, probably…"

* * *

Malika sat in an armchair in a strange apartment, terrified. Her skirt was hiked up above her knees, and the blouse she wore was unbuttoned—several buttons had been undone, and one had even torn off and flown somewhere. Bending over her was Mukhitdin, groping her with both hands. Shocked and terrified, Malika was in a state that made her unable to defend herself. At that moment, her entire life seemed like nothing but darkness and horror, and she felt as though she were dying, that her life was about to end in this nightmare…

When someone else entered the room—someone who had apparently arrived from out of nowhere, late at night in this empty apartment—Malika, powerless and almost voiceless in her despair, covered her face with her hands and gave a near-silent scream.

"Mukhitdin, what are you doing?!" came a menacing male voice from somewhere off to the side or above.

Malika still held her palms over her face, too afraid to see what was happening around her.

"You… you came… Why are you here?" Mukhitdin asked, his voice wavering. Judging by his tone, he clearly had not expected this person's arrival.

"I tried calling you, Mukhitdin. Why have you turned your

phone off?.. I came here on an urgent matter! I thought that I would have to apologize for bothering you… and then I walk in on this! It's as if I had a feeling something was wrong. So this is what you're doing, you scumbag?! I entrusted you with my apartment—so you could disgrace girls here?"

Malika heard someone strike a blow across a face—most likely a hefty, resounding slap.

"Get out of here, you bastard! Leave the keys, too! Understand? We're not just 'not friends' anymore—don't even consider us acquaintances!"

Malika was trembling all over. Yet sensing that it was not a second attacker but rather her rescuer who had arrived, she couldn't stop herself from bursting into tears.

A minute later, she heard the apartment door slam. That meant her assailant was gone…

The man who had saved her came over to her quietly and gently removed her hands from her face. When Malika saw who stood before her, she nearly fainted.

"Malika?! It's you?! How did you end up here… with that…? Poor thing… You do remember me, don't you? I'm Amin. My father is friends with yours, although you and I haven't really been introduced; we've only met a few times. Tell me, that guy—he didn't manage to… actually do any evil to you, did he?"

"No, Amin. Thank God, nothing happened! You… thank you… You came just in time. You saved me."

"It's as if I sensed something was wrong!.. Now, Malika, you don't have to be afraid anymore… This is my apartment. Go freshen up and tidy yourself. I have a car; I'll grab the documents I need and then drive you home. And please don't worry—nobody will ever find out about what happened tonight. But I promise you, if I get my hands on him I will punish that Mukhitdin. And you, please, do stay away from him! Who knows what else he might pull off… I see you're far too trusting… far too trusting."

Malika looked at Amin with warmth and, thanking him in a trembling voice, she burst into tears again.

10

Malika sat silently, alone in her room, having locked the door and asked her family not to disturb her...

She no longer had the strength to cry, and she was unused to complaining about her fate to others. Besides, she felt far too ashamed to talk about it now. She could hardly fathom how her closest friend—someone she had trusted for so many years, with whom she had always enjoyed a warm and easy bond—could act toward her in such a treacherous, vile, and contemptible way. A heavy sense of bitterness weighed on her heart. She was oblivious to everything around her. Many hours passed like that.

Unexpectedly, her gaze fell on her beloved seven-string guitar. Since childhood, Malika had studied both piano and guitar, but she had always had a special fondness for the guitar. Sometimes, with its magical sounds, the instrument reminded her of the ancient Eastern ghijak... Firuz-begim often spoke about the wondrous effect that sound and melody have on people's destinies... music, much like a fragrance, can bring enlightenment and show the way to success...

Like a recluse in her own room, Malika picked up the guitar and began to play. She had often improvised in the past, strumming and sometimes humming not only well-known melodies by the world's greatest composers but also brand-new motifs that sprang forth from her soul.

On this day, however, her heart was brimming with a sharp, throbbing pain. Malika knew that her wise and kind great-great-grandmother, Firuz-begim, would surely try to find words to comfort her. She had even heard her grandmother gently ask Malika to open the door so they could talk—clearly wanting to help her dear granddaughter! But Malika let neither her nor her parents in. Out of sensitivity, none of them insisted on breaking her silence. Something inside Malika almost wanted to keep hold of the searing, genuine hurt she was feeling—the very real and unfeigned pain.

As she strummed an unfamiliar melody (amidst the voice of her pain, she sensed how tender and lyrical the tune was), she began to feel something else stirring within her, something she had scarcely experienced before. It was an unusual state, one that intoxicated her, drew her in, bringing euphoria and bliss verging on a melancholy sort of enlightenment. Malika had no idea that this feeling was called a "creative inspiration." For her, it was entirely new.

She hardly noticed how the piercing anguish caused by a person's despicable and revolting act receded and faded into the background, making room for something beautiful.

And for the first time in her life, Malika composed her own song. In that moment, she forgot that she was singing to no one but herself, that only she could hear it—she simply didn't think about it. The song poured out from deep within as though it were soaring like the wind above the earth, enveloping all living souls with light, peace, and joy.

Deep in Malika's soul, another gentle sensation emerged, akin to a type of womanly love she had never known before—a love for him… Yet the figure she envisioned was not Mukhitdin at all. Oh no!

In her mind's eye, she saw a handsome young man with enchanting, river-green eyes, sporting a small beard and mustache. For a moment, it seemed there was something familiar about his appearance—something she recognized. But she didn't wish to distract herself by trying to recall when or where she might have seen that face before. Above all, she did not want to lose the rapture in her heart, that soaring feeling, and this tender flush of infatuation. She didn't want to lose the marvelous music pouring out of her like a crystal-clear mountain stream.

After Malika repeated the song several times, feeling truly inspired, illuminated, and as if cleansed of all her woes, she set the guitar aside. Deciding that, just for this first attempt, she would do without modern electronic means and rely on centuries-old methods, she took a notebook and pen and wrote down the notes. As for the lyrics, they seemed to find their place all on their own—she chose well-known verses about love by her favorite poetess, Nodira-begim:

My soul is a victim to your honeyed lips;
All my life is a sacrifice to your magical chains.
Separation destroys all who long to meet with you—
Their souls, their very lives are offered to your beckoning call.
And if it is not I whom sorrow and jealousy consume,
Then so be it: let my pain be a sacrifice to some new keeper.
Both sun and moon are but fables, mere illusions;
You are the sun—while I am a sacrifice to your crimson rays.
A torrent of diamond tears runs from my sorrowful eyes,
An offering to the rubies of your lips, those scarlet petals.
And for your slender form, my graceful cypress,
I remain, in my harsh destiny, your devoted sacrifice.

Malika finished writing her song, releasing all her pain and despair through it. Feeling renewed and healed of her wounds, filled with light and hope, she then drifted into a peaceful sleep.

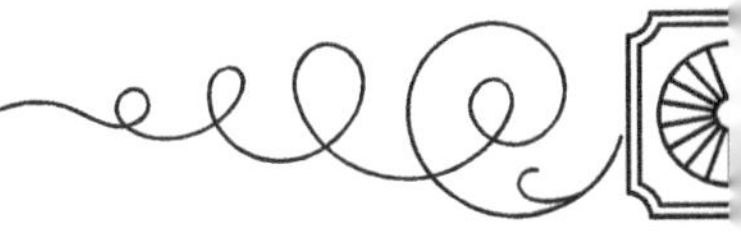

11

At Abdulla Rustamovich's "Fattaxov PC" firm, the workday was buzzing along as usual.

"Amin," Rano said in a lively tone as she entered her older brother's office—he was the company's commercial and financial director. "The 'Taj Mahal's Eternal Love' perfume by the French brand Romea D`Ameor has cleared customs and arrived at our warehouse. Tomorrow it'll be allocated among the retail networks, and of course, we'll supply the wholesalers too."

"Excellent!" Amin replied. "Rano, I wanted to share an idea with you. I respect your opinion, so let me just put it out there and you can mull it over."

"Sure, brother, I'm listening."

"France as a manufacturer is always remarkable—it's luxury, prestige, refinement, a benchmark of taste and style…"

"And 'fascinating' price tags," Rano added with a smile.

"Yes, you're right—and the corresponding prices. Usually reflecting top-notch quality. But you know our main clientele is from the East. And while today's European producers strive to account for the demand and specifics of every market in which their potential customers reside, you have to admit that manufacturers from the East might have an easier time understanding the mindset of Eastern customers—various cultural nuances, the worldview of the majority of people in, say, our Uzbekistan."

"I see… You mean to say it's time for us to consider partnering with luxury brands from Eastern countries?"

"You catch on fast," Amin said approvingly. "Because those cultural nuances apply to perfumes and cosmetics as well."

"You're referring to Arabic…?"

"Yes, Arab countries—and India! India came to my mind when you mentioned the fragrance 'Taj Mahal's Eternal Love.' After all, the Taj Mahal is in Agra, India, and it's a Wonder of the World built by our ancestors—the Great Mughals descending from Amir Temur, Babur…"

"That's fantastic, I got it. I'll definitely start building connections with manufacturers from those regions. I know they attended last year's trade fair in Cannes, and I've already begun corresponding with TFK—The Fragrance Kitchen—a niche Kuwaiti brand founded by Sheikh Majed Al-Sabah. They're hugely successful, and their entire range is presented in its own corner at the TsUM in Moscow."

Amin nodded approvingly.

"Great… as always, well done! Then, naturally, we'll talk it through with Father—his opinion is always valuable."

"Agreed. Meanwhile, there's something else I wanted to discuss with you, and it's important too."

"I'm listening, little sister," Amin said, smiling faintly, his eyes tinged with sadness.

"We've been so busy I haven't had a chance to ask about personal things. First off—how are you feeling? What did the doctor say about your headaches—are they serious?"

"The doctor prescribed a treatment. I got the necessary medications and have already started taking them. We'll see what happens. In any case, don't worry about anything, my dear sister! It's nothing fatal… If anything concerns me, it's your health issues. I know Mom's been nagging you about 'fitness and figure,' and I realize how much you hate that talk, but… you're a part of my soul, my guardian angel, and I'm worried about you too. So please don't be upset that I'm asking… Rano, might your occasional heart pains and blood pressure spikes have something to do with excess weight?"

"Please, can we not talk about that?" Rano said with a pleading moan.

She tried to mask her discomfort about this sensitive topic with a smile. She didn't want to upset her brother with a quarrel because of his benevolent interference in her life and slightly obsessive care for her. Besides, she had only just begun a personal conversation - and she couldn't interrupt it halfway without finding out the main issue!

"All right, as you wish," Amin yielded to his younger sister. He decided not to pick an argument with a woman, after all, it concerned her own life.

"Brother, so you don't dwell on it too much—and if this helps ease your mind— I'll tell you the reason behind some of my ailments. It's not overeating…"

"Oh?"

"Yes. At least I'm eating less than I used to, and anyways that's not the point anyway. Nor is a lack of exercise. According to the doctors, I have a metabolic disorder and, besides that, a genetic predisposition to being heavy. So please, neither you nor our parents should torment me by talking about it! Okay?"

"All right, I understand," Amin said soothingly.

"But right now, I want to talk about you, not me. I'm no less concerned about your fate than you are about mine. And there's another important question… I've noticed that lately you seem very down—often out of sorts. I'm guessing old emotional wounds still trouble you, that you can't forget her?"

"Her?!" Amin started, taken aback by her unexpected question. For some reason, Malika sprang to his mind—he had recently encountered her in his own house and had found her, in his eyes, the most extraordinary and beautiful woman he had ever seen.

"I mean your ex-wife, Madina," Rano clarified, somewhat puzzled by her usually sensible brother's uncharacteristic confusion.

"Oh! No… it's not about her."

"Then who is it?" his younger sister persisted. "You know you can confide in me; I'm not one for gossip, and plus you're my brother, and I tell you everything about myself, so you can share about yourself in return."

"But you're just a kid," Amin teased kindly.

"Stop that!" Rano said in mock annoyance. "I'm twenty-two. How am I a 'kid'? I'm a top manager in a large company! And not because of family ties, I might add, but because I've earned it. I see something is eating away at you, tormenting you, and obviously you're telling no one. Please share it with me! You'll see that you'll feel better. I promise no one else will learn of your troubles. So what is it?.. Who is she?"

Amin gazed at his sister with surprise and undisguised admiration. He was aware she was sharp-minded in business—she had always studied well, but he hadn't expected such insight into the private feelings he had never confessed, not even to himself. Indeed, she had "caught" him.

"What are you on about?" Abdulla Fattakhov's eldest son tried to deflect. "Who…?"

"How should I know who? That's for you to say," replied Abdulla Fattakhov's daughter with gentle but pointed waspishness. "I do see that you're suffering about something, and because our work here is going fine—thank God, no catastrophic problems—it must be something personal, maybe deeply personal. Amin, I don't want to be intrusive or tactless, but you aren't a stranger to me. It hurts me to see you like this."

"And how exactly am I?"

"Like 'nothing at all'! Lost, shattered, depressed. And I so want to help you! I know you well; you're a sensitive, gentle, and vulnerable person. You can suffer deeply for a woman—someone you like. So I'm asking: who is she?"

"You know…" Amin spoke pensively. "It's embarrassing to talk about, but unfortunately, you're absolutely right…"

At another time, Rano would have welcomed those words of praise—she would have felt good about being so astute. But not now. Seeing the clear sorrow in her brother's eyes, she felt a pang of empathy, a reflection of his sadness echoing in her own heart. Rano started to feel uneasy herself. Compassion and genuine sympathy for Amin swept over her.

Meanwhile, her brother continued speaking:

"I once knew a girl… Well, I didn't really know her, but I was acquainted with her… just not closely. She always inspired my sympathy and respect. It's just… I can't tell you everything just yet…"

"Oh no, that won't do. I can't help you unless you tell me. You know perfectly well: this conversation will remain between us forever! So…?"

"…All right, you convinced me. But don't breathe a word of it to anyone, Rano, got it? Especially not to Mom."

"Understood. I promise. I'm listening."

"Her name is Malika. She's the daughter of Doctor Said Yahyaevich, the ophthalmologist—Dad's friend."

"Ah, yes, of course—I know him. And I remember Malika; I've

seen her a few times. It's odd we've never become friends, because I get the feeling we're somewhat alike in character. She struck me as a bit withdrawn."

"Maybe. I don't know her well. But recently, I met her… well… anyway, doesn't matter where. I met her."

"And…?"

"We talked a bit. Actually, it was more that I… sort of protected her from some awful person who… well, he treated her dishonourably."

"Oh, so you stepped in?"

"Yes, I stood up for her honour… I don't mean that her virtue was compromised—absolutely not! She's so pure, so radiant, so decent…"

"Yes, that was my impression too when we met. She and her family came to visit us once! And when you and our parents visited their home, I couldn't go along—I was sick."

"That's right."

"But Malika, as I recall, really did seem lovely. So what became of her 'honour' then?"

"I simply prevented an irreversible disaster she was in no way to blame for—nothing more."

"You did the right thing, brother, I'm proud of you! But… then this sadness of yours… So that means…"

All at once, Rano understood.

"So, are you in lov—? I mean, does she… do you like her? Is that why you're so upset? Did you propose something—wanted to date—and she turned you down? Turned down my wonderful, kind, best-in-the-world brother?! You don't say! Perhaps I misjudged her after all…"

"Please don't say that. Malika is really good."

"Then what's the problem? I don't get it…"

"Her father visited ours the other day—they talked about betrothing Malika…"

"Really?! Why don't I know anything about this? Well, what are you so upset for? If you like her that much, isn't that great news?"

"Why do you insist on cutting me off before hearing the end? I regret telling you, now!"

"No, no, don't say that, brother. Forgive me," Rano pleaded, gentle and free of any arrogance. "I'm listening carefully. It's just that not everything is immediately clear, so I'm asking questions before I forget my train of thought."

Amin gave her a mildly reproachful look, though not in anger—he loved his little sister dearly.

"Fine, fine, I won't say another word! I get it: our father didn't give his consent to the marriage…"

"He did."

"…?" Rano just gave him a questioning look.

"Father decided to marry Malika off to… our brother Bahadir."

Rano looked at Amin again in surprise—this time, her eyes showed even more astonishment than before.

"And that happened before my recent encounter with her, before I started talking with Malika in a friendly way! After that meeting, I can't stop thinking about her. I tried to convince myself otherwise but can't… Naturally, afterward, I wanted to talk to Father and explain everything—to say, 'If it's all right with you, please let me—not my brother—court the lovely daughter of your friend, Said Yahyaevich…' But then I thought it through and changed my mind."

"But why?!" It seemed to be a day of endless questions and surprises for Rano. "Why give up so soon, why not fight for your happiness?"

"I reasoned that Bahadir probably suits her better and that she would be happier with him. And compared to her happiness, mine doesn't matter… I know my brother often resents me, envies me in business. Our relationship is still precarious. But I love him. He's my brother—my flesh and blood—and he's very dear to me. So I'll let him have this beautiful Malika. I don't doubt for a second that he'll be quite taken with her. You know why? Because a woman like that can't help but captivate and command enormous respect! And maybe right now he's not entirely worthy of her. But I believe in him. I'm almost certain that in time, marriage to Malika will change him—that Bahadir will become worthy, truly worthy of her, a man who can make her happy!.."

Rano fell silent. This time, she took a good while to process what Amin had said. Finally, when he finished speaking, she shared her thoughts:

"Perhaps, if I were a man in your shoes, I might have done things differently—fought for the one I love and not let anyone else have her. But you're a noble soul, so your logic is your own. And I do care about our little brother Bahadir. He may not be too dependable right now, but he's still family. So, I guess all we can do is hope your decision isn't a mistake. If Malika appeals to Bahadir, and he wants to marry her—which you believe is inevitable—and if Malika herself doesn't mind, since we're in the 21st century, not the Middle Ages, she'll likely be asked her opinion as well, right? Then may they be blessed by the Almighty and have a strong, happy marriage. As for you, dear brother, I'm sure you'll find your other half, destined by heaven, someday! In any case, no matter what decisions you or Bahadir make, you're both my brothers, and I'll always support you."

Amin looked at Rano with brotherly warmth and gratitude.

12

Tashkent, 2014.

"Hello, Mukhitdin! Hi, it's Galina Krikunova."

"Hi, Galya, I recognized your voice. What do you want?"

"How rude and impolite! What's with you? Did you wake up on the wrong side of the bed?"

"It doesn't matter. Sorry if I was rude. Just cut to the chase, please. I've got little time—I need to study for the entrance tests, read lots of theory, and on top of that, I should probably rehearse more for my performance exam on my instrument."

"What field did you pick?"

"Instrumental performance, strings, of course."

"Oh, great, good for you. And Malika—she's also applying to the conservatory, isn't she? Will she be taking the same exams?"

"No, I think she's going in for pop vocals. That track has slightly different entrance requirements than mine. But it'll be easier for her—she's won competitions multiple times, so she'll have certain privileges... But why are you asking me about Malika?!" He suddenly exploded. "You're her friend—go ask her yourself!"

"Fine. Don't get upset. I'll ask her. Honestly, it makes no difference to me—I was just trying to make conversation."

"I don't have time to chat."

"I thought... But, if you're busy..."

"Yes, I'm busy. I don't feel like talking."

"What's the matter?"

"Nothing. None of your business!"

"There you go again with the rudeness… Fine, I'll keep it brief. There's nobody else to help me—you might know this, I live alone. The chandelier in my room broke, so I bought a new one that really needs hanging today. But it's big and heavy. I can't sit in a room with no chandelier—just a bare lightbulb will be glaring in my eyes. And without a strong man's help, I'm out of luck!"

"Hire a 'handyman for an hour' on the internet."

"Thanks for the tip, but I'm not inviting some stranger over to my home, right? God forbid. He might even steal something…"

That broke the dam. Despite his foul mood, Mukhitdin burst out laughing.

"What's there to steal at your place? Are you that rich?"

"No, but still… even inexpensive things could be valuable in a home. Please! It won't take long—ten minutes at most, and I live close by. You were here once with Malika, so you must remember where I live…"

"I do. Apartment thirteen, right? To be honest, though, I really don't feel like going out."

"Mukhitdin, is it so hard for you to do something nice and help out a friend of your friend? Otherwise, I'll have to ask some other gentleman to help with this simple little chore. I always thought you were a real man who wouldn't refuse a weak girl who needs help!"

"Oh, all right, you got me. I'll get dressed and come over. Wait for me."

* * *

"Well, Galya, there you have it—your chandelier's all set. As long as you don't play basketball or ping-pong here, it'll last a hundred years."

"Thank you so much, Mukhitdin! You have a sense of humor…"

"Yeah, humor's all I've got left at this point… Alright, I'm leaving."

"No, no, you can't just leave! Have some tea and candy… And I've got a nice pot of borscht, too! Let me feed you. You must be starving, practicing day and night."

"I'm never hungry," said Mukhitdin curtly.

"Really? Strange. I thought you rarely eat anything—just look how thin you are! Never mind—come on."

Galina tugged him by the arm into the kitchen. He sat on a chair.

"Wash your hands right here in this sink. The faucet in the bathroom is leaking. Maybe sometime you could come fix it too?"

"What do you think I am, a worker from the local housing office?" Mukhitdin almost took offense. "And as for being skinny— it's just my build. I eat normally."

"I don't know, that's how it seemed. You don't dress well, don't pay attention to your appearance… By the way, you never told me about your parents—aren't they just regular folk?"

She walked over to the stove and turned on the gas under the pot of borscht.

"What's it to you?" he replied, surprised. "Planning to marry me or something? Asking all these questions."

"And if I am! Would you take me?" Galina gave him a mischievous grin, then feigned innocence, tossing back her long chestnut hair.

His brow furrowed. Galina quickly tried to dispel the tension:

"I know, I know—you're head over heels for my friend Malika! You'll marry her… if she agrees, right? I'm sure I'm right."

"What are you, stupid?!" he suddenly snapped.

"And did you know, Mukhitdin, that our Malika—"

"I'm asking you!" he became angry again. "Don't talk about her. I'd rather just go home."

"No, you're not going anywhere! Sit down. I have no idea why I can't say a word about Malika. What happened? Did you two have a fight or something?" Galina poured the warmed borscht into a bowl and set it before him.

"No. It's just that I… I did something awful… I really wronged Malika, understand?"

"Not yet. Eat, please, or it'll get cold."

"Thanks… Mmm, it's really good… You cook wonderfully!"

"Glad you like it, especially coming from you. You know, if you come over more often, I'll keep cooking like this—and offer you plenty of other things, too! I think you get my drift. No one's going to bother us here—since I live alone."

"Yes, I'm… too busy. Admission exams are in just a few days! I can't promise anything, so you best not wait. Anyway… I don't even know how I lost control like that with Malika—my head just wasn't on straight."

"Because of her? Wow! What did she do to hook you so?"

"You don't get it. Malika's really beautiful and an extraordinary girl."

"Yeah, yeah, I see. I just don't see what makes me any worse. Why is every guy so stuck on 'Malika, Malika'? Like they're glued to her! I know—she's sweet, kind, patient, and gentle, right?.. You men love it when a pretty-faced woman gazes at you silently, doesn't argue, doesn't scold, doesn't try to outshine you, always shows the utmost respect, yes? While still having her own quiet pride, never clinging to anyone? She must seem unapproachable—thus interesting and intriguing, right? And you decided you were man enough to capture that 'fortress'?"

"I told you—I lost my mind… And I'm not happy about it. I really hurt her. Now Malika won't want to see me or speak to me."

"That'll blow over. She's kind and quick to forgive. I don't know what exactly happened, but I'm sure she'll forgive you soon enough. You'll see. As for you… whether you can forgive her, I'm not sure."

He nearly choked while finishing his soup.

"Forgive her for what? What are you talking about?! Huh?"

"Mukhitdin, are you clueless? Don't you realise what she's always saying about you? Want me to open your eyes about 'your' Malika? She's told me more than once that you're a failure and she's the talented one. She says she'll be hugely successful in music while you remain some obscure, ordinary violinist, doing a handful of small concerts in tiny venues, or working as a modest music teacher… Keep that in mind—she thinks you're just a loser, a nobody."

Mukhitdin stared at Galina in stunned disbelief. He felt deeply hurt and unsettled. Tea and sweets were off the table now.

"Me?! Malika?!! That can't be! You're making it up… Galya, you're her friend and, as far as I know, her closest one. How can you say that about her?"

"It's simple. Everyone in this world, first and foremost, should look out for themselves, their own happiness. Mukhitdin, why would you need her? Look around—there are so many other pretty, affectionate girls, much better than Malika."

"You mean yourself, I suppose?"

"Maybe I do mean myself. Malika doesn't love you, but I've had a thing for you for ages. Why bother with her, especially after some unpleasant incident… Be my boyfriend!"

"I don't believe you. Malika could never even think something like that about me, let alone say it…"

"But she did! Don't believe me if you don't want to—your choice. That girl isn't worth someone like you! But I'll be here waiting. I can tell you'll come to me eventually."

Leaving Galina's place, Mukhitdin was shaken to his core.

Before meeting with Galina, he'd felt guilty toward Malika, but now he was convinced that she—Malika—was the one at fault, the cause of everything. He felt a profound hatred toward her, believing for the first time that he had been cruelly and wickedly betrayed—that his pride had been wounded—and by whom? The girl he loved…

"Could she really have said that about me? How do I come to terms with that? How can I believe it's true?!?", he thought in distress.

13

Malika scored very high on her admissions exams and was admitted to the conservatory on a tuition-free scholarship.

Mukhitdin, on the other hand, "bombed" his tests, failing to earn enough points to even enroll on a paid contract. He also performed poorly during his practical exam, stumbling over all the assigned pieces. After that, he fared no better on the tests. Nothing seemed to go right for him, and he walked around looking like he'd been plunged in ice-cold water.

In honor of his clever daughter's success, Malika's father organized a festive family dinner. This meant extra work for the Mumtazovs' housekeeper, Larisa, since everything had to be especially tasty, beautiful, and filling that day.

After dinner, Said Yahyaevich invited his beloved daughter into a separate room for an important conversation.

"Malika, my dear child, you've made your mother and me very happy. I have no doubt you'll continue to study just as brilliantly throughout your entire time at the conservatory…"

"Papa, it's not just my conservatory," Malika said with a laugh.

"Well, from now on you can consider it yours. We Mumtazovs, wherever we may be and whatever we do, never disgrace ourselves—we always have to show the highest standards and the very best results. You and I have spoken of this before, and I see that you're setting your sights on exactly that—striving to be the top student in your class. Understood?"

"Yes, I understand, Papa."

"But I don't just mean grades and scores. I'm talking about attaining true knowledge, skills, and mastery. You should become so proficient at your craft—like an old artisan who's inherited his trade from ancestors, right along with their genes—that you don't even have to think about 'technique,' which must become second nature to you, perfected to the highest degree. Then you can create real art that borders on the miraculous."

"Thank you for such valuable advice, Papa! I'll remember it. The teachers at my music college have said something similar. But you've expressed the meaning on a deeper level."

"Good. Now I want to talk to you about something else. You'll have to combine your studies with family life."

Malika looked at her father in surprise.

"Papa, but I am living in a family already!"

"Yes, but I mean your own family hearth. I know, my girl, it's tough to both excel in your studies and be married—especially for a young woman. But your mother and I will help you however we can. Financially, you and your husband won't have to worry about anything—at least, unlike many other students, you won't need to work while studying. That's already a big relief, right?"

"R…right…" Malika barely managed to utter, still reeling from the shock.

"Your job will be your family. You've turned nineteen now, daughter. Which means that a proper age for marriage has come forth. Of course, you're beautiful and smart, and I, as your father, am very proud of you. But in today's world, it becomes harder each year for a young woman to marry. Your mother's told me more than once how many pliable, attractive but single women she works with. No one will marry them at thirty or forty years old! They're not old ladies at all; they keep house perfectly, they support themselves, so they're self-sufficient in every way. But the main thing that is always valued is the youth of the bride. And as a parent, I have no right to let my only child 'age out' and become an 'old maid'! Do you understand?"

Malika nodded in silence, struggling to keep tears at bay. She had absolutely no desire to marry. Meanwhile, Said Yahyaevich went on:

"That's why your mother and I decided to introduce you to a young man from a good family. And just the other day, my good friend Abdulla Rustamovich Fattakhov offered to unite our families by marriage. He has a wonderful, very fine son!"

Malika looked at her father, baffled.

"Papa, may I ask a question?"

"Of course, my dear! Go ahead."

"Could we wait at least a year or two? After all, I've only just been admitted to the university. Soon classes will start, and they'll take a lot of my time and energy…"

"You see, I'd like to arrange your marriage before the school year begins. I don't think there's much point in dragging it out."

"Papa! Have you already decided everything for me?"

"No, not at all. If you absolutely can't stand the young man, I'll nullify all my commitments—despite my deep respect for Abdulla-aka… But please, at least meet him! They're a wonderful family, and their son already works, helping his father in business. He's got a good head on his shoulders… You do remember my friend's sons, don't you?"

Suddenly, Malika recalled Amin, who had rescued her not long ago—and she brightened, feeling some relief in her heart. He was such a kind person—intelligent, compassionate, friendly! Granted, he was no longer that young. But then again, he wasn't old either…

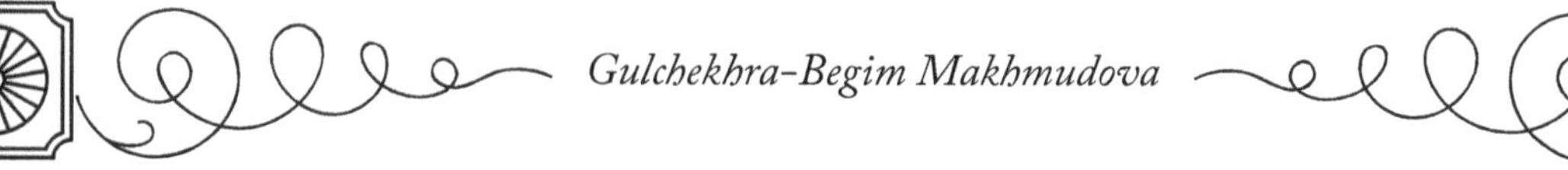

Could he be her prospective fiancé?.. Or maybe it was Mr. Fatta-hov's other son? She couldn't remember his name…

"So, this guy, what's his name?"

"You'll find out when you meet him and have a chat in a café—get to know him better yourself!"

"All right, fine. I agree, but only to see him and talk, okay?"

"Good, my girl. You're a sensible one—you understand your father. Trust me! Your Papa would never suggest something harmful for his beloved daughter."

14

When Abdulla Rustamovich came home from work, he quickly noticed that his wife, Mukhabbat, was out of sorts. She was setting the dinner table for him.

"Why haven't you laid out a plate for yourself?" Abdulla Rustamovich asked. "Have you already eaten without me?"

"No, I haven't eaten."

"Well then, sit and keep me company! You know I don't like to eat alone. After all, isn't the point of having a family to avoid dining in solitary gloom?" He smiled beneath his gray mustache.

"Family—exactly what I wanted to talk to you about," Mukhabbat began, speaking somewhat indirectly.

"All right, I'm listening. Is something wrong?"

His wife stayed silent. She lowered herself onto the chair beside him, frowned slightly, and fixed her gaze on a single spot somewhere off to the side.

"You're acting a little strange today. What's going on?" Abdulla Rustamovich asked, unable to bear the silence any longer.

"Our daughter, Rano, told me today about something you all kept hidden from me!" Mukhabbat replied, her voice tinged with hurt.

"What was hidden, and who's included in 'you all'? Could you speak more plainly?"

"'You all' is you—my dear husband—and also our sons, Amin and Bahadir! And what was hidden? You've apparently decided to marry off our Bahadir! You didn't even consult me, his own mother!

So my opinion doesn't matter to anyone and means next to nothing?.."

She didn't raise her voice, but her displeasure was evident. Indeed, she was close to tears.

Abdulla Rustamovich set down his fork and said wearily:

"Come on now—honestly! You're upset over a trifle…"

"The fate of my own son, something as important as his marriage—is that just a trifle?.. I have to thank my daughter for sharing this news with me, and she only found out for herself recently… Tell me plainly: when did all this start in our family?"

"You're talking in riddles again, Mukhabbat. Forgive me—I'm not a fool, but after a long day's work, my head's not so quick. Explain it clearly—what's 'started'?"

"Distrust. Remember how happily we lived in the first years of our marriage? We always told each other everything that was on our minds—our joys, our troubles, our hopes and hurts. What happened? Why does it feel like we've grown distant? Or rather, like you've grown distant, as if you're a stranger…"

"Don't be ridiculous," he said, smiling again good-naturedly.

"I've spent a lot of time thinking about it. And I've concluded that there must be someone else in your life! It's better if you tell me the truth: you've found another woman, haven't you? Who is she?"

Abdulla Rustamovich froze, staring at her in astonishment.

"What on earth? Have you lost your mind, woman? I don't have, and have never had any other woman! Look at me—old, entirely gray, overweight—who would want me except my beloved, most beautiful Mukhabbat, eh?"

"Really?.."

"But, of course! I just didn't want you worrying needlessly

about our son, and I was afraid you wouldn't agree to part with Bahadir… But if you like, he and his wife can stay with us! Only, promise me you'll stop spoiling him. Make sure he doesn't walk all over you. He's a grown man—he needs to live his own life!"

"But why are you out late so many evenings? I can't help worrying."

"I care deeply about my work, dear wife. In business, everything has to be supervised, kept constantly under close watch, because our competitors—of which there are more and more—never sleep! So, we have to work hard. Fortunately, the children are grown, and all three of them help me in their own ways. I'm very glad about that."

"I understand."

"As you know, I never forced them into this particular business; I gave them the opportunity and allowed them each to choose their own path. Only God can say if any of them will someday decide to change professions and pursue something else that maybe suits them better. Even then, I wouldn't stand in their way. But for now, they're helping me in my business, which is a big advantage for our whole family. While they're here, I can teach them a great deal—and not just about business. I'm talking about life in general. Of course, a day will come—and it's not far off—when each may want complete freedom and independence. Then who'll I leave all this to? I'm not getting any younger, you know. I'm hoping at least one will take over the reins of the company! I know that our youngest, Bahadir, once told me he dreams of it, as he has let it slip once. He's certainly not dumb, but he's still 'green,' not ready yet. Amin, of course, shows more promise than anyone, but right now, he can't single-handedly manage all the responsibilities nor run the entire business. He's clever, competent, thoroughly dependable, and I can always rely on him. He's currently helping me more than the others. But…"

"But what?.."

"Amin's a romantic, as you know, Mukhabbat. Sometimes he can be fooled, duped even, despite his intelligence. Nowadays, success in many companies' dealings often relies on all sorts of strategic and tactical ploys. For instance, a rival firm might send an undercover 'industrial spy'—someone who poses as a beneficial addition to our team—and Amin, with his guilelessness, wouldn't see through it. He'd befriend an enemy or competitor! And that guy could gain rapport and trust and find out all our commercial secrets. That's why I say he's also 'green' for running the company on his own. In that respect, Bahadir's disposition may be better suited. He's more…how should I say it accurately… well, more down-to-earth."

"Yes, our boy Bahadir is indeed a realist."

"Exactly. His head isn't up in the clouds, and he knows how to approach people with a healthy dose of caution—he's good at gauging their worth. If only he'd become more serious about life in general! Then he'd rise high—he could do more than run a single firm. He could lead an entire holding company, multiple enterprises, as their director and founder. That's why I decided to marry him off—and not just to anyone, but to a smart, admirable young woman who is also a beauty. I'm talking about Dr. Said Mumtazov's daughter, Malika. Of course, Bahadir doesn't know yet—I was planning to tell him this evening."

"Malika? Yes, I remember her. She's a wonderful girl, so polite and pleasant. But what makes you think she'll agree to marry our Bahadir?"

"To start with, she's an obedient daughter to her father. After

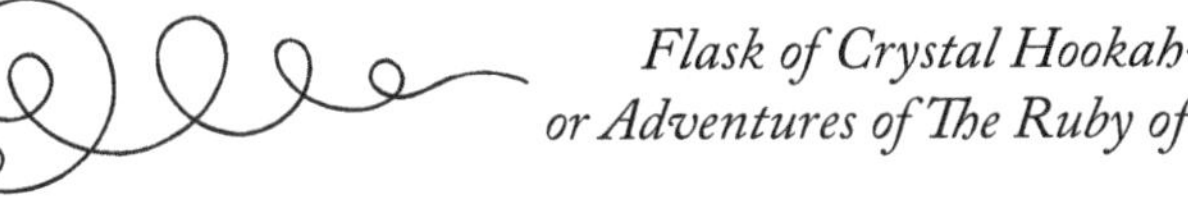

all, Said and I have been friends for years…" Abdulla Rustamovich smiled again.

"All right," Mukhabbat nodded. "but are there any more arguments in favor of this marriage?"

"Our Bahadir might be far from perfect, and I don't like his excessive habit of chasing after girls, but still—you know as well as anyone—he's kind and decent. And, as everyone says, and we can see for ourselves, he's also handsome—just like his mother!" Abdulla Rustamovich planted a kiss on his wife's cheek. "I'm confident Malika will like him well enough not to reject him. And I'm sure he'll be pleased with her too. But if he vehemently refuses, or if they simply don't click, then… I'll look for another good bride for him soon enough. One way or another, the time has come for him to marry. Twenty-one is the perfect time for it. I'm convinced marriage will do him good."

"Well, then I have no objections," Mukhabbat replied, smiling in turn.

Abdulla Rustamovich paused in thought, then added:

"You know, my dear, why is it better for the children of close friends to marry each other..?"

"Why?"

"Because it would shame them to ever betray or abandon one another! They'd feel embarrassed not only before their parents but, down the road, before their memory as well…"

15

Larisa Solodkina came to the Mumtazov family's apartment twice a week to clean and cook enough meals to last them for several days. She hadn't been working for them very long, but everyone was pleased with her, especially Sitora. It was Sitora who hired Larisa and dealt with her the most. Sitora believed Larisa had a cooperative, conflict-free, and unpretentious nature—traits not always found in people who haven't reached great heights in life. Larisa made things easy, comfortable, and dependable.

Sitora had always been careful with her personal belongings. Even around close friends she completely trusted—and certainly around housekeepers, including Larisa, for whom she felt great appreciation—she never left money or valuables in plain sight.

But today, Sitora was preoccupied, feeling scattered, and a bit absentminded. One of the boxes containing her jewelry was left out, resting openly on her vanity.

As Larisa went about her chores, she noticed her mistress's condition and approached her:

"Sitora Kadyrovna, forgive me if I'm overstepping, but... is something the matter?"

"No. Why do you ask?" Sitora, startled, broke out of her reverie.

"It's just that you seem out of sorts. Is everything okay with Malika? She hasn't come home yet."

"Yes, Malika... My daughter! She went on a date with her fiancé today... Her father took her. If I'm honest, I'm so worried about her."

"Please don't fret, Sitora Kadyrovna! Malika's a bright, beautiful, kind-hearted girl—nothing bad will happen to her!"

"Just the opposite, unfortunately. In life, it's often exactly the sweet and beautiful ones who face the most trials. It's true, though, that the wise among them do their best to sidestep any dangers… You see, Larisa, I'm just not ready to marry off my only daughter so soon!"

"But why…? Don't you want her to be happy?"

"Of course I do! I absolutely want her happiness. That's not what I meant. I'm not at all opposed to her getting married. Just not now! I don't feel ready to let my child go into another family, even if it's the family of my husband's friend. Nobody can ever replace your own parents. And can a mother-in-law really become a second mother to her new daughter-in-law? Never."

"But Malika can still come visit you, right?"

"She will, of course. But it's not the same. My girl won't be under my constant watch or protection… though she's hardly listened to me much for some time now. She's grown independent. Evidently, she's an adult, but to me she's the very best, she's so obedient and calm, and she loves her father and me dearly. She never backtalks to us. How will her new family treat her? Will they cherish and love her the way her father and I do? And this fiancé… who can guarantee he'll be worthy, that he won't mistreat my daughter or upset her?.. He comes from a respectable family; he's my husband's friend's son."

"Well then, why are you so worried? Everything will be alright!"

"If only I had your confidence. I've heard whispers about this young man being idle, a spendthrift, chasing every girl he sees…"

"But maybe Malika and this fellow won't like each other at all," Larisa suggested. "In that case, there probably won't be a wedding, right? So perhaps there's no need to worry prematurely…"

"Yes, that's what my husband said too: if they don't take to each other, they won't marry."

"There you go! And you were so anxious. Everything's bound to work out, I'm sure of it. Everything will be alright with your girl. Who knows—maybe he's not such a bad guy after all!"

"God grant that it's so. Thank you, Larisa—you're a good-heart-ed person. You've practically become one of the family. You're sensible, intelligent, and I've noticed you're fond of reading. It's good that you have spent so many years working in a library! How did you end up as a housekeeper?"

"I guess it's just how life turned out. The salary at the library was terribly small so I had to find another line of work… Thank you for your kind words, Sitora Kadyrovna. It's nice to hear, though I haven't really said anything special… Some people think I'm not very bright, just because I'm blonde. You know what they say about blondes."

"They're mistaken. Larisa, if you've finished everything around the house, feel free to head home early today."

"Wonderful, thanks! Oh, what a gorgeous necklace that is, if you don't mind my asking. I wouldn't normally pry, but I've never seen such beauty with my own eyes. Those are rubies, right? Genuine ones?.. Or are they spinels?"

"What necklace? …Ah, this? Yes, it's a genuine ruby necklace—gold with rubies and diamonds. It's going to be a gift from me, Said, and both grandmothers to our daughter. Firuz-begim passed it on to me today. When our hopes for our daughter's happiness come true, we'll present it to her at the wedding…"

"Really? That's a wonderful gift! Obviously, it's something of great value! Malika will be so thrilled; I'm sure she'll love it!"

"I agree. Rubies are indeed beautiful and expensive, but that's not the main thing. They're said to have many beneficial qualities. People say they bring strength, luck, and happiness. I really do want my daughter to be genuinely happy..."

"Yes, rubies have magical properties— it's the gemstone of power. The rulers of the East all wore ruby rings as tokens of power, success, and boundless energy... I read in the library that the throne of Shah Jahan held the largest ruby in the world, and afterward, the Queen of Great Britain turned it into a necklace... It's very similar to yours... It's amazing that a necklace like that should be here with you!.. I believe in 2012... well, maybe I'm mixing things up..."

"What are you talking about? I'm not following."

"No, no—nothing..."

16

Tashkent–Moscow, 2012

From childhood, Misha Leonidov, at the age of twenty-five, was used to fending for himself.

He had long understood that he was never particularly wanted by his parents. His father, Nikolai, worked as the chief accountant for several firms in Tashkent and for a time supported the family quite comfortably, even lavishly. But one day—far from a pleasant one for him—a routine prosecutor's inspection uncovered serious financial manipulations and a large shortage in the accounts of one of Nikolai Leonidov's main client companies. The director of that company, who had orchestrated the embezzlement, promptly washed his hands of the affair, thrusting the accountant squarely into the legal crosshairs. As a result, Nikolai was "locked up"—or more simply, wound up behind bars for a good, long time.

As for Misha's mother, the moment his father was jailed and the family income abruptly, dramatically dwindled (while expenses, as often happens, stayed the same), young and still rather attractive Natalia—spoiled by her life of luxury—had no desire to share her husband's sad fate. She took off with a new suitor to a seaside locale. She did so without a second thought, leaving her only son to fend for himself, with no intention of returning from those distant resorts to her native Tashkent. The neighbors immediately labeled her a "flighty loose woman" and a "cuckoo mother," which did nothing to make Misha feel better.

Misha could at least take solace in the fact that, after multiple sales and exchanges, one run-down, single-room apartment in a concrete building was left to him—almost devoid of basic conveniences but, all the same, his very own place on the outskirts of the city. He had to hustle for real in order to survive.

Like many abandoned children, Misha felt that everyone everywhere owed him something. So when he frequently grabbed whatever he found lying around that wasn't tied down, he felt not the slightest pang of conscience—such lofty notions were alien to him. In fact, deep down, he believed he needed to go on using all sorts of life's goods however he could. Yet the sensation of satisfaction and fullness never came, and like an addict continually chasing a bigger fix, Leonidov Junior needed fresh schemes to keep his spirit calm, to feel even a flicker of happiness. The idea that a truly fulfilling personal life could be built without deception, cheating, or theft never even crossed Misha's mind.

From early childhood, however, he had been a neat boy; so when he grew up, he never looked ragged or like your average thief or con artist. On the contrary, at first glance, anyone might have taken an immediate liking to him or, at the very least, felt genuine sympathy and possibly pity for his rough childhood. He had the manner of a poor but refined student—very tidy and very pleasant.

Misha never truly learned any practical skill—and he didn't like working. What he did love was thinking, philosophising, and talking up a storm. In other words: persuading, cajoling, and smooth-talking. His face—and especially his eyes—always looked so honest (which could not be said of his soul) that people believed him. Thus he managed more than one scam to his own advantage.

He tried out a variety of jobs and professions, eventually becoming a commission broker—or, in today's more fashionable parlance, a realtor. He learned the business in one firm until they threw him out for fraud and then started working "for himself." Leonidov bought and sold houses and apartments, earning decent money. But, thanks to his habit of living fast and burning through cash, he couldn't seem to save a thing.

Working in real estate led Misha to cross paths with his new boss and patron: head of a large company that operated a chain of stores, cafés, and restaurants—a man all his subordinates (and not just subordinates) simply called "the big boss," or just "the boss." The boss had a special nose for spotting people like Misha—he valued them.

Of course, as was typically the case, things started with one of Misha's deceptions. The boss, through his assistants, wished to purchase yet another suburban townhouse for his private pleasures, without his wife's knowledge. And though tricking the boss was next to impossible—since he himself specialized in tricking others—Misha still managed to push a far-from-ideal property located 120 kilometers from the capital onto this wealthy client, and at a sky-high price, pocketing a tidy sum.

The boss absolutely loathed being swindled. Furious, he demanded that they drag the insolent crook before him.

"You scoundrel, you punk, you worthless nobody!" the boss roared at Misha. "How dare you play games with me?! Who do you think you are?! You have no clue whom you tried to cheat!"

In actuality, Misha hadn't "tried" to cheat the boss—he'd already succeeded. But the boss refused to phrase it that way, as it would have diminished his own prestige. Misha, for his part, didn't like being yelled at or insulted in a loud voice, but to say that these tirades frightened him or stirred his conscience would be an exaggeration. As he listened, he was thinking about the tasty bun and

cup of tea he planned to enjoy while watching a soccer match on TV that evening. He was certain it would happen, no matter this raging uproar now.

"All right," the boss finally addressed one of his young assistants, a fellow named Gosha, "we'll take this… uh… 'entrepreneur' out of his apartment—which he'll sign over to me today—and we'll move him into some tiny dump. Then… Hey, you… What's your name?"

"Mikhail," came the subdued yet dignified reply.

"Mikhail, indeed. You'll work for me now. You'll get a small salary, just enough to scrape by. The rest of what you earn goes into my pocket, paying off your debt for the financial and moral harm you caused. Got it, brainiac? You owe me a lot now!"

Thus, the boss took Misha on as his personal realtor, because after meeting the swindler-agent, the boss decided to seriously jump into this profitable real estate business for himself and needed experienced people to run it.

"Boss, pardon me," Gosha said warily, "but I've got grave doubts about this 'specialist' here. It's clear he's a hard-boiled conman. Can we trust him?"

"I don't trust anyone," the boss assured Gosha. "And don't you worry—you're still my top guy, no one can replace you. As for that slick kid Misha, let him break his back working for me. Then we can toss him out afterward."

To ensure the wily scoundrel wouldn't flee from the boss, some beefy guards kept a constant eye on him. In other words, the boss's personal (or "pocket") agent was kept on a tight leash. Every one of Misha's deals was strictly watched and audited.

Things might have gone smoothly for the boss, since Leonidov pulled off a few very profitable deals on his behalf, if not for Misha's freedom-loving spirit and his insatiable lust for money. He wanted to free himself from this hated, drawn-out yoke as soon as possible.

So one day, entrusted with a large sum of the boss's money to purchase a "prime real estate" property, Misha managed to outsmart the security detail assigned to him (naturally, the boss didn't trust Misha with anything of value) and promptly escaped with the funds to Russia. Specifically, he headed to the grand and beautiful city of Moscow.

* * *

In Moscow, having arrived with the large sum of money he'd stolen from the boss, Misha Leonidov found himself unable to resist even bigger temptations than before. Restaurants, women, cars, and all sorts of entertainment were part of his standard routine. Soon the money, almost unnoticed, began to run out. And with it, all the girlfriends he'd acquired scattered like leaves in the wind.

Misha realized he'd have to "work" again.

But then, sitting around one day in the small apartment he was renting—no longer as posh as the place he could initially afford—he happened to hear on the news about the arrival in Russia's capital of a unique and, more importantly, extremely valuable exhibition from Kuwait: "Treasury of the World: The Jewels of India from the Age of the Great Mughals."

"Well, treasures are treasures, art is art—no big deal," he thought. Yet some inquisitive and forthright journalists, who had already dug up and shared the details with anyone ready to listen, mentioned that among the pieces was one particularly precious item—a gold necklace set with the authentic, ancient Temur Ruby and diamonds!

They reported that for a long time, this ruby necklace had been part of the British Crown Jewels, kept in the Indian Room at Buckingham Palace, but recently it had been purchased by the Kuwaiti Sheikh Al-Sabah. The organizer of the exhibition in Moscow was the sheikh's wife, Princess Hissa. Judging from the photographs, the ruby was so magnificent that you couldn't take your eyes off it and digging through the internet, Misha discovered its other name—"Hiraj-i-Alam," meaning "Tribute of the World"— and learned that this famed ruby weighed in at 352 carats (or 361 metric carats), an enormous size indeed.

Ever appreciative of beauty in all its forms, Misha felt a fire spark in his eyes—and elsewhere—upon hearing this news.

An "enterprising fellow," hardly devoid of certain talents, who desperately needed more money for the future happiness he envisioned, Misha decided to get down to business.

Of course, it wouldn't be straightforward to slip such a costly item from beneath the noses of the formidable Kuwaiti security detail and no less formidable Russian guards. Still, Misha always had a special knack for this sort of thing, along with an extraordinary cunning.

He knew that first, the ruby necklace would be taken to the Assumption Belfry of the Moscow Kremlin. Misha understood that stealing the jewel there was out of the question—far too risky, and he'd never been one to roll the dice so boldly. He preferred calmer, more reliable routes. So he decided to wait until the necklace was transferred to a smaller, lesser-known museum in Moscow.

That's precisely what happened. In this little museum, most of the attendants were elderly pensioners who, though trying to be vigilant—since they needed to justify being there—would hardly be a match for Misha's slyness and resourcefulness. In the end, by deceiving and outsmarting altogether more than twenty people who'd been guarding the treasure within the modest museum or along its route there, Misha managed to swipe it—just before the police could arrive.

He arranged the theft so skillfully that no one even suspected him. At least for a while, he could sleep with a sense of security.

The young man decided that keeping the necklace in any storage room or a bank was too dangerous, because it was surely already being sought after. Any storage clerk or bank employee would promptly alert the authorities about such a valuable find, obligations to client confidentiality notwithstanding—and without hesitation, they'd turn Leonidov over. Therefore, for the time being, Misha resolved to stash the necklace in a secret spot right in his own apartment and begin searching in earnest for a jeweler—or, better yet, a wealthy buyer—to whom he could sell this rare treasure at a hefty price.

* * *

Meanwhile, the head boss, furious that Misha Leonidov had slipped away, ordered his hulking henchmen to dig the slippery fellow out from "underground" if need be and drag him before the boss's very eyes, no matter where he was. Now Misha owed the boss even more than before, and the boss intended to personally "shake down" Mikhail by "cleaning up" that insolent mug of his, convinced that Mikhail fully deserved it.

It took some time, but the boss's men did track Misha down in Russia's main capital. When they found him, they pinned him to the wall—both literally and figuratively. Naturally, Misha had no desire to hand over the precious necklace with the Temur Ruby, which he had acquired at such great effort, so he did not utter a single word to the boss's henchmen about possessing this treasure.

However, before sending them off and entrusting Misha to their "care," the boss gave a quick warning that this young man might pull any manner of trick. He told them to search Misha's place thoroughly—whether it was a rundown shack or a hovel—and that is exactly what they did.

They did find something! Granted, they had been searching for money, but there was virtually no money in the house. Instead, they discovered a remarkably beautiful necklace with rubies and diamonds. The associates had doubts about whether this thing was really worth anything, because they knew nothing about its value and were not particularly knowledgeable about these matters. But when they called the boss and briefly described the find to him, he was so delighted and intrigued that he demanded they fly straight from Moscow to Tashkent—together with Mikhail and, above all, the valuable necklace.

"Try not to beat Mikhail too badly for his stunts," the boss said. "He's so weak, he might keel over and die if you overdo it. But remember, he's a sly one, and don't let him slip away with that necklace for anything."

Little did the henchmen suspect that their boss was extremely knowledgeable about gemstones and absolutely adored rubies, knowing practically everything about them. He had a couple of rubies, albeit small of his own at home. But he had never even dared dream of an ancient stone carved with the names of six Mughal emperors! All he did know was that if he ever sold the necklace containing the Temur Ruby, it would be valued far higher than his little rubies could ever be…

But when Misha and the necklace finally arrived, and the boss discovered where Misha had gotten it, he was aghast. Not even a seasoned character like him could have expected this, and not from a rascal like Misha! The boss had hoped the necklace had simply been lost and that Misha had stumbled upon it. But to keep a stolen piece—even if it was not stolen in another country—was dangerous. The boss had no intention of moving into a prison cell for permanent residency. Especially since the ruby necklace belonged to a world-famous figure of immense wealth—and thus, no small amount of influence! The Kuwaiti intelligence services had likely turned the entire globe upside down over this incident!

Yet something about it all puzzled the boss. Suddenly he remembered what it was.

First, numerous sources discussing this necklace claimed it was not really the Temur Ruby at all, but a strikingly similar, albeit less valuable, Ulugbek Ruby. But that was the lesser problem. Second, Russia's media had been completely silent about the theft! So…was no one even looking for the necklace?

That was more than strange.

The boss had a connection: David Iosifovich Vitstein, a savvy antique dealer and jeweler. The boss went to see him personally to figure out what to do and to get an appraisal of the piece Misha Leonidov had so cleverly obtained.

"Well, my dear friend," Vitstein said to the boss, having examined the item closely, "I'm afraid I must disappoint you. It's a counterfeit! An excellent, brilliant copy, modeled on a magnificent original from the Great Mughal era—the necklace with the Temur Ruby. The ruby itself—or, more precisely, as determined back in 1851, the spinel—dates to the fourteenth century, a gem of rare beauty and quality. But as you know, its primary value lies in the inscriptions on it, bearing the names of emperors and their wise sayings. And as much as it pains me to tell you, I assure you this piece here isn't the genuine article; it's just a replica. It was made in the twentieth century!"

The boss fell silent, turning the matter over in his mind. He kept his emotions bottled up—he did not want to reveal them to some jeweler, however friendly. He merely said:

"David Iosifovich, I trust that my visit with this neck…hmm… this necklace replica remains strictly between us? And here—this is your fee for your services and for your silence."

"Of course, my friend, of course!" the old man replied with a grin, hastily tucking a stack of crisp bills into his jacket pocket. "How could you even ask? My lips are sealed."

Returning to his office, the boss vented his entire fury on Misha, who had been brought before him.

"Where's the real one, you idiot?!"

"Excuse me, the real… The real what?" Misha asked, not quite following.

"The real necklace, you imbecile!!!" the boss roared. "Where is it? Where did you hide it?! You dared to dupe me yet again?!"

For the first time in his life, Misha was truly baffled—and regretted only that he had not consulted a jeweler himself to verify everything. And now—he was once again drowning in trouble, back in Uzbekistan, broke once more, and a "slave" to the boss…

Questions flooded Misha's mind.

"But…how is this possible?" he thought. "There's no way the Kremlin Museum would put a fake on display—it had to be the real thing! So, when and where did the switch happen? In that small museum? Unlikely… Maybe en route, when the necklace and ruby were being transported? Yes, that must be it—the Kuwaitis must have taken precautions. Their special agents stealthily swapped the pieces between two exhibitions! They kept the real treasure for themselves, hidden away somewhere highly secure! That's why there's no international scandal. Ugh, how could I make such a stupid mistake? What a shame! Now I'll be at Nasyrov's beck and call forever..."

Misha's head was spinning. He was dying to know what this "Ulugbek Ruby" was all about. And just how many giant rubies were there, anyway? He thought he would give anything to see and hold the genuine necklace with that precious ruby in his own hands!.. But at this point it was unclear – would it be Temur's ruby?.. Or Ulugbek's ruby?.. Or perhaps another gem linked to one of the great Uzbeks...

17

Agra, 1608.

Arjumand was by no means a naive, foolish girl who trusted anyone and everyone without question. She came from a noble, well-educated family. Despite her youth, Arjumand already knew that people can be unreliable—that they might deceive or disappoint you. She also understood that, at times, even those who sincerely wish to keep their word might fail due to circumstances beyond their control. And yet, for all that, she believed in her beloved, Shah Jahan, with her whole heart! If he had said she would be his wife, then nothing and no one could ever change that decision, because his word was as unbreakable as the Padishah's throne—indeed, as steadfast as the power of the Great Mughals.

Still, the prospect of waiting for her happiness all alone—unable to see or hear from her beloved—was unbearable! It seemed the entire city, all the people, already knew practically every word that had passed between Jahangir and Shah Jahan.

"Shah Jahan still loves me just as before—he told the ruler so!" Arjumand rejoiced. That was the only thing that comforted her. But the long separation weighed heavily on her.

From time to time, Padishah Jahangir took to traveling. And when he journeyed away from the palace, it seemed almost the entire empire would go with him.

This time, he decided to bring a large retinue and his gravely ill first wife, Taj Bibi Sahiba Bilqis Makani—a Rani, or princess of

Indian origin, and the daughter of the Rajput Raja of Marwar. Of late, Taj Bibi had been afflicted by a mysterious, debilitating illness, so she would have preferred to stay in Agra. However, Jahangir insisted that she accompany him. She traveled by elephant, seated beneath a canopy on a pitambar—a special throne-like platform fashioned from wrought gold and precious stones. Following her were other elephants and palanquins bearing the women of the harem, each attended by her own entourage of slave girls, servants, and eunuchs.

Also riding beside the Padishah was his favorite son, Shah Jahan. Ahead of them walked nine elephants, each bearing a rider carrying the banner of the Great Mughals—a lion ready to pounce within a golden circle. Next came four elephants flying green flags adorned with the image of the sun. Farther on were white stallions with golden saddles, stirrups, and bridles. One of the riders carried a banner embroidered with Padishah Jahangir's title, "Conqueror of the World." Another rider held a drum, beating it occasionally to announce the approach of the imperial caravan.

Several slaves ran in front of Jahangir's palanquin, sprinkling perfumed water to keep the ruler's path fragrant and less dusty.

Of course, state affairs could not be set aside, even during such journeys. Consequently, thirty elephants, eighty camels, and twenty wagons were laden with all sorts of important documents. Riding a short distance from the Padishah were four viziers, their horses likewise burdened with official papers—documents holding information the sovereign might need at any moment. Several times a day, the viziers also made new entries in the Padishah's autobiographical work, the Tuzuk-i-Jahangiri.

Walking on foot alongside the viziers were three other men charged with measuring the distances covered by the caravan, calculating how far it traveled between one waypoint and another. Another man carried an hourglass and a gong, striking the gong every hour to mark the passing of time.

Following orders from her father and grandfather, Arjumand joined the retinue of the Padishah's wife, protected by a modest guard. She complied without protest.

Arjumand believed this journey would help distract her from her dark thoughts. Moreover, she knew that her Shah Jahan was riding at the head of the caravan! Oh, how she longed to see him, to touch him. The anguish of his absence refused to leave her. Yet she still hoped: perhaps fate would grant her a happy chance to meet him. But that imperial splendor stretched on for kilometers, keeping her beloved so far away. How much longer could she bear such an intolerable separation?

* * *

Arjumand had no interest in chatting with the women who delighted in travel, nor did she wish to waste time idly with them. Her soul was overcome with sorrow and yearning. At last, she gathered her courage and asked her most trusted servant to slip away under the cover of night, moving ahead of the caravan to find Shah Jahan. Of course, his tent was guarded, and getting close to him was anything but easy. Yet the girl's love-struck heart held out hope for a miracle…

And a miracle occurred! A few hours later, just before dawn, her servant woke her.

"Aghachi, my lady," he said, "the prince is waiting for you in a secluded spot. Come with me!"

Arjumand raced to this meeting as though she were in a dream, scarcely aware of her own footsteps. Even though it was still dark, with only distant lanterns flickering, she recognized him at once—her beloved, her prince!

Shah Jahan hurried toward her.

"Oh, Arjumand!" he exclaimed softly yet fervently. "How I have missed you!"

She could not hold back her tears.

"Please, my dearest, don't cry…" he said. "Here I am, right in front of you! Though I risked my life to come, I'd gladly give it up for you. It's just that if my father finds out, he'll be furious. Right now, he's against our… well…"

The prince trailed off, loath to hurt her with the unvarnished truth. Though he knew she understood a great deal already, he felt it would be cruel to remind her of all the painful obstacles stacked against them.

"Arjumand, my dearest, my soul's delight, my happiness!"

He savored each fleeting moment of closeness to his beloved—kissing her hands, her eyelids, her forehead, neck, and hair, holding her tightly yet tenderly in his arms. "Forgive me for everything! You must think me all talk—powerless, not only over soldiers and servants, but over my own promises. But believe me: if it were in my power, I would fulfill my vow at once. I swear to you, that day will come when I keep my word! But not yet… Are you very angry with me?"

"No, no, my love. How could I be? I understand everything… I love you. So very much."

"You're an angel. And still, I beg you—forgive me! I thought you'd turn away, refuse to see me, since I haven't come for so long…"

"I would never turn away! But have been waiting for even the slightest word from you…"

"Alas, I couldn't send one. They track my every move; my life isn't my own. Even now they are probably searching for me, and we won't be allowed to talk long… I feared, more than anything, that you might stop loving me—that you wouldn't wait, that you'd grow disillusioned, forget me… or that, over this year we've been apart, you would marry someone else. After all, I know that your age is of the essence – you're already thirteen, am I right?"

"Yes, my prince. And you're sixteen—also of marrying age?"

"I am. I didn't want to tell you, but… soon they may force me to marry. Against my will! It feels like a death sentence, Arjumand! I've told my father I love only you, that I will marry no one but you—that you must at least be my first wife, the mother of my sons, my heirs. But father… Forgive me; he forbade it. I'm the Shahzade, and I have to obey the Padishah's commands, especially since he is my father. In our land, who can defy their parents? And I, all the more, cannot. What example would I set for our subjects if I disobeyed? Defiance and rebellion against authority is the start of chaos. We Uzbeks, the Great Mughals, always strive to keep order—at home and throughout the world. I'm required to marry a Persian princess—it's a matter of politics."

Arjumand could not bring herself to say how much it hurt to hear all of this. Of his impending marriage to another woman, even if it was forced, even if it was for the empire's sake. What if she told him the truth – that she would willingly become nothing more than his concubine, his servant? No, he would think her frivolous and lose all respect for her… Besides, she was from a noble family and had to maintain her dignity. Yet her love for him was so immense that she would have served him gladly! Little did she know that he felt the same depth of devotion, that he too was ready to be her slave forever…

She caressed his shoulders and pressed her lips to the faint stubble of his cheeks. He kept holding her in a fierce yet gentle embrace.

"My beloved, I don't know how to write poetry like my father Jahangir, but I want to share with you some verses by one of my ancestors, the great Mughal and great poet, Babur. I substituted my name for his, for it's as though these lines were written about us—about my love for you, my beautiful Arjumand! Here, listen:

Without my moon-faced beloved, the sunlight holds no brightness;
Sugar itself lacks sweetness without her, whose sweetness
I have praised.
Without that slender beauty—like a cypress arrow
piercing my heart—
Without my rose-cheeked one, the roses themselves have neither
fragrance nor color.
What purpose would paradise serve me? All I desire is to be with her.
Why seek another refuge in some other realm's garden?
They might behead you, O Jahan, for her sake,
But never could they sever this heart from its beloved!

"How beautiful…" Arjumand smiled through her tears. "It is lovely. Thank you… Do you truly love me so deeply, my prince?"

"I swear it!" he said, dropping to his knees at her feet and bowing his head, once again showering her hands with ardent kisses. "We shall be together—believe me! Otherwise, I am not Shah Jahan. I have no intention of breaking my promise. Just trust me, and wait. I do not know how long, but wait. One day, I will rule this empire, and you shall be my queen, and our son shall be the heir… Of course, I cannot force you. If you wish to marry someone else—"

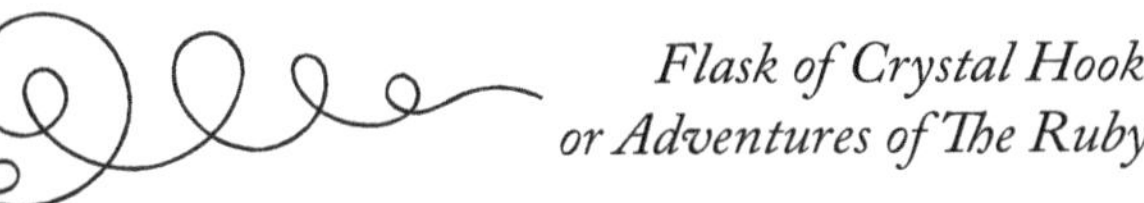
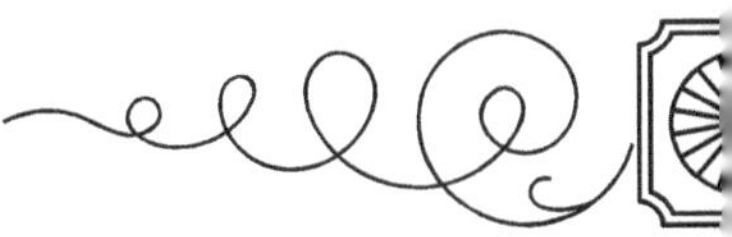

"Hush, Shahzade!" she softly covered his mouth with her hand. "Don't say such a thing. Without you, there is no reason for me to live. If they force me to marry another, I will die."

"Oh no, no! I would sooner die than see you come to harm. If people only knew how hard this is for me—how it torments me! But the time will come, my beloved Arjumand, I swear it, when we are happy!"

* * *

Suddenly, Arjumand's servant approached them.

"How dare you interrupt us?" she exclaimed—not angrily, but in startled surprise.

"Aghachi, I can see soldiers from the Padishah's guard galloping this way! I've already heard there's an uproar in the camp. Shahzade, it appears they've come for you! It seems your father has been looking for you…"

"Forgive me, my love! Hurry back to your tent so you're not subject to everyone's scrutiny and my father's wrath! Remember what I told you: wait for me and believe…"

And with that, Shah Jahan quickly slipped away.

The Padishah Jahangir's guards drew up to the prince and dismounted.

"Your Highness," one of them said, "may I ask why you are here alone, without an escort or even servants?"

"What insolence, soldier! How dare you speak to me so? Have you forgotten you're talking to the crown prince of the Empire?! I don't get it, how did you find me?"

"Forgive me, Your Highness. And do not be angered that we trouble you at such a late hour, but the sovereign has ordered us to bring you to him—immediately!”

"Has something happened?"

"Pardon me—I do not know… But our ruler is still awake."

"Very well, let us go."

He mounted his horse and rode off with the soldiers.

* * *

Shah Jahan asked the guard posted outside Jahangir's tent to announce his arrival.

"Your Majesty, His Highness Shah Jahan is here!"

"Show him in."

Shah Jahan gave his sword and dagger to the guard before entering. Even he—Jahangir's favorite son—was not permitted into the ruler's quarters carrying any weapon. Caution was never out of place.

"You called for me, Father?"

"Yes, my son," the Padishah replied. His face was taut, displeased, agitated. "Where have you been all this time?! Whenever you're urgently needed, you're nowhere to be found!"

Shah Jahan wanted to argue that he had spent countless hours—especially on this journey—right by his father's side, but he only asked:

"I've heard something happened, dear Father?"

"Yes, something has happened. A serious problem!"

The Padishah paused, taking his time as he sipped his strong wine. Shah Jahan sensed that his father had some hidden motive or plan—something not yet clear to the prince—and that he was stalling, unwilling to reveal everything at once. Shah Jahan had no right to hurry the Padishah; he waited patiently until his father

chose to say what he deemed necessary. Jahangir did not offer his son a seat, so the prince stood, half-bowed in deference.

"My son, can you tell me right now the chief symbol of authority of the Great Mughals?"

"Yes, Father: it is the Mur-Uzak, the Padishah's Seal."

"Correct, very good. But that's not what I mean. Do you know what makes our empire rich and powerful? What gives me, the ruler of this vast empire, the right to regard myself as the Shadow of the Almighty on earth—the Master of the World?"

"Perhaps the vast hoards of treasure that belong to you as the Great Mughal?"

"You're very close to the truth, my son. But to be more precise: not just a sea of riches and jewels, but…two particular stones, each so valuable that one alone could purchase the entire world! No king, shah, sultan, or tsar has enough wealth to buy them from me!"

"I understand, Father. You refer to Humayun's diamond, also called Koh-i-Noor—'Mountain of Light'—and the magnificent Temur Ruby."

"Again, you are correct. Precisely those two. And do you know where they are right now?"

"You entrusted them to me for safekeeping, but—"

"'But' what, Khurram?!" he snapped, addressing the prince by his childhood name, emphasising that he saw him as still a callow youth. "Where are these treasures, then? Pray tell!"

"Father, you took the Koh-i-Noor back from me in 1607, deciding that such a splendid diamond could only remain with you! After that, I myself saw…"

"What did you see?!"

"That you sent a courier to Bengal—and I had the impression he carried away—"

"You only think you saw! You dare accuse or suspect me, the great Padishah and your father, of something?"

"No, no, of course not, Father! I would never...I didn't mean that."

"Very well. Suppose I did indeed take it from you—do you have any document to prove it?"

"No, Father," Shah Jahan answered, hanging his head, dejected and cowed.

"Fine. Now tell me this: where is the splendid, crimson Temur Ruby, engraved with the inscriptions our illustrious ancestors commanded to be carved on that precious stone?"

"That ruby is hidden in the palace at Agra, in my quarters, in a secure place."

"A secure place, you say? A messenger arrived from our palace only minutes ago. He reports your hiding spot was broken into— and the Temur Ruby stolen!"

Hearing this, Shah Jahan fainted on the spot.

"A physician! Quickly, fetch a physician!" Jahangir shouted. He had not expected that his straightforward lesson—one intended to teach the heir to the Padishah's throne, the future master of the empire, to be vigilant, not to trust lightly, and to act with care— would affect Shah Jahan so deeply.

Naturally, Jahangir would never have allowed the two unique jewels, Koh-i-Noor and the Temur Ruby, to vanish. He had only wanted to show his son how vital it was to guard the Great Mughal empire's principal treasures as though they were his very eyes...

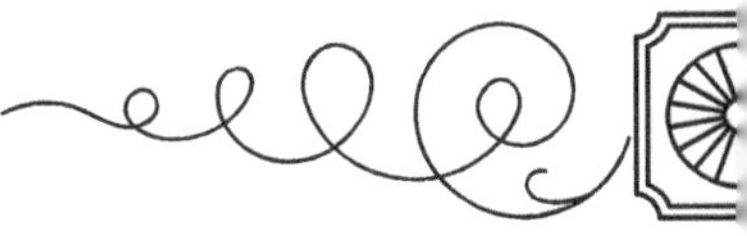

18

Tashkent, 2014

Said Yahyaevich was driving Malika to the restaurant that Abdulla Rustamovich had told him about over the phone. Of course, Said trusted his daughter, and he could have simply let her go on her own, but that day he wanted to show her a little extra kindness and surround her with fatherly care and attention. Besides, he was glad for any chance to see his old friend again, since Abdulla Rustamovich had also mentioned that, out of respect for the Mumtazov family, he would come to the meeting with his son.

Afterward, both fathers would leave their children to talk in private.

Malika both wanted and did not want this meeting. On one hand, she would be happy to see Amin Fattakhov again—if, of course, it turned out to be him! But if it was someone else, maybe his brother, she had to recall what he was even like. She was curious, though… merely curious. It wasn't as though she was about to marry this stranger right away! What kind of person was he? If she didn't like him, Malika thought, it would be no problem convincing her father to abandon this whole wedding plan.

As soon as she and her father pulled up to the restaurant, Malika recognized Abdulla Rustamovich from a distance. He was standing facing the road, talking to a tall, slender man who stood with his back to the road. Malika immediately realized that this man…was not Amin. She felt a slight pang of disappointment, and her eyes lost some of their sparkle.

They drove up to the entrance. The car stopped, and the father and daughter got out of it.

The tall young man had already turned around, but Malika still hadn't seen his face—an Eastern girl wouldn't normally stare a potential groom straight in the eye right from the start!

"Ah, my dear friend!" Abdulla Rustamovich warmly greeted Said Yahyaevich.

"Good evening! How's your health?" Said responded with the same warmth. "This must be Bahadir! Hello, hello, son! How are you? It's been a while since I last saw you."

So that's it—that name that starts with 'B'… So, Bahadir! Malika thought to herself.

"Good evening, Said-aka!" Bahadir said with a polite bow and a bright smile. "I'm so happy to see you! I hope you and your entire family are well?"

"Well, I should be asking you that! Have you forgotten who the doctor is here?"

He emphasised the end of his sentence theatrically, and all the men laughed heartily—not that anything was particularly funny, but rather because this warm, meaningful reunion filled them with genuine contentment.

Finally, they remembered Malika—though, in truth, none of them had actually forgotten her; in the East, one never entirely forgets a woman's presence, even if outwardly it may appear she is given a modest place with little attention.

"And here, Abdulla-aka, is my daughter Malika," Said said, in the same joyful tone.

"Yes, yes, of course, my friend!" Abdulla Rustamovich replied, still talking to Said rather than Malika. "A lovely girl! And just look how she's grown! Truly a bride in the making!"

At last, he decided to address the "lovely girl" who had "grown up" and was now a "bride".

"Malika, how are you, my child? I heard you got into the conservatory? Well done! Your father has been boasting about you; he's so proud! …This is my younger son, Bahadir. No need to say 'nice to meet you,' because you've met before, even if you didn't talk much. Today, you'll have a chance to get to know each other better…"

Malika hardly heard any of these pleasantries and reassurances. She was secretly looking at Bahadir, scarcely believing her eyes. It was like magic, like a fairytale. In that moment, she completely forgot all the worries that had been troubling her.

Standing before her was the very person who had appeared in her vision the first time she ever composed a song—a handsome young man with greenish eyes and a trimmed beard and mustache…

Once their fathers had gone, the young man looked directly at her and politely invited her to step inside the restaurant.

When they were seated at a table, just the two of them, Malika realized, as she looked at Bahadir, that she was utterly "lost" and would gladly follow him to the ends of the earth!

Bahadir, for his part, gazed at Malika—now a radiant, extraordinary beauty who had captivated him completely—and found himself unable to look away.

He understood, he felt, that she was forever his destiny and his happiness.

19

Gosha and Roma were meeting Mukhitdin at the Chelsea Pub. A CSKA vs. Zenit match was being broadcast. Gosha and Roma had arrived early, before the match started, while Mukhitdin was running a bit late. The friends ordered some light, non-alcoholic drinks and settled in to watch the game.

"Is Amin coming?" Roma asked Mukhitdin.

"I doubt it… I don't know!" Mukhitdin answered irritably. "I haven't seen him in ages."

"Got it. Same for me and Gosha. Think something's happened to him?"

"Like I told you, I don't know. I don't talk to him anymore!"

"Really?!" Roma was surprised. "You used to cling to him more than anyone else. Weird…"

When the match was over, Gosha turned to Mukhitdin interrogated him with questions:

"Mukhit, why do you go to that cheap café? Sure, it makes sense for me and Roma—we can't afford better. But your dad's loaded. You could be living the high life!"

"Yeah, my father's beyond rich. Could buy up anything. And in some ways, he already has. Only one thing he hasn't bought—and never will—is me."

"Man, come on… How can you talk like that about your own family?"

"To hell with him!" Mukhitdin spat out angrily.

"Take it easy, bro! After all, he's our boss. Don't forget that!"

"Oh, so you two are his loyal 'lapdogs,' right?!" Clearly in a foul mood, Mukhitdin remained upset, and not even an exciting match had managed to lift his spirits.

"What's up with you, man? You're acting like you're about to do something reckless—you've been tense all evening, and now you're throwing around insults. Lucky for you, me and Roma aren't proud or quick to take offense… But some people would've punched you in the face for calling them lapdogs! …Oh, my apologies, sir!" Gosha added with a note of sarcasm. "Hope you don't mind that we speak so bluntly, without picking polite expressions, do you?"

"It's fine," Mukhitdin relented, smiling at them for the first time that evening. "Alright, guys, let's drop it. I admit I overreacted. It's just—"

"Anyway," Gosha cut him off, "do you talk this way in front of Malika too? Or is that how you spoke to your teachers at the music college?"

"No, of course not. I can't really let my guard down with them—or at home, either. That's why I come to you guys. And Malika…eh… I'd rather not talk about it. Clear enough?"

"Gotcha," Roma nodded, though actually he did not get it at all, especially the part about Malika—none of that was clear to him. Still, he did his best to calm both friends and prevent any argument or fight. Gosha was actually calm, just teasing Mukhitdin a bit, trying to lighten his mood.

It seemed Gosha had been wanting to ask something for a while, but he hadn't dared. Now, when emotions were running a bit high, he finally spoke up:

"So tell me, Mukhit—does the boss not give you any money or what?!"

"How is that any of your business?" Mukhitdin bristled. "And let me remind you: he might be the boss for you, but not for me!"

"Fine, fine. You're all cool and independent! No need to get worked up. You don't want to talk, don't. I was just curious! Me and Roma, we make peanuts—"

"Don't exaggerate, Gosha—'peanuts,' really?" Roma cut in. He hated lies and often caught both Mukhitdin and Gosha stretching the truth. "You can't complain. You just bought yourself a decent 'Matiz' and you're about to move into your own place…"

"But compared to what's possible, that's peanuts," Gosha argued. "And compared to what he himself makes! I know for a fact that our boss is a millionaire—maybe even a billionaire! Mukhit, I can't believe you're not living in the lap of luxury. You have a mom, too—doesn't she look out for you? Why're you acting all Prince Edward?"

"You mean the one Mark Twain wrote about, who dressed up in rags?" Roma clarified.

All three guys, despite often speaking slang for "street cred," were actually fairly smart and well-read.

"Well, exactly. Mukhit, seriously, if I didn't already know who your dad was, I'd never guess you were 'golden youth'!"

"Try 'platinum,'" Mukhitdin said sarcastically.

"But you're his only heir… Me and Roma are sure your dad's an 'oligarch'!"

"You'd best keep your mouth shut if you plan to keep working for him," Mukhitdin warned Gosha just in case. "I'm not going to blab; don't worry, but it's better for everyone to be careful and not shoot off at the mouth wherever they go. Even I don't let myself say everything I want. And as for his…uh…assets, well, I never talk about them or show any interest—that's his business, his… 'values' so to speak."

"Yeah, I get it, but isn't it a bit short-sighted not to show any interest?" Gosha pressed on. "He's not taking all that with him to the afterlife, is he? You're his son! He's gotta leave it all to you. How can that not concern you?"

"I'm more concerned with my music, with my violin," Mukhitdin sighed. "I dreamed of getting into the conservatory, but it didn't work out. Now I have no idea what's next. My father said today he wants to send me to India to work."

"No way!" Roma's eyes widened with excitement. He'd always dreamed of seeing India's wonders—especially those gorgeous Goa beaches.

"He has a friend there," Mukhitdin explained, "Singh Bhojwani, a fashion designer who owns a big prêt-à-porter factory and a huge mansion in Delhi. My father wants me to live there for a while, to see real capitalism from the inside, learn a few things, and improve my English."

"Why not send you to Europe or the States?" Gosha asked. "That's way more 'glamorous' than India."

"There's no Singh Bhojwani—my father's trusted friend—in either Europe or the States," Mukhitdin clarified. "He's a smart, capable Indian businessman who knows a lot about life. He has his own philosophy, which my father shares."

"So we're not gonna see you before you leave, huh?" Roma asked, suddenly worried. "This is all so sudden…"

"It was unexpected for me, too. Of all people, I'll miss you two scoundrels the most!"

"When are you going?"

"Soon, guys. Very soon. Once I finish some important business in Tashkent, I'm off. At first I didn't want to go, but now, after talking to you, I'm thinking maybe this trip will do me some good…

Maybe I'll forget her…"

"Who?!" Gosha and Roma chimed in unison.

"No one. Just… never mind. The main thing is, I won't forget you guys. We'll keep in touch online."

"Make sure you don't forget to chat to us!"

"Sure thing. You know, talking with you has even made me stop being angry at my father…"

"Do you ever call him 'Dad'?" Gosha smirked. "You always say 'him' or on occasion 'father'… It's like you two aren't even related."

"That's how it is. But you guys—well, you're basically my own."

"Alright then, Mukhit. Don't forget us…"

"I won't. Take care, guys!"

"Bye and good luck to you! Crown prince…"

* * *

Gosha was rather afraid of the boss—like all his subordinates were. But this young man knew perfectly well that the boss valued his loyalty. Mukhitdin was right about that: Gosha and Roma were indeed as faithful to the boss as guard dogs. Years ago, when they were nearly penniless teenagers, the boss happened upon them at a local bazaar, where men capable of doing odd repair jobs or other manual labor went looking for temporary work. The boss took a liking to them, gave them a few tasks at his house, then offered them jobs at his company and helped them with housing.

They had to work very hard, with little rest, but at least they were no longer hungry, they had clothes and shoes, and in general lacked for nothing. The boss had no trouble underpaying hundreds of employees for months or even years. But sometimes he enjoyed grand gestures—always with an eye toward future gain. That was how things turned out with these two guys, especially Gosha. He was remarkably adept at handling all kinds of assignments from the boss, ranging from the "dirty" to the highly delicate.

Because of this, despite his perpetual, almost animal-like fear of the boss, Gosha could occasionally address him as if he were an old friend or even a son spoiled and favored by his father.

And so, today Gosha came to the boss with confidence. Without waiting for permission—or even letting the receptionist in the lobby announce him—he knocked on the door of the boss's office. Gosha knew the information he had would be of great interest to his employer.

"Boss, forgive me, but I've got important news!" Gosha declared.

The boss was on the verge of anger. At that very moment he was expecting one of the prettiest young female employees, intending to…have tea with her.

"What do you want?! Speak up, and be quick about it!"

"Remember, three years back you mentioned you wanted to find out what became of the real necklace with the Temur Ruby that once belonged to that Kuwaiti sheikh? Misha Leonidov tried to steal it, but the piece he got hold of turned out to be a fake."

"Well?" the boss replied irritably.

"So, yesterday I was out with some friends. We were hanging out in a café, having a few drinks…"

"I don't care about that in the slightest!" The boss cut Gosha off sharply.

"Right, sorry. Anyway, one of the guys there was an acquaintance who works customs at the airport."

"And so?"

"We ended up talking about the high life—about wealth, real

estate, all sorts of jewels. Turns out, my friend was on duty one day in February 2009, and he saw a passenger coming through customs from Moscow with a ridiculously expensive and dazzling necklace—rubies and diamonds, set in gold, all declared on his customs form. From the way he described it, it sounds an awful lot like ours!"

"'Ours?' the boss sneered. "Next you'll say mine… You're quite the proud tycoon, aren't you?"

"My apologies, boss… Anyway, Oleg said this treasure was carried by an Uzbek—a Tashkent local. Oleg can't remember the man's name, obviously, and back then he had no reason to make note of it. But for some reason, he recalls that the traveler was some well-known eye doctor. Maybe Roma and I could try searching for him here? In the end, there can't be that many high-profile ophthalmologists who flew in from Moscow at that time, right? And if we find him, maybe he's the one who's got the necklace—the real historic stone you want!"

"Well… suppose so. But how did the customs guys let him through?"

"He had some special permit to transport the necklace. According to Oleg, the permit was apparently from the Russian Ministry of Internal Affairs, and it stated that the piece had been gifted to that doctor by some… Arab sheikh! My friend also said he's never seen anything so beautiful in his entire life…"

"Listen carefully. Go team up with Roma and start 'digging' until you find this eye doctor for me! You can bring on as many of my men as you need to help. But watch yourself: don't mention a word of this to the doctor, and don't lay a finger on him! Just find him. Then I'll take it from there. I'll try to persuade him to sell me that valuable necklace. Not like I'd steal it from the doctor, after

all—I'm not Misha Leonidov."

"Understood, boss. Will do."

"Alright. Off you go. And be careful not to spook him."

As Gosha left, the boss thought to himself, *How I want that Temur Ruby!*

20

Agra, 1609

"Forgive me for asking, Your Highness, but why do you seem so sad?" inquired Mirza Ghiyas Beg, the Pillar of the State, bowing respectfully before Shah Jahan. "If it's because you still have not been granted permission to marry my granddaughter, Arjumand, then…"

"Oh, of course, that weighs most heavily on my mind!" the prince replied with a weary sigh. "After all, Ghiyas, you have been the Padishah's chief advisor for more than two years now, and my father both respects and values you. I do not understand why he keeps refusing to betroth Arjumand—raised under your care—to me…"

"The will of our sovereign is absolute, my noble prince."

"Yes, of course… But there is another serious matter that troubles me. I can share this sorrow with very few, lest the courtiers or the Padishah's subjects ridicule me and bring shame upon me! Yet I trust you. Nearly two years ago, our sovereign entrusted me, as his heir, with the safekeeping of two precious jewels—perhaps you have heard of them."

"Oh, esteemed prince! Very few, even within the palace, know of them, but your servant Ghiyas is aware of the matter and would never dare to reveal such a secret. You speak of the great, tear-pure diamond, the Koh-i-Noor, and the magnificent Temur Ruby, do you not? And you are looking for them because you believe they

have disappeared?"

Shah Jahan regarded the chief advisor with surprise and respect.

"That is correct. I see you keep well informed of the palace's affairs—and yet you are discreet. Commendable! But what matters now, Ghiyas Beg, is that I can find neither of those gemstones—they have simply vanished, as if into thin air! My father entrusted them to me, and I was duty-bound to protect them! Every time he summons me, I feel too ashamed to meet his gaze."

"Please do not fret so, Prince. Allow me to say that…nothing has actually disappeared!"

"What do you mean? How so? I have hired loyal men who have searched high and low for these two stones! And you say they have… not vanished? Could that be true?.. Where are they?!"

"Your wise father, our sovereign, merely wished to teach you—his heir—to be mindful and careful with the empire's wealth, especially with those two priceless gems that have no equal anywhere on earth."

"Is that so?!"

"Oh yes. He ordered his servants to 'steal' the Temur Ruby from Your Highness, so to speak, and he hid it away himself in one of his small secret chambers. As for Humayun's stone—the Koh-i-Noor—I heard Shah Jahangir tell one of his intimates that you, Prince—pardon me for repeating this—made a mistake: when the Padishah came to take the diamond from you, you did not ask him for a written acknowledgment, nor did you note in the official records that this diamond would no longer be in your safekeeping!"

"Ah! That is true. There were no witnesses, and I neglected to note that my father had reclaimed it for himself! But…where is the diamond now? It must still be with him, here in the palace. Although…I recall overhearing that someone took it somewhere…"

"You are quite right, Prince. The Koh-i-Noor has not been in Agra for some time. Back in 1607, Padishah Jahangir ordered one of his couriers to take it to…"

Ghiyas Beg abruptly fell silent, afraid to continue.

"Well?! Why do you hesitate? Speak!" Shah Jahan demanded impatiently.

"I am not entirely certain… Very well. He had it sent to Bengal. I beg you, Prince, say nothing of this—otherwise, I shall surely lose my head!"

"I promise you. Do not be afraid. Tell me everything you know."

"Hear me out. This is what happened at the time…"

* * *

Gaur, Bengal, 1607

"Madam, the sovereign instructed me to deliver this bundle to you personally!" announced the messenger, who had just dismounted from his foam-flecked horse and was gasping for breath from sheer exhaustion after many days on the road.

"I will have you fed so you can rest for a while—then you must set off at once on your journey back," Mehrun-Nissa ordered. "Meanwhile, I shall look at the gi— I mean, at the letter containing the Padishah's instructions for my husband, General Sher Afkun, and for me, his faithful companion. I will write a reply to our ruler on both our behalf, and you shall deliver it."

"As you wish, madam," the exhausted messenger replied submissively. "Whatever you say!"

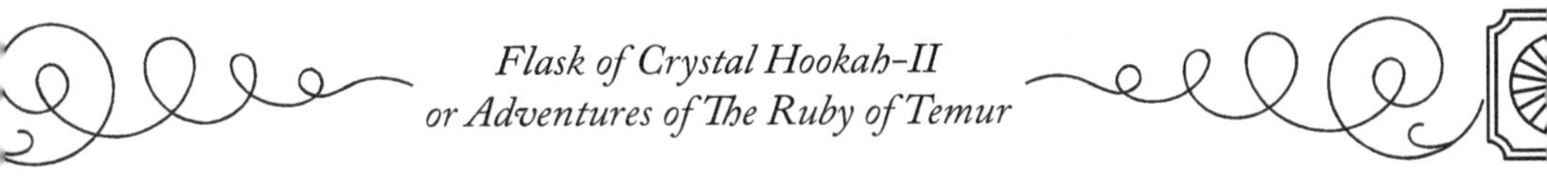

Such were the instructions he had received in Agra: to do whatever she commanded.

Mehrun-Nissa went to her quarters, locked the door from inside, then sat upon a soft divan and unwrapped the bundle. Inside was a lengthy page of verse from the Padishah. Skimming it, she saw that Jahangir was once again openly extolling his passionate feelings for her and calling her the "sovereign" and "ruler" of his heart. Also tucked inside was a small item—small in size yet immense in value and significance: the Koh-i-Noor diamond!

Mehrun-Nissa knew well that this stone, a gem of misfortune and death, was meant as a secret sign; she immediately understood its meaning. At once, she began composing a concise but pointed response to the Padishah:

"Oh, Conqueror of the World! Your servant Mehrun-Nissa will carry out all that you ask of her and all that you command her…"

The very next day, she contrived—by fair means or foul—to send her husband Sher Afkun out on a hunt, during which, by some "unfortunate coincidence," he was gravely wounded by an arrow. Bleeding heavily, the Great Mughal commander Sher Afkun died within a few hours.

On hearing this news, Mehrun-Nissa was overcome by grief and mourned deeply. She buried her husband with full honors right there in Gaur.

As for the diamond, she kept it with her—retaining it as a symbol of the Padishah's special favor toward her.

***

Agra, 1609

The news of Shah Jahan's upcoming wedding was a real blow to Arjumand. For two long, painful years she had waited in hope of becoming his wife. But alas…

On December 12, 1609, Padishah Jahangir sent fifty thousand rupees as a bridal deposit to the household of Princess Kandahari-Begim Sahiba, the daughter of Sultan Muzaffar Husain Mirza Safavi from Kandahar, which at that time was part of Persia.

In his book, the Tuzuk-i-Jahangiri, Jahangir wrote:

"The daughter of Muzaffar Husain Mirza Safavi, ruler of Kandahar, is betrothed to my son Khurram (Shah Jahan), and a council was convened to discuss the forthcoming marriage."

The astrologers and stargazers approved the union, determining an especially auspicious hour for it, and preparations for the wedding were underway.

Kandahar was of great importance to the Mughal Empire—an affluent city and a hub of trade routes. Over the centuries, Kandahar had repeatedly changed hands, depending on which ruler's army held the greater might. In the fourteenth century, the territory of Afghanistan became part of the Temurid Empire. In the sixteenth century, the last Temurid ruler, Babur, founded the new Mughal Empire with its center in Kabul, from which he launched victorious campaigns into Hindustan (India). Babur soon moved to Hindustan, and Afghanistan fell under the Shia Persian Safavid realm. Even during times of peace between Persia and the Mughal Hindustan, relations between the two states were tense. Many years before, when Shah Humayun was forced to yield Delhi to Sher

Shah, he found refuge in Persia. The Persian Shahanshah did not refuse him shelter and, under challenging conditions, provided him with an army, sending one of his younger sons along. As a result of a protracted campaign, Delhi was reclaimed for Hindustan.

At present, Kandahar belongs to Jahangir. He and the Persian Shahanshah did not greatly trust one another. However, the arrival of the Shahanshah's heiress in Agra symbolised the start of a new era in their relations. Both rulers aimed to show that they longed for peace. Jahangir was deeply convinced, however, that such peace could only be achieved if his empire maintained a dominant and prevailing position.

Meanwhile, Sultan Muzaffar Husain Mirza of Persia, sending his daughter on a long journey—no small distance to cover—gave her the following instructions:

"Kandahari, your marriage to Prince Shah Jahan will finally give us the opportunity to take Agra and all Hindustan under our control! I cannot abide the rule of this upstart Jahangir but you must do everything you can to win over both him and your future husband, the Shahzade. I will show you what must be done, how to make them bow to us and then I, the Sultan of Persia, shall be the master of Hindustan too!"

* * *

In an effort to stave off her gloomy thoughts and lift her downcast spirits, Arjumand went to see her aunt, Mehrun-Nissa. The latter had been widowed and had returned to Agra a year and a half earlier.

"Dearest Aunt, how are you?" Arjumand greeted her.

Though they lived in the same household, each was usually

busy with her own affairs, and they did not often converse.

"Oh, it's you, my dear!" Mehrun-Nissa had only just risen and was in a bright mood. "Come in, Arjumand, have a seat. Here are some fruits and sweets—help yourself. Did you come on some errand, or just to chat with your aunt?"

"I just wanted to know how you've been, whether all is well."

"All is fine, my darling. Thank you! And how are you? You don't look happy."

"Well…" Arjumand sighed. "It's hard to hide anything from you. You see, my parents believe the time has come for me to marry. They keep sending one suitor after another. But I don't wish to marry anyone but Shah Jahan! Dearest Aunt, I beg you to help me! You do have influence over the Padishah—and also over your brother, my father."

"Oh, you're exaggerating how much sway I have!" Mehrun-Nissa smiled with a sly twinkle in her eye. She understood perfectly that her niece, out of politeness, was actually understating the extent of her influence over Arjumand's father Asaf Khan, and grandfather Ghiyas Beg—and even more so over the Padishah, who was madly in love with Mehrun-Nissa.

Arjumand had no idea that her aunt was intercepting all of the letters she wrote to Shah Jahan—and all of his letters to her, his beloved.

Mehrun-Nissa approached her niece and embraced her tightly.

"You poor thing! You look so thin. You probably barely eat, do you? Please, calm yourself, my child. Don't worry—everything will turn out well!"

"How can it? Everyone has heard that my prince will soon marry… that Kandahari woman! What am I to do, how am I to go on living?"

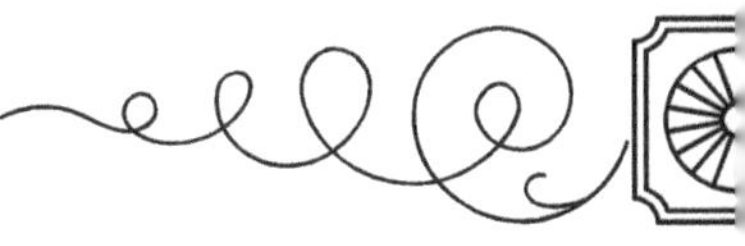

"Everything in life passes quickly, Arjumand. Your feelings for Shah Jahan will pass, too. He isn't the only man in the world, is he? Just wait—you'll see. Before long, your heart will cool toward him and you'll forget him altogether."

"No! I will never forget him!" Asaf Khan's daughter exclaimed. "Please, do not speak that way. I want no other—only him."

Suddenly, Mehrun-Nissa burst into laughter.

"Oh, so it's a great love, isn't it? How amusing. I have never felt such a thing in my life, and I have no desire to. Remember this, child: love makes people weak… and foolish! Lovers are easily crushed, easily tricked and exploited, their actions easily controlled, and they become vulnerable. But I suspect…"

"What is it, Aunt? Please, go on."

Just then Mehrun-Nissa's expression hardened, turning unkind.

"I'm quite sure that a love for the heir to the throne can't possibly be entirely selfless!" she remarked irritably. "Admit it—my dear Arjumand, you have big ambitions!"

"What do you mean, Aunt? I don't understand," the girl replied, distressed. "Believe me, I love Shah Jahan as a person, not as a prince! Were he destitute and of no lineage, I would love him just the same!"

"And what does your mother say?"

"She says the same as you and the Padishah: 'Forget him!' But those words cannot kill the feeling in my heart. I'm devoted to Shah Jahan and will always love him."

It appeared that Mehrun-Nissa softened somewhat.

"All right, all right. Why be upset? I merely wanted to know the truth."

"I always tell you the truth, Aunt!" Arjumand said, on the verge of tears at the sense that someone so close to her did not fully trust her. Something about Mehrun-Nissa's manner struck her as somewhat odd. *Doesn't she want me to be happy?.. No, that couldn't be!*

"Come now, calm yourself, my dear. I am on your side. I'll always support you."

"Oh, Aunt!" Arjumand's tears had dried by then, and she pulled herself together, deciding she had been wrong to think ill of her wonderful relative. "I just had a thought—did you bring back your magical Crystal Hookah from Bengal? I know that when you light it, breathing in its fragrant smoke, you can peer into the future and see what awaits us!"

"My star, that ancient Crystal Hookah truly is extraordinary. I always keep it with me. Like Aladdin's magic lamp, it can grant any wish, but tell me: why do you want to uncover what is hidden from ordinary human eyes? Knowing the future can bring much sorrow and drag one into dark, lingering thoughts…"

"Aunt, just don't tell me everything. Show me only which husband the Almighty has chosen for me! Is it Shah Jahan, or…?"

"Do you really want it that badly? Well, then…"

Mehrun-Nissa slipped off her shoes, padded soundlessly over to her Crystal Hookah, filled it, and set alight the wonderfully scented herbs. As the hookah began to emit its fragrant smoke, she circled around it in a rhythmic, Sufi-like dance, eyes wide open, humming softly in time. She continued like that for about an hour. Then she stopped, sat down, took the mouthpiece of the hookah, inhaled its liquid smoke, and, gently swaying in meditation, murmured through the haze:

"I see a distant future. In a vast area of grass and small trees, there stands one of Agra's treasures—a dazzlingly beautiful palace of white marble… People from every corner of the world come there just to see this wondrous palace, a marvel among marvels—unlike anything anywhere else… How is it linked to you? Those who visit it always remember and honor you, because that palace… bears your name!"

Arjumand listened, scarcely breathing, scarcely able to believe these wondrous words. Drawing smoke from her hookah again, Mehrun-Nissa went on:

"I also see far-off times. There is a young woman who resembles you, playing some sort of instrument and singing. They will also call her, as they call you, 'Malika,' which means 'Princess'…"

She paused, then resumed:

"Now I see the nearer future. The third and most beloved son of our Padishah Jahangir—the Shahzade Shah Jahan—will wed you, and you shall bear him many children…"

Until then Arjumand had been silent, listening. But now, trembling with the powerful emotions stirred by what she had heard, she finally broke the hush in Mehrun-Nissa's room. She spoke, snapping her aunt out of her trance.

"Aunt… dear Aunt! Oh, thank you!!!" Arjumand cried in excitement and delight, hugging her father's sister gratefully and kissing her on both cheeks.

"What did I say to you while I was 'on the other side'?" Mehrun-Nissa asked her niece with a smile. "Hold on… Yes, I recall vaguely…"

Her features changed again. It seemed she was annoyed with herself about something.

"Still, I hope you don't take all this fortune-telling and prophecy too seriously," she said in a strained, anxious voice, patting her niece's cheek.

"Why not? I believe all the good you've foretold, Aunt," Arjumand answered, still shaken by the magnificent destiny that had been revealed to her. "If all that is indeed the will of the Almighty, then I am simply overjoyed!"

"Well, well…" Mehrun-Nissa muttered, as though dismissing her own words, lost in her own thoughts.

"But I know for certain," her niece continued, "that happiness doesn't arrive on its own if we don't strive to create it. Will you speak to the Padishah about me and the Shahzade?"

"What? Oh, yes… Fine, I'll try, Arjumand. But know this—I promise nothing!"

When Arjumand left Mehrun-Nissa's quarters, her mind was whirling with all her aunt had said in her trance, amid the swirl of Crystal Hookah smoke:

"…They will also call her, as they call you, 'Malika'…"

21

Tashkent, 2014

Malika discovered that she and Bahadir had quite a bit in common despite their different areas of study. Unlike Malika, who aspired to be a professional musician, Bahadir was pursuing a degree in international management. But the most important thing they both absolutely loved was good music. Bahadir turned out to be a huge fan of many musicians and singers Malika had adored and listened to since childhood. They dove eagerly into conversations about their favorite music, marveling at how much their tastes overlapped.

Malika liked that Bahadir asked her right away to address him as a friend and not be formal about it. He was sociable and outgoing—she never had to probe him for stories.

However, beyond music, many of the topics he brought up bothered her a bit. More often than not, he'd tell her about… his former girlfriends. He told her what he liked about them, the ups and downs of his relationships, how they had flirted with or deceived him, and how he himself had deceived them. Innocent and unspoiled, Malika found it hard to relate to such tales. Nevertheless, she refrained from criticising him.

Bahadir was also generous to Malika, offering her small courtesies in his own way. It seemed to her, though, that his attention felt more like someone simply enjoying her company, rather than the kind of focused devotion a man might show if he intended a serious proposal—one that would bind them together for life.

It was clear that Bahadir liked her; he looked at her as a young, beautiful woman, with a purely masculine—and barely concealed—desire and "appetite." She sensed that, in principle, he might have wanted to start the kind of casual relationship he was used to having with other women, a relationship built mainly on satisfying his libido. Yet she also sensed that he held her in special regard—he respected her innocence and purity, making sure not to treat her like the others.

He invited her on walks along tree-lined paths, took her to theaters and concerts, and offered his arm to lean on as they strolled. Once, he even suggested she try on a rather expensive piece of jewelry. But for all the hints of courtship and the prior arrangement between their families, he was in no rush to propose marriage… Perhaps he never intended to at all…

This left Malika increasingly anxious, for her feelings toward him were growing deeper. That worried her—she did not want her love for him to end up outweighing his love for her. Nor did she wish to be tormented. She wondered if it might be better to break things off now, before her feelings turned into a bonfire of pain— before they grew so overwhelming and uncontrollable that she'd be powerless against them.

Moreover, Malika sensed that something weighed on Bahadir's mind. During their time together, he could be obviously and genuinely kind, yet without warning he would fall into prolonged stretches—sometimes whole hours—of inexplicable tension. Whenever she asked if something was wrong, he just brushed her off with a forced joke.

On one occasion, his behavior was particularly strange.

It started well, as usual: he invited Malika to a restaurant. They

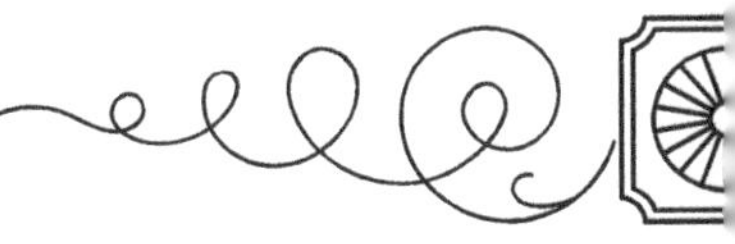

placed their orders and began talking. They had just begun eating when two individuals approached—a short, older man with a small, reddish beard, and a beautiful young woman of about twenty.

The moment Bahadir noticed them, Malika could tell he grew nervous. He invited them to join at the table, but they refused. The young woman looked at Bahadir as though she knew him well. Observant as she was, Malika caught onto that the girl knew him intimately well. Bahadir greeted her with a simple "Hi," acting, in Malika's presence, as though there was nothing special between them.

"Dear Bahadir," the older man with the reddish beard said, sounding polite but with an unpleasant undertone, "the boss has been asking after you for a while. Have you forgotten you have certain obligations to us?"

"Yes, yes, I remember, Veniamin Arkadyevich… But if we could, let's talk about it elsewhere, not here and not now! Set up a time for me to come, and I'll be there. Alright?"

"That's not quite alright, my friend. Come on, dear, you'll step out with us now, and your girl here can wait… Apologies, miss! Bahadir, you've made your order, haven't you? She won't get bored, we hope?"

"Y-y-yes, I have," Bahadir stammered for some reason, turning redder still.

"Well then… Hey, waiter!" The waiter approached, and the older man continued: "Bring the finest champagne to this table for the lady—on me! Quickly now… Leyla, let's go."

The waiter nodded obediently and hurried off with the order.

"Malika, I'll be back in five minutes, okay?" Bahadir said abruptly, clearly agitated. Without waiting for her response, he followed Veniamin Arkadyevich and Leyla out.

But he was gone not five minutes—not even fifteen or thirty. Malika waited patiently for about an hour, not wanting to offend him by leaving. Her calls went unanswered.

At last, Bahadir returned. He was alone—unable to talk properly, refusing to explain anything.

"Who were those people? What was that about?" Malika asked, distressed and worried.

"Nobody. Don't pay them any mind."

"What did they want from you? Do you owe them something?"

Bahadir jolted, as though he had been struck.

"Owe them?! No, of course not! How could you say such nonsense? Let's just go home."

"And that young woman—who is she? You obviously know her, right?"

"The girl? Oh, Leyla. Yeah… well, we… used to… We were just friends."

"Ah, I see."

"Have you eaten?"

"Yes. Do you really think food's the point right now?"

"Alright, then let's get out of here… please!"

The episode deeply unsettled Malika, but she avoided bringing it up again with Bahadir.

* * *

During one of their café meetups, Malika finally decided to have a direct, honest conversation with Bahadir, having seen that he was unwilling to take the initiative when it came to any significant questions.

"Bahadir, forgive me, but there's something serious I'd like to discuss with you…"

"Sounds ominous," Bahadir joked. But then, as though guessing what it might be about, he tensed and frowned. "Malika, if this is about marriage, I… I've actually been wanting to say… I'm sorry, but… Probably…"

"Bahadir," Malika cut him off, "please—since I started, let me finish, okay?" She gave him a warm smile. "Otherwise I'll lose my train of thought… I'm nervous, but I have to say it! You have no obligation to marry me! You're free—just like I am! Do you understand?"

Bahadir was taken aback. He hadn't expected such words from Malika. He looked at her closely, surprised, then grateful—truly, he was not ready for marriage…

From that day onward, they did not see each other.

***

Adulla Rustamovich noticed that his younger son had been in a strange mood of late. He mentioned it to his wife, and they decided to talk to Bahadir together.

"Son, we're your parents—who could be closer to you than us?" Abdulla Rustamovich began. "Tell us directly: what's going on? Did something happen? Why do you walk around looking so grim, like a storm cloud?"

"Nothing's wrong, dad, everything's fine."

"Then can you tell us whether you plan to marry Malika or not? Are you even seeing her?"

"Why are you asking about that, father?"

"Because before, you always talked about her—especially to your mother and sister—but now, you don't say a word. Don't tell me you've let such a wonderful girl slip away."

"No. Well… I'm not sure…"

"What?!"

"Alright, I'll explain everything… You took away my freedom of choice…"

"What do you mean, Bahadir? What's that supposed to imply?" his father asked, puzzled.

"Father, Mother, ever since I was a child, I've dreamed of marrying for love."

"Alright… So?"

"Please, hear me out!"

"Go on, then."

"I wanted to find my future wife by myself. Myself, do you understand? Of my own free will, not because you suggested it. Sorry if that offends you."

"So why didn't you find one?" Abdulla Rustamovich inquired.

"I haven't had a chance yet. I'm still young. Give me time, father—I'll definitely find her!"

"So Malika's not to your liking, then? She's a marvelous girl; it's rare I meet anyone better—except maybe my own daughter, your sister Rano, who's somewhat similar to her. You really don't like her?"

"I do like her. Very much, in fact."

"Son, are you trying to mock us?"

"No. Malika's wonderful. But you were the ones who brought her into my life, Father. Don't you see? You did. And I want to choose my own partner, so that I can be everything to her—her husband and her master."

Sitting off to the side, Mukhabbat chose not to intervene in this complicated father-son talk; she simply clutched at her heart.

"I can just imagine," his father's voice rose, betraying his growing agitation despite his usually composed manner. "The kind of wife you'd pick for yourself—no doubt as frivolous as you are! God forgive me."

"No, I'll find someone extraordinary."

"Alright, go ahead—just try. I'll give you one year, no more!"

"Why so little time, Father?"

"It's plenty enough. Besides, it's time you grew up, Son. The 'kid stuff' ended long ago! How long are we supposed to baby you? How many more years do we have to support you and let you fray our nerves? It's time to get serious!"

"I'm sorry, Father, but you're talking as though all your children are already married and only I remain single…"

"When it comes to Amin and Rano, Bahadir," Abdulla Rustamovich said calmly, "I'm more at ease. Yes, they're not married yet either, but I'm already thinking about their futures. They're serious, responsible, and reliable. Your mother and I know we can count on them when we're old. But you…"

"Ah, so I'm this worthless, good-for-nothing misfit you ended up with!" Bahadir flared. "Thank you so much, Father!"

Offended, he quickly threw on his coat and left the house.

22

One day, when Malika's parents were out, the doorbell rang. She looked through the peephole, thinking not to open it, but the visitor said:

"Malika, I've only come for a minute—to ask for your forgiveness. And to say goodbye!"

It was Mukhitdin.

But she had been expecting Bahadir, hoping that it was him. It wasn't…

Even so, since the young man had spoken that way, she opened the door. Yet she still had no intention of chatting with him in a friendly manner.

"Malika, hello," Mukhitdin began.

"Hello," she replied curtly.

"I know you're mad at me, and you're right to be. But believe me, I never meant to hurt you. I don't even understand how it happened… I just lost my head… I really like you!"

"Let's not talk about that!"

"I heard you're getting married…"

"Yes, I am. So what?"

"Congratulations…"

"No need. Is that all?"

"Forgive me, Malika, please, for…that incident…"

"Why should I forgive you?"

"Because you're the most wonderful girl in the world. I'm certain of it!"

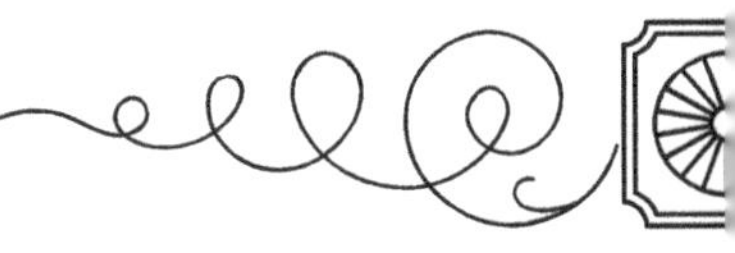

"…Fine… I'll try… But it'd be best if I didn't see you for a while!"

"Actually, I came to tell you I'm leaving. I won't be in Tashkent for a year or more."

"All the best."

"You're not even going to ask where I'm going? Don't you care? What about all those years we were friends?"

"Does it matter where you go? And our friendship—you stamped it out yourself, remember?"

"I'm off to India, Malika, to work and learn about business!"

"I wish you success and happiness."

"Thank you very much."

"Goodbye, Mukhitdin. Better yet—farewell."

"No, Malika, wait. We can't just part ways like this! After all, I… you know how I felt about you… And I still feel that way."

"That's all in the past, Mukhitdin. I already told you—or rather, you already know—I'm getting married…"

"I brought you a gift, since I'm leaving. It's both a keepsake and a wedding present. Forgive me if it's modest and unworthy of you. But if you accept it, I'll be grateful and very happy."

"I don't need anything."

"Maybe you mean to say 'you don't need anything from me, Mukhitdin,' right? But it's not nice to refuse a gift offered in true repentance and from the heart!"

Malika hesitated for a moment. She didn't want to accept it, but she hated hurting people.

"What is it?"

"It's perfume. In fact, it's exactly the type you like—oceanic notes. I think you'll enjoy it!"

Malika opened the box. Taking the bottle in her hands, she

breathed in the aroma.

"They smell wonderful! What do you know, you remember my taste… Thank you."

"I'm so glad you like it. By the way, this perfume lasts quite a while. So… am I forgiven?" he asked, brightening.

"Yes, you're forgiven.

> *If you answer evil with evil,*
> *You punish the one who wronged you.*
> *If you answer evil with good,*
> *You reward yourself…*

"Please remember these words by the poet Saadi… Have a safe journey, Mukhitdin, and may you be successful. Who knows— maybe we'll see each other again…someday."

"We most sure will, Malika! I'll write to you."

"That's really not necessary," she smiled softly, without any malice. "I don't know how my husband will feel about it! You probably forgot—I'm getting married!"

"It's fine. I'm sure he'll put up with us!"

23

Malika was lying in her bed when Galina entered after knocking loudly. She was carrying a bag of goodies.

"Galya…" Malika managed to say weakly.

"So, what's up with you, girlfriend?" Galina said. "I called, and your mom told me you were sick… How'd you manage that?" Her tone was sharp and pointedly concerned, as if she were speaking to a small child rather than an adult friend. And something in her voice sounded less than genuine, almost false.

If Malika hadn't been running a fever, she would have been surprised by Galina's words—"How'd you manage that?"—because her rational mind knew (and would have pointed out to her visitor) that falling ill can happen to anyone, since no one is immune to disease. But at the moment, Malika didn't care about any of that— she had no energy for logic or explanations. She felt awful.

"I've brought you some fruit, since that's what sick people are supposed to have!" Galina beamed, for some reason putting special emphasis on the phrase "sick people," as if there was some hidden joy in that word understandable only to her and invisible to everyone else.

"We… have… everything at home," Malika noted, her voice halting from weakness. "Why are you… spending money?"

"Don't talk nonsense, please! I never spend that much on anyone—you know that! So don't worry. Better tell me what's going on with you. What kind of illness is this? What do the doctors say?"

Malika found it hard to speak and really didn't want to expend her limited strength on conversation with anyone right now. Still, she couldn't be rude by ignoring her friend or pushing her away. Mustering what energy she could, she tried to maintain the conversation:

"They… still can't figure out… what's wrong with me…" Malika murmured. "They say… there's a focus… of infection… in my body…"

"Does anything hurt?" At that, Galina grew more serious; her previously somewhat false concern and show of caring seemed to shift into genuine compassion and real worry for her friend. "Malik, your father is a doctor, isn't he?"

"He's… an ophthalmologist."

"Yes, an eye doctor, I know, but still! What does he say? Couldn't he get you in to see some good specialists?"

"I… didn't let him… do that."

"What do you mean, you 'didn't let him do that'? Are you out of your mind? You're lying here, practically dying, and he—?"

"Galya, please stop shouting," Malika begged. "My dad… loves me… But I don't want… to upset him… or make him worry. He has… so much work… And right now… he's away on a business trip…"

"I see—so your dad doesn't even realize how bad you're feeling. Am I right?"

Malika said nothing, feeling guilty.

Galina was starting to lose patience:

"And what about your mom? This just isn't acceptable, Malika! And you still haven't told me: what hurts?" She stressed each word separately and was raising her voice now.

"My stomach… and my pancreas… badly. I'm taking no-spa and stronger antispasmodics. Trouble is… for some reason…

they're not helping… I feel worse…"

"I'm no doctor, just a nurse, but even I can see you need a proper diagnosis! You need a thorough check-up! Besides, I really don't like your complexion… And especially—" Galina took another careful look at Malika. "—the look of your skin. See that rash? It might point to some kind of poisoning… Think back to what you ate in recent days."

"The usual… Nothing out of the ordinary."

"Oh, please. I know you and your fiancé are always going out to cafés and restaurants! Maybe you picked something up there. Who knows what they're cooking with?"

"The food's fine… and I… haven't been to… any restaurants in a while. We don't meet up anymore… And why would I go alone? … My family feeds me at home."

"You're not meeting with who? Oh—your boyfriend! What was his name? Bahadir, I think? Good grief! So he dumped you, right? And now you're stressed out because of that, huh? Aha! So that's why you're sick!"

Malika stayed silent. She wasn't especially upset by what Bahadir had done and knew for sure she wasn't ill because of it, although she had liked him a lot. But she was too weak to argue with her friend or explain anything.

"So tell me! Why did he reject you?" Galina pressed on, not bothering to soften her blunt words or worry that her friend might find the subject painful. Then, realizing she might be going too far, she softened a little and added, "What a jerk! I have told you before, though, all men are scum…"

"Galya, please… Stop it."

"What do you mean, 'stop it'? He's not worth it. Forget him. Plenty of fish in the sea. And girls as pretty and smart as we are, well, there's only us. Let them chase after us."

Nothing in Malika's personality—despite her beauty—inclined her toward flirting openly with men or making them suffer, much less forcing them to "chase" her.

"But we haven't settled the issue of your health," Galina insisted, convinced she was right about everything. "Sure, your emotional turmoil might have weakened your body further and lowered your immunity, but I think it might not be the main cause. Like I said, I really don't like that rash on your skin… It looks like a symptom of poisoning. And your occasional cough might be another symptom. Your head is probably dizzy, too, right?"

"How… did you know? Galya, you… you're practically a 'professor' of medicine," Malika managed a small smile through her pain. "Why… didn't you… enroll… in medical school? Why did… you stay… a nurse… in the hospital?"

"Not everyone's as good at studying as you, Malika! You're the genius here! Your mom already told me—on the phone and in person—that right from the start of the school year, you became the best student in your class. People say there are already legends all over the conservatory about how you sing and about your extraordinary voice!"

Malika glowed despite the pain. She felt touched, replying a bit sheepishly:

"Who says that?... They exaggerate… I'm only… in my first year…"

"Well, listen up, 'Maria Callas,' here's the plan: tomorrow, when I go to work, I'll talk to our best doctors. I'll ask whichever one they recommend to see you first. Then, in all likelihood, you'll have to come in, do some tests, and undergo more thorough diagnostic procedures—an X-ray of your stomach or a scope, CT scan,

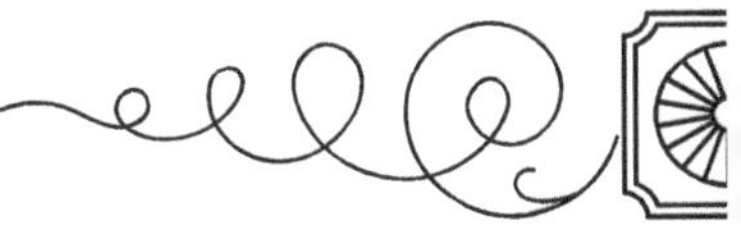

MRI—who knows… Basically, whatever the specialist says."

"All right, Galya. Thank you so much!"

"Nothing to thank me for yet. That's what friends are for. Now get better! And put that idiot who treated you like that out of your head! Got it?"

"He's not an idiot…"

"Oh really? Then what is he? And here you are defending him! I, on the other hand, would have just killed him right off."

24

Dr. Sadreddin Kasymov, an epidemiologist specializing in toxicology, had Malika admitted to the hospital immediately after his initial examination. Having prescribed the necessary diagnostic procedures and studied the initial results, Dr. Kasymov concluded that Malika, as her friend Galina had correctly guessed, had indeed suffered from poisoning by some kind of liquid substance—presumably an infusion made from poisonous plants. It could also have been poor-quality or adulterated cosmetics, or, much less likely, perfume.

The doctor instructed her not to use any herbal remedies, cosmetics, or perfume for a while, in order to confirm or rule out his diagnosis. He also prescribed all the necessary medications. In fact, within just a few days, Malika's condition improved significantly.

She did not believe that any real danger could come from makeup, let alone perfume, but, just to be safe, she followed the advice of the experienced doctor—even avoiding the perfume given to her by Mukhitdin, despite loving its scent and the boost it gave her.

One day, while riding the metro to get to the conservatory, Malika felt very unwell. She managed to endure her last class of the day with great difficulty. After returning home, she again had to take to her bed.

Dr. Kasymov came to examine her.

"Well, young beauty, frightening your mother again, are we?"

Malika tried to laugh, but her face contorted involuntarily in pain instead.

"Tell me in detail everything you touched yesterday and today," the doctor continued very seriously.

Malika did her best to recall it all. Meanwhile, Dr. Kasymov carefully inspected every item in her room, especially those on her desk. His gaze halted at a bottle of perfume.

"What's this, Malika?" he asked, his expression humorless. "Did you use it today? Be honest."

"Yes, Doctor. A friend gave it to me. I think it's some kind of Arabian perfume. The scent is lovely!"

"I see. But didn't I tell you, my dear girl, not even to think about using anything of the sort? Under no circumstances! Especially not until you are fully recovered! I've heard people say you're unusually compliant. So why did you ignore me—your physician?"

"Doctor… I'm sorry. I totally forgot your warning."

"You see? We spent so much effort and time flushing out your stomach and intestines, then restoring their microflora, and you're forgetting to be cautious!"

"I'm to blame. I acted as though I were perfectly healthy. How careless of me…"

Suddenly, a thought struck her:

"But there's no way these perfumes could have poisoned me, Doctor! That's impossible! You don't seriously believe—"

The epidemiologist/toxicologist grasped her train of thought and interrupted before she could finish:

"Indeed, I do. My dear, allow me to consider every possibility, because in life, anything can happen. I've personally seen cases where even close relatives poisoned one another—Heaven forbid, something you wouldn't wish on anyone! So, you say this bottle of perfume was brought to you by a friend?"

Malika said nothing. She wondered: Could that person—who

had come to her supposedly with the best of intentions, asking forgiveness and looking at her with such sincere eyes—have betrayed her a second time, so vilely, so criminally? Or maybe he simply, through ignorance, bought these fake perfumes cheaply at some bazaar or "gray market" shop—without knowing what sort of product it was. Yes, that must be the case! It couldn't be anything else…

"I only dabbed on a little bit of it once or twice today," Malika tried to justify herself and Mukhitdin.

"That's more than enough to cause poisoning if the perfume contains a toxin dangerous to humans—basically, a poison. Especially given that you already used them earlier, when the first signs of this illness appeared, right?"

"Yes, I did. Unfortunately…"

"Well, there you have it. But don't lose heart!"

While he spoke, Dr. Kasymov carefully placed the bottle of perfume into a small plastic bag.

"I'm taking this with me for chemical lab analysis. I'll check my suspicions. But I'll be honest: I'm ninety-five percent sure these very perfumes are 'guilty' of causing your distress…"

A few days later, it emerged that the perfume given to Malika by her "friend" was indeed highly toxic, containing a large concentration of methanol.

Thanks to considerable effort from Dr. Kasymov and his colleagues, Malika was able to get back on her feet relatively quickly.

25

"Gosha, get in here—immediately!" The boss's voice was clearly displeased.

Gosha did not make the "master" wait long.

"Yeah, boss, I'm listening!"

"No, I'm the one listening to you. You and Roma—did you find that ophthalmologist who came back from Moscow with the priceless necklace?"

"Not yet, boss. I'm sorry, but—"

"I don't get why you're dragging your feet! It's like a bunch of useless nobodies work for me! What am I paying you all that money for? It's as if there are so many prominent ophthalmologists in Tashkent—especially ones who flew from Moscow to Tashkent in February 2009!"

"Well, that's exactly the problem. We've been searching persistently and discovered all the famous doctors. We dug into everything about them—their wives, kids, workplaces—"

"And what? Why are you babbling pointlessly, Gosha? 'Dug in,' he says. Detective Pinkerton, my ass. I want results, you understand, results! Where are they?"

"It's just that the Uzbekistan Airways folk won't give us any info about who flew where and when in that particular year. They say it's confidential."

"Good God! Of course they're not going to hand over that info. Then find out everything about these doctors, track down their relatives, friends, housekeepers—if they have any—their cats, dogs, birds, whoever might know these details of their lives."

"Got it, boss, will do."

"Listen here. I didn't really want to spread the word about this necklace… But it seems there's no other way. I suspect you guys will keep searching for another year if you don't tackle it from a different angle. Tread carefully—hear me? Carefully, without running your mouths. Try to find out from the people around these big-name eye doctors whether they've got any special jewelry in their house—something they might have shown someone, bragged about… And as soon as you hear about a necklace with rubies of any kind—we'll check later if it's the stone we're after—right away put that doctor on our watch list and give me his coordinates personally. Clear?"

"Yes, boss, I understand everything! You really have a brilliant mind!"

"All right, spare me. I know myself well enough; I don't need your compliments. Just hurry up and get it done."

Gosha nodded obediently.

"What else do you need?!" the boss asked irritably.

"Well… Mukhitdin isn't replying to emails from the guys. I just wanted to know how he's doing, or if he'll be back soon."

"Not soon—nearly a year from now. He rarely calls me, too—he's very busy in India with work."

* * *

Late that evening, when Said Yahyaevich got home from his business trip, he was surprised that only his wife came out to meet him. Their daughter did not appear.

"Sitora, my dear, hello! Where's Malika…?"

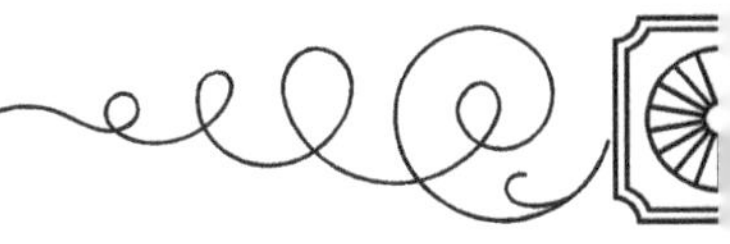

He hugged and kissed his wife.

"Welcome home, Said! As for Malika… Come on in, wash your hands, dinner's on the stove. I'll warm it up."

"Dinner can wait. You haven't answered me: Where's my daughter? What's going on with her?"

"She's… in bed, she's sick."

"What, still?! I hope it's nothing serious?!"

"No. Though at one point it was some danger. But the crisis was averted."

"What danger? What crisis?! Did you call for an ambulance or a family doctor?"

He walked quickly to his daughter's room.

"Malika, my darling daughter, my sunshine, daddy's home! Tell me—what happened?"

"Hello, Dad! Don't worry. Thank God, I feel a lot better now."

"No ambulance was needed," Sitora answered his question. "We have Galina to thank—she suspected Malika had been poisoned…"

"Poisoned? Food poisoning?"

"No, Papa," Malika said, "the doctors think it was external, through skin contact. I had a red rash—look, there's still some left."

"Said, on Galina's request, a toxicologist and epidemiologist came from her hospital twice—a very competent doctor. His surname is Kasymov. Have you heard of him?"

"No, I haven't. So what did this Kasymov say?"

"He said Malika might have been poisoned by some sort of liquid—an alcohol-based herbal concoction, or even perfume… Is that possible, Said?"

"Yes, wife, I think it is possible. If the perfume is 'made' with something toxic—like methyl alcohol—poisoning would be un-

avoidable… What?! Why are you both staring at me like that? There's already a lab test result, and my guess was right, huh?"

"Yes, exactly," Sitora nodded. "It was methanol—methyl alcohol."

"Where did this poisoned perfume come from? Malika, can't you buy a decent French fragrance with verified quality from a proper brand-name boutique? For example, from one of the 'Parfum Gallery' stores?"

"Of course I can, Papa. But this was a gift."

"From whom, exactly? I'd like to look that 'gifter' in the eye!"

" That's enough of that—don't torment our daughter. Let her rest and let's have dinner. I really need to talk with you!"

They headed into the kitchen. While they ate, Sitora brought up something that had been weighing on her mind for some time.

"Said, I realize this is a delicate subject, but I have to ask—I've stopped sleeping at night. I'm worried about our only daughter! That young man, Bahadir—unless I've misunderstood—treated her badly, unfairly."

"Why do you say that? Aren't they seeing each other?"

Sitora shook her head.

"Not at all."

"Maybe Malika pushed him away? Maybe she didn't like him. She's well within her rights!"

"No, she didn't push him away."

"Remember, I told you that Abdullo-aka and I agreed that if our kids didn't work out a marriage, neither of us would hold a grudge. We're old friends, and not even major issues like our children's happiness should destroy a long, strong friendship—right?"

"Yes, that's right. But I think something else is going on, Said. I'm afraid our girl has fallen for that rascal; he's gotten under her skin! And it looks like he's stopped meeting her or calling. If they were still talking, Malika would tell me; I'd know! Apparently they don't even call each other anymore. I can't fathom why. He doesn't call her, and she doesn't call him at all. If they'd met just once and instantly realized they weren't right for each other—then fine, they'd go their separate ways like two ships passing in the night. But you know, I told you they met for two weeks or maybe more— almost every day. And, as far as I know, he used to call her about five times a day. That means he really liked her, too! Now he doesn't call at all. What could have happened? I asked Malika if they had a fight. She said no, no fight. She won't tell me anything substantial."

"Please, dear, don't let it get to you. I know you're her mother, but you worry too much. I think we shouldn't meddle in their rela- tionship. You'll see—everything will sort itself out. After all, she's still young; her whole life is ahead of her! Our daughter is both smart and beautiful."

"I'm not sure… Maybe you're right."

"Of course I'm right. But if you want, I could carefully speak with Abdullo-aka about it. If he knows something, I'm sure he'll tell me!"

* * *

"So, Said, did you talk to Abdulla Rustamovich?"

"Yes, Sitora, my dear, I spoke with him—or rather, he spoke with me."

"Well then, what's the verdict? Is there going to be a wedding? Or are you about to tell me that he knows nothing about his son's decisions?"

"You are so perceptive, my wife! Indeed, the elder Fattakhov was confident that everything between the young people was fine and on track for a wedding. He was quite surprised to hear that things are not going well. What do you expect? He's a busy man, just like I am, he got bogged down with work, and basically wasn't keeping an eye on the situation. Modern youth don't listen to their parents anyway; they do everything their own way, as they wish! Besides, his son—let me tell you—is not a bad fellow, but he's complicated. Anyway, Abdulla promised he would definitely talk to him. As soon as he figures out what's going on, he'll call me."

"Let's hope he does… In that case, I won't worry. Especially since you said everything's going to be fine."

"Everything will be fine! Trust me. But there's something else I wanted to discuss… My dear wife, I hope you're still taking good care of that precious piece of jewelry that Firuz-begim gave you?"

"Yes, of course, Said! We absolutely plan to give that beautiful necklace to our Malika for her wedding! It's so wonderful that you met that esteemed Kuwaiti sheikh and that he delivered that necklace via you to my dear great-grandmother! By the way, I'm still waiting for you to tell me the whole story. I'm sure it's very interesting… How does Firuz-begim fit into this? Why did the sheikh give her such an expensive piece of jewelry?"

"Oh, I see, Sitora—the story of this gift is really bugging you! Well… You remember that at the start of 2009 I and a group of my colleagues—the best ophthalmologists of the CIS—took part in an international seminar in Moscow, right? Having seen in advance that the sheikh would be among the invited guests, I wrote to him by email and told him about myself. Knowing how much he devotes himself to charity, especially for the visually impaired, I decided to try my luck and ask him for help in the form of equipment for my eye clinic…

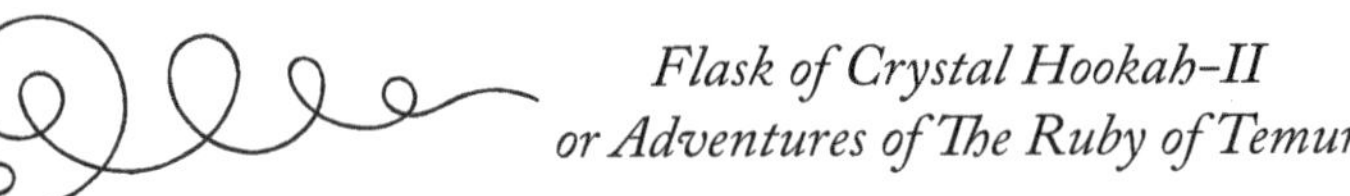

Sitora listened carefully to her husband. He continued:

"I was pleasantly surprised that Sheikh Al-Sabah not only replied to my email but also graciously agreed to sponsor our ophthalmology clinic! Naturally, I was overjoyed. As you know, we run on self-financing and mainly survive on the modest payments of those patients who can afford treatment—and we don't have many of those. A good number of them, as you're aware, we treat practically free of charge through charitable grants and sponsorships. Ours is not a commercial enterprise because for me, as head of the clinic, what's always mattered most is people's health, not money.

"Well, at one point in my letter, I happened to mention to the sheikh that my wife's grandmother once had a close personal acquaintance with his relative—the late Sheikh Al-Nahayan of the Arab Emirates. Sheikh Al-Sabah responded that the name of our Firuz-begim Alimkhanova was indeed known to him! I must say I was extremely surprised by that. He promised me he would tell me all about it in person when we met.

"When we finally met with Sheikh Al-Sabah in Moscow and had dinner together in his hotel suite, he gave me a detailed account of the whole story—one that our Firuz-begim had never mentioned, most likely out of her own noble sense of modesty...

"It all happened in the late 1980s and early 1990s in the waters of the Persian Gulf, but it started even earlier, in Russia. Here's what happened back then..."

***

Moscow, 1987

There was a big influx of tourists at the Cosmos Hotel—visitors from the Emirates, Kuwait, Syria, Jordan, and other Arab countries. All had come exclusively for eye treatment.

Professor Fedorov had already been informed of which high-ranking foreign guest he'd be dealing with that day. But as usual, he stayed completely calm. He was not in the habit of segregating people by social class or rank; his sole concern was their health—especially the condition of their eyes—because he was one of the best ophthalmologists in the world.

Fedorov was a man who feared nothing. He believed that a doctor who is fearful is not yet a doctor, and that a micro-surgeon's success requires the absolute absence of fear. The same as in wartime: only the one who doesn't fear death can emerge victorious. Fedorov used to say that a surgeon who's not scared, will not botch the operation, he can operate normally. The simplest and at the same time most challenging thing is to do away with fear... faith is crucial...!

Svyatoslav Nikolaevich loved performing surgeries. During surgery, he felt his own power over the process—like being in flight, gaining altitude, making tight turns. He often said he was continually walking a razor's edge yet somehow knew with a sixth sense he would make it across. He clearly felt the responsibility and value of what he was doing, and he knew that his patients—many of them nearly blind—would be seeing again the very next day.

Though during the actual operation Fedorov tried to keep his emotions in check, his nature was overall impulsive, at times even

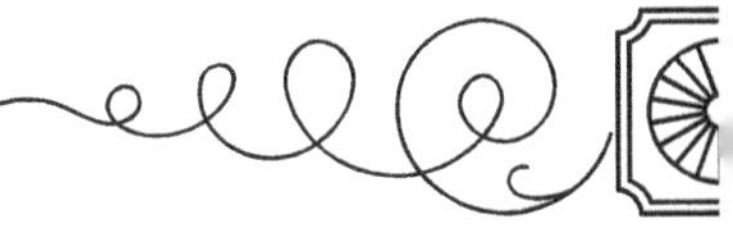

explosive. The great doctor knew that he likely could never have become a general practitioner; he needed to see immediate results. Right in his clinic, patients would toss aside their now-unnecessary glasses.

The Inter-Industry Scientific and Technical Complex "Eye Microsurgery," led by Svyatoslav Fedorov, operated independently, maintaining a network of branches in Russia and abroad, as well as specially outfitted aircraft and "floating clinics" in the Persian Gulf, the Mediterranean, and the Red Sea.

And so, on the 16th floor of the Cosmos Hotel in Moscow, an open diagnostic session had been set up for visiting Arab guests. Undergoing an initial exam, they would receive consultations from ophthalmologists, who would then refer them, based on a preliminary diagnosis, to surgeons at the main building of ISTC "Eye Microsurgery."

On one of these days, Arab Sheikh Al-Nahayan had arrived. He had reserved several rooms at the Cosmos Hotel because he was accompanied by his wife and several members of his personal security team.

After Al-Nahayan finished the diagnostic exam with the ophthalmologist, he was sent to Professor Fedorov as previously arranged. Fedorov examined the sheikh under a slit lamp and diagnosed a "mature cataract of the left eye." Studying the patient's outpatient chart, the renowned doctor said to his assistant:

"Nadenka, we'll operate on this patient on Thursday."

Then he turned to Al-Nahayan:

"Your Excellency, you see, your eye can be compared to the engine of an old car—pretty worn out and in urgent need of repair or replacement. We'll remove that cloudy old lens and install new intraocular lenses—an IOL. Your eye will work like the engine of a brand-new Mercedes!"

To Professor Fedorov's surprise, upon hearing these words, the sheikh did not shower the doctor with thanks; rather, he cast a stern, displeased look. He then began admonishing the translator for how the professor had dared to compare his eye to a car engine.

In order to smooth over the incident as quickly as possible—one that threatened to become quite awkward—the translator instantly improvised:

"Your Highness, most respected Sheikh, please don't take offense at anything. I'll explain everything to you in the car on the way back. Right now, may I suggest that you simply thank the professor for finding time for you in his extremely busy schedule? He has scheduled your surgery for Thursday."

Summoning his will, the sheikh composed himself and said through the interpreter to Fedorov:

"It will be an honour for me to entrust myself to your talented hands. I will thank God for bringing me to you."

On the appointed day, Svyatoslav Nikolaevich himself carried out the operation, making a small incision, removing the hardened, yellowish lens, and inserting the IOL. Then his assistant Nadezhda took his place, stitched up the incision, and patched the sheikh's eye.

The next morning, they checked the sheikh's vision and discovered it had improved by a full eighty percent. Delighted with the result, the sheikh left a note of gratitude in the guestbook for Fedorov, writing:

"You are a marvelous surgeon and a kind magician!"

Some time later, he invited the academician to his country to treat its citizens, promising to provide whatever he needed.

"Could I set up a floating clinic in the Persian Gulf?" Fedorov unexpectedly asked the sheikh, through his assistants. "You see, I have a principle: treatment must be brought as close as possible to the patient's place of residence!"

The sheikh readily agreed. How could he refuse such a request from the man who had granted him the second chance at the gift of sight? And now that chance would be available to his fellow citizens as well!

Fedorov understood that in dealings with foreigners—especially from Arab countries—one must exercise maximum tact and caution. Yet, being utterly fearless, he was prepared to take risks in that regard as well.

***

Leningrad, November 1987

"Hello, Svyatoslav Nikolaevich! This is Kharchenko speaking. The vessel for your Eye Microsurgery Center is ready; you can come to our Baltic Sea Shipping Company and inspect it. I've already signed the operational permit."

"Thank you from the bottom of my heart, Viktor Ivanovich. Which ship is being allocated to us?"

"The *Mikhail Suslov*. It's one of our newer, better-quality passenger ships. If you dislike the name, you can petition the minister for a rename."

"I see. Well, we'll keep it as *Mikhail Suslov* for now. Thanks again."

"If I may be curious: will your floating clinic have the same name as your main center?"

"No. This will be the *FLOKS* medical enterprise—an abbreviation for *FlotOkoServis* (Fleet Eye Service)."

"Excellent. Best of luck."

***

Bremerhaven, Germany, March–July 1989

From mid-March to the beginning of June, the *Mikhail Suslov* was refitted at the Lloyd Werft shipyard in Bremerhaven. The car deck was converted into a modern, high-tech medical facility, fitted with surgical modules costing one million marks each. Altogether, refitting the vessel cost around 27 million German marks.

It was planned that four groups of physicians would work on board simultaneously. The ship cruised the Black Sea and the Mediterranean, offering all the comforts of a cruise. Then, during port calls, onboard surgeons performed eye operations.

At the beginning of July, the ship arrived in Odessa.

A "top-level" decision was made to rename the *Mikhail Suslov* to *Pyotr Pervy* ("Peter the First"), with a political subtext behind it.

The ship had a capacity for 415 people. The clinic's small team carried out operations overseas, thereby freeing space at home for local patients.

This unique floating ophthalmology clinic brought in up to fourteen billion dollars a year.

***

The Persian Gulf, United Arab Emirates, Late 1989–1990

Arriving at the height of the navigation season, the *Pyotr Pervy* immediately began operating on its route, and at the end of the year headed to the port of Jebel Ali, where it remained until April of the following year.

Fedorov was pleased with his experienced and highly qualified colleagues who worked side by side with him. Svyatoslav's wife, Iren Yefimovna, had also intended to join him in the *FLOKS* floating clinic in the Emirates, but in the final days her plans changed due to urgent family matters, and she had to stay in Moscow. The *FLOKS* project leader was joined by his associates and friends: Yuri Cheglakov, Valery Zakharov, Nonna Yartseva, ophthalmic surgeons from the "Clinical Hospital" such as Yuri Kalinnikov, Elena Iliche-va, and other talented physicians.

Among the interpreters were Maria Shadmanova, Elena Byk-ovskaya, and Inna Shivaldova from Russia. Firuz-begim Alimkha-nova from Uzbekistan was also invited to participate in the project.

At first, Fedorov had doubts about Firuz-begim's candidacy. She was already of advanced age… But when the professor read her biography, he readily agreed to take her along. It turned out that of all those who had gathered with Fedorov to treat Arab patients, no one knew their language, psychology, and mentality as well as the former wife of the Emir of Bukhara, Firuz-begim Alimkha-nova. Moreover, a female mediator and interpreter was crucial for treating women, preferably someone not European, but thoroughly Eastern and highly educated. Firuz-begim was best suited for this role.

Nonetheless, the famous doctor could not have fully anticipated just how important, necessary, and valuable Firuz-begim's presence on the ship would be!

Even more so given that, according to Sheikh Al-Nahayan's aides, his beloved daughter—Her Highness Fatima—planned to visit the *FLOKS* floating clinic in January. It turned out she had been planning this for some time.

***

Washington, D.C., USA, a Few Months Earlier

Former FBI agent Jeb Hill knew everything about espionage and terrorism. While still in the service, he'd dreamt of obtaining highly valuable, confidential information—e.g., about VIPs, major politicians, and millionaires—that would allow him to become considerably richer. His line of work involved gathering crucial intel, blackmail, and the like. He'd had these ambitious plans in the making for a while, and after successfully pulling off a few deals to earn seed money, those plans led him…to the Arabs.

Hill knew there were lots and lots of wealthy Arabs, but he decided to play for truly high stakes. After some thought, he realized that the Al-Nahayan family itself would be his biggest financial target. Jeb started plotting how he could extract from the sheikh as much money as the sheikh himself was pumping out of his "golden" oil wells.

Hill recruited trustworthy accomplices and began preparing an operation that he secretly referred to, just within his criminal group, as "Sheikh."

Everything was carefully devised and prepared. The operation was scheduled for early 1990.

***

Persian Gulf, United Arab Emirates, Early 1990

Svyatoslav Fedorov and his colleagues performed one operation after another on the ship, almost without rest. The Soviet government took virtually all the profits from treating Arabs, but even so, Fedorov strove to do most of the surgeries for very little money, or even free of charge. As for the lodging and board of the vessel's crew and Fedorov's entire team, the host—Sheikh Al-Nahayan—covered all those expenses himself. Moreover, he did not draw these funds from the state treasury, paying for everything "out of his own pocket." But his means were so vast that, as the saying goes, he spent some—and just as much remained.

Thousands of people—both men and women—lined up to be operated on by Fedorov and his team. Dozens of ophthalmologists from many parts of the world arrived at the port of Jebel Ali to witness the skill of the Russian specialists firsthand, staying aboard the ship for several days. Despite this influx of visitors, there were enough cabins to accommodate them all.

In the operating block, special telemonitors were installed. There was nothing to criticize—the Fedorov team confirmed its reputation for excellence. Everyone who underwent treatment had their vision restored, at least in part, and for some, completely—depending on the severity and complexity of their condition.

In short, the success of the "Floks" clinic was astonishing and surpassed all expectations. The example of this one-of-a-kind floating ophthalmology clinic became a testament to innovation and a successful attempt to diversify the services of passenger shipping.

Sheikh Al-Nahayan insisted that some of the auxiliary medical staff be sourced from the top Arab hospitals and clinics. Fedorov did not object.

One day, Sheikh Al-Nahayan's daughter, Fatima, arrived with her personal security detail. Of course, a member of a family as prominent and wealthy as Sheikh Al-Nahayan's must have adequate protection—and Fatima certainly had it. However, as Fedorov's colleagues later learned, due to limited accommodations aboard the ship, her security detail here was only a third of its usual size. Still, she was accompanied by the most reliable, time-tested guards.

Prudence was warranted: just the jewelry Fatima wore was valued in the tens, if not hundreds, of millions of dollars. One of the most notable and valuable pieces was a necklace with rubies and diamonds, which she loved more than any other and often wore. She had brought it with her to the *Pyotr Pervy*.

Fatima Al-Nahayan was around thirty years old and divorced. Given her status and wealth, she had many admirers; among them, she was most closely acquainted with the son of the president of one of the Emirates' largest and richest banks—a man named Abbas—as well as with the son of Sheikh Al-Sabah of Kuwait, Fahad. Fahad had asked her to marry him and move to his country. Fatima refused, maintaining only a warm friendship with him. She never told anyone that for the past several years, she had been deeply in love with the handsome young Abbas.

Abbas, for his part, never proposed. He had always lived without wanting to take on any responsibilities, flitting through life like a butterfly. Because of that, his banker father never entrusted him with large sums of money or gave him serious posts in his organization. Abbas was very content with his friendship with Fatima—secretly, she was always taking care of him, paying all his

bills and debts.

When Fahad learned of this through his channels, he said:

"Fatima, my advice is that you should not even associate your-self with that Abbas! He's totally unworthy of you. He doesn't love you; he's just using you."

"How can you say that about him, Fahad? You don't know anything."

"I know all about him. I say this because… because I love you! That man, Abbas, is constantly in debt. He always finds a way to get himself mixed up in unsavoury situations. Why do you need such a… well… friend? He's a bona fide gigolo! Please, be careful with him. He'd sell you out for pennies without a second thought."

Fatima refused to believe him. She also did not know that Jeb Hill had already approached Abbas, buying from him information about all of Fatima's major plans and every important move she would be making over the next six months.

* * *

Fatima, who initially had no desire to be examined or even have her eyesight checked by Fedorov's doctors, finally confessed—after two days on the *Pyotr Pervy*—to the famous professor that she had decided she wanted to be sure she could entrust her precious vision to the Russian specialists, just as her father had done. It turned out she required a complicated and urgent surgery.

"We'll operate right here at the 'Floks' clinic, aboard this ship!" said Svyatoslav Nikolaevich. "I hope you don't object, Your High-ness?"

"I would prefer having it at home—or in one of the city clinics."

"Time isn't on your side, I'm sorry. Better to do it here, and as soon as possible."

"I understand. Very well, then—prepare me for the operation. I'll pay all expenses immediately."

"Thank you, but that's not our main concern. Right now, and above all for the sake of your own health, it's very important that you follow all my instructions and recommendations!"

"Alright, I agree," Fatima said, smiling. "Tell me what they are. I promise I'll be a good patient!"

The operation was scheduled for the following Sunday.

* * *

Prior to surgery, Sheikh Al-Nahayan's daughter—like all other patients—left all her belongings, including her jewelry, in her securely guarded luxury cabin.

When Fatima regained consciousness after the operation and began feeling somewhat better, she clearly heard commotion around her and sensed there was a disturbance.

"Did something happen?" she asked, as though sensing trouble.

They told Fatima that an excessively loud scream had been heard on deck. Everyone had been alarmed, since such a thing had never happened before in Fedorov's clinics—every single patient was properly anesthetized before surgery, so a scream like that could not have come from a patient's treatment.

In response to Fatima's questions, her guards brought a witness to the unpleasant incident, which had occurred exactly during Fatima's eye operation. The witness was one of the Russian interpreters, Inna Shivaldova. The poor girl seemed visibly frightened.

"What happened, Inna? I was told you know something, that you saw something. Please, tell me," Fatima asked politely.

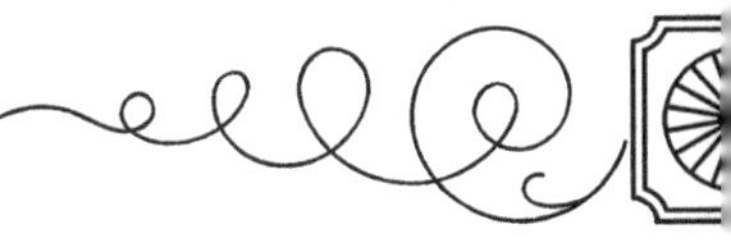

"Sheikha Fatima, I… I was walking down the corridor, and by pure chance ended up near your cabin…"

"Wait. You know where my cabin is located?"

"Yes, of course! Everyone knows, in fact. Besides, I'm an interpreter, I need to know these things all the more."

"Understood. Go on."

"I was surprised to see that your bodyguards weren't by the cabin."

"They weren't? Oh… Right. Most of them were with me in the operating room. Though… I had left one reliable guard, Abdul, by the cabin. So he wasn't there?"

"No, Your Highness."

"Strange. Where could he have gone?"

"I heard someone found him in the ship's restaurant, very drunk—he could barely speak and was practically asleep."

"Really?! That's so bizarre!" Fatima exclaimed, amazed. "Abdul never drank—he's a devout Muslim. I suspect someone deliberately got him drunk. They probably slipped him a sleeping agent in the alcohol, too. But I don't get why…"

"Anyway, Madam Al-Nahayan, during your absence for the operation, one of the Arab nurses was in your cabin. I think her name is Basima"

"What was she doing there?"

"I caught her going through your things."

"Going through my things?!" Fatima flared up angrily. "How dare she?!"

"And the main point, Madam, is that when I walked in, she was actually holding your favorite ruby necklace."

"My necklace? Wait, how do you know it's my 'favorite'?"

"Oh… I just… I assumed, because you wear it often."

"But you've only known me for three days—you can't really judge that."

"I'm sorry, Madam Al-Nahayan. I spoke without thinking. It just… seemed that way to me…"

"So what happened then, Inna? Did you react in any way when you saw that?"

"Yes, of course! I told Basima to put everything back immediately. And she answered that you yourself had sent her… to fetch your purse."

"But I was already in surgery at that time! And by the way, my purse was with me, hanging on a chair in the operating room."

"Yes, but she… she claimed you asked her to bring you your purse! When I expressed my doubt, Basima started shouting, acting hysterical, and threatened me. She seemed mentally unstable! I was so scared that, seeing a bronze statuette on your table, I rushed over to her and struck her on the head."

"You did what, excuse me? You struck someone… on the head? A nurse?!! But why? You could have killed her!"

"I… I certainly didn't plan to kill anyone. It's just that she seemed very dangerous. When I hit her, she let out a shockingly loud scream."

"Naturally… You're lucky the ship's security didn't call the police, because usually in such cases they do. So, Inna, where is that… what's her name again? Basima?"

"Yes, Basima. She's a nurse from Abu Dhabi's Second City Clinic. She was given first aid here and then almost immediately taken by ambulance back to her hospital. But I heard she's alive, just unconscious and slightly injured…"

"That is indeed an unpleasant story…"

"Oh, please forgive me, Madam, for… Perhaps I shouldn't have

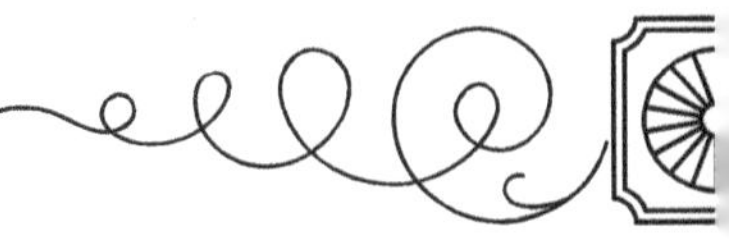

acted that way. I only wanted to protect your belongings—especially the valuables."

"Yes, of course, I understand."

"As soon as the nurse screamed, ship security rushed in. Right now all your valuables are back in place, completely safe and sound."

"I'm very grateful to you for that, Inna. You saved them for me! If not for you, who knows what would've become of my things and jewelry… Especially that ruby necklace—it's truly precious to me… You see, it's an antique, a rare piece, and really priceless. I'm confiding in you because I trust you."

"Thank you, Your Highness. You… you won't go to the police, will you?"

"No, Inna, of course not! We've settled the matter ourselves, right? Now I'm in your debt. On the contrary—tell me what I can do to thank you."

"Oh no, Madam Al-Nahayan… There's no need…"

"From now on, please call me simply Fatima."

"Alright, as you wish. Fatima, I don't need anything. It's a great honor just to talk to the Sheikh's daughter like this. The only thing…"

Inna reddened uncomfortably. The quick-witted Fatima helped her out:

"Yes, yes—I'm listening. Don't be shy; speak up."

"Fatima, if it's possible, I'd like to keep talking with you—it's such a pleasure, so valuable… Could I be your main interpreter here on the ship?"

"Of course. But as I understand it, Inna, you don't speak Arabic, only English?"

"I do speak some Arabic—though only a little."

"Well, well, don't be embarrassed. And how's your Russian?…

Oh, what am I saying? I'm still a bit foggy right after my surgery. You're Russian!"

"Yes, I'm Russian." Inna smiled kindly. "Though I didn't grow up in Russia."

"Really? Interesting. Where, then?"

Inna glanced at her wristwatch.

"Oh, I'm sorry—I just remembered I have to run. Professor Fedorov asked me to come by at two o'clock!"

"Certainly, go ahead. I won't keep you any longer. Once again, thank you for what you did, and since you'll be my chief interpreter on this ship, I'll see you soon!"

Inna gave her new, influential friend a warm smile and left quickly.

* * *

The weather in Abu Dhabi was splendid, ideal for both car rides and walks. The air temperature was moderate—neither any heat to speak of, nor cold. The day promised to be wonderful for everyone.

But Firuz-begim Alimkhanova—who had been endowed since youth with an extraordinary intuition—felt a special sense of foreboding. She was almost certain that something out of the ordinary would happen today.

Fatima had invited all the Russian women from the *Pyotr Pervy*—and, by habit, common among many foreigners, this group also included the Uzbek Firuz-begim Alimkhanova—to take a short tour of the city's sights with her. A whole motorcade of top-quality cars was provided to the guests for just this purpose. The women gratefully and willingly agreed to this little outing.

Svyatoslav Nikolaevich had given nearly everyone the afternoon off; there was still plenty of work to be done, of course, but at least the women deserved the chance to rest properly once in a while!

After the tour, some of the women went to the market, while a smaller group—which included Fedorov's ophthalmologists and nurses, plus the interpreters Inna, Elena, and Firuz-begim—accompanied Fatima to a restaurant owned by her father, located in the heart of the city.

It was a beautiful, cozy place that lent itself to a pleasant, relaxing time. One half of the restaurant was allocated to men, the other to women. Fatima, having worked up an appetite during the outing, decided to join her guests for a meal as well.

All the women were thrilled beyond words. They longed to spend more time with the Sheikh's daughter; until now, only Inna Shivaldova had been fortunate enough to have that opportunity.

Reflecting on this, Firuz-begim glanced briefly at the lucky Inna, who had so quickly earned the favor of the Arab Sheikh's daughter. At that moment, something about Inna struck Firuz-begim as odd—something unusual—but she couldn't pinpoint exactly what it was. The restaurant's atmosphere, the enticing smell of the exotic dishes they'd ordered… It was all so temptingly pleasant, so much so that Firuz-begim—like all her companions—immediately switched her focus to enjoying this marvelous break in delightful company.

Fatima had to step away from the table a couple of times—apologising each time—when her pager went off and she had to make a call. Her security team waited for her both inside the restaurant foyer and outside. But Fatima, not wanting to bother her guests or disrupt their conversation, had instructed the guards not to come too close to their table.

Suddenly, Fatima began feeling unwell. Excusing herself, saying she'd be right back, she got up from the table. Inna offered to accompany Fatima to the ladies' room:

"Excuse me, if I may, I'll go too."

"Inna, wait, I'll come with you!" Firuz-begim suddenly said. If anyone had been watching her face at that moment, they would have noticed it had gone very pale.

"What, you as well?!" Inna said, surprised for some reason.

"Yes. Why not?" the older woman replied seriously.

"But I know there aren't many stalls in there. And wouldn't it be inconvenient if we all left at once?"

"Inconvenient for whom?" asked Firuz-begim, feigning ignorance.

"Oh, well... it's just better if you stay here, please!" Inna said, standing up. She tried to sound polite, but for some reason her voice bore an undercurrent of pressure. Then she pulled a handkerchief out of her cosmetics pouch.

Sensing the tension and potential danger in the air, the sharp-minded Firuz-begim suddenly shouted right into Inna's ear:

"Inna!"

The startled young woman turned around, and in a flash... Firuz-begim grabbed the nearest cup of hot coffee and flung its contents straight into Inna's face.

Inna cried out in pain. She couldn't move and sank into the nearest chair. Everyone present was shocked by the bizarre, flagrantly uncultured, and seemingly inexplicable act committed by this older Uzbek woman.

Meanwhile, Fatima had already gone off to the restroom...

At that moment, Firuz-begim whispered something to one of Fatima's security guards, who had just rushed over to the women.

The guard, giving a signal to his colleagues, swiftly took hold of Inna and also a waiter who turned out to be her accomplice; together with the other guards, he escorted them both out of the restaurant.

When Fatima returned, already informed about what had happened, the women all sat back down at the table. They were all still greatly shaken and surprised, but things had calmed slightly. Firuz-begim then calmly and thoroughly explained everything, justifying her actions to those present.

The women were exceedingly curious to hear all the details from her.

* * *

"Respected Sheikha Al-Nahayan, the thing is that this seemingly modest girl, who introduced herself to all of us as an interpreter, is actually, as I've come to realize, an international terrorist. Possibly from America, but I'm not sure exactly. In any case, it appears so. And I'm convinced that she wanted to kidnap you."

"What?!" Fatima exclaimed in astonishment. "Kidnap me?! But why, for what purpose?!"

"For ransom, of course!!! And I 'spotted' this Inna, then slightly neutralised her…"

"But… Firuz-begim, how did you figure out that Inna is a terrorist?"

"To begin with, it's unlikely that her real name is Inna. As I said, I think she's not Russian. Didn't you notice that when she speaks her 'native' language, she has a clear accent? Fine, even if she grew up outside Russia, there are still words in the Russian language that she couldn't possibly pronounce with an Anglo-American accent if

she hadn't lived in the States… Either way, she's young, and maybe that's why she slipped up several times. Although I fully assume that the people who sent her are far more experienced than she is, because they seem to have planned everything quite meticulously and thoroughly."

"Where did she make mistakes that let you 'spot' her?"

"You may know that I once belonged to a very influential, also royal, family… So back then, I happened to encounter more than one spy and infiltrator. I observed these people more than once. Almost all of them have a similar psychology and behavior. The thing is, they try so hard, right from the start, to gain the trust of their potential victim that they forget to show any sense of restraint. That affected politeness and 'kindness' always seem to me feigned and false, which raises my suspicion. And today, here in the restaurant, when we all sat down at the table, I saw her face was cold and indifferent, as though nothing worried or delighted her, as if this meeting didn't touch her at all—even though I already knew she wanted it more than anyone else! And her whole body was tense, taut. That's how an animal looks before pouncing, or how a person looks before some crucial, dangerous, and difficult act—usually involving an attack. At a moment when all of us here were so at ease, naturally relaxed and at peace, I found it very striking and unusual that only one person among us showed such a strange combination of facial expressions and body posture."

"All right," said one of the doctors, Olga. "That's all very sensible. What next?"

"As I mentioned, she made a few 'slips.' For example, at one point during conversation, Inna struggled to say in which country she was born and got confused about it twice. You must agree that's not entirely normal! Another thing: this whole story about the

supposed theft of Her Highness's belongings and jewelry, which everyone heard about, seems like pure fiction and a fabrication by this so-called 'witness to the incident.' How did she end up there? Why did she even enter Fatima's cabin? She never explained that to anyone! The only conclusion is that she herself orchestrated the entire situation—falsely luring Nurse Basima into our mistress's cabin, completely framing her, and then knocking her out so she couldn't testify against her! By the way, it's been a few days since that incident, and I managed to find out what became of the nurse who was taken to the hospital after the injury Inna inflicted on her—supposedly 'to save Fatima's property.' Well, did you hear that the nurse disappeared?"

"What do you mean, 'disappeared'?" Fatima asked in surprise. She had been distracted by urgent matters and, though she inquired about the poor girl's health on the actual day of the 'emergency,' had forgotten to check on her fate afterward.

"Gone, just like that! But that's not all," Firuz-begim said. "Of course, we're all delighted about this excursion. However, it was Inna who appealed to Lady Al-Nahayan for it! And not by herself, not directly—apparently so as not to expose herself unnecessarily—but through Doctor Yartseva. But it was Inna who needed at all costs to get Fatima out into the city. Kidnapping the Sheikh's daughter on the ship would have been impossible or extremely difficult, and at other times—before and after Fatima's treatment—it would also be tough, because then Mistress Al-Nahayan is accompanied by very large, powerful security. At this point, with us, the criminals thought her safety wouldn't be so 'impenetrable.' But they didn't take into account the main thing…"

"What was that?" asked the interpreter, Elena.

"Us! In any case, we would never have let anything happen

to Fatima, and we would have managed to protect her from any kidnappers, right?"

All the women completely agreed.

"She slipped something into your juice unnoticed, Lady Al-Nahayan, which suddenly made you feel ill. I realized this chain of events simply couldn't be a coincidence! And the moment Inna pulled out her handkerchief, I already knew she was a criminal, and it crossed my mind that the handkerchief might contain chloroform, which she would need in order to put you, madam, to sleep in the restroom. Also, I noticed how she exchanged strange glances from time to time with one of the waiters, who was then taken away along with her. They had secret signals. And I wouldn't be surprised if it turns out that someone among your security, Lady Al-Nahayan, was also involved in all this sordid business."

"I'm astonished…" said Fatima.

"I knew," Firuz-begim continued, "that if I went with both of you to the restroom—the very place Inna didn't want me to enter—I wouldn't stand a chance alone against a strong young woman. So on the spot, I came up with the plan to stop her right there, at the table. I hope she'll forgive me for slightly messing up her face… Possibly even for life. But I simply had no other choice!"

Firuz-begim gave a good-natured smile.

"That criminal ruined everything for herself," noted the Sheikh's daughter.

All the women looked at Firuz-begim with genuine respect and admiration, while Fatima regarded her with immense gratitude as well.

***

Tashkent, 2014

Said Yahyaevich took a sip of tea and looked at his wife with a mysterious expression.

"Well, Sitora, Sheikha Fatima Al-Nahayan, in heartfelt gratitude to our Firuz-begim for saving her from the hands of that kidnapper-terrorist, presented her with… a precious ruby necklace!"

"What, really—that very one? The one worth millions?"

"Yes, indeed, the very same one that she treasured and loved so much. In truth, our benevolent Firuz-begim didn't even want to accept it… But with this gift, Fatima wanted to show that her life, her safety, and her relationships with good people—her new friends from Uzbekistan and Russia—were far dearer to her than any wealth.

"That's a wonderful story! But then how did that necklace end up with the Sheikh of Kuwait instead of with Firuz-begim at that time?"

"I don't know all the details, but I do know this: in those Soviet days, they wouldn't have allowed Firuz-begim to bring such an expensive gift back to Tashkent from abroad. So by the will of fate, the necklace ended up in the hands of the person I was fortunate enough to meet in Moscow in 2009—Sheikh Al-Sabah."

"That's the same one you told me about earlier?"

"Yes, exactly. He's a very decent man. He said that, at the request of Sheikh Al-Nahayan's family, he spent a long time searching for Firuz-begim but couldn't track her down. Then… I myself got in touch with him and happened to mention her, and he was overjoyed! After all, on the largest ruby set into that precious necklace, at the request of the Sheikh of the Emirates' daughter, and on her behalf, back in 1990, a heartfelt inscription was engraved, addressed to Firuz-begim Alimkhanova. That's how Sheikh Al-Sabah came to know her name… He brought the jewelry with him to our conference and graciously handed it over to me—together with all the accompanying official documents—so that I could take it to Tashkent and deliver it personally into Firuz-begim's hands. And you know, that's exactly what I did. And now your dear grandmother wants to make our daughter Malika happy by giving her that precious piece on her wedding day! That's worth a great deal…

"I can't argue with that, Said."

"And there's only one thing I regret, Sitora: that I never had the chance to know Fatima Al-Nahayan personally, nor Professor Fedorov—who, sadly, passed away so suddenly…

"As an ophthalmologist, there's so much I could have learned from him personally, and working with him, I'm sure, would have given me enormous pleasure, and my patients even better health. And I'm convinced we would have developed an excellent personal relationship. After all, as this story I've just told you shows, true, kind human relationships can't be measured by any amount of money…"

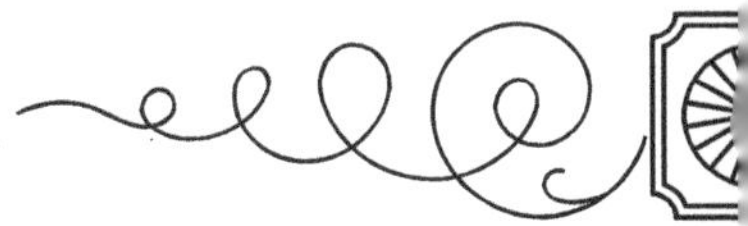

27

Bahadir had been used to believing since childhood that he had an entire sea of friends. Despite his quick-tempered and, on the whole, complicated nature, he was always sociable, kind, and generous, which genuinely made people enjoy "hanging out" with him. He had yet to learn how to distinguish between casual acquaintances or friendly interactions and genuine, true friendship.

Already a young adult, Bahadir would most often see his buddies in bars, restaurants, clubs, and less frequently at the institute. Being openhearted by nature, he told them practically everything about himself: his family background, who his parents were, their financial situation, what he wanted to become, what he dreamed of, what he aspired to—everything.

However, Bahadir noticed that not all of his pals were genuinely and truly interested in knowing in detail his whole "backstory," what made him tick, what worried him, what upset him, or what made him happy.

It was only really important and interesting to one person— Rudik Khayrullin.

There were circles of friends with whom Bahadir Fattakhov shared an interest in studying international management, economics, and the financial sphere as a whole. There were others with whom he could simply unwind, listening to pleasant, familiar music, discussing it, and sometimes dancing in nightclubs. And there were still others with whom he liked talking about cars—which he was passionately fond of—and all sorts of other equipment, as well as the latest computer and other modern technologies. Ever since childhood, Bahadir had been so fascinated with tinkering around with all kinds of "hardware," chips, and wires that he sometimes wondered at having enrolled in an economics major (his father's insistence) rather than going into programming or equipment engineering. By age sixteen, he could easily fix almost any computer problem, regardless of model or classification, and he could disassemble and reassemble a music player or any other complex gadget without difficulty.

It was primarily on this basis that he immediately grew close to Rudik, who lived on the same street as Amin, Rano, and Bahadir. Rudik was considerably less skilled with technology than Bahadir, but he often went together with Bahadir to neighbors or other acquaintances to fix something, though he himself contributed little to the repair work, mostly just observing closely how quickly and precisely Bahadir worked. For Bahadir, tasks like that were child's play; he fixed everything easily and took great satisfaction from the results of his capable hands.

And Rudik possessed remarkable qualities that are rare these days: he never took offense at anything, and he never felt any envy at all… This was especially evident in his dealings with Bahadir. On the contrary, if Bahadir had some kind of problem or felt down for whatever reason—misunderstood, upset, or hurt by someone—Rudolf could always empathise, support, and encourage Bahadir, never letting him get depressed, lose hope, or give in to despair.

Bahadir noticed that when he was around Rudik, he felt smarter, more talented, stronger, and more successful. Once, back in their youth, some drunken hooligans attacked Rudik in the courtyard, and since Bahadir was athletic and well-trained, he easily took care of Rudik's attackers.

From that day on, Rudik treated Bahadir as his powerful protector and benefactor, finding it a great pleasure, honor, and even happiness to walk around and be friends with him.

All this boosted Bahadir in his own eyes, making him feel more important.

"Baha, you're the best friend in the world!" Rudik would say in sincere admiration.

Rudolf never hesitated to speak directly to Bahadir about all his troubles and needs and never felt embarrassed about asking his strong friend for help, plainly and simply.

Rudik never skimped on lavish praise, lauding Bahadir and marveling at him in front of all their companions and acquaintances. At first, Bahadir felt awkward about this blatant, undisguised flattery, but he eventually got used to it and even came to like it a lot. And on any day Rudik might forget to "sing praises" to Bahadir, it would feel as though something was missing.

Bahadir's mother, Mukhabbat, had been aware of her younger son's friend named Rudik ever since Bahadir's childhood. For the first few years, she was generally tolerant of their friendship, watching Rudik on the occasions he visited them—sometimes for dinner, tea, lunch, or to ask Bahadir for a little "loan." Naturally, Bahadir did not have money of his own at that time—he started earning later—but his father, Abdulla Rustamovich, would often reward each of his children with small "bonuses" for good academic performance or on holidays, giving them some spending money for "cola and ice cream."

But as the boys got older, Mukhabbat noticed that Rudik's requests also noticeably increased. He began borrowing larger sums from Bahadir, still never returning them. What's more, Bahadir, being good-hearted and naive, would frequently and willingly help his "best friend" in all sorts of ways. This led Mukhabbat to regard this "best friend," who she felt had latched onto her son like a leech, with growing wariness and even suspicion.

* * *

On that day, the already twenty-five-year-old Rudolf called his younger, but "senior" in their relationship, and highly respected friend Bahadir and suggested a meeting, saying that there was an important topic that would be good to discuss.

"What's this about, bro?" Bahadir asked, curious. "If it's about my love life, then right now, after the breakup with Malika, I'm in no shape—"

"No, no, Bahadir!" Khayrullin assured him enthusiastically. "I've got a fantastic business idea. Trust me, you'll like it!"

They agreed to meet at a cozy little bistro they both loved.

Seated at the table, Rudik made a show of reaching for his wallet in his back pocket.

"Don't bother, I'll pay," Bahadir stopped him out of habit.

"Come on, Bahadir, that's a bit awkward! After all, I'm the one who invited you."

"Cut it out. I know you're working now as an engineer in a big company and earning a decent salary, but I'm aware you've got a sick mother." (Out of politeness and compassion, Bahadir avoided saying "alcoholic mother.") "She needs a lot of care. Meanwhile, I have zero financial trouble, as always. So, I'll pick up the tab. Go ahead, order whatever you like, don't hold back."

"How about a couple of skewers of shashlik and a hundred grams of vodka, eh, Bahadir?"

"I'll gladly have shashlik, but I won't be drinking, sorry—I've got an important seminar tomorrow. I still need to prepare. Maybe some other time… I'll have tea with lemon."

"Tell me, Baha, how are you? Is everything okay? Still pining for that girl… What was her name?"

"Malika. Yeah. I can't get her out of my head."

"She really got to you, huh… Well, call her, what's the problem?"

"I think I offended her… I ended up pushing her away. And I'm still not ready for a serious relationship with anyone—even her. My father gave me a one-month deadline to find a fiancée on my own. But I don't want anyone."

"Really? That happens… But then why'd you meet up with different girls?"

"I was hoping to forget Malika faster, you see? And I thought I could find a wife on my own without my parents' help. But so far I haven't managed."

"Tell me, Bahadir, is it really necessary to marry at twenty-three?" Rudik gave a broad grin. "I'm twenty-five, and I've got no shortage of girlfriends. I'm living it up and have no intention of getting married! Why rush? Can't it wait at least three or four years?"

"I'd be happy to wait, but my father insists I marry. He figures it'll 'talk sense into me,' as he calls it, make me more 'serious' and 'level-headed.' That's why he set me up with Malika… And truth be told, she's a good girl. Really pretty, just enchanting. I've never met anyone like her in my life. There's something about her, Rudik— like her beauty radiates from her pure, kind, luminous heart…"

"Awesome. If she doesn't work out for you, maybe I'll take a crack at her. If she's that special, right? Let me have a shot—no use letting a good thing go to waste."

"No, man. And don't joke like that about her ever again, got it? Don't you dare! I won't allow it."

"Sorry, Bahadir—sorry, I'm an idiot. Spoke without thinking. You really are hung up on her! Well, in that case… I think the proposal that brought me here will be perfect for you. If you show up to Malika—"

"She's not mine at the moment—"

"No matter, she will be yours, I'm sure of it! You're a stud, Baha, and a clever guy. If you go to her not 'empty-handed' but with the promise of a bright future full of money, I figure she'll gladly receive you—with open arms, as they say. Even for the 'saints' and 'angels' on Earth, it's nice to be wealthy and enjoy all sorts of good things in life, right?"

"Well, maybe. So what's your idea?"

"I'll tell you. You know I'm working at the local branch of the Italian company Vit-Alma, which manufactures and globally supplies plastic household goods, right? As an engineer-technologist and production setup specialist, I buy equipment for our firm at good prices and deal with top-notch tech-equipment manufacturers. Meanwhile, you're in the international division of your father's company…"

"Wait, I'm not following—what does my international division have to do with it?"

"It's that, Bahadir, we'll bring in reliable foreigners. Specifically—Europeans. I'll handle everything with the best equipment, if you don't mind. And you'll be our chief investor and general director—so you won't be under your father's thumb anymore! So, what do you think?"

"What kind of joint venture is this? You haven't said, Rudik."

"Well, here's the thought: the two of us, together, start our own joint venture to produce perfumery and cosmetic goods—a home-grown Uzbek brand, manufacturing in Tashkent together with 'your' French partners and 'my' Italians, but named after world-famous Eastern figures like Biruni, Temur, Ulugbek, Bibikhanum, Babur, Shah Jahan, and so on. We can compile a technical and financial feasibility study plus a business plan, and present it to our foreign partners so that they'll support us and invest. And this business is sure to be highly profitable—I guarantee it! So, what do you say?"

"It's pretty interesting, actually. But I'm not sure we can pull it off…"

"Baha, just trust me! I'll take care of all the paperwork—I'm good with documents. Remember, you mentioned there's a Frenchman your father's company has cooperated with for years? What's his name?"

"Jean Marshal?"

"Exactly. You said he's been wanting to set up a joint venture in Uzbekistan, because in their oh-so-praised Europe, equipment, labor, even factory space rent, all cost huge money. And here, it'd be cheaper for him. I think he'll be happy to sign on and become a partner."

"We'll see. But as far as you're concerned, these foreigners would end up owning the enterprise, right? Not us?!"

"No, not at all. Like I said, you'd be the main owner! Nobody else deserves it. I'll set it all up in the paperwork, so don't worry about that! I've even come up with a name: JV 'Bakh-atir'—as in 'Bahadir's Perfume'! Sounds cool, doesn't it? And it's got a ring similar to your name?"

"That does sound pretty awesome… Wow, you're something else!"

"And I'd serve as your right-hand man in this project—your deputy. Sound good?"

Bahadir didn't reply. He mulled over Rudik's words, trying to weigh everything.

"So which Italians do you plan on bringing in? Are they reliable—can we trust them?"

"Of course! Actually, it's just one Italian… but he's tried and true, worth a hundred investors. If you're curious, his name is Francesco Valdoni. He supplies imported equipment to our firm, Vit-Alma."

"Do they really make the best equipment in Italy?"

"But it's not just Italian, Bahadir! Francesco works with equipment from all over the world. As do I, for that matter. He's sharp and reliable—believe me."

"Well… actually… I still have debts."

"Gambling debts? Yes, I know—you mentioned them. That's exactly what you'll pay off!"

"So, Rudik, does this mean we won't have to invest anything?"

"How could you not? Of course we'll need to invest! But these investments will be modest. And really—there's no such thing as big business without a decent investment, and you know that better than I do. But you'll make it all back quickly; all the money you put in will return to you with high interest, and you'll easily be able to pay off your gambling debts! Please, trust me!!! Have I ever deceived you, Baha?"

"The idea itself is really interesting. I like it. Maybe, Rudik, I'll take the risk. But give me a little time to think, all right?"

"No problem, it's a deal! And don't forget about your Malika!"

"To tell you the truth, Rudik, I never expected to miss her this much… There's only one thing I don't quite like about her—she's

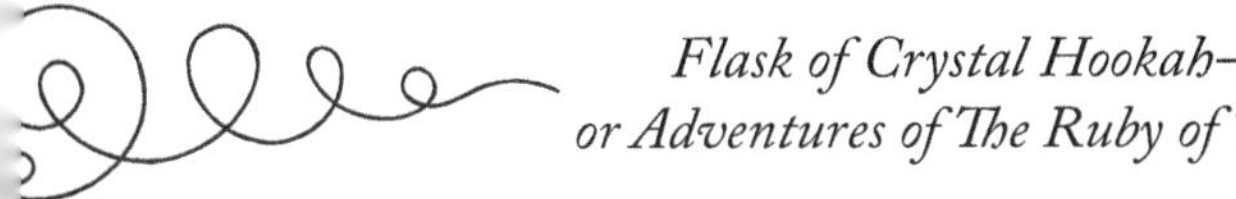

too 'proper,' too pure, and beside her, I feel like some kind of monster or worthless person."

"Come on, Baha, what do you mean 'monster'? I've told you many times—and I'm ready to repeat it—that you're the coolest person in the whole world! She'll understand that too. Besides, I think that as a real Uzbek man, you'll completely bend her to your will, your strength, and your authority. And as a true Uzbek woman, she'll submit to you entirely—if she really loves you."

"I'm not sure, Rudik, whether she loves me or not," Bahadir sighed. "That word 'love' is so... heavy. But I did see the spark in her eyes when she looked at me and talked to me. Whenever we met, she was never cold or indifferent toward me; she always showed genuine concern for my life. Even when she saw things in me that she probably couldn't like, she still never judged me for them—she accepted me as I am..."

"You see? That's great."

"Of course, I'm a fool—what more do I need? It's clear that only a wife like Malika suits me! She's so understanding and compliant, ready to put up with anything. It's easy and comfortable for me to be with her; I don't feel any strain at all! I don't have to adapt myself to her or pretend to be better than I really am... And besides, my father asked me the other day to make a final decision about Malika."

"Then go for it—marry her! Though I won't hide it: as your close friend, I'd be really glad if you stayed single a little longer so we could hang out more. Especially since I'm not sure how your future wife will feel about our joint venture..."

Bahadir gave a somewhat sad smile.

"You talk like this JV already exists, Rudik! It's not even established yet. And if it does happen, I won't be asking Malika's permission, and she won't interfere in anything."

"Oh, that's right! Spoken like a real man. Listen, Bahadir, is that girl from a pretty well-off family?"

"Her family... Her father is a well-known doctor in the republic—he runs a private clinic."

"That's not bad!" Rudik whistled. "Have you been to their house? Any gold, expensive real estate, jewelry?"

"What are you getting at?" Bahadir asked, surprised and suddenly anxious. "Why do you need to know that? I haven't seen anything myself, but I heard that Malika's great-great-grandmother was once the wife of the Emir of Bukhara."

"Wow! No kidding! Do you have any idea how wealthy that Emir was? I heard all his women had loads of jewelry. And if you say Malika's ancestor was his wife, that means your Malika is a very rich heiress! Her fortune would be really useful for our new business."

"Listen, Rudik, I've never been and never will be a gigolo. I won't ever depend on my wife's purse!" Bahadir said angrily. "Besides, marrying for money is low, indecent, and humiliating for a man—even in this day and age."

28

"Hello, Malika, good afternoon! How are you? This is Amin, the son of Abdulla Rustamovich, your father's friend. You remember me, don't you?"

"Of course, Amin. Good afternoon! I'm… all right, thank you for asking. And how are you? Is everything okay? Your parents are well?"

"Yes, yes, everything's fine, don't worry! I just wanted to see how you're doing, how your studies are going. I imagine you like it?"

"I like it very much." She smiled absently into the phone.

"I've heard about your achievements, Malika. I was told that you took a prize at the republican vocalists' competition. Good for you!"

"Oh, that was back in college, more than a year ago already."

"I'm sure there will be many more competitions in your future, and you'll definitely keep winning!"

"Thank you. But please, don't flatter me too much…"

"Oh, come on, Malika! I didn't mean to embarrass you. On the contrary—I just wanted to say something nice. I'm sorry it didn't come out right. You know, Malika, maybe you'd let me make it up to you by inviting you to dinner at a restaurant? That's actually why I'm calling."

"Me?.. What for, Amin?"

"Oh so, that's how it is, is it?" He pretended a mock anger in a warm, good-natured tone. "Is it really so hopeless in our day and age for a still young and rather interesting man to invite a lovely young lady to dinner—just in a friendly way?"

"No, of course not! It's not at all hopeless if it's on friendly terms… It's just that, after that incident…"

"What incident? Oh—maybe you mean that awful meeting with Mukhitdin? Yes? I see—you feel uncomfortable around me after that, is that it? But that's all the more reason, Malika: I want us to remain good friends, without any awkwardness or discomfort! Please, accept my invitation! Refusal is not allowed."

Malika remained silent for a few moments.

"All right… I agree to have dinner, but only out of great respect for you and solely on friendly terms…"

"Oh yes, Malika. And you know, it will be… a joy for me to have you as a friend—or better to say, a 'companion,' yes?"

"Well… yes, it seems so."

"Wonderful!"

"I'm glad. Tell me the restaurant's address."

* * *

Amin was waiting for Malika at the restaurant entrance with a stunning bouquet of flowers. It seemed he was very nervous and had dressed with special care, looking impeccable from head to toe—in short, he appeared absolutely splendid.

Malika was touched by this. It had been a long time since she had received even this kind of attention and effort from a man, just to please her.

All the same, not even the smallest spark of passion, desire, or attraction toward this handsome, grown man lit in her heart. No matter how she tried to fight it, she could picture only one person—Bahadir. Perhaps that was why she smiled so warmly at Amin: the moment he offered her the flowers with trembling hands, she mentally replaced him with Bahadir.

"Malika, good evening! You look lovely tonight—like a heavenly flower in some magical dream garden… Please forgive me. I'm sure that if it's all right with you, we'll have dinner together again—strictly as friends, of course. I wouldn't presume anything else. But right now, I have a duty… In fact, someone else is waiting for you!"

When they stopped by one of the cozy window tables, Malika was so startled that she nearly fainted. Sitting there, no less elegant and impeccably dressed than Amin, was his younger brother, Bahadir Fattakhov!

***

Amin apologized once more, courteously said his goodbyes, and left. Bahadir stood up to greet Malika. From the vase on the table, he picked up a bouquet just as extravagant as the one Amin had given her and confidently offered it to Malika, without a hint of shyness.

In that instant, she thought he didn't seem as nervous as she or Amin. But that impression soon faded. Maybe it was drowned out by a different kind of anxiety he was feeling… Malika couldn't analyze or perceive it clearly.

Bahadir placed their order. While the waitress brought the food and light drinks, he watched Malika attentively, catching her shy, gentle, and naively happy glances.

He too longed to feel happy and realised it was entirely possible in her presence. She attracted him as a woman, and he felt drawn to her… Yet something seemed to stop him from surrendering fully to this happiness.

He abruptly demanded, in an almost harsh tone:

"So, why didn't you call me, huh? Feeling too proud?"

She was surprised by his sudden 'accusation,' but it didn't offend her.

"I was waiting for your call. I was afraid to bother you. I thought maybe it just wasn't meant to be…"

"How can you jump to that conclusion about 'meant to be' or not? I was thinking, weighing things, trying to find the right way forward, don't you see?!"

"Yes."

He was certain she would now turn the same question on him—why hadn't he called her, not even once?

But she said nothing.

Bahadir was amazed. This remarkable girl, unusually gentle and thoroughly unassuming, seemed even more attractive to him now.

"All right, Malika, it's up to you, but I realised I can't live without you! You understand?" He asked for the third time if she understood, as if he were talking to a child who needed things repeated, despite knowing very well she was nothing like that. Malika thought maybe it was just his way of making sense of everything happening.

"Yes, of course."

"And you're not angry with me?"

"Me…?"

"Yes, Malika. I thought maybe you wouldn't want to see me again; that's why I asked my brother to invite you here. So, you're not mad?"

"No, no, not at all. I'm not angry."

She gave him a warm, tender smile. He gazed at her, unable to look away.

"All right, then… So, Malika, will you marry me?"

Bahadir slid closer to her and impulsively grabbed her hand.

"Why are you quiet, Malika? Did you get flustered? It's me, right here—everything's okay! You hear me? I'm proposing to you, right now, offering you my hand and heart. What do you say? Let's not delay the wedding. We can hold it very soon!"

Although he wasn't really asking her anything—more like deciding for both of them—she dissolved into an ecstatic, blissful smile, unable to contain the pleasant rush of emotion, and wrapped her arms around her beloved gently and tremulously.

Bahadir pressed her firmly to his chest. Then, lifting her chin slightly and looking straight into her exquisitely beautiful eyes, he kissed her on the lips passionately and fervently.

"So you agree?" he asked, recognizing her silent answer and smiling happily. "Well, thank God!"

29

Agra, 1610

Kandahari-begim traveled for many months before reaching Agra. At last, in October of 1610, she was wed to Prince Shah-Jahan of the Great Mughal Empire.

The wedding was grand and magnificent. On that day, the bride and groom received an outpouring of extravagant compliments. The celebratory gathering took place in a splendidly furnished mansion which, by tradition, belonged to the mother of the reigning emperor. It was located within the mighty walls of Agra Fort, adjacent to the padishah's palace.

Slave-girls, specially trained for the occasion, prepared Princess Kandakhari for her first wedding night. She was thoroughly bathed and anointed with various ointments and fragrances. The shahzade was likewise made ready for this night.

But he had no desire to think about his young wife! All his thoughts remained fixed on a single woman—his beloved Arjumand…

The prince and princess lay together. The slave-girls brought a certain part of her body closer to the prince. But suddenly he… sharply turned away, knocking two of the slave-girls to the floor.

"Get out of here!" he cried angrily at them. The slave-girls, genuinely astonished by such behavior—no one had ever acted like this with Shah-Jahan—rubbed their minor bruises and withdrew quietly and obediently from his chambers.

Thus passed many, many nights in which Shah-Jahan never once touched his wife. Whenever he needed mere physical fulfillment as a man, they summoned a concubine; by the prince's order, her face was always covered. Once he had satisfied his body's demands, the prince would send the concubines back to their quarters and promptly forget they existed.

He wished only to remember and love that one woman, holding her form and face in his mind.

Oh, Arjumand!!!

* * *

Agra, 1611

Padishah Jahangir had already assisted in sending his first wife, Taj-Bibi Bilkis-Makani, to the next world—she had been poisoned during the padishah's journey—and, not without the help of Mehrun-Nissa, he also disposed of her husband, Sher Afkun. It seemed that now nothing could prevent him from being with that captivating and beguiling daughter of Giyas Bek, the Pillar of the State! And yet he suffered, feeling helpless, unable to do anything, because nearly four years had passed since Mehrun-Nissa had been widowed, and she still refused to become Jahangir's wife!

Everyone around him was amazed.

"Which astrologer is advising her?" the padishah wondered. "I ought to bribe him!"

"Aunt, why are you delaying your remarriage?" Arjumand asked her one day. Although she felt sorry for her young cousin Ladilli—Mehrun-Nissa's daughter, who had lost her beloved father—time did not stand still, and her mother, still not old and still beautiful, needn't remain alone forever. "Don't you want power and wealth?"

"My dear, you must understand: I know all too well the ways of rulers! Usually, whatever they desire, they obtain—whatever it may be—on the spot. But once they have it, they lose all interest in the object of their recent longing. I won't allow or tolerate being treated that way: taken up and then cast aside. The longer I keep the padishah at the necessary distance—without shrinking or stretching it too much—the more he yearns, and the deeper and stronger his feelings for me become! In the end, I shall be more desirable to him than the throne itself! It's easy for me to keep Jahangir under my control, because I am not..."

Though Mehrun-Nissa did not finish her sentence, Arjumand knew exactly what she intended to say.

Eventually, there came a day when Mehrun-Nissa finally yielded to the padishah's pleas and agreed to marry him. Preparations for the celebration commenced.

"You don't love him at all, daughter," said her mother, Surayya, shaking her head as she helped the bride select outfits. "Of course, Shah Jahangir is extremely wealthy... But without love, where's the happiness in that? And to become, no less, the padishah's twentieth wife! What joy is there in that? Perhaps your father, Giyas Bek, could speak with our sovereign again and convince him to leave you in peace and not take you as his wife?"

"Why would I do that, Mother? There's no need. Don't worry about me," Mehrun-Nissa reassured Surayya. "You'll see—I'll climb to the highest rank of honour! Love is nonsense; is it really the most important thing in life? The padishah is already in my power, and I'll control him even more, become his mistress in truth, and he'll be my servant! Whatever I want—any whim—I'll have fulfilled with pleasure! Everyone will revere me, speak my name

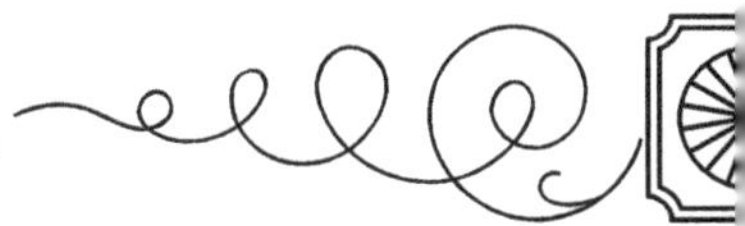

with respect, and I'll become the padishah's chief wife!"

"Oh, Mehrun-Nissa!" her mother cried. "Don't talk like that! What if someone overhears you by chance?... Are you really thinking of poking your nose into politics too, running matters side by side with the men as their equal? Where has that ever been seen in the East—that a woman might dare involve herself in politics? But I know you: you're fearless and bold, you love power! And your brother, Asaf-khan, isn't much different—he's obsessed with his career, now a chief advisor under the padishah, serving the ruler alongside your father. Well, perhaps you too will rise high and achieve even more in life... Who can say!"

* * *

The wedding of Jahangir and Mehrun-Nissa was splendid and extraordinarily lavish. The padishah spared no expense, and the people of the empire feasted—eating, drinking, and celebrating—for many days and nights.

As for Arjumand, at the wedding she noticed only one person: her precious Shah Jahan. And he, as though bound in chains, could not tear his eyes from her.

Just as he had asked Arjumand, she continued to believe and wait...

Jahangir was overcome with happiness and bliss. He forgot about affairs of state, indulging more than anyone else in wine and surrendering himself to sweet delights with his passionately beloved wife. He showered her with gifts and jewels of every kind.

"And where is my Koh-i-Nur diamond?" he asked Mehrun-Nissa. "Are you keeping it safe?"

"Like the apple of my eye, my dear. Let it remain with me for now—that's safer!"

Jahangir deferred to her in everything. Mehrun-Nissa was right: the power over the ruler of the empire—and thus over the empire itself—was now practically in her hands.

***

Lahore, Shah Jahan's Residence, 1612

"Your Highness, your brother Sultan Shahriyar-mirza has arrived to see you," a servant informed Shah-Jahan.

"Oh really?.. What does he want here?"

The question wasn't really for the servant—how could he possibly know the purpose of this visit? Shah Jahan paused for a moment.

"Very well, send him in."

Prince Shahriyar entered his elder brother's chambers and pressed his right hand to his heart, bowing deeply. As Shah Jahan approached, Shahriyar knelt and kissed the hem of the second master of the Lahore palace—after the padishah himself.

Shah Jahan briefly considered opening his arms to embrace the brother he had not seen for quite some time, but after weighing something in his mind, decided against it. At the same time, he kept a sharp eye on his brother's hands and belt for any sign of a dagger. Of course, anyone entering the prince's chambers was carefully searched, but Shah-Jahan knew that when it came to Shahriyar, no extra precaution could be considered excessive. Convinced that at least for the moment his life was safe, he relaxed, smiled at Shahriyar, and offered his hand. Shahriyar kissed it and then rose to his feet.

"Greetings, my brother! How is your health? All is well?"

"Yes, Shahriyar, all is fine, praise be to the Almighty! In fact, I'm preparing to marry for the third time. Our sovereign and father has finally allowed me to wed my Arjumand-begim. You may offer your congratulations."

"Congratulations, honourable shahzade. But I know nothing of your bride. Is she also a princess?"

In these words—and especially in the younger brother's tone—Shah-Jahan sensed a faint barb. Clearly, Shahriyar had already been informed that Shah Jahan's new bride was not of royal blood. Though Shahriyar himself had long since forgotten he was a bastard, born to Padishah Jahangir by a mere slave-concubine, he nevertheless viewed the fact that Shah-Jahan's chosen bride was 'no princess' as good reason for scorn and mockery.

However, Shah-Jahan pretended not to notice the irony.

"She is the daughter of one of our padishah's closest associates, the chief advisor Asaf-khan, and the granddaughter of his chief counselor, Itimad-ud-Daulah Giyas Bek. She is worthy of respect," he replied in a tone that allowed no argument. "Moreover, Arjumand is exceptionally beautiful and clever; in my opinion, she surpasses all the treasures on earth!"

"I'm happy for you, shahzade," said Shahriyar, as courteously as possible but without much warmth. He considered adding another cutting remark about his brother's obvious, boyishly passionate infatuation, but decided not to provoke an open conflict and held his tongue.

"So why didn't you invite your own brother to the engagement?"

"I assumed you were too busy for such occasions."

"How could I possibly be too busy for my dear older brother! If you at least invite me to the wedding, I'll be sure to attend."

Shah-Jahan paused for a few moments.

"Is that so! You didn't come to the first two. But fine—come. You're invited."

"Excellent, brother. I'll definitely take advantage of your invitation!"

Shah Jahan gestured for his brother to sit. Showing the impeccable manners befitting an emperor's son who might one day ascend the throne, he refrained from asking outright what had brought his guest. He knew Shahriyar would tell soon enough.

Shahriyar settled on a soft chaise lounge and, aware that he should not test his elder brother's patience for too long, spoke:

"My lord, we both know our dear and blessed father—may Allah grant him many years of life and good health—is nonetheless mortal. Sultan Husrau-mirza, the padishah's first son, is blind and infirm—may Allah forgive his sins! The second heir, Sultan Parviz-mirza, is weak-willed and drinks heavily; is he fit for the throne? I doubt it. As for our younger brothers—Shahzade Jahandar-mirza and Shahzade Garshasp-mirza—I do not even take them into account, as I trust those foolish weaklings have no ambitions to rule the land! And our sisters, of course, don't matter here. So that leaves only you and me... But I, brother, by all considerations, am more deserving! It seems our father has made this plain to me."

Shah Jahan merely smirked at such unprecedented arrogance and insolence.

Shahriyar paused, apparently considering how best to articulate his real purpose. It looked as though he was carefully weighing each word.

"My lord, I rely on your wisdom and greatness! Perhaps you agree that the padishah's throne is, in its own way, a huge burden of responsibility and beset by countless difficulties. Shah Jahan, I beg you, think it over: do you really want that? I promise that if you renounce your future claim to the throne in my favor now, I will guarantee you a safe life, with all possible comforts and honors!.. Yes, I know you were granted the privilege of pitching the red tent—the prerogative of the crown prince—which was denied to us, your brothers. But even so… Wouldn't a peaceful life, far from politics and the governing of the state, be better? I say this so you may choose the easy way—step aside from the succession!"

"'The easy way?'" Shah Jahan smirked. "So there could be a 'hard way,' too?"

"I wouldn't want it to come to that, brother. I don't want to fight you!"

"Shahriyar, listen to me," Shah Jahan said, struggling to contain his outrage. "Never again dare to suggest such a thing! The time will come, and I will be the ruler of the Great Mughal Empire. Remember that! Now… please leave. I no longer wish to see you."

"Well then… If that's how it is, I'll go. But understand, my lord, that you've made this choice yourself. There will be no peace or friendship between us anymore—only war. I will fight for the padishah's throne. Yet I warn you, as a brother I once loved, from now on you must be on guard and fear for your life! I am not threatening you, but it would be better for you not to stand in my way… I wish you a happy wedding, my brother!"

With that, Shahriyar rose abruptly and stormed out of Shah Jahan's chambers.

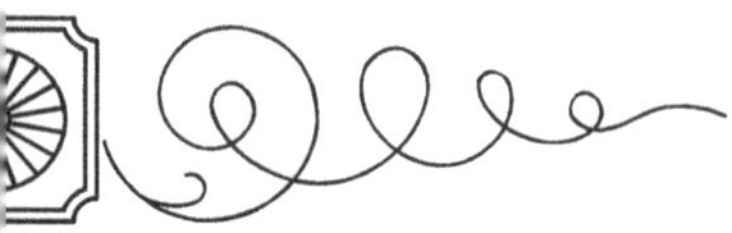

30

Tashkent, 2014

The door to the office of the chief doctor at Tashkent's premier ophthalmology clinic, headed by Dr. Said Yakhyaevich Mumtazov, swung wide open. Normally, no one dared enter this office without knocking, but the established rules—applicable to everyone else—did not bother this particular visitor. He wasn't one to ask permission before coming in; he simply entered.

He was a man of around sixty to sixty-five, broad-shouldered, slightly heavy but well-kept, with excellent posture, a touch of gray in his hair, a measured yet very confident stride, and a well-groomed face. Almost anyone who met him instantly understood that he was far from poor and had experienced the benefits of power, high status, and wealth.

It wasn't that he flaunted his position or spoke condescendingly to others—he didn't. Yet in his demeanor, which was by no means ostentatious, in his calm, soft-spoken voice, and in all his mannerisms, one sensed he was like a king who had graciously descended to mingle with mere mortals and granted them the happy privilege of seeing and hearing him. Next to this "king," no one ever dared utter any proud or rebellious "no," nor did anyone ever contradict or challenge his opinion, even if it was completely off the mark. In every situation, he was accepted as unconditionally right.

Taken aback, Dr. Said Yakhyaevich rose from his chair at once to greet this guest, who from the very first moment seemed more

like the owner of the place. Although Dr. Mumtazov could not afford particularly luxurious attire, he was interested in fashion and knew enough about it to notice that the visitor was dressed to the nines: wearing a very expensive dark-blue Brioni suit and a light-gray Armani shirt.

"Well, good day to you, Doctor!" the man said warmly and graciously, with great dignity and a tone that evinced clear self-respect. He glanced around. "I see it's quite nice here—furnished rather economically, but tastefully."

"Thank you." Even Said Yakhyaevich himself hadn't expected to feel momentarily disoriented and almost shy in front of someone. "Forgive me, but to whom do I owe the honour…?"

"Murad Nematullaevich Nasyrov, head of the 'Minor' chain of shops, cafés, and restaurants. You know, back in the day, I had my eyes treated by the late Svyatoslav Fedorov. I've heard you were his student and worked with the professor…"

"Oh no, no, I wish that were true, but I'm afraid those rumors are, unfortunately, an exaggeration."

"Really? Well, no matter. When my eyesight began to deteriorate again, I decided to come to you, since you're known to be a top eye specialist. I'm sure you'll help me!"

"All right, let's see what we can do. Please go to the reception desk, open a treatment file, and they'll tell you what diagnostics are needed. Then our clinic's specialists will decide on your course of treatment."

"I'm afraid you misunderstand me. I've come here specifically for you. You, personally, must examine and treat me."

Under other circumstances, Dr. Mumtazov would have immediately objected to being told what he "must" do. But the visitor's tone permitted no hint of contradiction or doubt.

"My apologies, Murad Nematullaevich, but I personally almost never perform treatments anymore—only in the most urgent and rare situations. I manage this entire clinic; I'm mainly an administrator."

"Young man," said the stranger (who was only ten or fifteen years older than the nearly fifty-year-old Said Yakhyaevich), "I've done my research on you. You remain one of the finest ophthalmologists, not only in Uzbekistan, but in the entire CIS—and possibly the world."

"Oh, come now—I think you're exaggerating…"

"Please don't interrupt; just hear me out. I never exaggerate anything!" the guest declared in a forceful voice. "You mentioned 'urgent and rare' cases—let's assume mine is exactly that. As for compensation, don't you worry. You'll earn from this single course of treatment what you typically make in an entire year at your clinic."

A sheen of sweat appeared on Dr. Mumtazov's forehead.

"Thank you for your flattering words, respected Murad Nematullaevich. We do have a pricing schedule for VIP service."

"Great. Then let's not waste time on lengthy conversations! I want to start treatment as soon as possible!"

He all but commanded a man who, until this moment, considered himself the sole authority here—and who was meeting this visitor for the very first time.

From a young age, Said Yakhyaevich had been drawn to people endowed with inner strength, authority, and power. Even if something about them rubbed him the wrong way, he was used to deferring to them. Now, as head of the ophthalmology clinic, he did everything possible to ensure that this VIP patient was satisfied. Indeed, Murad Nasyrov's eyesight improved markedly within just a few days.

Dr. Mumtazov neither expected nor demanded any special thanks from Nasyrov. Naturally, first Nasyrov paid the required sum at the clinic's cashier, and then, as many patients do with many doctors these days, he slipped a considerable extra amount into an envelope—which, during another private meeting with Said Yakhyaevich, he stuffed into the pocket of the doctor's white coat. No matter how much Dr. Mumtazov tried to refuse the additional payment, his new acquaintance wouldn't hear of it.

Moreover, after the treatment concluded, Nasyrov invited Dr. Mumtazov to dine at one of his restaurants. Despite his reluctance—Said longed to spend that evening at home with his family—he found it awkward to decline. It turned out that this influential "boss" Nasyrov had a vast network of solid contacts throughout the city, which could prove very useful to an administrator-doctor whenever he encountered various sorts of bureaucrats.

"Said, I've heard you're marrying off your daughter," Nasyrov remarked unexpectedly during dinner.

"I beg your pardon, but how did you find out about that?" Dr. Mumtazov asked, surprised.

"Oh, there are no secrets from me!" the restaurant owner laughed. "I always find out whatever I want about whomever I want. Besides, just about everyone in your clinic is talking about it. After all, the wedding of the chief doctor's only daughter is probably an event for them, too... I believe your daughter's name is Malika, correct?"

"Yes, indeed. You seem very well informed!" said Said Yakhyaevich, even more astonished.

"Well, I have a proposal for you: hold the banquet right here in this restaurant."

"Thank you… But most of the wedding arrangements are the groom's responsibility—and his parents'. As for me, I've already bought everything the young couple will need for their future life together…"

"That's all right, Said. Just speak with the groom's father and tell him you have a good friend who can offer a great restaurant hall at a discount. You do like the atmosphere and our cuisine here, don't you?"

"Yes, very much. But… Murad Nematullaevich, in that case, I'd be in your debt…"

"Come now, don't say that! This is nothing. And I won't hear any objections! You've restored my eyesight, Dr. Mumtazov! I'm forever in your debt. So please, accept my offer."

When they said their goodbyes, for some reason Said Yakhyaevich thought, *"It's all wonderful, and this important, businesslike man could certainly be of help to me. Still… something about him doesn't feel right. I just can't put my finger on what…"*

* * *

The wedding of Bahadir and Malika was set for late September. Preparations were in full swing, and both the bride and groom were given a week off at their universities.

Bahadir was on edge and not too pleased that his share of the wedding expenses was minimal, since most of the costs were covered by both fathers. On the other hand, although his pride was slightly wounded, he fully realised he couldn't possibly afford the wedding on his own. He hadn't forgotten about his debts—or rather, the aging and dangerous "tough guy" from the casino, Veniamin Arkadyevich, constantly reminded him of them.

During the wedding preparations, Malika grew very close to Bahadir's sister, Rano—a sweet, kind girl who helped the bride and groom choose their attire (the bridal gown and a classic three-piece suit) and navigate all the necessary procedures and formalities for legally registering the marriage. Whenever the couple needed her, Rano was always there.

Rudik Khayrullin was the groom's best man, and Galina Krikunova was the bride's maid of honor.

"Malika, you're so lucky," Galina said shortly before the ceremony. "You're marrying such a good-looking guy! But keep in mind that your very best friend is still single. So if things don't work out with your fiancé—soon to be husband—and you suddenly decide to leave him, remember there's someone here who'll be happy to 'pick him up'!"

Malika frowned and adjusted her beautiful wedding hairstyle in the mirror.

"Oh, why the scowl?" Galina laughed. "I'm only joking! I don't want your Bahadir. I prefer… Mukhitdin."

"What? Mukhitdin?!" Malika was stunned.

"Yes. Why are you so surprised? You never needed him, anyway. For that matter, I did everything I could so he'd fail his entrance exams and stay here with me…"

"With you?"

"With me, girlfriend—with me! But he just got up and left for a whole year."

"Don't worry—he'll come back."

"I hope so… The only downside is my Mukhitdin isn't as wealthy as your fiancé Bahadir, and his father's no businessman. Yet I have just as much right as you do to live beautifully and bathe in luxury! Make sure you don't lose your Fattakhov! And don't forget about your close friend here, who, by the way, needs your support."

Malika decided Galina was just teasing to cheer her up before the wedding.

Meanwhile, Rudik was also "advising" his friend:

"Baha, you did the right thing by deciding to marry this wealthy bride, Malika! Now you'll be able to pay off all your debts easily…"

"Quiet, Rudya—keep your voice down! Nobody should know that I gamble or that I have debts—none of my relatives, and especially not Malika! You got that?"

"Of course, Bahadir, no worries! Relax and don't stress about it. The main thing is, we can start our own business! You haven't forgotten, have you?"

"I remember the business and your Italian guy with his equipment. But just know that I'm marrying Malika because I love her and I really like her! It's not about her inheritance."

"Great, fine, Bahadir! Love whoever you want—it's none of my business. But money never hurt anybody, right?"

"Oh, Rudik… you really are…"

"What—too money-minded? It's not me, buddy—it's our lives that are to blame!"

"I meant to say you're just a little too practical…"

* * *

The wedding was beautiful and luxurious. Murad Nematullaevich did not let Said Yakhyaevich, his daughter Malika, or his old friend Abdulla Rustamovich Fattakhov and his son Bahadir down. The restaurant, the refreshments, the hall décor, the concert program, the entire service—all were truly excellent. Everyone left satisfied, and social media was buzzing with an abundance of photos

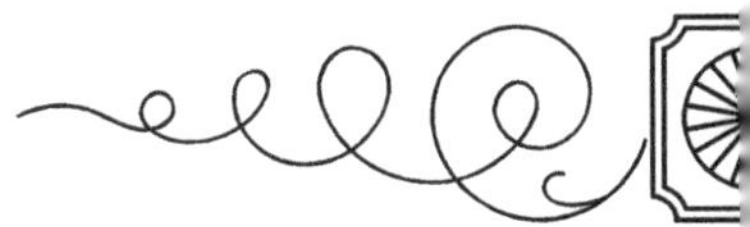

and enthusiastic reviews of both the wedding and the newlyweds.

Only Dr. Mumtazov, deep in his subconscious—by a sort of "sixth sense"—felt that he was now somehow indebted to the prominent businessman Murad Nasyrov.

Bahadir was dazzled more than ever by Malika's beauty: in her wedding dress, adorned with a marvelous ruby-and-diamond necklace, she herself was like a precious and enchanting treasure! On the whole, Bahadir was glad he had married this particular girl. It gratified his pride that all the guests kept remarking on what a "delightful and clever" bride she was and what a "handsome couple" she and Bahadir made.

Malika, for her part, was genuinely happy to have married the man she loved.

Their first night as husband and wife was magical and intoxicating; they lavished one another with tenderness, bliss, and affection.

Both mothers, Sitora and Mukhabbat, lay awake for a long time, filled with concern about the future of their beloved children.

Abdulla Rustamovich fell quickly and soundly asleep, at ease about his younger son's destiny.

Said Yakhyaevich tossed and turned, unable to sleep for most of the night, wondering whether the luxuriously organized wedding—with huge discounts on the banquet hall and splendid catering—was simply another lavish show of gratitude for curing the eyes of that somewhat untrustworthy "fellow," Murad Nematullaevich, or if that man would eventually ask something more of him, Said Mumtazov, in return… Or maybe Nasyrov was merely angling to become his friend or confidant? But why would he do that?..

31

Murad Nematullaevich summoned his closest, most trusted 'gofers,' Gosha and Roma, to his office the very next day.

They appeared before the 'boss' at once, in response to his order.

"Listen closely, boys," Murad Nematullaevich began. "I've gone to all this trouble of 'befriending' Dr. Mumtazov purely so I could get closer to him and find out for myself whether he and his family really do own that golden necklace with rubies and diamonds."

"You mean… that piece, boss?"

"Yes, possibly that. People like them—like most middle-class nobodies who have no real sense of true wealth—are so naive and trusting! They show off their treasures without realising how easily they can lose them. But even they only displayed that piece—the necklace with Temur's Ruby—at the wedding. Any other time, they probably keep it locked away somewhere safe. I really need it. But I am not a thief, so I have to come up with a sensible, appropriate way to coax that jewel away from the doctor—and I need your help. Especially you, Gosha. You're a sharp kid, so put your brain to work."

"Thanks, boss. I will do my best. But this isn't exactly a simple job… If you hadn't gotten acquainted with the doctor, then if the necklace disappeared, no one would ever suspect you…"

"You little pup—don't you know I don't make mistakes?! I had to find out for certain whether he really has the necklace. But first off, you bunch of street punks would never have been invited to such a wedding, where the bride actually wore it. And second,

I've stopped trusting 'strangers' on this. Luckily, my own eyes work great now! And yesterday at the wedding, I saw that piece with my own eyes. I must say, it's extremely beautiful and clearly worth a fortune…"

"So what do we do, boss?" Gosha asked, feeling guilty for not having come up with anything yet.

"Let's think. At first, I just wanted to buy it from the doctor, but then I reconsidered—if I offer him money for the necklace, he'll likely refuse, even for a lot of money."

"Why?"

"Because, Roma. Haven't you heard the story of how that jewel got to the doctor from some Arab sheikh? Yes, I'm sure Said values it more than life itself. Even though he, his wife, and some grandmother of theirs gave it to his daughter as a wedding gift, Dr. Mumtazov still expects that piece to stay in their family forever! It's important to them. They don't see it as just a giant pile of cash—they view it as some spiritual heirloom. Got it?"

"Yeah, boss, I hear you, though I'm not sure I get it completely. I could always swipe it quietly…"

"Don't even think about it! I'm not about to bail you out of prison afterward."

Suddenly, Gosha had an idea, though he was afraid of the boss and didn't speak right away.

"Boss, I have a thought…"

"Well?! Speak up—stop stammering! What is it? What did you come up with?"

"How about this… You still have that one necklace, the replica of the original, the one Misha Leonidov got in Moscow, right?"

"I still have it, sure. So what of it? What good does that do us?!"

"As far as I understand, it looks a lot like the necklace that now belongs to that ophthalmologist, Said Yakhyaevich's daughter, right? We can simply swap one for the other… at first, just to verify that the bride's necklace—the one you mentioned, Malika—is actually genuine. A theft would be too obvious, but a switch might go unnoticed for at least a while, and nobody would suspect anything. Meanwhile, if their necklace turns out to be fake too, we can just swap them back again the same way!"

"'If it also turns out to be fake…!'" the boss mimicked Gosha. "God forbid. But what if this necklace of theirs—whatever the Mumtazovs are called—happens to be real? If they realise it's missing, there'll be an uproar! I don't need that headache!!!"

"Don't worry, boss. We'll stash it so well that no one finds it, and no one finds us, either!" Gosha assured him.

"Huh, you're a brave one, I see… But overall, it's not a bad idea—good job," Murad Nematullaevich praised Gosha. "So how do you plan to pull off this switch without the owners realising?"

"I've got a pretty good plan. Please, just trust me! Very soon, you'll have the ruby necklace in your hands… Ah, too bad your Mukhitdin isn't here. He's got such skilled, practically 'golden' hands—he would've been a huge help!"

"Yeah, well, the last thing I need is my son getting involved in something like this. Better that he's not around. You two handle it yourselves! And make sure not even a single rat catches wind of my involvement, got it? I'm not involved!!! Understand?"

"Sure thing, boss, don't worry! We'll do it right. Isn't that right, Roma?"

Roma nodded, used to following Gosha's lead in everything.

"Boss, just give us a couple of weeks."

"A couple of weeks?! That long?"

"Sorry, but for a job like this, it's not very long at all. We need

to do it carefully, cover our tracks, so neither of us—and especially not you—gets exposed," Gosha explained succinctly.

"All right. Go to it. I expect results. That ruby necklace… must become mine!!!"

32

Lahore, 1612

"Is it true what I've been told, then, that your name is Askar, and you are the finest warrior?"

"Yes, my lor—"

"Shhh!" The second speaker's voice was hushed, their face hidden by a hooded cloak, making it impossible to tell if it was a man or a woman; yet from the tone, it was instantly clear this was a person of power and wealth. "Remember, no one must learn of me or this conversation between us! I pay you in gold dinars—keep your tongue behind your teeth or I will shorten it swiftly! Now listen carefully.

The commanding voice fell silent for a moment. The hood turned from side to side, checking to make sure no one was watching. Satisfied that the coast was clear, the person of power and means continued:

"You need not kill him yet. Merely frighten him so that the ceremony is disrupted, and so he has no taste for claiming sovereign greatness and power... The rest is none of your concern. All you must know is where and when to carry out my order! If necessary, you may stab the guard who protects him."

"But if the guard dies, there'll be a great uproar..."

"Pay no mind to that. Have pity for no one! It will serve as an excellent lesson for all... So, Askar, have you understood me, and will you carry out my commission as required?"

"Yes, I understand. I will accomplish it perfectly—have no doubt!"

* * *

"Shahzade, forgive me, but…" Muhammad was clearly troubled by something; for a long time, he hesitated to confide in the favorite son of the Padishah.

"What is it, my loyal vizier?" Shah Jahan asked. "Speak up! I give you permission."

"My lord, I'm worried. Is it wise to hold a grand wedding in such turbulent times? You have enemies. They might use the commotion and the crowds around you to do you harm…"

Shah Jahan placed a hand on Muhammad's shoulder.

"And what do I have you for? Surely you can protect me, can you not?"

"You are right, master. However… last night I had a strange dream. In it, I saw something like hills or mountains in the distance, which suddenly turned into huge, or even gigantic, beautifully-formed horses, sheep, and lions—truly majestic beasts, large as mountains. They were far away, but clearly visible; their exotic appearance seized my full attention. Then, one of the lions sprang forward and, in the blink of an eye, appeared right beside me. Without warning, it roared at me and leaped… And that's when I woke up. What could it mean?"

"It was nothing more than a nightmare, Muhammad! Do not be afraid. You're a brave warrior. However great and powerful our foes may be, together we will triumph!"

"May God grant it so, shahzade. But… there is something else…"

"What is it?"

"Perhaps I am too bold, my lord…"

"Speak freely! We are friends, and I will hear any truth from you."

"Your bride… She isn't that young—she's already seventeen!…"

"Well, Muhammad? I'm twenty. I'm still older than she is. Let me tell you this: if she were thirty, she would still be so lovely and full of youth to me that I cannot look away. I assure you, over the years I've known her, she's become even more beautiful, even more enchanting than when I first laid eyes on her and fell in love forever! Her face shines like the sun by day and the moon by night; her smile fills my soul with indescribable joy. She is my destiny—my love and my life… I hope, at least, you're not against this marriage?"

"Certainly not, my master, how could I be!" Muhammad shook his head vehemently.

"I know how you honor your lady Kandakhari-begim, how loyal and devoted you are to her, for you once served her father and have known her a long time. But I ask you to be honest and fair. You must show respect to all three of my wives—they are all your mistresses. Yet to Arjumand-begim, offer the highest regard!"

"Yes, shahzade!"

"As for marrying in these times… Do you not know that the astrologers chose this year as auspicious for my wedding to Arjumand? Long ago they assured us that the stars favor a successful celebration. So do all in your power to ensure the wedding proceeds calmly and joyfully!"

"As you command, my lord! I stand ever ready to serve you faithfully."

With that, Muhammad bowed obediently.

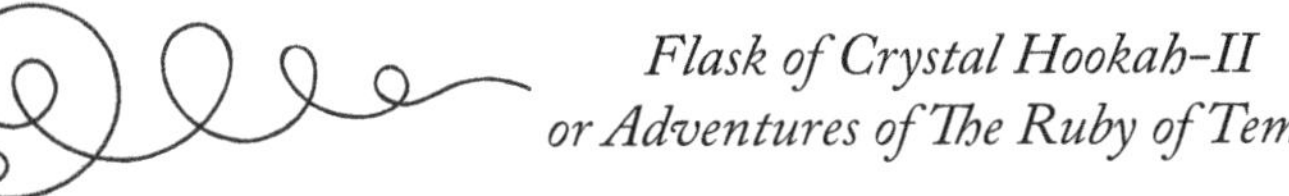

***

Agra, 1612

Padishah Jahangir and his wife Mehrun-Nissa arrived for the ceremonial part of Shah Jahan and Arjumand-begim's wedding.

The ceremony proceeded in grand style, with luxury and splendor… All the guests were brightly and festively dressed; flags and garlands fluttered from the horsemen's spears; the elephants were covered with gold-embroidered blankets. At the head of the entire procession of guests marched musicians blowing into long trumpet-like instruments (which would later be called *karnay*), the sound imitating the roar of elephants in battle to strike fear and secure victory over enemies… At weddings and celebrations, these instruments were used to drive away evil forces and to summon glad tidings and blessings…

The groom was arrayed in a gold-embroidered blue robe and a silk turban stitched with gold thread. The bride wore a tunic covered with a white veil. Around her neck shone a marvelously beautiful gold necklace, even visible through her veil, set with rare rubies—a gift to the new bride from the Padishah himself.

The entire notable aristocracy of the empire, led by Jahangir— this included Arjumand's father, Asaf-khan, Prince Shah Jahan, and all their closest attendants—processed in the company of slaves, musicians and dancers, acrobats, caged exotic animals, astrologers, and dervishes, making their way toward the grand congregational mosque. The bride proceeded separately, accompanied by her mother and her aunt Mehrun-Nissa, as well as her attendants. She regretted that her future husband's mother, Taj Bibi Bilqis Maka-ni—born Rajkumari Shri Manavati Baiji Lall Sahiba—was no longer in this world and could not rejoice in her and Shah Jahan's happiness.

Beneath the mosque's dome, two male witnesses—one from the groom's side and one from the bride's—came forward. Sheikh Yakub-khan Ahmad began the wedding ceremony.

"Faithful believers, today we perform the nikah," said the sheikh, "the sacred rite uniting man and woman into a single family, so they become one in spirit, soul, and body. According to the Muslim faith, nikah is the Law of Allah, the cornerstone of the union between man and woman, needed to continue the human race, to bear children, and to uphold the family. Islam makes this foundation significant and completely rejects the baseness and scorn of marriages born of wicked motives. Nikah follows in the paths of the prophets and the sunna of Muhammad for future generations, preserving the purity of man and woman's noble names, affirming humanity's supreme status above all creation. Nikah stands guard over the faith and morality of Muslims!"

He glanced over the bride, the groom, and their witnesses; seeing that they were fully prepared for the rite, he went on:

"Witnesses, pay close attention: we shall now pronounce the *ijab*—the proposal to the bride and groom. You must respond, and let your answers be honest and pure before the Almighty. So then, Shahzade Shah Jahan Bakht Bahadur-mirza," the sheikh addressed the groom and his witness, "I give to you, as your lawful wife, the daughter of the honorable chief advisor Nawab Abdul Hasan Asaf-khan—Arjumand Banu Qadsia-begim Sahiba—free, unmarried, chaste, not in the category of mahram! Do you take her as your wife?"

"I do," replied the groom's witness on his behalf.

"Arjumand Banu Qadsia-begim Sahiba," the sheikh turned to

the bride's witness, "I give you, as your lawful husband, the son of our most esteemed sovereign, the ruler of Hindustan and of the world, Abul-Fath Nur ad-Din Muhammad Jahangir—Shahzade Shah Jahan Bakht Bahadur-mirza! Do you take him as your husband?"

"I do," responded the bride's witness on her behalf.

"Groom, do you consent to this marriage?"

"I consent," answered the groom's witness.

"By sharia law, at the conclusion of a first marriage for the bride, her consent is not required," Sheikh Yakub-khan remarked. "Nevertheless, given her noble lineage, we may ask for her consent anyway… So then, Bride, do you consent to this marriage?"

"I consent," the bride's witness replied on her behalf.

"Bride, do you grant the groom the dowry in the amount of one thousand gold dinars?"

"I do," replied the bride's witness.

"Groom, do you accept the dowry from the bride in the amount of one thousand gold dinars?"

"I do."

"Groom, do you grant the bride the dower in the amount of three thousand gold dinars?"

"I do."

"Bride, do you accept the dower of three thousand gold dinars from the groom?"

"I do."

"Groom, do you agree to all the conditions of the marriage contract?"

"I do."

"Bride, do you agree to all the conditions of the marriage?"

"I do."

"Groom, do you swear fidelity to your wife according to sharia?"

"I swear."

"Bride, do you swear fidelity to your husband according to sharia?"

"I swear."

"We have given the bride to you as your wife, Groom!"

"I have taken her as my wife!" said the groom's witness.

"We have given the groom to you as your husband, Bride!"

"I have taken him as my husband!" said the bride's witness.

"From this moment on, you are considered husband and wife—amin!" the sheikh proclaimed.

"Amin!" responded everyone present at the ceremony.

* * *

"Look, Askar—the wedding festivities are in full swing, but Padishah Jahangir and his wife are seated some distance from Shah Jahan. Wine is flowing freely, people are eating and drinking a lot—so no one will have time to help him! This is the perfect moment for us…"

"Maybe we shouldn't ruin the celebration after all? What if they catch us?"

"Askar, carry out the order without talking back—just the way we were told—and be brave!"

"Of course, I'll do it exactly as ordered. But right now, so many people are congratulating the shahzade; all I see are unfamiliar faces and a crowd of backs. I don't want to spill innocent blood. I'm a warrior, not a murderer!"

"All right, let's wait a bit longer. But we mustn't lose our chance! We need the crowd on our side, or else… nothing will come of it."

"We'll just wait for the right moment—then we'll do what needs to be done!"

* * *

"Kuchkar-bai, pour me another…! And you—you rotten trickster—you drop by my house way too often when I'm not around. What did you want with my wife? Answer me, you scoundrel! My neighbours told me everything."

"Nothing of the sort happened, Mirzabek! It's getting really late—you should head home already; many of the guests have left. You've had more than enough to drink."

"Ah, so now you think you can teach me and tell me what to do?! It's bad enough you compromise my wife by having tea with her in my own house when I'm gone, but you have the nerve to act all high and mighty! I don't know what else you two get up to… But I won't tolerate such shame! I'll show you right now!"

With those words, right amid the peak of the wedding feast, the hulking Mirzabek slammed his fist into the face of the slimmer, more refined Kuchkar-bai.

"Are you crazy?! You idiot, have you lost your mind?" Kuchkar-bai flared up in response to the insult and fought back, defending himself against Mirzabek.

The men, swearing at each other and grabbing one another by their clothing, staggered away from the table, still striking out.

Something glinted suddenly in Mirzabek's hand.

A few remaining guests rushed over to break up the brawl. Seeing the disturbance at his master's celebration, Muhammad—the loyal *atalyk* of Shah Jahan—raced to the scene as well. He prevented Shah Jahan himself from joining in.

In the blink of an eye, Muhammad thought he saw a knife hilt inlaid with sparkling stones, and then he was nearly blinded by the flash of polished metal. But for a moment, the throng of men blocked his view of whoever was holding that knife.

Suddenly Muhammad saw that it wasn't Mirzabek—the man being confronted—who raised the knife. It was someone else, much younger, warrior-like, who lifted the blade right above the belly of his heavyset opponent. Muhammad bravely threw himself forward to help Kuchkar-bai, but immediately gave a loud cry and, clutching his chest with a bloody hand, collapsed to the ground, dead on the spot.

The men, stunned by what had happened, stepped aside at once.

"It was him—Mirzabek!" Kuchkar-bai sputtered, dazed. "I saw him with that knife, the one he stuck in our shahzade's atalyk! Faithful believers, what is this? The atalyk saved my life! If he hadn't intervened, I'd be lying in a pool of blood in his place! But now he's…gone."

"It wasn't me!" Mirzabek shouted indignantly. "I swear, I didn't even touch him!"

Only now did Prince Shah Jahan—distracted by a conversation with his relatives—notice the confused, suddenly silenced crowd. He rose and approached them. When he saw his servant lying in a pool of blood, pain and fury filled his gaze:

"Bring a physician here at once!" the shahzade shouted.

One of the guests happened to be a doctor. He quickly checked the dying man's breath.

"Forgive me, Your Highness, but there's nothing I can do for him. He isn't breathing."

"Let all know," roared Shah Jahan, "I will learn the full truth of what happened here, and anyone responsible will be severely and justly punished!!!"

Shahriyar, this is your doing! thought Shah Jahan, deeply shaken, after they carried Muhammad's body away. *You planned to kill me at my own wedding?! If not for my faithful, dear Muhammad... You send assassins with daggers against me? But know this: you will not get away with it so easily!*

A death at our wedding! Arjumand thought in horror. *Such a terrible omen...*

Nevertheless, the love of the two newlyweds was so strong that even such a tragic event could not prevent them from savoring the intoxication of their first wedding night.

Shah Jahan insisted on disregarding the usual Muslim custom for the first night, whereby the consummation of the marriage takes place in view, behind a screen, with close relatives present to witness the bride's innocence. The blood on the sheet, resulting from the bride's loss of virginity and defloration, was normally shown to everyone as a symbol of her purity and chastity...

Instead, the young couple secluded themselves in lavish quarters, without any observers, defying customary laws. This act would soon become the talk of the court—the fierce love binding Shah Jahan and Arjumand-begim...

33

One evening, when the Mumtazovs' housekeeper, Larisa, was running especially late and stood alone at the bus stop waiting for the bus—which came only rarely at that hour—a brand-new white Matiz pulled up. The driver honked at her.

She hadn't been flagging it down—she was wary of taking taxis and hated to spend money on them. Still, she leaned over and peered into the open car window.

"Miss, hop in, I'll give you a ride wherever you're going!" the young driver said.

"No, sorry. I don't have money for a taxi…"

"Did I say anything about money? It's free of charge—I'll drive you anyway!"

"No, I can't. It's awkward… You go on."

"And what, you're just going to stand at this bus stop till morning?"

"Why till morning? My bus should be here soon!"

"Are you aware what time it is, Miss?"

"Don't call me 'Miss'… I'm older than you!" Larisa said, feeling flustered.

"So what? Beautiful women have no age! Come on, get in—it's nearly night. I'll drop you off in no time!"

"…All right. You've talked me into it!"

She sat in the front seat, and they took off.

"I'm Jorik. And you?"

"Does it matter?"

"Does it not? Lovely Miss, tell me."

"Larisa."

"Larisa—that's a wonderful name! Has anyone ever told you you're really very attractive?"

"Oh, stop it, Jora. Are you a taxi driver by profession?"

"No. I'm… a handyman 'who fixes everything out of boredom.' Ever heard of someone like that?"

She laughed.

"No, can't say I have. You've got a sense of humour. So, when you've got the time, you 'gypsy' ride around in your car?"

"Yes, exactly. And I guess you have a husband waiting for you at home right now?"

"Actually… I'm not married."

"You don't say?! Seriously? Miss, that can't be!"

"Why not?"

"Because I've just had fantastic luck, Larisa—after so many fruitless searches, I've finally found the 'girl of my dreams'! And she's a blonde, no less!"

"You're teasing me, Jora… I'm no 'girl'—I'm an old maid."

"Don't ever say that! And I wouldn't dare to think of mocking you. On the contrary, I'm more serious than ever. I'm completely captivated by you!"

"Oh, come on…"

"Larisa, looks like we're here already… But I can't just let a woman like you go so easily! Here's my phone number—call me anytime, day or night. Of course, if you gave me your number, I'd call you myself!"

"That's not necessary, I think. We joked around—and that's enough."

"There you go again, Larisa, you don't believe me! But I mean every word sincerely, with all my soul… So, tell me—what time will you be going home from work tomorrow?"

"I'm not sure yet. Probably a bit earlier than today—or about the same time."

"Then let me give you another ride! Is that okay? May I?"

"Why? I'd feel uncomfortable."

"Don't worry, not at all! It's alright. So?"

"We'll see…"

"I'll definitely swing by that same bus stop and wait for you, all right? You see, Larisa, I really like you!"

* * *

A little over a week passed since Larisa and her new friend first met. Now Jora gave Larisa a ride home almost every day, often stopping by "for tea," and later sometimes even staying at her place until morning.

That weekend, following Jorik's suggestion, the newly minted couple—who weren't exactly the same age—went for a walk in the park.

"Larisa, you were telling me about your work…"

"Yes, what about it?"

"Oh, nothing. I'm just curious… You mentioned your boss doesn't lock the drawers of the dressing table, right?"

"Yes, Jora. Why are you asking—"

"And you're sure about that?"

"Well, I've seen her open them without any keys more than once. They trust each other, and me, too…"

"Smart girl, my blonde beauty, very observant! Now you'll be even smarter when you fetch me that piece of jewelry I told you about from one of those drawers and swap it with the one I give you.”

“But, Jora, then they’ll immediately stop trusting me… I’m afraid! What if my employers suspect something? I really don’t want to lose this job.”

“They won’t stop trusting you, don’t worry.”

“But once they notice it’s missing, they’ll suspect me. Who else would they suspect?”

“Listen, Lara, are you sure the bride—what’s her name…”

“Malika.”

“Right, Malika—are you sure she didn’t take that jewelry with her to her husband’s house and left it instead with her parents and grandmother?”

“Great-great-grandmother.”

“Whatever! You’re certain the necklace is still at the house where you work, not somewhere else?”

“Yes, absolutely. I’ve seen it myself. My boss often takes it out of the dressing-table drawer to admire it.”

“Why wouldn’t the newlywed wife bring it to her husband’s home?”

“I don’t know. I guess they decided together it’d be safer—after all, it’s a very expensive piece.”

“Got it. You’re doing great, Larisa, my beauty.” He put his arm around her.

“Stop it, Georgiy—people are watching. This is awkward!”

“You know what I’m gonna do afterward? I’ll sell that expensive necklace, and we’ll run off abroad together, buy a house or apartment, and start our happy family!”

“You said ‘family’? Really, Jora?”

“Of course, Lara—absolutely! I love you. Now hurry up and

swap those two necklaces, and don't mess anything up, got it? Be careful!"

"All right, darling. If you say so. I'll do anything for you. Even though I'm a bit scared."

"Don't be! You've got me. But don't tell anyone about us for now, okay?"

"Why not, Jorik? Why can't I tell anyone about you?"

"Because people are envious. Someone might get jealous and try to ruin our happiness. You wouldn't want that, would you?"

"Of course not. I trust you completely and will do exactly as you ask."

"Excellent, my clever girl!"

And he embraced his "old maid" tenderly once more.

The very next day, the expensive ruby-and-diamond necklace was in the hands of "the boss," Murad Nematullaevich Nasyrov.

34

Rano had an unusually gentle, good-natured, and friendly disposition. She knew how to love, how to forgive everyone no matter the offense, and she found it easy to connect with good people. She and Malika turned out to be very similar in many ways; they quickly bonded and became like true sisters. They cooked for the whole family together, cleaned the house together, and often went shopping or to the bazaar for groceries together.

Rano tried her best to do pleasant things for the young couple and supported their relationship as much as she could. Bahadir and Malika were in the midst of their "honeymoon," often staying up until midnight, especially on weekends, talking with each other or surrendering themselves to passionate love.

Understanding this, the kind and caring Rano gave them the chance on weekend mornings to linger in their bedroom a bit longer. On such days, she would go out herself to buy fresh dairy products—delivered by car from a village to their suburb—and then prepare breakfast for everyone on her own.

One Sunday, a week after Larisa and Jorik's walk in the park, Rano, as usual, went out to buy milk. Her mother, Mukhabbat, was already awake. She was surprised that her daughter was taking longer than usual.

When Rano returned, Mukhabbat noticed that something seemed to have unsettled her.

"Did something happen, my dear?" asked the mother of the Fattakhov family as she helped Rano carry the bags to the kitchen.

"Yes… maybe, Mama. I just saw, from a distance, a strange woman who was looking at me very oddly… Our neighbors in the line for groceries told me they've seen her before, lurking near our house, always asking questions about us!"

"Goodness!" Mukhabbat gasped. "Who is she? What does she want from us?"

"I don't know. She looks tanned, like our Amin, maybe even darker. She resembles a Gypsy or maybe a Lyuli. They say she was asking if this is really where our family lives."

"Well, that's just what we needed! So, did you talk to her?"

"No, Mom, I didn't get a chance. When she saw me, she quickly left."

"What was she wearing? Did she look like a beggar?"

"No, not at all! Even though, as I said, she looks like a Lyuli, from what I could see she was very decently dressed—actually, I'd say fashionably, and with good taste. She carried herself with proud posture, had a graceful walk—and to me she seemed quite beautiful and, as you might say, 'well-bred.'"

"Call her aristocratic, why don't you?"

"What if she was, Mama?.. Still, I'm wondering what she wants from our family… Could it be… she's looking for Father?... Wait—could it be… does my father have someone else?!"

"Don't talk nonsense, Ranosha—calm down! Your father has no one else and never has. There's absolutely no reason not to trust him. So, I'm certain this has nothing to do with him…"

Suddenly, it was as though a realisation struck Mukhabbat. She gasped, clutched her heart, and quickly rose from the table to leave the kitchen.

"Mama! What is it? Are you unwell?"

"No, no, nothing, dear, I'm fine. Don't worry."

"You're not explaining anything… Do you recognise this woman? You know who she is, don't you?!"

"Tell me—was she tall?"

"Yes, as tall as our Amin."

"And about forty-five years old?"

"How do you know?... Mom, are you hiding something?! Is there some secret here? I want to know!"

"Don't get worked up, daughter—there's no secret. More than likely she's looking for some relatives of hers, and she got the wrong address. Maybe they just share our surname, and she came here by mistake. You see, she left already!"

With that, Mukhabbat went off to her room, holding on to her heart.

"All right, then! Let's just pretend I believe there are no secrets…" Rano said broodingly, though her mother was no longer listening.

* * *

A few weeks passed. Amin left on a work trip, and Bahadir announced that he and Malika would stay in his brother's apartment until he returned—"to feed Amin's fish." Bahadir convinced everyone in the family that this arrangement would be more convenient for the young couple, and at the same time, he did not miss the chance to drop a hint to his father about buying a separate apartment for him and Malika. Abdulla Rustamovich gave no response—pretending he hadn't caught his son's drift.

Malika had grown to love her husband's parents and didn't want to leave their home, even for a day, but Bahadir persuaded her, and she gave in. They gathered their things quickly and be-

241

gan living in Amin's apartment for the time being. No sooner had Malika crossed the threshold than she remembered the unpleasant situation she had found herself in there a few months earlier—on account of her "friend" Mukhitdin. Mustering her willpower, she tried to set aside those negative memories. She told herself that she would be living here now with her dear, loving husband!

However, as soon as they moved, Bahadir started coming home very late almost every night. Malika worried, though she decided not to complain to anyone, preferring to talk things over with her husband herself. Yet he brushed her off and joked around, insisting that he was stuck at work, attending company events, or out with friends.

"You know, darling, you're still in school and not working, so I put in a lot of effort to secure our family's future!" Bahadir said once.

Malika couldn't argue with that, but her uneasiness only grew.

Bahadir himself seemed to have changed, as if someone had replaced him. He increasingly spoke rudely to Malika, answering her questions with short, dry, and often sharp replies. He had less and less interest or energy for intimacy with his wife.

Malika began to have suspicions.

Maybe there's someone else?! The young wife thought anxiously. *Who could it be? That woman I saw at the restaurant once—Leyla, was it? Or somebody else? No, no—what am I thinking? I know my husband loves me!*

Still, Malika was at her wits' end. Through Rano, she discreetly learned that Bahadir left his father's firm not late at night, as he had told her, but by seven in the evening as usual. Where did he go after that? She was at a loss. But she continued to keep her worries to herself and didn't confide in either her own family or his.

One day, her husband's behavior crossed all bounds. He arrived home extremely drunk and badly injured, obviously beaten by someone. Malika wanted to call an ambulance and the police.

"Don't you dare call anyone!" Bahadir shouted at her. Though drunk, he still grasped what she intended to do and wouldn't let her. "Don't even try! I'll… wash up… take a shower, then… you can… what was it?… treat my wounds yourself!"

"Of course, I'll treat your wounds. But I'm not a doctor or even a nurse! Maybe I should ask my friend Galya to come over—she's a medic and can do everything properly… Though, what am I saying? It's almost two in the morning; I can't bother anyone at this hour. But why can't we call an ambulance or the police?"

"Shhh! Quiet, woman! Don't make a scene. Everything's fine."

"Oh, yes, everything's wonderful! Except for the fact that my husband comes home at daybreak, dead drunk, and brutally beaten. So much for our 'honeymoon'—it's over!"

"Malika!"

"What else, my misery?"

"I love you!"

"Yes, I can see how much you love me… Can you at least explain what happened? Who did this to you?!"

While she spoke, she gingerly dabbed iodine on his wounds.

"Hooligans."

"Hooligans?! Just like that—random street thugs? What did they want from you? Do you walk around carrying large sums of money?"

"Are you stupid, wife? Where would I get large sums of money? Think about what you're saying."

"But it seems to me that you earn a pretty decent salary at your father's company. Though I haven't seen a trace of it lately…"

"You are all such a pain!"

"Who is 'you all'?"

"All women."

"Oh, I see. Looks like you know a lot of women, right? Some sort of expert on the female sex."

"You can't talk to me like that! You must respect me!"

"Right, got it. Come on then, respected one—sleep it off, sober up, and tomorrow morning I'm not letting you go anywhere until you explain what's going on with you."

* * *

The next morning, Bahadir woke up early. His whole body ached terribly. Moreover, though he couldn't recall everything that had happened the previous night, he still vaguely felt guilty toward his wife.

Malika was already standing at the stove, cooking breakfast for him. He came up from behind, wrapped his arms around her, and kissed her gently.

"Good morning, my love."

"Wash your hands. I'm about to feed you."

"I don't get it! Where's my usual 'Good morning, dear'?"

Malika said nothing, looking at Bahadir with mild reproach.

"All right, all right, I know I behaved badly last night. Malika, please, forgive me!"

"Go ahead, eat. I made your beloved omelet with fresh kuku herbs… And I'll forgive you if you tell me in detail what happened to you yesterday! I'm really worried…"

"There's no need for you to worry…"

"What are you saying? How am I not supposed to worry? My

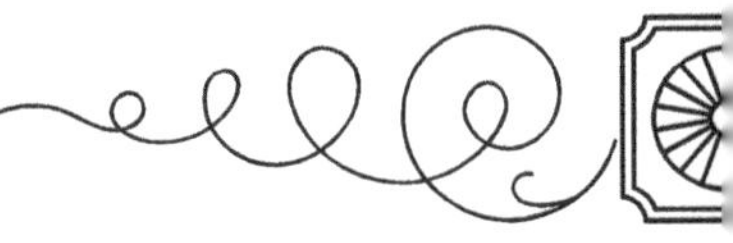

husband gets beaten half to death and comes home at almost two in the morning, barely able to stand, and I'm not supposed to worry? Bahadir, be honest—how can you treat me like this?"

"No one should treat you like this, Princess Malika… But I—got cornered, 'shaken down.'"

"What do you mean? You owe someone money, yes?"

"Yes. A lot."

"I see. Then why not ask your father for help? He's in serious business, and he's your father—he'd definitely help you."

"You don't understand anything! There's absolutely no way I can tell my parents, or Rano, or Amin—anyone at all. I didn't even want to tell you. And I especially can't tell my father! You have no idea how much money we're talking about!"

"So why did you even borrow the money?"

Bahadir lowered his gaze.

"I wanted to buy a new car, an import. And my father wouldn't give me the money."

"Is that the Opel you're driving now?"

"Yes, that's it. You've been in it, you know it's a cool car. But it's very expensive."

"All right, fine. But wouldn't your parents have helped you—at least with a loan or given you some funds upfront from your future salary?"

Bahadir couldn't look Malika in the eye. He hated lying to her; he felt disgusted and ashamed. But he didn't want to admit that his father, Abdulla Rustamovich, had actually given him the full amount as a gift for that Opel. Because if he owned up to that, he'd have to confess everything else, too—something he absolutely didn't want to do.

"You see, Malika, the person who lent me the dough…"

"The money," Malika corrected him.

"What did you say?"

"Please say it correctly: 'lent me the money.'"

"Right… anyway, he's a very dangerous and frightening man. Unfortunately, I didn't realise that when I first met him, when he offered me the loan."

"How much do you owe?"

"Fifty thousand euros."

"How much?!"

"Malika, you didn't hear? Fifty thousand in foreign currency."

"What, are you crazy?! Does your car cost that much?"

"No, plus some other important expenses. I spent money courting you…"

"You're trying to tell me that the brief, modest way you courted me cost that much money?!"

"Malika, please, don't torture me. Bottom line, this guy turned out to be extremely aggressive and impatient, and he doesn't want to wait any longer. He gave me just three days, and he said if I don't come up with the money, he'll kill me!"

"Don't scare me like that, darling! How could he kill you over money? He's bluffing."

"I'm afraid he's not."

"That's horrible! I can't comprehend how anyone could kill a person over some money," Malika said, genuinely baffled—unaccustomed to the sins and vices of the world.

"Listen, wife, you do love me, right?"

"Why do you ask? You know I do."

"I'm begging you—help me!"

"Me? Bahadir, I'm ready to help you any way I can! But what can I really do? Let's call the police!"

"What's the police going to do? We can't call them—under no circumstances! He warned me that if I go to the authorities, he'll make sure there's 'nothing left' of me."

"This is a disaster. How could I have married someone who gets himself into such terrible messes?!"

"Malika, you've got to do something! I urgently need money!!!"

"All right, my dear, I'll tell my parents everything—I'm sure they'll help."

"No!!! Didn't you hear me? I said you can't tell anyone! Your parents will immediately go to the police, and that won't work. All you need to do is ask your father for money, no explanation. He's a businessman, the head of a private clinic, so he's definitely not poor."

"Even so, I can't just not explain anything. As a businessman, he'll absolutely ask me why I need such a huge sum. What would I say? How do I explain myself? I've never asked my dad for money like that before…"

"Just lie to him—tell him you want to go on a honeymoon trip with me."

"Lie? To my own father?!"

"Sure. What's the big deal?"

"Bahadir, try to understand—I can't deceive anyone, especially my parents! Besides, my dad will definitely find out there is no trip. Though, honestly, I really would like to go away somewhere with you…"

"I would too, believe me! But…"

"But you won't spend the money on our trip—am I right? You need it to pay off that enormous, terrifying debt!"

"Yes, sweetheart, exactly. You know, if I'm honest, I kinda figured I was marrying a girl with a big dowry…"

"Ah! Forgive me that my father isn't some Arab sheikh who presented you with an oil rig as a dowry! And I'm sorry, but I can't lie to my dad, and I won't."

"So, you don't care at all about your husband, huh? That's it?"

"I'm terribly worried about you, but this is your fault for getting into such a bad situation! I'm at a complete loss as to how to help…"

"Then… bring me your ruby-and-diamond necklace—you wore it at our wedding! I can sell it! If I'm not mistaken, it's very valuable—enough to cover the debt. Then this guy who's threatening me will finally leave me alone!"

"Sell it? My grandmother's gift—from my parents, too?! Incredible!"

"I don't get why you didn't bring it with you here. What, you don't trust me or my family? I'm sort of offended…"

"What makes you think I don't trust you?"

"Well, you did leave the piece at your parents' house."

"So? This has nothing to do with not trusting you or your relatives. If you want, I can go to my parents' house tomorrow—I actually need to pick up some warmer clothes from there anyway, it's starting to get cool at night—and at the same time I can grab the necklace. But you plan to sell it. How will I ever look my parents in the eyes?"

"So I guess some trinket is more important to my wife than her husband. What if they kill me?"

"All right, let's hope for the best. Tomorrow I'll go and get that necklace from home!"

"That's my clever girl! Thank you, my love. Don't worry—I'll figure something out later so I can get it back to you and your parents. But right now, I need saving—do you understand?"

"I understand. But it's better you don't promise me anything."

35

Sitora noticed that her only daughter was troubled.

"Malika, my girl, are things not going well with your husband? Please, don't keep it to yourself—tell me everything!"

"No, Mama, that's not it. Everything is fine!" Malika tried to hide the truth, though lying never came easily to her. "It's just… just… I'm worried about Rano and my mother-in-law! They've been a bit uneasy these past few days. Rano said she saw a strange woman near their house who was asking about their family, but she never went inside—the moment she spotted Bahadir's sister, she just "disappeared"… It's all very odd. If someone has business, they can just come and speak openly—why do it so secretly? That's why they're on edge. Who knows what this stranger wants from them…"

"I see. But it seems to me that alone wouldn't have you so anxious… Something else happened?"

"No, everything's all right! It's just… Mom, I'd like to ask you for something…"

"Of course, my dear. I'm listening."

"May I take the ruby necklace with me—your wedding gift? It's mine now, isn't it?"

"Of course. It's in my room, in the second drawer of the dressing table. You knew that, didn't you?"

"Yes, I did, but I'm asking permission anyway… I'm polite, right, Mom? Oh, here it is—yes, exactly in that spot!... Oh!!!"

"What is it, Malika? What's that 'oh' about?"

"This… Mama, this is not the necklace!!!"

"What do you mean 'not it'? What are you saying?"

"Just look at it for yourself! I clearly remember that our necklace had four rubies, and one of them—a large one—bore an inscription in Arabic…"

"That's the dedicatory inscription from your great-great-grandmother's time, given by the daughter of an Arab sheikh."

"Yes, I know the story—Father told me about it. But look at this piece. It's also pretty in its own way, yet it has only three rubies, and none of them bear any inscription. The rubies seem duller, their shapes are different. It's bizarre."

"Bizarre?!" Sitora exclaimed. "No, my dear, I'm afraid this isn't supernatural at all—it's straightforward theft."

"Theft? In our home?! But how is that possible? Do you think, Mama, that thieves have been here? That's horrifying—I don't even want to believe it."

"Not quite a week ago—maybe a little more—I saw our necklace here in this drawer myself, the one with the Arabic inscription! Where could it have gone? …Larisa!"

Larisa came—indeed, she ran right in—at her mistress's call. Seeing the agitation and anger on Sitora's face, she shrank back, tense. Normally, when her employers called her, she would immediately ask what they needed or how she could help. Now, however, the housekeeper fell silent like a fish, as if she were afraid of something.

"Larisa, tell me—do you dust my dressing table? Well? Cat got your tongue?"

"Y-yes, Sitora Kadyrovna, I… Every time I clean, I dust the whole house… Y-you… you know that."

"I asked specifically about this dressing table!" Sitora said even more sternly.

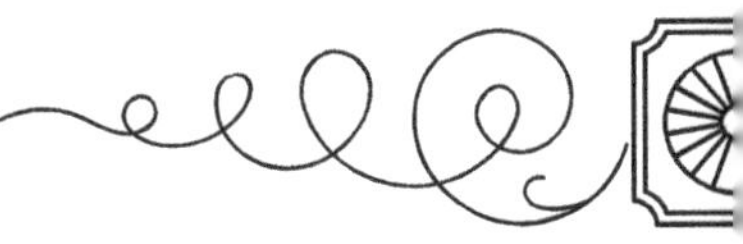

"I… y-yes, yesterday I dusted it. The dressing table…"

"And do you clean inside the drawers?"

"Inside? No, of course not. Never, unless you tell me to."

"But you must have seen that there was a valuable piece of jewelry here, correct?"

"There was? Yes? I—y-yes, Sitora Kadyrovna. I saw… the jewelry."

"A necklace with rubies," Sitora emphasized every word, speaking to Larisa as though the latter were a dim-witted student or someone slow of mind who needed things spelled out. "My daughter's great-great-grandmother, Firuz-begim, and Said Yakhyaevich, and I all gave it to Malika as her wedding present. You do know that, don't you?"

Larisa flushed, on the verge of tears from stress and fear.

"S-Sitora Kadyrovna, you're not… suspecting me of something, are you?"

"And what makes you think I'm suspecting you? Is there a reason I should suspect you? That means you know what happened?"

"N-no, I don't know anything…! I… I don't understand what's going on! I've served you faithfully for so long, and now you… I…"

"The necklace is gone, Larisa. Who else am I supposed to suspect? We don't have any strangers in the house. Apart from you. So I figured maybe you took it—there's no one else for me to suspect at the moment!"

Larisa trembled all over and actually began to cry out loud.

"Why are you shouting at me, Sitora Kadyrovna? It's right there, next to you!"

"This is an entirely different necklace!!!" Sitora exploded. "And you know that perfectly well, don't you? You're just making a fool of me!"

"Please, Mama," Malika couldn't stand it any longer and intervened, her compassionate heart unable to bear the ordeal Larisa was being subjected to. "Don't rush to blame Larisa for everything. Maybe she truly has nothing to do with it! Let's check to see if anything else of value is missing from the house. Maybe some thieves really did break in. Heaven knows we don't need that on top of everything else... But we have to be sure."

Sitora, whose fury had somewhat subsided after yelling at the housekeeper, took her daughter's advice and started walking through the rooms, checking carefully whether all their other belongings were in place.

"See, nothing else is missing—just the necklace!" she reported irritably to Malika, who had been with her the entire time, helping her search. Malika had meanwhile sent Larisa off to the kitchen. "So you see, you're ruling out the possibility that Larisa might be involved, but I'm not so sure you should."

"Mama, please, calm down. We'll figure it out."

The two women returned to Sitora's room. Malika picked up the necklace again, the one she still found foreign and unfamiliar.

"Mama, I think if our necklace was swapped, we have to ask why. Wait, I think I get it. Probably the difference is in the quality of the stones and the piece's overall value. I'm certain the necklace Fatima Al-Nahaiyan gave our Firuz-begim Alimkhanova is worth hundreds of thousands of dollars. But this one... this might be worth only a thousand or, at most, two thousand dollars. So the motive behind the switch seems obvious!"

"You know, the Kuwaiti Sheikh Al-Sabah has a necklace similar to ours—you know, the one we gave you? It also features rubies and diamonds of the very highest quality. And, by the way, one of its largest rubies—a famous 'Temur Ruby'—also bears an Arabic inscription. Those writings are considered priceless because they bear the names of our medieval ancestors—the Great Mughals, Uzbek rulers, many of whom once ruled in India! Incidentally, it was our former librarian, Larisa, who told me about all this. Evidently, she's long been interested in rubies!"

"That's fascinating, Mama, but let's come down to earth. What do we do about our necklace?"

"Well, you do what you like, but I'm going to call the police right away! Let an investigator figure it out and find what's been stolen. I'll personally reward him for it. And I've already informed our security that Larisa won't be leaving tonight—she'll be staying here in the house."

"Oh, Mama, you're still at it! But Larisa is your loyal worker, and I honestly don't think she's guilty of anything! She's always served you so faithfully. How can you suspect her?"

"You just don't know, my daughter, what big money can do to people!"

"All right. But in any case, Mama, wouldn't it be better to wait until Papa gets home from work before calling the police?"

"No, my dear, I can't wait! Don't you understand? Our family heirloom is missing—something that's worth a fortune, besides its personal value to us. That's it—like it or not, I'm calling the precinct."

Malika knew there was no point in arguing with her mother, especially under these circumstances.

"*So, this is how I 'helped' my husband get the money…*" she thought sadly.

***

Murad Nematullaevich often took the necklace out of the hidden wall safe in his opulent mansion's study. He simply couldn't tear his eyes away from it. While, as a man, he had little interest in jewelry "baubles," and even the gold-threaded diamonds left him indifferent, the rubies commanded his full attention. He knew they were extraordinary stones—possessing not only exquisite beauty and high value, but also substantial energy and possibly even magical power: the power to grant their owner immense authority and fabulous wealth. Although Nasyrov already had both in abundance, his restless nature was never satisfied; he always wanted more.

All the same, the idea of selling this unique necklace of precious gems for a high price had crossed his mind more than once. That reminded him of his Indian friend—a major businessman named Raj Singh Bhojwani. Nasyrov knew Bhojwani had a passion for treasures of all kinds, including priceless natural stones. Murad Nematullaevich thought that if he could persuade the Bhojwani to buy the piece, the Indian would almost certainly pay any price. That, at least, was what Nasyrov hoped.

On the other hand, he was loath to part with rubies like these—especially the one bearing the Arabic inscription. From everything he'd gleaned, it was likely the famous "Temur Ruby," renowned worldwide. Judging from descriptions and photos he'd found online, it certainly looked the part! Murad had no desire to sell such a rare gem hastily and possibly under its true value, so he weighed his options carefully, not wanting to make a rash decision.

Naturally, he couldn't display the necklace to just anyone. So he again phoned his old friend, the talented jeweler David Vitstein. He needed to be absolutely sure of the authenticity of this

new necklace—obtained without the knowledge or consent of the Mumtazov family via Larisa and "Jorik." Murad Nematullaevich reassured himself that when it came to grand objectives, all means were permissible. There was no room for needless emotions or sentimentality.

He dispatched Gosha and Roma to reconnoiter the jeweler's apartment. The information they returned with did not please Murad Nematullaevich.

"Sorry, boss," Gosha said, "but David Iosifovich's neighbor told us the old man left for Israel for good, to live with his daughter. She'd been trying to get him to move there permanently for a while…"

"This doesn't please me at all," Nasyrov said with a scowl.

"What do we do? Shall I look for another competent, reliable jeweler?"

"Go ahead, Gosha. Just keep your mouth shut—otherwise, you know you'll be setting yourself up."

"Understood, boss. Don't worry; I won't say a word to anyone about the necklace… Oh, boss!"

"Yes? What is it now?"

"Larisa told me she's read a lot about those rubies and learned that back in the days of the Great Mughals—Shah Jahan and the others—this extraordinary stone had another name: 'The Ornament of the Palace.' It was set into the royal throne in the shah's main quarters. Maybe that's why it was called that?"

"Possibly. 'The Ornament of the Palace'—it does have a nice ring to it. And by the way, Gosha, I have to hand it to you. You pulled off quite the trick framing that con man Misha Leonidov, operating under his alias 'Jorik,' and orchestrating everything so skillfully. Even I'm impressed."

"Thanks, boss. When meeting Larisa, I even disguised my appearance to imitate him. You probably noticed that Misha and I look somewhat alike—he's lighter-haired, I'm darker. But whenever I went to see Larisa, I'd dye my hair differently, alter my walk, my voice, my mannerisms. I'm sure that if she's ever cornered, she'll insist she was seeing Misha, not me! That's exactly what she believes, after all…"

"Let's hope she doesn't give you away."

"She knows nothing, I'm certain! I never once told her my last name."

"Well, as I said—good work. Now hurry up and find me another jeweler, someone who knows how to keep his mouth shut."

* * *

"Hello, Mr. Bhojwani? This is Nasyrov, from Tashkent. Hello!"

"Oh, Mr. Nasyrov, hello, how are you? Doing okay?"

"Good! And you—everything all right? I'm calling on business. But first, of course, I wanted to ask how my son, Mukhitdin, is doing… Is he behaving himself?"

"He's doing great! He's working—very capable and clever, though in other matters he's very independent and freedom-loving. But it's fine: he's still young."

"Yes, my son takes after me—we're both Nasyrovs, and just as freedom-loving."

"I think, Mr. Nasyrov, that he's inherited your business acumen, too! He's a real tiger."

"That's good, Mr. Bhojwani. I'm glad about that. Send my regards to my boy! And please remind him to call his mother and me more often."

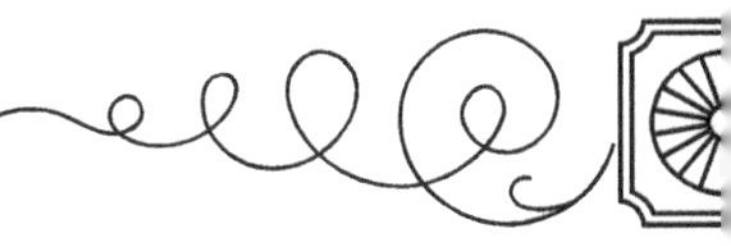

"Okay, will do. He's at the factory right now. Do you want me to call him over?"

"No, no need. Let him call home some evening when he gets the chance. I'm phoning you about another matter. Tell me, might you be interested in a treasure from the era of the Great Mughals? You're a connoisseur of history, so I won't explain who they were."

"Of course I know! But which treasures exactly? And why do you ask?"

"Well… there's a chance I can get hold of the Temur Ruby…"

"What did you say?! The Temur Ruby itself?! That's impossible! It was, if I'm not mistaken, until recently part of the British Crown jewels, and now some Arab sheikhs own it. It must be worth hundreds of millions, if not billions, of dollars!"

"Yes, you're right. But there's a possibility that it somehow made its way to Uzbekistan… Don't forget, after all, that the Great Mughals were largely Uzbek, and modern Uzbekistan is essentially their historical homeland! So let's just say there are certain anonymous volunteers who were interested in transporting this jewel here."

"If that's the case, I'm absolutely delighted! I'd be thrilled for you if you managed even just to see, let alone hold in your hands, this unique precious stone! But, pardon me, I'm not sure yet what this has to do with me."

"Would you, theoretically—just speaking hypothetically—be willing and able to buy this ruby?"

"Would I be able to? Well, maybe… Depends on the price—whether it's realistic or symbolic—and on who's selling. As for whether I'd want to… That's not even a question. I'd dream of it, Mr. Nasyrov, dream of it! It's a true wonder of the world!"

"I understand you, Mr. Bhojwani. In that case, please await my call about this matter in the very near future."

"Deal! I must admit, you've surprised me, dear Mr. Nasyrov... I can hardly believe my ears. The Temur Ruby! Unbelievable!"

36

"Hello, Malika. Where are you, my love? Still at your parents' place? Why are you so late?" Bahadir's voice, judging by its tense tone, betrayed his nervousness. "Everything okay?"

"Um… I'll come home and explain everything, all right? Sorry, I can't talk now. I'll be a bit later. There's food in the fridge—heat it up yourself, okay?"

"Of course. Take care of our issues there, and come back soon! I miss you."

Malika looked again at the investigator—Police Captain Ravshan Umarov.

When Umarov first arrived, his gaze had been dull and indifferent, but after an "inspiring" conversation with Sitora that hinted at a generous "incentive" for his work, he had visibly perked up.

"Our investigative team is trying to figure out the situation," the captain said, wiping his sweaty forehead with a not-so-fresh handkerchief, as he spoke to the women. "You're right: there's no sign of forced entry through the front gate or any of the main doors, nor any clear trace of thieves having entered the house. Now, regarding the missing necklace: Ms. Sitora Kadyrovna, I'll definitely need you to provide a detailed description, all right?"

"Yes, of course," the mistress of the house agreed.

"But I must warn you—it won't be simple to find it."

"I realise that. But I did promise you a worthy reward if you make a real effort!"

"Yes, yes, I remember…" he blushed and again wiped the sweat from his brow. "As for this other necklace you found in the dressing-table drawer, our expert examined it carefully and checked for fingerprints…"

"And?"

"Apart from your prints, Sitora Kadyrovna, and those of your daughter Malika, it contains only one other set of prints. They all belong to…"

"I can guess—my housekeeper!"

"Not at all. Her prints aren't on it. But the ones that are did appear in our electronic database. They belong to a certain Mikhail Leonidov."

"And who's that?" Sitora asked in genuine surprise. "I've never heard that name. Malika, maybe you know him? Have you ever met someone called… what was it, Ravshan? Oh, yes, Mikhail Leonidov. Malika, does that name ring a bell?"

"No, Mama! I don't know anyone by that name."

"This is so strange! Who is he, and why would he rob us? Most importantly, how did he even find out about our necklace? Unless… Larisa… Larisa, come here, please. Do you know someone with the last name Leonidov?... Mikhail Leonidov?"

"I forgot to mention," Captain Umarov interjected, "that according to our information, in the criminal underworld he has a so-called street name, and goes by—'Jora' or 'Jorik.'"

At the sound of this alias for the criminal, Larisa involuntarily flinched.

"N-n-no, I… I don't know…" the woman stammered in a trembling voice.

"They call him that," Ravshan continued, "because, rumor has it, he's fascinated by the biography of Marshal Georgy Zhukov. Collects everything related to him, including valuable war trophies

and various WWII-era treasures…"

"So that's what it is!" Sitora exclaimed. "Then it really could be him…"

"Mama, I think we've already exhausted and worn out poor Larisa," Malika interjected calmly. "It's obvious she has nothing to do with this… Please, Larisa, go on and attend to your duties in the house."

Larisa glanced fearfully at the investigator. He, too, made no objection; he'd already questioned her, and the questioning had led nowhere.

The Mumtazovs' housekeeper needed no further urging—she darted out of the room where the investigator stood, faster than lightning.

* * *

When Malika returned to Amin's apartment and told her husband everything that had happened, he was beside himself with anger.

"But why didn't you at least take that other necklace?"

"First of all, it's currently with the investigator, and the forensic experts are still examining it…"

"The forensic experts!" Bahadir echoed his wife mockingly. "Why did you even need all these forensic experts?!"

"My mother was the one who called them, not me. I was against it, but she wouldn't listen… And second, that other necklace is worth peanuts—maybe a couple thousand dollars. That wouldn't be enough to save you, right?"

"Why not? That's still something! I'd add whatever I've managed to scrape together from my friends, plus my salary…"

"Ah! So you did get a salary this month…"

"Yes, but I told you I had to set it aside to pay for my debt! That's why I didn't mention it to you."

"I see. Well, pardon me. I just didn't think—"

"You just don't think about anything!"

"That's not fair, Bahadir."

"All right… you forgive me, too. I'm just on edge—try to understand!"

"I do understand… Your debt problem hasn't gone away. Could you finally tell me who's blackmailing you? You're my husband; I should know."

"What for? Could you protect me from this guy?"

"Yes, darling, I'll do whatever I can."

"I can't tell you. I'm afraid—for you and for… well, you can figure it out yourself…"

* * *

The following evening, Malika had prepared dinner and went into one of the rooms to call her husband to the table. What she saw upset and worried her:

Her husband was rummaging through Amin's personal papers.

"Bahadir, what are you doing?! Are you looking for something? But these are all your brother's things! So, while he's away on business in Paris, you…"

"Please, stay out of it, okay?"

"How polite. Then again, that's just how you've been lately—rude and abrupt. I only came to say dinner's ready. I thought we could eat together, but I've lost my appetite. So help yourself to what's in the pot."

"Fine! I'm not doing anything terrible, just looking for my documents," Bahadir lied automatically, out of habit. "See, not too long ago I gave Amin my ID—he needed to sign something. I'm just looking for it now!"

Malika looked sadly at her husband, said nothing, and left.

* * *

"Hello, Jora—I mean… it turns out your name is Mikhail, right?.. It's Larisa! I'm calling you from a neighbor's phone. For some reason you're not answering my calls… Oh, you're busy, lots of work? I see. I've missed you so much!.. Yes, my situation… how should I put it? Actually, Jorik—sorry, Misha—I can't get used to calling you that… Why did you hide your real name from me?.. Misha, the thing is, I'm scared! How can you not see why?! The police are all over my employers' house… Well, what other case could it be?! Of course it's that one!!! Please, don't play dumb and pretend you don't 'get it'… What should I do? They could figure out it was me! You're so sure I'll be okay? Well, my mistress does sense something; she's suspicious of me. She must have a grandmother's intuition—she's that sharp. But her daughter Malika, this 'angelic soul,' is totally on my side, defending me. That might change, though, if she learns the truth, and then I'm done for! Listen, you lie low for now, got it? Or the cops will track you down in no time!.. The stones are safely stashed away? Good. Please don't vanish on me, Misha—call me! You'll call, right? Okay, bye. Kisses."

***

Sitora flopped onto the couch and placed a hand on her husband's knee.

"Said, I think that even though the investigator seems good—he's not stupid—we can't rely too much on the police. They won't be able to find our necklace quickly! Let's tell Grandma, Firuz-begim, everything. I have a feeling her unique prophetic gift could really help us right now!"

"You just miss the fragrant smoke of the Crystal Hookah, my dear?" Yakhyaevich teased gently.

"What makes you say that?"

"Because everyone knows she only uncovers these 'mystical' riddles and secrets with the help of her hookah! But you know, I don't believe in all that mysticism and miracles. I'm a scientist—practical, and in every way down-to-earth."

"I know exactly what you're like, my darling husband! Even so, I think we should tell her about the theft."

"That'd only make her worry! Don't forget it was initially gifted to her, and she simply passed it on to Malika for the wedding. Her involvement won't help now."

"You think?"

"Of course."

"All right, then let's do it like this: if a week goes by and the investigation doesn't move forward on finding our precious necklace, I'll tell Grandma everything. Agreed? I've got a strong feeling that Firuz-begim, better than anyone, could show us where—and with whom—we need to look for our treasure!"

"All right, wife, you've convinced me. You can talk anyone into anything."

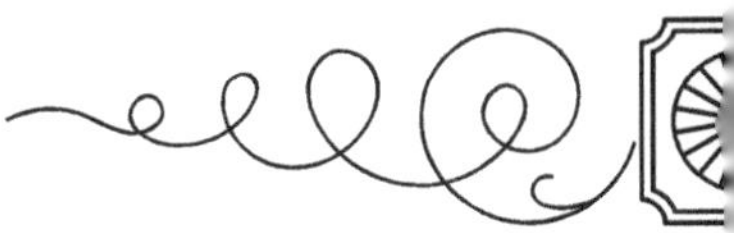

* * *

"Veniamin Arkadyevich, hello! I've come to see you."

"Ah, look who's here—and without security! Bahadir! Well, come on, have a seat. Will you have some tea?"

"No thanks. I'm here about the debt."

"I figured as much, dear boy. Of course, about the debt! What else can you do, sweetheart, but to pay it?"

"I've found an apartment I could give you to settle part of it…"

"Really? Excellent!" Veniamin Arkadyevich stroked his reddish beard in satisfaction. "And whose apartment might it be, if you don't mind my asking? I hope everything's above board—no shady business?"

"No, of course not! It's my brother's apartment. I have all the paperwork. I just need a bit more time to transfer the title into my name, and then naturally, I'd sign it over to you. Plus, I'll need to produce a fake deed of gift, showing that my brother 'granted' it to me."

"You see, Bahadir, what a smart guy you are! A real champ! Go on, do your thing."

"So… will you wait a little?"

"I'll wait a little," Veniamin Arkadyevich replied sarcastically, mimicking Bahadir's tone. "But as for our 'boss'—I can't say. Still, I'll try to persuade him! Two weeks—will that be enough?"

"I'm not sure, but I'll do my best."

"You better do, darling! Otherwise, it's harakiri! Understand?" He laughed, revealing teeth yellowed by age and cigarettes. "But don't drag your feet too long—my boss doesn't like that. That's the first thing. And now the second, the most important. Even with that apartment, you realise it's still not enough. How do you plan

to repay the rest?"

"My wife has a family heirloom…"

"Oh really?! Well, that's interesting. What kind of heirloom?"

"A necklace—very, very expensive."

"Is that so!" The bearded man whistled. "And what's the plan?"

"I was going to take it… sell it—and give you the money."

"Five hundred bucks, right?"

"No, why five hundred? It must be worth two or three hundred thousand in green—at least. I'm not sure exactly…"

"Not bad."

"But…"

"But?"

"It's gone missing. Just the other day—it was stolen!"

"Well, well! This is getting interesting!" For some reason the red-bearded man burst out laughing. Then, as if thinking something over and making quick calculations in his head, he suddenly turned serious:

"And what's that to me, Bahadir, all these stories?"

"Well, they're looking for it. Maybe they'll find it… then…"

"…then you'll sell it and give me the money. Or hand over part of its value. Got it. So, you're a grown man, handsome, you're studying, you work… right? And I hear you've even gotten married. True?"

"Yes. But what's that got to do with—"

"Yet you still act like a clueless child. Painful to watch, really! You spin these fairy tales that have no grounding in real life or real money."

"But I'm telling the truth…"

"Pipe down, youngster, and listen to me. You deal with your brother's apartment— that's on you. And about the necklace—forget it. Your relatives will never get it back, understand? But there's another option. And in my opinion, it's your best one."

"Really, Veniamin Arkadyevich? I'd be so gratef—"

"Shut up and don't interrupt. In the next few days, you're going to bring your young wife to our b— I mean, to the 'boss.'"

"Malika?! But why?!"

"Well, it was his idea. I'm just passing it on."

"What—he knows my wife? That's weird. How?"

"Don't act dumb. Our boss knows everything about everyone. He saw her once, and he really liked her."

"Wait—so… Excuse me, I'm not following. Are you saying my wife is supposed to—"

"You know exactly what I mean! Are you a baby? Don't you know how these things work? But this is just for one night—for now. The boss promises to forgive you half your debt in return. Half, you understand?! That's a cool twenty-five grand off your tab! And if you let her go to him for good—he'll wipe your entire debt."

"Have you all lost your minds?! Bastards, scum, degenerates! My wife?! Never! Not in a million years! Got it? I'd rather beg in the streets."

"You won't make it that far."

"What?!"

"You won't even get onto the streets—you'll never get there. You'll collapse along the way. And your beloved young wife will be left a widow. Is that what you want? …No? Then think, sonny. Think!"

"I'm not even going to consider it! Over my dead body! You can go f—"…

***

"Mama, I really, really need your help! Urgently!"

"All right, sweetheart, of course. But what happened this time? Why do you sound so agitated and nervous?"

"Mom, if possible, I'd prefer to explain everything face to face."

When they met in town, Malika said:

"To put it briefly, Mama, my Bahadir is in trouble. He's in despair, not himself, and it pains me to see him like that. He won't tell me everything, but one can guess plenty… I have to help him, you understand?"

"Not quite yet. But I'm listening carefully!"

"I have to speak with someone… someone very bad, maybe even dangerous, who's threatening to hurt my husband!"

"My goodness! Let me call that investigator of ours—Ravshan Umarov!"

"No, Mama, no, we can't do that! These people are so dangerous that they'd take any contact with the police as a direct threat and, accordingly, a reason to carry out drastic actions against Bahadir! We absolutely can't allow that."

"I understand. And you want me to go with you to meet them? Darling, that's extremely risky! Couldn't there be another way?"

"They won't dare do anything to us, especially in broad daylight and in a public place. They already know we exist. They've surely looked into our addresses, phone numbers, everything about us. It's pointless to hide from them. In my opinion, we should do the opposite: go and talk to them openly. Not to fight—let's face it, we can't fight them, it's beyond our power—but to find out, calmly, what they want and whether we can work this out with minimal losses."

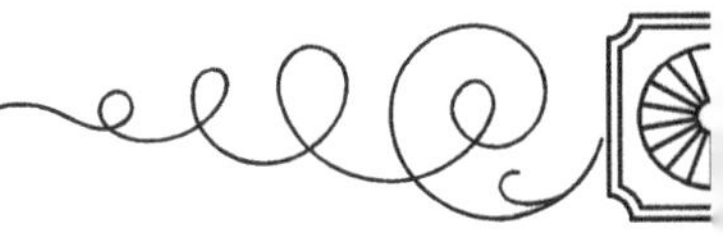

"Then let's go. I'm ready. You're my life, and if necessary, I'll shield you with my own body!"

*If they offend me—I might put up with it,
But if they hurt my child, I'll tear them to pieces…*

* * *

The waiter politely greeted the two women entering the restaurant. Malika remembered she had once been here with Bahadir.

"Whom do you need? Veniamin Arkadyevich? Let me call him!"

Within a couple of minutes, an older man with a reddish beard approached their table.

"What can I do for you? Ah, my dear young lady, it's you! Of course I remember. Malika, right?… How lovely that you've graced our modest establishment…"

"Hello, Veniamin Arkadyevich," Malika responded curtly.

"You remember my name? You truly are quite charming!" He beamed broadly. "And your companion… My goodness, you resemble each other so! Is this your mother? Delightful!"

"If you don't mind, let's skip the flattery and theatrics," Malika cut him off, even more coldly. "We need to speak to your boss."

"But I am the boss."

"It's pointless to give us that nonsense."

"All right, but the boss is very busy right now… Could you wait? I'll have them bring you something tasty—on the house!"

"Don't bother. You'd best fetch your 'boss' right this moment—or I'll call a close friend at the Republican Prosecutor's Office. And trust me, I'll find a reason for you to have serious problems here. For example, I might mention your underground casino… Would you like that? I'm not joking. Believe me?"

Whatever inside information Malika possessed and the tone in which she said it made the man—experienced, dangerous, and worldly though he was—promptly comply.

Within a minute, the "boss" emerged from his office, approached the table where Malika and Sitora sat waiting, and took a seat across from them. He was the owner of this restaurant and an entire chain of businesses, as well as—incidentally—one of the main facilitators of Bahadir and Malika's wedding… Murad Nematullaevich Nasyrov.

He settled comfortably on a chair opposite the two women, who were on guard and ready for battle. Then, eyes wide, he stared not at Malika, but at her mother.

"Sitora?! Is that really you? Impossible… Well, hello, my dear!!!"

"Murad?! Never expected this… What a meeting indeed… After twenty whole years! For what it's worth, this is my daughter Malika."

"This young woman is your daughter?!"

Normally so self-possessed, Nasyrov was momentarily stunned with astonishment.

37

By nature, Misha Leonidov was as slippery and elusive as an eel. He could wrap anyone around his finger—even someone as "serious" as the boss—and eventually slip out of his clutches to freedom.

There were only two areas of Mikhail's life where he almost never resorted to deceit. First, he was always honest with himself—his beloved self—never indulging in false fantasies or empty dreams that had no chance of coming true. Second, Misha made every effort to be honest with the women in his life; and because of his good looks and sharp mind, there were a great many of them. He never promised any of them an "eternal familial bliss" in lawful matrimony. All of them knew perfectly well that, where Misha was concerned, pinning hopes on marriage was useless, pointless, and downright silly, because he would immediately, openly, and directly warn each new girlfriend not to expect that, and these women stayed with him simply because they found it comfortable, interesting, and pleasant. Many were not even bothered by the fact that Misha was a genuine gigolo who, quite shamelessly and without any pangs of conscience, often lived entirely at their expense, exploiting their kindness and generosity.

Still, to him, these were "honest" relationships. In all other spheres, Misha was an out-and-out liar, trickster, and swindler.

Nasyrov knew the rules of business, capital management, and human resources quite well. But he knew very little about the real estate market into which he had "plunged" through Misha, just like many people—rich or otherwise—who lust for profit and what they imagine to be "easy money." Misha, on the other hand, already knew this field fairly well and had some useful experience in it.

Even though Nasyrov had assigned some musclebound "overseers" to keep an eye on Mikhail, in reality neither they nor the boss himself could keep watch on a sly, resourceful guy's every move around the clock for several years. Moreover, the boss, burdened with countless affairs, simply could not devote so much attention to one person—especially someone who was neither close to him nor a member of his family, just some hustler, con artist, and scoundrel who had once fooled him in a big way and now owed him a substantial amount of money.

Of course, Murad Nematullaevich could have long ago ordered his personal guards to get rid of Mikhail and bury him somewhere in a "quiet forest clearing," but the boss saw that, as his unofficial, "pocket" employee—and specifically as a realtor—Leonidov was bringing him quite a tidy profit. Abandoning that "extra" large profit simply wasn't in the boss's nature.

The key to Leonidov's success as a broker was that, when buying and selling houses and apartments, he used every cunning trick in the book—sometimes even illegal, fraudulent schemes—making clients come to him instead of going to his competitors, readily handing over their money.

In short, thanks to Misha, real estate funds flowed regularly and steadily into the boss's pocket. As a result, the boss grew ever more satisfied with Mikhail and gradually loosened the invisible "vice" clamped around the young man's arms and legs.

Thus, armed with two seemingly innate habits—deceiving others and stealing—Misha devised a cunning plan that would free him forever from the boss's octopus-like "tentacles" without endangering his life or well-being.

He realised that simply running away would be unwise: the boss's goons could hunt him down anywhere and drag him out "from under the ground" if they had to, returning him right back there as well. Mikhail definitely did not want that. He loved life and loved himself. Even just getting beaten up would have been utterly unacceptable to him. He lacked the physical strength to fight back, but he did possess a sharp mind. So, he thought everything through—carefully weighing what would be necessary for full and absolute freedom, since he had no desire to remain in Nasyrov's grasp indefinitely. Misha understood that he shouldn't run but act more cleverly and wisely. He came up with a complex scheme that would free him from Nasyrov entirely—but it required time and patience to pull off.

Since a realtor's work often involves long, tedious negotiations, persuading clients, and boring paperwork, the "watchdogs" assigned to Misha were soon lulled by all this dreary broker intolerable boredom. Besides, Misha managed to convince each of them (they took turns on duty) that having to witness every step of his work would be pure torture. Indeed, after seeing enough of those dull proceedings, they were only too willing to believe him. They understood that the boss didn't need to hear every detail, and it was impossible—as well as pointless—to watch Leonidov every minute, including his dealings with clients.

In short, both the boss and his overseers grew more trusting. Misha would have been a fool not to take advantage of that, especially when he yearned for freedom with all his heart! So, he did.

Mikhail secretly began doing more and more deals "on the side," thereby earning substantial "off-the-record" money. He'd tell the boss that a particular transaction had fallen through—a common occurrence in real estate—and at the same time would finalise the most profitable transactions for himself, often using the boss's money to do so.

He succeeded in convincing Nasyrov that he needed a reserve of funds to "promote" the business—transportation, newspaper ads and flyers around the city, buying off clients, and most importantly, purchasing the cheapest properties, which could then be resold at a hefty profit. In other words, he promised good returns.

Misha shuffled the funds so skillfully that even the most competent accountant or economist would have been baffled by the flow of off-the-books money. And, since the chief accounting department for the boss's chain of stores, cafés, and restaurants had grown thoroughly sick and tired of the endless real estate deals—some successful, some not—and all the paperwork and re-registration that came with them, Nasyrov instructed Mikhail to deposit the necessary sums into the company account himself. The boss's head accountant, Lidiya Petrovna, only checked the figures afterward.

However, the chief accountant couldn't possibly know the actual transaction amounts; she only saw what was in the official paperwork. And the paperwork looked "clean" and "transparent," thanks to Misha's meticulous efforts. As for the unreported profits, Misha funneled the bulk of those proceeds into his own anonymous account, which he had opened in secret from everyone. Not a living soul knew about that account except Leonidov himself and a couple of bank operators (and the bank bears no liability for client misdeeds, functioning only as a financial intermediary). In short, it all appeared completely legal and aboveboard.

Hence, by making use of the boss's capital, Mikhail carefully and methodically transferred a significant portion of the profits from real estate transactions into his personal anonymous account.

But after a while, that still felt insufficient to him. Now flush with funds, Misha hired Sergey, one of the most expensive hackers around.

"Sergey, I know for a fact you're the best hacker in town," said Misha Leonidov. "I've got a job for you—a request, really. You'll need to break into certain corporate and personal accounts I'll identify. It doesn't matter whose they are. Let's just say they belong to one company. You'll invisibly 'crack' those accounts and transfer the company's and its owner's funds into my personal account. Got it?"

"Yes, Mikhail, I understand. No problem."

"You'll also need to hide all record of our monetary transactions from everyone who uses these accounts—basically, erase any sign of your involvement. In the computer database of this person and company, on their website, and in all their documentation, the funds you remove must still show up as being there—in other words, on the company's account and the owner's personal account. Meanwhile, they'll really be with me… Is that possible?"

"Yes, these days everything is possible, Mikhail, especially for the fee you're offering. Don't worry; we'll handle it."

As a result of all these prolonged and exceedingly cautious machinations by Mikhail Leonidov, his "all-powerful" boss, the wealthy "oligarch" Murad Nematullaevich Nasyrov, found himself—without the slightest inkling—practically bankrupt.

38

"Mama, why are you putting so much on yourself?" Rano took from Mukhabbat's hands a large bag containing a variety of groceries from the nearby supermarket. "I already said I'd do all the shopping myself! And I'm trying to do that as best as I can. Yesterday, Father went to the bazaar and brought back fruit and vegetables. What else do we need? After all, Bahadir and Malika are still staying at Amin's place, and Amin himself is still away in France on business. It's just the three of us here—how much can we possibly need?"

By habit, as soon as she came in from outside, Mukhabbat went to wash her hands in the bathroom. Afterward, she headed to the living room, dropped heavily into an armchair, and covered her face with her hand.

Her daughter walked over to her.

"Mama! What happened again? Are you feeling unwell?"

"No, Ranosha, don't worry. Everything is fine. It's just…"

"What…?"

"I ran into that woman—remember the tall, dark-skinned one you mentioned…"

"Of course I remember. Honestly, whenever I think about her, I still get goose bumps all over. There's something about her—something majestic, but at the same time kind of frightening… So did you actually speak to her?"

"Yes."

"That's why you feel like this! Did she do something bad to

you? The nerve of her… You shouldn't have gone up to her!"

"No, no, she didn't say or do anything that should worry me. But in the past, at one point, I did endure a lot of trouble because of her."

"What do you mean, Mama? You actually know her? I suspected as much! Who is she?"

"My daughter, you don't need to know this just yet. Don't burden your bright head, all right? What matters is that I talked to her, and she won't bother us anymore, at least for the time being…"

"For the time being? What's that supposed to mean?"

"Well… for as long as… The thing is, she wants Amin very much—she insists on meeting with him. Demanding, even. I didn't want that, but she's insisting. Once my son returns from his trip, I'll tell him everything. He's an adult now; let him decide for himself. Whatever he decides, so be it. And I… What else can I do now?…"

She covered her face with her hand once more and was lost in her own thoughts.

Although Mukhabbat Fattakhov's daughter was very curious to learn the secret involving her brother Amin as well, she realized now was not the time to pester her mother with more questions. After all, she thought, once her brother came home, everything would surely become clear and be resolved.

* * *

Catching Misha had become quite difficult by now, so Gosha decided to call him.

"Mishka, hey there, buddy!" Gosha still acted as if he were on friendly terms with Leonidov. "Any news? I heard you're in the boss's good books these days. Well, that's impressive—you're doing

great. Keep it up!"

Gosha spoke in the tone of an "older brother" who believes he is far more important, successful, and clever than the "younger sibling," condescendingly praising what he views as trivial, almost childish achievements.

"Thanks, Gosha. Sorry, I'm really busy. Is it something urgent? Speak up."

Gosha hadn't expected such brisk insolence from Mikhail. Who did he think he was, talking almost like a superior to Gosha—who was, after all, the boss's right-hand man?

"I just wanted to talk, have a chat. Thought I'd invite you out for a drink tonight—go to a bar, have some music, pick up a few girls. You know, just cut loose a bit. We're practically the same age, like brothers. But if you're that busy…"

"Gosh, don't take it personally. It's just that my deals keep falling through one after another, you know? I'm trying to scrape together at least some profit for the boss."

"Yeah, I get that, man. But by the way, I'm calling you on the boss's orders, too. You know our new café in Yunusabad?"

"I've heard of it. Supposed to be really fancy. So what?"

"The boss asked me to tell you that he wants to meet with you there tomorrow at exactly six in the evening. He says he has something very important and pleasant to discuss. I'm guessing he wants to thank you for something and maybe reward you with a personal gift, who knows. He does that sometimes. And you did land a few profitable deals for the company recently. So, he wants some private time with you to show his appreciation. Also, Misha, I think the boss plans to entrust you with a delicate matter. I'm not sure what—it's something he'll tell you himself. But don't worry; I'm sure it's all good."

For a moment, Gosha's phone went silent, as if suspended in a brief pause.

"Misha, why aren't you saying anything? Can you hear me?"

"I hear you, Gosha. I... Sorry, I was just thinking. Got it. Thanks."

"So, will you come? I have to let the boss know your answer today. But personally, I wouldn't advise turning him down."

"I understand. Of course I'll come—like I really have a choice."

***

"Hello, is this the police station? I need Captain Umarov. Is that you? Good. I have urgent, very important information. It doesn't matter who I am. Just call me a 'concerned friend.' You're looking for Mikhail Leonidov, right? The one suspected of stealing valuables? And you can't find him, correct? He's a thief and needs to face justice for that ruby necklace he stole and for other crimes! It's entirely possible the necklace stolen from the Mumtazov home—the one you're after—is in Leonidov's possession. How do I know? That's not important. Listen carefully: Mikhail will be at the newly opened café Minor at Yunusabad today at six in the evening. Oh, you know that place? Perfect. Yes, yes, for certain! You can nab him there without any trouble..."

39

"Sitora, you look wonderful—after all these years you haven't changed at all!" Despite his stature and importance, Murad Nematullaevich beamed and seemed almost childlike in his delight. "Wait, I remember lending my restaurant for your daughter's wedding. So why, dear friend, didn't I see you there?"

"I hardly left the banquet hall that evening, Murad," Sitora replied. "I sat modestly with my relatives—that's probably why we never saw each other."

"Well, I'm very happy to see both of you here and now. So, you must be Malika, Sitora's daughter, right? You really are stunning— just like your mother…"

Until that moment, from the time Nasyrov took a seat at their table, Malika had been at a loss for words. She simply didn't know how to behave around this man to whom she and her mother had come as though to an "enemy," someone who demanded the unimaginable from her and her husband… Now, hearing him speak to her in a slightly sugary tone about her beauty, she felt uncomfortable.

She frowned.

"Come on, now… You must be angry with me because of what my assistant Veniamin said to Bahadir, right? I know Bahadir is your husband. You haven't forgotten it was I who arranged your wedding?"

Malika thought that from now on, he would always be reminding them of that.

"So, Malika… Your husband owes a debt, and it's very large. There's no real danger to him, so you can stop worrying. But a debt is a matter of honor, isn't it? My dear ladies, it still needs to be repaid. Forgive me—I'm just an old man."

"What kind of debt?" Malika asked sharply, still on her guard. "Is he gambling with you—cards, maybe? Some illegal casino, right? Is that how he lost to you?"

"Shh, quiet! What is it with you, child, have you lost your mind? What casino? Where do you get these wild ideas? When I heard that horrible word from my assistant, I almost fainted. We don't have, and cannot have, any casinos. They're prohibited by law in our country. Didn't you know? I'm just a humble, honest businessman who loves good food, and I have only a few cafés and little restaurants. That's all!… Well, girls, you really do surprise me—suspecting and accusing me of something like that! It's beyond comprehension and rather hurtful…"

He laughed in a strangely unnatural way.

"Forgive us, Murad," Sitora intervened. "But why does Bahadir owe you money?"

"And why, my dear ladies, should you trouble your lovely heads with these purely men's affairs?"

"All the same…" Malika insisted. "My husband's problems are my problems too."

"Oh, so that's how it is. Well, in that case, he needs to explain everything to you himself, right?"

Malika said nothing.

"All right, if it worries you that much, I'll try to answer your question. It seems he wanted to buy a car—something along those lines. I don't even remember the details anymore. He borrowed money from me a while back and hasn't managed to pay it back.

And what about me? How am I supposed to live? I need money as well! I have plenty of expenses, you know…"

He forced another unconvincing laugh, then continued:

"But since it turns out, dear Sitora, that Bahadir is your son-in-law, I'm willing to wait. It's a lot of money, and I understand you can't repay it quickly… I hope you can manage in about a year, yes?… But, under one condition."

"What condition?" Malika's voice tensed again.

"We need to see each other more frequently now. At least, we can't lose contact."

"How does Bahadir know you?" Malika pressed, still distrustful.

"How? Let me think… From your wedding day, of course. Yes, I remember it now. He approached me himself and started talking. A fine young man—he made a great impression on me. He reminded me a bit of my own son. He told me how he wanted to buy a foreign car, and I thought, why not help a good person, newly married at that? I'm such a generous soul—I help everyone. So, I couldn't refuse your Bahadir either…"

At that moment, a waiter arrived with a tray full of gourmet dishes.

"All right, dear girls, no more questions. Look, they've brought you a whole array of delicious specialties. Now I need to step away for a while—please excuse me. Enjoy your meal! Sitora, my dear, this isn't goodbye. You and I absolutely have to meet one-on-one. Will that be acceptable—say, right here next Monday? Yes? Excellent. Malika, my dear, don't be offended. Your mother and I used to be very close, and we both have plenty of memories… Goodbye, lovely ladies. Relax, eat, and don't think about anything else. After all, life is so beautiful!"

After he left, Malika tugged on Sitora's sleeve.

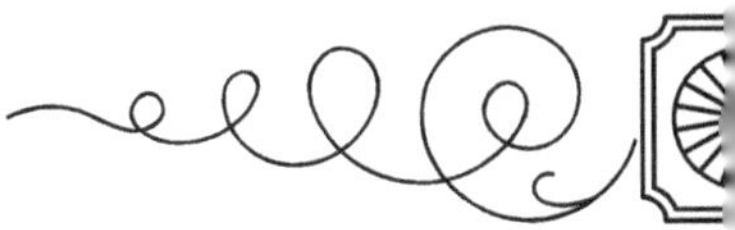

"Mama, please, can we go—right now? I don't want us to owe him any more than we already do."

"Of course, my dear, of course…"

* * *

"Malika, good evening, my dear." Bahadir hugged and kissed his obviously tired wife, who had just arrived home. "Where were you for so long? Why didn't you answer my calls properly? You just shouted, 'I'll tell you everything later, Bahadir—later!' and hung up. What is all this about?"

"I met and spoke with your extortionist—Veniamin Arkadyevich. And then with Murad Nematullaevich. You know him, don't you?"

"Who did you talk to?! Malika! Don't scare me… Not that! My wife, you've killed me! Why? Who asked you to do that? I only told you about these dangerous people so you'd be cautious… and you went straight to them…! What did he do to you? Did he touch you?"

"Are you silly? Do you imagine I'd let anyone just do something to me or 'touch' me? Besides, I wasn't alone there."

"Who were you with?"

"With my mom."

"With who?!"

"With my mother—your mother-in-law—Sitora Kadyrovna."

"Thank God, of course, you weren't alone! That was wise. But still, the two of you must be crazy! Going to see Nasyrov in person! I have no idea how you even managed to find him… or how you got away from him? He's a dangerous man! If I'd known, I'd never have told you anything about my problems!"

"You had no choice. We're a family—you and I are one."

Bahadir nodded gloomily. He felt a bit angry with his wife and jealous too; he didn't entirely trust that no one had tried anything with his beautiful wife at that meeting. Although—she had said she was there with her mother. Once that sank in, he relaxed.

"Don't worry," Malika went on. "It turned out he's an old friend of my mother's…"

"What?! Who?!"

"You're not hard of hearing, Bahadir, so why the questions? They hadn't seen each other for about twenty years, apparently—so they knew each other even before I was born. But they recognised each other right away and were really happy to meet again. Especially him, that Murad. I had the feeling he was once in love with my mother, even though he's significantly older than she is. It's just, you know, the way he looked at her—as if she were a real queen!"

Bahadir now looked at his own wife Malika as if she were a true queen.

"So, did you manage to straighten out my situation?"

"You're quick to get to the point. No, not entirely. But Murad Nematullaevich gave us a whole one-year extension. And right now, there's no threat to your life whatsoever."

"My clever girl!" Bahadir, pleased, kissed his wife again. "But where will we get that kind of money, even in a year? I can't wrap my head around it."

"Listen… I didn't mention this to you at first…"

"More surprises?"

"Bahadir, it's not really a surprise. Or rather… The thing is, my main professor of pop vocal performance at the conservatory sent my paperwork to a Moscow international singing contest. If I manage to at least take third place, I'll receive a good cash prize.

Of course, I never wanted to go there just for the money. But since you're in this predicament, I have to help you somehow as your wife. What do you think?"

"A contest? In Moscow?"

"Yes."

"What's it called?"

"'Superstar.' Does that matter?"

"If you go there, does that mean you'll be away from Tashkent for a long time?"

"If, God forbid, I get 'flunked' early, I'll come right back, and we won't lose anything except the cost of my tickets. But if the Almighty helps me and I'm lucky enough to get through all the rounds, it could take three or four months. I'll fly home to Tashkent every so often."

"Maybe I should go with you, Malika, and stay there the whole time? I can't bear being without you."

"Where would you stay? Have you thought of that?"

"And you—where will you stay?"

"Contest participants get cheap dorm rooms, and we can manage that financially. My conservatory administration will also help out where they can. If I win… Bahadir, this is our chance. Please, let me try… You won't regret it."

"I understand, though honestly, I feel a bit humiliated, relying on my wife's money to solve my problems… And I don't want you leaving; I don't want to be apart from you even for a single day."

"Thank you, my love. Still—think it over. My professor says I have the qualifications to make a good impression and take at least third or maybe even second place. And if I'm really lucky, maybe first…"

"What about your studies?"

"They'll let me go. I'll catch up later and take exams externally."

"You amaze me, my darling! All right, we'll see. I'll think about it…"

***

Rudik Khairullin decided to call his friend and partner Valdoni in Milan.

"Ciao, Francesco! How are you?"

"Ah, Rudik from Tashkent, buongiorno! Any good news?"

"I spoke with my friend, Bahadir Fattakhov. He's agreed to take part in our project—you know, setting up the joint venture to produce perfume and cosmetics."

"Perfetto, excellent! But… Rudik, are you sure your scheme will work?"

"Absolutely."

"Still, you should double-check everything carefully, all right?"

"Of course. I've already discussed it with Bahadir, and he's contacted his father's regular French partner—a perfumer from Paris named Jean Marchal. Jean will be one of our main investors."

"Good. Make sure the whole thing doesn't fail!"

"Don't worry, Francesco—it won't. I have experience with this kind of deal. We'll talk about the rest of the details later."

"All right. Don't let me down, Rudik—I'm counting on you. And please, don't breathe a word about our plans to anyone…"

"Of course, amico, don't worry. Everything will be molto bene—or, as we say, very good!"

"Grazie, Rudik. E allora, ciao!"

"Ciao!"

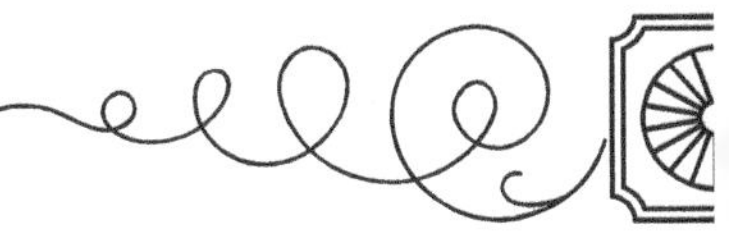

* * *

Toward the end of the workday, Gosha went into the boss's office at his summons.

"Tell me everything you know," Nasyrov said. "How do things stand at the moment?"

"Boss, Captain Umarov is digging in the dirt with his nose, looking everywhere for our—or rather, pardon me—your necklace with rubies and diamonds… You know, the real one we took from the doctor and his family. First of all, he's been checking every jewelry shop and workshop. That's why, forgive me, but I took the liberty of suspending our search for a jeweler for the time being. I figure it's too risky right now—whoever the jeweler might be, he might turn us all in out of fear… Are you going to punish me for this?"

"Why would I punish you, Gosha?"

"Well, I disregarded your order and acted on my own…"

"You're responding to circumstances—that's a different matter. Although… Gosha, you know perfectly well I don't tolerate or forgive insubordination, correct?"

Gosha realised he had overstepped and began trembling with fear. He knew what the boss was capable of, how easily he could "wipe someone off the face of the earth."

"Y-yes, Boss. My fault. Forgive me…"

"Relax! I'm joking. I forgive you. After all, your main goal has been to protect me, to watch out for my safety, and you still do. In fact, your brain work does more to protect me than all my bodyguards combined. So well done! You did right by not telling any jewelers about our treasure. All the jewelers we know are rotten scum—though they love bribes, and won't miss an opportunity to take them. But they'd just as soon 'sell us out' to the authorities the minute they got the chance. No, for now, we must lie low. Meanwhile, I'll find a way to confirm whether that piece of jewelry is genuine! … Now tell me something else: Will Mikhail show up for the 'meeting' at the restaurant?"

"Yes, it's almost six o'clock now. I'm pretty sure he's already there, waiting like a fool for you. And that investigator, Ravshan Umarov, has been tipped off. I think he won't pass up the chance either—who wouldn't want a reward and commendation from their bosses? He'll arrest him."

"He'll detain him first."

"What did you say, Boss?"

"He'll just detain him. And presumably charge Leonidov with switching out the two necklaces—meaning, stealing the Mumtazov necklace, the one in our possession now. Suspicion points to him alone, thanks to those 'fingerprints' you so cleverly left on the necklace Misha brought from Moscow! What a fool he is—he never even thought to wipe off his prints! The poor sap set himself up. But that's no concern of mine anymore. I've already found a competent realtor to replace Mikhail, and now that's who will handle all my transactions. But listen, Gosha: those fingerprints alone aren't enough to pin the theft of our supposedly real necklace on Mikhail, not unless it's actually found to show who took it. So, when Mikhail ends up in custody, you'll scare him through our contacts there, make sure he keeps his mouth shut about us and takes all the blame himself! That includes even in court, if there's a trial. And there will be a trial—I guarantee Misha that much! I need him to take the fall in our place, get it? Especially keep me out of it. So just promise him he'll do the minimum time, get parole or amnesty since it's his first offense, and that once he's out, he'll get a hefty reward for his troubles. Got it?"

"Yes, Boss. Understood."

"Do we still have someone at the restaurant keeping an eye on things?"

"Everything's set there, Boss! Misha swore to me that he'd be there for the meeting, absolutely. The poor idiot has no clue about our plans."

"Gosha!" Nasyrov couldn't hold back. "How many times do I have to teach you that everything must be checked thoroughly and brought to completion every single time?"

"Well… Roma's there, having dinner. He'll update us afterward. But, Boss, everything—"

"Whose phone is ringing? Gosha, it's yours! Answer it already—those rings are driving me crazy!"

"Hello? Yes, Roma. What? Speak louder, there's a lot of background noise… What?!"

"What's he saying?" asked Nasyrov, abruptly shifting his gaze to Gosha's phone. "Is everything okay?"

"What, Roma? Say it again! What do you mean he 'didn't show up'? … Boss, Mikhail didn't come to the meeting after all…"

"How could he not come?!" shouted Nasyrov. "Have you all gone mad? And the captain—is he there? Who's the police going to arrest now? Our 'bait' got away!"

"Roma, what else?… They've looked everywhere, tried calling him? Mikhail is nowhere to be found? That's impossible—I was able to reach him easily just yesterday! He's completely out of touch? Could he have slipped away?… What?! The chief accountant called? How so—'almost nothing left'? Are you sure?!"

Gosha was speechless, staring at the boss in horror.

"Well, I'll be damned," Nasyrov hissed with bitterness, suddenly putting it all together. "He cleaned out my account?… Looks like this Misha really wasn't such a fool. Far from it!"

40

Amin, who had just flown in from his business trip, met with his father, Abdulla Rustamovich, in their company's office, inside the director's office. That same evening, Bahadir and Malika had gathered their things from his apartment and moved back in with Bahadir's parents.

"My son, I'm so glad to see you!" Abdulla Rustamovich hugged his eldest. "You know we're expecting you at our place for dinner this evening—your mother's already busy cooking up a storm. We'll celebrate your return!"

They both sat down near Abdulla Fattakhov's desk.

"Father, of course I'll come. I hope our work doesn't hold us here too long today…"

"No need to worry, son. I promise. Listen… maybe it's just me, but you seem to be glowing, looking so self-assured since you got back. Am I right? Are things going well for us in France?"

For a few seconds, Amin was silent, as though lost in thought.

"Well, Father… how shall I put it… not exactly…"

"Did you speak with our partner—Monsieur Jean Marchal?"

"Yes, yes, we had a brief conversation about future collaboration, but he was very busy; he's dealing with some personal issues, so we weren't able to—"

"Son, excuse me for interrupting. But please remember: Marchal is extremely important for our business, and no matter what, we cannot afford to lose his firm—ever! Try to handle him tactfully."

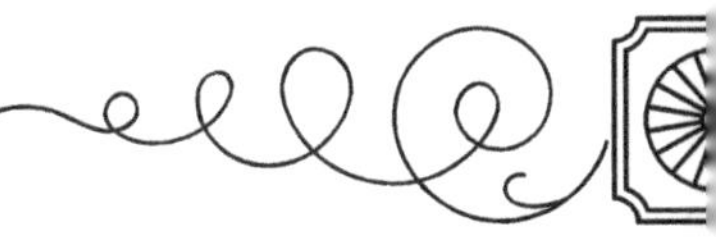

"I understand, Father. All right. What I wanted to tell you… if I seem confident, it's only because… Well, actually, I'd like to say that I'm going to come see you this evening, but not alone…"

"Ah, yes—you mentioned briefly that you plan to get married. I must admit I'm surprised and intrigued. Who is she? Did you meet her over there in France?"

"I met her on the plane. She's from here—an Uzbek—and she was also traveling to Nice on the same flight for her own business. Our seats in business class happened to be next to each other—and I'm now certain it was fate, the hand of God. The moment I saw her, and especially once we started talking, I felt this tremor inside me… I've never experienced anything like it. Of course, there have been women I liked, and you know how much I loved my wife. But this woman, Dilshoda, has completely enchanted and disarmed me. She's beautiful, bold, and determined."

"I'm very happy for you, my boy."

"Thank you. And by the way, she really helped me with our business matters…"

"Oh? Does she work in perfumes too?" asked Abdulla Rusta-movich.

"No, no. She's an international-affairs lawyer."

"A lawyer? In international affairs?! Wait… You went on that trip at my request… Tell me honestly: did something bad happen over there?!"

"Father, I just didn't want to say anything right away so you wouldn't worry. But, to be frank, yes—something did happen. The situation is rather unpleasant, to say the least. It's just that…"

"Stop dragging it out. Speak up!"

"Please, don't get too upset. The fact is, our partner factory near Nice—the one producing the main batch of perfumes we've

ordered and paid for—has been declared bankrupt by the EU authorities. The factory is being shut down. A liquidation commission has already started work."

"What are you talking about, Amin?! I've already transferred a huge sum to that enterprise… and we have a contract! They… Are we not going to receive our shipment?!"

"We're fighting for it, Father. In fact, it was Dilshoda who advised me to file a lawsuit as soon as possible so we can claim the merchandise that rightfully belongs to us. I'll explain everything in detail. As you know, there's a serious economic crisis in the West. The dollar's unstable; the euro's also gone down, and consumer purchasing power is dropping—which means reduced demand for goods. Unfortunately, this affects our sector too: perfumes and cosmetics. Many companies are going under."

"I know all too well, son, that many countries with large perfume-buying populations have started local production of their own perfume and cosmetic goods. Often, distributors who have pre-ordered products from European manufacturers refuse to buy them in the end, and the producers go bankrupt due to overproduction. They have stock they can't sell because so many foreign buyers cancel… And then there's the EU law: if a company's net assets are less than its charter capital, the latter has to be lowered. If reducing the charter capital makes it fall below the legal minimum, the company must liquidate."

"That's right. It's an objective situation, and no one's deliberately cheating or duping anybody. In our case, that factory can't pay its taxes on time, and according to French law, overdue tax payments qualify as bankruptcy, leading to confiscation of all assets. Maybe after some time, they'll manage to pay their clients if funds remain. If the business is insured, the insurance company pays out a settlement to all clients, but that can take years…"

Abdulla Rustamovich clutched his chest.

"Father! What's wrong? Are you feeling ill?"

"Son, look in that top drawer… there's some validol…"

Right away, Amin took out the medicine and handed it to his father, who slipped a tablet under his tongue.

"Father, please, don't work yourself up too much!" Amin fretted. "I just couldn't stay in France any longer without talking to you in person about this, because I don't think this is something we can resolve over the phone. But I'm ready to fly back there any time to do whatever it takes to get our shipment back. The main thing is that the batch earmarked for us is still there, and the liquidation commission hasn't seized it yet—though there are snags…"

"Son, try to understand, this is a substantial order, and we invested a lot of money in it. Of course, I believe eventually we'll get our money back. But the question is when. And as I've explained to you more than once, in business, money has to move quickly or there's no point in it and no reason to acquire stock. 'Time is money'—that's no empty motto, it's the cold hard truth. That's exactly how it is! I can't stand seeing capital just sitting idle, not circulating in trade. It drives me crazy!"

"I understand, Father… but please, try not to worry too— Father!!! What's happening? Do you feel worse? I'll call an ambulance right now! Stay calm, please! Everything will be all right. Hello, ambulance? My father's very sick. Yes, it's his heart. No, it's not a residence; it's our company office. Write down the address. Please, hurry!"

* * *

Malika was running a bit late for class. In recent days, she had been feeling weighed down by the confusing and difficult circumstances that had befallen her family. On one hand, both literally and figuratively, the beloved ruby necklace, so important to her parents, had vanished. On the other, there was the unclear situation involving Bahadir and his enormous debt, which, sooner or later, had to be repaid to that strange and even somewhat intimidating man, Murad Nematullaevich. Malika was convinced he was somehow tied to criminal activity, though she was afraid even to think about how.

How had her Bahadir ended up stumbling into such an unpleasant situation in the first place? How did he manage to get mixed up with such a dubious group of people, who, from the outside, seemed respectable enough? And all for the sake of some car! To her, it hardly seemed worth it—no amount of comfort or expensive things could possibly justify paying such a price. That's what ran through her mind. She also thought that her father, Said Yahyaevich, was just as trusting as a child… But why would he get tangled up with such a terrifying figure? Why allow him to get involved in his only daughter's wedding? Or… could it be he was forced to accept his involvement?

Malika felt a wave of unease wash over her.

No, that can't be! It's not all that bad. Her father was acting calm enough—at least he wasn't fidgeting around like Bahadir—so maybe he owed Murad nothing. Thank goodness, that was at least some relief. But what did her mother have to do with Murad?

Questions swirled around in her head, making it spin.

Anyway, Bahadir could have bought that car later, not right after the wedding…

Suddenly Malika noticed a glaring inconsistency in this whole chain of events. In other words, it seemed someone was clearly "stringing her along," tricking her, because something simply didn't add up. But just as she tried to think it through, she walked into her scheduled classroom.

Malika had this remarkable habit of focusing exclusively on her studies while in class, fully devoting herself to theoretical and practical knowledge. Normally, she was able to forget everything else during a lecture—but this time it didn't work… She couldn't hear the teachers; her thoughts kept straying far outside the classroom and even beyond the conservatory walls.

She now realised something clearly: Murad Nematullaevich had said Bahadir had borrowed money from him a long time ago, then also claimed it happened at the wedding. Yes, Bahadir had indeed bought his car a long time ago—but their wedding was only recently!... That was the point: Bahadir had owned his foreign car well before the wedding! How to make sense of that without getting lost?...

If that was the case, Bahadir couldn't have first met Nasyrov at the wedding. That would mean they had been acquainted long before that… So Bahadir must have borrowed money from Murad at some earlier time. But why from him? Where did he meet Murad, and how did he learn about him? People like Murad Nasyrov don't just meet with anyone, they certainly don't socialise freely with everyone. Could it really be that Bahadir was gambling, lost a bet to Murad, and ended up in debt? Why else would he keep it all from her?

It was all so very unclear and, frankly, frightening…

41

Murad Nematullaevich was sitting in one of his restaurants on Amir Street, drinking tea and waiting for a special visitor.

"Boss, you called?" Roma stood at attention in front of Nasyrov, as usual avoiding direct eye contact.

"Yes. First, I want your version of what happened. Tell me how Umarov behaved that night."

"You mean the police captain?"

"Yes, Roma. Don't play dumb and pretend you don't know him."

"Well… he came with his task force. They arrived quietly, in civilian clothes. They sat here waiting for Misha Leonidov for about half an hour or maybe a bit more."

"And then?"

"When he didn't show up, they left just as quietly, without making a scene. They'd been told not to cause a stir or scare the customers."

"Fine. Now, the second point. Tell me why, whenever something happens in the accounting department, my chief accountant doesn't call me, but instead calls you, snotnose?"

"Boss, forgive me. She said she couldn't reach Gosha, and she was afraid of your anger. She called me to ask for my advice…"

"Advice? From you?! Who do you think you are?!"

"I'm nobody, but she asked if we could figure out together how best to tell you about… well, the disappearance of the funds from all the accounts… She was really scared, panicked, so she decided to call me first."

"I know how Lidiya Petrovna coddles you and Gosha, calling you 'poor boys', as if you're poor. I've already taken good care of you both, but she's got it into her head that she's some sort of 'mother hen' to you, and now she thinks she has to protect you."

"Allow me, boss, shall I ask her to call you right away?"

"No need. Do you really think that learning someone stole a huge amount of money from me, I could just sit calmly? I've already called her—right after Gosha phoned you. We spoke briefly, and I told her to come here for a serious talk… or rather, an interrogation. Either way, I'm going to tear a strip off her for not safeguarding my money, for letting someone snatch almost all of it from right under her nose."

"Boss, but Aunt Lida isn't to blame. Truly, she's not. Please go easy on her!"

"Quiet! Are you gonna start telling me what to do? I have an important meeting now, and when Lidiya shows up, let her sit and wait as long as necessary. Understood?"

"Yes, Boss, whatever you say. I'll see to it. Besides, she wouldn't dare approach you until you give the word…"

"That's right. Now get out of here."

As soon as Sitora entered the main hall of the restaurant, Nasyrov thought that maybe it would have been wiser for both of them to postpone this meeting until his finances were straightened out and he was in a better mood. But what could he do now—he had invited her several days ago. He couldn't just send such a guest back home!

"Hello, dear…"

"Please, Murad, don't call me that. If my husband hears, he won't like it at all."

"Don't worry about that, dear. He won't know anything unless you tell him… And you look marvelous! As always. I must say I'm a bit surprised you accepted my invitation and came. Even though I'm… dealing with some serious matters right now… But of course, they can wait. I'm delighted you're here."

"It's nothing like what you might be imagining, Murad."

"Sorry, I'm not sure I understand. What exactly did you think I 'might be imagining'?"

"I want you to know: this meeting of ours is strictly 'business,' if you could call it that."

"You've piqued my curiosity, Sitora. Have you decided to go into big business? Restaurant management, perhaps? Looking for advice?"

"No, that's not it. I already have my own business—though it's not large. I'm a fashion designer, in case you've forgotten. Cafés and restaurants are of no interest to me."

"I see. So what is it, then?"

"Tell me honestly: is my son-in-law Bahadir in real danger?"

"Ah, that's what this is about." Nasyrov smirked. "Here's the menu. Order yourself something good; let's have lunch together."

"No, thank you."

"What do you mean, no?"

"I don't plan on ordering anything."

"As you wish. Though in my opinion, that's a shame."

"Murad, I beg of you, just tell me the truth: what do you want from that boy?"

"Some 'boy'—he's pulled off some very grown-up 'tricks.'"

"Can you tell me exactly what he's done?"

"You really want the truth?"

"Yes, I do."

"Why? You're not going to like it."

"Bahadir is my daughter's husband. Murad, they love each other, and I have to help him."

"I see. Let's talk about your daughter first."

"What? Why? What does she have to do with this?"

"If you tell me the truth, it might affect your son-in-law's fate."

"What truth, Murad? What are you talking about?"

"I've done the math. Malika is almost twenty, right? And you left me exactly twenty years ago. I'm still hurt by how you treated me. Even though we weren't together long, I loved you very, very much, and you knew that. Why did you leave me? What makes that eye doctor so much better than I am? You really humiliated me…"

"Murad, how else was I supposed to act when I found out you were married and that your wife was expecting your child?"

"I would never have abandoned you. I could have supported you and our daughter for the rest of my life. Because Malika is my daughter, isn't she?… Why are you quiet? You don't have to say anything—I've already figured it out myself. She looks like me."

"No, she looks like…"

"What? Why did you stop talking? Ah… nothing to say?"

"All right, fine. But you have to understand: I couldn't agree to be just your 'companion,' instead of the wife I'd dreamed of becoming when we first met and you courted me so elegantly. I fell in love with you then, like a foolish young girl—which I was—completely trusting in you… But when I accidentally learned there was already a stamp in your passport with someone else's name on it, and that this other woman was expecting a child, I was devastated. And Said—he'd been courting me for a long time, patiently waiting for me to say yes. He's a wonderful man who truly loved me then and still does."

"Well, isn't that just idyllic? Bravo to your doctor friend. Congratulations to him. Does your husband know his daughter isn't really his?"

"Murad, please, let's not talk about that… He more or less—"

"Sitora, let's start over, the way we used to be. When I saw you a few days ago, everything inside me shook, I lost my head—as if those twenty years had never passed… You mean so much to me, understand? I feel I still love you just as strongly as I did before."

"Don't, Murad, please…"

"But I can see that you still like me, even though I'm no longer young. Am I right? I'm a confident man who knows life, someone with both feet on the ground…"

"You said you have problems right now…"

"Ugh, these problems, curse them. Don't worry, I'll figure it out—wouldn't be the first time. The main thing is for you to be by my side; that'll give me the incentive and strength to fight. You understand?"

"And how do you imagine this? I have a husband who loves me dearly, and I—"

"What about you? You want to say that you love him too? No need to lie."

"Yes, I love him… Please, Murad, let Bahadir go."

"Who's holding him captive or tying him up, as you put it? What are you talking about?"

"I can sense the boy is trapped, that he's caught in a net. And knowing you a little, and the circumstances too, I suspect those are your 'nets.'"

"Don't talk nonsense. He simply owes money for a car, that's all…"

"What car? My daughter told me everything. His father, Ab-

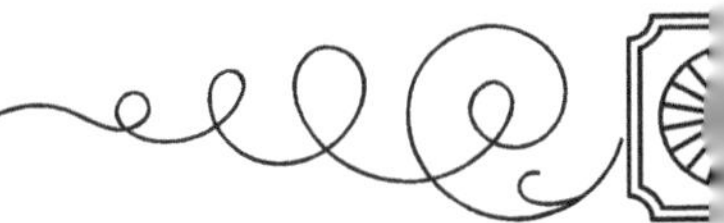

dulla, gave him the money for that foreign car a long time ago. There's no way he could have borrowed it from you, let alone just recently, and at the wedding. It's just some made-up story—a lie, really."

"All right, Sitora. But don't be so harsh with me, or I might take offense. Let's assume you're partly right. Still, everyone should take responsibility for their mistakes, wouldn't you agree? Your Bahadir made serious mistakes, which I can't just forgive like that. But… there's one condition, if you want me to free him from this huge debt and let him go without a fuss. If you fulfill it, no one will ever lay a finger on Bahadir again. Agreed?"

"What condition?"

"You and Malika—both of you must become my second family. Permanently. I'll buy you a beautiful, comfortable house, and we'll spend plenty of time together there. You'll leave your ophthalmologist. How you handle it is up to you. And the three of us—you, me, and our daughter—will begin again and finally be happy."

Sitora stared at him in horror and disbelief.

"Murad, this is madness! Why would you want that after twenty years… and you have a wife… You said you have a son too!"

"Don't let that trouble you. In the end, divorce hasn't been outlawed. Of course, I won't abandon my son—that's the one thing you'll have to accept. But Mukhitdin's a smart kid, he has his own life, his own career. I'm sure he won't get in our way."

"And if I refuse?"

"I wouldn't advise that. Believe me, you could regret it terribly."

Sitora looked at him, angered beyond words, but forced herself to remain calm. Finally she asked:

"How long do I have to think about it?"

"None at all. I need a quick answer! But fine… I'll give you exactly one week. Not a day more. I don't have the patience for any longer. One week from now, you must give me your answer. And be aware, my dear, that your son-in-law's life depends on what you decide."

Sitora froze in shock.

"His life? What are you talking about?"

"Yes, his life. Because if you refuse me and he can't pay back the debt, then he'll have to say goodbye to life. And his death will be slow and agonising—believe me. At best, he'll end up in prison for a long stretch, where he'll probably catch tuberculosis and die just as slowly and painfully."

"Murad, what's happened to you? You're a horrible man."

"No, my dear, I'm still the same person—just one you never really knew. But I spoke the truth when I said I still love you and need you. I'm asking you, don't drag this out. I think you understand me."

42

Gosha knew that if he just called Larisa, anger and hurt might make her hang up right away. Deep down—very deep down—he felt ashamed that he had so brazenly deceived a good woman who hadn't deserved such treatment. But he consoled himself with the thought that he had no choice: business was business.

Though Larisa was older than he was, he didn't find her objectionable at all. If he hadn't been under the boss's tight "supervision," so dependent on him and preoccupied with important matters, he might well have continued their little fling, pleasing both sides and not requiring any commitment…

But right now, Gosha had no time for that, and he was more on edge than ever.

The boss's affairs were going badly; he was on the brink of total ruin, and as the boss's main right-hand man, Gosha felt a special responsibility to guide both the boss and his people out of this global catastrophe. So their minds were occupied almost entirely by that. And precisely at such a moment, Gosha had to go see Larisa—and not for romance. That cheeky movie-like story about "love" no longer mattered to him; what he needed was to prepare one of the "backup airfields" for the boss's cover.

Larisa was at home. When the doorbell rang, she looked through the peephole, but apparently the visitor stood off to the side, so she couldn't see who it was.

"Who's there?" she asked cautiously.

"It's me," came a low voice, too quiet for Larisa to immediately recognise as Gosha's.

"'Me' who?"

No answer from behind the door, only a second knock.

Reluctantly, Larisa opened up. The moment she saw her pal, a wave of anger washed over her, and she tried to slam the door shut, but Gosha held it firm with his foot.

"Larisochka, my sweet darling, please hear me out! I'll explain everything."

As we know, many women possess a remarkable capacity for forgiveness, especially when it comes to those they love. Larisa was no exception. Though still hurt, she let her "suitor" step inside the apartment.

"I know, I know I'm guilty," Gosha began talking at once, "I know I'm scum and a wretch. Please forgive me for not even calling you all this time. You can't imagine the serious problems I'm facing!"

"How would I know that, Zhorik… I mean, Misha… I'm confused by all your names! How can I guess if you never tell me anything about yourself or share what's going on?"

"Larisochka, my blondie, well, here I am at last, and I will tell you everything. I brought you some chocolates. Shall we have tea?"

Larisa looked at him with both reproach and love…

"All right, I'll put the kettle on. But I need less sweet stuff—how many times do I have to say it? You'd do better to help me out sometimes by doing the market shopping, lugging heavy produce back home, after all, you've got a car! As it is, I do everything my-self, with these two hands…"

She was close to tears. For a moment, he genuinely felt sorry for her.

"Okay, Larisa, I promise, I'll help you."

"You only ever make promises… How about money?"

"What do you mean 'how about money?'" Gosha pretended not to understand.

"Well… can you help me out?"

"Are you short on cash, dear?"

"I'm managing for now, but trouble could come soon because I might get fired any day now!"

"Why would they fire you? The police proved you had nothing to do with that necklace theft, and you weren't at fault at all."

"Even so, I told you how my boss has been giving me the stink eye since that incident and doesn't trust me like before. She hides all her valuables now. It's a miracle I haven't been fired already. Honestly, I suspect she's keeping me around on a short leash, under scrutiny."

"Come on—no need to give up or worry. It'll all work out."

"Easy for you to say… Zhora… I mean, Misha…"

"Better just call me Zhora—or Gosha…"

"So, aren't you 'Misha' now?" She was thoroughly confused.

"Call me whatever's comfortable. Misha was just for cover."

"Oh, all right. Zhorik, you promised you'd sell that expensive ruby necklace and that we'd take off forever somewhere far away! Then you disappeared…"

Gosha wasn't exactly prepared for that "accusation." He'd long forgotten what promises he'd made.

"No, Larisa, darling, I didn't 'disappear,' I've just been extremely busy. You see, I have a lot of work-related problems."

"What problems? You're just a driver. Did you… hit someone?!"

"No, of course not, silly. And I've told you before, I'm not only a driver; I can do a lot of things. One of my jobs has problems—sorry, but I can't talk about it in detail right now. I have to handle it myself."

"Is there anything I can do for you?"

"Yes, sweetheart. Soon you might have to put that necklace you took back in Sitora Mumtazova's dressing table."

"What?! Are you out of your mind? So you want me not only to be fired in disgrace but also thrown in jail? You want to see me lose everything, is that it? So that I'll lose my job, my salary?!"

"Not necessarily… but if it comes to that—maybe you'd take the blame on yourself? Then I'll 'pull some strings' so you don't get punished, don't worry."

"Blame for what? What do you mean, 'pull some strings'? What are you talking about?! And tell me why you didn't sell that jewelry so we could go away somewhere, like you promised?"

"Give it time…"

"Time for what, Zhora, for what?! You want to return the necklace!"

"No, no, Laris, that's not certain. We'll only have to do that if it turns out to be a fake."

"What do you mean, a fake?"

"As in, not an actual precious treasure, but a 'dummy.' That could happen too…"

"And what about all your promises?"

Gosha said nothing.

"You know what, my dear? Get out of here! Go on, get lost, quick!"

"Wait, Larisa, let me explain…"

"I don't want to hear a thing. You treat me like I'm stupid! I see now why you came. You only need me for your 'business,' right? I was so naive, happy you finally remembered me—I believed you! I thought you actually loved me. My mother always warned me never to trust men! And here we are. All of you are liars, tricksters.

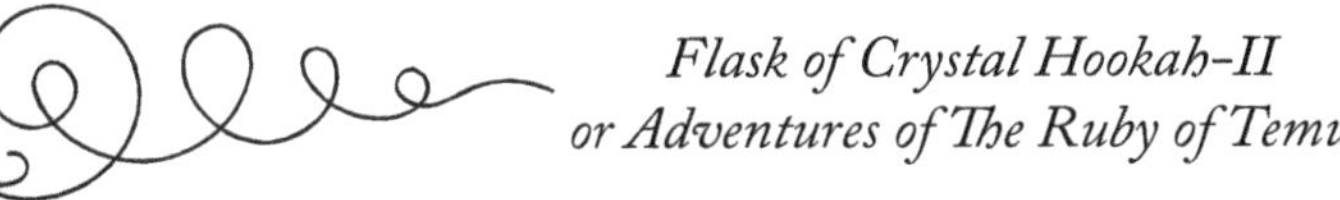

I'll never forgive you! Go away."

"Larisa, just—" Gosha tried to defend himself as he was forced toward the door.

"That's it, you rotten cheat. Goodbye! And don't ever come back. I'm done helping you in anything, ever again!"

Gosha looked at his lady friend with vexation, then silently left the apartment.

43

Firuz-begim quietly entered the study, where her great-granddaughter Sitora's husband, Said, was sitting at a desk, poring over scientific journals. Seeing the esteemed elderly woman, Said started to rise politely to greet her.

"Sit, sit, my son," Firuz-begim said kindly. "I'd like to sit down for a bit myself, if you don't mind—here, in that armchair. Ah, how my legs hurt! Old age is no joy, but it's a great achievement and a gift from the Almighty… If only you doctors could someday find a cure for all ailments at once. I know—just the daydreams of a chatty old lady… There, I'm settled. Well, that's comfortable enough… Said, my son, I have something to discuss with you. I'm almost certain you won't listen to me, but please indulge me as I will speak. Honour the old lady."

"I'm all ears, Firuz-begim!"

"Sitora told me about what happened in our house recently—about the missing necklace…"

"We'll definitely find it, don't you worry!"

"Please hear me out first. I saw the police here myself. I just didn't want to interfere when they came, so I stayed in my room… Said, my hookah helped me—yes, you know I have my own methods of sensing and uncovering secrets, and now I know who's holding our necklace!"

"You do? But the police… They still haven't managed…"

"Yes, yes, I heard the captain is trying to track down the thief. But believe me, he'll find no one of consequence! He may, in fact,

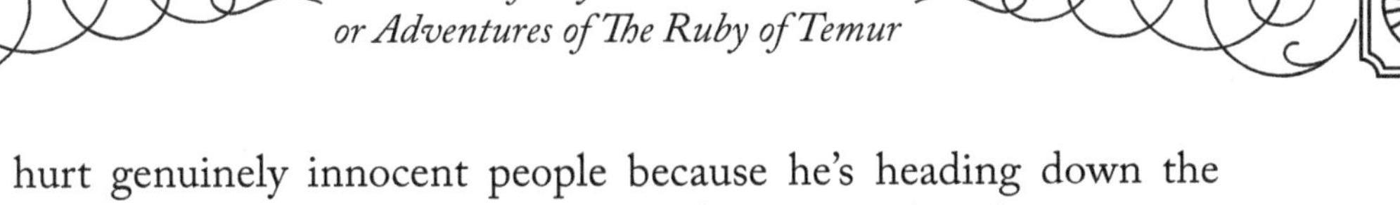

hurt genuinely innocent people because he's heading down the wrong path… Meanwhile, the necklace was taken by one very prominent and wealthy man—someone you've gotten to know fairly recently—who's also more than willing to help and patronize you… Well, he didn't take it himself, obviously; he did it through others, figureheads. And I doubt the police will ever catch him."

"And who is this 'prominent man'?"

"That, my son, I won't tell you, because I know you're not yet ready to hear me or believe me. It'll be better if, with some hints, you figure it out for yourself—if you draw the right conclusions on your own!"

"A prominent man? Wealthy? Ready to help? Who else could it be…? Wait a minute—could it be my new acquaintance, Murad Nematullaevich?"

"In truth, I don't know his name. I only know certain details by which I recognised him."

"No one else comes to mind who fits your description… But listen, that can't be! He'd never stoop to such a thing! He's the one who helped us with the wedding… Firuz-begim, of course I'm grateful for your wish to help Sitora, Malika, and me, and please forgive me, but—"

"You see, Said, I told you that you wouldn't listen. Fine, let's just pretend I never told you anything. Try to find the thief yourself if you can—may the Almighty help you. I'm not angry at anything; I only wish you luck. But please, be careful, my son. The man I described is very dangerous… And God willing…

'Relief always follows hardship—
One need only have the patience…'

That's what my beloved poet Saadi once said," the old woman whispered, stepping slowly out of her son-in-law's office.

* * *

"All right, Lidiya. What is it you wanted to tell me? I'm waiting for your explanation of everything that's happened!" Nasyrov was barely restraining himself from shouting at the poor accountant right there in the restaurant.

"Murad Nematullaevich, please forgive me for raising a panic and causing a false alarm…" The chief accountant of the Minor chain trembled with fear before her boss.

"What? A 'false' alarm? Did I hear you right? Does that mean everything's fine with our money?"

"Yes, it seems—"

"'Seems'? Or is it actually fine? I don't understand! Why did you then—"

"If you'll allow me, Boss, I'll explain everything in order."

"Yes, of course—that's exactly what I'm expecting!"

"Well, the thing is, the night I sounded the alarm—which was also the evening, I heard, when the police staged some kind of 'raid' at one of our restaurants—I received an email from the bank that services us. It said a very large sum had been withdrawn from our account…"

"What?!" Nasyrov couldn't hold back.

"Please don't be upset, Murad Nematullaevich. Let me say right away, to make it easier for you to hear me out: it was some kind of mistake! So, the email from the bank suggested that I verify it myself by clicking on a link at the bottom. Supposedly, that link would lead me to the login page for our company's online bank. It

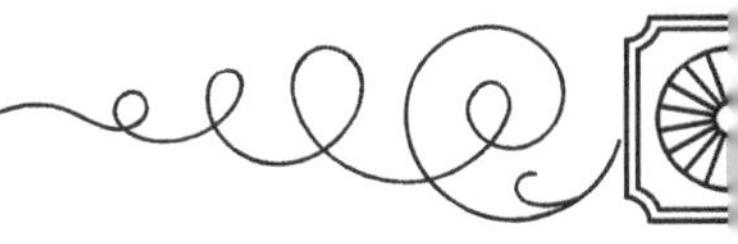

was convenient, so naturally I did it. I needed to see the situation with my own eyes!

"All right, go on."

"So on that page, in the fields for login and password, I entered our encrypted credentials like usual. It wasn't difficult, as I've done it many times before. You know we can now handle deposits and transfers online, without physically going to the bank.

"Yes, of course, I'm aware."

"But at that moment, I was horrified because what I saw on our account weren't our large funds but just pennies—everything else was gone…"

Nasyrov, listening to Lidiya Petrovna, went pale with fear, but she continued:

"To be honest, I found it odd that the bank's email arrived so late, after business hours. Naturally, I panicked—and, forgive me, made you anxious too! But it turned out to be for nothing. The next morning, when I got to work, I decided to check the company account again, and I couldn't believe my eyes: all our funds were there, just like before! Furthermore, that same morning, I received another email from the bank—apologising to our organization for the error in the previous email. But we can forgive them, can't we? Everyone makes mistakes. The most important thing is that the money is still in our account."

"All right, Lidiya, I get it," Nasyrov said, wiping the sweat from his forehead. "You just about gave me a heart attack. Now go—out of my sight. Be more attentive in the future!"

"Yes, of course, Murad Nematullaevich!" the woman mumbled, relieved to have 'dodged a bullet.'

"So, does this mean Misha Leonidov was completely innocent?" Nasyrov thought to himself once the chief accountant had gone. "He didn't take any money from me? Then where did he go? Did he run away for some other reason? I haven't wronged him lately. Maybe something happened to him? Poor guy... Turns out I was wrong about him. And he made me so much money, too—he could still be useful... I'll have to find him!"

* * *

"Morning, Mister Nasyrov, this is Bhojwani from Delhi."

"Hello, Mister Bhojwani! Any news?"

"Well, actually, I'm expecting news from you. You promised to call me about the ruby... Have you forgotten?"

"No, of course not! I've just been swamped with work. My apologies."

"I see. But tell me, have you verified whether the stone is genuine?"

"I still haven't had the chance, unfortunately."

"I think I can help. You know that this ruby spent many centuries here in India. And you know that I'm not just a fashion designer, but also something of an Indologist. I have a simple idea that I believe you'll like. Do you have photos of Temur's Ruby?"

"Yes, I do. Right here on my iPhone. Well... I'm still not entirely sure it's the real thing, but at least I have pictures of the necklace featuring one large, interesting ruby."

"Could you email me the photos of that necklace right now?"

"Absolutely. I should have thought of that sooner. Not a problem. Give me one minute... There they go. Did you get them?"

"Yes, they're opening now. I see the necklace—honestly, it's magnificent. And I see a luxurious, very large ruby along with three others that are a bit smaller. They're all set into a gold chain inlaid

with diamonds mounted in gold. Mister Nasyrov, this is… this is stunning! You know what, I can't be one hundred percent certain without seeing it in person… but I dare say this might be exactly what we're looking for."

"I'm glad to hear that, Mister Bhojwani. Shall I send it to you?"

"Let's try. And to avoid problems, I propose the following plan, Mister Nasyrov. You know that in just a few days my clothing line will appear at an international fashion week in Europe, right?"

"Yes, I heard something about that."

"I'll arrange it so that my trusted person—and if you like, it can be your son Mukhitdin—will come from Europe straight to Tashkent for a day or two. Then, when he travels back to me—his study period isn't over yet—he can discreetly attach the necklace to one of the dresses as if it were an 'inseparable accessory.' After all, I always adorn my creations with accessories, so no one should be suspicious. That way, the necklace will make its way from Tashkent to me in Delhi. Do you agree?"

"That's a brilliant idea, my friend! And I'll get to see my son— I've been missing him."

"I'll send the deposit for the necklace with Mukhitdin. A Visa Platinum is acceptable, right?"

"Perfectly acceptable."

"Great, Mister Nasyrov. So, it's a deal?"

"Yes, I believe we have an agreement, Mister Bhojwani. Good-bye!"

* * *

When necessary, Misha Leonidov knew how to act quickly. Right now, he realised he'd reached a moment in life where, to avoid getting caught, he had to do everything both wisely—thinking through every smallest step—and with lightning speed.

The scheme suggested to him by Sergey, a master of his craft, was evidently well-tested and proven—if not by this local hacker genius himself, then at least by his equally skillful colleagues abroad. The programs Sergey used were mostly exclusive and very expensive, developed by top American computer specialists.

Without going into all the details, Sergey briefly explained to his client Mikhail how it usually worked and what he had done with the information Leonidov had provided.

"At the email address of the company whose account number you gave me along with other useful data," Sergey said, "I sent a special email. It carried the logo and contact details of the very same bank that services both the company and its owner. It was easiest to start with the company's account. If I understood correctly, my email was opened not by the owner, but by an employee—perhaps the head accountant."

"Yes, yes," Misha confirmed. "All those responsibilities lie with the chief accountant, Lidiya Petrovna. What was in your email?"

"It contained a 'trap' for the recipient—a link to what looked like the bank's website. For me, forging a near-identical webpage is child's play. The site in question, which in fact had nothing whatsoever to do with the real bank, still looked very much like it. By following the link, that woman effectively landed on her company's 'personal account' page on the bank's website… But of course, it was fake—just a dummy page. And to access any 'personal account,' you naturally have to enter a login and password—which is exactly what she did, unknowingly handing that information over to me."

"I think I'm beginning to understand!" Leonidov exclaimed in amazement, though it was difficult to surprise someone of his experience in fraud.

"Within a matter of seconds, right before her eyes, I 'zeroed out' the account, which must have given her a real shock. But, as you asked, I carefully erased all traces of my actions afterward. You've probably heard of programs that, once launched, 'wipe' any record of operations on the target computer. I already had practically total unseen control of her machine, so its entire database, the hard drive—everything—was at my fingertips. So the operations I carried out that evening, through mine and effectively her computer, were 'wiped away,' hidden as though they never happened. However, the transaction itself was complete. The money was already transferred to your accounts, and on her computer (though not on the bank's), it appeared as if nothing had been withdrawn—as though I hadn't done a thing."

"My, my! What a dangerous program that is… and your entire scheme is, too. Sergey, I'm impressed by your work. You're a true pro!"

"Yes, and in the banks themselves, the transfers showed up exactly the way you needed. By the way, aren't you curious why I opened several different accounts for you?"

"No, I have a general idea: so that another talented hacker like you can't grab all those big sums at once, right?"

"Exactly. Having multiple accounts is safer and more secure. You may have heard the saying among millionaires: 'Don't put all your golden eggs in one basket.' And under no circumstances repeat the mistake of that woman, who was apparently no computer expert. She might be a good accountant, but she clearly knows nothing about online security."

"So how did you manage to withdraw money from that personal account belonging to the bo… the person I told you about and whose account name I gave you?"

"You mean the owner of that same company?"

"Yes. How did you handle that part? Because, if I'm not mistaken, that man never received your 'bank' email, nor did he try logging in through any fake link, correct?"

"Yes, he never got that email and never used the link. It would've been risky to use the same method twice. Plus, I wasn't sure this savvy businessman wouldn't be suspicious of some 'bank notification' arriving outside working hours, late at night."

"Makes sense."

"So here's what I came up with. I know for certain people like that access the internet most often from their phones—smartphones, specifically. And that 'magnate' is no exception. I assume with 90-percent certainty or more that he also uses his online banking on that phone from time to time to check his finances. And you gave me his phone number, from which, again, he accesses his bank account."

"Yes, I remember giving you that number without even knowing how you'd use it!"

"I deployed a malicious Trojan virus into your acquaintance's smartphone via an SMS, infecting his entire system. The SMS was a 'trap message,' supposedly from the bank, stating that one thousand dollars had just been deposited into his account—an account that was accurately named."

"One thousand dollars? Why that amount?"

"Well, I basically picked it out of thin air. Under the circumstances, that seemed like a reasonable figure. If I'd mentioned a larger sum, he might have gotten suspicious; if it were smaller, he might not have bothered checking. My goal was to get him to open his online banking account as quickly as possible via his phone,

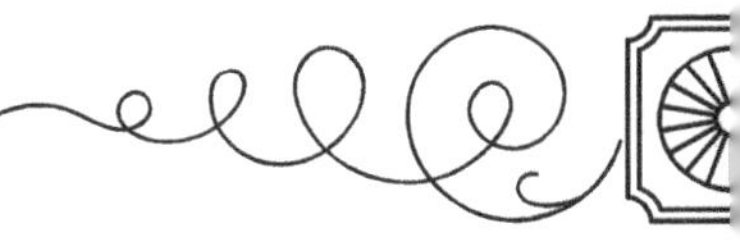

typing in what?"

"His login and password? Or in other words, the 'key' to his account?"

"Exactly. The situation with him is a bit different, though. At the moment, he can't access his online bank at all. Once you leave, I'll restore his access remotely. But then he'll immediately see that his account is empty. Which is why, right now, there's no way we can let him use his smartphone as usual. It's possible he might hire a good programmer who'd uncover our ruse. True, our names would remain hidden regardless. But, Misha, for your own safety, you need to leave the country as soon and as far as possible!"

"Yes, that's exactly my plan. Thank you very much for your help! I withdrew the agreed amount from one of the accounts— and here, Sergey, is your share, as promised."

"Excellent. Everything's correct. Thanks."

"No, thank you. May I ask one more question?"

"Of course, go ahead."

"Why didn't you just keep all the money for yourself? Why not 'dump' me? You could have done that—you're obviously such a master. Or should I be worried?"

"No, Mikhail, don't worry. I'm not planning to set you up or turn you in to the authorities. And I didn't take it all for myself be-cause I don't need that much. I like the thrill, the virtuoso nature of this work, and I'm happy with what I earn… let's call it 'honesty.'"

The very next day, Misha transferred part of his newly gained, enormous fortune from his accounts onto new ones he'd opened in different countries under his own name, and took some in cash. After that, he bought a plane ticket and calmly flew off to the Mal-dives to begin his new, wealthy life there permanently.

44

Amin visited his father in the hospital after work. Although Abdulla Rustamovich's condition had stabilized, the family received more upsetting news: the head of the Fattakhov family was diagnosed with a massive myocardial infarction.

Before heading home, Amin decided to drop by his parents' house, where his mother and sister were waiting for him. Mukhabbat was so worried about her husband that she felt as though it was her heart—and not his—that was severely ill.

Amin thought that Rano also seemed unwell—he hadn't noticed anything at the office, but in their home setting, he could definitely notice it: Rano's cheeks were hollow, and she looked pale and distressed…

"She must be really worried about our father," Amin thought. He decided not to pester his sister with questions about her health. Besides, another piece of news—one Rano shared with him and their mother—completely threw him for a loop: she wanted to adopt a child from an orphanage.

"Why not have one of your own?" Amin asked in surprise.

"You can see how unlucky I am with marriage," Rano sighed sadly, "and by eastern standards I'm already at the age of an 'old maid.' I don't want to just 'conceive' a child with someone outside of marriage. So I'm thinking of taking in a 'stranger's' child—yet making them truly mine, my own, forever."

"That's a fine idea, daughter," her mother said, unexpectedly agreeing without argument.

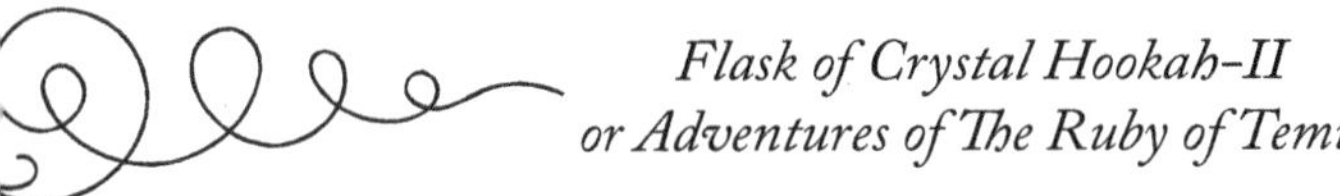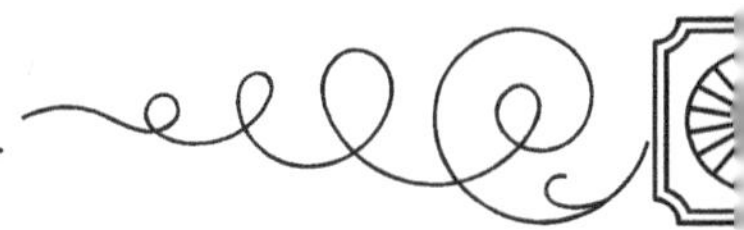

When Amin was leaving the house to head back to his own place, he ran into a well-dressed, unfamiliar woman by the gate. Just then, his mother had stepped back inside to grab the bundle of homemade baked goods she'd prepared for him and left in the kitchen.

"Hello, my son," the stranger said. "You must be Amin, right?"

"Hello… How do you know me?" Amin asked in surprise. "Have we met before?"

"Yes, we certainly have. I've known you since the day you were born. Because you—are my…"

She didn't finish. Mukhabbat appeared behind the gate. On seeing this neatly groomed, dark-skinned woman—whom she clearly recognised—Mukhabbat became extremely agitated:

"What do you want with my son? Leave us alone! Please, go away, just go!"

"But wait, Mukhabbat, I only wanted to—"

"No, he doesn't need to hear a word of it! We want nothing at all from your family! I beg you, please leave us alone and go away!"

"Mother, but why?" Amin ventured. "Pardon me, but… may I at least know who you are?"

"All right, Amin, I don't want to cause a scene," the stranger said. "Let's see each other some other time. You do come here often, don't you?"

"Well, yes… but—"

By then, the woman wasn't listening. She disappeared as suddenly as she had come.

"Please, my son, don't meet with her," pleaded Mukhabbat. "I'm begging you! And don't ask me anything for now. I promise, when I can, I'll explain everything."

"Mom, all right, if you insist… You know I'd do anything for your sake. But still—who is this woman? How does she know me? I don't understand…"

* * *

Bahadir decided it would be best for him and Malika not to inconvenience Amin any further and to rent a small apartment so they could live on their own as a young couple. That's exactly what they did, with some help from Bahadir's mother, Mukhabbat.

On one cold evening in November, Bahadir sat in the kitchen, drinking tea and waiting for Malika to come home for dinner; she was running late at the conservatory, rehearsing with her teacher and musicians for the competition.

Suddenly, the doorbell rang loudly and insistently.

"At last!" Bahadir muttered to himself, because it was unlikely that anyone outside the door would hear it. "All right, all right, I'm coming! Malika, can't you be patient? And where are your keys?"

He opened the door. Standing outside was a man in a police uniform—a completely unexpected sight for Bahadir.

"Good evening. Are you Bahadir Abdullaevich Fattakhov?"

"Yes, that's me. What's this about?"

"I'm Captain Ravshan Umarov of the Criminal Investigation Department, Tashkent Main Internal Affairs. May I see your documents?"

"My documents? … Sure. Come in. Are you our new local officer? I've never seen you before. Is this a passport check?"

Bahadir took out his passport and driver's license, showing them to the policeman.

"Citizen Fattakhov Bahadir, you are under arrest on suspicion of large-scale theft."

"What?! Are you out of your mind?"

"Careful, citizen! Don't be rude to me, or I'll add 'insulting a police officer in the line of duty' to the charges."

"But how—what happened? I don't understand a thing…"

"You'll come with me. I'll explain everything there."

"On what grounds are you arresting me?"

"I have a warrant. Let's go!"

* * *

At the police station, the interrogation continued.

"Captain, may I at least call my wife? She's going to worry!"

"Later, you'll call her later. Right now, you have to answer a few of my questions."

"But why on earth do you think I've stolen something? This must be a mistake!"

"Citizen Fattakhov, witnesses saw you sneaking into the Mumtazovs' house at night—"

"Witnesses? Whose house? Did you say my wife's parents' home?!"

"That's right. You're suspected of stealing a jewelry necklace with rubies and diamonds."

"But… that's totally stupid!"

"Watch your words, citizen. I'm on official duty."

"Sorry, Captain, I didn't mean to offend you. Still, think about it—why would I do that?! Why would I need some women's jewelry, and from my own wife's family, no less? That's really absurd!"

"Don't be so sure. That piece is worth a fortune. Obviously, you wanted to sell it on the sly, without your relatives finding out."

"For what purpose?!"

"To settle your gambling debts, of course! By the way, you can be charged just for that. Aren't you aware that gambling for money is strictly forbidden in our country and punishable by law?"

Bahadir hung his head. *Could it be that… That was definitely it! It must have been a set-up by them! Those awful people. Now, it was clear…*

"All right, young man. Here's some paper and a pen. I suggest you write down a 'full confession' right away, and I'll be lenient about your insults. I'll process it as 'voluntary admission of guilt.' I promise it'll help in court. It'll reduce your sentence."

"In… court?! So there's going to be a trial, and prison time? But I swear, I haven't done anything—"

The investigator took a necklace out of his desk drawer. It bore the fingerprints of Mikhail Leonidov, as well as those of a few Kuwaiti guards and a couple of museum employees in Moscow. He handed it to Bahadir.

"Do you recognise this item?"

Bahadir took it, examining it closely.

"Well… My wife Malika wore something similar on our wedding day! But, I think… the one she had looked nicer… From what little I remember, anyway—I was pretty distracted that day, getting married and all. I believe the central stone was larger than the one in this piece."

"So 'you believe'? Maybe it's precisely the same necklace your wife wore, which therefore belongs to her parents. In fact, your father-in-law, Said Yahyaevich Mumtazov, has documentation for it! Were you aware of that?"

"No, I had no idea."

"If you had known, you wouldn't have stolen it, right?"

"Seriously, Captain! I didn't steal anything!!!"

"Don't shout. I can hear you just fine—I've got excellent hearing. We'll see what the fingerprint test shows. If we find yours on it—"

"They will be there, because I've just touched it for the first time, right here in front of you! Wait… so you set me up! That's underhanded and dishonest!"

"Listen to him! A thief lecturing a law officer on morals. Sergeant, lock him up! Straight to the holding cell!"

45

Agra, 1612.

"Dearest, why did you decide to have that Indian merchant, Mahesh Prasad, executed?" Emperor Jahangir asked his wife, Mehrun-Nissa, as they reclined together late at night. "Don't you think that's rather harsh?"

"But he's a thief, Your Majesty," Mehrun-Nissa replied calmly. "And a thief must be punished at once, to teach others a lesson."

"You used to praise him, saying he was one of the best merchants and brought you fine fabrics and sweets from other lands…"

"I never imagined he would dare to steal some of my trinkets…"

"Are you absolutely sure it was he? His guilt was never proven."

"That's beside the point. I might have endured it somehow. But the real issue is that he somehow managed to snatch the Temur Ruby from me!"

The padishah laughed, shaking his head.

"My dear, you have it all wrong. Remember at the wedding of your niece, Arjumand-begim, to my son Shah Jahan? She wore a necklace set with rubies."

"Yes, something like that... But I had so many worries then, I paid no attention to what bauble was on her neck."

Jahangir nodded.

"Wait…" Mehrun-Nissa came to her senses, suspecting what her royal husband was implying. "Are you telling me that the precious Ruby of Temur, which you yourself promised me for all

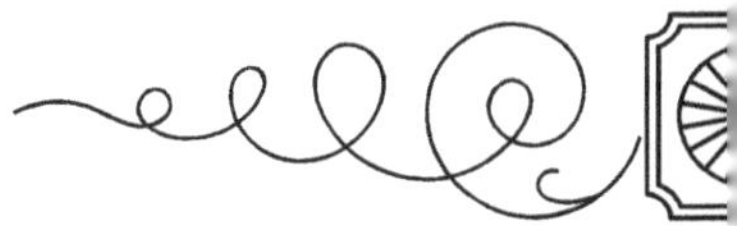

time—that most glorious of gems—was set into her wedding neck-lace? That it graced the neck of that unworthy girl, Arjumand?!"

"How can you speak of your own niece like that? As far as I recall, you used to speak fairly well of her and treat her kindly. What changed?"

"Don't you see, husband, that from the start I opposed their marriage? Any man who is with his beloved—who loves him in return—grows far stronger and more successful! Now Shah Jahan is a great threat to you and your throne! And yet you give them priceless gifts of incomparable worth! You yourself said that Ruby is a symbol of the Great Mughals' power! I'm distraught…"

"But with you, I've also become much stronger, haven't I?" the ruler remarked. "And I still have plenty of precious stones—far more than you think."

"But none so mesmerising or imbued with power as Temur's Ruby, right?"

Jahangir fell silent for a moment.

"Well, you're right about that," he said slowly. "Still, I'm certain my son, Shah Jahan, is entirely loyal to me. He'd never—do you hear? never—turn against his father! So please, my dear, stop wor-rying about every little thing. Your lovely face shouldn't be marred by frowns."

He smiled at his wife. She did not reply, remaining in a gloomy mood.

"So, we're not going to execute that Indian merchant, are we?" he asked. "I'll order his release."

"As you wish… It makes no difference to me anymore."

There can be no good outcome for us from that union between Shah Jahan and Arjumand-begim! Mehrun-Nissa thought.

***

Shah Jahan grew up amid luxury and wealth. He had everything he could possibly desire, and he quickly lost interest in even the most magnificent and extraordinarily expensive jewelry, gold, and precious stones. He simply did not know the true value of such treasures…

That was the case until he encountered the greatest treasure of his life—Arjumand-begim. Only she remained consistently dear to him. Before meeting her, he had never known what it meant to love; he had never been "afflicted" by passion, consumed by it entirely. The prince had been convinced that love was nothing more than a myth, an invention of romantics and poets. Only now did he realise how powerful and real this feeling could be. His tender love for Arjumand took hold of the prince's entire soul…

Every devout Muslim is obliged to fulfill his marital duties on the night from Thursday to Friday. Shah Jahan, however, visited his wife's chambers far more often. He could not be away from Arjumand for long; he constantly sought to see her, to hear her gentle, calm voice that he felt was so familiar and precious.

He loved everything about his wife. He felt that the depth of her grey eyes hid some undisclosed secret, an unanswered riddle. When Arjumand grew sad or became exhausted after her charitable activities for the poor—events she organised regularly—he would hold her close to his heart, doing his utmost to restore that joyful, blissful smile to her lips, along with the sweet dimples in her rosy cheeks.

And when Shah Jahan himself fell ill, Arjumand would stay by his bedside for hours and days on end, hardly leaving him at all. Her cool, gentle fingers touching his feverish brow would bring him in-

stant relief, driving away the illness and clarifying his thoughts. But most of all, both Shah Jahan and Arjumand cherished the nights spent together in rapturous bliss. Shah Jahan gave his beloved the tender name Lala—"crimson drop of a ruby."

This happily enamored couple greatly irritated Mehrun-Nissa. She used all her cunning and influence over Emperor Jahangir to send Shah Jahan to the rebellious and warlike principality of Mewar, west of Agra, to quash yet another Rajput uprising, hoping finally either to subdue and bring them under complete control—something Shah Jahan's grandfather, Akbar, had failed to achieve—or to wipe them out entirely, leaving "not a single stone upon another."

* * *

Outskirts of Lahore, that same year.

"They took us away to this summer residence—and did not even allow us to attend the prince's wedding!" said Shah Jahan's first wife, Par-Parkhiz, speaking to his second wife, Kandahari-begim, with barely concealed vexation. Then she turned to a servant. "Hey, whatever your name is—bring us biryani and doi-maach in yogurt! And hurry!"

"Yes, madam."

Par-Parkhiz spoke again to Kandahari-begim.

"I do like this Indian food… Now, what was I about to tell you? Ah, yes. My husband, Prince Shah Jahan—"

"Prince Shah Jahan is my husband!" Kandahari interjected.

"As I was saying, Prince Shah Jahan married that dowry-less Arjumand purely for profit!"

"Why do you think that?" Kandahari-begim asked in surprise.

327

"What 'profit' is there in it?"

Once the servants brought their food, Par-Parkhiz continued:

"That Arjumand has an aunt who recently wormed her way into becoming the emperor's wife. I don't know how she managed it, but they say this Mehrun-Nissa—whom the emperor is increasingly calling 'Nur Mahal'—has completely bewitched Shah Jahangir. Rumor has it he wants to make her his chief wife, above all others! Right. So, that rotten family of theirs is scheming to secure their place in the state and maintain power over the country and its people forever! Nur Mahal, Arjumand's auntie, will help our husband, Shah Jahan, become ruler of the empire! And Arjumand's father—he's the kush-begi under the emperor. If nothing stops him, he might be made grand vizier any day now…"

"That seems unlikely," Kandahari-begim protested. "Such a position has to be earned. As for that pauper Arjumand, I saw with my own eyes at the betrothal how lovingly my husband gazed at her! And at the wedding, I heard he asked his father for a ruby necklace for his bride."

"Is that so?! What does he see in Arjumand? She's so demure… I can't stand her!"

"Well, it's obvious enough with you, Par-Parkhiz. You're the daughter of a high-ranking nobleman, and your family is very, very wealthy. Shah Jahan wasn't going to let that chance slip away. Though the imperial treasury is anything but poor, it doesn't belong solely to the emperor and his family—it's meant for the entire land," said Kandahari, almost reciting lines of verse. "So whether you want to or not, you even marry someone unattractive if it brings you closer to the throne…"

"Don't you dare say that!" Par-Parkhiz fumed. "It's not like you can imply that he married you for love either! And you yourself

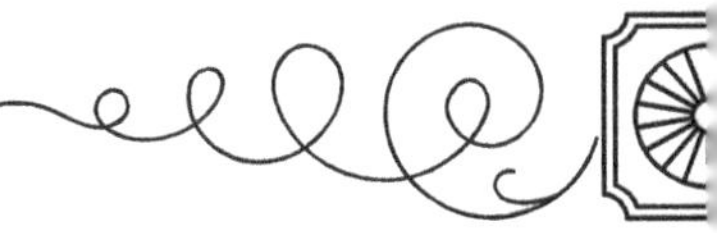

aren't poor. So presumably he had his own calculations for you as well. But now, with his new wife, we mean nothing to shahzade!" Par-Parkhiz declared confidently.

"You just said it yourself, Par-Parkhiz, that this marriage with Arjumand was for his personal gain. Maybe he doesn't actually love her either. She'll be the same as us—or maybe even less in his eyes. The prince will amuse himself for a bit with his young bride, then forget all about her!"

At that, Kandahari-begim fell silent in thought.

"We'll see," said the older wife, not pausing her meal. "People say they've loved each other for nearly five years, and all that time they waited for the emperor to let them marry… And you, Kandahari-begim, from what I can tell, aren't criticising or cursing the new bride. Maybe you want to befriend her, share her grief and joys?… Are you completely stupid?! She's the number-one enemy to both of us… And why aren't you eating?"

"I can't swallow a thing. Think about it—what's the point of all this talk? Empty words don't suit me. Better to demonstrate who truly deserves respect and love, and who doesn't!"

"All that's a waste of time—you won't succeed,"

"You never know. There are ways… and tricks to punish her."

Par-Parkhiz eyed Shah Jahan's second wife in bewilderment and curiosity.

* * *

Shah Jahangir ordered that Asaf-Khan, the kush-begi, be summoned.

When he arrived, the padishah said:

"Minister, I have a task for you."

"I am listening, my lord!"

"Let the Royal Mint instruct its finest artists—especially Abd-us-Samad—to use my most recent and best portraits as sketches for new coins and medals bearing my likeness."

"But, Majesty, forgive me… the Qur'an forbids—"

"Silence and listen!" the padishah cut him off sternly. "Are you presuming to teach me? My orders are not up for discussion—otherwise a head will roll."

"Oh, everyone knows you are kind, my lord, and you would never—"

"And you exploit my kindness, is that it, Asaf-Khan? Be careful not to take advantage of it. I don't care that your sister, Mehrun-Nissa—whom I have named Nur Mahal—has become my lawful wife. I want dinars, tankas, and other gold and silver coins to bear elegant calligraphy, and in place of the zodiac signs, my portrait!"

"As you wish, Your Majesty. I only hope that—"

"What else?!"

"I only hope the people will not be upset by such an innovation."

"Then make sure they do not stir up trouble!" the padishah said angrily. "Why should I have to explain or justify my decisions—my will—to my subjects? Let them obey swiftly and without question!"

"As you command."

"And another thing. Tell the painters who create my portraits that from now on, they must depict me exclusively with a halo—an aureola around my head, signifying the padishah is Allah's representative on earth. I command that, through art, my greatness be made known to the entire world!"

Asaf-Khan, once more, bowed submissively before the emperor.

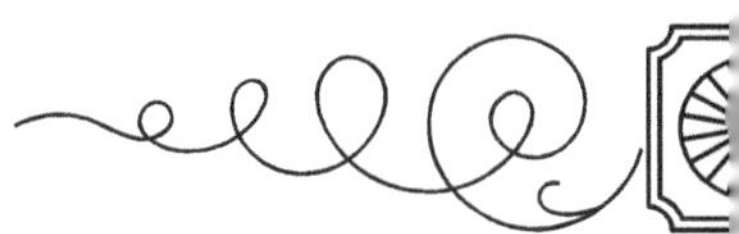

***

Mewar, 1613.

Throughout all of Hindustan, only the people of Mewar still maintained an army that steadfastly resisted the Great Mughals. Even among them, however, many had been subdued or turned into allies by the Mughal forces.

Shah Jahan had not wanted to bring Arjumand, who was already pregnant, on his campaign—marches were always so difficult for women, and especially expecting mothers! Yet his beloved wife would not hear of staying behind.

"You swore we would never be parted for even a moment!" she told him before they departed. "I will always be by your side, wherever you may be, and I will follow you everywhere."

"But the campaign will likely be long and grueling. I can't risk you and our child. Besides, you hold high status now—you are a princess, the wife of the heir —and have every right to remain in the palace, in the most luxurious quarters you wish. Yet you want to come to the battlefield with me…"

"I cannot bear to be separated from you for so long!" Arjumand protested. "I have already endured five long years of waiting and loneliness. Besides, this child will only remind me that you're not there. I simply can't stand that."

Arjumand did not tell her husband that only recently she'd felt so unwell she feared losing the child. A physician had shared terrible news with her:

"I'm afraid, Your Highness, that someone… may have poisoned you."

"Poisoned me?!" Arjumand had repeated in horror.

"Yes, I'm quite certain it was rat poison."

Fortunately, thanks to the physician's diligent care, Arjumand recovered soon after.

"I don't even know whether I'll return alive, let alone victorious," Shah Jahan said grimly and anxiously.

"Never speak like that! You are a victorious prince, and I believe in you! You will most certainly conquer the Rajputs of Mewar and win the people's admiration! It's clear my aunt, Mehrun-Nissa, wants something else entirely—that's why she sent you here instead of Mahabat-Khan. She wants you defeated and disgraced, for that would only strengthen her power in the land… But you will undoubtedly win! Don't let yourself think otherwise."

"In any event, even if I do prevail, she'll lose nothing," Shah Jahan said with a sardonic smile. "She'll just tell everyone that she is farsighted and skilled at picking the right generals."

For many months now, Shah Jahan had been in Mewar, accompanied by his pregnant wife, Arjumand. They traveled with a large army; behind them lumbered elephants and horses laden with an equally large store of provisions.

In the beginning, all went rather well, and the people of Mewar surrendered easily. But then came a day when one rebellious Mewar prince barricaded himself in his towering fortress. With him was a small army and a year's worth of supplies.

Shah Jahan was no more successful in laying siege to this fortress than his grandfather, Emperor Akbar, who had fought long ago and suffered heavy losses against Mewar's defenses. The princes of Mewar were highly cunning and courageous. In most cases, they wanted nothing to do with being subjects of the Great Mughals or paying perpetual tribute. So Shah Jahan, thinking constantly and circling the fortress day after day in search of a weak point, realized

he could not subdue it by force or by outnumbering the defenders. Only wit, guile, and military strategy would suffice.

In the end, victory came, and the obstinate prince surrendered.

There was no limit to the prince's elation and joy.

"Send word to my father that the Mewaris have been defeated!" he proclaimed proudly.

Shah Jahan galloped to the tent where his beloved wife awaited him, eager to share his triumph. But he was met by the physician, who was in Arjumand's chambers.

"Your Highness, forgive me," said the doctor, "but your wife has just lost the child… It was a girl; she was stillborn."

Arjumand wept in grief.

"It's all right, my dearest," Shah Jahan tried to comfort her. "Don't cry! It hurts me to see you suffer. We have our whole future ahead of us—we're still young, full of strength, and love each other so much! You'll see: we'll have many, many children yet."

Through her tears, Arjumand smiled at him tenderly.

46

Gosha had recently been feeling worn out. First there were the boss's problems—which, luckily, seemed to have resolved, but not without plenty of stress—and then his falling out with Larisa… Naturally, all this had taken its toll on him. So Gosha suggested to his friend Roma that they spend the entire evening and half the night "hanging out" at their favorite pub to relax and recharge. Roma had no objections.

"Ah, too bad Mukhitdin isn't here with us—we could really cut loose!" Roma remarked once they'd gotten their beers with chips and settled in comfortably. "Of course, in any of the boss's cafés or even restaurants, as his employees, it would cost us less—they'd give us the best service at a good discount. But…"

"But there's no soccer there, and none of that total freedom we appreciate so much," Gosha finished his thought. Then, for a few seconds, he closed his eyes and tilted his head back, savoring the sweet moment.

"Right, man, you got it!" his friend confirmed.

They watched an exciting match with strong players and several goals, lifting their spirits even more, and in their excitement they each ordered a double shot of whiskey.

"Ah, might as well go all out!" Gosha said, getting carried away. "Nobody can say a thing to us here and now! It's awesome—freedom!"

They drank and snacked on the lemon wedges that came with the strong liquor, then both asked the bartender to repeat the order.

"Listen, I have an idea," Gosha said, clearly getting into the swing of things. "How about we just say exactly what's on our minds right now, huh?"

"Nah, bro, that's not a good idea."

"Oh, come on, Roma, don't be such a prude."

Roma was a little unsteady, but still fairly in control.

"That's not why, Gosha. It's not about our moral image! Although, remember, the boss told us that wherever we go, we have to keep in mind we're 'the face of his company' and must always conduct ourselves 'appropriately'? Which means what?"

"What?" asked Gosha, already pretty tipsy.

"This! That he won't forgive us if we get smashed like little piglets—"

"Like who?"

"I mean, like pigs. And if we shame him in the process. And also—sorry, Gosha, but you can't just say whatever you want, wherever you want, anytime you want."

"A-a-ah! What? Are you nuts or something? That's not what I meant! I'm just saying we can talk about our own lives, our own problems. Let's just tell each other the plain truth today, all right?"

"Oh, I get it. All right. Since you suggested it, you go first."

"I think I'm a jerk, Roma."

"What? Gosh, I'm not following… Where is this coming from?"

"Well, with Larisa I acted like a total scumbag. She didn't deserve that. She's really mad at me now, and I don't blame her."

"So you've got the hots for her or something? Man, you're something else!"

"Oh, no, come on! It's just… I feel sorry for her, honestly. I lied to her, I took advantage of her."

"Yeah, you do love to lie. I've told you more than once that it's nasty, and lying to women is especially low. They trust us—bastards that we are—and care about us. But at least you're admitting you were wrong. That's something. Well done, man—I respect that."

"But that doesn't help her in any way, does it?"

"That's true. So what do you plan to do?"

"Nothing, really. I haven't got the energy to deal with it."

"Then just forget about this Larisa of yours."

"I would have a long time already. But it's not so simple. I feel ashamed, Roma… What about you—why are you so quiet? Is everything okay on your end?"

"You know, I'm not much better than you. Ever since I left my hometown, Ferghana, I've only called my mom three times and haven't visited once. Sure, Aunt Lida is a good person—she looks out for both of us as much as she can. But she'll never replace my real mother!"

"True. She won't."

"And so on one hand, I'm ashamed of myself in front of my mom, and on the other, I'm embarrassed to admit to anyone— especially you, my friend—that I, a grown young man, miss my mother so badly, like it hurts! Sometimes I feel like I could just howl. But how can I get away? Do you think the boss would let me take even a day off work? Not a chance. We don't get vacations or real weekends."

"Come on, Roma, that's nothing to be ashamed of. It's totally normal. I miss my mom too, and I even miss my alcoholic father, who's passed away. We're human—there's nothing strange about that… Listen, we agreed this would be our evening of truth and confessions, right?"

"Right. You're the one who wanted it!"

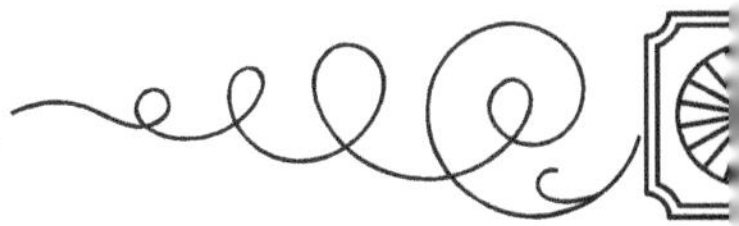

"Exactly. I just wanted to let myself say anything I want for at least an hour… And I'm telling you, man, our boss is one shady character, a real bastard."

"Shh! What are you doing?"

"Relax, there's nothing to worry about. He's not here, and none of his 'minions' are either. His inner circle is basically us two. Oh, well, and Misha. But Misha's just vanished, and no one knows where he's gone. Probably the jerk pocketed some of the boss's money from all those real estate deals and took off before anyone could catch him! He's disappeared, nowhere to be found. But whatever, to hell with him. Anyway, we can speak freely right now."

"But if Mukhitdin were here, you wouldn't be speaking so freely!"

"Yes, Roma, that's true. Even though Mukhit's a pal, and even if he can't stand his father, I still wouldn't dare say stuff like that in front of him. Lately, I don't trust him so much. Have you've noticed how he's changed—and not for the better? Ever since going to India, getting involved in that profitable business with that advanced millionaire Bhojwani, he's practically stopped communicating with us online. I mean, of course, who are we to him now? We're just some regular nobodies, while he's this big-shot! He's even ditched his music. See, it's in his genes: he's just like his old man."

"Shh, Gosha! Don't shout. What if someone hears us…?"

At that moment, Roma suddenly felt almost sober. Gosha, on the other hand, was still "three sheets to the wind."

"Hear us? Didn't I tell you, Roma, there's nobody here but us. Chill out. Another thing I wanted to say—have you noticed the boss still singles me out from the crowd? I'm special to him! He trusts me completely, and I always know all his business."

"Are you serious, Gosh?"

"Sure I am."

"I get the feeling the boss is hiding things from us. Like we don't know the half of it…"

"Well, here's what I think. Mukhit's gone far away, likely for a while. He might even never come back to Tashkent. He's comfortable over there, abroad. Meanwhile, I'll become like a son to the boss and inherit all his wealth!"

"Ha, isn't that a bit much? You're biting more than you can chew! If Mukhitdin heard you say that, he'd never forgive you. Careful."

"But Mukhit's not here, is he? Why are you so scared of everything? And you're not going to tell him or anyone else about my plans, right? I promise, Roma, bro, I'll definitely share that fortune with you."

"Wait a second, old boy—whose fortune did you say?"

"Mine! I told you—The boss will surely adopt me! Then when he's on his deathbed, he'll pass all his capital on to me."

Roma nearly choked, coughing.

"And why in the world would he do that?!"

"Because! Because I'm his best assistant."

"Well, I'm not going to blab about your nonsense to anyone, but keep in mind that there are ears everywhere. Hey—hang on…"

"What is it, Roma?"

"I just—thought I saw something. Let's get out of here, Gosh, it's time. We have work tomorrow."

"Oh, that work again! I'm so sick of it! All right, let's go."

They paid their tab, stood up, and left their favorite café—a place where there supposedly were never any "outsiders" or "extra" people.

"Roma, how I want to be filthy rich… to live in the Caribbean,

the Canaries, or the Seychelles…"

"You're dreaming!"

"What are you looking at?"

"Whoa! Yep, for sure. Gosha, I think we might be in trouble!"

"What do you mean? Can you explain?"

"Back in the café, I thought I glimpsed someone close by I recognised a few times. But I couldn't place her. Help me out here. It's that girl, she used to hang around Mukhitdin a lot! Beautiful chestnut hair… I think she's a nurse."

"You mean Galya?"

"Yeah, exactly—Galya, Galina. She's a friend of that girl Mukhitdin was in love with for so long…"

"Malika."

"Even drunk you remember, Gosha! Right, Malika.

"Well so… What?! Galina was here right now?!"

"Yes, Galina was right there, just now, in the café. She could've heard our entire conversation! And I just saw… how Mukhitdin's car drive off."

Gosha whistled.

"Oh, come on, Roma, that's impossible. You're spouting nonsense. Why so jumpy? Get a grip! Mukhit's in Delhi, not here! … Let's go home. I need to figure out if I should try to make up with Lariska…"

***

"Hello, daughter! It's Papa," came Said Yahyaevich's voice. It sounded unusually serious—he usually spoke to Malika more gently. But she knew that if her father was less than soft with her, something important had happened.

Malika grew alarmed:

"Papa! What's wrong? Did something happen to Mama? Or

to Grandma?"

"No, no, my dear. They're fine, thank God. But you still need to come here at once. We need to talk—and it's definitely not something to discuss on the phone."

She hadn't had time to tell her father—and didn't want to upset her parents right away—that something had happened to her as well, something she still couldn't explain. Nearly a full day had passed with no sign of her husband, Bahadir, and she hadn't been able to reach him on the phone.

Malika had already called his office. The phone was answered by Amin. Bahadir's older brother and, at the same time, his supervisor—and also their sister, Rano, both of whom were just as worried as Malika about Bahadir's sudden disappearance. They had no idea what to think or where to call. Right after Malika's call informing them that she hadn't seen her husband since the previous day, the conscientious and responsible Rano began phoning every major hospital in the city. She just couldn't bring herself to call the morgues.

But there was no sign of Bahadir in any of the hospitals…

Amin had suggested maybe calling the police—what if, god forbid, there had been a traffic accident? Rano's response was that they shouldn't call straight away but that they might first check Tashkent traffic reports online, which she immediately did.

Neither "Fattakhov B." nor any nameless injured party showed up in the day's accident logs, thank goodness.

Malika, of course, didn't just sit on her hands. That day, she'd asked to leave school early and told her professor she wouldn't be at rehearsal—she hurried home and began calling all their mutual friends and acquaintances, especially those who knew Bahadir. Nobody could say anything definite.

"Where could he have gone?" Malika wondered in horror.

She was already overwhelmed with anxiety, and right then her father called, making it clear that he, (or perhaps the parental home in general? Malika didn't know yet) had some situation of their own.

* * *

"Papa!" Malika flung herself into her father's arms and couldn't hold back her tears anymore.

Said Yahyaevich hugged his daughter, too.

"Papa, where's Mama? She's not home?"

"Yes, Malika, your mother is still at work—she has a delegation from Italy today. That might be for the best, because first, you and I need to talk seriously, and it can't wait. Please, my child, let's sit down. Are you hungry?"

"No, Papa! How can I think of eating right now? You've really scared me! This day has been nothing but trouble… I'm not doing too well myself…"

"What happened to you?"

"I'll tell you later—let me hear you out first."

"All right. Basically, Malika, about an hour ago, Investigator Umarov called me. You remember him—he came regarding the theft of our—well, your—necklace."

"Yes, I remember…" Malika looked at her father with wide eyes, trying to guess where this was leading. "So…? Why did he call?"

"He told me something strange, something I honestly don't quite understand…"

"Papa, please, don't keep me in suspense!"

"I'll try… It's just hard to say. Captain Umarov claims he's found the person who stole our valuable piece—and already taken him into custody…"

"Well, that's good news for you—for all of us, really… But, Papa, if that's all that you wanted to tell me, then… why are you so upset? Isn't that good, that he caught the thief? Or isn't it…?"

"Daughter, the investigator said that apparently… the thief… I can hardly bring myself to say it!"

Malika felt her frayed nerves ready to snap on this difficult day. "What about this thief, Papa?"

"…that it's your husband, Bahadir Fattakhov."

Malika jumped up from the chair, as though scalded.

"What? Papa! How can you say that? Do you actually believe this… this captain? He's lying! That's utter nonsense—complete idiocy!"

"That's not all, child. Sit down, please! There's more. He's holding Bahadir at his station, for now in the booking cell, as the main suspect in this theft, until all the details are clarified."

"Papa, wait. I'm confused right now. Who is he holding? … My Bahadir?! And here we've been searching everywhere for him! What's that investigator doing? Does he think Bahadir's a criminal?!"

"Calm down, daughter, don't shout!"

"Papa, I'm so sorry—my nerves are shot. But Bahadir's parents don't even know yet that he 'disappeared.' His brother and sister and I have been searching for him everywhere all day! We were scared to even think… we started to fear the worst … And he's at the police station at the hands of that captain Umarov! Couldn't Umarov have at least given Bahadir his legal right to make a phone call? Then we wouldn't have been searching so desperately for my

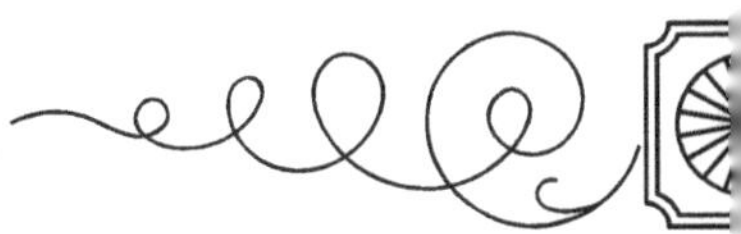

husband everywhere, calling all over town! The only places we didn't call are the morgues. What kind of person is he, anyway?"

"You should tell me—what kind of person is your husband?" asked Said Yahyaevich unexpectedly, anger and disappointment in his voice. "His father—my friend, Abdulla Rustamovich, whom I've known for years—is a wonderful, honest, and very decent elder of our community. But it turns out I don't know his younger son at all. Who is he, really? What is he like? What does he do outside work and studies? Maybe he really is a thief? Maybe he helps himself to things that 'aren't nailed down'?"

"Papa! How can you say that? Why are you talking like this?... Bahadir is not like that! He would never do something bad!"

"But you yourself shared recently that your husband has big debts. Isn't it possible he quietly took and quickly sold this expensive necklace just to pay off his creditors?"

At those words, Malika suddenly recalled her conversation with Murad Nematullaevich about how he'd lent Bahadir money—supposedly "for a foreign car." That's when small but agonizing doubts began to worm their way into the young wife's heart regarding her husband's "crystal-clear honesty"...

It seemed after all that he'd been deceiving her for a while.... Admittedly: where did those debts come from, and why were they so large?... And what was the real involvement of oligarch Murad Nasyrov—a businessman with an outstanding reputation, who had cunning, guileful eyes that she found impossible to trust? Why would he lend money to this "simple" young man—a non-partner, not a friend, not a relative, just some random guy?... Maybe he wanted to secure the trust of this young man's father-in-law, Said? But for what reason?! Or, as she had suspected and feared, were gambling debts involved?...

Malika was filled with turmoil and panic. She felt ashamed in front of her father on her husband's account, and she had no idea what to say...

* * *

When Malika returned home, she got a call from Amin.

"Hello, Malika, any news? Did you find out anything new about my brother? Rano and I are really worried."

"Yes, Amin! Thank you for calling at just the right time... I don't know what to do. It turns out Bahadir is... at the police station! He's been arrested..."

Amin let out a low whistle.

"You're kidding! I don't understand—why? For what? Do you know anything?"

"Yes. They suspect him of... It's so absurd I can't even bring myself to say it!... Basically, they're charging him with theft—from my family! Can you imagine?"

"That's definitely some kind of misunderstanding, and obviously something fishy going on. I know Bahadir well—he may have his flaws and weaknesses, but stealing isn't one of them! We're a decent family, and he would never disgrace our parents. What's he supposedly stolen?"

"My precious necklace—the gold one, with real rubies and diamonds. Remember, I wore it at our wedding?"

"Yeah, I recall something like that... But the idea that Bahadir took it is totally ridiculous! Malika, here's what we'll do. I have... well, my girlfriend... Actually, I recently met a very capable, brilliant woman whom I trust completely. Her name's Dilshoda, and she's a lawyer... True, she usually doesn't handle 'local' issues, but she has lots of friends in this field—top professionals. I'll ask her, and she won't refuse. Together, we'll absolutely find the best defense lawyer for Bahadir!"

"That would be great… Because I was supposed to fly to an important competition in Moscow soon…"

"Really? A singing competition? That's fantastic news; I'm happy for you. You'll do great."

"What's there to celebrate, Amin? My husband's in jail—how am I supposed to go anywhere now?... It's impossible…"

"I understand. But this is obviously a setup, so I promise we'll hire an excellent lawyer, and with everyone pitching in, we'll get Bahadir out quickly! Then you can safely go to your competition with peace of mind."

"Do you really think so?"

"Of course! Trust me, Rano and I won't abandon our brother. Everything will be fine. Just one favor, Malika: please don't say anything about this to our parents yet, all right? Father's in the hospital with a serious heart condition, and this kind of news could make things worse. And for Mother as well. It'll be better if, once this is all resolved, I tell them about it afterward if it's necessary. Ok?"

"Of course I won't say anything. May God grant your father a swift recovery!"

"Thanks, Malika."

"And please, don't tell my mom either."

"All right. But why not?"

"Because if even my dad's thinking badly of Bahadir, then Mom, in her emotional state, might not get to the bottom of things and force me to divorce him. I can't let that happen!"

"I won't let it happen either, don't worry."

"I know for a fact that Bahadir can't be guilty of something like this!"

"Malika, I believe your husband's going to be fine, and soon he'll be home."

"God willing. I really want to believe in that… Though I suspect proving his innocence won't be easy…"

***

Gosha stumbled into his apartment completely drunk, barely aware of his surroundings. By force of habit, he headed for his bedroom and flopped onto the bed still wearing his jacket and shoes. Through his boozy haze, he heard someone's quiet footsteps in the apartment and caught a strong whiff of smoke.

Vaguely, Gosha sensed that his place was on fire—that the relentless flames were about to consume him. But he felt so exhausted and relaxed that he couldn't fight it. During a brief flicker of consciousness, he thought: "I think I saw some long strands of hair on the floor—definitely a woman's… Larisa, my dear, did you decide to burn me alive? Why? It seems, you never forgave me!… And why did you dye your blond hair chestnut brown…?"

Just then, there were loud, hurried footsteps in the stairwell outside.

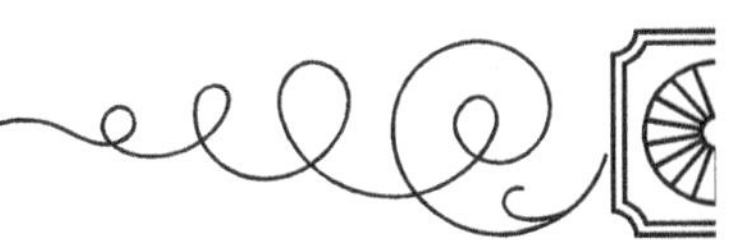

47

Tashkent, January 2015.

A little more than two months had passed since the most re-cent events. Once Murad Nematullaevich learned from the bank that he truly had been robbed, he logically deduced that it must have been Misha Leonidov—no one else could have done it, as everyone else either feared or respected him too much. Nasyrov tried to locate Mikhail, but so far had gotten nowhere.

It was some consolation that Leonidov, as it turned out, had not taken everything from Nasyrov. He had stolen only the com-pany's financial liabilities, certain non-current assets belonging to the company, and various financial current assets that had been kept in the bank. However, he had not touched the company's real estate—its industrial and non-industrial facilities, residential and administrative buildings, land, production equipment, and so on. Although the company's so-called "capital accounts" had shrunk noticeably, most of the firm's highly liquid assets and valuables, as well as securities—shares and stakes in other companies, accounts receivable, production stock, and some other tangible assets whose value the owner could trust—remained in Murad Nasyrov's pos-session.

Even so, the boss's mood remained bleak. Nasyrov still faced difficulties and problems in his business. To escape the crisis, he would have to do something—maybe urgently reduce staff, cut employee salaries, or sell one of his apartments and at least one low-profit venue – a restaurant or café.

Adding to these problems was Sitora, whom he had encountered again after twenty years. Something flared up in him—a feeling one could hardly call "love," since in truth Nasyrov had never learned how to love genuinely, and was used only to possessing whatever he strongly desired. But Sitora did not reciprocate his interest. She certainly was in no way planning to move in with him, let alone bring her daughter along.

Sitora had wanted to tell him that he was mistaken about Malika—that Malika was not his daughter—but she decided not to argue or explain. Let him think whatever he wished; perhaps it was even for the best...

Back in her youth, when she discovered that Murad was married with a family, she had decided to leave him—and at around that time, she met Said. Their relationship moved swiftly; they fell in love, and within a month (or even less) after her final break with Murad, she married Said, formalising the marriage—something she had never had with Nasyrov–and Sitora became pregnant... by Said.

In later years, Sitora disliked recalling her affair with Nasyrov. She was ashamed of that youthful mistake... Around him, she had always felt less like a partner or a friend and more like one of his "fine possessions," yet another beautiful "trinket" such as the ones he used to give her from time to time.

After her last meeting with the oligarch at his restaurant, Sitora ran her life story through her head once again and clearly saw that nobody in the world was dearer to her than Said and Malika. Now she also valued Bahadir, for he had become a very close and important person to Malika, their only daughter.

When Sitora learned what terrible fate had befallen her son-in-law... at that point, she knew nothing about his partial culpabil-

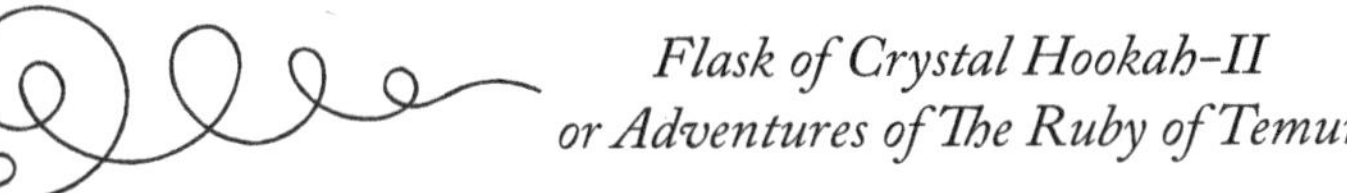

ity—about his gambling in a casino—she reflected on it and quite soon concluded that if Bahadir Fattakhov had ended up behind bars, Nasyrov must certainly have had a hand in it. The oligarch had plainly lent his filthy hand to the situation.

Malika's mother remembered how Murad had threatened her and her daughter that if they did not agree to his "proposal"— which, in reality, was an absolute command, an order from a master to his slaves—then the young man would be "ground to dust." That meant he would either be eliminated outright or, "in the best case," be made to serve a long sentence, as people say, "locked away."

And so it came to pass.

"And that Captain Ravshan Umarov!" Sitora was astonished. "He fears neither God nor the law; on his 'protector's' orders—his wealthy patron and sponsor—he threw an innocent man in pretrial detention and is preparing to send him to prison, and then more. And he's happily going on with his life! A disgusting person. I wonder how much Nasyrov paid this detective for Bahadir…"

Sitora began thinking about how she might help Bahadir. Initially, she wanted to tell her husband, but Said knew nothing about her past with Nasyrov or about the two recent conversations she'd had with him. Twenty years earlier, all he knew was that his fiancée had left some disreputable, married businessman and that was it. Said had no idea what this businessman's name was, and he didn't want to disturb the soul of his beloved with excessive curiosity and questions. And now, thought Sitora, it's even more impossible to tell him anything: as almost any Eastern man, he would torture himself with jealousy, and might suspect his wife of an infidelity that never took place. She could never let that happen!

So Sitora called Malika in Moscow and asked her not to mention to anyone that she knew Murad Nasyrov. Malika was surprised, but she obeyed her mother's wishes.

"Mama, I'm already preparing for the second round, the main competition of 'Superstar'! I really don't have time for extra conversations with anyone, even family. But I'll keep your request in mind."

Malika really had passed a grueling audition, where tens of thousands of both seasoned and novice participants—most of them quite talented—tried out, and she had made it into the final hundred participants of the main "Superstar" show competition.

"My dear, you hang in there. Try not to worry about anything. Although I'm very anxious about Bahadir's fate. I'm sure he's locked up now because Nasyrov is taking revenge on us—for rejecting him! As I've said many times, Amin, Rano, and I are doing everything we can to prevent this from going to trial and to get Bahadir released soon. His friend Rudik, and even your father, in short, everyone is trying to help in every way they can."

"Dad shouldn't worry," Malika replied with a touch of irritation not specifically aimed at her mother. "He doesn't even believe Bahadir is innocent, and he has enough issues of his own. So…"

"Daughter, don't be upset with your father! Perhaps he said something harsh to you in the heat of the moment. But now he's going around, feeling guilty that you don't want to talk to him! And who do you have that's closer than your parents?…"

* * *

Malika was genuinely hurt by her father—after all, he had suspected her innocent husband! Yes, as already mentioned, Malika herself had occasionally entertained fleeting doubts about Bahadir's honesty, but she tried to drive away all such negative thoughts.

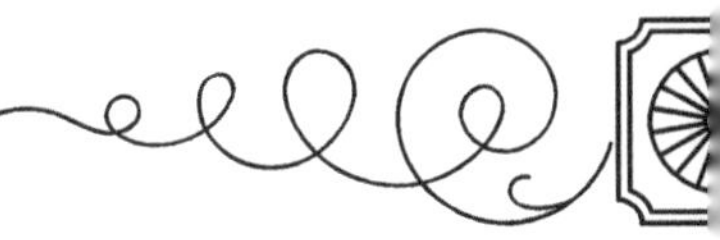

In her eyes, he simply could not be a bad despicable person, let alone a criminal.

For his part, Said Yahyaevich felt upset about having offended his only, much-adored daughter. In hopes of making amends and atoning for the hurt he had caused, he resolved not to speak or even think poorly of Bahadir anymore. Like the rest of the family, he began looking for ways to get the young man out of trouble.

Unaware of the full circumstances and details, Said could think of nothing more promising than calling his influential acquaintance, Nasyrov, to ask for help…

"Hello, Murad Nematullaevich. This is Doctor Said Mumtazov."

"Greetings, dear Doctor Said Yahyaevich. How are things? What can I do for you?"

"If possible, I'd like to come see you. It's not something I can discuss over the phone."

"Certainly, come on over. Would it suit you to meet at noon. Yes? Good. I'll be waiting."

Said Yahyaevich arrived at Nasyrov's office.

"Some tea or coffee?" Nasyrov offered politely, playing the gracious host.

"No, thank you. The thing is, you see," Said began right away, "I assume—or rather, I know—you have good, strong connections and considerable influence… The problem is that my son-in-law has been uhh—well, he's been detained and is currently sitting in pretrial custody. But my daughter is absolutely convinced he's done nothing wrong!"

"Wait a moment, my friend—what is he being accused of, or, to be precise, suspected of? There's been no trial yet, correct?"

"Yes, you're right, there hasn't been a trial. And my son-in-law—you should remember him, we hosted the wedding for him and my daughter at your restaurant—my son-in-law, Bahadir Fattakhov, is being charged with theft… But it's such a strange and confusing affair."

"Oh really! How interesting… Sorry, I mean it's a truly extraordinary incident, and I can imagine how badly this must have shaken you and your entire family! My sincere condolences…"

"Thank you."

"So what exactly happened? What was stolen? And why did they detain specifically your… what was his name? I'm sorry, I've gotten a little rusty."

"Bahadir"

"Oh, right, right, Bahadir…"

"The police are saying he had obvious motives and that…"

"Sorry to interrupt, I'm not quite following: What was stolen and from whom?"

"That's the strangest part: it was stolen from our own house! A piece of jewelry went missing… a necklace set with rubies and diamonds."

For some reason, Nasyrov stiffened slightly, his forehead glistening with sweat.

"Astonishing… Must be quite valuable?"

"We didn't buy it ourselves, so I don't know its price, but I'm sure it's very costly."

"And do you yourself suspect anyone, Doctor Said Yahyaevich?" At this moment, Nasyrov avoided meeting the doctor's eyes, so as not to betray his anxiety.

"No, I'm no expert in such matters. I can't imagine who could have done it, since we never have strangers in our home! For a while, my wife was pointing the finger at our housekeeper, but I just don't believe Larisa could do something like that!"

"Larisa? Hm…"

"She's perfectly normal, conscientious, and does her job properly. But that's not even the main point. Honestly, I can't believe my son-in-law could be a culprit of this theft!"

"Really? You're completely sure he's innocent?" Nasyrov smirked.

"Well… not entirely sure… but my entire family insists on it. Besides, he's a rather refined young man, not the type to steal, even if he might have had some motive…"

"A motive? I'm only asking because it could fundamentally change the situation."

"They say he has certain debts… I haven't gone into the details. We've had a visit from a district police investigator—Captain Umarov—who's handling our case. He's the one who detained Bahadir, claiming to have proof of his guilt. He cites the motive and 'something else': apparently, the necklace that was planted on us in place of the real one, which my wife gave to Umarov for the investigation, bears our son-in-law's fingerprints, at least according to the captain. But… I'd like your opinion on whether this could be faked. Could it be that the investigator has been 'bought off' by the real perpetrator?"

Nasyrov grew visibly more tense. Then, adopting a friendly smile, he remarked:

"Well, as the special agent in that Jackie Chan film, 'Who Am I?', once said, you'll find chameleons and shapeshifters in nearly every institution… As for the possible motive, that definitely provides a strong reason to suspect your son-in-law. I'd imagine that a major motive for—let's put it gently—appropriating an expensive piece of jewelry, even from one's own young wife, might be the desire to resolve a serious financial issue as quickly as possible. Such problems are typically large debts—maybe to a utilities office, some organisation, or a private lender who can't or won't wait anymore. Your young man got himself in a sticky situation: he took the necklace, sold it, used or planned to use the proceeds to pay off the debt. And having been freed or partly freed from the clutches of his creditors, he promptly wound up in the talons of the law. Ergo, it's quite possible that he committed the crime! …"

For several seconds, silence reigned; Said Mumtazov said nothing.

"What's on your mind, Doctor? … Do you still firmly believe in your daughter's husband's complete innocence?"

Heavily, the doctor lowered his eyes and remained silent once more.

Nasyrov came to his rescue:

"All right, let's shift the topic slightly. The necklace itself—no one has found it yet, right?"

"How do you know all this, Murad Nematullaevich?" asked Said Mumtazov with a melancholy smile. "Yes, the police have been looking for nearly three months, ever since it was reported missing—and still, nothing… But why do you ask?"

"Well, would you like me to speak with this captain? Perhaps I can influence the investigation—who knows, your Bahadir might confess, or a different suspect might be discovered as the real thief…"

"You're a genuine guardian angel. Of course I won't refuse your help. To be frank, that's exactly why I came to see you…"

"Excellent."

"But please, let's not push for any forced confession, or make him go to prison!"

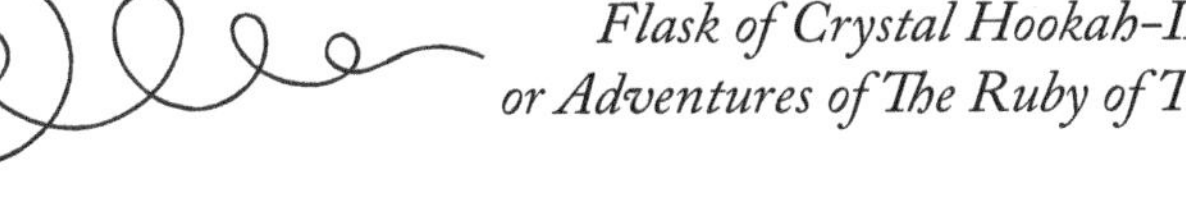

"Don't you worry. They'll figure it out. Please write down the investigator's full name so I won't forget it… I promise I'll do everything I can to help!"

"And you'll help to get Bahadir out? Is that even realistic?"

"Well, if it turns out he's innocent, then… But let's not get ahead of ourselves, Doctor, all right? I can't make any concrete guarantees regarding your son-in-law, but of course, I'll do whatever I can!"

From the look on Said's face, it was clear he was not only satisfied but deeply grateful. The businessman's willingness to assist in solving his problem now commanded the doctor's esteem and respect.

"I was wrong to think poorly of this man, to suspect him under Firuz-begim's influence," thought Said as he left Nasyrov's office.

* * *

"Hello, Roma? Hey, it's Misha…"

"What?! Who? Misha, is that you?… Holy cow! Where did you disappear to, buddy? The boss has been hunting all over for you!"

"Eh, I just had to take off in a hurry… So how are things over there?"

"Well, how should I put it… Mixed. Listen, the boss believes you've cleaned him out. I'm not sure if that's true or not… But where are you now? Where are you calling from?"

"That's not really important… So he's looking for me after all?"

"Oh, yeah—big time. If you don't want to get caught and feel his wrath, you'd best not show your face around here. I hope you've found a safe hideout?"

"Don't worry about it. Nobody will ever find me."

"So, Misha, I guess things are going well for you?"

"You could say I'm living the good life, enjoying myself."

That much was true. Mikhail had indeed bought a luxurious villa overlooking the sea in the Maldives, plus a couple of fancy cars (he felt any more would be pointless). He'd also hired a whole staff of helpers for everything he needed.

"I see… So it's true—you withdrew a huge sum from the boss's accounts… You've got guts! None of us would ever dare do something like that, but you…"

"My relationship with him is different from yours or Gosha's. It was never all that smooth…"

"Yeah, I know."

"Speaking of which—how's Gosha?"

"Gosha's not doing so great. Someone set him on fire—he's badly burned."

"What?! So… he's dead? Sorry to hear that."

"No, no, he's alive, fortunately. See, on that particular day, I had a weird feeling that my friend might be in danger. For some reason, late at night, I decided to swing by his place, even though earlier we'd been at a café and then gone our separate ways. Probably my intuition kicking in… I called the fire department and ambulance in time—otherwise we wouldn't have saved Goshka. To this day, I have no clue who would do that to him—burn a guy alive while he's drunk and clueless, unable to save himself…"

"Maybe it was an accident—he got careless with a flame? You said he was drunk—he could've messed around with matches or a lighter…"

"Could be… Hard to believe, though. Gosha thinks it was his girlfriend setting him on fire out of revenge!"

"You don't say… Sounds like a dangerous, vengeful type. But

maybe it wasn't her… Man, you folks have it rough—like a Mexican soap opera!"

"Tell me about it, Misha. So what are you up to? You've got plenty of money to live on, right? I guess you're lying low somewhere, living it up?"

"No, that's not me. Actually, I'm serious about learning the ropes of big business. I go to all sorts of seminars and training in finance. I want to become genuinely successful."

"Wow. I'm a bit jealous…"

"All right, Roma, take care of yourself. Say hi to Gosha for me, but not to the boss."

"Sorry, Misha, but I have to tell the boss you called. I don't have a choice."

"Huh, so you're a loyal servant to your master, eh? I get it… Do as you like, do what you gotta do. I'm calling from a disposable phone anyway—he'll never, ever trace me. You won't be hearing my voice again. This call is over. If only you knew, Roma, how good it feels to be far away from Nasyrov and all of you—his henchmen!"

Roma was about to say something else—he wanted Misha not to resent him for his loyalty to the boss, for having to report their conversation. But all he heard was a click and a dial tone. The number was displayed on his phone, yet Roma—no more tech-savvy than Gosha or Misha—still understood that giving the number to Nasyrov and his goons would accomplish precisely nothing. Leonidov himself made it sound like he was quite sure of his advantage; he'd made it clear they'd never be able to track him down. The battery in that disposable phone, which Misha had likely already tossed, would die soon enough—and there would be no way to pinpoint not just the street or district, but not even the country he was currently in…

And Misha wasn't lying: he truly was studying how to invest and grow capital wisely at the finest, priciest business schools. He now had bold dreams, plans, and goals: to climb high in his career and become one of the richest, most successful people on the planet… and beyond that—to acquire the remarkable treasure, the "Ornament of the Palace," that opulent golden necklace set with Temur's Ruby and diamonds. He'd become just as infatuated with that piece as Nasyrov was.

Having substantial funds and colossal means now, Mikhail understood that if necessary, he had to be prepared to give everything he had in order to buy that necklace—wherever it might be!

Even if it was still with the Ruler of Kuwait…

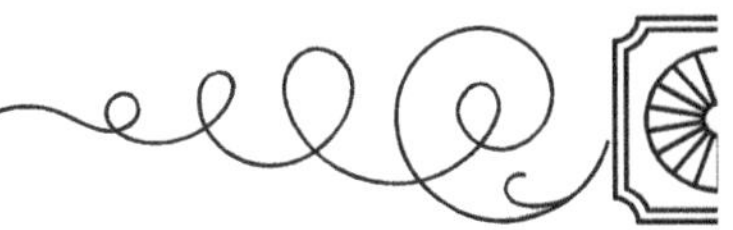

48

Roma had Gosha admitted to the Republican Burn Center, because a regular hospital or clinic would never be able to handle such extensive burns. Roma himself also needed a specialist's help—though far less severe—after pulling Gosha from the flames, he had suffered a few minor burns.

In a twist of good fortune for them both, they ended up under the care of one of the center's top physicians: an experienced burn surgeon, Farhad Nabiev. He was in his sixties, lean, fit, strict, and very serious—attributes that fit well with the demands of his profession.

"Roma, you have first-degree burns," said Dr. Nabiev after examining the two friends. "But your buddy, as we've determined, has a mixture of second-degree burns, and mostly third-degree—some of which are verging on fourth-degree. That, I'm afraid, is extremely serious…"

"Will… he survive, Doctor?"

"We can only hope, young man. Altogether, he has burns over sixty percent of his body, which is substantial. While I prepare Gosha for the first surgery, the nurses are applying dressings with panthenol and aloe vera. That will ease his terrible suffering somewhat. He's still unconscious—hasn't come around yet—and that state partly protects him. Even so, the signals his brain sends to our monitors indicate that his body experiences searing pain from time to time. If he were awake, he might have died from the severe pain alone—his heart wouldn't have handled the shock."

Roma turned pale. He was truly alarmed.

"Doctor, I really don't know anything about any of this. What does it all mean? I guess that having a relatively mild skin injury, like I do, is straightforward. But how bad is Gosha's condition, really?"

"Well, first of all, Roman, a burn doesn't affect only the skin. In general, a thermal burn can come from hot liquids, steam, or intensely heated objects. In your and Gosha's case, the burns were caused by direct exposure to open flames."

"And what do these different 'degrees' of burns mean?"

"Burns are classified into four degrees, depending on the depth of tissue damage. First-degree burns—like yours—are characterised by redness and some swelling of the skin. You did well, apparently being quite careful when you entered that burning apartment to rescue your friend. Only the outer layer of your skin, the epidermis, was affected. Usually, recovery in such cases comes within four or five days—so once you start using the treatments I've prescribed, including medical ointments and gels, you'll be fully healed very soon."

"I'll do everything necessary, Doctor. Thank you!"

"No need to thank me—it's my job. Now, let's talk about something more serious, because your friend's situation is far worse. And I assume that matters a lot to you?"

"Yes, very much so. To be honest, I'm really worried about him."

"You're a good friend; in that sense, Georgy is lucky. A large portion of your friend's skin is afflicted with both A and B types of third-degree and fourth-degree burns. In other words, there is permanent tissue damage forming a gray or black crust, and, even worse, charring not only the skin but the deeper layers: muscle, tendons, and bone…"

"That's awful…"

"It is, unfortunately. One can't envy your friend. Deep burns often leave severe scar tissue, and when they involve the face, neck, or joints, disfigurement is common…"

"So from now on, people are going to recoil from him…" Roma said dejectedly.

"No need to lose hope so quickly, young man. Gosha's body is young, strong—maybe things will go better than expected. But you need to know: necrotic tissue partially liquefies and sloughs off over several weeks, and in such cases, healing is extremely slow. That's what awaits—or may await—your friend."

"But, Doctor, you promised to help him!"

"Of course we'll do everything in our power. You see… if your friend were, let's say, a heavier-set woman with large hips and lots of skin folds, we could graft some of her own skin onto the damaged areas. But he's a slight young man. Of course, we do have donor skin available, but you realize that grafting large quantities wouldn't be free. It isn't a cheap material—donor skin, or donor organs, for that matter! And neither you nor the patient's relatives have that kind of money, do you?"

"No, unfortunately not. What do we do, then, Doctor?"

"We'll see what happens. I hope either you or we can find a solution."

* * *

Both Lidiya Petrovna and Roma did their best to visit Gosha in the hospital as often as their jobs allowed.

At first, the biggest challenge was getting the additional medicines necessary for someone who had suffered such severe burns,

361

along with the right kind of diet—quality food that was not cheap. Neither Lidiya Petrovna nor Roma had enough money to cover all of it.

But time passed; nearly three weeks had gone by since the fire, and Gosha finally regained consciousness. Only then—once he was fully lucid and had all his memories back—did things become significantly easier, because Gosha started paying for his own treatment.

Initially, after realising what had happened to him, Gosha didn't want to live at all, but gradually he pulled himself together, felt a renewed desire for life, and tried to savour and appreciate each moment. Despite several successful surgeries brilliantly performed by Dr. Nabiev, Gosha still felt awful physically, often moaning from unbearable pain. Not only had a large percentage of his skin been burned, but parts of certain organs were also destroyed (for instance, his right kidney and the muscles in his right thigh were damaged). Which is why he needed donor organs as soon as possible. Gosha knew that otherwise, he wouldn't last long.

After questioning the friends who hadn't abandoned him in his hour of need, trying to figure out exactly what had happened, Gosha asked Lidiya Petrovna during one of her visits:

"So, the boss didn't help me at all?"

The kindly woman sadly shook her head and wiped away an involuntary tear from her plump pink cheek.

"You mean, not a single cent toward my treatment?!" Gosha wasn't supposed to raise his voice—he had to conserve his strength—but he just couldn't hold back the anger and pain that welled up inside him.

"There, there, Gosha," Lidiya Petrovna tried to console the young man. "Look on the bright side: thank God you're alive! You

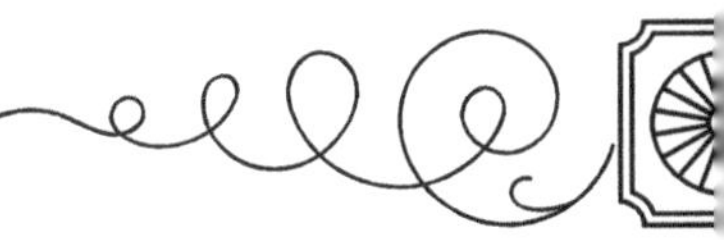

should thank Roma—he practically pulled you straight out of the fire; he saved your life. And then the firefighters arrived and put out the flames in your apartment."

"But what's left in there that wasn't touched by the fire?" Gosha asked in despair. "Of course…At least the door there… it still locks, right?"

"Yes, thank God," the woman replied briefly.

"So, the boss… He gave absolutely nothing, huh…?"

Lidiya Petrovna looked at Gosha with a guilty expression and shook her head again, speechless. She felt deeply uncomfortable and pained that her boss hadn't done anything at all for his best assistant—a young guy who had not yet 'grown into his own'—stranded in such dire straits.

"That's weird," Gosha murmured in surprise. "After what I did for him… Well, what's there to say!"

Roma dashed in, brought fruit and new medicines, then dashed out again. He hardly ever stayed long—he had too many responsibilities now, including some of Gosha's tasks at work. Besides, it pained him to look at his friend, now barely recognisable and horribly disfigured by fire and fate…

Money for treatment was desperately needed. Gosha told Roma where his "rainy day" cash was hidden—a not-so-small sum he had saved up for quite some time. Roma already had a spare key to Gosha's apartment.

Roma moved in circles where slipping a hand into someone else's pocket or emptying someone's apartment—even a best friend's—was not considered shameful or disgraceful, let alone taboo. On the contrary, some of the guys he and Gosha knew would even brag about such "feats." So when, at Gosha's request, Roma went to retrieve Gosha's hidden money—primarily to fund Gosha's treatment and recovery—he felt a burning temptation to pocket at least part of it for himself.

Just as Roma was about to leave Gosha's apartment, someone rang the doorbell.

Quietly and cautiously, moving stealthily, Roma tiptoed over to the entryway and peered through the peephole. Standing outside was a blonde woman of about forty. Roma recognized her almost immediately—he'd seen her photo at Gosha's place.

It was… Larisa!

"Who is it?" Roma decided to ask—though a moment earlier, he had no intention of talking to anyone or letting anyone in, or letting anyone know that he was in the apartment and had taken something. But an uneasy feeling had crept over him.

What, thought Roma, *has she really returned to her crime scene?!*

"Oh my! Who are you?" said a voice outside. "My name is Larisa; I'm a friend of Gosha's. I have a key, but I can't get it to fit and open the door—you've locked it from inside…"

Roma had no choice now, so he opened the door. Indeed, the blonde woman held a key identical to the one he had. She looked fairly pleasant up close, and it was clear she had to be at least forty. "An old maid," Roma recalled Gosha's description of his girlfriend.

Roma said hello, then fell silent, not knowing how to proceed.

"And you must be Roman?" Larisa helped the slightly flustered young man out. She was very friendly. "I figured it out right away. Gosha's told me a lot about you! You're his very best friend, right? But…hold on, where is Gosha?"

Roma stayed quiet again, thinking that she didn't look like any sort of cunning femme fatale… There was no way she could have "acted" that well; her expression was entirely guileless. So maybe she wasn't the one behind the arson?… Roma was unsure whether to tell her everything at once—clearly she didn't know anything!

"I just wanted to surprise him. We had a fight over a month ago, and I was really mad at him. But all along, I kept thinking I should come over and return his keys. I kept putting it off—maybe I wasn't ready to break things off for good, to put a 'final end' to it, because…I still… Well, never mind. I wanted to make up with him. But I guess he must have found another woman by now… right?"

She gave Roma a meaningful look, as though he, as Gosha's best friend, was the ultimate expert on Gosha's personal life.

Roma remained silent and uneasy. Finally, he made a decision:

"No, Gosha's seeing nobody. He has no time for that right now…"

He faltered. Should he tell her or not? But what if she fainted on the spot? Probably no smelling salts in the apartment…

Yet at those words, Larisa looked a bit bolder and even a bit happier.

"Really?" She beamed. "Has he…mentioned me at all?"

Roma wanted to say that Gosha had only begun speaking again a couple of days ago, and that no, he hadn't specifically mentioned Larisa. But Roma suspected Gosha was thinking about her…

"Larisa, do you have some time?" he asked unexpectedly.

"Well… yes. Why do you ask? Where's Gosha? He's still at work, just running late, right?"

"No. But it seems to me he's waiting for you…and will be glad to see you. Come on—let's go together."

"To Gosha? Of course! But where? You said he'd be happy to see me?"

"Well…you'll see soon enough. Please try not to worry."

"What happened?" Larisa's smile vanished as quickly as it had appeared. Some mysterious womanly intuition—dampened and misled only by her lingering grudge toward Gosha—now kicked in, alerting her to the seriousness of the situation. Larisa suddenly felt that something serious had happened. "Please, tell me plainly, Roman, where is Gosha?... What's going on with him? Is it something bad?"

Roma wasn't prepared to put it all into words. He just hurriedly slipped on his shoes and left.

Larisa didn't say anything during the taxi ride. She spent the entire trip silently weeping without knowing why. "She must really love him," Roma concluded.

He started feeling sorry both for this "old maid" who was head over heels for his young, disfigured friend and for Gosha himself, who now could only be saved, apparently, by the money he had stashed away—prophetically, it seemed—for a "rainy day."

When they got out of the taxi, Roma was still hesitating, unsure what to do next.

"Wait, Roman…this is…a hospital!"

So far, Larisa had only seen a large white medical building. As they walked closer, she noticed the sign: "Republican Burn Center."

She stopped abruptly, her tone leaving no room for objection:

"Right, start talking this instant—what's happened to Gosha?"

Roma was forced to lay out the basic facts. He glossed over his own "heroics" in saving his friend, merely saying that "the firefighters arrived in time—if they'd been much later, Gosha wouldn't have made it."

Larisa was in shock. But when you love someone… She dashed headlong down the first pathway she saw in the hospital courtyard, forgetting to ask Roma which ward or floor Gosha was on. After a moment, she realised she might be going the wrong way and waited for Roman.

A few minutes later, they were outside the patient's room. Roma was about to stride right in, forgetting that Larisa might need at least a moment to brace herself for this meeting and to put all those past grudges behind her.

Finally—after a very short yet apparently intense mental and emotional reckoning—"Gosha's girl" worked up the resolve to enter his room.

Gosha wasn't expecting her at all. He hadn't groomed himself, hadn't brushed his teeth, hadn't covered the charred, scorched, and ruined parts of his body… Everything hurt like crazy…

"Goshinka!" Larisa hurried to his side and tried to hug him. Her movement was clumsy—she was too shaken. "You…um, how are you?"

That was all she managed to say. Larisa was still in a state of shock. Not only had she failed to recover from the sudden news Roma had delivered about his friend, but now, seeing with her own eyes how drastically her loved one had changed, it was like a fresh jolt of electricity coursed through her. It took no small effort for the woman not to recoil at the sight of how disfigured a man dear to her was. Somehow, though, she felt no revulsion—no impulse to pull away. On the contrary, her heart contracted with compassion. Her feelings for him hadn't diminished in the face of this dreadful sight; in fact, they seemed to blaze up in a new way.

Gosha didn't greet her. For some reason, his eyes glistened. In moments like these, people often claim they have "a speck of dust" in their eye to hide their sentimentality. Without a word, he lifted one still barely functional hand, took Larisa's hand, and pressed it fervently to his lips.

Then he shot Roma a look of reproach and annoyance, acting as though Larisa no longer existed, as though she wasn't standing right by his bed.

"Why'd you bring her here?" he demanded.

Roma fell silent for a few seconds, then found an answer:

"Well, she showed up at your place on her own—she was worried… You'd vanished… I couldn't just turn your girlfriend away! And besides…it wasn't her who, uh…did that to you."

"Did what to me?" Gosha pretended not to understand; he repeated the obvious to mask the excitement and searing sadness he felt, along with his anxiety about the future.

"I mean, it wasn't Larisa who started the fire in your place!" Roma, deep in his subconscious, knew these explanations were redundant—that Gosha had already understood that he was talking about that evil fire! At the same time, he sensed both of them—exhausted, battered souls—needed this somewhat awkward, not-so-informative conversation right now.

"Oh…all right," Gosha mumbled.

He let go of Larisa's hand a while ago and wasn't looking at her anymore—neither with tenderness, as when he'd kissed her hand, nor with resentment over her long absence and anger at him. Instead, his gaze held no emotion at all, as if she were invisible or a piece of furniture.

"Roma, I'm tired, I want to sleep," Gosha addressed him pointedly, as though ignoring Larisa entirely and not talking to her. Finally, he extended a small courtesy to his visitor: "Please, everyone, just go!"

Gosha turned his face to the wall. In seconds, tears were flowing down his cheeks.

At that moment—though she couldn't see his tears—Larisa

seemed to sense them by that special "sixth sense" or intuition so many women have as a heaven-sent gift. She instantly perceived that his harsh, dismissive tone was nothing more than a shell behind which hid a wounded, vulnerable being. And right now, more than ever, that being needed help, support, and protection. And above all, he needed it from her! She guessed that the poor burn victim simply did not want to, did not give himself the right to torment and burden anyone, and especially her, Larisa, with himself, evoking in her only pity and condescension. He didn't want her to be tied to a disabled man or let her life be stunted by his tragedy. It was enough that tis life was already ruined...

"Gosha, I'm staying here," Larisa stated firmly. "I'm not going anywhere, and not even you can drive me away! We'll make sure you get better! Do you hear me? …Roma, you can go."

Roma nodded and made his way to the door. Suddenly, he turned back:

"Oh, Gosh, I almost forgot—I brought your money! Totally slipped my mind, sorry… Here it is in a little packet—every last coin. See? I'm putting it in the top drawer of your nightstand. If you need anything else, brother, just say the word! I'll do anything for you."

* * *

Larisa kept her word. She tended to Gosha diligently and faithfully all throughout his hospital stay and continued caring for him once he was discharged home after several successful organ-transplant surgeries.

Larisa moved in with him.

Little by little, Gosha stopped feeling embarrassed around her.

He could no longer conceal that he was deeply, wholeheartedly in love with this woman—who, in turn, clearly cared about him. Gosha realised that if they accepted each other just as they were, if they both needed and cherished each other so deeply, then what difference did it make that she was so many years older? And did it matter anymore that he would never be handsome or any sort of "knight in shining armor?"… When love is real, everything else is just a trivial detail.

49

"Good evening, Mr. Nasyrov! This is Bhojwani. How are you?"

"Good evening, Mr. Bhojwani."

"I'm fine, everything's all right. But I have a serious matter to discuss with you, Mr. Nasyrov. Do you have time?"

"Yes, sir. Has something happened?"

"Yes. If you don't mind, let's switch to Skype—I'd prefer we speak 'vis-à-vis,' so we can see each other."

"All right, that's fine."

A few minutes later, they were looking each other in the eye via Skype.

Bhojwani spoke first:

"Mr. Nasyrov, we're both businesspeople, and if you don't mind, I'll skip the lengthy preface. Your necklace is not authentic!"

"Are you saying… How could that be? That's nonsense. After all, everything suggests it belonged to the Kuwaiti sheikh! Are you saying the rubies and diamonds aren't real? I can't believe that!"

Still, Nasyrov knew his Indian friend well enough: he was an honest man who wouldn't lie, not even for a large sum of money.

Bhojwani immediately tried to reassure Murad Nematul-laevich.

"Hold on, Mr. Nasyrov—I didn't say the rubies and diamonds themselves were fake. The point is, no, they're all quite expensive and fairly high-quality stones—believe me. The real issue is that even the largest ruby in the necklace you sent me via Mukhitdin isn't the Temur Ruby. And so this piece is worth much less than that particular one, the original. It's good that I didn't transfer the full amount to you, only an advance, or I'd have suffered significant losses. Though I have no doubt about your honesty and that you'd have returned everything. Do I have that right?"

Nasyrov felt uneasy. The conversation made him uncomfortable—he felt awkward over the situation. But he couldn't afford to lose this friend and partner, so the Uzbek oligarch kept his composure, trying not to show his negative emotions to the Indian, or even feel them if possible.

"Yes, of course, my dear friend," Murad Nasyrov replied courteously after a pause. "If I understand you correctly, you want to return the necklace to me and have me refund your money?"

"Do not hurry, I beg you," Bhojwani said calmly. "I propose this arrangement: first, you try to find for me that very necklace whose centerpiece is the Temur Ruby. If you succeed, I'll return the one I have now, pay extra for the genuine piece, and then, if you agree, we can negotiate the total price of the deal. But if you can't obtain the original with the Temur Ruby, then I'll keep the one you've already sent me—a fine piece—and pay you nothing more. You won't owe me anything either. Agreed?"

"May I ask why you need this, Mr. Bhojwani?"

"I'll tell you. Simply put, I happen to like the appearance of the necklace you sent in exchange for my payment—it's an exquisite piece, crafted by a talented jeweler with taste and refinement. Of course, I'd dearly love to have first and foremost the necklace we've been discussing for all these months. But I have a hunch it may still be safely in the keeping of Sheikh Nasser al-Sabah. And in that case, it might be impossible for us to get hold of it... You see? That's why, if we can't acquire the real one, I'll be content with the piece destiny handed me through you—a perfectly decent variation

on the ruby-and-diamond necklace. What do you say to that?"

Nasyrov hesitated. He had been counting on receiving the second part of Bhojwani's payment! He hadn't expected such a screw up with the jewelry.

"Would you allow me some time to think?" he finally asked.

"Of course. It's your right. But I have another important question."

"I'm listening. I hope it's nothing too serious this time?"

"Well, that depends. You know, Mr. Nasyrov, that I was raised in the Hindu faith, taught to remain calm in all things. But I bear responsibility for everything I own and for everyone placed under my management. My duty compels me to ask you: Mr. Nasyrov, do you know where your son Mukhitdin is right now?"

Murad Nematullaevich was taken aback. That was a strange question—Mukhitdin was supposed to be in Delhi with Bhojwani!

"I'm sorry, I don't quite follow…"

"I see. So he's not with you. The thing is, for several days now, Mukhitdin has disappeared… At first, I didn't want to trouble you unnecessarily. I thought maybe it was some minor confusion, something we could clear up here, that we'd locate your son on our own. But we can't find him anywhere. Are you sure he didn't fly back to Tashkent?"

"No, he didn't come back… Oh my God! I entrusted him to you! I was certain—Hey… Bhojwani, where is my son?!"

"I don't know, my friend," replied the Indian. "But please, don't you worry so… Perhaps he just went off on a trip with friends? It sounded like he was planning to go somewhere; maybe there's no phone coverage there, and he's 'out of network range.'… I need him too—he's been a big help in my business. So why would he leave without telling anyone?"

"Yes, he can be difficult… I'll come to you—tonight, if there's a late flight!"

"For now, I don't think that's necessary, Mr. Nasyrov. What if he's not even in Delhi? You'd just be wasting your time and money. We'll keep looking for him on our end. The moment I have any information about Mukhitdin, I'll let you know immediately!"

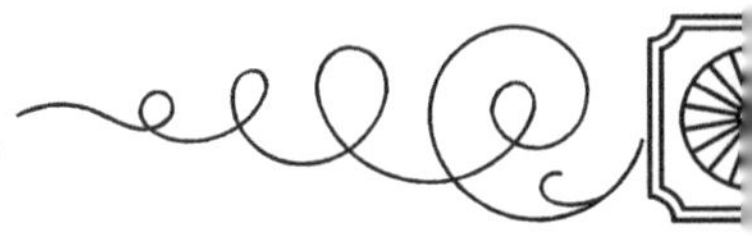

50

Mukhabbat brought ginger tea with honey and lemon to her husband, Abdulla Rustamovich—who now only worked half-days in the office and spent most evenings flat on the couch. The heart attack had really taken its toll.

A loving and attentive wife, she cared for him as much as possible, hoping he would worry less about his aches and the troubles at work—and about his younger son, too. Abdulla Fattakhov couldn't find peace, given Bahadir's detention and the prolonged difficulties with his shipment that had been seriously "stuck" in France—no matter how hard he and his children tried, they still couldn't recover the full order. His only comforts were the two women who meant the world to him: his wife and his daughter. "We'll soon have an adopted granddaughter, too," he thought. "Rano's getting all the paperwork done for the little girl she's taking in…"

Suddenly, the doorbell rang. Mukhabbat gave her husband a questioning look and rushed to answer it. She was surprised, because Rano was already home—exhausted from work and other concerns, she had gone to bed early. And Amin had called to say he was all right and wouldn't be dropping by his parents' place tonight.

Who could it be at ten in the evening?

Mukhabbat opened the door and… gasped, clasping her hands in amazement. Standing on the doorstep was a malnourished, thinly, and pale Bahadir!

"My son!" she cried out in delight. For months, she had only been permitted to see him twice, and then only through glass. The most recent visit was more than a month ago. "You've gotten so thin! My dear boy…"

"Hello, Mama. Let's not make a fuss. I'm fine."

Bahadir stepped into the house at once and gave a firm embrace to his mother, who had flung her arms around his neck.

"Mama, where's Papa? He didn't come to meet me… Is he at home?"

"Yes, yes, he's home. It's just that your father…he mostly has to lie on the couch, you see…"

"What happened?" Bahadir asked anxiously. "Is Father ill?"

"Yes, he's been unwell… But how did you manage to get released?"

"I had some help. I'll tell you later, all right? I want to see Father!"

"Of course, son. Go on in. Just be gentle—don't move too quickly, all right? Your father can't take excitement. His heart…"

Bahadir gave his mother a serious, understanding look. He felt he was very serious about everything now, more than ever before—or so it seemed to him.

But of course, they couldn't avoid agitating Abdulla Rustamovich at least a little. Weakened, unable to rise from the bed, the elder Fattakhov reached out with unsteady arms, hugging Bahadir warmly. That evening, through tears, he could only manage two words a few times: "Son! My son…"

Bahadir stroked his father's back and arms.

"Easy now, Father—it's all right. I'm back. I've been cleared. Dilshoda—Amin's girlfriend—helped me, along with Amin and Rudik. They all fought for me, and hired a lawyer. Everything's fine. They didn't even take it to trial, so in the end, it worked out. And I really am innocent!"

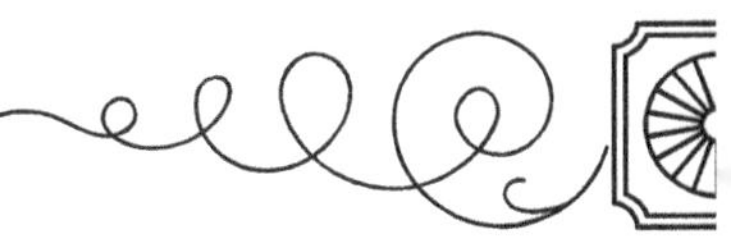

He kept quiet about how hard the lawyer had worked to prove Bahadir had never gambled in any casino—that those rumors were pure fabrication and slander. But what had happened had happened. And having tasted such a bitter lesson, Bahadir had decided, for Malika's sake and for his parents, to abandon his destructive fascination with games of chance forever. He wanted a new life—clean and happy.

He'd planned to ask his mother a question, worried that maybe Amin and Rano had lied to soothe him, telling him what he wanted to hear. But he knew his mother would never lie—she'd be gentle, yet direct, without playing coy.

Finally, Bahadir summoned his courage:

"Mama, has Malika… did she ever call you from Moscow?"

"Of course she called, son!" Mukhabbat answered at once, without the slightest hesitation—so obvious that she couldn't have prepared any special response. "Not just once, or twice, but many times. The poor girl must be spending all her money on phone calls to us! I keep telling her we'll call her back! But still, each day she phones once or twice to ask how you are, how you're holding up. And it can't be easy for her over there! She's working hard… She loves you, like a fool! Got it?"

"Yes, Mama, I understand," her overjoyed son replied, his face lighting up.

"Thank God—life seems to be getting back to normal," Bahadir thought serenely as he lay down to sleep in his parents' warm, bright, cozy home.

51

After Bahadir returned home, Abdulla Rustamovich slowly began to recover. Still, he did not yet have enough strength to work full-time. Meanwhile, business at the company was far from good, and Abdulla Fattakhov understood this. But he hoped his children could somehow "steer" their shared enterprise away from collapse and ruin.

Dilshoda and Amin still planned to marry, yet they had decided to live according to traditions of modest morality, respecting the counsel of their elders and, as proper Uzbeks, not living together before the wedding. They merely met almost every day and spoke on the phone several times daily.

To help Amin, Dilshoda—a capable and promising lawyer specialising in international affairs, with experience in foreign economic structures—came to his office and asked him once again to describe the situation in detail. In her heart, she was absolutely certain that Amin in no way sought to exploit her knowledge or contacts for personal gain—indeed, he had repeatedly offered to find another lawyer and free her from any obligation. Yet the young woman very much wanted to be of use to her fiancé and his family.

Amin invited his brother Bahadir and his sister Rano to his office for the discussion. They both arrived and greeted Amin and Dilshoda.

"So what's the goal of this meeting?" Bahadir asked, immediately indicating how busy he was.

"Both of you know my fiancée is an experienced attorney

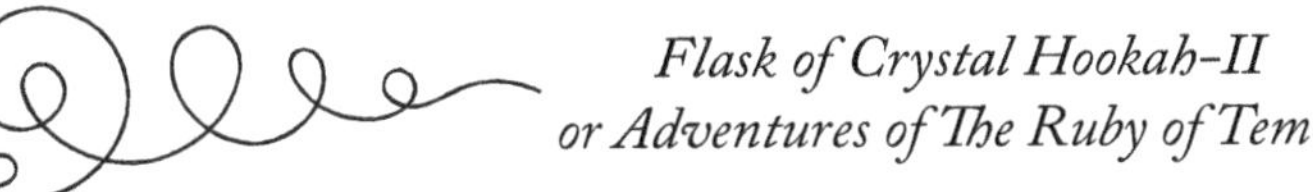

specialising in international 'external' business," Amin replied. "I want to give her a thorough account of all our problems, hear her thoughts, and see how she can help us."

"Forgive me, brother, but my sister and I know well what our problems are," Bahadir countered. "You can briefly fill us in on your plans later. Right now, we have urgent tasks at the firm: we need to ship out another batch of products to the Samarkand branches, and we must keep an eye on that!"

"I need to check all the invoices," Rano added. "That's important."

"Yes, yes, I understand," Amin said, yielding to his siblings. "All right guys, head out and work. I'll update you both afterward."

He turned to Dilshoda.

"We have several problems, my dear," Amin sighed. "I'll start with the first one, which seems most critical right now. The perfume factory in France that was declared bankrupt still hasn't finished producing our goods. Months have passed. So the most sensible option now is to try as quickly as possible to retrieve our money and finish producing our brand at a different factory."

"So, among the items seized by the liquidation committee, there's a brand specific to your company?"

"Yes. My father invested a lot of effort into creating a new men's fragrance called *Avicenna*. It's dedicated to Uzbekistan's cultural heritage!"

"That's wonderful."

"Indeed. But you have no idea how difficult it was to register that name internationally. And the product label says 'Made in France,' which matters to customers and distributors…

"Dilshoda, I won't dive into every detail of our perfume business, but I'll outline the main points you should know to fully understand our situation. Our firm represents world-famous perfume and cosmetic brands on the Uzbek market, as well as skincare products… But that's not our focus right now."

"Yes, Amin, let's discuss the stalled goods shipment. I can tell you that the liquidation committee is the one with authority to grant your firm the official permit allowing you to collect all the ingredients of your perfume products from the bankrupt factory and hand them over to another facility for further production."

"I see. So, the claim wasn't filed in court?"

"No. I submitted a request-claim directly to the Chairman of the liquidation committee, awaiting their reply."

"Got it. Thank you for helping! I really hope that the permit arrives soon, and we can finish producing our products at a different factory… I won't go into how perfume is made in France—fascinating, but a long story…"

"Perhaps someday you can tell me all about it—as a woman who appreciates lovely aromas?"

"Certainly, if you'd like."

"Listen, Amin. Our ambassador to France is an old classmate of mine. I'll try to contact him and ask for assistance. He's extremely busy, and it's really a last-resort idea, but it seems we have no other choice."

"Yes… You know, if I were to recount everything that's happened to us lately, you'd be horrified—especially by the sort of people skilled in cunning deceit, theft, and fraud. Unbelievable things happen! For example, workers at factory warehouses somehow manage to cheat us—and not only us, mind you, though with no offense to 'great Europe' intended!"

"Really? What do they do? Where's the scam?"

"They pack the perfume bottles for clients in such a way that

the large boxes hold fewer items than listed on the invoice. By external appearance and weight, you'd never guess! Only when the goods—sealed and marked in factory pallets for transporting fragile cargo—arrive at our firm's warehouse and we open hundreds of boxes do we discover that nearly every box is short by about 5–7 bottles…."

"How is that possible? That's pure theft!"

"Exactly. Sometimes airport workers—baggage handlers, typically cheap labourers from Southeast Asian countries—open the pallets and, instead of the perfumes, stuff them with heavy stones to match the weight. When the shipment arrives in Tashkent, the pallets look intact, and their weight matches the invoice. Yet inside the boxes, instead of perfume, there are stones… And you can't prove anything to anyone!"

"That's awful… My goodness, you don't live a dull life. This seems like some circus full of tricks and stunts… But you mentioned other problems as well?"

"Ah, yes, there are so many things piling on us! One major part of our shipment from L'Oréal had to go from a Moscow warehouse to Tashkent in container trucks via Kazakhstan. We'd never shipped our goods through Russia and Kazakhstan before, but we thought it might be cheaper… Despite all our years of experience, how could we know we'd 'get burned,' dealing with a shady carrier?"

"'Carrier'? Who was it?"

"A shipping company called *Buibay*. At the initial meetings, the company owner, Ildar, seemed like a very trustworthy person! Unfortunately, our first good impression was mistaken. In the trucks carrying perfumes—which, by contract and plain common sense, must be handled with extreme care—he decided to cut corners by loading his contraband, unregistered medicines as well. So guess what: because of these undeclared meds, the entire shipment got held up at customs. Now Ildar demands a huge sum from us to get them to drop the case quickly."

"That's blatant daylight robbery!"

"Exactly. I haven't told Father anything about this because of his heart condition—he's already had one heart attack, and another blow would be too much… But I'm worried: the company is taking a serious financial hit!"

"Amin, I assume you didn't sign a formal contract with these truckers? It was just a verbal agreement and trust?"

"Yes. But we never sign contracts with forwarding companies—only arrange insurance. Who could've expected this outcome…?"

"Wow, that's complicated. Still, I've got a couple of influential contacts in Kazakhstan. If they can't help, we'll look for other options—pursue it in court with lawyers, and in the meantime try to cover the merchandise cost with insurance."

"What are you talking about? … Insurance payouts can take years! I'm at the end of my rope. I feel desperate."

"No, no—don't let it get to you! You are not alone. You've got your brother and sister… I'm here too… So don't lose heart, don't give up! I believe in you, my dear. You're strong and capable. With God's help, you'll overcome every obstacle, solve every problem, and come out on top!"

"Thank you, my love. I can't help remembering these lines by the poet Nasir Khusraw:

> *'The notion that money buys all things*
> *Holds true only to a point…*
> *With money you can buy all things,*
> *But never love or happiness!'*

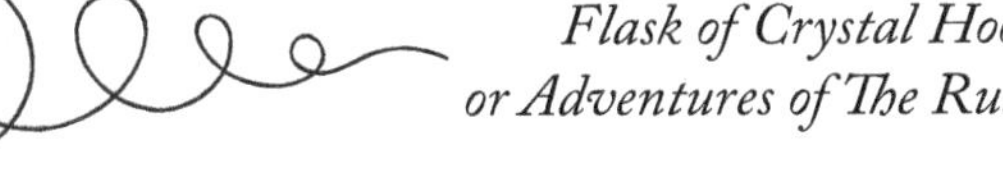 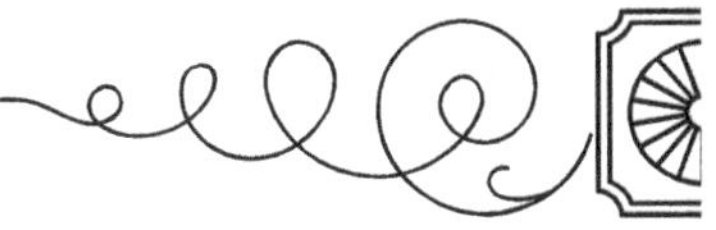

"And know, my dear, that now every one of your problems is mine, too. And together—well, we're surely invincible."

"I'm so glad, Dilshoda, that I have you and that you're by my side…"

52

Sitora had an idea—she decided to purchase a shipment of fabrics for her collections from India, a country famous for its outstanding fibers and weaving mills.

Of course, Sitora already knew that India primarily produced fabrics from cotton and linen—both grown in abundance there—as well as cashmere wool. She knew that, in various parts of India, weavers had long practiced embroidery, and around the eleventh century began embroidering with gold thread, later with silver and silk. The motifs for these embroideries were often drawn from nature, especially flowers and birds, or from mythology and legend.

About a week after the event that made the entire family happy—her son-in-law Bahadir's return home—Malika's mother flew to Delhi. Naturally, she had phoned ahead to representatives of several weaving mills whose products she had seen and read about on their websites. These mills were expecting her arrival.

After visiting two mills, Sitora bought natural linen fabrics, but she still couldn't find what she needed most: top-grade cashmere and a bit of Indian damask, a silk fabric of Chinese origin. Though these were listed on the mills' websites, it turned out that large consignments of those fabrics had recently been sold, and they were now preparing to produce new lots, which would require waiting at least a week.

Sitora did not have that kind of time—she couldn't leave her family and business for so long. She only regretted that her dear daughter Malika was currently away, in Russia, at the competition.

But Sitora accepted this forced separation, knowing it was necessary for her daughter's future happiness and artistic growth.

Since she had not found everything she needed at the two mills, Sitora called a third one with which she had not made arrangements beforehand while she was still in Tashkent. As it sometimes happens in life, a strange twist of fate subject to God's will carried her…right to a mill owned by none other than… Raj Singh Bhojwani.

A man named Ajit, the sales manager, answered the phone. He warmly invited her to visit the mill in person and pick whatever she fancied, promising they would negotiate prices when they met.

Sitora confirmed her visit for that same day, and there she was greeted by a very hospitable Ajit.

The lady from Uzbekistan needn't worry at all! One thing Ajit could say right away: if she purchased a large shipment, Mr. Bhojwani's company would offer her a significant discount. All the more so because it seemed Mr. Bhojwani had some very friendly ties with her country…

No, thank you—the lady wasn't tired and would like to see the products immediately. Yes, indeed, she had heard something about the "Bhojwani" brand but had never personally met the trendsetter of modern Indian fashion, nor had she seen his collections in person. Moreover, she was pleasantly surprised that his company also produced fabrics of the highest caliber. Did they currently have the quantity of cashmere and Indian kamka she needed?

Yes, absolutely. The lady would be satisfied…

Sitora really did like everything at the mill. The fabrics were simply magnificent. She bought several smaller rolls and also paid for their delivery to the storage lockers at the airport.

There was one surprise: in one of the factory's workshops, she thought she overheard an employee mention the Uzbek name "Mukhitdin." But she had no time to ask him who that might be— was it a countryman of hers, or did India also have such names? She was already expected for an appointment—by none other than Mr. Bhojwani himself.

The Indian businessman and fashion designer cordially invited Sitora to sit on a sofa and offered her some coffee. She thanked him.

"Mrs. Mumtazoff, it's a pleasure to meet you!" Bhojwani beamed. "I love Uzbekistan, and long ago I visited your country. It's truly a wonderful land! I even have a friend who lives in your capital—he's also a businessman. Granted, not in weaving or design, but a different field… Anyway, that's not important. I just wanted to say I'm very happy you came, and it's an honor for me to receive you here at the company office. By the way, your English is quite good."

"You're very kind, sir. Thank you for your compliments. Many businesspeople in my country now speak English. As for my visit to you, I should say it's an honour for me as well—to be here and get acquainted with you."

"Thank you, my lady. I'm flattered. Pardon me, but could I ask how long you've been in fashion? I'm only asking because judging by the fabrics you've chosen and by the particular models of mine that, according to my managers, caught your eye—and about which you gave verbal comments—it seems you have an exceptional, refined sense of taste!"

"Thank you, sir," Sitora responded, heartened by this compliment from a luminary of the fashion world. "Yes, I've been in the business for over ten years. Of course, that's enough time to gain some experience, and though fashion is considered unpredictable,

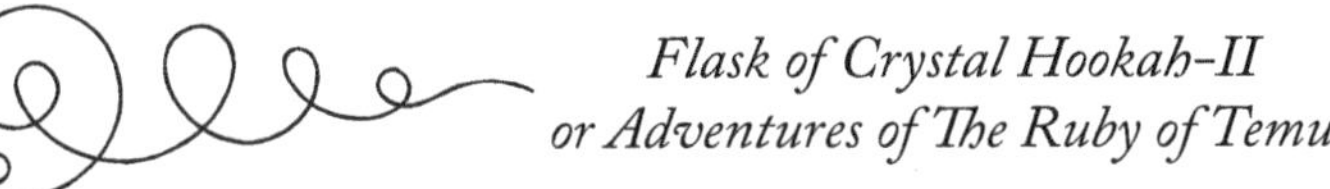
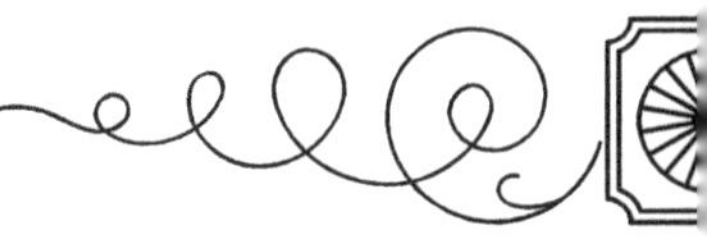

I still believe I have a clear idea of what I want and what I need for my future work. Like you, I appreciate classic business attire for both men and women—everything strict, graceful, and elegant."

"Splendid, my dear lady, truly commendable! I'm only surprised we haven't met yet at international exhibitions. Why is that?"

"Mr. Bhojwani, you're a master of fabric creation and haute couture, while I work in the prêt-à-porter segment."

"I see. But have you never wanted to branch into high fashion? I'm certain you'd do remarkably well!"

"No, that's not for me…although one should never say never…"

"Absolutely! And I'd always be willing to help you however I can."

"Thank you, Mr. Bhojwani—that's wonderful to hear!"

"Would you like me to show you one of my latest designs, which hardly anyone has seen yet? It's a *habit de fête* dress, or as you say, an 'evening out' gown. I'll let you in on a secret—there's a very unusual and expensive accessory on it. But you'll see for yourself in just a moment!"

"I'd love to," Sitora exclaimed, even more delighted by the company owner's trust and friendliness.

Bhojwani made a quick phone call to his assistant, and while they were bringing the dress, the two designers continued chatting over coffee about their profession.

When they brought in the mannequin with the "evening" dress, Sitora glanced at it and…nearly fainted from astonishment! Its "accessory" was… none other than the very necklace with rubies and diamonds that Firuz-begim Fatima al-Nahayan had presented and that had been passed on to Sitora via her husband Said by the Kuwaiti sheikh!

"My lady, what's the matter?" Bhojwani exclaimed in surprise, seeing her unusual reaction.

"Forgive me, sir… But…may I know where you got… that necklace?"

"Oh! It came from Uzbekistan. A friend of mine—yes, that same businessman I mentioned—sold it to me. It's quite a fascinating piece, wouldn't you say? You like it, yes?"

"The thing is, Mr. Bhojwani…this necklace is mine—or rather, it belongs to our family! My husband actually has documents proving it. There can be no mistake, because I recognise that large ruby so well—it strongly resembles the famed Temur Ruby…"

"Yes indeed, it does… My, my… What a story! My lady, somehow I believe you. Although strictly speaking, I should ask you for that ownership document for this remarkable jewelry piece…"

"Please believe me, the document exists—authentic, bearing the signature and seal of Mr. Al-Sabah himself, the Sheikh of Kuwait. I have it in my phone's photo gallery—look, here!"

"No need, I have said, I believe you even without it… But just how my buddy Mr. Nasyrov has deceived me!"

"Excuse me, did you say…Nasyrov?! You mean Murad Nasyrov, owner of that chain of cafés and restaurants? Are you talking about him?…"

"Well, yes, that's ri… But how do you know? Do you know him? I thought Tashkent had millions of inhabitants, and not all of them know each other!"

"Of course. Nonetheless, I know Nasyrov well—and have known him for quite some time. One more apology—just to clarify, Mr. Bhojwani: so he gave you this necklace? Presumably as a gift?"

"No, he sold it to me, at a high price. Money's not really the issue, though. I admired the craftsmanship… I couldn't have known that the piece, as you say, is yours…"

"Yes, it belongs to my daughter—or our family, in general… But now what do we do? You paid a fair sum for it! And now I can't ask you to return it…"

"No need to ask—take it, my lady, it's yours! I won't allow a wonderful woman like you to be humiliated by begging or pleading."

"Sir, honestly, I don't know how to thank you. You're an incredible person! We spent so long searching for it, even involving an investigator, and as a result someone—my own… But that's not important. Thank you so very much!"

"Think nothing of it. All is well."

With a swift, practiced motion of a fashion designer's hand, Bhojwani removed the necklace from the dress and handed it to Sitora.

"The only thing I find puzzling, my lady, is how Mr. Nasyrov got hold of it in the first place. Did he steal it from you?"

"I'd dearly like to know that, too… But anyway, Mr. Bhojwani, I thank you from the bottom of my heart! I'll send you the ownership certificate today by mail…"

"Excellent."

On the flight from Delhi to Tashkent, Sitora suddenly remembered she had forgotten to declare the expensive necklace. Yet for some reason, the customs officers hadn't stopped her.

"How wonderful!" she thought. "Although, it's somewhat odd…"

53

Roma had become a sort of "headquarters" go-between or unintentional informer not only for Misha Leonidov but also for… Mukhitdin.

For many months—ever since Murad Nasyrov's only son went to India for an internship—Mukhitdin rarely called or wrote to his old friends, Roma and Gosha, and even more rarely responded to their calls or messages. Now, he had decided to call Roma himself.

After a few words of greeting, Mukhitdin, purely as a formality, asked how Gosha was doing. When Roma told him what had happened to Gosha—that he'd been badly burned in a fire—Mukhitdin abruptly changed the subject, saying only:

"Well, nothing to be done. Let's hope he recovers."

Though Roma, who was generally good at not holding deep grudges against anyone, could more or less accept that Mukhitdin had been absent from their lives for so long, he was taken aback by the cold indifference with which the boss's son reacted to Gosha's plight. He felt offended on Gosha's behalf.

What bothered him even more was the moment he realised—just two minutes into the conversation—that the real reason Mukhitdin had called was not to hear about his friends' fates but only to ask for news about his ex-girlfriend, Malika.

"You remember her, right, Roma? I used to talk about her a lot."

"You're talking about the one who got married almost half a year ago?" Roma clarified.

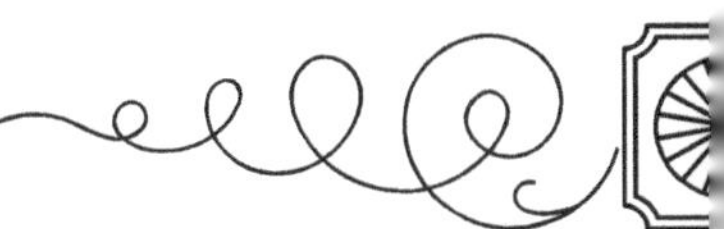

"Well…yeah," Mukhitdin grudgingly confirmed.

"Of course I remember her. You showed us her photo. It's hard to forget such a pretty girl. The word is she's doing fine. Her husband was apparently detained for something—he ended up in pretrial detention—but he's been released. They're living normally, maybe even well. Oh, and I recall overhearing something! Your father mentioned to someone that she's in Moscow right now, taking part in some prestigious singing contest that'll be shown on the First TV Channel. But sorry, that's all I know about her…"

"Got it. Well, that's something."

"So, Mukhitdin, should I at least pass on your regards to Gosha from you?"

"Yeah, sure, pass it along. All right, that's all. Bye."

And with that, deciding there was nothing more to be said, he hung up.

* * *

Sitora crossed the threshold of her home feeling satisfied and happy. She was delighted that their family heirloom had finally been found and that, by some quirk of fate, she herself had brought it back!

Said Yahyaevich had wanted to pick her up from the airport himself, but unfortunately his back had acted up badly—so he sent a driver from the clinic. And now Said, hobbling because of radiculitis, came out to the gate to greet his beloved wife, hugging and kissing her warmly.

Sitora went to see her great-grandmother a bit later. Firuz-begim hadn't managed to come out and welcome her great-granddaughter; nowadays, she more and more often lay on her couch, covered with warm kurpachas. Their meeting, too, was wonderful. The only thing that surprised Sitora was that Firuz-begim showed no real excitement at the jewel's recovery and return.

"She's becoming indifferent to everything," Firuz-begim's great-granddaughter thought sadly. "unfortunately, it's clear that our dear granny really has grown very old…"

The husband and wife talked over dinner and tea till almost midnight. Suddenly Said said:

"Forgive me, my dear—but would you let me see that ruby necklace again? I only got a glimpse of it today. Just think how much unwanted trouble it caused our family! They nearly put Bahadir away for years… And of course, the boy wasn't to blame! I was wrong to hurt our daughter Malika with my suspicions. But all right—thank goodness all that's in the past! I've heard many a time that rubies, in general, bring power and wealth, happiness and good fortune. So I figure our troubles were temporary, maybe not even caused by them at all. Now everything should be just fine for us! Will you show it to me?"

"Of course," Sitora replied, beaming with a smile.

She took the jewelry out of her cosmetic bag and handed it to her husband.

Said Yahyaevich lifted it gingerly, a mysterious sense of excitement welling up inside him as he admired it. Then suddenly… he turned to his wife in astonishment, eyes wide.

"Sitora, excuse me—where did you say you got this piece?"

"Well, how so? It was kindly returned to me by an Indian fashion designer, now my business partner—Mr. Bhojwani. He said someone recently sold it to him. Why?"

"Sold it??? Who? Look—this is a total fake, worth maybe twenty or thirty thousand som at best."

"Please, don't be kidding like, Said!" Sitora gasped, clutching at her heart.

"I'm not joking at all. Look closely! Besides the fact that the rubies obviously aren't star rubies, they're not even genuine. I, for example, can see it clearly. You would have noticed too if you'd examined it without rushing… My wife, I'm afraid your Delhi partner didn't treat you very nicely."

"I can't believe it! He couldn't have… You see, dear, he's actually a reputable, well-known man. And incredibly wealthy, a millionaire. Why would he do this?"

"I don't know. I can't be certain… In any case, this is definitely not our necklace. It's a fake."

So that's why Firuz-begim reacted that way… Sitora remembered.

"Yes, now I can see it myself. But how strange this is, my dear husband! Maybe Mr. Bhojwani himself was deceived?"

"That's possible… All right, I'll have to ask some of my contacts to help find our treasure. Actually, I've already told one pretty influential person about it. Let's see if he's discovered anything."

Sitora tensed up involuntarily. Some woman's intuition, deep in her subconscious, told her it might be someone not so good—or entirely trustworthy.

"Who is that person, Said?"

"Oh, my dear wife, please don't clutter your mind with this stuff! Don't be upset. I'll handle it myself, all right? And I promise: we will definitely find our—or rather, Malika's—necklace! Go get some rest. I'm sure you have to go back to work tomorrow."

"How do you know?"

"Are you kidding? In over twenty years, I've learned everything about my wife—this incorrigible workaholic!" said Said Yahyaevich

with a fond smile.

The next morning, waking up earlier than usual, the head of the household made a phone call from his room so as not to disturb her and so she wouldn't inadvertently overhear.

"Yes, hello?" came a brisk voice on the other end.

"Murad Nematullaevich, good morning. This is Doctor Mumtazov."

"Ah, my friend! Good to hear you. How are you?" Nasyrov replied.

"Honestly, not so great. At least our son-in-law's been released."

"I'm glad—very glad for him and for you."

"Yes, thank you. But there's still the other matter you promised to help me with. Remember? Finding our family necklace with the rubies and diamonds."

"Yes, yes, I recall something of the sort. Sorry, I've been snowed under with business! Problems piling up too…"

"So you can't help?"

"Why not? I'll give it a try. Have you seen or heard anything about a piece resembling yours since then?"

"Well, my wife brought back a very similar one from Delhi. Only it turned out to be a blatant fake, and quite a cheap one at that. Not a single genuine stone. But we need our actual piece, because it's a memento of certain people and events important to our family!"

"Yes, I understand your situation and sympathise…"

"And then, Mr. Nasyrov, think about it: what significance would any other, even if similar, piece hold for us? We need ours!"

"Yes, correct. All right, Said Yahyaevich—I'll see what I can find out through my channels: if anyone's seen a necklace fitting your description. I'll get the police involved, too."

"But maybe the police—that might not be necessary?" recalled Said Yahyaevich nervously, remembering recent events.

"Don't worry, I have my own people there. Everything will be fine!" Nasyrov assured him calmly.

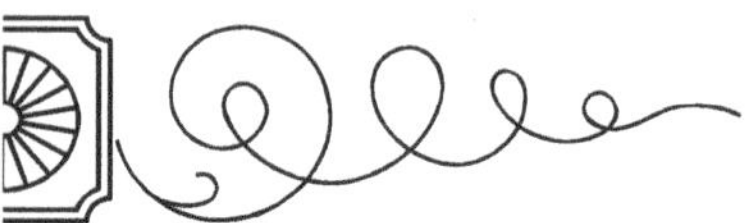

54

Jagir (a feudal holding) of Hisar Feroz, 1613

Arjumand struggled to recover from the loss of her first child, Khuralnissa—a name given when she was laid to rest in the earth. Even the comfort of the cozy room of the princess, in the palace once granted by Padishah Jahangir to his beloved son Shah Jahan, did little to ease her physical and emotional suffering and pain.

Shah Jahan frequently visited her, and during these visits they would talk. In his presence she strove to appear strong, sometimes even joking and laughing—she did not wish to upset him. She understood that even a husband who loves with all his heart might soon grow weary of a perpetually tearful, distraught, and sorrowful wife. A man, after all, has his own troubles.

Meanwhile, Shah Jahan called for his physician, Rashid-khon. The doctor observed that the prince was clearly not in good spirits.

"My servant told me that my wife was deliberately poisoned! Tell me, Rashid-khon, what made you conclude that her poor condition—and the loss of our child—is due to poison?"

"Your Highness, I was the one who examined Princess Arjumand! The symptoms she displays, and the state of her blood, can only result from a large dose of rat poison."

"You mean to say that my beloved might have died?"

"Alas, that is so, Shahzade," the elderly doctor sighed heavily.

"Such wretched, insignificant scum around us! Do they not understand that I am the son of the Great Moghul, ruler of this entire empire, heir to the throne, and that I can wipe them from the face of the earth? Do you know, or perhaps suspect, Rashid-khon, who dared commit this act? For I will find him, whether they are buried in the earth or hidden in the heavens! I will find them and punish them."

"Remember, not long ago when misfortune struck and your daughter died, I traveled to Agra to fetch special remedies for Princess Arjumand? When I returned, I reported that your father, Padishah Jahangir—may Allah bless him—had summoned me to his palace…"

"Yes, I was surprised that you stayed so long on that trip."

"The Padishah wished to know in detail what had occurred, for the news of the tragedy in the family of Prince Shah Jahan had reached his ears. However, I did not mention my suspicions concerning poison. But when, in passing, I mentioned that Princess Arjumand was gravely ill and exceedingly weak, your first wife, Kandahari-begim—who, at that time, was in the palace with Mehrun-Nissa's harem—became very joyful and radiant, as if I had delivered some wonderful news. Then, I, your humble servant, took the liberty of conveying my suspicions to His Majesty. Padishah Jahangir was incensed and ordered his servants, without explaining anything to anyone, to call everyone out into the palace garden. Afterward, the padishah's attendants meticulously searched every room—even the private chambers of your family members—to see if anyone had hidden any poison among their personal effects."

For a moment, Rashid-khon fell silent, uncertain whether he should reveal the entire truth to Shah Jahan.

"Come now—don't keep me in suspense! Who turned out to be the culprit?!" Shah Jahan couldn't hold it in anymore.

"The servants of the ruler found poison in the quarters… of

Kandahari-begim, your eldest wife," the doctor answered.

At these words, Shah Jahan was beside himself with anger and fury.

… A few days later, after arriving in Agra, Shah Jahan dissolved his marriages with his first two wives—he had come to understand that even Par-Parkhiz might pose a threat to Arjumand. Besides, he had no need for her either. In accordance with the law, he pronounced the word "divorce" three times before each of them, sending Kandahari-begim back empty-handed to her parents in Kandahar, while Par-Parkhiz was allowed to return to her family, albeit with lavish gifts.

Henceforth, nothing further endangered the life or health of Shah Jahan's beloved—and now sole—wife, Arjumand.

* * *

Province of Rajasthan, Ajmer, 1614

Jahangir wished to celebrate his army's victory in Mewar with grandeur, so Shah Jahan and Arjumand had come to Ajmer. While they waited here for the Padishah's arrival with his royal retinue, Arjumand gave birth to the baby Jahanara—conceived in Hisar Feroz, as if the Almighty had granted a splendid, glorious substitute for the first child who had hastily departed this world.

In the Darghah Mosque, Shah Jahan offered thanks to Allah both for his victory over the Mewar princes and for the birth of his beloved daughter. Yet Arjumand's heart was heavy, for Jahanara was a girl—not a boy—and that meant she would never be destined for the throne. Even as the daughter of a prince, she would be denied the right to an education in the future. What could one say about

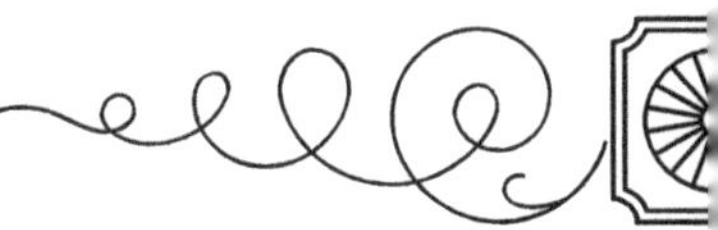

common, non-noble girls! Such were the laws: all rights belonged solely to men, and, alas, nothing could be changed…

Unwilling to remain in the confines of the small city fortress, the Padishah pitched his tent on the shore of Lake Sagar.

"We have gathered here to mark one joyous occasion: my dear son, Shah Jahan Bahadur, has brought us good news," proclaimed Jahangir. "I have secured a great victory over the lords of Mewar! They have bowed their heads before me—the ruler of Hindustan—and now, without doubt, these lands are mine!"

"What is it that displeases you?" sneered Mehrun-Nissa, noticing Arjumand's downcast expression. "Everyone already understands that this victory was won by Shah Jahan. But do not forget that everything in this empire belongs to my husband—and in every war and battle he may count himself the true victor!"

Of course, Arjumand's aunt had already made it known to everyone that sending Shah Jahan to Mewar was her personal, great achievement.

Meanwhile, Jahangir continued:

"Shah Jahan has been entrusted with our highest confidence and the honor of leading our army on campaign, fighting to strengthen our dominion." Then he cast a look at all present, a look filled with solemn importance. "Therefore, I hereby bestow upon him a new military title and grant him permission to wear the red turban reserved for the heir to the throne!"

Father and son embraced warmly. Shah Jahan felt proud and pleased—especially by the heartfelt affection shown by his father.

"Now, surely—Shahriyar will never be the future Padishah!" he thought.

***

Hisar Feroz, the same year.

"Arjumand, my dear, what have you done with the precious necklace that was given to you at our wedding?" Shah Jahan asked in surprise. "What is this? Did you attach the beautiful Temur Ruby to my red turban of the heir? … But why?"

"Because, my beloved, that great stone will bring you luck, glory, and power," Arjumand replied calmly.

"Do you truly believe that?"

"Of course! I believe in the power of this ruby, and I believe in you, my Padishah…"

The life of Arjumand and Shah Jahan in Hisar Feroz was peaceful and prosperous. The lovers relished a respite from the intrigues of the Padishah's court. While Shah Jahan had grown accustomed to courtly life, Arjumand had never been able to accept or understand it. Therefore, she was happy to live in her husband's jagir—a place of honour for any Shahzade, as only the heirs to the throne resided there.

Arjumand loved her husband boundlessly, passionately, and sincerely, and she strove to be near him as often as possible. He, too, loved her and was always delighted by her company. Their meetings were not merely for intimate pleasures; they found joy simply in being together—whether sitting in silence or discussing everything under the sun.

Everything was perfect—until… one day, the heir's turban of the empire, the red turban adorned with a beautiful red ruby, mysteriously disappeared!

It was completely unclear where it could have gone. All the

servants and any possible witnesses were questioned. The heir's turban had vanished, as if it had never existed at all…

Yet, just three days later, it reappeared in the Shahzade's room—exactly where the prince had left it last. Strangely enough, the precious Temur Ruby was still in its place! This odd incident Shah Jahan called "pure mysticism," the interference of unclean forces, and very soon everyone completely forgot about it.

***

There, 1615.

At last, he was born—a son, the heir!!! Padishahzade Sultan Muhammad Dara Shikoh… He was a fair-skinned, smiling, remarkable boy in every way. Arjumand even felt as though giving birth to him had caused her hardly any pain at all. Such a light and lovely infant, whose very arrival filled his parents with indescribable joy! He had Shah Jahan's eyes and Arjumand's tender skin.

The mother of Dara refused to entrust her son to wet nurses—who would consider feeding the prince a great honor and receive handsome rewards and an esteemed position in the harem. Yet Arjumand feared that through the nurses' milk, their very nature, their character might seep into the child's soul; so she chose to nurse her first son herself.

Shah Jahan soon entered and kissed the baby, inadvertently tickling his little face with his beard. Dara smiled warmly.

"He is my heir forever!!!" declared the prince, beaming with joy. Carefully, he placed his son back into his cradle and then asked, "And you, my dear, how are you feeling? Are you in any pain?"

"Thank you, I'm very well," Arjumand replied, her face lighting up. She hardly wished to acknowledge her own ailments. "But… you know, my love, what troubles me is…"

"What is it? Speak, dear! If there's anything I can do for you, I will do it without hesitation."

"No, I'm not speaking of myself right now," Arjumand said thoughtfully as she caressed Shah Jahan's face. "I know my aunt Mehrun-Nissa very well. She will scarcely be able to come to terms with the fact that she now shines in the full glow of your glory. Yes, she still possesses the Mur-Uzak—the seal of the Padishah— which grants her great power even now. Yet she may be frightened for her future… When the Almighty eventually takes the soul of your father, Padishah Jahangir, and when you, Shah Jahan, ascend the throne in his stead, what will become of her? Will she be cast out—or… for then she will no longer be able to rule the country and hold sway over all!"

"You are right, my dear Arjumand," he agreed. "Moreover, I believe she is afraid that my servants might kill her as my rival! But… fear not, I will not do such a thing. After all, she is your own blood. When you next see her, you can soothe her."

…Meanwhile, as unrest once again broke out on the Deccan Plateau—disturbances that, even since the time of Akbar, had subsided only briefly—Mehrun-Nissa, whom Jahangir had dubbed "Nur Mahal" (Light of the Palace) and "Nur Jahan" (Light of the World), hatched a dark scheme. Without a moment's hesitation, she suggested to her husband Jahangir the name of the one who should ride out to war against the enraged, rebellious princes of the Deccan.

That name was—Shah Jahan…

* * *

Hisar Feroz, Deccan Plateau, 1616

Arjumand was in her quarters, unable to calm her worries. She was pregnant again and not feeling well. And yet, she had absolutely no desire to be separated even briefly from her beloved! But she simply didn't have the strength to go with him…

"You act like a child," she scolded her husband seriously, "treating war as if it were just some entertaining game. You get swept up in the thrill of battle and sometimes forget altogether that it can take your life once and for all! I'm afraid for you…"

"Don't be afraid, my love! Understand that on the battlefield, everyone must constantly see their commander and so I must be in the front lines! Otherwise, the army will waver, and the soldiers will scatter. Of course, fighting in the Deccan will be no easy task, but I know I'll return victorious. You'll see: all will be well. Just take care of yourself and our children."

In the end Arjumand did follow Shah Jahan to the Deccan. Her husband had not yet returned from the battlefield when she gave birth to another son—Shah Shuja. Exhausted by childbirth, the wife of Shah Jahan placed the newborn in the care of wet nurses.

No one—no one but Arjumand—had expected that Shah Jahan would emerge from that grueling Deccan campaign not merely alive and well, but triumphant!

* * *

1617

Mehrun-Nissa no longer regarded Arjumand as an ally the way she once had, having realised that her niece would not submit unconditionally in all things to the aunt who ruled in place of the Padishah. So the Padishah's wife came up with a sinister plan to sow discord between Arjumand and Shah Jahan.

"The best way to accomplish this," Mehrun-Nissa thought, "is by foisting another wife on the prince! Of course, he won't listen to me on this matter—or on anything else. But he would not dare refuse his father. So once again, we'll do it through Jahangir."

And the outcome was that Shah Jahan found himself with another wife—Hasina-begim, daughter of Nawab Shah Nawaz Khan Bahadur, granddaughter of the Subahdar of Gujarat, Nawab-Mirza Abdur-Rahim Khan.

When Arjumand heard of this, she nearly died from sorrow, pain, and jealousy.

Her burden was eased only when, on his very first wedding night, Shah Jahan went not to his new wife Hasina's quarters, but rather into Arjumand's!

"My dear, that marriage was merely to satisfy Father," he whispered tenderly in her ear, holding her tight and showering her with warm kisses. "But I have always loved you, I love you now, and I will love you forever!"

* * *

Agra, 1618

It was a great relief for Arjumand to leave the stifling heat of the Deccan behind and return to the cool, familiar city of Agra.

"Why do you keep getting pregnant endlessly?" asked Mehrun-Nissa with mild irritation after the two women exchanged the usual family hugs. Both concealed that chill in their relationship, especially on the side of the Padishah's wife. "Look, your belly is round again, like a pumpkin. Why do you have to be in bed with your insatiable husband so often? Couldn't you at least occasionally refuse him? For instance, I lie with Jahangir no more than once a month! Seems like you must really enjoy those carnal pleasures, hmm? And as for him—what a strange nature, his fertility is like some prized bull…"

"Please, Aunt, don't speak that way about Shah Jahan! After all, he is a prince, and I love him dearly."

"Oh, go ahead and love him, who's stopping you? But I dislike that you stopped singing and playing your instrument a long time ago… And then—why must you follow him wherever he goes? It's so hard for you! You even hurried off after him to the far-off Deccan and war! While pregnant! What a whim…"

"We swore never to part from each other, so we can't go back on our promi—"

"Swore, they did… So what? And how many times will you give birth? I feel sorry for you—you're not looking well, you've put on weight, you have circles under your eyes. All right, let's leave that. One more thing I want to say, girl: you've been doing too much charity for the poor. Why? Don't you think you're overstepping yourself? You're not the Padishah! Think over my words."

Arjumand lowered her head—she did not want to quarrel with a relative, though of course, Mehrun-Nissa was neither her mother nor her father, nor should she be giving her such orders. And the truth was, Arjumand did still sing and play—but only for her husband…

The grand ceremony was held in the reception hall, the Diwan-i-Am.

"My son, I congratulate you on our glorious victory in the Deccan and present you with the title of 'Shah Sultan Khurram Bahadur,'" announced a pleased Padishah Jahangir as he approached Shah Jahan and kissed him. "Do you like this title? The Deccanis now fear us and desire peace. And look, our treasury is overflowing—the entire Deccan is paying me tribute!"

The Padishah clapped his hands. A servant came over, and he ordered him to bring a tray heaped with precious stones. Scooping some up with his fingers, Jahangir showered Shah Jahan with them—diamonds, rubies, pearls, sapphires, emeralds—as if with sand. This was *darshan*, a blessing from father to son and an expression of his love.

"I also give you my most prized item—the very first copy of my book, the *Tuzuk-i-Jahangiri*! Value it, my boy. Perhaps you won't like everything in it. But I was honest and truthful, and I'm proud of that! Incidentally, it says quite a bit about you in there as well."

"Thank you, Father, for this honour and trust!" Shah Jahan replied, brimming with delight.

"So why is there a worthless piece of glass on your noble red turban?" sneered Mehrun-Nissa at the heir prince.

Shah Jahan bristled. He could barely restrain himself in front of his father and the crowd so as not to snap back.

"What do you mean, Mehrun-Nissa?" he asked very quietly, so none of the onlookers could hear.

"I mean your turban—haven't you noticed? It hasn't been your real turban for quite some time now! And that isn't the Temur Ruby on it, but a cheap imitation…"

Indeed, Mehrun-Nissa had managed to spoil Shah Jahan's celebration.

"But…did she spoil it—or my Arjumand?" the prince wondered morosely.

When Shah Jahan was finally alone with his wife, he could not hold back:

"How could you? Why did you attach a worthless stone to my red turban in place of the precious Temur Ruby? Maybe in truth you switched my turban recently as vengeance for my marriage to Hasina? But you know perfectly well I only married her at Father's insistence. I don't even go to her quarters! Why have you disgraced me before everyone? You've turned me into a laughingstock! I looked like a foolish boy."

"My darling, please, darling—" Arjumand felt deeply hurt by her husband's accusations, by his doubts about her, but she did not want to reproach him. "I swear I did nothing wrong. I attached the genuine Temur Ruby to your turban!"

"Are you sure? You're not lying?.. Strange. Forgive me if I'm wrong. I'm upset not so much about the turban itself, though it is important to me, but rather at the dishonor I felt. Those shameful jibes from your aunt… But where, then, has my turban with the ruby gone?"

"So that means it really was swapped for another one? But who? and why?!"

"I suspect, wife, that if Mehrun-Nissa knows all about it, then most likely it was done on her orders. Or at least with her knowledge! And the motive is clear: to pass on what belongs to me as heir to someone else…"

Yet life carried on, and Arjumand bore another Shahzade. Shah Jahan named him Muhy-ud-Din Muhammad Aurangzeb. For some reason, Shah Jahan never cared for him—he paid him little attention, giving all his fatherly affection only to his "true heir," Dara…

* * *

1619

"Rashid-khon, I beg you, please give me some sort of healing elixir!" Arjumand was close to tears. "All these frequent pregnancies have worn me down. I'm exhausted…"

"I can give it to you, Princess," the physician sighed, "but your health, already fragile, will be further undermined. It would be even harder for me to treat you afterward."

Still, she insisted, and the physician gave her the elixir. It did help Arjumand… but only for a short while. Indeed, her health deteriorated. Yet she could not refuse her husband when he sought closeness with her.

And so one day, when Shah Jahan came to her, excited and aflame with desire for her, she—feeling very ill—softly asked him to leave her alone.

The husband betrayed no reaction, but he was hurt. That very night, he went to Hasina's quarters…

Within a few months, Hasina gave birth to Shah Jahan's son—Shahzade Sultan Jahan Afruz…

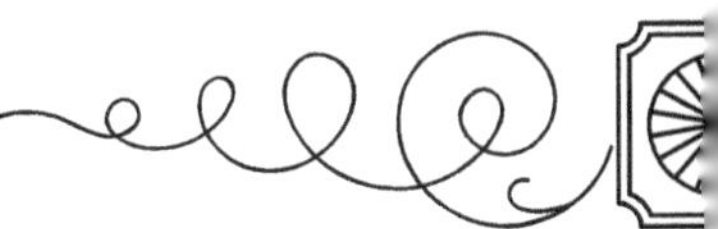

And after some time, Arjumand—who had not yet fully recovered from her previous births and pregnancies and who managed to become pregnant a little after Hasina, because she never denied him again—gave birth to her next shahzade – Sultan Umid Bakhsh.

***

Agra, 1621

A messenger brought Arjumand sad news: her beloved grandfather, "Pillar of the State" Giyas Beg, had died. Arjumand was terribly upset.

Shah Jahan and Arjumand immediately set out for Agra.

Arjumand's father, Asaf Khan, and his sister, Mehrun-Nissa—both having lost their father—held each other tightly, doing their best to console one another. Giyas Beg had been a steadfast support to his daughter, and now she feared that without him, her influence on the Padishah—and thus her power in the empire—would diminish significantly...

Mehrun-Nissa's daughter, Ladilli, who in childhood had been friends with Arjumand and still regarded her like a sister, invited her over.

Uncharacteristically for the usually reserved Ladilli, she burst into tears.

"What's wrong, little sister?" Arjumand asked, quickly getting up and gently patting Ladilli's head in concern.

"Mother is marrying me off to that wretched man—Shahryar! Maybe you don't know, but at court they call him Na-Shudari, 'The Worthless One.'"

"What?! You can't be serious! That's dreadful..."

"Arjumand, please speak to my mother, explain everything! I love someone else. I don't want to marry that hideous prince-bastard!"

Arjumand lowered her head. Even if she wanted to, she could not defend herself or her husband in front of Mehrun-Nissa, let alone Ladilli… The poor girl, timid since childhood, would never dare speak against her mother's wishes; she would endure in silence.

"All right, I'll try," Arjumand finally said, unable to refuse her little "sister." "But—I'm sorry in advance—I can't promise anything… You know your mother wields such great power now, and to argue with her decisions… Besides, the man you love is probably a commoner, not equal to Prince Shahryar. So, alas… Although this marriage also saddens and frightens me…"

Arjumand understood that while Ladilli was indeed considered old for marriage by Indian standards, Mehrun-Nissa—sensing a threat to her boundless authority—would stop at nothing to reinforce her position.

Shah Jahan likewise disliked Mehrun-Nissa's arrangement. He saw his brother as an ambitious fool, incapable of anything worthwhile. And after all, was it not on Shahryar's orders that his loyal mentor Muhammad once lost his life?… Then again… perhaps it was the schemes of the cunning Mehrun-Nissa at work even then? And maybe she was the one involved in that tragedy? And now it was plain that through Ladilli, she planned to manipulate Shahryar and help him become Padishah after Jahangir's death. Well, that wouldn't do…

"No, my dear," Arjumand said, as though reading his mind. "My aunt wouldn't dare attempt such a thing. Everyone knows that you are Jahangir's first and most beloved son!"

"But how long will I remain so in his eyes?" Shah Jahan responded with a sad smile. "It seems to me your aunt is gradually extinguishing and uprooting all my father's love for me…"

55

Tashkent, February 2015

Mukhitdin did not see fit to inform his patron and his father's friend—Raj Singh Bhojwani, an Indian businessman—that he had flown to Moscow, taking with him all the savings he had amassed, which were considerable. He also took with him, just in case, the expensive ruby-and-diamond necklace he had stolen from Bhojwani. In the event of difficulties, he expected to sell it at a favorable price for a tidy sum, enough for an even more luxurious life.

Already rather adept at working with garments, Mukhitdin had managed, with great care, to detach the precious accessory from one of Bhojwani's mannequin outfits and to attach to it the cheap replica he had commissioned and prepared in advance.

Sitora ended up phoning Bhojwani. Restrained—trying not to let her obvious anger spill over onto her colleague—she explained to him that the necklace provided to her by the acclaimed fashion designer had turned out to be a worthless fake.

Hearing this, Bhojwani was sincerely upset. Though he never allowed panic, confusion, or agitation into his Hindu heart, that did not mean he was devoid of normal human feelings. The Indian man felt deeply uncomfortable about the misunderstanding and apologised repeatedly to Mrs. Mumtazoff for what had happened, promising to do everything in his power to find out where the real necklace had disappeared to and who had so shamelessly taken it. The word "steal" was simply not in the vocabulary of the honourable raja—he could not comprehend such a notion. He never locked his house nor hid anything from anyone, as he was used to trusting people and always tried to see only the good in them when possible.

Almost immediately after this phone call with the lady from Tashkent, Bhojwani made inquiries and learned that, apart from himself, access to the gown had been granted to only two people—his own daughter Indira (named in honour of the great woman, the daughter of Jawaharlal Nehru) and, in addition, one other: Mukhitdin, son of the Uzbek oligarch Murad Nasyrov…

And, of course, one did not need to be a police investigator or a private detective to deduce who had taken the jewelry. It was precisely Mukhitdin who had vanished so abruptly, without informing anyone, and only after his departure did the unsuspecting Lady Sitora arrive, retrieving the fake piece, all the while believing it to be the precious family heirloom.

Raj Singh Bhojwani was both annoyed and saddened that, during all his time spent with him and his noble family, Mukhitdin Nasyrov had not become a better person—he had never learned to behave in a morally upright way… Witnessing the young man's considerable ability in business and the art of styling, Bhojwani had hoped that he would also grow to be someone of decency. Alas, it turned out he was mistaken…

The Indian designer decided, for the moment, not to phone the elder Nasyrov, but rather to think about how best to break the news of this unpleasant incident—the probable culprit being his son.

Meanwhile, Mukhitdin flew to Russia's capital and went straight to one of the city's finest elite hotels, the Metropol Moscow.

Settling into a deluxe luxury suite, Mukhitdin began to plan his next moves. He either wanted to reclaim Malika at any cost or, if that proved impossible, to do everything in his power to take revenge on her and ruin her life.

He fully understood, however, that accomplishing this would be no simple task. He remembered how, back in India, he had learned about a powerful sorceress and went to visit her so that for a large sum of money she would cast a spell making Malika fall in love with him.

But the moment the old witch saw Mukhitdin, she told him at once:

"Young man, you've come here in vain. The girl you want so badly for yourself will never be yours! And all my magic is powerless against her, because she is protected by the Almighty Himself and by the angels of her noble ancestors—and the love surrounding her is strong, mutual, and invincible…"

* * *

Here at the "Superstar" competition, Malika felt more deeply than ever how much she adored performing in front of an audience—be it a small crowd or, all the more, a large one—how the stage attracted, captivated, and fascinated her, and how passionately she wanted to keep sharing her gift with listeners and spectators.

For the single winner—whoever took the Grand Prix—there awaited not only a substantial cash prize but also a magnificent reward that any artist, be they new or already famous, would dream of: a free concert tour across the largest pop-music venues of the CIS. This was an extremely enticing opportunity for the contest participants. For most, however, it was probably just a dream.

Malika Mumtazova had already caught people's attention during the preliminary rounds. Possessing a powerful voice and

brilliant technique, the jury members simply could not pass her by when deciding who advanced to the second jury round. Out of ten thousand hopefuls, she was chosen among the fifty participants entering the first stage of the main competition.

And so, the day arrived when this wonderful young representative from Uzbekistan would appear before the principal judging panel of the international contest: four outstanding luminaries of Russian and foreign music. They were famous individuals—just one glance or a single word from them could strike fear and awe into contestants who had never known a stage of such magnitude. Here, more than talent was required: courage, strength of will, firmness of character, and the ability to keep one's composure at a very emotional moment.

Two of the judges—a man and a woman—were Russians from Moscow: composer Yuri Antonov and singer Zhanna Rozhdestvenskaya. The third was an American of Russian origin from Los Angeles, the legendary producer and composer Walter Afanasieff. The fourth guest judge was the renowned "Indian Madonna," Alisha Chinai—the singer who had pioneered pop music in India.

Malika did not know beforehand that an Indian artist would be part of the jury. It felt to her like some kind of "sign from above," because this student from the Tashkent Conservatory had prepared for the first stage of the main "Superstar" competition… a new song called "Taj Mahal"! She and her mother Sitora wrote it together, with the sensitive guidance of Firuz-begim…

Malika stepped onto the stage and sat down at the piano. The music began. Then she started to sing about the love of two people who had lived in distant India in the seventeenth century. At the same time, Malika knew she was singing this song primarily for *him*, her beloved Bahadir!

They had spoken by phone only a handful of times during these weeks of competition. Bahadir himself had begun calling her again as soon as he realized that his wife had never, not for a moment, abandoned or betrayed him. During his darkest hours, she had remained loyal to him with all her heart, ever by his side, bound together so closely in spirit… And now Malika felt certain that even if Bahadir was not actually watching the main Russian TV channel, he was still, in some sense, hearing her—and that his soul resonated deeply with her song…

With her lovely voice, Malika filled the great television-studio auditorium, and indeed the entire world, singing:

> *Wonderful love arrives to last forever.*
> *So Shah Jahan was in love with Arjumand-begim…*
> *The mighty Taj Mahal joined their hearts as one…*
> *For the Shah, such love was both joy and sorrow.*
> *Because fate would soon wield a cruel blade:*
> *For Arjumand's days… they were already numbered.…*
> *Yet you can still hear the song of that great love:*
> *No one shall ever part two souls in love!*
>
> Chorus:
> *We are one, forever we are one,*
> *I am yours, and you are mine alone.*
> *This world—it's made just for us!*
> *Dear Shah Jahan, I'll be your Arjumand for all eternity.*
>
> *As the pride of all the earth, that mausoleum stands,*
> *Raising their sacred romance to the heavens…*
> *Taj Mahal so grand, it gleams and enthralls,*

In every stone—only her face, Arjumand!
And let the tale echo through the centuries,
Of that eternal love living on, defeating death.
In trembling hearts, let words ring out anew,
Of two who were faithful… And not to be forgotten.

Chorus:
We are one, forever we are one,
I am yours, and you are mine alone.
This world—it's made just for us!
Dear Shah Jahan, I'll be your Arjumand for all eternity.

Malika's wonderfully beautiful and powerful voice filled the huge TV studio hall. Yet the most striking thing was not merely her vocals or even her brilliant, virtuosic self-accompaniment on piano. Everyone could sense exactly what she was conveying—the message of her soul, her feelings and experiences. The story of Shah Jahan and Arjumand-begim's great love, and all the pain and suffering they had endured, came alive through this marvelous song and moved every listener.

No sooner did Malika finish than the entire hall fell silent for a moment—so profound was the impact made by the piece and by her performance…

It was the Indian guest judge who broke the silence, having had the meaning of the song's words simultaneously translated. Yet she could already feel the beauty of the melody and the depth of the performer's soul.

"That…was absolutely magnificent. Bravo!!!" Alisha Chinai said into the microphone.

And at once the entire audience rose to give Malika a standing ovation. It was clear from the very first round that this young woman was among the brightest favorites of the audience, and caught the attention of both the jury, and the producers. Each of the renowned producers, of whom there were several present, was already thinking about how they might work with this talented Uzbek performer, a born singer and songwriter, during and after the show.

Of course, all four judges said "Yes" to her performance, granting Malika a well-deserved pass to the next stage of the competition.

Meanwhile, India's top female singer made a note in her own notebook to be sure—once the competition was over and the young woman from Uzbekistan was free—to invite Malika to a recording studio in Mumbai and record a few tracks together. Their voices were extremely different in timbre, so if they did a duet, perhaps with a hint of male rap as backup, the result would sound thoroughly modern and beautiful. As for the songs themselves, Ms. Chinai already had a few ideas. And perhaps they could try recording a few tracks for film as well, maybe for an Uzbek–Indian co-production shot in Bollywood…

* * *

"Malika, my darling, your father and I watched you on television!" Sitora exclaimed excitedly and anxiously into the phone, trying to make sure her daughter heard her well. "You did such a wonderful job! We're so proud of you!!! Everyone—friends, neighbors, relatives—has been calling us. Everyone is sending their congratulations and celebrating your success! As for me—I'm especially happy, because you performed our song!"

"Yes, Mama, thank you, it means a lot. Please convey my deep gratitude to everyone for their moral support, for believing in me. I still have quite a few challenges ahead. I can't relax now—I'll have to do a lot of work with the producer who takes me onto his team, and keep performing in the competition."

"My daughter, maybe I should come out to be with you and support you?"

"No need, Mama—I don't think that's necessary. But Bahadir could come…"

"He misses you terribly. But you two talk on the phone now, thank God, and you know all about that… Couldn't you fly to Tashkent for just a couple of days?"

"Unfortunately, not at the moment—it's not possible. I'm doing all of this for our family, for all of us… Please make sure my husband understands that! You can explain to him, right? If he found a way to come to Moscow for a couple of days, then…"

"I'll certainly tell him. It's just that I've heard there are serious problems right now at his father Abdulla Rustamovich's firm. Amin and his fiancée are trying to get everything sorted out. But it's tough. From what I gather, they really need Bahadir at the company."

"Yes, of course—I understand. Then he shouldn't worry. The moment this competition is over for me—and that could happen at any moment, if I get cut—I'll head straight back to Tashkent."

"My dear, you hang in there, please! Best of luck to you! We're all sending you kisses and cheering you on! And no matter what happens, remember that—both for your father and me, and for your husband—you are the best! And listen carefully to what your mother is telling you, Malika: we love you very much and believe in your success!"

"Thank you so much, Mama. I really needed to hear those words… Kisses!"

56

Bahadir's closest friend, Rudik Khairullin, had been keen to help him get out of prison as soon as possible for a reason: he had long been waiting for the younger Fattakhov so they could open their joint venture with Italy and France to manufacture perfumery and cosmetic goods.

Now that Bahadir was free, more or less caught up on urgent matters, he could devote more time to this project, which he believed to be quite promising.

He called Rudik—who promptly came over. But not to the office, as it was still too early to involve all of the other Fattakhovs in this matter, let alone any potential witnesses visiting their firm. Instead, Rudik came to the apartment that Bahadir and Malika were renting.

Bahadir greeted his friend warmly and treated him to tea.

"Rudik, once again—huge thanks for all the effort you've put in for me together with my brother Amin and his girlfriend!" Bahadir said, visibly moved. "If not for you all, I don't know what would've become of me…"

"I understand, Baha… But please, don't thank me—we're close friends. You haven't forgotten that, have you?"

"Certainly not… Rudik, you know, those people have been calling me again these past few days, reminding me about my debts, threatening me! That Veniamin Arkadyevich, that Murad Nasyrov… They're real monsters! I'm almost certain they were the ones behind my landing in jail. I'm scared. They could kill…"

"Don't dwell on the worst-case scenario, Baha. By the way, this project is exactly what will help you!"

"You think so?"

"Well of course! I'm confident." Rudik replied with a sweet smile. Then his expression turned serious, tense even. "Bahadir, let me remind you we have to hurry up with establishing our joint venture. We've really dragged our feet—first there was your wedding, then you were locked up… Sorry if that sounded tactless, reminding you of that unpleasant time… But basically, both you personally and your company need to get out of debt, right?"

"My company? You mean my father's firm? Between you and me, I'm guessing if, God forbid, anything happened to him, he'd leave the company to Amin, not me!"

"Anything could happen. But if you don't want that to happen, you have to act. Understand that the money you'll earn through our joint venture will help both you personally and save 'Fattaxov PC' from bankruptcy. Then, who knows—by coming out as a triumphant hero, the most successful and wealthiest family member, you might end up heading both our new JV and 'Fattaxov PC.' You remember how I proposed we call the JV 'Bakh-atir,' i.e., 'Perfume by Bahadir'?"

"Yes, I remember… That's…great, I really like it!"

"Wonderful."

"Will our perfumes have aphrodisiacs?" Bahadir ventured playfully.

"With pheromones and anaphrodisiacs!" Rudik bantered right back. "But let's be serious, all right?"

"Sure. So what's the plan?"

"Here's the gist. You and I need to create a joint venture in Tashkent to manufacture perfumery and cosmetic products—to-

gether with Europeans, but with an Uzbek manufacturing brand, bearing the names of our nation's renowned sons and daughters. I know this Italian, Francesco Valdoni—he's a producer and global supplier of large-scale plastic household goods and imported equipment. I've already spoken with him. For our small factory under JV 'Bakh-atir,' he's willing to supply equipment on favorable terms so we can turn out top-notch products!"

"I really want to hope that it really happens…"

"Trust me, it'll be just right! You and I—me as an engineer-technologist and an expert at setting up production, and you as an international specialist—we'll attract reliable European investors to this project. I'll handle the quality equipment side, and you'll be our principal founder and general director. Sound good?"

"Me??? A general director?! That's tempting…impressive."

"I've already drawn up a feasibility study and a business plan. And this project will be really profitable, I told you that too."

"And, as I remember, I suggested at that time that we involve Jean Marchal, a longtime partner of my father's and my firm, a perfumer from Paris."

"That's right, Bahadir. You see, what a clever boy you are, you remember everything!" Rudik laughed a small laugh into his mustache. "Thanks to their investments, our partners will have their own interest in the joint venture and will receive a good part of the dividends. But the main owner, Bahadir, will be you personally! And I will be your 'right hand' in this project, your deputy. You don't mind, do you?

"Of course I don't mind. And am I really going to be the general director?"

"Of course! Have I ever lied to you? Now, my dear friend, we'll need a little help from Amin. Please speak with your brother yourself—he shouldn't realise I'm involved in this, because, well, he… let's say he might not trust me. Talk to him so that he arranges a bank loan. For that, he'll have to put something up as collateral—I'm thinking he can figure out what. Perhaps he can pledge Fattaxov PC's assets to the bank."

"Hold on, Rudik, isn't that risky? We'd be putting my father's firm on the line…?"

An old memory of a conversation with his mother flitted across Bahadir's mind:

"Your Rudik is slippery" Mukhabbat had said. "I don't like him, he's untrustworthy. I hope you're careful with him!… I think he could easily trick you—even betray and sell you. You never know what to expect from someone like him!… Be careful, son, I warned you…"

Bahadir thought, "Nonsense. Those are just prejudices. After all, a mother is a mother—she's jealous of everyone close to me, even my friends!"

"Oh, come on!" Rudik exclaimed, shaking Bahadir from his stroll down memory lane and back to reality. "It'll be fine. You're like a little kid, for goodness' sake—so fearful! Don't be, Bahadir… What's to fear? Did you know perfume and cosmetics rank second in global profits? Amin will pay back the bank on time, he'll manage. Where's the problem? By the way, the account in Italy is open, and I know all the banking details."

"What account?"

"Keep up! The account where you and Amin, and Jean Marchal, and any investors we find, will send money for equipment! That's how this all gets rolling."

"Ah, right."

"You understand that the success of any manufacturing venture hinges on the quality of the equipment. That I guarantee personally. You can trust me!"

"Of course."

"Then stop overthinking it! I'll handle everything, set it up properly. You'll just do the managing, and once all is running smoothly, issue your directives… So, then, my priceless friend, you'll get it cleared with your brother and with Marchal?"

"Yes. In the next few days, I'll talk to them both."

"Great. You're a real star, Baha! Honestly, I respect you so much!!!"

* * *

For several months, Rano had been feeling uneasy. She was worried about her father's deteriorating health and the fate of their family business. A competent economist, she could see that under the current circumstances, "Fattaxov PC" was not coping with all the emerging difficulties. Moreover, although she wasn't entirely sure, she felt that if her father, Abdulla Rustamovich, were to completely step away from the business, her own brothers would begin to quarrel and perhaps even, in a sense, fight among themselves for the right to lead and hold primacy in their father's company.

Additionally, when Rano adopted a girl from an orphanage—and Malika had been of great help to her in this matter when she was still in Tashkent—Rano managed to cover up the fact by obtaining the necessary medical certificates, proving that she… wasn't entirely in good physical health. For it turned out that Rano was rapidly developing diabetes…

The one-year-old little Samira, whom Rano had adopted, was wonderful—a cheerful, smiling, tender girl. Her young "biological" mother had renounced her at the maternity hospital. And all the Fattakhovs came to love the little one very much. Rano, in particular, had grown especially attached to her. Having never fully realised her great potential for love and care due to the absence of a husband, she devoted a great deal of attention to the adopted child, becoming a wonderful mother to her.

Her main problem now was to somehow control her type 2 diabetes, and, despite the fact that she had begun regularly taking insulin injections as prescribed by her doctors, to prevent her parents from guessing that the doctors had given her such a serious, definitively confirmed diagnosis…

* * *

Bahadir had called his brother beforehand and said that he would like to meet him face-to-face, without any outsiders.

"Come, of course! I'm waiting for you, little brother," Amin replied warmly over the phone.

When Bahadir arrived, Amin offered him a light dinner and some tea. But he declined. Amin was surprised that Bahadir seemed somewhat tense.

"Has something happened to you?" the older brother inquired sympathetically.

"No, why would you think so? Everything's fine. Thanks for your help."

"Oh, don't mention it. We're family, after all. And how is Malika? Do you call her?"

"Yes, Amin, my wife and I talk on the phone often," Bahadir said without much warmth—as he almost always did when speaking with Amin. "Everything's fine with us. Soon, Malika will begin

426

working full-time with one of the best music producers and will continue to participate in the international 'Superstar' competition."

"Excellent, I'm happy for her!" Amin said with a warm smile. "She's so smart. Do you even know how lucky you are with your wife?"

"I know," Bahadir grumbled discontentedly. He really disliked it when some other man praised his wife—even if it was his own brother.

"But do you have some important matter to discuss with me?" Amin steered the conversation. He did not want to irritate, upset, or anger his beloved younger brother.

"Yes, I do. Amin, the thing is, I've been offered the chance to start our very own enterprise, our company, on very favorable terms!"

"Wait, I don't quite understand. And 'Fattaxov PC'—whose company is that? Isn't it ours?"

"Well, that's another matter… After all, it is our father who is still in charge there! We do everything the way he dictates. And after father, I know you, Amin, will become the boss there…"

"Why do you assume everything for everyone already, Bahadir?!"

"Don't argue—I know. You're our eldest heir, after all. And father loves you more than he loves me."

"Please, don't make that up. It isn't so. In our family, we all love you."

"I don't know. But I've been offered to head a new company, in which I will become the principal founder and its general director!" As he said this, Bakhadir even brightened up, his mood improving. "In fact, all the necessary documents have already been officially registered—in my name. All that remains is to set up production."

"Really?! How interesting… But may I ask: what does that have to do with me here?"

"But you'll be able to help me with this, won't you? And I will, without a doubt, share with you both a part of this business and the profits! They will be ours collectively—we're brothers, after all. And, by the way, thanks to this, we'll pull our father's 'Fattaxov PC' out of the crisis! What do you say, Amin?"

"Suppose, Bahadir, I'll help however I can. But what exactly do you require from me? And can you tell me who offered you this business?"

"No, I'm sorry, I won't say that for now; you don't need to know. But everything there is secure, the people are trustworthy!"

"Really? Well then. God willing, let it be so, you know best…"

"This will be a joint enterprise—with Italy. It is precisely our partner from Italy who will supply us—under contract, of course— with high-class technological equipment for the production of perfume brands in Uzbekistan at prices affordable to the average consumer! And as for how you can help me… well, by taking out a bank loan… a secured loan… some kind of collateral will be need- ed… But surely you'll come up with something? You can risk the assets of 'Fattaxov PC', which are in your hands… I won't be giving you any advice on this—after all, you're a financier and you know how it's done!"

"'Risk'—you said it right, Bakhadir. And it's a serious risk."

"Oh, come on, Amin, stop it! I know that Father's firm is al- most bankrupt. What do we have to lose there?"

"You don't say. Our—" he emphasized that word— "firm 'Fat- taxov PC' has both tangible and intangible assets, as well as some liabilities… And then—what will father say?"

"Brother, you must not mention any of this to father this time!"

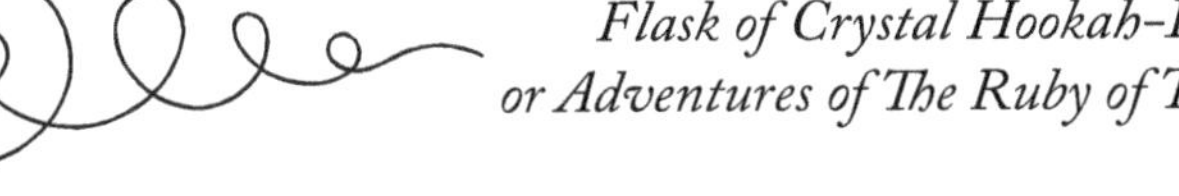
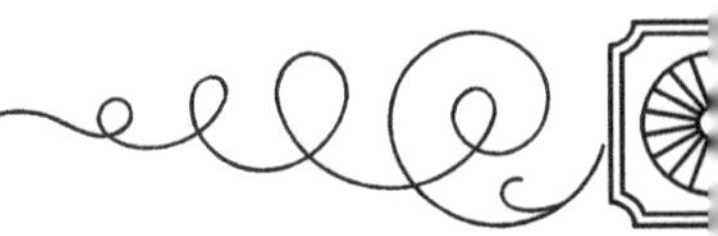

"Why is that, Bahadir? You already know that father won't approve of this, right? From that I conclude that it's shady, and in general—not worth pursuing."

"Why not? Parents are always overly protective of us, their children, and they don't always trust us completely. Especially in business, where large sums are involved. You, my older brother, know and understand all this no less than I do…"

"Yes, you're right, little brother… Indeed, Father is often overly cautious with us, like with children… But maybe he's right about something?.."

"I don't think so. And also, Amin, we just need investments from Jean Marchal."

"Yes, but father asked me to work very carefully with this gentleman, Bahadir! Marchal is extremely important as a partner for 'Fattaxov PC'…"

"But we won't screw him over! In the end, the monsieur will still be satisfied! Business sites and production facilities in our country are far more profitable and interesting for any European than those in Europe—including in France, where everything comes with outrageous prices, an economic crisis, and unthinkable taxes!"

"Well, I can't disagree with you there. But… Still, I think I'll have to decline for now. I'm sorry, Bahadir, and please, don't be offended."

"'Please, don't be offended!'" Bakhadir mockingly repeated Amin's words with anger. "Know this: if you refuse, then you will no longer be a brother to me!"

"Why do you have to say that right away? 'Not a brother'… Calm down, Bahadir, there's no need to be so harsh."

"You always lecture me like I'm a school kid. Everyone just keeps instructing me—both our parents and you! Instead of helping me for real. If you don't want to, just say so!"

"Why wouldn't I want to? You're my younger brother, and I love you—you know that…"

"You say that all your life. It's time to show by your actions that it's true. If you do as I ask, then I'll believe in your sincere brotherly feelings for me!"

"You speak like a hurt child… It's time to grow up, Bahadir. Alright, I'm sorry, I won't lecture you… Okay. I'll think about what can be done and try to help you. But there's no free money right now—not for me personally, nor for our parents, nor for 'Fattaxov PC'. Therefore, I'm afraid that, after all, we'll really have to take out a bank loan! And use our father's entire firm as collateral…"

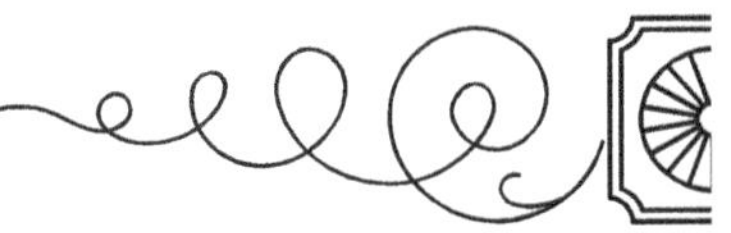

57

Murad Nasyrov wanted to appear "cool" and "all-powerful" in front of Said Mumtazov. He understood that the doctor, despite his naive honesty and guilelessness, could still be of use to him. All the more so because his eyesight could deteriorate again, and there was no better ophthalmologist or eye clinic in the country. Of course, as a last resort, if it came down to it, he could seek treatment abroad. But as a businessman, Nasyrov knew better than most how much they "rip people off" there, especially foreigners. No, he definitely did not plan to ruin his relationship with Said Yakhyaevich. The question was how to obtain that—cursed be the name—necklace for him, the one that Gosha and his girlfriend Larisa had snatched from the Mumtazovs on Nasyrov's orders, which was now in Bhojwani's possession. How could he possibly get it back? He couldn't just steal it or buy it back from him now!

All the same, Nasyrov decided to try his luck and call the Indian just in case.

"Hello, Mr. Bhojwani! This is Nasyrov."

"Good evening, Mr. Nasyrov. Any news? Has Mukhitdin been found?"

"No, unfortunately not. That scoundrel, my son, doesn't pick up the phone when his own father calls! He may not love me, but he still ought to show some respect… And his mother and I worry—wondering where he is, what he is doing…"

"I'm sorry to hear that, Mr. Nasyrov," the Indian responded politely but reservedly, not especially flattered by such a show of trust and "outpouring of the soul."

Nasyrov, however, managed to notice that the tone in which his acquaintance from Delhi was speaking to him now wasn't as friendly as before, as it usually was.

"Forgive me, dear sir," Nasyrov asked, "have I done something to offend you?"

"No, not at all, Mr. Nasyrov. We are friends, of course. But your son… Well, never mind, I don't know why I'm bringing it up. You're not to blame for anything; there's no point in discussing it."

"No, wait, Mr. Bhojwani! Tell me, what did Mukhitdin do to you?"

"I feel awkward talking about it. I'm afraid you won't believe me, and you'll condemn me for telling you all of this…"

"What is it? I beg you, my friend, speak openly, don't worry about my reaction, and don't spare my parental feelings! I must know what my child is guilty of…"

"Well, all right. The thing is, we've had a necklace go missing—the same one I bought from you… And the problem isn't that it was expensive, it's simply the very fact that it disappeared—it's rather unpleasant…"

"Mr. Bhojwani, I understand, and I'm truly sorry—believe me… But why have you decided that this vile, disgusting, and I would even say shameful act was committed by none other than Mukhitdin? Could you not have made a mistake?"

"No, unfortunately. We investigated thoroughly, checked everyone and everything. All the evidence points to him. And I had wanted to give that necklace to my daughter—she loved it so much…"

"Then perhaps she…? But no, what am I saying? She has no reason to do that! Your daughter surely knows and understands

that—pardon my bluntness—in any case, all your wealth will sooner or later come to her."

"Yes, you're right. Besides, believe me, my Indira would never be capable of doing such a thing! Mr. Nasyrov, forgive me for bringing it up. I see that I'm troubling you for no reason…"

"No, no, not at all! I just wanted to know all the details. And now, after what you've told me, I see that it really could have been my wayward son… My dear sir, please know that I am deeply, deeply ashamed of him, that brazen brat! And I'm very sorry it happened. If you will allow it, sir, perhaps I can reimburse you for all your losses…"

"No, no, Mr. Nasyrov, there's no need for that. This has nothing to do with you. Under no circumstances do I expect any reimbursement. But if you could find your son and ask him to return the jewelry to me… I'm even prepared to offer a decent reward for it. Or if, for instance, you could find me another one, similar and in no way inferior to the original… You remember, we once talked about it—or rather, you yourself mentioned the famous Temur Ruby? Then I would be extremely happy… If it's possible for you, of course."

"Of course, my friend, of course! I'll think of something. So, you say that our—excuse me, your—necklace is now in Mukhitdin's hands?"

"Yes, Mr. Nasyrov. Forgive me for reminding you of it…"

"Oh, come on, that's nonsense, don't apologise! I promise you that I'll find my son as soon as possible, no matter where he's gone."

***

Investigator Ravshan Umarov had not been in a good mood lately. His routine work had grown tiresome, and he'd observed that almost every investigator—and indeed many police officers in general—lived a life in which they were rarely at home and seldom seen by their wives and children, constantly forced to deal with criminals, thieves, and conmen—the dregs of society. Of course, among the people he dealt with there were also decent individuals, not to mention numerous claimants and witnesses to various incidents. Yet even these brief encounters could not drown out the heavy, unpleasant impressions left by lengthy dealings with parasitic gangsters.

The only thing that, apart from occasional drinking sprees and nights out with hired girls, brightened Ravshan's life was money. And often, big money. Umarov loved money more than anything. No one knew exactly how much he had—and he himself wasn't sure, since money flowed to him in torrents, much like throngs of pilgrims to a sacred shrine. From childhood, Ravshan had possessed a knack for "making" or finding money. People, for one reason or another, would frequently offer him an opportunity to take some—and he always took it, gladly and without a second thought about such cumbersome notions as the pang of conscience, shame, or honor. Yet he was adept at hiding all this from his superiors and even his colleagues, ensuring they wouldn't envy him or "rat him out." And perhaps for that reason, money was always at his side; he never scorned a single coin, considering none of it "excess" as he cherished, respected, and truly loved every sum in his pocket.

Before long, Ravshan effortlessly found himself in the company of the "serious" people—those whom the criminal world often

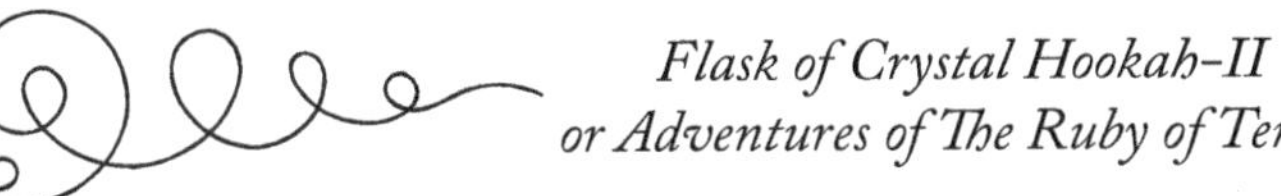
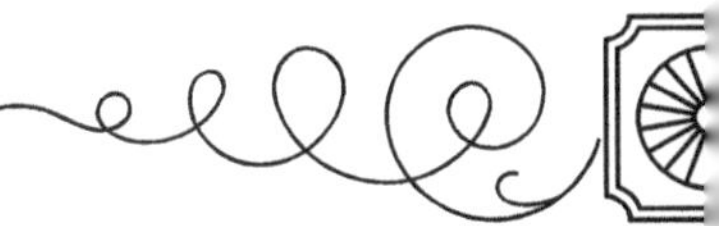

called "bosses," "godfathers," or "protectors." Even while still merely a senior lieutenant, then a police captain, and later the head of an investigative unit, he quickly established himself to such an extent that gangsters and thieves began to regard and refer to him not as just another criminal authority, but specifically as Ravshan Umarov.

However, this posturing did nothing to impress one truly "cool" and most dangerous authority—Murad Nematullaevich Nasyrov. Upon meeting Ravshan, he made it very clear who was "in charge" and to whom one simply had to obey.

Thus, Ravshan became Nasyrov's personal "track dog," faithfully and obediently serving the boss, for which he regularly received substantial monetary rewards.

This went on for several years—until… one day, Nasyrov began facing major business problems engineered by Misha Leonidov. The boss could no longer, on his own, sufficiently and regularly bribe everyone—including Umarov—since he was already doling out money to many who, one way or another, helped him keep his affairs afloat and upon whom his perpetual freedom, quite literally, depended.

Of course, Ravshan was aware of Nasyrov's casinos and his other "skeletons hidden in his closet," and Murad Nematullaevich knew that Ravshan was well informed on the matter, but Nasyrov now had far fewer opportunities for payoffs and kickbacks than before. He explained this "temporary" situation to Umarov in a rather curt manner, and the captain understood, agreeing to wait as long as necessary for those "better times" that he believed would inevitably come for them all.

However, now Ravshan had to resort to… taking more bribes from other people.

Then, one day—after the capture and setup of Bahadir Fattakhov and his subsequent fortunate release and return home—a young man was brought before Captain Umarov. He had been detained, allegedly, according to the victims' accounts, following a fight.

Umarov quickly realised that this young man, Tulkun, was essentially innocent; he had merely defended an unknown girl in a chivalrous manner when, late in the evening in a park, drunken hooligans attacked her. Tulkun fought alone and did not employ any forbidden tactics—the hooligans resorted to those. As a result, the noble youth suffered several heavy blows, leaving his face and entire body bruised. Yet he never even considered seeking help from the police—it would have been beneath his dignity. Meanwhile, the most brazen of the hooligans, Vasya, reported to a friendly officer that some guy—whom he noted could be found here and there—had severely beaten him. There were witnesses and even a doctor's report documenting the injuries inflicted by Tulkun on "poor, defenseless" Vassiliy.

In the end, Tulkun was locked up in detention. Captain Umarov spoke with him on three separate occasions, hinting that if the young man contacted his relatives and they paid a fine on his behalf, then the investigator would release Tulkun—not under any conditions, but completely free, so that he could roam at his leisure. Essentially, it was very difficult—if not impossible—to let him go at the moment, but if Tulkun managed to "help himself" by convincing someone to pay for him, then perhaps something could be arranged, and he would be set free.

All this, it seemed, confirmed the truth that the Lord's wrath is held in check for a time, sparing the wicked. But eventually, there comes a moment when that cup overflows—and then such people are doomed, for divine retribution inevitably catches up with them...

And so it happened with Ravshan. He had grown utterly tired of begging for money from Tulkun—a well-dressed young man clearly not from a poor family—who had been holed up with him for nearly two days. The captain had refused to grant an appointment to Tulkun's mother, Mahira Hamidova. But now he decided to let her in—not for a meeting with her son, but into his office so that he could speak with her in person and make it clear that a ransom for her son was both necessary and inevitable. Ravshan never dealt with such matters over the phone; he was always careful to avoid exposing his own secret transgressions.

Mahira turned out to be an attractive, beautiful, well-groomed, and very neatly dressed woman just over forty.

"Clearly, she's from a wealthy family," Umarov deduced.

She and her husband had two children—the elder, Tulkun, and the younger, Sharaf. Her husband's name, she mentioned, was Aziz. Umarov was immediately a bit surprised at the dignified manner in which she carried herself in the investigator's office; she neither begged nor pleaded nor demeaned herself, but instead asked very seriously and, to his surprise, calmly inquired what exactly her son was being accused of, why he was being held for so long, and on what grounds.

When Captain Umarov presented her with all the "grounds"— which any reasonably competent lawyer would immediately recognize as having been hastily patched together—Mahira pointed out that her son should be released immediately, for she was convinced there was absolutely no evidence of his guilt. On the contrary, she had found the young woman Tulkun had rescued. She could confirm that it was those inebriated hooligans who first harassed her, and then attacked Tulkun and beat him mercilessly. The girl was even distressed that the hero had not been given any medical help at the time.

Ravshan kept twisting the matter, trying to imply to the visitor that he had the power to lock her son up completely and for a long time. And to prevent that from happening, she needed to "support" the investigator. Only then would he be willing to release the young man. After all, police work is tough, and that should be understood—one must offer every bit of "voluntary" cooperation…

Mahira Hamidova listened to the captain very attentively, periodically glancing at her phone. She did not give him the bribe he requested.

The next day, for some reason, Ravshan Umarov was summoned to the district prosecutor's office. He had heard that a new chief had just been appointed there, though he hadn't yet caught his name. But his colleagues were saying that this man was honest, fair, principled, and completely incorruptible.

"And why am I being summoned? For what reason?" Umarov wondered in confusion, finding the whole situation both perplexing and intriguing. "Ah—they probably want to promote me. It's about time, too. I've been stuck as a captain for too long; it's high time I became a major!"

When Umarov entered the district prosecutor's reception area, he asked the secretary to announce his arrival.

"Please, sit here and wait a moment," said the secretary.

Ravshan sat down and, glancing casually at the nameplate on the prosecutor's door, nearly sank into his chair—he was ready either to collapse right there… or to run away.

The nameplate read: "Aziz Sharafovich Hamidov, Chief Prosecutor of the District."

That very day, Ravshan Umarov was removed from his post, dismissed from the force, and immediately detained on several charges under the Criminal Code of the Republic of Uzbekistan.

One of the prosecutors' investigators, acting on orders from above, opened a criminal case against him. The case included an audio recording, submitted by Mahira Hamidova, in which a citizen Umarov R.D. was heard extorting a bribe at his workplace—while on duty, no less.

Not that the young employee of the prosecutor's office, Tulkun Hamidov, couldn't, in fact, behave like a true hero. Certainly, he could—and indeed he did—and he saved people when necessary. It had been decided by him and the other operatives not to take undue risks. Thus, the typical incident, allegedly involving Tulkun, the "passerby" girl, and the "hooligans," was, in reality, a carefully planned and orchestrated operation by officers from the Internal Security Department. It turned out that although Umarov had been quite skillful at concealing his misdeeds, all secrets would eventually come to light. For some time now, his extortion and bribery had been known to both the Ministry of Internal Affairs and the capital's prosecutor's office. The district prosecutor, Aziz Hamidov, was tasked with exposing the "werewolf in uniform" and bringing him to justice as swiftly as possible, with the help of his wife—also an officer—his elder son Tulkun, and Tulkun's girlfriend.

During a careful review of Umarov's entire operation, something else rather intriguing was suddenly discovered: the former investigator-turned-criminal was directly linked to a major underground group engaged in blackmail, money laundering, arms trafficking, and… the gambling business for profit. It remained only to use Umarov as a means to reach the chief "ringleader" of this criminal machine—the "spider" oligarch masquerading as an ordinary, respectable businessman.

Yet neither the police nor the prosecutor's office knew the name of this "spider."

Meanwhile, Murad Nematullaevich Nasyrov, busy with his myriad business problems and new schemes for getting rich—and having temporarily forgotten about his "friend" and "backup" Ravshan Umarov—had no idea that Ravshan had already been taken down. And that now, he himself wouldn't remain free for long. For although Nasyrov had not yet sensed it, the ground was rapidly slipping from under him…

* * *

"Mukhitdin, son," Murad Nematullaevich texted his son, "I can't get through to you. There's a deal. For the necklace—which I know for certain is in your possession—you can get a handsome sum from me! Call me back. Your father."

And the "loving" son called back.

"How do you know about the necklace, Dad? Ah— I get it, Bhodjwani ratted me out!"

"Don't speak that way about your patron—even if he's a former one, assuming you're not planning to return there. Still, that man has done a lot for you, and you must respect him. Don't be an ungrateful whelp…"

"Dad, did you ask me to call just so you could lecture me?"

"No, son. I want to help you—financially. You don't have anything to live on, do you?"

"Why not? I have money. I made a good living in India."

"That's wonderful, Mukhitdin. But do you still intend to sell the necklace at a profit?"

"Suppose so. And then?"

"May I know: why did you even take it?"

"I wanted to sell it, but it didn't work out in India. So, I brought it with me to Russia."

"You're in Russia now? In which city? And why?!"

"In Moscow. And why… Dad, really, it's my own affair."

"I can help you sell the necklace. Please send it to me by express mail. Pack it first in a metal box—like one from cookies or candies—so that customs will let it through. And under no circumstances skimp on a sturdy outer packaging! It will all pay off, I assure you. In about five days, at most a week, I'll send you a good sum for it."

"I don't trust you. How do I know you won't cheat me?"

"How dare you talk to your father like that, kid?! What impudence!! Don't you dare speak to me in that tone!… Why don't you love me? Do you even know who I am? I'm your own father, and you're my blood, my son! Yes, I didn't beat you enough when you were a child…"

Just as Mukhitdin, hurt and angry at those last words, was about to hang up, he heard:

"If you don't show me the proper respect, son, I'll deprive you of your entire inheritance."

The young man, quickly weighing everything and running it through his mind, held his tongue.

"Alright, Dad, forgive me. I'm just not in the mood right now… Could you send me the money in advance?"

"Actually, I need to sell the necklace first…" Nasyrov mused. "But whatever. What wouldn't I do for my son? I'll send it to you today. How much do you want?"

Mukhitdin named a sum.

"Wow! I'm actually glad, son, that you're not that stupid… Give me your exact address."

"That's not necessary. Send the money via Golden Crown to

my full name, and text me the transfer number. I'll ship the necklace to you tomorrow."

"Just, please, Mukhitdin, don't treat me like Mr. Bhodjwani!"

"What do you mean—don't 'dupe' you?" chuckled the younger Nasyrov.

"And that too. But I mean this: please, don't swap the necklace for another! I need exactly the one you have right now. It belongs to the family of my friends, the Mumtazovs, and it's very valuable to them. I must return it to them."

"Which family? As in Malika Mumtazov?!! Then why did you sell it to the Indian?"

"At the time, it was necessary. But now it needs to be handed over to the Mumtazovs—or returned to Bhodjwani. I'll think about it. But I'm a bit surprised: do you even know Malika, Mukhitdin?"

"Yes, we know each other… Prepare your money, Father! As soon as I receive it, I'll send you the necklace."

"Agreed. And don't disappear—call once in a while. Your mother and I worry."

Well, would you look at that! So the necklace belongs to Malika… Mukhitdin thought.

***

Of course, Nasyrov immediately sent the money—the entire considerable sum that Mukhitdin had named. The father didn't even want to imagine what would happen if his son failed to send the Mumtazovs' necklace… He decided to trust him.

"I'll have to sell this very same necklace to Bhodjwani again—for the second time!" thought Murad Nematullaevich.

He called the Indian and reminded him that not long ago,

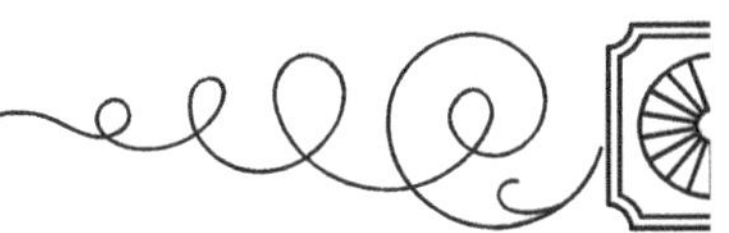

Bhodjwani himself had offered, if needed, to buy back that precious item.

"And where is the necklace?" inquired Bhodjwani, sounding curious. "Is it with you?"

"No. It's currently with someone… someone you don't know…"

"Isn't it with Mukhitdin?" the Delhi man said, genuinely astonished.

"No, no, my son lost it," Nasyrov quickly fabricated. "But I've found its 'ends' in a completely different place—and that other place requires payment…!"

That was a lie. But essentially, Nasyrov had spent his whole life deceiving and swindling people—only on a grand scale. He never liked lying about trifles. Yet he wasn't willing to betray his own son, even though he suspected that clever Mr. Bhodjwani would likely figure it all out on his own and, as usual, never let on.

"Mr. Nasyrov, when can I get the necklace?" asked Bhodjwani.

"As soon as you transfer the money for it."

"And what about the Kuwaiti sheikh's necklace and Temur Ruby? Remember?.."

"Yes, yes, of course, I remember everything. I'm looking for a way to get it, Mr. Bhodjwani; I've thrown everything into the search. But it's difficult—you must understand…"

"Maybe then you'd not rush to send me this necklace? Especially since I had planned to present it to a charming lady acquaintance who mentioned that this precious ornament belongs to her family—and I just remembered that she, like you, lives in Tashkent. Wouldn't it be easier for you to deliver it to her yourself—of course, at my expense? Besides, she said she was acquainted with you…"

"With me? That's strange. But who is she?"

"Mrs. Mumtazoff."

"Ah— yes, yes, I recall something…"

It can't be! Nasyrov was astonished. *Sitora Mumtazova has already visited my Indian and met him! Unbelievable. How on earth do people manage to do everything these days?*

"So, will you deliver it?"

"Yes, of course," Nasyrov agreed briskly.

"And after you do that, I'll transfer the money for it to you."

"Pardon me, dear sir, I didn't quite catch that: you won't transfer it immediately?"

"No, sorry."

"Don't you trust me anymore, my friend?"

"Oh, come now, Mr. Nasyrov! Of course, I trust you completely. As soon as I learn through my channels that the necklace is now directly with the Mumtazoffs, I'll try to pay you for this kind service as quickly as possible! But I can't do it just yet. However, I'll send you my Commitment today—a formal document confirming our deal."

"Alright, I understand, Mr. Bhodjwani, agreed."

"Excellent. Good luck, my friend!"

Nasyrov was somewhat annoyed with Bhodjwani—he'd noticed that the man had become considerably more cautious. However, the owner of the cafés and restaurants found solace in one thought:

I was, in any case, planning to call Sitora's husband, Said Yakhyaevich, and offer him the same deal as Bhodjwani—to buy back their necklace for a decent sum. But now I have every legal basis to do so…

***

Bhodjwani did not mention to the Tashkent oligarch what Mrs. Mumtazoff had said about him, nor that he, Bhodjwani, knew who had illicitly taken the necklace from Sitora and her family. Singh decided that it was none of his business and, moreover, that he should not jeopardise his relationship with an old friend and partner.

Meanwhile, he called Sitora and warned her that their necklace might once again be in Mr. Nasyrov's hands, adding that Bhodjwani had asked the Tashkent businessman to hand the necklace over to her. Bhodjwani also subtly hinted that although he had promised to pay Mr. Nasyrov for this service—and was bound to do so—Nasyrov might try... to extract money from the Mumtazoffs' family as well.

Grasping the nature of Nasyrov's likely clever ploy, Sitora warmly thanked her colleague from Delhi:

"Mr. Bhodjwani, thank you very much! I will certainly take all this into account. I promise you that we won't pay anything to that man... I just have one request for you, which I believe will not be difficult to fulfill."

"I'm listening attentively, madam, and I'm ready to do everything in my power."

"I am immensely grateful that you are once again willing to spend and bestow generous gifts upon our family. But I beg you—and I ask you as well—not to pay Nasyrov another cent for this necklace! I implore you, no monetary transfers to him! Let him first return our necklace, and you—come up with something, stall if you must, but do not pay. I can't reveal everything, but believe me, by taking this step you will neither deceive nor let anyone down. It is the wise and proper course."

"But I can't, madam! I have already sent Mr. Nasyrov a commitment certified by lawyers and signed by my own hand. It is now a matter of my honor to pay for his services."

"As you wish, Mr. Bhodjwani. However, I know that this man is crooked… Therefore, I insist that you not send him a single cent."

"Well then, dear madam, I'll think it over. And perhaps I'll heed your request…"

"That would be wonderful."

* * *

"Hello, Said Yakhyaevich! This is Nasyrov."

"Hello, dear Murad Nematullaevich. My health? Fine, thank you. And yours? I'm glad to hear you're well. I'm listening—surely you're calling on business?"

"Yes. Remember, you asked me to help you locate your necklace?"

"My daughter's…"

"Pardon, what did you say?"

"The necklace now belongs to my daughter, Malika."

"Ah, yes, let it be so. In any case, I'm calling because I have found it! But… it is your family's, and you mentioned it is very valuable to you, correct?"

"Absolutely correct. And why do you ask, Murad Nematullaevich?"

"You see, the necklace has somehow ended up in the hands of complete strangers, and I fear we will have to buy it back… I mean, you will have to, because, you know, I'm currently facing serious business problems and simply have no available funds."

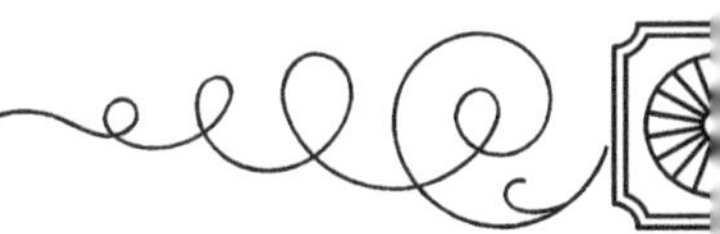

"I understand. Of course, we'll consider it! And where is the necklace now?"

"It is, for the time being, with… these people. They quoted me a price for your family's heirloom… I tried to argue, to bargain, but alas, it was all in vain. Unfortunately, these people turned out to be very greedy and selfish…"

"Yes, yes, I understand. Well, it happens…"

"I contacted them again today, Said Yakhyaevich. They promised that as soon as you pay the full amount, they will return the necklace to you."

"I don't understand: return it?"

"Forgive me, I misspoke. I meant they will hand it over to you—through me."

"Excellent. But please understand, Murad Nematullaevich, with all due respect—I need guarantees. The sum is substantial."

"What guarantees? I am here. I am your guarantee! Do you not trust me?"

"I do trust you, Murad Nematullaevich, like a member of my own family. Let's do it like this: 'In the morning—chairs, in the evening—money.'"

"But the classics had it the other way around, my friend: 'In the morning—money, in the evening—chairs.'"

"Never mind, we'll just rephrase that literary masterpiece a bit. As soon as you bring us our necklace, …our mutual friend, Mr. Bhodjwani, will immediately reimburse you in full for all the hassles concerning it! After all, that's exactly what you agreed upon with him, isn't it?"

For several seconds, Nasyrov was silent, astonished by the doctor's awareness.

"Yes, of course, Said Yakhyaevich… Exactly so. Goodbye."

"All the best. We look forward to hearing from you soon about our necklace!"

At that moment, Nasyrov felt as though he were a heavyweight, knocked out in one blow in the ring by both the Mumtazovs and Bhodjwani.

58

Both the beauty of Malika's voice and the level of her musical talent—including her performance technique—were so exceptional that even the most seasoned producers were astonished by her. Every one of them wanted to recruit the singer into their team. And each one understood, felt, and saw that unless unforeseen, undesirable, force majeure circumstances arose or a special directive came from above, this modest and enchanting girl from Uzbekistan could not only reach the finals of the competition but also claim one of the top spots.

And although the "Superstar" competition was international, Malika Mumtazova might still face difficulties simply because she wasn't Russian and did not live in Russia. But… "time will tell," the producers mused.

After the preliminary rounds, each producer was left with twelve vocalists.

Ultimately, Malika was claimed by the brilliant composer and impresario—author of countless popular hits—Konstantin Melodiev.

Moreover, Malika proved to be an obedient and agreeable student, capable of working in harmonious tandem with any professional, and despite her gentle demeanor, high culture, and delicacy, she always maintained her own opinion with a clear and resolute stance. Yet she never placed her own views or ambitions above the cause or above respect for others, especially for her elders, mentors, and masters. Therefore, it was both easy and creatively stimulating for Konstantin Valeryevich to work with her.

Mukhitdin spent many hours contemplating how to restore the once warm relationship he had with Malika, although he was angry with her—angry that she had married another man and, most of all, that, according to her friend Galina Krikunova, who had long been enamored with him, Malika had labeled him a "good-for-nothing loser" and spread it to everyone. Thus Mukhitdin thought… Yet for some time now he had begun to suspect that Galya's account might have been overly exaggerated, for as far as he knew her, Malika could never have behaved in such a manner—it was simply not like her.

Mukhitdin knew exactly where and how to find Malika. It wasn't difficult at all, since she now attended rehearsals and filming sessions every day at one of the main studios of central Moscow television. The real challenge lay in getting in there and influencing her attitude toward him.

He was aware that perhaps Malika might have suspected that the perfume he had given her before leaving for India had been poisoned with methanol. And he knew from Galina—with whom he continued to correspond regularly, and whom he had even incited into setting fire to Gosha's apartment—that all because Gosha fancied himself as someone important, nearly as if he were the son and heir of Murad Nematullaevich Nasyrov, when in fact Nasyrov had only one son and heir—Mukhitdin! He knew from Galina that after the perfume poisoning, Malika had been gravely ill and had barely recovered. But he felt no shame.

After all, he loved her! It was just that she, stupidly, refused to see or understand it!!!

Malika continued advancing in the competition. At nearly every performance, the entire hall erupted in applause for her.

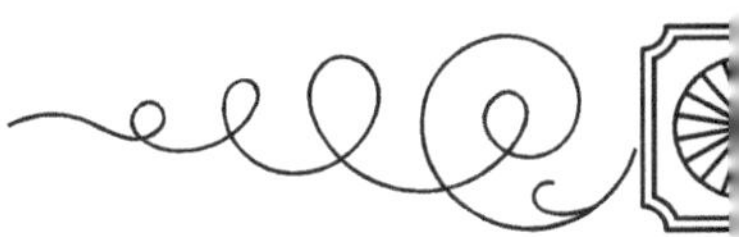

Meanwhile, Mukhitdin was devising a plan to "win" her over. How irresistibly he was drawn to her—how he longed to possess this delightful girl, reminiscent of a princess from the days of Mumtaz Mahal!

But he knew he had to act cunningly and cautiously.

At first, Mukhitdin considered derailing Malika's progress in the contest—perhaps by once again attempting to poison her or even by attacking her and inflicting an injury, then discreetly abducting her, especially since in Moscow she was alone, without friends or relatives. Or perhaps he would try to bribe one of the judges.

But after weighing all the pros and cons, he changed his mind. A different plan had taken shape.

The younger Nasyrov decided not to hinder Malika's progress in the contest—preventing her from reaching the pinnacle of the musical Olympiad—but rather to do everything in his power to facilitate her success. His reasoning was that if Malika failed to advance, she would most likely soon return to Tashkent, home, to her husband. But if she did progress further—and especially if she won—she would surely remain in Russia for a long time, sign a contract, and work with producers seriously and for an extended period. That would mean she'd stay away from her husband and… who knows—perhaps even with him, Mukhitdin?

To execute his plan, Mukhitdin had a considerable amount of money—especially now, after his father had helped him by sending the payment for the Mumtazovs' jewelry.

However, Mukhitdin ultimately did not keep his promise to the elder Nasyrov—he never sent the necklace to Tashkent.

Instead, he conceived the idea of personally presenting it to Malika as a "gift…"

***

Bahadir tried to call Malika periodically; he missed her, but work—both with his father's firm and especially with the new joint-stock company "Bakh-atir," named in his honor—and other problems were increasingly occupying him. Consequently, his calls to his wife became a bit less frequent, and their conversations grew brief and tense, reduced mostly to the two phrases: "How are you?" and "I'm fine."

Malika, too, was extremely busy and exhausted, yet she always tried to find warm, kind words for her dear husband. Still, she sensed that Bahadir was gradually drifting away from her. However, she refused to believe the worst or burden herself with such worries. Her mind was entirely consumed by music—endless, hours-long rehearsals and contest performances.

Meanwhile, Mukhitdin was seeking ways to get closer to the object of his secret passion. But after everything that had happened, he couldn't approach Malika directly—he was afraid she wouldn't accept him. He decided to act more cautiously and through indirect means.

Getting past producer Melodiev proved no easy task, for the maestro of music was almost always surrounded by security and assistants who did everything they could to protect his peace and shield this exceedingly busy man from bothersome onlookers and overzealous fans.

Nevertheless, Mukhitdin managed to break through to Konstantin.

"I have a sponsorship proposal that should greatly interest him as a producer," Mukhitdin told one of the celebrity's assistants.

"Ah, so you're here on business—he's needed by you as a producer?" the woman clarified.

"Exactly right! See what a clever woman you are—you understood everything perfectly!" beamed the younger Nasyrov. "And I'm only here briefly, purely regarding financing."

Konstantin greeted the young stranger very reservedly but courteously, agreeing to give him about five minutes for a conversation.

Mukhitdin explained the purpose of his visit. He wanted to help in every possible way the promising young singer Malika Mumtazova—one of those that Konstantin was currently mentoring in the "Superstar" project.

"May I ask, why such interest in this particular performer?" Melodiev inquired. "Although, of course, I guessed that you, too, are from Uzbekistan. Do you know Malika personally?"

"Yes, yes, we're friends."

"Then why didn't you speak with her first, and come directly to me?"

"The thing is, Konstantin Valeryevich, I'd like to give her a pleasant surprise! She doesn't even know about my coming to Moscow yet. And please, do not mention it to her for now. I'd like to remain incognito for a while. However, I can finance her advancement in the contest. I have that kind of opportunity."

"I understand. But I can't accept your money. That's not how we do things here. If you want to become Malika's personal producer—if you're capable, of course, since that requires specific knowledge, experience, and a good grasp of show business—you're free to invest as much as you want in your friend! And believe me, then no amount of money will be enough. Any amount. Moreover, I must tell you that within the framework of this contest, Malika is already performing so brilliantly and talentfully that she doesn't need any additional financial injections. As her producer, I'll do everything necessary to ensure Malika secures one of the prize positions—that's why we're rehearsing so intensively now… As for your assistance to her as a performer, there's another option: you could contact the contest organisers and offer them your sponsorship services. They'll most likely not refuse you."

"But then my money wouldn't go toward promoting Malika Mumtazova, but rather to advertising the contest as a whole?"

"Yes, exactly so."

"No, that's completely unacceptable to me! I don't need self-advertising like other sponsors, nor the promotion of the entire project on television or elsewhere. I'm not interested in the other performers at all. Only Malika matters."

Konstantin instructed one of his assistants, Vitalik, to escort the guest to the organising committee. However, Mukhitdin had no intention of meeting with any of the "Superstar" organizers. He wanted to see Malika and decided to act directly and straightforwardly.

Vitalik, however, knew where and when Malika Mumtazova could be found. She was already well known on central television. Not only was she the indisputable favorite of the contest—one of its brightest stars—but she was also a very cultured, polite, attentive, and kind person, even toward ordinary people. And Mukhitdin asked Vitalik to do something for him.

"Excuse me, Malika, I have some joyful and pleasant news for you!"

"Pardon me, but do we know each other?"

"Well, not really. But I work here in television. My name is Vitaly."

"Ah, nice to meet you. So, what is your news, Vitaly?"

"The thing is… your husband has come to see you!"

Malika startled and became anxious.

"What?.. And where is he?! I must see him right away!"

"Do you have a moment?"

"Yes, I think I can step away for a little while."

"Then come with me; I'll take you to him."

Malika informed Konstantin Valeryevich's assistants that she'd be out for a few minutes and went after Vitalik. On the way, she called Bahadir. For some reason, he didn't answer, which greatly surprised her.

Malika ran toward him like a doe to a cherished stream. She realised that she missed Bahadir in an indescribable, maddening way! How she longed to embrace him tenderly and kiss him! She was overjoyed that he had managed to come to her.

Vitalik led Malika into one of the empty dressing rooms. As she entered, Vitalik quickly muttered,

"Well, I'll leave you alone now! I suppose you'll find your way back on your own…"

Stepping into the room, Malika was stunned. Seated in the chair before her was… Mukhitdin!

"And where is… my husband?" she asked in astonishment and confusion.

"Hello, Malika! How are you? Your husband? He isn't here, as you can see," said her former friend, whom she hadn't seen in what seemed like an eternity—ever since, before his departure to India, they had said goodbye in her courtyard, and many things had happened since then. Malika was so flustered that she couldn't immediately recall just how much harm that "friend" had done to her.

"Hello, Mukhitdin," Malika replied cordially, regaining her

composure. "What brings you here?"

"I came to see you, dear!" he declared, emphasising the word "you" loudly.

"What does that mean? If you merely intended to see me, then… we'll chat for a bit—and then you'll leave. But if…"

"I won't go anywhere without you! I'll go with you—or you come with me. Choose whichever is more convenient for you. Where do you live in Moscow? In a dormitory? Well, I've got a fantastic setup—I'm staying in one of the best hotels here. So, we could even check into my room together right now."

"Sorry, are you out of your mind?! I'm married, you know. And I love my husband very much."

"Malika, that doesn't matter. Understand, silly, that I love you more than your Bahadir ever could. What kind of man is he? But I… I can make you happy. I have money, Malika—lots of money. And I could become your personal producer, since I know a thing or two about music—unlike your loser of a husband…"

"You shouldn't speak of him that way! Bahadir is very…"

"Why doesn't he get out of his enormous debts if he's not foolish? And—on top of that—he sent his young wife to another country so she could earn money for him, allowing him to settle his creditors on her account! A fine man, I must say! I know everything. After all, your husband owes not just to anyone, but to my father! You understand?"

Malika recalled an unpleasant conversation with Murad Nasyrov about Bahadir, as well as Mukhitdin's attempt to assault her and poison her with perfume laced with methyl alcohol.

"First of all, it's not for you to judge him. And secondly, I'm not going anywhere with you. Please, Mukhitdin, leave me alone! Better yet, forget I ever existed. My husband and I are fine, and…"

"It's hard to believe. Why are you here, while he's back in Tashkent? He didn't even come here for a day to support you, to cheer you on?! He probably doesn't help you financially at all! It's more like quite the opposite, in fact. Am I not right?... With me, you'll be snug as a bug."

"Finally, understand that I do not love you, and you and I can never be together. You and I—we are very different people, and being with you… is even frightening and unpleasant to me."

"Oh, is that so?!" Mukhitdin blushed with anger.

"Yes, well, sorry. I have to go. Goodbye."

She turned toward the exit. At the doorway of the dressing room, Mukhitdin shouted after her:

"Well, look. No one has ever humiliated or hurt me like you have, Malika! You're treating me very wrongly, and you'll regret it dearly! I will take revenge on you, Malika! And I, you fool, was even going to return your family's precious necklace to you… Now—you'll never see it again!!!"

But Malika walked away far, and she could no longer hear his words.

A few moments later, Mukhitdin emerged, extremely dismayed, irritated, and angry. He did not bother to chase after Malika.

* * *

Galina Krikunova frequently called Mukhitdin. He himself rarely called her, especially when he was in Delhi—and he mostly phoned when he needed something from that "friend of his friend." But when she called him, he usually answered, not dodging the conversation or hiding. It wasn't out of decency at all—simply, the younger Nasyrov realised that this sly girl, who was truly in love with him, might prove useful to him more than once, and it was best not to upset her too much.

And indeed, without Galina, he wouldn't have been able to punish and "break" Gosha—after all, it was she who had set fire to Gosha's apartment. Admittedly, Mukhitdin had no intention of killing or maiming his father's assistant; he merely wanted to scare Gosha thoroughly so that he wouldn't dare to encroach on someone else's inheritance.

Everything would have been fine, but Galina was jealous. She had long known that Mukhitdin harbored more than a passing infatuation for Malika. For as long as she could, she had endured it, fearing that her own complaints and jealous outbursts might drive Mukhitdin away and inadvertently lose him altogether. Yet inside her, everything was boiling and seething; she was beside herself. And when she learned from Mukhitdin himself that he had flown to Moscow—not to see just anyone, but specifically Malika—a fiery lava of hatred and anger for the potential rival ignited within Galina.

Meanwhile, Malika, who had maintained a warm and close relationship with her dear friend, had no inkling or suspicion of anything amiss—not of Galina's jealousy toward her from Mukhitdin, nor, for that matter, of Galina's burning and uncontrollable hatred.

Galina saw that Mukhitdin was determined to obtain Malika at any cost, to possess her and be with her. But Malika's friend was not one to give up easily. She began to look for ways to thwart Mukhitdin's relationship with Malika—and she devised a plan of action.

59

Tashkent, March 2015

Amin did everything as he had promised Bahadir—he prepared a sound business plan to justify a loan at one of Tashkent's banks, documentarily assuring the bank of his reliability as a client, and secured a large preferential secured loan for the creation of the joint-stock company "Bakh-atir." Taking a conscious risk, he provided the bank—without his father's knowledge— the documents for the assets of Fattaxov PC as collateral.

Bahadir got in touch with Jean Marchal and outlined the proposal to him. Intrigued, Jean traveled from Paris to Tashkent so that, if everything proved good and truly reliable, he could sign the contract. In the agreement between the Uzbek and the French sides, the conditions for Mr. Marchal's investment in the joint-stock company and his receiving a certain percentage of the profits after production began were to be specified. The experienced French businessman understood that the venture was, in a sense, risky and that it would take time to turn a profit.

Jean did not call his own lawyer, as Rudik had kindly provided him with a local one.

"Everything is in order, monsieur—there are no errors; you can sign the contract with confidence," said the lawyer Rudik had arranged for the negotiations.

Marchal hesitated for several minutes—doubting, rereading the contract, asking questions of his prospective partners and the

lawyer, wondering whether either side might let him down—and, in the end, he resolved to sign the agreement.

"I will send the money as quickly as possible," assured the French investor.

Marchal departed, and he transferred the money almost immediately.

Bahadir and Rudik then began constructing a very small factory for the joint-stock company "Bakh-atir." In any case, Rudik supervised the process closely and regularly reported to Bahadir on the progress, noting that construction was well underway.

"And the bulk of the investment needs to be sent right away to our equipment supplier in Italy," Rudik emphasized. "You understand—without equipment, these walls are nothing but useless rubble. We need proper machinery for production.

"By the way, our partner from Italy, Francesco, promised to find an affordable perfume laboratory with experts who have a good 'nose' for scents—we need original formulas for our new fragrances! These European specialists will devise the recipes and formulas, and the actual work will be done here—that is to say, transformed into exquisite perfumes."

"I'll first consult with Amin to see if we can transfer the money to Italy now," objected Bahadir. "After all, he's a financier and knows these matters better than I do."

"Of course, Amin will always be the boss! Fine, so be it! But who are you, Bahadir? You're practically handing over all the power and decision-making to your brother, waiting for his permission on what can or cannot be done. You're a grown man now, you have your own family after all. It's time to be more independent! 'Can we now transfer the money'… Why do you need your Amin's opinion on that?"

"He isn't mine."

"Exactly. He helped us get the loan—thanks to him, and that's that. Let him go his own way, sorting out his father's company and handling his own problems! Now, as the general director of the new joint-stock company, you can manage things yourself—and I'll help you do that."

"Alright. You're right, of course. The best always goes to my brother. But this company is mine! You know, Rudik, I've decided: go ahead and transfer the funds to your Italian partner—do it today!"

"To our Italian partner, boss, our partner. Francesco Valdoni from Milan."

"Very well... our... So, construction is already underway, and soon the equipment will arrive from Italy, and we'll launch production! That's fantastic, Rudik. We'll have our own exclusive and completely unique line, and we'll be the first to release Uzbek perfume brands with European quality! That's so cool!"

"Of course it is, Baha," Rudik chuckled softly.

* * *

Galina personally knew Malika's parents—Sitora and Said Yakhyaevich—as she had been Malika's closest friend for many years. She went to see them.

"I need the address of Bahadir's parents. You see, Malika called me from Moscow and... anyway, you know how caring and attentive she is—so wonderful, always thinking of people, especially the elderly. She asked me to buy some fruits and nuts for them at the bazaar and deliver them as a gift on her behalf. Malika said that when she arrives she'll settle everything with me. But I assured her

461

I would do it entirely selflessly! Although times are hard for me now—nurses' salaries, as you know, are so small…"

"What a good girl you are, Galichka," praised Sitora, serving the unexpected visitor tea with sweets. "A true friend—you fulfill all of Malika's requests and help her in every way you can! Our daughter is very lucky to have you. But still—you shouldn't have to cover all these expenses on your own. We'll help. Isn't that right, Said?"

"Yes, of course," nodded Said Yakhyaevich. "After all, the Fattakhovs are not strangers to us—they are our relatives. Moreover, Abdulla Rustamovich is my long-time dear friend. Here is their address. And please, allow us to help you with the money and the shopping! Or if you prefer, my driver can take you to the market for convenience."

"No, no, it's not necessary—that would be too much. I want to help the old… I mean, elderly myself."

"They lack nothing, except perhaps a little attention…"

"Of course, of course—it's all just for the sake of attention. So, I wanted to say that you don't need to drive me there; but a little money… perhaps I'll take some—so as not to offend you."

And Said Mumtazov handed Galina some money for her visit to the Fattakhovs.

"Thank you," Galina beamed. "Well then, goodbye—I'm off."

"All the best, dear girl!" said Sitora warmly. "Do come by more often."

* * *

Later, Galina thought that it made no sense to spend the entire sum given to her by the Mumtazovs on treats, so she kept more

than half of it for herself...

She then went to the home of Abdulla and Mukhabbat Fattakhov with a modest package of fruits.

"Hello! My name is Galina; I am a close friend of your daughter-in-law Malika," she said as Mukhabbat opened the gate and stared in surprise at the completely unfamiliar, red-haired girl with bright make-up. "Malika asked me to bring you these treats. She's worried about your health!"

"Oh, how nice—so thoughtful. Please, come in... Abdulla! We have a guest from Malika... Although Malika hasn't told us anything about you."

Galina entered the house and handed the packet to the hostess.

"She just isn't up for everything right now. You know, she's completely absorbed in that silly music show in Russia. I've told her more than once: 'Malika, stop this nonsense, especially in a foreign country! You have a husband in Tashkent, and both your parents and his need care—your attention is what's truly important!' And she wouldn't listen at all. It breaks my heart to see how some people only think about themselves!"

Both Fattakhovs listened to this outpouring of a stranger's soul with astonishment and interest.

"Do you think that over there in Moscow, our daughter-in-law... how shall I put it... is involved in something... er... frivolous?" Mukhabbat nearly choked. "But she said that it's a very serious contest for singers, broadcast on television. Though we don't watch it—we have neither cable nor satellite; we stick to the Uzbekistan channel out of habit. So, does that mean it's just some sort of show? Could it be that she even dances—like... like in a club where women or men... are undressed?!"

Just the thought of it made Mukhabbat feel uneasy. She began to imagine all sorts of things—and immediately believed them. And she was horrified.

"Well, no, probably not..." Galina hastily tried to calm Malika's agitated in-laws. "It seems she doesn't dance that much..."

"That much? So she does dance sometimes?!" blushed and tensed Abdulla Rustamovich. "Unbelievable... And she always pretended to be so good, so proper, like an innocent little lamb. But in reality!" he began to shout. "When she comes back, I'll deal with her! I'll quickly knock all this nonsense out of her, and I won't even care that she is the daughter of my close friend!"

"Wait, Abdulla. I can't quite believe all this... It doesn't seem like Malika! Could all this really be true?"

"It's the plain truth," Galina lied shamelessly. "Would I deceive you? Excuse me—of course, you are elderly and shouldn't worry so much—I'm a medical professional, so I know. But I wanted to tell you about her 'innocence'... I'm just afraid you won't listen to me and understand..."

"Why not?" growled Abdulla Rustamovich from his chair. "You're not a fool. Spill it, dear—what else has my daughter-in-law done that's wrong?"

"In short... I don't even know how to say it. My tongue just won't cooperate... She has started meeting regularly with our mutual friend in Moscow. His name is Mukhitdin... And I have seen them... kissing like lovers!"

"Is she out and about, then?!" roared Abdulla Rustamovich. "Well... 'daughter'... I will!... Disgracing my son? Cheating on him?!! When she returns here—I'll kill her!!!"

"What a disgrace..." Mukhabbat whispered in astonishment, completely bewildered by such 'pleasant' and 'innocuous' news.

"Please forgive me for bringing you such bitter news... I under-

stand how embarrassed you must be about your daughter-in-law…
I feel ashamed for her myself… I don't even know what to say!"

"You are blameless, Galina," replied Bahadir's mother. "On the
contrary, thank you for warning us, for opening our eyes to her!
What a disgrace…"

"What was it I wanted to say…" Galina stood and headed for
the door. "She wouldn't listen to me, and she rarely listens at all. But
you, as her husband's parents, will surely take action… Otherwise, I
worry about our Malika, very much…"

"How can she be 'our' daughter now?!! When she returns—I'll
kick her out! I'll kill her!!!" roared Abdulla Fattakhov, clutching his
heart. "It's all well that Bahadir doesn't know yet. But he will find
out anyway! And as for that Mukhitdin—I'll drag him up from
under the earth and punish him!"

"What's the use of looking for him? Here's his phone number—write it down if you wish."

Galina dictated it, and Mukhabbat recorded Mukhitdin's
number.

Suddenly, Abdulla Rustamovich let out a loud groan and began sliding off his chair.

"Ah… oh-oh…" he moaned.

"What's wrong with you, Abdulla? Dear… Are you feeling
unwell again? Galina, call an ambulance! It seems my husband is
having another acute heart attack."

"I'm already calling… What was your address again?… Ah,
right… Yes, miss. Alright, let them come as soon as possible… They
said the ambulance will arrive shortly. Well, don't worry and take
care, okay? I'm off then."

Perhaps I went a bit too far, thought Galina as she left the
Fattakhov house. *But it's nothing to be afraid of. Both Malika and*

Mukhitdin will get what's coming to them!

The ambulance doctor later gave Abdulla Fattakhov a preliminary diagnosis of a second myocardial infarction.

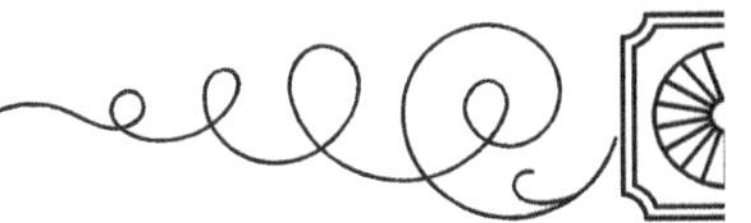

60

There was a knock on the door of Mukhitdin's hotel room. But he wasn't expecting anyone and didn't bother to get up. He sat on the couch, drowning his sorrows in expensive whiskey—he felt like nothing mattered except drinking and sleeping.

Yet someone wouldn't stop knocking loudly. A woman's voice from outside pleaded for the door to be opened immediately.

"I'm coming, I'm coming," Mukhitdin grumbled reluctantly and with irritation. "Who is it?"

"It's the maid. You ordered coffee to your room—I brought it," came the reply.

"I didn't order anything; get out!"

"But how? Aren't you Mr. Nasyrov? You placed an order, and it's already been paid for."

"Strange… Fine, then—hand over your coffee and scram as quickly as you can," Mukhitdin replied "politely" as he opened the door. Standing there on the threshold was indeed the maid, but she wasn't holding any coffee—and she was accompanied by three tough-looking men who immediately barged into his room.

"What does this mean?!" Mukhitdin demanded, indignant. "Who are you? What do you want?"

"Don't worry, we're only here to take what we need—and then we'll leave immediately," one of the thugs said. "Guys, check every drawer, and I'll look under the mattress. Hey, kid—where is it?"

"What—'it'?" Mukhitdin asked, confused. "What exactly are you looking for? I don't have anything."

"You're just drunk— so maybe a bit forgetful. Let us remind you properly!" the second thug said, waving his fist in front of Mukhitdin's nose. "The necklace—gold, studded with rubies and diamonds. Got it? Remember now?"

"Ah—necklace… But I don't have it! I sent it to Tashkent to my father."

For some reason, all three burst into loud, hearty laughter.

"Alright, alright," said the third thug, "the boss warned us that you, buddy, are quite the fantasiser. I figure it's because you've got too many convulsions in that big brain of yours and so you think too long. Don't think—just grab the ornament and hand it over to us quickly."

"Yeah, or we'll straighten out all those twists until your mind is as flat as a board. You want that?"

"N–no, I don't want that, please don't!" Mukhitdin, now sobering with fear, stammered.

Reluctantly, he retrieved from the hotel safe the necklace that belonged to the Mumtazovs and handed it over to the first thug.

"That's the smart move! You should've done that from the start. Honestly, we kind of 'swindled' you a little. None of us would have laid a finger on you—unless you had really resisted or tried to run. And that's all. But anyway—the boss ordered us to be gentle with you. After all, you're his son."

"Whose order? 'The boss's'? My father's?!" Mukhitdin sputtered.

"Well, what did you expect, pal?" replied the second thug. "Of course it's from Murad Nematullaevich—your parent. He sends his regards. Now tell us, how long can you keep putting off the delivery he so desperately needs? He's not a little boy to be toyed with. He transferred the money to you on time—and even more than you asked for, right?"

"Are you trying to deceive your own father, kid? That's not right. Well then, goodbye. Be well!"

And with that, all three thugs disappeared as suddenly as they had appeared.

That very evening, the Mumtazovs' necklace was already in the hands of Murad Nasyrov.

* * *

"Rudik, I've already transferred the bulk of the initial deposit of our joint-stock company 'Bakh-atir' to Italy," Bahadir said as Rudik entered his director's office. "And I think I need to fly to Italy urgently…"

"Come now, Bahadir, you'd be better off waiting here for all the equipment documents to arrive and for customs clearance, while I handle the control over the equipment's assembly and shipment in Italy myself."

"Alright, agreed… fly out on the next available flight."

"Can I count on the company to cover your tickets and per diem?"

"Of course, Rudik…"

"Great, thanks!" Rudik headed for the door. "Shall I go to accounting? I'll tell them that you approved releasing funds to me."

"Hold on, I haven't finished. Sit down for a minute. I'm sorry, I can't give you money right now—we don't have any extra. Once you return, if you hand in your airline tickets at the company's accounting and submit the hotel bills and all other necessary expenses—after the fact we'll try to reimburse you. But for now—it just won't work. And you boasted that you found some rich investors?"

"Yes, some very bad-ass ones. They're local 'new money Uz-beks.' Actually, one of them is a real oligarch."

"What's his name? I hope it's not Murad Nasyrov?"

For some reason, Rudik fell silent.

"Well, why do you care for his name now, Bahadir? We haven't signed the agreement yet. I must first meet with him, have a preliminary discussion, agree verbally on everything—and then, naturally, I'll invite my priceless boss, the general director of our joint-stock company, Bahadir Abdullaevich Fattakhov, to sign the contract! And the money will start flowing to us like a stream! But right now, I'd like to buy the tickets with our company's funds…"

"My company, Rudik—mine. After all, I'm the principal founder. And remember, my brother Amin, who found us the initial capital for the office, for registering the documents, and so that everything could get started."

"Yes, I remember. And I'm just here on the side, your mere lackey."

"Don't speak like that! You know how much you mean to us—you're my deputy and my closest friend and assistant… And as for the investments we've already received, Rudik, those still need to be worked, and then repaid to all the investors with interest. I think we're still far from steady cash flow and great wealth."

"Well, don't be such a pessimistic nitpicker! Life is wonderful, and everything's fine—we'll get rich! By the way, what about the money from Jean Marchal? I hope you sent that to Italy as well to my… I mean, for Francesco, for the equipment?"

"Yes, I sent it. A small portion."

"Why only a small portion?!" Rudik began to get nervous. "Why are you doing that? What are you thinking?! You promised to send everything!!! And now we won't have enough for the purchase."

"First of all, I never promised you that—you're mixing things up again. And secondly, don't worry about a thing: I pressed our economist, and he calculated everything and assured me that the funds already transferred are exactly enough for the down payment on all the necessary machines."

Rudik fidgeted in his chair, then abruptly stood up.

"Yes, I wanted to ask you, Rudik: how's our construction? Is it going on?"

"It's in full swing," Rudik replied irritably and discontentedly. "I've already told you. How many times must you have to ask the same thing? I'm not a parrot that just keeps repeating things!"

"Well, don't get angry or take it personally. I must check everything thoroughly. That's why I'm the director and a founder. Tomorrow, please, present me with a detailed report for every sum of money allocated to construction. All right? I'll cross-check it with the accounting documents."

"Everything is in order there. What's the need to double-check? Do you think I'm a thief?"

"Alright, Rudik, don't talk nonsense and, I beg you, don't get worked up. It's hard to recognize you sometimes. You're always so soft, kind, friendly—but now… Of course, I don't think you're a thief, and I trust you as I trust myself. It's just a formality. You yourself said I'm the boss. That means I must lead not only on paper but also in practice. Right?"

"Yeah, right," Rudik muttered, then added much more gently, "I'm sorry, Bahadir, I lost my temper—I'm just a bit tired."

"That's understandable. We've embarked on such a huge venture. A national production!"

***

The next day, before going to work, Bahadir decided to visit his father in the hospital. Abdulla Fattakhov had undergone surgery, was still in intensive care, and was extremely weak.

"Dad, hello—how are you? You don't need to say much; just move your lips or nod—I'll understand. What's wrong? Why did you have to scare us all again?"

"Everything's fine, son… Don't worry," his father whispered, barely moving his lips. "Please, you… support your… mother."

"Of course, I will. I'll visit her this evening."

"No, you'd better go now. Please…"

"Understood. I'll leave immediately. Get well soon!"

Bahadir hadn't always been the most obedient son. But this time, seeing his father's condition and fearing to lose him, out of respect and love, he left the hospital and immediately went to see his mother. On the way, he called Rudik several times, but Rudik didn't answer.

Strange, Bahadir thought. *Maybe he's still asleep? It's high time to be at work!*

Amin, Rano, and Bahadir's mother wasn't feeling well either. The illness of her husband and the bad news about her daughter-in-law had taken a toll on her.

Mukhabbat wanted to gently break the news to Bahadir, but as a warm-hearted woman she couldn't keep such heart-wrenching information to herself for long—and she was convinced that it was best if her son heard it from her directly.

"Sit down, dear," she said.

They shared tea and a delicious cupcake—Mukhabbat was an excellent baker—and talked for a while. About fifteen minutes

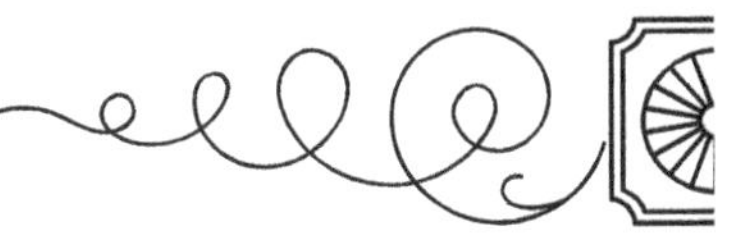

later, Bahadir stood up.

"Mom, I have to go; it's time for work. Dad just asked me to…."

"Yes, yes, I know. I've went to see him early this morning. Sit a little longer—I won't hold you up."

"Did something happen? I mean, aside from Dad's heart attack and surgery?"

"Yes, I think something did. Tell me, have you been calling Malika lately?"

"Malika? Is there any news from her? Is something wrong?" Immediately, Bahadir felt uneasy. He felt ashamed for not calling his wife more often—as if he'd abandoned Malika to cope with all her difficulties alone. "Well… I do call her occasionally, of course… But, honestly, I can't do it so often…"

"So essentially you've left your young, beautiful wife unsupervised?"

"What exactly happened, Mom? Can you explain it clearly?"

"Son, I'm not sure I can believe it… But yesterday a friend of Malika's came by and said that…"

Mukhabbat sighed heavily.

"What friend? What did she say? Mom, please, don't torment me—just tell me!"

"Apparently, your Malika is… cheating on you with another man. Her friend actually saw it."

"What's her name?" Bahadir frowned.

"Galina. Do you know her?"

"Well, only very superficially. Ever since Malika married me, I don't think she talks to this Galina often—maybe only on the phone. But it's not like I'm not spying on my wife…"

"You're not a spy—but you really should keep a closer eye on her. You're newlyweds; your marriage isn't that solid yet. So please, son, sort this out for yourself! The guy she's allegedly with—call him Mukhitdin."

"Mukhitdin? That scoundrel! I've heard about him—my wife mentioned him. But she absolutely can't stand him; he's tried making a move on her more than once, and she's always turned him down. What connection could they possibly have? It's all nonsense… Besides, Mom, you know very well that Malika is an angel. She would never betray or cheat. That's just not like her!"

"Maybe, dear. I want to believe that too. But you really need to check for yourself. Here, take some money from me—go to Moscow, see your wife, and find out if everything is really alright, and whether what people are saying is true!"

"Well, 'people are saying' sounds like an exaggeration—it's just one friend's word, isn't it? Alright then. I don't need the money; I'll handle it… I'll fly to Moscow."

* * *

There was no word from Rudik—not that evening, nor the next day, nor the day after. At first, he didn't answer the phone, and then his line had become "unavailable." On the fourth day, troubled by the strange situation, Bahadir went to see Amin at their father's firm.

Bahadir now visited there much less frequently, since he was busy with his own joint-stock company. But from his phone conversations with Amin, he learned that the situation with the shipment from France hadn't improved. The cargo still hadn't arrived in Tashkent, and the French representatives of the L'Oréal brand, claiming that their goods were "stuck" somewhere along the way.

They were still blaming not the Kazakhstani transporter-thief but the most aggrieved party—"Fattaxov PC." They were demanding that the Fattakhovs pay a colossal VAT. In short, those problems had yet to be resolved.

But what troubled Bahadir most now was the force majeure affecting his joint-stock company—a situation that clearly arose because of Rudik, who had, as it seemed, vanished into thin air.

"That's it—your buddy has completely 'dropped' you!" Amin said, smiling sadly at his younger brother. "I had a feeling this might happen, Bahadir, because, forgive me, I never trusted that Rudik guy. Just like our mother warned you! She warned you about him quite some time ago…"

"I remember. But maybe he just hasn't had a chance to call?"

"Then why can't you reach him? It's always 'unavailable.' Write him an email, a Facebook Messenger, message him on Agent or Odnoklassniki—whatever! There's the internet in the twenty-first century!"

"I've already written to him wherever I could. He's not answering. He hasn't been active on social media these past few days. I wouldn't be surprised if he deleted all his accounts. But—it just doesn't add up… Rudik isn't like that; he couldn't!"

"You're still such a trusting boy, Bahadir. He's exactly the kind of guy he is—you just never wanted to see it. I'm afraid you've been swindled, brother; you've been taken for a ride. And that means we're all in serious trouble now—both your joint-stock company and, worst of all, father's firm. I practically put it up as collateral! And that's disastrous. How are we going to repay the loan?"

"Well, we'll wait and see," Bahadir replied, his tone unexpectedly enigmatic, and for the first time in a long while, he smiled at his elder brother.

61

"Hello, Said Yakhyaevich? Good evening—this is Nasyrov."

"Good evening, Murad Nematullaevich. I thought I recognised you. How's your health?"

"Well… tolerable. I did promise I'd return your family necklace, didn't I? And well—I've found it."

"Really? That's wonderful. And where has it been all this time?"

"Never mind that. Will you be at home? Have you gotten off work yet? Right, I figured that, perfect. Then one of my men will be arriving shortly, saying it's from me, and handing over the ornament."

"Thank you, Murad Nematullaevich. Tell me, how can I ever repay you for this?"

"Please, don't mention it. What accounts can there be between friends? You owe me absolutely nothing. Couldn't I just do something for a friend entirely selflessly?"

Alas, apparently not—you know that Bhodjvani will pay you handsomely for returning this piece of jewelry! I know it all too well…

"Yes, of course you can—that's very noble," replied Dr. Mumtazov, his irony artfully concealed. "Thank you."

Within a couple of hours, the family necklace—with its rubies and diamonds—was finally home. Now Firuz-begim, Sitora, and Said had only to wait for Malika's return from Russia—her homecoming being their most cherished treasure, one that had always meant more to them than gold, or diamonds and rubies, or even life itself…

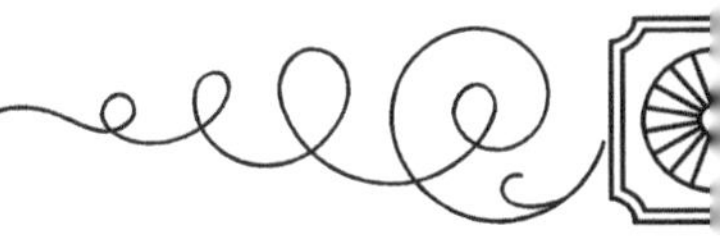

* * *

Abdulla Rustamovich was on the mend, convalescing at home. His sons never mentioned any work or business problems to him; when he inquired, they answered evasively and briefly, usually summing it up with "everything's fine."

However, Amin was deeply troubled by the new problem that had arisen because of Rudik.

Meanwhile, Bahadir decided to visit his factory to see how construction was progressing. He had long wanted to go, but had never found the time. Now, something was urging him to make the trip—and Rudik's sudden "disappearance" had been gnawing at him. What he saw shocked him! Not only had construction not even begun, but there wasn't a single worker on the premises—only an empty, filthy hangar. "I'm such a fool!" Bahadir thought bitterly. "Both this disgraceful affair with Malika and Rudik's actions prove that you can't trust people... And under no circumstances should you bring friends or relatives into your business—because it always becomes awkward to strictly and meticulously control all their affairs. I was so afraid of offending Rudik—and what did that lead to? It led to him shamelessly and brazenly fleecing me. And I inadvertently put my own brother in a bind—now he has to repay money to the bank... Alright, let's think about what to do next..."

* * *

Malika was anxious because Bahadir wasn't calling or even answering his phone... She recalled the words of her teacher, Boris Petrovich, with whom she still occasionally spoke on the phone:

"The success that has already caught up with you—and the success yet to come—will force you and everyone close to you, including your husband, your parents, and your friends, to reexamine and rethink your relationships... Be prepared for that."

Indeed! That's so true... the girl thought bitterly. Yet it was better to believe in Omar Khayyam's saying: "If God wishes to make you happy, He will lead you along the most difficult road, for there are no easy paths to happiness..."

She was also troubled by the fact that her wonderful friend Rano—whom she had heard about from Bahadir just a couple of weeks ago—had fallen ill. And another cause of nervousness and anxiety was Galina Krikunova.

A day before the semifinals of the contest, Galina called Mukhitdin in Moscow from Tashkent. This time he treated her sharply and rudely—he was not in the mood.

"Why do you call me so often?" the young man asked. Galina got the impression he had drunk quite a bit; his words slurred and his thoughts muddled. "Why are you on my ass like a leech? I'm not Alain Delon. What do you want from me?! Can you say it? Do you need my money? I'm not as rich as my... never mind, you don't need to know. Leave me alone, understand? I love someone else! Ugh... I hate her, that bitch. That Malika—may she be... but she's better than you, like the sky is better than the earth... the earth... no, even better... than the underworld. Got it? You're not even worth her notice! That's it, don't call me anymore. I've had enough! If I ever need you, I'll call you myself."

He abruptly hung up.

Krikunova was in a trance from that conversation, from the words of "her" Mukhitdin.

Just wait, my dear! Soon Malika's husband and his parents will

*find you, and then you'll get what's coming to you!!! I've no empathy for
you—you'll get your just deserts...*

In despair, she immediately called Malika.

"Malika, hello! I hope you remember me?"

The unsuspecting Malika was genuinely glad to hear from her.

"Gal, hi. Of course I got it. How wonderful that you called just
now—I really need your support! How are you, my friend?"

"You still think we're friends?" Galina suddenly burst into
laughter. "Don't make me laugh! And why should I support you?
You're always like this: thinking only of yourself, and nothing else.
I heard you're getting all cozy with my guy over there in Moscow!
Don't you have your own husband?"

"What?... With which guy? I don't understand. Gal, who are
you talking about?"

"Don't play dumb. My Mukhitdin—I know he flits around you
like a bee around a flower. He's clung to you as if you were dripping
with honey, and he just won't let go! I don't understand one thing:
what does he have in you that he can't find in me? You're just a
singer, an actress! So what?"

"Gal, please stop. You'll be ashamed of such words later."

"Shame? Me?!! You should be ashamed—stealing other wom-
en's suitors! I thought my Mukhitdin would go off to India and
completely forget about that Malika. But look at him—she's in
Moscow, and he's followed her there like a calf on a leash!"

"Gal, wait. But I don't need any Mukhitdin at all."

"Look, your husband is going to give you and Mukhitdin a
piece of his mind! I told Bahadir's parents everything about you
two love birds..."

"Whom? What did you say? Why? What for? I haven't done
any..."

"Just shut up already! Because! And if you don't like that young man, then drive him away from you. Why give him hope? Must all the blessings of life go only to you? Where's the justice in that? Mark my words—you won't be happy."

"What are you saying? And why?... Gal, have a heart!" Malika felt herself growing uneasy; her legs began to buckle. She was horrified—what had happened to Galina? What had become of their once strong and, as she believed, reliable friendship?

"Listen, if I have inadvertently wronged you in any way, please forgive me..."

"Oh, oh, oh! How high-minded and conscientious of you... How I hate you! All my life, everyone's attention goes only to you. Malika—a beauty, Malika—a genius, Malika—a great talent! The kindest, most sensitive, and most responsive girl, an angel! And all the men only have eyes for her—they can't get enough. And what about me? Am I any worse than you? Well, tell me! You don't know. That's what it is... The only consolation is that I can cause you as much pain as you've caused me."

"Pain?... Why, Gal? Stop it. I'm hanging up now."

"No, you listen. Yesterday they brought someone to our hospital... you know who? Guess!"

"Bahadir?!" Malika gasped. "That's why he isn't answering the phone and isn't calling me! What's happened to him? Tell me, Galina, what happened to my husband?"

"What will become of him, you fool? Don't freak out—he's fine. He isn't answering your calls because your husband is convinced of your infidelity!!!"

"Infidelity? Him? Mine?... With whom?!!"

Inside, Malika thought, *That poor girl must be completely off her rocker—that's what happens when you have no success on the personal front...*

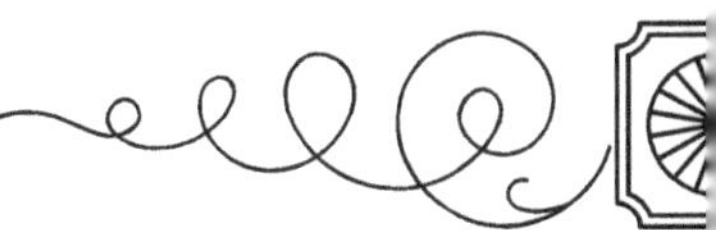

"It's with Mukhitdin, you dummy!" retorted Krikunova. "I've told everything to his parents. And they must have passed it on."

"Oh, Gal, what have you done! Why? After all, Bahadir's father has a weak heart—he won't be able to take it. Moreover, you know as well as I do that nothing of the sort is actually happening—it's all lies, you've made it all up!"

"But they all believed me, Malika!... So you want to know who is seriously ill right now? I'll tell you: your friend Rano, Bahadir's sister."

"What?! What's wrong with her?!" Malika shrieked, horrified by the word "seriously."

"Ischemic heart disease together with a severe form of diabetes. There's nothing that can be done for your Rano anymore. At any moment, she could lapse into a coma from which she might not recover. And you, her friend Malika—you're very far away; she has no husband, her parents are also ill, and I've heard that her brothers are deeply entangled in some serious business problems. And be thankful to me for warning you out of my own kindness! But I repeat, this is only so that you feel as much pain and hardship as I do right now!!!"

Then, without another word, Galina abruptly hung up.

Malika was shocked, devastated by everything she had heard. The malice in her friend's words did nothing to surprise her; instead, with a roar in her mind, her favorite quatrain by Saadi sprang to life:

> *"The sage, like musk—even if unwilling,*
> *Spreads his fragrance all around;*
> *The fool, like a drum, resounds—*
> *Just because he is empty."*

Her first impulse was to run to her producer and announce that she would catch the next flight to Tashkent and refuse to participate any further in the TV project. However, after careful thought, Malika realised that she could not allow such cowardice to prevail, and summoning all her willpower at the semifinals, she delivered a grand performance...!

* * *

Rano knew that diabetes itself, by and large, is not a fatal disease. However, to prolong one's life it is essential to adhere to several mandatory and important conditions: complications must be avoided, one must be constantly monitored by a good endocrinologist, follow a strict diet, and, most importantly, try to avoid stress.

And although this attractive, vivacious young woman tried her utmost to stick to her diet—even though her metabolism had long been almost irreparably impaired, and she was under medical supervision and already taking insulin—there were still problems. For one thing, having a job, elderly parents, and a one-year-old daughter whom Rano was raising without a husband, she could hardly follow any treatment regimen strictly and consistently. Occasionally, there were lapses... She loved all the joys of life and was always at the center of the city's most interesting events, surrounded by friends; she especially found it easy to connect with boys, engaging them in lively, heartfelt conversations... Rano devoted herself completely, helping her loved ones not only through her actions but also with kind words, understanding, and support...

Rano had already begun to feel her condition deteriorating, but she told no one and did not wish to worry anyone. It was only

immediately after the quarterfinal and a few days before the semifinals of the "Superstar" contest that Rano managed to reach Malika by phone—who knew nothing of her illness—and congratulate her on a brilliant performance, which Rano had watched on television with delight. Out of delicacy, Rano refrained from mentioning that Bahadir, upset with Malika, had deliberately chosen not to watch the broadcast.

"I'm so proud of you, my friend!" Rano exclaimed in a bright, cheerful voice that day. "I was overjoyed for you—you did such an amazing job! And you even sang a song in our native Uzbek language with a national melody over in Russia… You've once again glorified our great country. I'm sure they'll award you a medal of order for that."

"Oh, come on, Rano! What medal?" Malika replied, blushing. "It's not like I'm putting all this work in for medals. I do it simply because I love our homeland so much, and I love my people—and especially all of you, my dear ones! I miss you so much, it's indescribable… By the way, Rano, did you receive my parcel with the medicines? Yes? Good. And for whom are they, if you don't mind me asking? Ah, you'll tell me later? Fine, as you wish… You're not hiding anything from me, are you? You're not sick yourself? Are you sure? Alright… If you need my help, just say so!"

Thus, Rano, sparing her friend's feelings, did not mention a word about her own illness—which had, like an octopus, already spread its cunning and dangerous tentacles over her life.

*　*　*

That same evening, Rano asked Bahadir to come to their home. "Brother, perhaps while Malika is away, you could live with us at our parents'?" Rano suggested. "And Dad is still weak; he could really use your attention."

"I understand you, little sister," replied Bahadir. "I can't promise I'll move in permanently, but I'll think about it, okay? And today I'll definitely come over."

And late that evening, just as he had said, he crossed the threshold of his parents' house.

The four of them sat together enjoying tea and delicious pastries—as used to be the case in the Fattakhov family in old times (now only Amin was missing). Everyone was pleased by the warm family gathering and in good spirits. No one wanted to think about or recall any problems or misfortunes that evening.

After tea, Mukhabbat offered for Bahadir to stay the night. He agreed. Rano then asked her younger brother to come into her room for a little chat before bed.

"Bahadir, I can see something is really bothering you," Rano began. "It must be the difficulties… because of Rudik's disappearance?"

"And you already know about that?" Bahadir smiled sadly. "So Dad knows too… That's very bad."

"Amin has told me. But Dad only knows that your friend Rudik went away somewhere—he overheard it by chance. But he doesn't know anything about what that 'friend' did."

"I'm worried that if Dad finds out that my brother and I have ruined his company, things will go terribly wrong. Dad will be furious. But that's not the worst part—I'm afraid for his heart. He could get so upset, because this company is his 'child,' and it means so much to him. And he might have to let it go, perhaps even sell it at an auction."

"Don't worry, Bahadir. God willing, everything will work out…

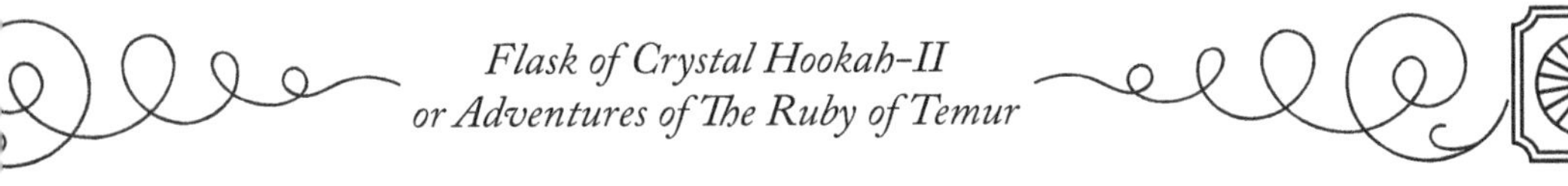

But I know of one more serious reason why you're walking around as if you're underwater, gloomier than a storm cloud."

"Is it that noticeable? Perhaps I'm acting rudely, not very politely, right?"

"No, not at all. You've always been and remain a kind and well-mannered person. I heard that Galina has been saying awful things about your Malika to our parents! It's terrible…"

"Please, Rano! I don't want to hear anything about… about Malika right now."

"Don't say that, Bahadir. After all, she's your wife, and I know you love her."

"Yes, but she's cheating on me!!!"

"You shouldn't even entertain such thoughts. That's exactly what I wanted to talk to you about. Listen… Oh—"

Rano suddenly clutched her heart, and her face flushed red.

"Sister! What's wrong with you? Are you feeling ill?!"

"N–no. Nothing, don't be alarmed. It'll pass… I just need to take my medicine…" Rano found the necessary pills and swallowed them. "Alright, it seems to have passed. As I was saying, here's the thing: Galina's words are pure lies and slander. Your wife is like a pristine mountain spring, a clear stream. By nature, she is faultless—as if she were an angel. And you're very lucky that such a wonderful woman married you and loves you. I know her well; we are steadfast and true friends. Of course, she isn't perfect, and like all people, she has her weaknesses. But compared to Galina, those weaknesses can be considered sacred virtues."

"Rano, don't defend her!"

"Please, just listen to me and believe me. I know Galina well enough—she has no qualms about lying, defaming, and slandering someone, especially if she's simply jealous. Malika has a very negative attitude toward Mukhitdin, whereas Galina, on the other hand, fancies him. That's probably why she has instigated this dirty intrigue. Of course, if you wish, you can go to Moscow and check everything out for yourself. But, God willing, Malika will soon return victorious to Tashkent—and you'll see for yourself that she has always been completely faithful to you, and you have nothing to suspect!"

"Thank you, sister!" Bahadir beamed and brightened. "Honestly, you've brought me back to life... I love Malika so much, and I was so worried about all this. I'm just a fool! I'll probably do as you advise—simply wait calmly until the contest is over and my wife comes home. After all, if she loves me, then no matter what 'mountains of gold' are promised to her, she'll come back immediately, right?"

"Of course, absolutely! Don't you doubt it. You two make such a wonderful couple…"

62

Agra, 1621.

In April, the wedding of Ladilli and Shahriyar took place—and, as is customary in the East, it was lavish and sumptuous. Mehruhn-Nissa had spared no effort to ensure that her daughter's wedding was even more extravagant than the wedding of Shah Jahan with Arjumand-begum.

The entire city was perfumed with the scents of countless lamps and hookahs burning everywhere; every house was adorned with garlands of flowers, and on every street tents laden with refreshments had been set up while cauldrons of charitable feasts bubbled away. Music played and drums beckoned the people to celebration near the mosque, where gold and silver coins were tossed into the crowd by the handful. Many guests remarked that on the groom Shahriyar's head was a red silk turban decorated with a large and extraordinarily beautiful ruby.

In the chambers of Arjumand and Shah Jahan in Agra, Asaf Khan paid them a visit.

"It has been only a few weeks since the death of our father, Giyas Bek," he said, "and my sister's attitude toward me has worsened markedly. She remembered whose side I'm on—in which 'camp' I belong, so to speak. Now she does everything she can to compromise and sully my reputation before the Padishah, plotting against me—her own brother—at nearly every turn! But I will not relent, for my daughter is dearer to me than my sister."

"Thank you, father!" Arjumand embraced him tenderly. "Shah

Jahan and I now cherish your support so much."

"I have always been confident in your loyalty to us," said Shah Jahan's father-in-law warmly. "If, as I hope and believe, I become Padishah, I promise you will be among my closest advisers—perhaps even vizier. But now… my father is ill, and only the Almighty knows how much time he has left. Which of his sons will he ultimately choose?"

"Whichever one he chooses—she, his wife, will decide," Asaf Khan replied with a rueful smile. "For example, he immediately approved the marriage of Ladilli and Shahriyar. He even told me that I was very fortunate—saying that my sister is the beloved wife of the ruler and her daughter a princess!"

"And what? He didn't even mention Princess Arjumand, my wife?!" Shah Jahan asked gloomily. "No? Then it seems my father is showing me disrespect!"

"Don't try to find meaning in what he didn't say, shahzade. Perhaps it's just a coincidence. However, one thing is clear to Mehruhn-Nissa—Arjumand and I are not like Ladilli and Shahriyar; we won't tiptoe before her and obey her every command without question. I believe it is best for us to wait for better times. Any sudden moves might startle her, and that would be entirely undesirable for us. We'll watch silently as events unfold. I, my prince, will speak in your favour before the Padishah."

…A few days later, Shah Jahan received an order "from the Padishah," which clearly meant—per Mehruhn-Nissa's design—that he was to set out at once for the south of Hindustan, to the Deccan, to once again subdue the rebellious and insurgent lords there.

***

Shah Jahan was informed that in the Deccan, indeed, unrest had broken out again. The Padishah was right about one thing: it is difficult, if not nearly impossible, to subdue discontented southerners at such a great distance from the capital. Yet he could just as well have sent Mahabat Khan or, at worst, his other son Shahriyar—instead of the heir to the throne! If not for Mehruhn-Nissa's insinuations that it should be Shah Jahan himself who goes…

And what reward would he receive from his father in the event of victory and the complete crushing of the rebels?… A brief "thank you" whispered in a secluded corner, in private, without witnesses? Would all his past victories and achievements be remembered? No?… Yet only two or three years ago everything was completely different—his father loved and held him in high esteem! But now… if he were to fail, Mehruhn-Nissa would triumph and rejoice. Shah Jahan imagined what she would say to his father:

"How can a man who cannot even manage a single small province rule a great empire!"

And the news from Asaf Khan about what is happening in the palace, in the capital, will reach Arjumand and I only after many months, Shah Jahan thought sadly. *No, I must speak with my father. Perhaps he will change his decision?*

For some reason, Jahangir long refused to see his "beloved" son. Finally, seeing Shah Jahan's persistence and humility, he consented and invited him to his presence—but not into his working office or private quarters, but into… the place for ablutions—the ghusl-khana. Meanwhile, preparations were in full swing in the palace for Jahangir and Mehruhn-Nissa to depart for Lahore, and from there, for the cool Kashmir, which the Padishah adored. In Agra Jahangir felt unwell, often gasping for breath—he could not tolerate the climate.

"Dear father, do you truly wish for me to go for an extended period to the Deccan and serve as your governor there? And what about my jagir, Hissar Feroz?"

"Your jagir?!"—for some reason the Padishah immediately exploded in anger—a reaction he had never before shown when speaking with Shah Jahan. "Since when has anything in my empire become yours?! It seems you are in a great hurry to take my place, son!"

"No, no, father! Please forgive me; I merely misspoke," hastened Shah Jahan to calm him. "I had not thought to…"

"You should think carefully when you speak to your master. You were given an order! Instead of following it unquestioningly like a dutiful subject, you come to me, disturb me, interrupt my pleasant rest, and ask foolish, pointless questions. And I have already given Hissar Feroz to my beloved son Shahriyar. By the way, are you aware that the red turban and the Temur Ruby are now in his possession?"

Shah Jahan was deeply surprised and shocked; his father, though long the Padishah, had never before spoken to him in such a tone. Yes, that woman—Mehruhn-Nissa, who had undoubtedly fanned the flames of their relationship on many occasions—seemed to poison everything around her; even the very air had grown heavy and foul. A sinful thought crept into Shah Jahan's heart: might she one day treacherously do away with the Padishah himself?.. And—what about his turban? More importantly—how can he now reclaim the principal symbol of royal authority, the precious Temur Ruby?

"Father, you gave my wife the ruby! Why is it now with Shahriyar?"

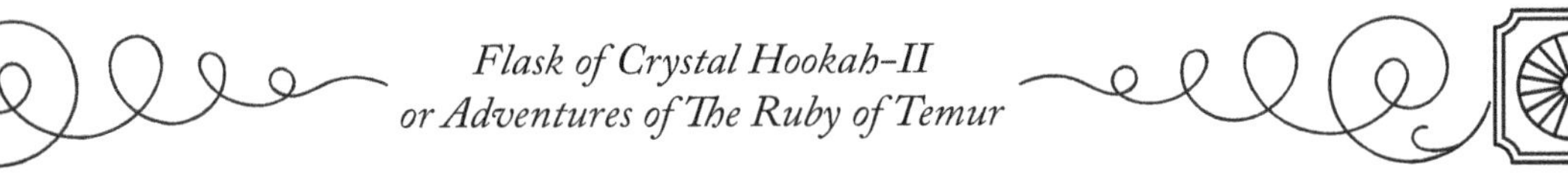

For the moment, Jahangir decided not to answer that question. However, noticing the dismay and deeply troubled look on his son's face—suggesting that he had perhaps overstepped—he softened slightly.

"Alright, my son, come here and embrace your father in farewell. You depart tomorrow."

"As you wish, father," Shah Jahan replied, utterly crestfallen. "So it appears there is no hope of remaining in Agra after all. Then, if you will allow me, I have one request. May I?"

"It depends on what it is. Well, speak!"

"Allow me to take with me to the Deccan my entire family—and my elder brother Khusrau as well. He has lived here in the palace for many years, blind and chained to a guard. This journey might at least cheer him up and brighten his dismal life."

"Very well. Let him go! I have endured that traitor for so many years already! How long must I care for him? Given my frail health, it has become a burden. In short, I grant you permission to take him with you, Shah Jahan!"

Jahangir did not see fit to personally see his two sons off—he excused himself on account of his own poor health. He merely conveyed his wish for their safe journey.

Strangely enough, Khusrau-Mirza did not want to go; he resisted, although he had never before openly clashed with Shah Jahan. He felt that the sudden care and concern Shah Jahan was showing him were not without reason… His dear brother knew full well of Khusrau's endless hatred—both toward him and toward all the other brothers. Yes, Shah Jahan was clearly up to something… But Khusrau had no choice; he had to go.

And Arjumand was pregnant once again. Shah Jahan, as he re-entered her chamber, noted that she remained as beautiful and desirable as ever, and that her smile brought him immense joy.

***

Decan, Burhanpur, 1621

Arjumand had just lost her newborn daughter. What a terrible fate… Again—her child, scarcely born, had died. All those arduous marches! Journeys to such distant lands, away from the familiar comforts of home…

"Kill that wretch Mehruhn-Nissa, little brother!" Khusrau said to Shah Jahan one peaceful day, when, with no battles raging, they were sitting together after dinner in one of the former princely palaces once captured by the Mughals. "You are braver than that—I know you can do it! Were I as clever as you, I would now be at the head of these imperial troops, ready to charge into battle at a single command. Although… I think, in my opinion, you could command an even larger army… someday."

"What are you trying to say? Speak plainly!"

"Well… perhaps you might even be deprived of that right! All our deprivations are because of her…"

"I am the first among the Padishah's sons!" retorted Shah Jahan. "And why do you want to get rid of his wife?"

"Ask yourself: are you really the first for her? For now, some woman of foreign blood, not of royal descent, is deciding everything! If it were not for her influence over the ruler, you would still be his most beloved son to this day. Isn't that so? Send the cavalry immediately—let your soldiers kill her!"

"You still haven't answered my question. What would her death give you?"

"Her death would cause my father great suffering, brother. A father who made me unhappy, who has always despised me. He

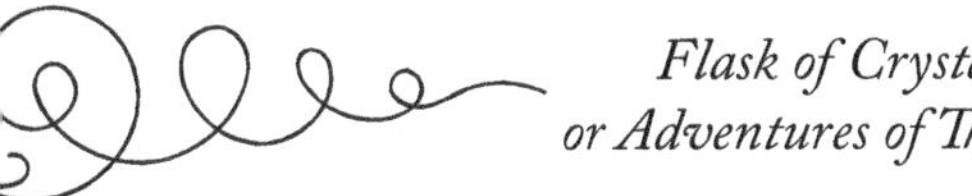

will weep and shout in pain—just as on the day, by his order, I was deprived of my eyes. And finally, he will die in agony and torment!"

"You really are a cruel, merciless one. It seems I understand: you need her life—to save your own. Or—to ascend the throne, is that it?"

"What are you saying?! How can I compete with you, my sighted brother? I'm not even thinking about that," Khusrau immediately lied. In the depths of his missing eyes one could see fear.

A few days later, after long deliberation, Shah Jahan resolved to murder… his brother Khusrau.

Through the servants, Arjumand learned of this. She was meant to speak with her husband…

"My beloved, but why?! Please, my husband, I beg you, do not do this!"

"You do not understand: he still has support, and he might usurp the throne in my place and destroy us all. You do not know how cruel and ruthless this Khusrau is."

"Very well, suppose so. Then exile him, or better yet, shackle him in chains and fetters! Or, if you wish, lock him away in the most dreadful dungeon. But do not kill him!!!"

"What is this? Do you harbour tender, affectionate feelings for my brother?" Shah Jahan growled, his expression sullen.

"Please, do not speak that way, I beg you! You know I love only you. But Khusrau's death would be a curse upon us—it would fall upon our children and our entire destiny! If you kill him, you will be the first to break the sacred law of Temur. Remember, your great ancestor proclaimed three centuries ago, 'Do not harm your brothers, even if they deserve it; do not kill your kin.' All the Mughals have always observed that precept. Babur passed it on to Humayun, Humayun to Akbar, Akbar to your father Jahangir. And you know that they obeyed those words even in the most difficult and, it seemed, hopeless situations. It was that very law that once saved Khusrau from the punitive hand of your father. The same blood flows in your brother as in you—do not spill it, for, God forbid, it might defile us and our descendants!"

"No, nothing bad will happen. I have listened to you, my wife, although this is none of your business. And the throne will be mine, and mine alone."

"At such a cost? That is horrible. I do not want that!" she gasped, choking on the terror that had overtaken her. "His blood could ruin us. Spare your brother! Make him renounce all his claims to the throne. And then—what will become of Shahriyar and Parvaz? Will you kill them too? They can defend themselves; they have armies! Think at least of our children! What kind of inheritance is that, one stained with blood?"

"Understand, it is for them that I think. If I do not begin protecting them now from anyone who might threaten their future, believe me, there will come a day when both you and I—and all of them—will be slaughtered by whoever ascends the throne, whoever he may be. Such is our reality, as it has been for centuries. Forgive me…"

That very night, by Shah Jahan's order, his soldiers entered Khusrau's quarters and slew him. He did not resist, accepting his dreadful fate in resignation. He was buried as a common man—not as a prince. The Padishah was told that Khusrau had suddenly died from acute abdominal pain.

The spirit of Khusrau began to haunt Shah Jahan's life, and soon his son by Khasina also died. After this tragic event, Shah Jahan divorced her…

***

Burhanpur, 1622

Soon, Padishah Jahangir sent Shah Jahan a letter informing him that the Shahanshah of Persia, Abbas, had treacherously led his troops into Kandahar—which now belonged to the Mughal Empire. He wrote that a powerful counterstrike must be delivered using the army that he, Padishah Jahangir, can lead. "Shah Jahan must immediately march the army north!" ordered Jahangir.

Shah Jahan continued fighting the relentless lords of the Deccan; many of his men perished. How he longed for Agra—he dreamed of entering it as a victor, even better, as the new Padishah. Yet even here in the Deccan—after all, this was his own land—if he left now, he would lose it all, and then be forced to submit completely to his father. And worst of all, there was Mehruhn-Nissa.

"I see her hand in this," he said sadly to Arjumand. "Of course, the Shahanshah of Persia is a scoundrel, but why does Father want to send specifically my army there?"

"You are the most experienced of all his generals," she replied.

"But there is also Mahabat Khan! Moreover, he wrote to me: 'with my army, which I can lead.' In other words, he does not trust me to command the army on my own against the Persians. Yet if we set out on this campaign, I fear I will lose everything I have."

"Husband, if you do not obey Father now, it may be even worse. You must make this crucial decision: to march on Kandahar or not. I will support you regardless and remain by your side wherever you are. Perhaps you could tell the Padishah that you only wish to wait out the rainy season?"

"I must please Father—and at the same time be strong and

courageous. Yes, I think I will do just that: I shall march north once the heavy rains cease. But he must allow me to command the entire army! And he must grant me a jagir in the Punjab. That would help me defend against Mehruhn-Nissa and my brothers…"

Upon receiving word from Shah Jahan that his order had been postponed, Jahangir became truly angry. He no longer called the shahzada "son of exalted destiny" but instead labeled him a "wretched man," a "scoundrel," and a "coward." He ordered Shah Jahan to remain in Burhanpur while the army was to be sent immediately to Kandahar.

"How can this be?" Shah Jahan lamented. "Without an army, I will lose all my strength!"

"But if you do not obey Father even in this, you will only enrage him further," Arjumand observed. "Yes, my aunt Mehruhn-Nissa is unleashing her venom. Today, send your trusted courier with a letter to the commander! Beg him most graciously to forgive you! After that, we can slowly move on to Kandahar."

They waited a very long time for an answer from the Padishah. Meanwhile, Arjumand became pregnant once again. She was constantly nauseated, her head spun, and her whole body grew weak.

Finally, Shah Jahan's courier returned. All was very bad—the Padishah refused to see him at all. Mehruhn-Nissa had ordered that he not be allowed into the palace. From that moment on, Shah Jahan's name became cursed and forbidden. Shahriyar became the main and sole claimant to the throne, the "heir" of the Great Mughals.

Shah Jahan decided to go to his father himself; his father was already on his way from Lahore to Agra. Arjumand refused to let him leave, despite her worsening health and the fact that each day it became harder for her to bear the child.

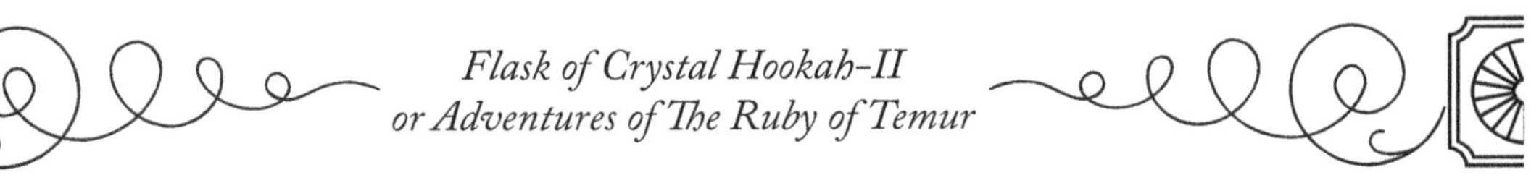

When Jahangir learned that Shah Jahan was marching to Agra with an army, and once again yielding to his wife's malign influence, he decided that his son was going there for one purpose only—to seize the throne during his father's lifetime. Now the Padishah no longer called the prince a "scoundrel" but instead branded him a "treacherous conqueror" and a "usurper."

"Why does he speak of me so?... I have never been, nor do I ever intend to be, a usurper!" Shah Jahan despaired to his wife, sharing his anguish. "I know my time has not yet come—why would I hasten it?"

Meanwhile, dreadful news arrived: Kandahar, which had belonged to the Mughals since the time of Akbar, had been completely captured by Abbas. The fall of the fortress city further enraged the Padishah, who was already unfriendly toward Shah Jahan. Jahangir declared his son "the cause of our defeat" and "an insubordinate traitor." His fury knew no bounds.

✳ ✳ ✳

Various Regions of Hindustan, 1622

The ruler of the entire empire, the Great Mughal, spurred on by his unkind wife, began a full-scale war against his own son—one who had loved him and, in truth, had never betrayed him. This war lasted four long years. The Padishah's army was led by Shah Jahan's former teacher, General Mahabat Khan, an expert on military affairs.

Another unnamed daughter of Shah Jahan and Arjumand did not survive childbirth… Shah Jahan tried to soothe and console his wife whenever he could. He would come to her and speak tender words of love, stroke her hair, kiss her hands, cheeks, neck, and lips—thereby lending her strength and breathing health into the weakened, exhausted body of his lover.

Shah Jahan himself was in complete despair, disillusioned by the constant assaults from his father and relatives…

General Mahabat Khan arrived at Shah Jahan's camp to speak with him before the decisive battle.

"My prince, allow me to warn you: the strength of your army will not be enough to defeat the army of the Padishah that has been entrusted to me! Mehruhn-Nissa continuously provides us with everything that might be needed for both battle and all other purposes! I have received an order from her—alas, now a woman rules over me!—an order to attack you and completely crush you. I'm sorry, but I must bring her victory. You cannot overcome us! And if, shahzada, you surrender without a fight, Mehruhn-Nissa promises to spare you and not to kill you."

"What a great mercy!" Shah Jahan smirked. "And what did my father order you?"

"To preserve your life, for you are his blood."

"Then know this: as his blood I will never capitulate!"

"I confess, no other answer was acceptable, Your Highness! Had I heard you agree to surrender, I would have been disappointed and ceased to respect you. But you gave me no such reason, and I am exceedingly glad. A great warrior is one who does not surrender even when he knows full well that he cannot win an unequal battle!"

"God knows how it will be."

"Yes, God knows. And still… your chances of defeating us are negligible. So, brace yourself, shahzade. Tomorrow I promise you a very difficult day."

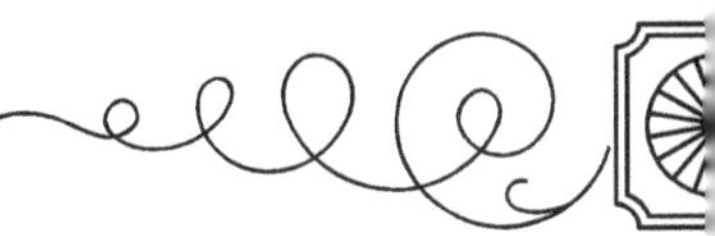

The next day, almost the entire army of Shah Jahan was shattered, leaving him with very few soldiers. The prince decided that in such a situation it was time to flee from Mahabat Khan. It was humiliating and shameful, but at least… you remain alive. He ordered his servants to prepare Arjumand and the children for a long journey. There was only one question: where to go?

The mighty army of Mahabat Khan could reach them anywhere.

* * *

Shah Jahan and Arjumand-begim were accompanied by only five thousand cavalry loyal to the prince. The rest of the army had dispersed as if it had never existed. The Shahzada could no longer keep men at his side—he had no means to pay them, and many had abandoned him.

"The majority of them will surely join Mahabat Khan," Arjumand observed sadly. "Mehrun-Nissa won't be stingy; she will pay generously to anyone who tracks down and betrays the 'unruly' son of the Padishah! We must be extremely cautious."

Shah Jahan could not but agree with her. Truly, the Creator had given him a wise wife…

The journey was exceedingly arduous, and Arjumand along with the children quickly grew weary. Seeing them, no one would have believed that the family of the great empire's ruler's son was traveling in battered carriages! And while Dara and the girls always stayed close to their parents, Aurangzeb was perpetually lost in his own thoughts, as if entirely alone with himself—withdrawn, serious, unsociable, even sullen. He did not get along with his brother.

It was no easy task for Shah Jahan to flee from Mahabat Khan carrying such a burden—his wife, children, and the remaining loyal servants. Yet not for a moment did he consider abandoning them along the way to save himself alone.

”Go on ahead, dear, don't wait for us," Arjumand offered her husband. "Without us, you'll find a safe place much faster! As for us with the children—we'll manage somehow, quietly. I believe that God will not forsake us, and that if the general's soldiers do find us, they won't dare lay a hand on us."

”No!" the prince replied resolutely. "Of course, God always helps and will help, and I want to believe that your life and the children's lives will be safe. But you are out of favor with those in power—because of me, since you are my wife and always by my side! I will not take a single step without you. We need only to meet good people, those capable of siding with me and not considering me an 'usurper'… Yet a man in my position, alas, may be ambushed by traitors at every turn. Whether we survive depends on what takes root in human hearts. For when they encounter us, each will think: 'What do I gain by helping the fallen prince? What benefit will come of it? Is he worth supporting now? If he someday becomes Padishah, then yes, unquestionably! But if not—if he is executed…' And that thought will haunt them day and night. I might promise them enormous riches and honors, but seeing our wretched state, they may decide that it is all nothing more than the product of my unwholesome fancy."

Shah Jahan was continually seeking trustworthy allies and cities that could offer a haven of peace.

And yet a kind man was found—one unafraid to extend proper hospitality to the prince and his family—Lord Mevara Karan Singh. In the past, after his victory over the Mewars, Shah Jahan had spared his life and that of his family. It turned out that the prince remembered and truly valued that debt.

”You may remain in my palace, Jag Mandir, for as long as you wish!” declared Karan Singh to Prince Shah Jahan.

”I thank you from the bottom of my heart, my lord! You render me an inestimable service. But I shall remain with you so long as it is safe for both my family and yours. For now, we need rest.”

* * *

Various regions of Hindustan, 1622–1625

They spent several wondrous months in the cool Jag Mandir, in complete tranquility and an almost regal comfort—until one of Shah Jahan's loyal warriors led Mahabat Khan far to the south.

But the cunning and experienced general soon realised that he was being deceived and, turning his army northward, immediately set out in search of his protégé—whom he was eager to place into the hands of his father, the Padishah, who was dissatisfied with his son, deeming him a "scoundrel" and an "usurper." Mahabat Khan left part of his detachment at Ajmer and began rapidly moving toward Udaipur.

”My scouts have reported that Mahabat Khan is only a day's journey from us," Lord Karan Singh said with alarm to Shah Jahan.

…Over these years, the prince had to confront the relentless general twice more—including in Bengal, in the region of Kavardha. Trial followed trial…

***

Kavardha, 1625

At last, Shah Jahan could no longer withstand the endless persecutions that had drained his strength.

A Letter to the Master of the Great Empire, Hindustan, and the Whole World, to the Lord of the Rivers and the Inhabitant of Paradise, to the Great Mughal Padishah Jahangir—from the most unworthy of sons.

I beg your forgiveness, dear father! For my mistakes I have already borne a just punishment. You were right to consider me an ungrateful offspring—one who did not show due respect to his venerable parent, who had repaid great kindness with evil. In just over three years, I have come to fully comprehend the gravity and depth of my guilt. And I understand that I can no longer persist in obstinacy and resistance! I accept all your conditions, my master, and I beg you for magnanimous clemency toward me and my family; I beg for life and peace. I am tired of enmity and dream only of embracing my beloved father and living forever in complete harmony with him. I entrust to you my life and the lives of my children, that you may dispose of them according to your highest and most merciful will.

Your Shah Jahan

The prince sealed the letter and handed it to a messenger.

"Ride as quickly as possible!" he ordered. "I will eagerly await a reply from Father."

The reply took a long time to arrive, for Jahangir was far away, in Kashmir.

However, the response eventually came. It was penned in Mehrun-Nissa's own hand—her power over both the Padishah and the empire now utterly immeasurable and boundless.

She forgave him and Arjumand alike. Yet Shah Jahan had to agree to her demands: a modest post as governor–subadar in Balaghat—the most distant from Agra, "God-forsaken" and the poorest of provinces. Moreover, Shah Jahan was to send his adolescent sons, Dara and Aurangzeb, to her as wards…

Shah Jahan immediately consented to her terms. A few days later, a retinue of a thousand horsemen arrived to escort the young princes to the palace in Agra.

Arjumand-begim was beside herself with despair; she would not see her sons for a long time.

***

Agra, the same year

Jahangir was delighted with his slightly grown-up grandchildren; he had not seen them for a long time and now examined them attentively. The Padishah came out to greet them in his now customary, entirely ordinary state—quite inebriated. The courtiers could plainly see that he still regarded his son Shah Jahan as a "good-for-nothing offspring," for some reason he had not yet departed from Burhanpur for the "useless" Balaghat.

"And how is your mother faring?" asked Mehrun-Nissa—Arjumand's aunt—with a tender smile as she addressed the sons. "She did send me her greetings and kisses, right…?"

63

Tashkent, April 2015

Rano didn't even get to watch the semi-final featuring Malika. Completely bewildered and anxious, Mukhabbat had called an ambulance that very night—the night of the contest's semi-final round—because her daughter had suffered an unexpected, and in her view strange, seizure.

Rano was breathing, but she was unconscious…

The next morning, Rano's parents and both of her brothers were in the hospital room.

"What's wrong with her, doctor?" asked Abdulla Rustamovich, the on-call endocrinologist at the hospital, deeply concerned about his daughter's grave condition. "Explain to us why she still hasn't woken up."

"I'm afraid I have very disheartening news for you. Your Rano has slipped into what we call a 'diabetic coma.'"

"W-what?! W-what kind of coma?" the head of the family gasped, clutching his ailing heart.

"Diabetic. Did you not know that your daughter has type 2 diabetes?" the doctor exclaimed in surprise. "Usually such a diagnosis is hard to hide. And besides, judging by her blood tests, she's been on insulin for quite some time now. Has she really not mentioned anything to you?"

Rano's parents were in shock, overcome with panic and anguish for their daughter.

Amin and Bahadir then continued the conversation with the doctor in his office.

"Doctor, please explain what can be done now and how we can help our sister. We'll get any medications that might be needed; we'll take her to any other hospital—just tell us what to do."

"Now, now… she isn't transportable at the moment," sighed the doctor, Sherzodovich, heavily. "You've already paid for her stay here, and no additional medications are required—at least not for now. Or perhaps, anymore…"

"What?!! What does that mean? Are you saying you're already preparing her for burial?!" Bahadir exploded in indignation.

"Not I, young man," the doctor replied calmly. "I'm afraid that she herself began treatment too late, thereby inadvertently dooming her… In any case, I think you understand. It happens. At first, people—failing to recognise a serious disease in its barely noticeable early symptoms, when diabetes is so easily controlled—attach no importance to the illness or its treatment. And when they finally realise, alas, it is often too late, and the disease becomes unmanageable. Type 2 diabetes, which has developed in your Rano, is accompanied by an increased production of insulin. Its development in her is most likely due to obesity, the untimely arrival of insulin in her bloodstream, reduced sensitivity of her cells to insulin, and also 'urban factors'—stress, a sedentary lifestyle, improper diet, and possibly even pancreatic disorders."

"Oh my, so many factors! We are such…" Amin shook his head in dismay and regret. "I never even knew that my own sister was so seriously ill…"

The endocrinologist continued:

"Perhaps I won't burden you with all the medical details, but here's the gist: in some patients, the cells lose their sensitivity to insulin—and that is exactly what has happened with Rano. As a result, her body's cells cannot activate the mechanism to absorb glucose."

"So what are you going to do? How do you plan to treat our sister?" Bahadir asked grimly and anxiously.

"The disease is already at an advanced stage," the doctor observed. "I don't know where she was examined, but her diabetes clearly wasn't diagnosed in time, and, apparently, the necessary treatment wasn't started immediately. Or perhaps she suffered extremely severe stress…"

"I understand everything!" Bahadir exploded. "'Diagnosis,' 'stress,' 'complications'—all excuses! Instead of actually helping the person and curing them, you're just spouting demagoguery!"

"Young man, unfortunately, diabetes is so insidious in the way it develops complications that by now treatment is largely ineffective. And as for your sister… Perhaps it's already too late, do you understand? She's lost consciousness, which most likely means that she… Well, I'm sorry."

"What, doctor?" Amin asked, barely holding back tears. "Why aren't you saying more? Tell us—will she… live?!"

"For now, yes. But she is already… in a coma. Prolonged, excessive elevation of blood glucose levels leads to an accumulation in the body—and especially in the brain—of ketone bodies and acetone. This 'ketoacidosis' is a dangerous phenomenon that leads to a comatose state. I won't hide that there is a risk… of a fatal outcome. But, of course, I assure you that we will do everything in our power to fight for her life…"

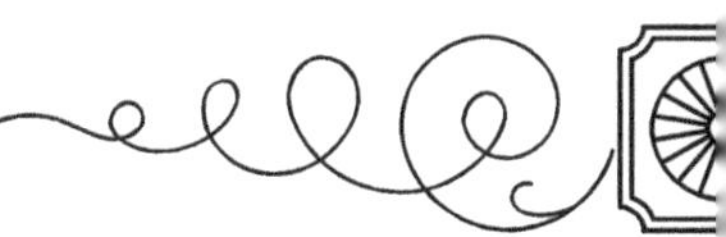

* * *

The next day, after her successful performance in the semi-final and triumphant advancement to the final of the "Superstar" contest, as planned the ever-obligatory Malika called on Rano's phone. The call was answered by her mother-in-law, Mukhabbat.

"Hello, Ranosha? Hi, my dear!"

"This isn't Rano. This is her mother. Who is this?.. Oh, it's you, Malika. You shameless one! Aren't you ashamed to call us?"

"Mom?! I don't understand… And why did you pick up? Where is Rano?"

"My Rano is gravely ill—she's in a coma," Mukhabbat said, her voice broken and weakened by endless tears. "What do you want from us? All you bring us is nothing but misfortune!"

In truth, Mukhabbat didn't really mean it that way; but in her emotionally uncontrolled state she had vented all her bitterness and loathing at life onto her daughter-in-law.

Malika wanted to say, *Mom, why are you doing this? What have I done to deserve such accusations?* but at that moment she wasn't in the mood for quarrels or debates about who was right and who wasn't.

Her very best friend—the blood sister of her beloved husband—was in a coma…

It all seemed so dreadful. Malika could no longer speak—and neither could Mukhabbat. Both women, each lost in her own thoughts, felt such acute, searing pain in their hearts, such an ineffable sorrow, that tears choked them both.

All three of the men in the Fattakhov family were equally distraught over Rano. Nothing could console them—even though they were all, especially the sons of Abdulla Rustamovich, deeply mired in serious work-related problems. They were tormented by the thought that their beloved, kindest sister in the world… might soon leave them forever.

And Abdulla Fattakhov himself had reason for particular distress and self-reproach.

Just a few days ago he had sharply scolded his eldest son. Both women—Mukhabbat and Rano, who were at the house at the time—heard every word.

"Why, why did I, an old fool, raise my voice at Amin? I made my only daughter nervous, upset her… She was surely already on edge because of the situation with my daughter-in-law, Malika, just like all of us… And then Rano was troubled by my outburst at Amin—because he mortgaged my company, got into huge debts, and nearly drove us into bankruptcy… I was so angry that, in the heat of the moment, I even told him in his face that he wasn't my son… My poor little daughter! I never meant to upset her… For her it was pure stress… But I knew nothing! I had no idea she was so gravely ill…"

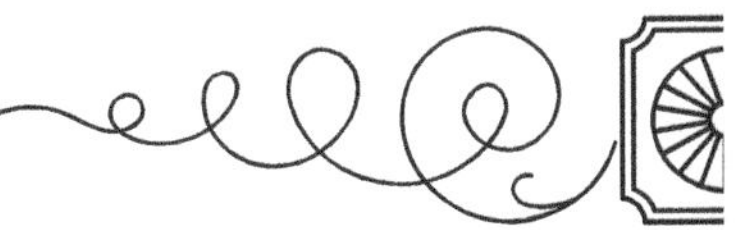

64

Galina Krikunova had caught a slight cold and went to the nearest pharmacy to pick up some medicine. Tashkent isn't exactly a small city, and still, there's always a chance of bumping into someone familiar in the most unexpected place.

That's exactly what happened this time. At the same moment Galina entered the pharmacy, a young man—whom she didn't know very well, but whose face seemed strikingly familiar—stepped in. He was standing a few places ahead of her in line, asking about painkillers.

And then, all of a sudden, Galina remembered where she'd seen him before: yes, of course—once when she was with Mukhitdin, and another time at a café where he was sitting with a guy named Gosha. Back then, Mukhitdin had asked her to tail that Gosha, to surreptitiously get him drunk, and then to set a small fire in his apartment. She hadn't learned the name of Gosha's friend, but now, under the circumstances, finding an excuse to introduce herself to this young man was not difficult at all. And she knew exactly why she needed to do it.

Galina decided that the cold tablets could wait—they weren't scarce—and in no case could she afford to lose this young man! She left the pharmacy a few seconds ahead of him, and as the young man was leaving, the resourceful and cunning girl "accidentally" dropped her purse right in front of his nose onto the tiled floor. The polite young man immediately stooped, picked it up, and handed it back to her.

"Oh, thank you so much!" Galina said warmly, and then immediately launched into her premeditated "approach," disguised as a heartfelt confession: "I got all flustered and couldn't manage to get the medicine I needed… I'm just… seriously ill."

Galina even let a few tears escape—just enough to evoke the needed measure of compassion and sympathy from him, but not so much as to irritate him.

"What's wrong with you?" asked Roma—because it turned out that he was indeed the one—"Can I help you with anything?"

"Oh, no, I mean… Hold on! You're an acquaintance of Mukhitdin Nasyrov, aren't you? I feel like I've seen you with him somewhere… Or am I mistaken?"

"No, no, you're not mistaken. I do know Mukhitdin. Although…" Roman wanted to add that Mukhitdin had been acting like the worst bastard lately… but he held his tongue. It would have been awkward to dampen the mood of an already upset young lady with negativity.

"What, pardon?"

"Oh, nothing, nothing at all. I just didn't know he had such sweet acquaintances!" Roman replied.

"Thank you. And don't you remember me? My name is Galya!"

"No, unfortunately, I don't recall. But it's nice to meet you. I'm Roman. So, how's your health? I ask because maybe you need some help too."

"Me too?"

"Yes, just as with my good friend, for whom I picked up some medicine. He's very sick. But first, let's talk about you. What happened? You haven't told me yet."

"Shall we talk somewhere else? Do you have a little time?"

"Well… I still need to deliver the medicine."

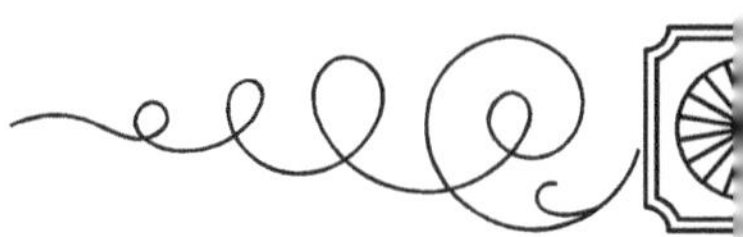

"Yes, to your friend—I remember. And what about him?"

"Some bastard nearly burned him alive!" Roman blurted out, agitated. His new acquaintance immediately appealed to him. "I mean… I wouldn't mind a bit of conversation—maybe have a cup of coffee or something. How about I call a taxi now and we ride together? I'll just quickly drop off these pills to Gosha along the way, and then we can find a decent café. Deal?"

"I don't object," Galina replied, containing her delight that everything was going exactly as planned—even though inwardly she felt a deep indifference toward this pleasant but rather gullible and not particularly shrewd young man.

At the café, Galina suggested that Roman order—not only coffee and pastries—but also fifty grams of cognac each. Her calculation proved correct. Roman had a few drinks, and soon his tongue was loosened. Meanwhile, Galina subtly steered the conversation toward the subject that interested her.

"Oh, that Mukhitdin turned out to be the very last bastard—just like his old man!" Roman, now a bit "warmed up" by the alcohol confided. It turned out he wasn't much of a drinker, so he got quite sloshed. "They think that if they're rich, oligarchs, then they can do whatever they want—that they can just treat people like garbage! Both of them, you know, treat us like trash… But aren't we human, huh? What do you say?"

Roma was still working for Murad Nasyrov, and in his sober state he would have kept his thoughts to himself instead of blurting out all that had long been building up.

"Of course we're human, human!" Galina agreed readily, glancing around to see if anyone was eavesdropping. "So you're saying, they're… oligarchs?"

"Absolutely! Just think about it. The head boss—well, as we

all call our master Murad Nematullaevich—owns an entire chain of cafés and restaurants. But that's not enough for him. He even runs an underground casino, where he rakes in unbelievable sums of money! Many so-called 'big shots' owe him loads. He wallows in luxury, yet it's never enough for him. He also secretly runs all sorts of shady financial operations, swindling and embezzling on a grand scale! But he's clever and cautious, and he's never been caught. And he even employs his own 'black realtors' to work for him... And I have to work with such a man..." he sighed. "But what can I do? He took me in when I was young and completely penniless. He helped me. And at first, everything was fine, but then—suddenly— he started treating Gosha and me like his slaves. I'll be in his debt for life. Yes, I'm used to the good life—plenty of food, fine clothes. I can't live without any of that anymore. You know? But now Gosha is totally out of it—and I'm left working for both of us..."

"Listen, what about his son, Mukhitdin? You say he's just like his father?"

"No, initially Mukhitdin was a great guy—we used to be bud- dies. A few years ago, against his father's will, he even took up the violin, wanted to become a famous musician rather than a wheel- er dealer or a thug like his old man—a mere 'money bag'... But then something happened to him... maybe because of some girl... Mukhitdin fell into a terrible depression and couldn't even play his instrument anymore. And then he went to India to intern in business. They say he managed to turn his life around there, learned a thing or two, and even made some money."

"And what, his father didn't give him money?"

"He did. How could he not? He was his only son, after all. Mukhitdin had everything. It's just that for some reason he never liked his father and was always speaking ill of him... And dur-

ing that trip to Delhi, when I hadn't seen Mukhitdin for several months, he changed a lot. He stopped talking to us—stopped communicating with Gosha and me… Imagine how hurtful that was: just the other day he called from Moscow and didn't even ask about Gosha… To him, to this Mukhitdin, nothing mattered—as if he couldn't care less that Gosha got totally burned! That he needs help, that he needs care… And yet he was working for his father! By the way, the elder Nasyrov—also a miser and an egotist—didn't help Gosha at all either. At least it's good that Gosha's girlfriend, Larisa, is constantly by his side, loves him, and takes care of him. And when she doesn't have time to buy groceries or medicine—I step in to help. It's not hard for me; after all, he's my friend! You understand?"

"Yeah, sure. You're a real champ, Roma!" Galina exclaimed, feigning sincere admiration. In truth, she was equally "indifferent" to poor Gosha—even though, by Mukhitdin's orders, she had been the one to set him on fire. "Do you know his address?"

After asking that, Galina paused for a moment, thinking something over. Roman began to nod off.

"Huh? Whose address?" Roman mumbled drowsily, clearly tired from the long conversation.

"Mukhitdin's! Where does he live in Moscow?"

"Ah, ah. He said he lives at the Metropol Hotel," Roman awakened. "I heard it's one of those 'cool' hotels, very expensive! I'm not sure exactly which room he's in, but if you like, you can easily find out… And why do you need it, my friend?"

None of your business, darling! And you were a bit too quick to call me 'friend', Galina thought to herself, though she didn't say it out loud.

Feeling a bit sorry for the chatterbox, and after Roman—who, as was his habit, paid the bill for both himself and the lady—stepped out of the café, Galina escorted him out onto the street, got him alone into a taxi, and sent him on his way home.

The needed information had been obtained. Now all that was left was the smallest matter: to find Mukhitdin and, at any cost, wrest control of him for herself...

* * *

Nearly three weeks had passed since Rano lost consciousness and was hospitalised. Friends and relatives took turns keeping vigil by her bedside. The only one missing was Malika. Yet not a single day went by in Moscow—so far from her loved ones—without Malika thinking of and remembering her faithful friend Rano. In fact, Malika had even composed a beautiful, uplifting, life-affirming song in Rano's honor, which she vowed to present as a gift when she could come.

Still, Malika had pleaded with both the contest organisers and the producer to allow her to leave for at least a couple of days to visit her gravely ill friend. But the project's founders explained that, as the clear favorite of the entire project, she had no right to do so. Otherwise, they warned, they would not only sever all creative and business ties with her but also ensure that her career would never take off in the future.

Reluctantly, Malika had to comply.

"Besides, think about it: if your friend is already in a coma, how can you possibly help her?" added the channel director, reflecting his own logic.

Malika also understood that a coma was not necessarily a death

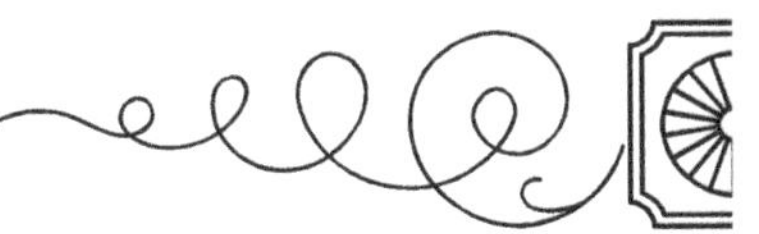

sentence—if one could reach Rano, perhaps her consciousness might return… So at night, she would call the hospital, and the on-duty staff would hold the phone right to Rano's ear… Through tears and sobs, Malika would talk to her, recounting their shared life stories… begging her to come back to life, to her family and loved ones, and most of all to her daughter, who had only just discovered the warmth of having a mother and her true love…

But… in the meantime, the attending physician and the entire panel of professors assembled at the hospital reported that Rano's condition was deteriorating, that the treatment—unfortunately—was no longer effective, and that her organs were not responding at all to any infusions… It was time to disconnect the life support machine…

The family was horrified at the very thought…

By Rano's bedside, Dilshoda recited every prayer she knew. Abdulla Rustamovich, Mukhabbat, Amin, and Bahadir all sat by the rapidly fading Rano, trying to reach her, hoping that, at least subconsciously, she might hear them with her soul—and that their kind, loving words might somehow save her, help her return to life… For they knew that miracles could happen, and they believed that every life and every death ultimately followed the Creator's will…

Each one recalled the many wonderful moments they had shared with this utterly beautiful, radiant, pure, sweet, sincere, and remarkably kind young woman…

Her parents wept bitterly, remembering countless minutes and hours when their daughter had prevented them from toiling with heavy chores at home—always finding ways to ease their burdens and give them a chance to rest. Now, Mukhabbat reproached herself, thinking that perhaps her daughter had overexerted herself at times… But no matter how much one may wish it, you can't shield your loved ones from all the hardships of life… Parents always do everything they possibly can for their children—even sometimes beyond their own strength.

Abdulla Rustamovich also worried about his adopted granddaughter. "Of course, we'll raise and nurture her," he thought. "But my wife and I are no longer young, and our sons have their own families. What will become of the poor little one if, God forbid, she is orphaned for the second time?"

Amin remembered how, as a child, Rano had delighted when he took her to the park with its attractions, treating her to cotton candy and ice cream. More than anything, his little sister loved the swings that rose only a little way up and moved in a circle—with the tree canopies just underfoot and the vibrant, multicoloured scenery of the park filled with the cheerful voices of children and adults all around. And even as Rano grew up, she never lost that childlike tenderness, naivety, and kindness… Despite her unfulfilled dreams of romantic happiness and the fact that no man had ever loved her as a woman, her soul never grew hard, callous, or embittered…

Bahadir realised: he would be deeply grateful to his sister his entire life. He would forever remember how, when their parents didn't understand him, she would often stand up for him, protect him, and care for him… grateful for always trying to be a peacemaker between him and their older brother Amin, between him and their parents... He cherished the times when, together with Malika, Rano had done everything in her power—both possible and impossible—to help him despise gambling and free himself from the long-standing, soul-draining "disease of the gambler," using love, care, attention, and engaging conversations about art, culture, and all things beautiful to distract him from his "gambling

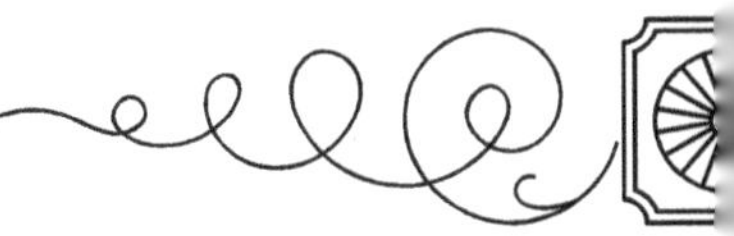

withdrawals." He remembered how Rano always thought of others before herself, constantly caring for people near and far…

Every member of the family and all their friends sat in silent shock, coming to the painful realisation that, as hard and frightening as it was… they must prepare for the worst—that Rano might never awaken, might never speak with them again, never laugh, never smile at each one of them with her bright, warm, and charming smile… Yet none of them, sitting by her hospital bed, could bring themselves to say "goodbye" to that radiant soul. No one wanted to turn off the last hope for her life—the machine that kept her breathing.

Rano's loved ones believed that even when a person knows that waiting for improvement is pointless and futile, one still continues to hope… as the wise King Solomon once said: "Rescue those who are already doomed to die…"

Sometimes, hope works miracles.

But if it is God's will to call someone to Himself, to Heaven, there is little point in complaining; one must simply accept it, for He knows best who will be better off and where.

And in that same month of April, Rano's soul left for the Almighty forever… for Heaven… for that parallel world… And from there she will always watch over and bless all her loved ones with a smile, especially her daughter Samira, whom she never had the chance to truly cherish…

Bahadir was still resentful toward the blameless Malika. Yet, being a decent man and deciding that it would be wrong not to tell her a word about the death of his sister and her close friend, he swallowed his pride and called his wife.

He spoke in short, dry tones:

"Malika, hello… We buried our Rano yesterday… If you can… Although…"

At first, he had thought to add, "If you can, come over," but then he decided it was unnecessary—there was nothing more that could be done for Rano now. And he thought that, in the end, Malika had herself to blame for lingering in Moscow for so long—a strange city, a foreign country, and without a husband—engaging in this singing business…and that she had come to despise herself.

Bahadir hung up the phone in silence. Malika did not press to continue the conversation with her husband… Her heart ached so deeply for Rano that tears and cries seemed to be choked in her throat as one lump.

"How can it be, Rano?" Malika thought. "You had become a true sister to me… How can this be?"

After leaving the dormitory and stepping out onto the street, Malika ran into a quiet, deserted place and, no longer able to hold back her emotions, burst into bitter, desperate sobs at the top of her lungs…

65

At Gafur Ibragimov's office—the trusted notary of Abdulla Rustamovich—the safe housed the wills of all his VIP clients, including Abdulla Fattakhov. Several months ago, barely sensing a sudden deterioration in his health—even before his first heart attack—the father of Amin, Rano, and Bahadir sought out this experienced lawyer and, with his help, drafted his will.

In that will, the principal and equal heirs were designated as Amin, Rano, and Bahadir. To his wife, Mukhabbat Fattakhov, he bequeathed their house by means of a gift deed and opened in her name a rather decent bank account on which good interest was steadily accruing. She had never asked for any of that—she was not materialistic—but it was his will, and she did not dare disobey.

However, following the ensuing critical situation—and especially after Amin had driven Fattaxov PC to bankruptcy, and after the tragic passing of Rano—the head of the family decided to rewrite the will, annulling the previous version. He once again called in his trusted notary.

Mukhabbat's share remained unchanged. The notary merely transferred into the new will everything she was to receive upon her husband's death. The only significant addition was a clause stipulating that, after Mukhabbat's own passing, the entire estate of Abdulla Fattakhov would pass to his granddaughter Samira, the adopted daughter of Rano, who is still just a little one. Mukhabbat signed her consent to this.

That left only Amin and Bahadir.

The principal founder—or, in other words, the owner—and general director of Fattaxov PC, after the departure of its original creator and manager, would be Bahadir Abdullaevich Fattakhov. Bahadir, like his mother, was also bequeathed a bank account with a decent annual yield. In addition, he received a collection of expensive antiques.

As for Amin, he was left with nothing more than his small apartment—once purchased for him by his father—and, if he wished, the right to continue working in the company as its financial director, along with a small percentage share of the company's profits.

And that was it. No additional bank accounts, no extra savings…

One evening, after dinner with his wife Mukhabbat and once they'd put their little granddaughter to bed, Mukhabbat cautiously decided to ask her husband how he had arranged the inheritance for Bahadir and Amin.

Abdulla Rustamovich had not wanted to reveal the entire truth to her, fearing that she might be upset over Amin and begin insisting on his rights. At the same time, however, he was used to the open, trusting relationship he shared with his beloved wife and had never hidden anything from her—especially on important matters.

After all, he thought, *Mukhabbat is dear to me; we've been together for so many years, and she should understand and support me in everything!*

And so he explained in detail what he had done, asking her not to argue with him about it.

"Who could possibly argue with you, Abdulla?" the matriarch sighed sadly. "But simply, when you married me with our little son, you promised that you would never leave him without attention or an inheritance… and that you would never ever reveal my secret to Amin or any of the other children! After all, we have always been one family…"

"Yes—until your son betrayed me!" exploded Abdulla Rustamovich.

"What did he do?" she demanded.

"He nearly set in motion the collapse of my entire life's work—my company. We are on the brink of complete bankruptcy!!! That's why I changed the will, rewriting our company in Bahadir's name. I can trust only him."

"I love Bahadir—he is my son too—but you've undeservedly hurt Amin. I'm sure that in the way he's handled your business, he never intended any harm! He is a serious and responsible man. And if he had to act as he did, it can mean only one thing…"

"Well then, according to you, what does it mean?" Abdulla Fattakhov demanded angrily.

"It means that, most likely, he simply couldn't have acted otherwise!!!"

Abdulla Rustamovich looked at his wife in astonishment.

* * *

Mukhitdin just couldn't seem to find anything interesting to do. After everything he'd done, he couldn't go back to India. He needed to get down to business—but he didn't really feel like it. And for now, his money allowed him to not work.

One April night, he decided to have some fun and "let loose" at a club known for its expensive booze and gorgeous strippers. Besides, Mukhitdin knew that if the mood struck, he could even "rent" someone there for money.

The younger Nasyrov was drinking, dancing, and generally enjoying himself.

Then suddenly, Mukhitdin noticed a familiar young man sitting at one of the tables. Due to his excessive weight, the guy looked much older than his years—but Mukhitdin knew exactly how old he was, because he recognised him as his peer and former classmate, Anvar Tukhataev. Back in school, like many kids, Mukhitdin had been afraid of "fat Anvar"—the bully, the underachiever, the terror of the whole school, the "desperado" type whom not even the principal could control. The teachers could barely put up with Anvar's insolent, brazen mug. But they couldn't expel him either—the school practically belonged to him due to its district. And although Mukhitdin himself had never been an angel, he'd never hung out with dangerous kids like Anvar.

But now, after all these years, out of boredom and curiosity, Mukhitdin wanted to find out what that guy was up to these days—if he'd even improved at all.

He walked up to Anvar.

"Hey! Hope I'm not bothering you? You're Anvar Tukhataev, aren't you?"

Anvar stared at Mukhitdin in surprise, but after about five seconds he gave him a hearty slap on the shoulder:

"Ooh, it's Nasyrov, the musician boy! Hey, bro! What brings you to Moscow?"

Mukhitdin hadn't expected that this guy—who had never been his friend—would remember him at all, or greet him so casually, as if they ran into each other all the time and had only been apart for a couple of hours.

Mukhitdin was about to excuse himself, feeling that this person was someone best left alone as before. But then a thought

occurred to him that he found intriguing. Besides, Anvar clearly wasn't about to let "brother" go so easily—after all, he hadn't seen him in a long time.

"Come on, sit down here next to me. I'll tell the waiter to bring us something stronger. Hey, Ruslan! Come here!"

A waiter approached.

"See, Ruslan, this is my buddy! You know, we haven't hung out together since we were back in school! We should mark this reunion. Come on, bring us the best stuff you've got!"

The waiter nodded obediently and left.

"Maybe… maybe I shouldn't, Anvar? I think I'm going to head off…"

"Where? Are you out of your mind, bro? We just met. No, that's not how things work around here. You see, this is my club—I'm the owner, and here I decide who goes where, who's allowed in and who isn't, and who just sits quietly waiting for my orders. Got it?"

Anvar smirked so menacingly that Mukhitdin felt a chill.

"Yeah, got it," Mukhitdin replied reluctantly.

After all, he needed to carry out the plan that had flashed through his mind.

"Now, tell me, little musician, how's it going? Still playing your violin? Have you become famous, made it big? Although… I don't think I've heard much about your successes…"

That question struck a nerve for Mukhitdin. He frowned and said nothing.

"Come on, relax, Nasyrov! Why are you so serious, really? I only asked out of courtesy—I'm a cultured guy, you know! So what if you haven't 'made it'? And what's the big deal? What do I care about your violin, and frankly, I couldn't give less of a…! Oh, whatever. And besides—not everyone's as lucky as I am! So learn a thing or two while I'm still around."

Anvar smirked unpleasantly again—so much so that Mukhitdin winced. But he decided not to show that he was already intimidated by this dubious character, this old classmate. He resolved to keep the conversation going to see if he could push through his plan.

"And you… I'm just here to chill!" Mukhitdin thought, deciding to start from a slight distance. "I love hanging out in clubs… Though this is my first time in this one. I didn't know it was yours!"

"Now you know—and from now on you'll come only to my club!"

Tukhataev stated this not with the casual tone of an invitation for tea at a friend's place, but almost imperiously, leaving no room for objection or resistance.

"I've got plenty of good girls," Anvar continued. "Look over there, dancing? All mine. I can hook you up with any one of them for the night—free, in honour of our long-standing friendship! But from the second night on, let me warn you straight—it'll cost ya."

Mukhitdin began to desperately try to recall when in his complicated life their "long-standing friendship" had even begun. But he couldn't remember.

"Are these all… whores?" Mukhitdin wondered. "That many?"

"Hey, watch your terminology! Not 'whores' but 'beauties of the night'—haven't you heard that term? That is my main business."

"Listen, Anvar," Mukhitdin thought—now was the time to put his plan into play—"could you… not for official duty, but for… well," Mukhitdin paused, then continued, "could you decide the fate of one girl? I want to help her!"

"No problem, hop, let's help her!" Anvar replied, his Uzbek "hop" still evident in his speech despite having lived in Moscow for a long time. "The girl needs a job, right?"

"Exactly! Get her a place, if you can, Anvar! But make sure she doesn't see the light of day…"

Anvar whistled.

"An unmanageable girl, huh? Is this your girl? Does she refuse to submit to you?"

"Sort of. But there's one catch: first, she has to be brought to you. I can't do it—she won't see me, she doesn't trust me."

"Good, that's the way it should be. Look at that clever girl! But for me, Anvar, complications don't exist. You want my guys to drag her here by force, right? Hop. And then?"

"Do with her whatever you want. The main thing is that she stops seeing life as a fairy tale. You can even… well, do, you know…"

"Do 'what'? Who do you take me for, bro? I'm not about to get involved in any murder business—don't even ask! Oh, how much you clearly despise this girl!"

Mukhitdin sat there, fuming. Why had he ever gotten involved with this Anvar in the first place?!

"Alright, listen, musician, here's an idea. I send some of the girls abroad, to the rich—sometimes even to sheikhs. I have connections everywhere; everything's taken care of. If you want, I can do the same for yours… wait a minute! Is she at least not a freak? That's important. And her age—how old is she?"

"She's very young, barely over twenty. And truly very beautiful."

"So why, you crawling bastard, do you want to ruin a rare beauty? You animal, Nasyrov—you're even worse than I am! But fine. Tell me, where can she be found? We'll take care of it. I'll ship her off to some third-world country—let's see who ends up buying her. But don't even think about expecting any commission from her 'sale.' Understood? Especially since with unmanageable ones it's always more difficult. Deal?"

"Deal." And Mukhitdin reluctantly shook hands with the "brother" scoundrel, already well aware that he himself wasn't much better than that guy.

66

Demoted Ministry of Internal Affairs Captain Ravshan Umarov—dismissed on criminal charges—was being held in the investigative detention center of the Tashkent City Police Department. He knew that if his case went to trial and he were convicted—and he was well aware that there was plenty to convict him for—then, no matter which penal colony he ended up in, his fate as a former policeman would be far from enviable. He hoped that Murad Nasyrov would somehow learn of his grim situation and help secure his release—not because Ravshan had bailed out or covered for the oligarch on more than one occasion, but purely for his own safety. However, things were not going well for Umarov, as his case was under the most stringent scrutiny by one of the city's most formidable prosecutors.

Meanwhile, Nasyrov neither heard nor suspected that Ravshan had been imprisoned. He searched for him for a long time, but the captain had seemingly vanished into thin air—he wasn't answering his cell phone for some reason. At Umarov's workplace, no information was provided about former "officials"—such details, especially when a person is under investigation, are usually classified.

When the businessman eventually found Umarov's home number and called, Ravshan's wife—frightened and having learned from bitter experience not to say more than necessary, especially to strangers and particularly over the phone—claimed that her husband had been sent on an urgent, long-term business trip abroad. Murad Nematullaevich was surprised: why hadn't Umarov mentioned any of this, warned him before leaving, or even made a phone call? That's not how partners do business! It all seemed very strange. But, preoccupied with his own problems, Nasyrov didn't think much of it or suspect that his friend was in serious trouble. Thus, Nasyrov himself remained unaware that his own freedom now hung by a thread.

Meanwhile, the investigation into Umarov's case did not stand still. The investigator assigned by the district prosecutor, Aziz Khamidov, discovered that large sums of money—far exceeding his salary—were in the former captain's accounts. Moreover, one of his colleagues informed the investigator that Ravshan had, on several occasions, met and spoke on the phone with a certain business strongman whom he sometimes, almost in jest, referred to as "the boss." The investigator soon concluded that this "boss" was a very lucrative "honeypot" for Umarov.

And when Umarov was finally hounded with interrogations on this subject, he decided to inform the prosecution about this influential man—his partner in several criminal cases and financial frauds. In return, he asked for leniency in his punishment by having the measure of restraint altered.

* * *

Malika was deeply troubled. Her husband—the man she loved—rarely communicated with her and didn't believe her, and in his eyes—and in the eyes of his parents—she had been viciously defamed. And by whom of all people! By Galya, a friend she'd known since childhood... Yet the greatest pain for Malika was the sudden loss of her friend, almost sister, Rano.

Her parents, though they loved and longed for Malika without blaming her for anything, were far away and couldn't come to offer proper support. And great-grandmother Firuz-begim hardly heard anything and couldn't speak normally on the phone.

Still, Malika felt that Firuz-begim was lighting her magical hookah and, in her own way, praying for her beloved granddaughter—asking the heavens to grant her victory, strength, and patience to overcome all hardships and to become truly happy. That thought strengthened, saved, and inspired the young woman.

Oh, if only Bahadir were here with her—even if only in thought and in spirit!

But she remembered that the toughest phase of the competition was tomorrow, and that there were obstacles she would have to overcome with every ounce of her strength.

Malika had managed to catch a cold, and her throat was terribly sore. Because of that—and in addition to all the troubles and sorrows that had befallen her—she developed a fever. Moreover, she knew there were people for whom her winning the contest was entirely undesirable. All of this made Malika nervous and anxious.

Yet she was mistaken in only one thing. After each of her performances, the flow—or rather, the unarmed army of her admirers, her viewers—grew more and more. Over the long course of the contest, her following had grown to enormous proportions.

Malika Mumtazova and her exquisite voice were already known in many corners of the world! And when, just before the contest, she visited the forum on the competition's website, she was astonished to read a multitude of kind reviews and words of support addressed to her—from her viewers!

That filled her with a soaring spirit. It was as if, in her subconscious, she heard the melodious voice of her dear grandmother Firuz-begim reciting the verses of the rabbi poet of the Bukhara jews, Elisha Samarqandi:

> *Love grants sight to the blind,*
> *Grants joy to the sorrowful.*
> *It transforms the mad into sages*
> *And endows fools with wisdom.*
> *Love bestows strength upon the powerless…*

"So why am I dropping my bundle?" she thought. "No, there's no way that I'm giving up now—I'll fight until the very end! So many people believe in me… As the French say, 'Do what must be done, and let whatever will be, be.' The main thing is not to lose one's dignity, to conduct oneself as honourably as possible—and to remain human!"

Of course, she was also morally supported by her producer, the talented composer and truly good man Konstantin Melodiev. In the run-up to the final, he had rehearsed extensively with Malika, believed in her, and hoped that, despite her malaise and weakness, she would not let him or herself down.

"Come on, girl, show your class—you can do it!" Konstantin said warmly and confidently.

The next day, when it was Malika's turn to take the stage, she gathered every bit of willpower, ascended the steps onto the platform, and… staggered. Her head began spinning, and she nearly fell to the floor.

Konstantin Valeryevich, like all the producers of the "Superstar" contest, was seated in the front row at one of the seats of honour. He quickly took charge of the situation, preventing a surge of noise and panic from erupting in the hall: he grabbed the microphone that lay beside him and, as if teaching everyone a lesson in strength

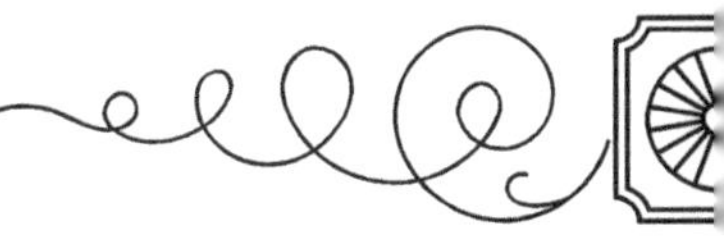

of character, spoke calmly and firmly:

"Everything is all right, friends—the artist is just a little nervous. But everything's fine!"

The murmurs in the hall instantly died down. Melodiev's words had an effect on everyone—and on Malika herself—as if they were a conductor's baton guiding the first violin; they rallied her, and, in truth, helped her quickly recover and fully focus on her performance.

Striving to walk slowly, unhurriedly, and with determination, Malika approached the microphone stand and addressed the audience:

"Good evening, dear friends! Each one of you is so precious and important to me that—truly—seeing you now makes me very nervous… There come moments in life when you must express yourself in words or through some creation born from your soul… An ancient Eastern poet once beautifully said:

> *There is no greater wealth than skill,*
> *It is more reliable than any treasury.*
> *There is no finer possession in the world*
> *Than that which is fashioned by a hand with soul…*

Some in the audience, upon hearing this introduction to the song, applauded timidly. Yet such a lackluster response did not stop Malika. She had long forgotten that she was physically unwell; her entire soul was now immersed in the song.

And then Malika began to sing:

> *In a tranquil world amid carefree bustle we live,*
> *Every day we march forward—both toward and away from our*
goal!

We will open doors for those who never have,
And soaring above the world, we shall enter our spiritual astral.

In the fleeting, transient process of life,
Against the vivid hues of existence,
In dreams of true victory—
We all stagger on day after day…

Put your love to babies' hearts.

We are all given the freedom of thought,
We must make our own choice.
Whether luck smiles on us or not in life…
And only love will save our world, will save our world!

From the kindness of our hearts, the world will bloom in our hands.
Each one of us longs to see the joy of happiness in our children.
Day by day, fate grants each of us a chance.
We believe in hope; we believe in the fairy tale that will save us.
The world will blossom again in smiles,
If we pour our love into children's hearts!

Put your love to babies' hearts.

With faith in ourselves, through fear and pain,
We shall preserve the world, warming it with love…

Had the hall not been dimmed and if every spotlight had been turned on, one could have seen that the faces of most in the audience were wet with tears. Both the moving, humane, peace-promoting

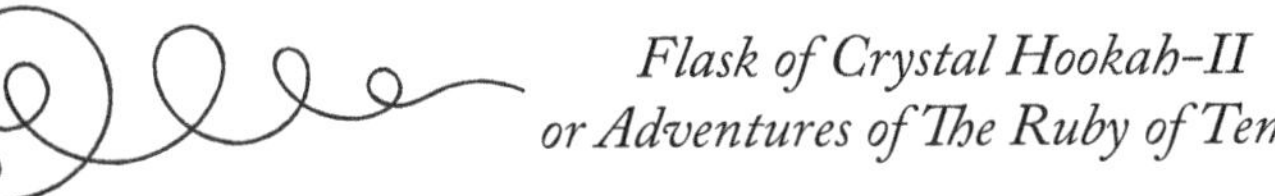
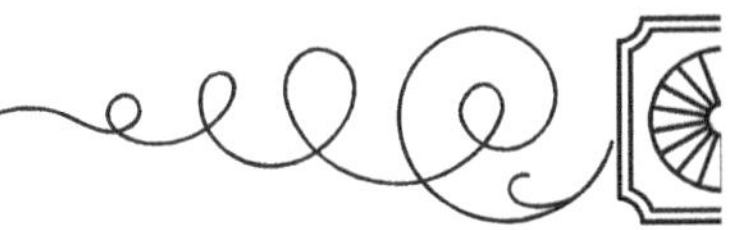

song and its extraordinarily sincere performance—so raw, as if exposing a torn nerve from the very depths of the heart—touched the people so deeply that it was, for them, a "moment of truth." In that instant, many present felt that everything essential had already been said and that now, as if hypnotised and entranced by the catharsis born within, they could simply, silently, and thoughtfully go home…

Yet after a few sparse, feeble claps, the hall suddenly exploded with thunderous applause and shouts of "Bravo!"

No flashy, boisterous show could move the audience as deeply as an open, utterly sincere conversation from the heart—a heart-to-heart, as if sharing secrets, as if whispering directly into each person's ear. A conversation about the eternal, about the value of life and true love… Malika was not acting; she wasn't playing a part—she was living her song. She simply sang it as its author, as an ordinary person… and in doing so, she won the hearts of millions.

The results of the audience vote could not, even if one wished, be falsified. Out of all the votes cast for the five finalists of "Superstar," nearly seventy percent were, by all accounts, for Malika Mumtazova alone!

This was not merely a victory—it was the true triumph for the singer!

Even more surprising was that Malika, having received the Grand Prix—the "Golden Star" statuette—from the general producer of the TV channel, chose to hand over the rights to a touring schedule throughout Russia to the contestant who had taken second place—a talented singer from the city of Vladimir, Ivan Sashkov.

"I must return to Uzbekistan, to my family," explained the contest laureate. "But I will be coming back here periodically, so that, as the producer told me, I can record an album!"

Fortunately, all the means were now at hand for that, since in addition to the statuette, the winner was awarded a substantial cash prize. Money was by no means important to Malika, yet she knew it was necessary for her husband—to free him forever from the bonds of that criminal businessman, Nasyrov...

Immediately after the live broadcast, Malika received a call from her parents. They were immensely proud of and overjoyed for their Malika, warmly congratulating her on such success.

"When will you arrive, daughter?" boomed Said Yakhyaevich into the phone.

"Papa, I'm not sure yet. Tomorrow I'll buy a ticket, and then I'll call you and let you know."

"Alright, my little one, my sunshine—we'll be waiting for your call!" said Sitora, almost in tears. She missed her only daughter terribly and, of course, wanted nothing more than to see and embrace her as soon as possible.

The very next day after the contest, Malika bought a plane ticket to Tashkent.

That night, as she fell asleep like a defeated soul in a dormitory room, she could never have imagined that the next day she would awaken... in an unfamiliar, shabby room with worn, dirty walls, amid someone else's grimy, poorly scented gray linens, on a narrow bed that wasn't her own. Next to it stood two more beds. On them lay a couple of girls around her age—quite attractive, yet emaciated, with haggard, drawn, and unhappy faces.

For a time, it seemed to Malika that this was all nothing but some sort of nightmarish dream.

"What is this?"—coming to herself, she asked in astonishment and horror of the girls who had awakened, or perhaps not yet fallen asleep at all. "Where am I? What is this? What has happened to all of us?!"

67

Amin was deeply upset by the unpleasant conversation with his father. Even after Rano's death—when the fractured family gathered for memorial services and other events—he scarcely spoke with the elder Fattakhov, still not having fully forgiven him. Moreover, Abdulla Rustamovich had yet to show his usual warmth toward his son.

Nevertheless, Amin was determined to restore justice and, at the very least, try to track down the swindler Rudik on his own. Even Bahadir now had no doubt that Rudik was nothing but a fraudster—a cheat and a shameless scoundrel!

Amin sent an official letter to the Milanese bank, the very institution into which the money had been transferred, and requested information on whether the funds were still in the account or if they had been withdrawn. The reply came swiftly by email: the account in the name of Rudolf Khairullin had been zeroed out and closed.

It was now imperative to urgently locate Francesco Valdoni. After all, he worked in Italy at the company "Vit-Alma"—how had neither he nor Bahadir thought of that earlier?

Amin then wrote to them as well. A couple of days later, he received a reply:

"Dear Signor Fattakhov, regarding your inquiry concerning Signor Francesco Paolo Valdoni, we must inform you that he is not currently employed with us. We do not know where he can now be found. According to our records, he left Italy not long ago. To our sincere regret, we are unable to offer you further assistance…"

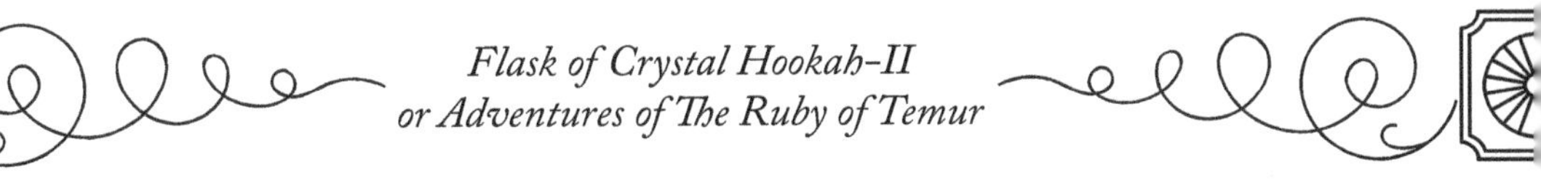

Amin realized that they were not having much luck with this matter. And here, alas, came a complete dead end. But where on earth could Rudik be found? Has he vanished forever?

***

Galina Krikunova wasn't about to leave Mukhitdin alone—not after she learned that the guy she'd long been attracted to, whom she had once even been ready to snatch away from Malika, not knowing that he wasn't available to her, turned out to be the son of a rich man, an oligarch.

Galina was cunning and deceitful, though she had never been noted for great intelligence. Thus, as she savored her revenge on both Malika and Mukhitdin, she failed to foresee or calculate that her attempt to undermine Malika's reputation within her husband's family—and to sully Mukhitdin's already not-so-bright image in the eyes of Malika's relatives—would not improve her own chances of winning Mukhitdin over. On the contrary, it might only drive the desired man further away from her and allow him to grow even closer to Malika. If Malika were to remain at peace, in love and harmony with her own husband, she would never have let Mukhitdin Nasyrov near her. And now—who knows what might happen? After all, Mukhitdin is still not indifferent to Malika!

Only now, after yet another unsuccessful attempt to reach Mukhitdin by phone, did Galina begin to understand this. "I've really done it to myself," she realised.

Determined to take a serious step, she went to her superiors at the hospital, requested an urgent unpaid leave, and flew to Moscow—to the person without whom she could no longer manage…

For Mukhitdin, Galina's visit came as a complete surprise.

"Oh, it's you." he said wearily and with a note of displeasure when Galina entered his room. "I can't believe you came all this way! So, why have you shown up? What are you doing here?"

"Wait, Muhit, please don't be rude—just listen," the girl replied humbly.

He twisted his lips in a scowl and lazily gestured toward a chair. She sat down.

"Mukhitdin, may I ask why you haven't returned to Tashkent for so long?"

"That's none of your business, woman! Why are you sticking your nose where you're not wanted?"

"I figured as much—you're lingering here because of that foolish Malika! I don't understand what you need her for, what you see in her. Fine, let's say you even manage somehow to persuade her to come here. And suppose she does come—even though, in my opinion, she has never liked you and has never held you in any high regard—she will never make you happy! Understand this at last! A man—especially one as refined and pampered as you, accustomed to attention—needs a loving woman, one who will satisfy him in every way!"

"You mean yourself again, right? But you don't satisfy me 'in every way'; you make me feel sick. I'm sorry!"

"You've got that nonsense hammered into your head. I know for a fact that I'm not ugly, and that I do appeal to you a little, too. After all, even before India—in Tashkent—you nearly got close to me. And now you, like a fool, have fallen again for this Malika! And you refuse to recover. And that's all because that little 'thing' dared to refuse you once more! You men get all worked up when the one you like pushes you away! But mark my words: I won't be chasing after you forever. If you let me slip away now—such a sweet, loving woman—you'll be left gnashing your teeth for the rest of your life!"

Deep down, Mukhitdin knew she was right and had nothing to say in rebuttal.

"Would you like some tea? Or something stronger?" he suddenly asked in a somewhat hospitable tone. In truth, the guy realised that perhaps this cunning, yet devoted, "snake" might prove useful to him in the future… and it seemed he had already figured out for what…

"I wouldn't say no to tea!" Galina rejoiced at the unexpected change in her beloved's mood.

"I'll order it right away—along with some pastries. You must be hungry from the journey, right? Just give me five seconds."

After they had tea and a snack, Galina asked:

"Muhit, I know that the international contest—which, by the way, Malika won—has just concluded. Fools and simpletons usually get lucky. But surely she will be returning home to her husband in the next few days. What are you planning to do now?"

Mukhitdin grew angry.

"But I already told you it's none of your business! I'm fed up. I do have a plan."

"What kind of plan? Are you planning to keep her near you by force? That Malika—the free-spirited woman who doesn't love you? She will never agree to that. Like it or not, she'll ruin your life. Because to her, you are nobody—certainly not her hero!"

Oh, she shouldn't have said that…

Until this very moment, Mukhitdin had been mulling over in his mind how to take revenge on stubborn Malika with the help of his former classmate—the gangster and thug Anvar—how Anvar would ship her abroad as a slave for some Arab sheikh, and how Malika would remain a miserable martyr for the rest of her life, far

Gulchekhra-Begim Makhmudova

from home…

But now, thanks to the idle chatter of Galina—who was almost desperate to have him—an entirely new plan had taken shape in his mind.

Indeed—he must become, in Malika's eyes… her hero!

***

The poor girls in that dreadful, ramshackle apartment knew all too well the fate that awaited them—they had accidentally over-heard about it back at Anvar's club. And now they had told Malika.

She was horrified. Slavery?! Oh, no, not that!

Where are you, dear Bahadir? Save me! thought the dismayed Malika.

And why had she refused work in Russia? At least now there would be some decent people here who needed her, who wouldn't let her be bullied, who would look for her—and surely find her! But now everyone was convinced that she had already flown off to Tashkent or, at the very least, was peacefully resting in a dormitory or strolling triumphantly around Moscow. Or… Even her famed and kind producer probably wasn't thinking about her fate at all…

What was she to do?

The apartment where the captives were held was unlocked by a spare key provided by Anvar, which was turned over by a woman of about fifty with an unpleasant face marked by a huge scar and a lame leg. She brought food for all the girls—a batch of poorly fragrant stewed cabbage and boiled potatoes. Malika couldn't, or rather wouldn't, eat.

"Eat, you silly girl!" the woman commanded. "You'll need your strength! You're merchandise, after all. And I'll be in trouble if the

merchandise doesn't look good. They even said to prepare meat…
But this will do for you. Now, come on, take a plate!"

"Ma'am, please let us out of here!" Malika pleaded. "I'll thank
you! I have money—just not here, at home…"

"Are you out of your mind, kitten? I just can't! I'd get in trouble.
No, no—don't even ask! And I don't need your money; they flesh
out for me anyway…"

Malika thought that the word "flesh" suited not only the
scarred, ugly face of the woman and the grim, strange apartment,
but the entire atmosphere of the place.

After a little while, the "owner" of this "business"—Anvar himself—showed up.

"Wow, that one really is a fine specimen!" the thug said as he
looked at Malika, licking his lips like a cat eyeing a bowl of cream.
"Maybe I should keep you for myself? Hey, little girl, do you want
to be with your uncle?"

He grinned menacingly. Malika's heart clenched. She wasn't a
coward, but that malicious smirk on his fierce face made her tremble like a trembling aspen leaf.

God forbid—she would never want to end up with someone
like that! Admittedly, becoming a sex slave to some old, fat, unattractive Arab rich man would leave no trace of joy either.

*Mom, Dad, Grandma, where are you?! Bahadir, my beloved, where
are you?!*

* * *

Seeing that Amin had grown despondent and didn't even want
to speak properly with her, a distraught Mukhabbat decided to visit
her son at his apartment on a day off.

Amin was alone. He warmly greeted his mother, hugged her, and kissed her. Then, settling her in the kitchen, he immediately put on the electric kettle and began preparing a spread of treats for tea. He was very well-mannered and couldn't help but pay proper attention to his elderly mother who had come to see him.

"Mom, who is with Samira?" asked the attentive Amin. "Is she all right? If she needs anything at all, just say the word—I'll take care of it."

"Don't worry, our little one is growing up fine! Right now, she's with her grandfather—he's watching over her," Mukhabbat beamed. It pleased her that her son cared so much about his tiny niece.

"That's wonderful—to know she's doing well; I'm happy about that!" replied Amin.

"My dear son," Mukhabbat kept looking into his eyes as they sat together at home and along the way, thinking about what words might best comfort him and ease the pain caused by his worsening relationship with his father. "Please, don't be angry with your father!"

"Mom, but he blurted out in a fit of rage that I'm not his son! And he said it with such hatred…"

"Oh, don't even think that way! He just got carried away. Don't take it to heart!"

"How can that be, Mom?" Amin nearly burned himself while making tea. "I understand that perhaps I unintentionally upset him because, in a way, I let him down in business. But, for God's sake, I'm not to blame for anything. Unfortunately, I can't explain everything right now—just believe me, at least you do."

"I do believe you, my son, I truly do."

"But can any business or work be worth more than our relationships with our loved ones? Isn't our family the most important and priceless thing of all?! I would never treat my future children that way—I would make sure they always know I love them more than anything in the world!"

"Good for you, my Amin! But you know what your father always says: 'Work is, first and foremost, a responsibility to people.' And that's very important, don't you agree?"

"Yes, Mom, of course. He's right about that. I've never forgotten that for a single second and have always tried not to let anyone down! I will do everything to set this right, and our company will surely rise again and become successful. But how can someone, even in a moment of emotion or sorrow, say: 'You are not my son!' Huh?"

Amin was clearly very agitated; it hurt him to remember those words.

Mukhabbat, who had been looking straight into his eyes, for some reason now averted her gaze.

"Or… Wait, Mom… So is it… true? Am I not really your son?!"

"My dearest, my only, my true son!" Mukhabbat found it hard to speak, nearly bursting into tears. "But only… not the biological son of Abdulla Fattakhov. I'm so sorry…"

"And you've hidden that from me all these years? Oh, you're unbelievable!"

"My dear, understand—it was better for everyone that way."

"Then why don't I remember my biolo-… well, my real father? Who is he?"

"You were only two years old when we split up with him. And later, while visiting some mutual acquaintances, I met Abdulla Rustamovich. He had his own business only years later, back then he was just a simple accountant and wasn't married. I really liked him, and from that very day he started courting me. Moreover, he didn't mind at all that I already had a little child from another man… Of course, I liked Abdulla very much too…"

"And then you married him…"

"Yes, half a year after that we got married, and Abdulla adopted you. He accepted you unconditionally right away! And he promised me that under no circumstances would he ever tell you or any of the children born to us after you that you weren't his blood son… But apparently, due to illness and his distress, he lost his temper and couldn't keep his word. Please forgive him, just as I forgave him. I think that now he's most angry with himself for, even though he didn't mean to, hurting you."

"And my father… Is he alive?"

"No, my son, he's dead… His ancestors came from India to Uzbekistan long ago, and were the third generation who lived here… Your father Jahangir always longed to return to his homeland, and one day, after leaving an exhibition during the Days of Uzbek Culture in India, he never came back… He abandoned us without explanation. And apparently he died there, but I don't know the details… Although his sisters still live here in Tashkent… Do you remember that dark-skinned woman who visited us several times? That is your real aunt, the younger sister of your father Jahangir. Your father's family wants to keep in touch with you. And who knows—perhaps it's time for you to meet them… As for me, they have never loved me and never will, although I never did anything bad to them. I suppose I'm too simple for them, while they are aristocrats—they are of India, descendants of the Baburid, with the blood of Padishahs… I have your aunt's address. I didn't let her come here—I was afraid it might disturb the peace and happiness of the Fattakhov family. But if you wish, you can certainly visit her.

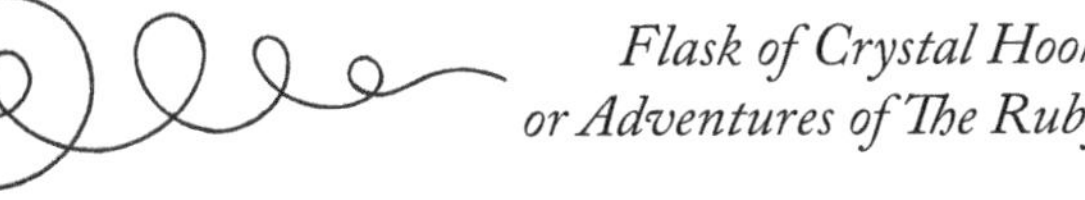

Now that everything is revealed, I won't try to stop it."

Amin listened to his mother very attentively. In him, realism and romanticism were always intertwined, and although he was now a completely grown and mature man, deep in his soul he still remained a child, capable of believing at any moment that his life might one day transform into a magical fairy tale.

Just think! He, Amin—the descendant of princes, Temurids, and Baburids… His ancestors were Babur, Shah Jahangir, Mumtaz Mahal, and Shah Jahan—about whom he had read so much! It was astonishing… At the mere thought of it, Amin's spirit was lifted, as if wings had sprouted on him.

"You know what, Mom?" he smiled. "I'll tell you this… Everything will be all right between us. And, God willing—simply wonderful!"

Mukhabbat beamed too, pleased that her visit to her son had not been in vain…

"May God grant it, my son, and praise be to God!" she cooed, patting his head.

68

Burhanpur, 1626

"Do you really think she wouldn't dare to get rid of them—our sons—or harm them?" Arjumand asked Shah Jahan, her tone seemingly calm and measured.

In truth, however, the princess could hardly sit still. She was anxiously fretting over her sons, and fallen out of favor because of her husband, and now held hostage by her aunt Mehrun-Nissa. So far, things with them had been quite fine, but who knows what might come…

"Let's think," Shah Jahan mused aloud. "My father is in very poor health right now, and how long he has left—only Allah knows. I myself wouldn't wish it upon anyone, for he is still my parent, yet let's be realistic: most likely, he will soon pass on to the next world. As for Mehrun-Nissa having any official rights to the throne, as we sometimes see in Christian countries—that is simply out of the question in our land! The heir to the throne, and especially the ruler of the empire, must be a man—a prince by blood, a hereditary Mughal!"

He glanced at his Arjumand, pleased that his beloved wife listened with such keen interest.

"That means her position is growing much weaker than it once was, doesn't it?"

"Undoubtedly."

"But there's something else that I should know, isn't there?"

"Exactly. You know, most of the courtiers, nobles, and officials are secretly against her! She is disliked by everyone! Eastern men have never taken kindly to being subordinate to a woman—especially not one as malicious, deceitful, and greedy as she is! Even if, as I've said, she herself was, so to speak, a 'padishah'—perhaps then they might have tolerated her out of fear of God, who raises and overthrows the rulers of the world. In short, she is very much disfavoured at court. And there's one more thing: my inept and worthless little brother Shahryar, her son-in-law—whom she practically dragged by the ears to the throne for years—has repeatedly shown his obvious weakness and foolishness in both political and military matters, and hardly anyone supports him either. Strangely enough, Mehrun-Nissa's backing has only harmed him!"

"Then what if you arrive in Agra? Won't the people be ready to support you?"

"I'm sure they will. Many are concerned about the future, and I am already receiving letters of greeting. You know, my poor brother Parvaz, who—thankfully—never aspired to power, wrote to me not long before his death?"

"What did he say?"

"He wrote: 'O Lord of our empire, my beloved brother Shah Jahan!'… How sad that the wine ruined him—he could have been a true friend and support to me."

"You know, my dear, power isn't beautiful for everyone. It can poison, damage the heart and mind, and destroy all that is human in a person…"

"Perhaps, but I hope that such a fate does not befall us!" Shah Jahan laughed. "And I tell you all this merely to assure you that at present our children in Agra are in no danger. You'll see: your aunt now fears us. And therefore, on the contrary, she will do everything in her power to regain both your favour and mine. After all, she wants to secure her own survival in the very near future!"

* * *

Kashmir, Burhanpur, Lahore, 1627

Arjumand's father, Asaf Khan, had sent a messenger to Shah Jahan accompanied by an army of five thousand horsemen. The news from the minister was expected yet still stirring: that in the autumn, Jahangir had died in Kashmir. Now at last, he could truly "enjoy" the cool breezes of his beloved city!

In the two years that had passed, Shah Jahan had managed to forgive his father—or perhaps he truly pitied the old Padishah, who had lived a rather unhappy life.

The messenger proved to be a man completely devoted to Shah Jahan, and he reported the following:

"Your Highness, I beg you, do not identify me to Minister Asaf Khan! But he has omitted something in his report. The matter is this: he decided as if his star had risen and he began to act with unexpected resolve and independence. Since now, at the moment of the Padishah's death, neither you, Shah Jahan Bahadur, nor your brother, shahzade Shahriyar, are in the capital, Asaf Khan has rallied the majority of the influential courtiers in Agra to his side and proclaimed as the new Padishah the fourteen-year-old son of Prince Khusrau-mirza—Sultan Davar Bahshah!"

Thus, for a very brief time, Asaf Khan became the de facto ruler under the young Padishah. This greatly displeased Shah Jahan, but Arjumand—well aware of her own father—convinced her husband

that it was merely a strategic manoeuvre which would ultimately help him, Asaf Khan's son-in-law, Shah Jahan, to ascend the throne.

Meanwhile, in Lahore, Shahriyar—who was attempting to cure his antics and was being fanned by the once again rousing and unyielding Mehrun-Nissa—was mustering a vast but untrained mercenary army using state funds. Mehrun-Nissa had sent a letter to her "pocket" son-in-law, the shahzade, demanding that he immediately bring his loyal troops to a state of combat readiness.

"Shahriyar has once again publicly declared his claim to the throne," Shah Jahan confided to Arjumand. "All of this is the work of Mehrun-Nissa's intrigues! Of course, how can she stand by idly as such vast power slips from her grasp? For a woman like Mehrun-Nissa, elusive power is especially alluring! Forgive me, dear, that I speak so unkindly of your aunt…"

Soon, Asaf Khan and Davar Bahshah led the imperial troops to Lahore. Asaf Khan defeated Shahriyar's inexperienced army, forced Shahriyar himself to surrender, and ordered him to be blinded. He then ordered that his sister Mehrun-Nissa be placed under house arrest and took with him the sons of Shah Jahan—Dara Shikoh and Aurangzeb—who had been under her care.

After the victory over Shahriyar, Asaf Khan received a letter from Shah Jahan—now en route to Agra—with an order to send the "Padishah" Davar Bahshah to his eternal rest. Asaf Khan did not fail to carry out this command from his son-in-law.

At the end of December, in the Great Mosque of Aziragha, Shah Jahan read the prayer, after which a servant proclaimed him Padishah of all Hindustan.

There was no time to delay. Shah Jahan and Arjumand, immediately setting out with a large army, proceeded to Agra—where the coronation was to take place and where he was to remain to rule the country! But now, along the way, they no longer had to hide. It was a splendid and proud procession of the sovereign, the ruler of this country which had until recently been hostile to them! Henceforth, all who encountered Shah Jahan paid him the due homage and respect—as to their rightful master.

Of course, the land and life around did not change overnight; they remained the same. But the heart of the new Padishah was filled with joy and exultation. Here he was, master of all, subordinate to none but the Almighty God—and to no one else!!! This feeling was unusual, pleasant, incomparable to anything else…

"Your friends—and even your most loyal retinue—will begin to fear and tremble before you!" Arjumand remarked as she looked at her husband.

"Well, so be it!" replied the ruler of the empire, Shah Jahan, contentedly.

She, the daughter of Asaf Khan, could feel the curious gazes of the crowd as well: she was the wife of the Great Mughal, his pillar and steadfast companion, the love of his life. Now she was being adored in a way that had never before been experienced in her life. Yet she was entirely untouched by any notions of vanity or ambition in her soul. On the contrary, she longed to return home, to her private quarters, and to hide away from all those intrusive, curious, cautious, sycophantic, or reverential gazes. And her husband had not become a tyrant in her eyes—he remained simply the same beloved, dear man she had always known.

***

Agra, 1628

Asaf Khan had received an order from Shah Jahan to send Shahriyar to his eternal rest. Naturally, Arjumand learned of this quickly. Compassionate and humane, she was opposed to all this bloodshed.

"Order them detained and simply exile them!" she pleaded with her husband once again. "My aunt wrote me a letter. She is asking you to make Shahriyar the governor of Lahore or Punjab—at your discretion, but do not kill him! She is worried about her daughter, Ladilli. She says you can send Shahriyar as far away as you wish."

"But he will return—all of them, my rivals, can return from any exile!" Shah Jahan shook his head. "By the way, you want the truth? In his place, I would have done the same. I would have gathered my own army and come back to fight another claimant. No prince would ever refuse the chance to become Padishah, and especially not the Great Mughal!"

"Then imprison them all… Give Shahriyar a little time, and he will forget all his ambitions, if he hasn't already… Please, do not repeat the terrible mistake with Khusrau, for you and Shahriyar—of one fraternal blood—they are kin…"

"Rulers have no kinship," replied Shah Jahan. "If Khusrau were alive now, I would not have become Padishah—and perhaps you, I, and our children would not even be alive! Oh, no, my love!!! Moreover, these are not even his ambitions but those of Mehrun-Nissa. How unlucky he has been with his mother-in-law, eh?" Shah Jahan sneered darkly. "You must understand that she will never cease; she simply hates you and me! If I show any mercy to Shahriyar, soon any proud and ambitious scoundrel will decide that he has the right to rise against me and my authority!"

"But the duty of a ruler is to be a father to his people."

"I know. That is what my ancestor Akbar taught—that a ruler must have a large heart. But Shahriyar is plotting evil against me, the Padishah! And therefore he must die. Forgive me. By the way, your father has already taken my red turban adorned with Temur's precious ruby from him—and handed it over to me!"

"You haven't forgotten about it, have you?"

"Of course not—it is a symbol of power and my victory… And now I must also decide what to do with your treacherous aunt, who has caused so much harm to both you and me!"

Arjumand's face was troubled; her kind heart was pained and dismayed by all of this.

"Do not be afraid, my beloved. I remember that she is your relative, and I promised you that I would show her mercy! Although I am not entirely sure that she would do the same for us…"

* * *

Without delay, Asaf Khan carried out the order of the new Padishah—he commanded his soldiers to put Shahryar to death. After that, Shah Jahan granted Asaf Khan the position of Mir-i-Saman—the first minister.

Mehrun-Nissa, meanwhile, was removed from power and spent the remainder of her days in exile in Lahore until her death in 1645. There she lived a quiet and tranquil life with her widowed daughter Ladilli. Mehrun-Nissa devoted herself to reminiscence, writing numerous poems and verses under the pseudonym Makhfi.

She bequeathed her Crystal Hookah as a keepsake to her niece,

552

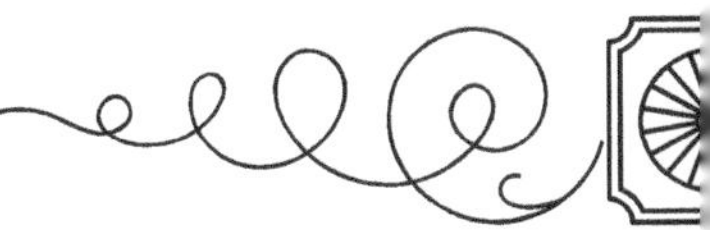

Arjdumand-begim.

Jahangir's wife solemnly buried her husband in Lahore, having built for him a beautiful mausoleum. Later, she too found her final refuge there in Lahore—in the mausoleum of Shahdara Bagh that she had constructed, not far from Jahangir's tomb. Also, from her own funds, she commissioned the construction of the Itimat-ud-Daulah mausoleum in honour of her father in Agra. On her own tomb, she ordered an epitaph to be carved: "On the grave of this poor stranger there shall be neither a rose nor a lamp; No butterfly will scorch its wing, nor will any nightingale sing its song…"

* * *

Agra, 1629–1630

Arjumand devoted much of her time to charity and aiding the poor, and she took great pleasure in it—especially now that she had far more opportunity to do so.

Her husband understood her passion and supported her. He, too, strove in every way he could to care for his people and his beloved country. He even entrusted her with the Padishah's Mur-Uzak seal. Although she initially refused it, he insisted:

"Take it, my beloved, I beg you," he would say, "so that you may keep me from all evil! And I want to tell you something important: henceforth, your name—as my father used to call you—will forever be Mumtaz Mahal, 'Adornment of the Palace'! Let future generations remember you by that name."

Furthermore, Shah Jahan placed the symbol of his power—the Temur Ruby, as well as the Koh-i-Noor Diamond—on his new Peacock Throne.

Yet his most prized possession, his dearest treasure, remained his beloved Arjumand-begim… Mumtaz Mahal… Adornment of the Palace.

***

Agra, 1631

A difficult fate, frequent childbirths, and the death of several of her children had finally taken their toll on Arjumand-begim. While giving birth to her fourteenth child, weakened beyond recovery, she passed away.

Shah Jahan's grief knew no bounds. He wept for a long time and cried out loudly, secluding himself in their marital chamber for forty days and forty nights…

His sole thought now was to immortalize her memory, to convince the world that his beloved was still alive—that she still dwelt in this world!

***

Agra, 1632–1653

Devastated by the loss of his beloved wife, Shah Jahan ordered the construction of a majestic mausoleum in the capital of his empire on the banks of the Yamuna River—a structure built of the most exquisite white marble, to be known as the "Taj Mahal," a name derived from that of Mumtaz Mahal. There, the ashes of Mumtaz Mahal were interred, and many years later, Shah Jahan himself was laid to rest in the same sanctuary.

Even during the construction of this tomb for his beloved, Shah Jahan would silently address his great ancestors—Amir Temur, Babur, Humayun, and Akbar—and envisioned the Taj Mahal in the likeness of the great monuments: the Gur-e-Amir in Samarkand, the Bagh-i-Babur in Kabul, Humayun's Tomb in Delhi, and Akbar's mausoleum in Sikandar…

For twenty-two long years, Shah Jahan oversaw its construction, inviting more than twenty-two thousand artisans from every corner of his empire, as well as masters from Central Asia, Persia, and the Middle East. Under the bright daylight, the marble of the Taj Mahal gleamed white; at dawn, it took on a pink hue; and on moonlit nights, it shone with a silvery glow.

He dreamed and dreamed of the day when Arjumand-begim—known forever as Mumtaz Mahal—would be remembered for her courage, kindness, love for humanity, and unwavering fidelity to her husband.

And he hoped that the great, boundless love between two hearts would never be forgotten…

69

Bahadir had been eagerly awaiting Malika—and out of childish pride, he hadn't phoned her himself. He didn't follow the contest closely, hardly watched it on television, and had no idea exactly when Malika would return home.

Maybe I should call her parents and ask? he thought. *Surely they're keeping a close eye on the broadcast of the contest and know everything! …No, I won't; after all that my father has told them, it would probably be awkward.*

Abdulla Fattakhov had indeed already quarreled with the family of his friend Said Mumtazov over his doubts regarding Malika's moral purity.

Suddenly, Bahadir's mobile phone rang. The number was unfamiliar—most likely an intercity or international call.

Malika, my love, you—finally! flashed through Bahadir's mind.

But it wasn't the wife of the younger Fattakhov at all…

"Hey there, Baha!" came the instantly recognisable, upbeat voice of Rudik. "How are you doing? I guess you've completely lost track of me?"

Rudik, like a sly gossip, cheekily snickered into the receiver.

"Rudik! Where are you? How could you?!! Where did you vanish? We've been looking all over for you…"

"Don't babble, please, Baha! I'm calling to explain everything. I hope you're not still waiting for me in Tashkent? Because that would be very foolish!"

Truth be told, Bahadir—without mentioning it to Amin—deep

down still waited and hoped that one day his long-time friend's conscience might finally stir…

"Bahadir, thanks to me, all your money—whoosh!"

"What? What… I don't understand…"

"Listen up, don't be stupid. The money was there—and then it all got washed away! I even left Francesco, who was in on it with me, with nothing. The poor fellow hoped that for his help I'd initially hand him a solid chunk of cash. Yes, he did help me, really: I needed to fly to Italy, and tickets aren't cheap, and if you remember, you gave me nothing for the journey. And then I needed to settle down here properly. He thought I'd give him at least thirty percent of that money—well, from my account, the very one on which you sent the money from your JV, thinking it would go toward buying equipment. Yeah right! Like I dashed off to buy the equipment. Fat chance! And that Italian Valdoni—also a naive fellow—hoped that we'd become rich together; he had already quit his job and I simply swindled him out of everything!!! Now let him live on pennies repairing machinery. That's exactly what you simpletons deserve…"

"But you were going to help me with the enterprise—you wanted to become my right-hand man!"

"Nothing of the sort I ever intended. I could care less about your whole JV!!! I've been nothing but your shadow all my life, Bahadir. And I must confess, I grew terribly tired of that! And now I'm my own man—both the 'right hand,' the boss, and the owner! How about that? I'm not excessively rich, but I'm well provided for—it will last me a long time…"

"It's disgusting to listen to you, honestly. So, you're not in Milan anymore…"

Rudik burst out laughing into the phone.

"I bought a small house in Bolzano—it's an excellent alpine

resort! Right now, I'm driving my convertible on a ride through the Alps. The air is simply wonderful, exquisite! It's pretty steep up here, true, but the car is a beast! Oh!!! Just don't be a bore and don't envy me."

"What's there to envy? Rudik, you're simply a fool. Everything you stole from me, everything you took by cheating and fraud—it won't bring you any happiness. Listen to me and come to your senses… You'd be better off returning to…"

"Are you out of your mind, Baha? I'm doing just fine here. Why would I return?… Ugh… What do you mean, anyway?… Don't talk nonsense. Oh! Why has it snowed so much today?! Damn! It's as if an entire avalanche has come down here… A nightmare."

"For instance, you could at least return the our partners' money that you have stolen from me and Amin. Or else…"

"Well, what else, dear?" Rudik wheezed, his voice strained as if he were dragging his convertible further up the mountain. "What are you going to do to me from so far away and without evidence, Bahadir?! Will you complain to your parents? Or turn me in to the police?"

Rudik then burst into loud laughter again. Suddenly, a crash and the screeching of metal were heard on the line…

"Hello, Rudik! Are you there? Hello!"

Someone moaned softly. Then the connection abruptly cut off.

"Poor guy…!" Bahadir thought. "Surely something must have happened to him there. He's brought trouble upon himself!"

Bahadir now understood that Rudik had never truly loved anyone and was, in his own miserable way, a mean-spirited fellow… Yet despite all of Rudik's sins and misdeeds, Bahadir couldn't help but feel genuine pity for him…

* * *

The necklace adorned with simulated rubies and diamonds that had been stolen by Misha Leonidov from the family of Sheikh Kuveyt at a Moscow museum, and subsequently taken "for the duration of the investigation" from the Mumtazovs, had for some time lain in the office of the former district office of internal affairs captain, Ravshan Umarov. Back when investigator Umarov held Bahadir Fattakhov in detention, he had planned to present this necklace in court as tangible evidence of Bahadir's guilt in the theft from the Mumtazov family. But the case fell apart, and the contrived piece of evidence proved useless… In principle, had everything been done by the book, this trinket of glass beads should have been returned to the Mumtazovs. Or at the very least, Umarov himself should have sent it to the district office of internal affairs' special evidence storage—a secure evidence locker. However, when the poorly fabricated "Case of B.A. Fattakhov" burst like a soap bubble, the counterfeit necklace was carelessly tossed deep into the drawer of his work desk and completely forgotten. Who needed it anymore?

Then one day, an operative—tasked by his superiors to clear out the former office of the now-dismissed Umarov—inspected the drawers of his desk to remove unnecessary junk. To his surprise, he discovered in one of them what he deemed a "precious" ornament. For some reason, the operative did not show the item to the experts; he evidently feared that the experts might inadvertently mention the found trinket to the higher-ups, thereby thwarting any chance of "communising" it from there. No, of course, this operative was by no means a thief. But the ornament was ownerless, having lain abandoned in the desk of a former employee… The operative thought, "Surely such a treasure shouldn't be allowed to vanish into thin air! It would be far better to sell it and finally live comfortably, like a human being…"

However, that very evening, as the operative—having stowed the ornament in his pocket—boarded a bus and, after a long, exhausting day at work, peacefully dozed off in his seat, a young, petty pickpocket passed by. The operative was in plain clothes, and the pickpocket had no idea that he was in the presence of a police officer. Seizing the opportunity, the nimble-fingered pickpocket swiftly helped himself to the "precious" item. He then delighted for a long while that his haul had turned out so well and lucrative! And once again, that counterfeit necklace began to "travel the world."

As for the genuine, most precious necklace—adorned with the Temur Ruby along with three other sizable gems, more precisely, spinels and diamonds—it most likely remained in the possession of Kuwaiti Sheikh Al-Sabah.

A third necklace, transmitted through that same sheikh via Said Yakhaevich—for Firuz-begim, from the daughter of the UAE sheikh, Fatima Al-Nahayan—rested quietly in the cargo hold of Sitora and patiently awaited its new mistress: Malika Mumtazov.

And the fake necklace, which Mukhitdin had ordered from some craftsman in Delhi—the very necklace he had attached to a mannequin dressed in Bhojwani clothing and which incidentally ended up with Sitora Kadyrova, who was visiting Singh Bhodjwani—was, following Bhodjwani's example, repurposed by Sitora as an accessory for one of the dresses on a mannequin…

But now, it was not thoughts of those unappealing stones and the necklaces made from them that preoccupied Sitora most. Her precious "diamond," her daughter Malika, had not called for several days and was not answering her phone at all! That was what greatly troubled Sitora.

"Could something have happened to my child over there?!" her heart pounded in panic, thought Malika's mother. "And I don't know… If something's wrong with her, I simply couldn't bear it!"

Something had to be done; they couldn't just sit idly by.

That very evening, she shared her worries with her husband.

Immediately, Said Yakhaevich dialed his daughter's mobile number himself. However, she did not answer.

"Said, we need to do something! Please, call Bahadir or Abdulla Rustamovich right away."

"Tell me, how am to talk to them? They've disappointed me so much! How could they think and speak ill of my beloved daughter—of that little angel?! Abdulla, with whom we have been friends for over thirty years, would never allow himself to do such a thing; he would never speak ill of people without verifying the facts!"

"Darling, now is not the time to dwell on past grievances. We must urgently find out—perhaps someone from the Fattakhov family knows something about our Malika? I'm so worried…"

"Yes, I too am very troubled by the fact that we haven't been able to reach our daughter."

Said Yakhaevich then dialed Bahadir's number.

"Hello, sonny, this is Malika's father calling. I hope you're not too busy?"

"No, not at all, Said Yakhaevich. Hello," Bahadir answered politely.

"Bahadir, did Malika call you after the contest?"

"No, she didn't. And is the contest over already, then?" Bahadir inquired.

"Don't tell me, as her husband you aren't even aware of that?.. Oh, come on! And, by the way, Malika won the Grand Prix over there, and Sitora Kadyrova and Firuz-begim and I are so proud of our little girl! And you—look at you—you seem to know nothing about her. I'm sorry, my son, but you simply can't be so indifferent—she's your wife, your family. You're now even closer to her than her own mother and I! Don't you care at all whether she is safe and sound?"

Bahadir fell silent. He despised being reprimanded, but he didn't dare contradict his father-in-law. Besides, he understood that, by and large, his father-in-law was right.

"And we're terribly worried," continued Said Yakhaevich. "We fear that in a foreign country—in a city unfamiliar to her—something terrible might have happened to Malika. She hasn't answered her phone or called for several days, and that is completely unlike her! Do you understand? It appears that we are in real trouble, my son—truly in trouble. And I don't know what to do; frankly, I'm at a loss. Perhaps we should even put her on an international wanted list?"

"No, Said Yakhaevich—such measures are usually reserved for criminals. And as for her… perhaps we should just file a report with the police…"

"But she's not in Uzbekistan right now; she's in Russia! What good would such a report do? How is our police supposed to locate her in Moscow?.. What are we to do, Bahadir?!"

"I need to think about the best course of action. Please, give me some time. But I promise you one thing: I will absolutely find my wife! Do not doubt it. Most likely, I'll even fly to Moscow myself—once I settle a couple of important and urgent matters first."

"Alright, my son. All our hope now rests with you!"

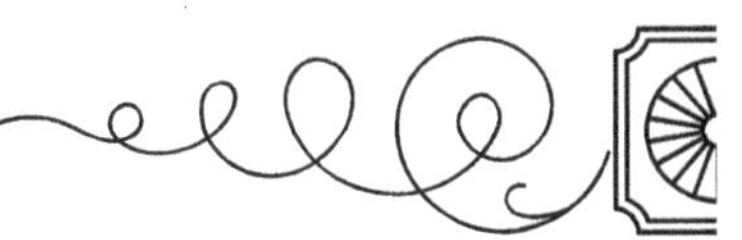

***

Later that day, Bahadir called the office of Nasyrov. He wanted to know if he could visit tomorrow. From his modest savings, he had set aside a sum he intended to hand over to Nasyrov—to help ease the tightening noose around his neck, because Veniamin Arkadievich had been calling him periodically, reminding him of the debt.

However, at Nasyrov's office no one answered the phone. Bahadir tried calling again, but all attempts were in vain. Then he recalled that for about five days now, Veniamin hadn't been bothering him at all. That struck him as strange.

On the same day, while listening to the local news, Bahadir happened to hear that both the former owner of restaurants and casinos—the oligarch Murad Nasyrov—and his assistant Veniamin Zverev had been detained and were under investigation… and that the prosecutor's office was levying very serious charges against both of them, especially Nasyrov, under Article 278 of the Criminal Code of the Republic of Uzbekistan," organising and conducting gambling and other risk-based games."

Bahadir sighed with immense relief! Could it be—freedom?.. Praise be to God.

Nevertheless, he was extremely worried about Malika, not thinking of her for even a minute, and hurried off to Moscow. Yet before he departed, one important matter still awaited him.

70

Amin had begun communicating with his Aunt Nur-begim and her two full sisters—also his aunts on his father's side—Zeynab-begim and Nurkhol-begim.

All three women were dark-skinned, quite beautiful and dignified. They all shared similar temperaments—restrained in their emotions and expressions of affection. Their genuine happiness at seeing their nephew was shown not through overt tenderness or words of familial love, but simply by never refusing him communication: they would call him regularly and, from time to time, take turns inviting him to visit. On a couple of occasions, all three had even visited Amin at his home. When they saw his future bride, Dilshoda, seated at his table, they accepted her in a rather reserved yet favorable manner.

"Once you truly come to love your kin and understand the full value of your heritage," intoned the aristocratic Nur-begim in a didactic tone directed at Amin, "then my sisters and I will reveal to you the secrets by which we, the descendants of the Great Mughals, have always stood at the pinnacle of prosperity and success."

She was convinced that she had the right to say so, for as it turned out, she was the CEO of a very respectable charitable organization dedicated to helping sick children. Moreover, both of her sisters were renowned physicians with professorial titles—luminaries in the field of medicine.

"Oh, how I wish I had known you earlier!" Amin lamented. "I would have certainly introduced you, my dear aunts, to my beloved sister Rano. It's a pity that it's already too late…"

One April evening, after Amin had returned home once again from a visit to his father's sisters, his phone rang with a call from Bahadir.

"Brother, hello! It's good that you're home. May I come over? We need to talk," Bahadir said.

"Of course, Bahadir, come over. Although it's rather late now—how will you get home afterward?… Actually, wait, you can spend the night at my place! And tomorrow we'll go together to work at Fattakhov PC. Is that alright?"

"Yeah, I'll probably stay the night, thanks. But the thing is, I already must… Anyway, I'll come over—and I'll tell you everything when we meet."

"Alright. I'll be waiting for you."

When Bahadir arrived, he declined the dinner Amin offered and immediately launched into the conversation that weighed heavily on him.

"Amin, the matter is that my Malika has disappeared… No one can find her."

Amin instantly grew tense and serious.

"Go on, Bahadir—I'm listening carefully!"

"Every one of us—both I and Malika's parents—has tried repeatedly to call her, but she never answers. I even got her phone number from the dormitory's entrance. The gatekeeper told me they thoroughly searched for Malika! She was supposed to have moved out long ago, yet she suddenly vanished without taking a single thing with her—even leaving her passport in the room, in a little cabinet! You understand, Amin, that this is very bad. She's a normal, decent girl—she couldn't simply 'go out for a stroll' for five whole days!"

"Of course. And has it really been a full five days since she disappeared?"

"Unfortunately, yes."

"Then why are you still sitting here, Bahadir? Forgive me for butting in, but I believe you should be in Moscow—you must find her!"

"Of course, I understand that myself. That's why I started talking to you on the phone—but I didn't get around to saying that I would fly there on the first available flight tomorrow."

"That's the right idea. Tell me, how can I help you with this?"

"Wait, brother. Nothing is needed—and I have the money. On the contrary, I want to tell you that I owe you! I learned from our mother that you ran into trouble with Father because you pawned the assets of his company! But I remember very well that I personally asked you for that favour—for the sake of my JV. And I was pleasantly surprised that you didn't betray me to my father, not even a word. But it turns out I inadvertently set you up. That's not right. And I don't want to be a lowlife—especially not toward my own, beloved brother!"

Amin could hardly believe his ears.

"What? What did you just say?"

"I said: to my dear and beloved brother! Please forgive me for everything, Amin. I was such a stubborn and uncompromising egoist that I'm now ashamed of myself."

"Don't say that. You're a good and kind guy!"

"You don't know everything. There was a time—back when my wife and I still lived in your apartment—do you remember that? I was then looking for the documents for that apartment because I wanted to sell it without your knowledge—to pay off my personal debts. I'm very ashamed of that now… Thank Malika—she didn't let that base affair come to fruition."

"Alright, Bahadir. Let's drop it! Thank God that it's in the past. I'm very glad that you've come to realize and repent, and that your Malika is a good girl. But what worries me most now is: where will you get the money for your trip to Moscow?"

"I have the money—both for the trip and even for saving Fattakhov PC!"

"How so?" Amin asked, still not fully grasping. "But from where?! I don't understand anything…"

"The thing is, when Rudik asked me to transfer all the investment funds to his account in Italy, I thought and… I didn't transfer everything! A significant amount, yes, but not all. The money provided to us by Monsieur Marchal remains with me—for a reserve, so to speak, in case of 'force majeure.' I don't even know why I did that, since I trusted that rascal… By the way, perhaps one should no longer speak of him like that…"

"Do you still doubt that your Rudik is a cheat and a swindler?" Amin asked in surprise.

"It's not that, brother—please, better not to say such things," Bahadir said sadly. "I don't doubt it, it's just… about those who have gone—you know the saying: never speak ill of the… I don't want to believe it, but I think Rudik… In short, I feel that he's in trouble…"

Then Bahadir told Amin about a recent conversation he had with Rudik, who was in Italy, and about the presumed accident of his car caused by a massive avalanche.

"What a mess!" Amin whistled. "And I even feel sorry for him…"

"Yes, it's a terrible matter… So, brother, I have temporarily 'frozen' the operations of my new enterprise 'Bakh-atir' and transferred the funds invested by Jean Marshal to the Fattakhov PC account. This will help us close the credit on time and save our father's firm from complete bankruptcy..."

"Excellent, well done. But how will we repay Marshal his investments and dividends?"

"Well, not immediately—there's still time. Today I visited our parents—to ask for their blessing for the journey—and I told our father everything. He will help us settle with Marchal; he has some excellent ideas for that account. So, don't worry about that money. And I confessed to Dad, brother, that you are in no way to blame—you simply nobly saved me and my new venture!"

"Why did you do that?" Amin shook his head.

"It's all right, don't worry! Our father nearly cried, saying that he had deeply hurt you and that... he is proud of you and—indeed, of all of us, his children, he loves us very much. By the way, my mother immediately—and my father, though not right away, eventually—supported me in my decision to go search for Malika!"

"And you?"

"Me?!"

"Yes, you. I hope that you truly believe her?" Amin smiled.

"Well... y-y-yeah, I'm trying, in a way."

"It seems to me, Bahadir, that once you fully believe her, you'll be able to find and rescue her! I sense that she very, very much needs your help!"

"Her father told me the same."

"See! That's why I think it's best not to delay any longer but to wholeheartedly trust your wife and accept the truth."

"The truth? ... What truth?"

"The truth that she is a wonderful, pure, and very faithful person to you, and that she loves only you..."

"Yes, I get it. Thank you for everything! Our parents and you are a great support to me."

"Alright, let's get some sleep, dear little brother, and tomorrow morning I will personally take you to the airport!"

71

In Moscow, the first thing that Bahadir did was drive to the dormitory where Malika lived. As the legal husband of the contest's participant—and winner—he was admitted into her room without any argument. There, he really did need to search the room thoroughly. What if he might find something that could help him in his search for his wife?

The room was quite neat and tidy, except for an unmade bed.

That's strange, Bahadir thought. *My wife would never leave her bed unmade. Or maybe she was abducted in the middle of the night— while she was asleep?!*

Bahadir looked under the bed, just in case. And suddenly, he discovered an object nearly the size of a palm. To his surprise, it was his wife's smartphone! Finding it under such circumstances was a stroke of luck. But it was puzzling—why hadn't the other people searching for Malika found it? Clearly, they hadn't looked hard enough.

Bahadir was unaware that in Moscow, the only person truly anxious about Malika's fate at that moment was her kind-hearted producer, Konstantin Melodiev. Many others, especially her new fans, weren't searching for her because they had no idea where she was supposed to be—whether in Russia or already in Uzbekistan. Meanwhile, Melodiev had involved the Moscow police, specifically the missing persons division, in the search.

Bahadir noticed that for several days, numerous calls to Malika's cell phone had come from Melodiev. The maestro, knowing that his protégé was still in Moscow, had been persistently calling, hoping that perhaps the girl would answer, intact and unharmed. Konstantin had no idea that her mobile had remained in her dorm room.

The missing persons unit had begun searching for the Uzbek citizen Malika Mumtazova, but so far all efforts had been fruitless. Consequently, Konstantin even had to involve one of his lawyer friends in the search.

Bahadir found Melodiev's number in Malika's phone and called the musician.

"Hello, Konstantin! This is Bahadir, Malika's husband."

"Hello, Bahadir. I'm afraid I have no good news—I have nothing uplifting to tell you. Our girl has vanished, disappeared without a trance. And how did you get my number? I hardly give it out. Ah—wait a minute! I'm guessing you found Malika's mobile? I've been calling it from time to time."

"Yes, I found it—in her dorm room. Konstantin, she left completely without her belongings! Almost all her clothes, her toiletries, and even a large sum of money—presumably the prize for her contest victory—remained there! I fear that she was somehow abducted—right while she was asleep, straight out of the dormitory!"

"Goodness… What a state that dorm must be in. How could someone sneak in at night, abduct the residents—girls, at that! What a disgrace. I will certainly report this to the appropriate authorities. By the way, after her grand victory at the international contest, there may be opportunists with a taste for easy money. After all, Malika has a 'golden' voice and enormous talent. And I wonder: what if someone figured out that there's a lot of profit to be made off her?"

"So, you're saying that this 'someone' is the one who abducted her?"

"Well, he or his helpers and conspirators… You know what, Bahadir? I'll pass that idea on to the competent people who are also now searching for your wife. Perhaps they'll uncover something along those lines. Alright?"

"Okay, thank you. And I'll try to search for my wife by other means."

* * *

Anvar Tukhataev had already arranged for the sale of Malika to a sheikh from Saudi Arabia; he had received an advance payment for her and was preparing the beautiful girl for shipment early tomorrow morning. Anvar had moved her to his opulent villa outside the city and assigned two women to attend to her, ensuring that she ate a hearty and appetising meal and that she looked appropriately presentable for sale.

Yet Malika had no appetite at all. After all she had endured—and despite her triumphant success on the "Superstar" project—the prospect of being sent even further away from her home and loved ones, and moreover, being treated as a submissive, utterly powerless slave, filled her with mortal dread!

As she contemplated her bitter fate, she suddenly remembered her granny Firuz-begim's tales of the Great Mughal Shah Jahan, who, after the death of his devoted and beloved wife Mumtaz Mahal, spent many years in harsh confinement, locked away in his own palace by his own offspring…

She also recalled the novels by Anne and Serge Golon about the enchanting Angélique—especially "Angélique and the Sultan." Images of the arduous trials endured by that delightful French-

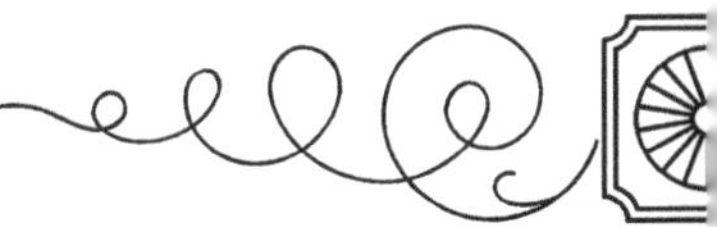

woman in the sultan's palace in Morocco flooded her mind. Malika thought that a similar fate might be awaiting her... But, unlike the heroine of those adventure romances, she was neither a marquess nor a princess, and she could hardly expect leniency or mercy from her future "master."

Yet the greatest anguish for the lovely Uzbek girl was the thought that she would now be separated by an unfathomably vast distance from her loved ones and kin…

The mere thought of her bitter fate was unbearable. She had to try to escape. But how?... Sinister, overbearing chaperones, swirled all around her and the guard outside her room was ever watchful. Every attempt to break free would surely end in complete failure.

All she could do was wait silently, humbly, and patiently for a miracle—a sign of help from the Creator…

* * *

Amin, having seen Bahadir off, did not return home. Instead, he stopped at a café, enjoyed a light breakfast, and then drove straight to work.

About an hour later, Abdulla Rustamovich arrived at the firm. Due to his health problems, the head of Fattakhov PC did not come to work every day. However, he knew that now only Amin was left "at the helm" and that he must help him—at the very least, be present in case any difficulties arose.

After learning from his secretary that his elder son was already at work, Abdulla Rustamovich himself approached the door of Amin's office and, for the first time in his life, knocked quietly.

"Yes? Come in!" Amin said, thinking that perhaps an early client was waiting behind the door.

The head of the Fattakhov family entered and greeted Amin with a warm smile. Amin politely stood up.

At that moment, Amin saw that the visitor was not the "cool" businessman or the ostentatious owner of the company, but simply a man who had come solely to greet his son, to speak with him heart-to-heart, and to wish him a good day...

"Hello, my son!" began Abdulla Rustamovich, his voice a little agitated and timid yet trying to sound calm and steady. "How are you? Is everything all right?"

"Yes, chief, hello!" replied Amin. He recalled that at the firm it wasn't allowed to address him as "papa." Moreover, what kind of "papa" is he now? And what sort of son is Amin to him?

"Oh, come now, come now, my son. Why this fuss? After all, there's no one else here but us, and there's no need to observe sub-ordination. Except, perhaps," Abdulla Rustamovich deliberately stressed nearly every word, "one can still show filial respect to one's parent."

Amin moved to a chair next to the table and courteously slid it aside so that "the boss" could sit.

"Thank you very much, my dear... Please, have a seat beside me."

Amin silently complied and sat down.

"How splendidly you've grown, my boy—so well-mannered, kind, and handsome! And do you remember when you were so little, and your mother and I would go together to parades and parks? I used to carry you on my shoulders and think, 'There he is, my little one—so tender and weak, in need of a father. And when he grows up, I myself will need him just as much and will want to lean on him!' And now, indeed, it has turned out that I can rely on you completely. You are smart, strong, serious, responsible..."

"Please, Abdulla Rustamovich…" Amin murmured.

"Yes, my son, ever since the day when, in foolishness and a fit of anger, I exploded at you, you have never called me 'papa' again. I never imagined that—even though I was completely to blame—that it would hurt me so deeply… Please, forgive your old man!"

The elderly Fattakhov could scarcely hold back the tears welling up.

Almost instinctively, Amin reached out and placed his hand on his father's shoulder.

"Well, come on. Don't be so…"

"You already know, my son, that your mother once told you that you were born… back when she was married to another man." It was evident that Abdulla Rustamovich found it difficult to speak of this. "As far as I know, you're now in touch with the sisters… of that man, Jahangir, aren't you? Of course, continue to speak with them—I have no objection; they are your relatives! May Jahangir's soul rest in peace… We are all servants of the Almighty. I, too, do not have much time left… Two heart attacks are no laughing matter, as you well know."

Amin knew this but did not wish to interrupt. Despite the heaviness of the moment, the atmosphere in his office felt good—very light, as though a sense of freedom had descended upon them both.

"But from the moment I first saw you—when you were only two years old—I loved you immediately! I thought then, 'There you are, my son. You will be just like me!' And it turned out exactly so. Often, men find it hard to accept, forgive me, a child that is not their own. But I accepted you right away and loved you. Perhaps because I have always loved your mother so dearly, her child was instantly to me my own, my dear! Do you understand? And since then, I have loved you all your life… It was just on that day—when we were discussing the problems of the firm, when I first learned that, without consulting me, you pawned all the major assets of our company—that I was simply furious, so angry with you! I exploded and said things I shouldn't have—things that did not truly reflect what I think and feel. I know you are not at fault."

"By the way, father," Amin said as he rose and picked up a document—a payment order for the Fattakhov PC account—from the table, "here is the money that Bahadir transferred to pay off our bank debt! That should, in theory, be enough to solve the problem."

"Thank you, my son, very good. But that is not the main thing now. The main thing is that you forgive me and understand that you are, to me, my dear boy—and that is forever, for all of my now ancient life! Do you understand?"

"Yes, father, but you are not ancient yet!"

They both smiled at each other. Amin then approached his father, leaned in, and embraced him warmly. The elder Fattakhov returned the embrace just as warmly.

"I love you, my son."

"Thank you, papa! I love you and Mother very much! I love our entire family."

"May God provide for Bahadir's wife—then, I believe, everything will be all right. We will host your wedding for Dilshoda. I promise—it will be a beautiful and dignified wedding. You do want that, my son?"

"Yes, father, I dream of it very much."

"And I will do everything for you, my son, just as you wish."

"Thank you so much!"

"That's good. Now let's get to work; today we have many important tasks. And together we will await good news from our Bahadir."

***

While sitting in the apartment of one of his father's friends, Bahadir decided to carefully review once again the entire contact list on Malika's smartphone. Suddenly, he stumbled upon one number from Tashkent—someone had called Malika not too long ago.

Maybe it's her teacher from the conservatory, Boris Petrovich? Bahadir thought. *Ah, no—no. Look, all his numbers are saved in her phone under his first name and patronymic. Then who else could have called Malika from this unfamiliar number? It's unclear. Well, why guess? I'll just call this number.*

He dialed the number. A young woman answered the phone.

"Hello. I'm listening. Who is this?" she said.

"Hello. Excuse me, my name is Bahadir. I'm Malika Mumta…"

"Ah, Bahadir! Well, hello. How wonderful that you called! Do you even know who you're speaking with right now?"

"Honestly, no—I can't even guess."

"I'm her close friend Galya. Remember, I was at your wedding with Malika!"

"Galina? Ah, yes—we were introduced, and indeed I've heard so much about you. Really…" Bahadir hesitated. "To be frank, not all of it was good. You came to my parents' house and said something rather unkind and unpleasant about my wife… Isn't that so?"

"Yes, she was a complete fool!!! And such a liar, too. It's awful, of course."

"What? Pardon me—I didn't catch that. So, you mean your words…"

"Lies and nonsense, from the first word to the last. But I'll need to explain everything to you, Bahadir. You see… Wait a minute, where are you calling from? It seems to me this isn't a Tashkent number."

"Yes, it's not from Tashkent. It's a city number of one of my acquaintances in Moscow."

"So, you're in Moscow now?!" Galina laughed unexpectedly. "Well, that's something!"

"Of course—I'm out here searching for my wife! I didn't get a chance to mention that she's disappeared…"

"What do you mean, 'disappeared'?! Completely vanished?! How horrible. The thing is, although I'm originally from Tashkent, I'm in Moscow now as well. We could meet somewhere and discuss everything. I believe I might be able to help you somehow."

"Do you know where Malika is and who abducted her?!"

"Well, no—not exactly. But I'll tell you what I've heard, in case it helps… Sound good?"

"Why should I trust you?"

"Because it's absolutely in my interest for your wife to return to you!"

Bahadir paused, weighing the pros and cons.

"Alright, suppose so. I think it wouldn't hurt if we talked just once."

"Excellent. Then let's meet in an hour at the bar of the 'Metropol-Moscow' hotel."

72

Mukhitdin didn't know that his father was facing prison. And even if he had known, it wouldn't have disturbed him much. For a long time now, he was only concerned with his own well-being, success, and comfort. Because of that, he rarely and sparingly even communicated with his mother, who still saw in him a tiny, "unfeathered" fledgling—incapable of anything in life. But Mukhitdin was determined to prove to the world, to his parents, to himself, and to stubborn Malika—who didn't believe in his extraordinary abilities and, as he felt, regarded him as a talentless nobody—that he was strong, smart, and capable of much. That he could even shape other people's destinies no worse than his father could! And that is exactly why he did not reject the idea of subjecting Malika to such a cruel and harsh trial. He understood that voluntarily, without extreme measures, she would never want to be with him or allow him to stay with her.

Initially, Mukhitdin had only intended to punish Malika mercilessly—by sending her "to the ends of the earth" via Anvar. But now his plan had changed fundamentally: he now intended to find out from the bandit Tukhataev the initial route along which she was being sent, and then try to somehow rescue her!

To Galina, he lied that he had already completely forgotten about Malika. Yet, seeing his preparations and his nervous fuss, she realised that was most likely not true at all.

Of course, Mukhitdin wasn't a fool and understood that Anvar would never reveal all the "cards" of his "business" or divulge all the information. So, after changing clothes and applying makeup in his room with the help of Galina, who was forced to assist him, Mukhitdin spent long hours—without Anvar noticing—lingering in his strip club, carefully extracting from the staff the details he needed regarding the shipment of the girls.

Mukhitdin was lucky: there turned out to be talkative, tip-hungry waitresses, as well as one of the bartenders and a cleaning lady. They told the unfamiliar, bearded Asian man—who generously paid them—that one extraordinarily beautiful Uzbek girl was being transported by an off-road jeep to the city of Yeysk on the Azov Sea, and from there she would be ferried by a special steamer to Saudi Arabia.

In fact, Anvar and his longtime associates had a well-established pirate trade route for human trafficking along a long chain of straits and seas: the Kerch Strait – the Black Sea – the Bosphorus – the Marmara Sea – the Dardanelles – the Aegean Sea – the Mediterranean – the Persian Gulf.

This was not a cheap or quick method of transporting slave girls, but it yielded enormous profits, as the Arabs paid handsomely for beauties from Russia and other former Soviet countries. The main advantage for the human traffickers was that along this route they were hardly controlled by anyone.

Also, the bearded and wealthy Asian man learned in the club that the poor girl was currently held in Anvar's suburban mansion—she was being prepared for shipment. The needed address could easily be obtained—for a handsome reward...

And now Mukhitdin had to figure out what to do next...

***

In the bar, Galina explained to Bahadir that once again, Mukhitdin's hormones had "gone to his head" and that he was about to "heroically" rescue Malika—essentially, to save her from himself.

"That little scoundrel!" Bahadir couldn't hold back. "I swear, if I ever catch him! And how does Malika feel about him? Does she love him? You said something…"

"Stop addressing me so formally; we're both young and about the same age," Galina replied.

"Alright. You told my parents that she's been fooling around with him."

"First of all, I didn't say it exactly that way, and secondly, I already explained that I did it solely to get back at Mukhitdin, and that I set Malika up—purely out of jealousy!"

"I see. So, Galina, your Mukhitdin will most likely try to find the place where they are hiding Malika. And did he say who and on which day they would whisk her abroad?"

"No, he was only supposed to find out that today, and we haven't seen each other yet; he left early. Perhaps I'll see him later this evening when he returns to his room."

"Let's reason this out. He will reveal that place or the date and time of Malika's departure to you, nor, especially, me. Why would he do that? Right?"

"That's right. So, what's next?"

"But even if he plays the hero, he's only setting himself up, the fool—and surely he won't be able to handle those bandits on his own!"

"Right… Oh, Bahadir, I'm afraid for him!!! And yet I love him… Of course, I will do everything in my power to dissuade him from going there tomorrow, but the way he treats me… I doubt he'll listen. Maybe I should get him drunk and try to hold him back through cunning? Why are you so quiet?"

Bahadir was thinking.

"No, that won't work, because then the bandits might either take her away or, heaven forbid, kill her—and you shouldn't be indifferent about that, because—did you forget?—you still have to repent to her! Moreover, Mukhitdin surely is stronger and, sorry to say, smarter than you, and in such a serious moment he won't even touch food, let alone drink or get physical! Besides, he might realise that you, to some extent, suspect his plans and know that you'll try to thwart him. As I see it, you most likely won't be able to hold him back."

"What if they kill him there, in that house or somewhere along the way?! That guy from the club, whom Mukhitdin mentioned, is completely off his rocker—a total scoundrel! And in his house, by the way, is your wife!"

"I remember that, Galina. You do have Mukhitdin's phone number, don't you?"

"Yes, I do. But why would you need it? I'm sure I'll see him today anyway…"

"We've already discussed this—even if Mukhitdin finds out the address of the bandit holding Malika, he won't give it to you."

"So you plan to call him yourself, right? But then, he definitely won't give you that address, as you yourself said."

"I know. I have a better idea."

* * *

Bahadir, who had been staying at the apartment of one of his father's old friends—the engineer Denis Alexandrovich—could not sleep for a long time that night. He tossed and turned, thinking about Malika and worrying, knowing that tomorrow would be an extremely, extremely difficult day. Finally, he fell asleep.

In his dreams, long and frantic chases filled his mind; then he saw Rudik speeding in a convertible, overwhelmed by a powerful alpine avalanche. Next, he dreamt that he himself was running away from that very avalanche. Then came a vision of Malika—she too was running, fleeing from some malevolent force…

After that, an old woman, Firuz-begim, appeared in his dream. She whirled around in her sacred dance beside an antique hookah, then ceased her dancing, sat down on a carpet in the Mumtazov household, and, gazing directly into Bahadir's eyes, said: "Husband of Malika! Be brave and courageous! She loves you very much, and you love her very much—so you will succeed! Just don't look back, don't turn around; only look forward—and fear nothing! You will succeed; you will rescue Malika from captivity!"

Before dawn, another, new dream came to the young man. In this dream, he found himself in a magnificent palace, reminiscent of the Taj Mahal in Agra. Bahadir entered vast, regal quarters, where upon a throne sat… the Sheikh Kuwait, Al-Sabah. With a single, beckoning finger, the Sheikh summoned Bahadir to come closer.

Bahadir approached and greeted the Sheikh. The Sheikh, in a thoughtful tone, said:

"Bahadir, what do you intend to do with the money your wife has earned for you? Will you go gambling with it again?"

"No, sir. I have decided that I will no longer play games of

chance! It is unworthy. I promised both my sister and my wife that I would never again sit at a gaming table."

"Well, that is commendable. So you will give the money to your wife, and it will be used for sensible and worthwhile purposes?"

"Yes, respected sir, I will certainly do so."

"You have earned yet another compliment. Now listen carefully and look here."

The Sheikh extended his hand, in which he held a small velvet jewelry case. He opened the case, and from it shone hundreds of "stars."

"Do you know what this is? This is a precious necklace. It was made by the English in the nineteenth century, but the stones set in it are much older. According to legend, the Temur Ruby alone was first cut in the fifth century BCE, and since 1398 it was owned first by the Amir and then by his descendants—the Temurids and Baburids. Do you see how magnificent and wondrous this stone is, once adorning the very throne before you! And how fine the other spinels are, not to mention the numerous diamonds! Take the necklace in your hands."

Hearing the authoritative command of the Sheikh, Bahadir obeyed. He rose, approached Al-Sabah, and, bowing slightly in a gesture of respect, carefully and reverently took from his hands the ornament—an item worth millions or billions, yet essentially priceless. Bahadir had never seen anything more magnificent, brilliant, or elegant, crafted with such incredible taste and aesthetic beauty.

"Would you like it to be yours?" the Sheikh asked. "Very well—take it for yourself. And you shall live in comfort for the rest of your days, never lacking for anything—especially if you resist the temptation to sell it, and instead keep it. You must know: it is so rich and unusual, and it grants you such power that people, upon

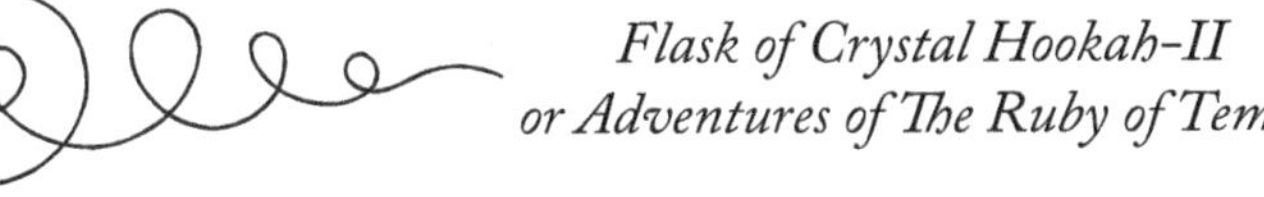
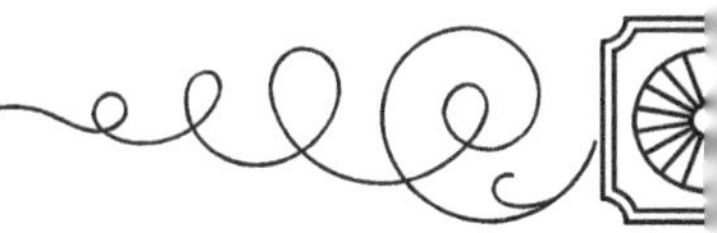

merely laying eyes on it, will give you everything you could ever desire!"

In his dream, Bahadir's eyes seemed to light up, and his heart pounded even harder. To have everything one desires and to want for nothing! Oh, how enticing and pleasant that was!

"But I have one condition," continued the Sheikh. "Actually, this isn't really my condition—it is what the Great Mughals have bequeathed to us. First, you must solve a riddle. Here it is: what is the true Adornment of the Palace?"

Bahadir pondered for a moment.

"Can't you guess? Think about it. And for now, let me tell you this—secondly: Bahadir, take this treasure for yourself, but… forever renounce your wife!"

Bahadir was dumbfounded. What is this honourable man saying?

"Yes, yes," the Sheikh said mysteriously. "You will have to make a choice: either this golden necklace with its rubies and diamonds—along with it, all the wealth and treasures of the world—or Malika, which, it seems, translates from Uzbek as 'Princess'… One of the two. Choose right now! If you do not make your choice immediately, tomorrow it will be too late—you will be left with nothing…"

Was this truly a test among tests?! How could he possibly forsake Malika?!

And… Bahadir awoke.

In the morning, he thought: *Even if one possessed all the riches in the world, would one be truly happy without love, without one's cherished wife? But the truth is… nothing and no one is dearer to me than Malika! She is, for me, the most important and precious thing on earth; she is the very Adornment of the Palace of my heart, of my entire life!!! And here is my answer to the Sheikh: I renounce all treasures—for the*

sake of my beloved Malika, my Princess!

The choice was made.

Bahadir called Amin from his mobile, telling him that everything was all right, that he was on the right track and knew where to search for his wife.

"Little brother, please be careful!" Amin urged him. "I understand—Malika is out there. But still, don't rush in alone; leave it to the experienced men in uniform!"

"I'll do my best, don't worry. And please support our parents as well…"

Bahadir gathered himself, thanked Denis Alexandrovich for his hospitality, and left—confident in his victory and certain that today he would meet his one and only and rescue her without fail.

73

Bahadir only wanted to reassure Amin. Meanwhile, he remembered well what his father had once taught him: in times of hardship, one must rely first and foremost on one's own strength and only lightly on "Lady Luck."… His father often reinforced those words with the wise verses of Omar Khayyam:

It is always easier to destroy than to build.
To offend is simpler than to forgive.
And it is always more convenient to lie than to believe,
While pushing someone away is far easier than loving them.

Bahadir had already arranged, through Konstantin, to enlist the help of the Russian police. Yet he knew that although they were professionals, they might make it in time—or they might be too late in extracting Malika. The police had tracked Mukhitdin's cell phone and pinpointed exactly where he had gone!

According to the tracking signals, the house of the bandit and human trafficker was located in Solntsevo. Bahadir hurried and reached the location before the OMON unit did—the special squad still needed to obtain all the necessary permits for deployment, and that was the snag: so far, there wasn't any compelling evidence proving that the hostage was indeed being held in that house.

The house stood a good distance apart from the surrounding buildings and was enclosed by a wrought-iron fence. Inside the yard, two or three guards were on duty.

Bahadir noticed there was a jeep near the entrance, and some kind of preparations were underway—large quantities of supplies were being loaded into the trunk of the vehicle, clearly for a long journey. Bahadir did not know what Mukhitdin knew—that the route for transporting Malika as a slave was supposed to lead through the Krasnodar krai to a distant Arab country. He thought that his wife might simply be kept here under the most deplorable conditions, perhaps in some dank basement, and tortured like a true prisoner.

Are they really planning to leave, those scoundrels? Bahadir thought in dismay. *Taking my Malika along as a captive? Not gonna happen! But where exactly is she? In which room of the house? I need to find out...*

And then Bahadir noticed that, from behind the rear wall of the mansion, the head of a dark-haired young man was cautiously peeking out. Bahadir squinted to get a better look. And the young man—was an Uzbek! Bahadir had never seen Mukhitdin himself; he had only heard much about him and did not know what he looked like. However, that wouldn't have helped much now—the face was too distant to discern clearly. Still, it wasn't hard to surmise that it was none other than Mukhitdin Nasyrov.

Goodness, what a daring fellow, Bahadir was surprised. *He's already inside, even though the gates are closed. And how did he get in? Maybe he scaled the fence in the dark last night or early in the morning? But the fence is rather high, and besides, the owner—the bandit—has guards! It's strange that this guy seems not to fear them at all... Although—perhaps he's very athletic, like Chuck Norris or Jackie Chan? And what makes me any different?*

Cautiously, so as not to alert the guards, Bahadir tried to find a way to climb over the high fence with its very narrow openings.

But no matter how hard he tried, he couldn't manage it. Then he decided that he must rely on his wits and ingenuity—perhaps like that Mukhitdin—and continued to observe and study the situation.

Two burly men—not security personnel, but also armed with weapons at their waists—were loading supplies into the vehicle and occasionally chatting among themselves. It was hard to catch every word as the wind only carried isolated fragments to Bahadir's ears. Yet he listened intently, hoping to glean some valuable information from them.

Suddenly, with pauses between, he caught fragments of conversation: "Yeisk," "Azov Sea," "Saudi Arabia."

But why would they need Saudi Arabia? My God, what a fool I am! How didn't I guess it immediately? But if what I think is true, then it's simply terrible... They want to sell Malika—apparently to some Arab—and transport her by land to the Azov Sea, and then...

What would come after was already clear enough—and just the thought that his own beloved wife would become not only a slave but even a sex slave drove Bahadir into a rage.

One of the roughnecks lit up a cigarette, and suddenly Bahadir recalled the dream in which Firuz-begim had foretold by the hookah, "You will save her!" That thought gave him strength. Of course, he realised something had to be done immediately!

But what? Should he call Konstantin? Or immediately contact the police—Major of OMON Alexey Ratnikov, who had given Bahadir his number just in case? No—if he did that, the bandits would hear, and that might alert them. After all, they might notice that someone is watching them, even if it is just one person—and then perhaps a second. After all, Mukhitdin, unbeknownst to himself, was now not his rival but an ally in the fight for Malika's freedom! If a commotion erupted in the area, things would only get

worse for Malika. And Mukhitdin would be "taken out" immediately as well.

It was also not the time to step away from the house to make a call—he might miss something important. No, he definitely shouldn't call right now. But he had to somehow warn the police that the hostage was definitely about to be taken away—eventually, very far, beyond Russia's borders! And the special forces needed to start moving, to begin their action! But how could he warn them? Finally, the anxious Bahadir realised that he could send Major Ratnikov an SMS message. He did so. Major Ratnikov replied that he understood everything and that their unit was already on its way.

They won't make it on time—one of those scoundrels has already jumped into a jeep and started the engine! Bahadir thought in despair. *I can't wait... I must come up with something myself...*

Meanwhile, Bahadir noticed that Mukhitdin... had suddenly disappeared from view.

Could it be that he's managed to get inside the house? So quickly? Bahadir wondered even more. *And why am I not there now?!! How am I supposed to get in?!!*

Quietly and cautiously, so as not to be noticed, he began to circle around the long fence, hoping to find even a small opening through which he might slip into the yard.

* * *

There were two overseers who never left their post together, at least one of them always remained "on duty" near the captive Malika. Suddenly, on that late morning, both found themselves ravenously hungry. They tied Malika, just in case, to a chair with ropes so that she wouldn't attempt to escape from her prison, then

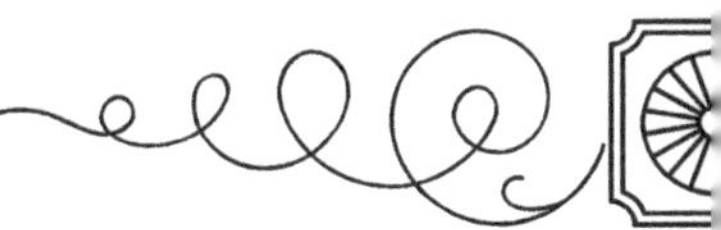

left the room on the second floor, locked the door behind them, and both descended downstairs for breakfast.

Now is the perfect time to run! Malika thought.

However, she had become so weakened that no matter how hard she tried, she couldn't free herself. And then, unexpectedly, salvation came from a source she never anticipated. Ever since that man had revealed his sinister and treacherous face, Malika never imagined there would come a moment when she would be so grateful to him! But sometimes, people do change for the better…

The cell door burst open… and Mukhitdin—apparently having managed to open the lock—rushed into the room. He immediately approached the still-frightened young woman and, with swift, confident movements, began cutting away the ropes with a small knife.

"Mukhitdin! How are you even here?" Malika gasped in surprise. "How did you know where I was?"

"There's no time for explanations, Malika, my dear!" Mukhitdin replied in a serious yet warm tone as he skillfully freed her from the ropes. "Let's run from here!"

Oh, if only it were Bahadir, flashed through Malika's mind. *How I wish it were him!*

Mukhitdin nearly pushed the weakened, former friend out of the room into the corridor, but then he paused for a couple of seconds. He swung open the window and, with a deft flick of his hand, tossed a small packet of light pyrotechnic devices down into the courtyard—over by the guards and slightly away from the jeep. Then he immediately dashed out into the corridor, returning to the frightened woman.

"We'll be caught," Malika fretted as they raced down the stairs.

"They won't catch us," Mukhitdin assured her, gripping her hand tightly. "Don't be afraid; I'm here—you're not alone now! I've thrown a smoke bomb down below. It will distract everyone for a while, and we can slip away from this dreadful house!"

"Mukhitdin, you really are a true hero," Malika marveled as they burst out into the yard through the rear service door of the mansion, finding themselves beyond its back wall.

"Thank you, Malika. I'd do anything for you, you know. But we must hurry!"

"Now, where to?" Malika asked, still disoriented.

"Over there—quickly, come on!" Mukhitdin commanded boldly and confidently, pointing to a small gap hidden beneath one of the lattice sections at the rear of the fence, partly obscured by green, leafy branches.

Barely managing to crawl through the narrow opening to freedom, they suddenly collided with Bahadir, who had been trying to gain entry into the yard through that very same gap they'd just discovered.

Malika was stunned. She had dreamed of him, though she had never truly expected to meet her husband here.

"Bahadir, my dear," she exclaimed, embracing him warmly and tenderly.

"Malika, my beloved!" Bahadir replied with heartfelt embraces and passionate kisses. "How I've missed you—you can't even imagine!"

Both of them, like children, were so overjoyed by this long-awaited reunion that they forgot all caution and the need to run as far and as quickly as possible! They didn't even notice the loud whistle nearby.

Suddenly, someone fired a shot from behind. The young couple barely had time to register what was happening before rivers of blood began streaming from Bahadir.

"Bahadir!!!!!" Malika screamed in horror.

Nearby, the roar of engines was heard, followed by heavy, rapid footsteps approaching from the front of the house.

"Attention: Surrender! The premises are cordoned off—you are surrounded!" ordered Major Ratnikov to the bandits and everyone present in the house and yard. "OMON is in operation! Come out of the building one by one, with your hands raised!"

Malika screamed and cried out for help. Major Ratnikov ordered two soldiers to run over and ascertain the situation. Within a minute, they returned.

"Permission to report, Comrade Major!" one of the soldiers said.

"Report now. What's happening? Who is screaming and crying?"

"There's a girl—a hostage—from the back side of the building. There is a man with an Asian appearance holding her; he is severely injured…"

"Is that Mukhitdin? That seems unlikely. Or… no, not that… That is her husband, Bahadir Fattakhov! What childishness! He didn't listen to me—he went in on his own, and now he's been hit by a bullet! These are bandits… Oleg, tell Kuznetsov that I order an immediate examination of that man, and have him call an ambulance right away—he knows the drill."

"Understood!"

Oleg immediately ran to a vehicle to fetch the OMON medic.

"Where is that Mukhitdin whose phone we have been tracking?" the Major muttered to himself. "This is interesting! He must be found—he is important."

"Comrade Major, this fellow tried to escape, but I caught him," said another quick and experienced soldier, Yerokhin, who never failed to apprehend a soul on the spot.

"Good job, Fedor!" the group leader praised him. Then, turning to the Asian man who was trying to hide, he asked, "You must be Mukhitdin, right?"

"Yes," the young man replied, his tone sour and spiteful through gritted teeth. "How do you know me? And why am I being detained? I was rescuing a girl!"

"We'll sort it out, my friend. In any event—sorry—it looks like you'll have to come with us."

At once, Mukhitdin's defiance melted away; he slumped, almost sobbing like a child:

"Officer, please, let me go… I'm innocent! You can ask Malika—the girl, that's why I'm here. I only went into the building for her!"

"Very well, kid! If you're innocent, why are you so nervous? Just write up an explanation at the police station—they'll talk to you, and then you'll be allowed to go home. That's that! Why are you twitching so much?" Then, turning to his soldiers, Alexey said, "Alright, everyone, have we detained everyone who was in the house and the yard?"

"Affirmative!"

"Have you thoroughly searched the entire building? All floors, rooms, corridors, cellars?"

"Affirmative, Comrade Major! Even the maids have been detained for questioning."

"Excellent. Now, let's transport everyone to our station; the investigator will sort it out there. And what about the owner of the house? Has he been detained?"

"No, Comrade Major, he wasn't in the house. But his people told us where to find him."

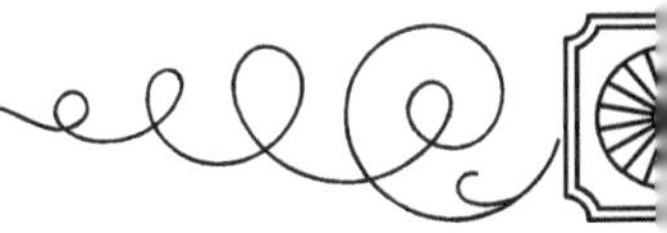

"Understood. If we know his whereabouts, then we'll detain him as well. There was an order to arrest him, too."

74

Anvar was apprehended at his club. He did not expect the arrival of OMON, and although his assistants resisted the officers with armed opposition, the special forces group ultimately overpowered all the bandits, rounded them up, and transported them to the station.

In this complex, multi-layered case—concerning human trafficking, the abduction of a hostage, a citizen of another fraternal state no less, and even an attempted murder—the police department, on the orders of its superiors, almost immediately handed the matter over to the Moscow Prosecutor's Office.

During interrogations, by comparing facts and conducting other investigative activities, it emerged that the Russian citizen Anvar Tukhataev had been engaged in the illegal trade of people and various forms of contraband for seven years. This was a crime punishable by severe sentences. However, Anvar, in an attempt to exonerate himself, not only handed over his entire chain of "partners" involved in this "business" but also betrayed the very person responsible for his capture—Mukhitdin.

The investigators then turned many questions toward the Uzbek citizen Mukhitdin Nasyrov, who had also been detained in connection with this case as a witness. Why did he break into the bandit's house—a house with which he had exchanged phone calls and SMS messages on several occasions, including on that very day? That remained unclear at first. One might suppose that Tukhataev would never have given the girl to Mukhitdin for noth-

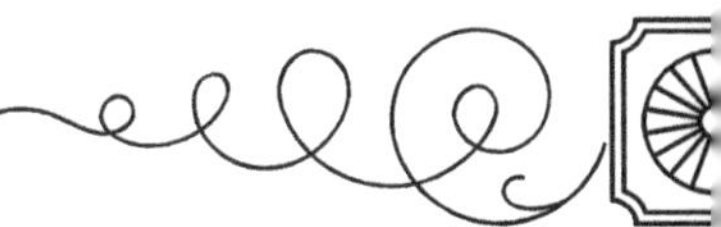

ing, but if Mukhitdin—supposedly acting out of the most noble motives—truly intended to rescue her heroically, then why, judging by the SMS logs from both sides, did he repeatedly call and text the owner of the house? How did he manage to locate a back entry so quickly, to open the spare door of the house, or to enter the room where the girl was hidden? And why did none of the guards rush after him in pursuit?

In answer to all these questions, the young Nasyrov obstinately repeated only one thing: that he had no malicious intent, that he had only wanted to help his longtime acquaintance.

However, after the cellular company provided the investigator with a transcript of the SMS messages, everything became clear: the kidnapping and subsequent "rescue" of the hostage in Anvar's house had, in fact, been nothing more than an elaborate ruse staged before the trusting Malika.

The women who worked in Tukhataev's house testified that they did not know this Mukhitdin at all. Meanwhile, the owner of the house—while leaving early in the morning for his club—had warned his staff that at a specified time they must leave Malika alone and have both of them exit the room after loosely tying her to a chair with a rope.

The guards later reported that Anvar had given them clear orders: no matter what that man, Nasyrov, did on the premises of his house, they were to pay no attention at all, acting as if his intrusion went unnoticed. In other words, he was to enter the house as if sneaking in—a trespasser and "savior" of the hostage—through a purposely made opening in the lattice of the back side of the fence.

During a subsequent interrogation, Anvar Tukhataev confirmed all this information:

"Yes, I asked my people to do that—and they carried out every one of those instructions," he stated.

"So you are saying that you had an arrangement with Mukhitdin Nasyrov regarding his so-called 'rescue' of that girl, Malika?"

"Yes, officer, exactly so," the bandit confirmed. "The thing is, he merely wanted to look like a 'Batman' in her eyes. And I helped him with that. After all, he is my former classmate; we studied together at school in Tashkent."

"I see. But I don't think, Tukhataev, that you helped him for nothing. Tell me honestly—why did you do this? Did he pay you a lot?"

"Not at all. In fact, he… doesn't have as much money as he boasted at first," replied Tukhataev. "Officer, if I reveal everything I know, will that be taken into account in court?"

"Yes, I promise," said the officer. "So what were you getting out of it?"

"Mukhitdin promised me that he would provide his Russian girlfriend for sale abroad—Galina—who, at that very moment, while he was 'kidnapping' Malika Mumtazova, was sitting in his hotel room, waiting for him like a loyal friend. Meanwhile, a jeep with my men was about to depart from my house to take her… very far, to Yeysk, and from there by sea to Saudi Arabia. And you know our route already—you've probably been questioning both Malika and my people. Otherwise, how else would you have learned so much about my 'business'?"

"Actually, it was your Mukhitdin who told us all about you in detail—essentially, he gave you away first! And you, as it seems, do not want to speak the whole truth about him."

"Damn him! I'd kill him," Tukhataev sneered.

"Wasn't it you who kept Malika imprisoned in your house, and were you not preparing her to be sent abroad to be sold to an Arab sheikh in Saudi Arabia?"

"Yes, at first—her… But that was at the request of Mukhitdin himself, so that he'd be free! He came to me and asked me to remove her, so that she wouldn't be alive. She did something that had greatly upset him, and it seems he wanted revenge. But I told him I wouldn't do murder; however, I could sell her abroad as a sex slave. That idea interested him, and he agreed. But I immediately told him that he would not get any money for that."

"And did he accept that option immediately?"

"At first, yes. But then, two days before we were to dispatch this Malika, he called me, agitated, and said he wanted to change the terms of our deal—that he had a better, more suitable option for me. He said: 'Anvar, I know these Arabs won't be impressed by Asian beauty; they will only be interested in a Russian girl! I have one just like that, also pretty. I'm keeping her for now in my hotel room.' And I had already received an advance for the goods, officer, and I absolutely needed to send a beauty to the Arab in time, whoever it was. I asked Mukhitdin, 'Are you absolutely sure that your Russian girl won't run away by the time we come for her?' He assured me that she wouldn't—that she can't live without him, she loves him… I tell you, this Mukhitdin is a rotten scoundrel—a real lowlife. Galina loves him, yet he hands her over to gangsters and is ready to sell her abroad! And as for Malika, he wanted to run off far away, marry her, and live with her. He somehow decided that after such a 'feat' she would not refuse him. By the way, I didn't know she wasn't single. Had I known, I wouldn't have even gotten involved with her! After all, it was her husband that found my house, and called OMON!"

"Yes, she is married," and noted the interrogator, "and her husband, Bahadir Fattakhov, is now in the hospital, wounded. By the way, do you know who shot him? Do you have any idea?"

"No, I don't. I wasn't in the house at that moment. And frankly, officer, I don't try to hand that on me! Mukhitdin and I never had any arrangement regarding any shooting!"

Later, it was Mukhitdin's turn to be interrogated who was protesting that he wasn't being released.

"You are being detained under several articles, citizen Nasyrov," the investigator announced, producing the relevant provisions of the Criminal Code of the Russian Federation. "A trial awaits you, after which you will most likely be sent to one of the prisons in your country. Now, tell me—who shot Bahadir Fattakhov? And also, what was that whistle that was found in your pocket?"

"I used the whistle to summon a guard employed by Anvar Tukhataev. I do not know his name. But he fired—not at Bahadir…"

"How come? What exactly are you saying?"

"I was in that house long enough to arrange a deal with one of the guards—for a decent reward. I needed help, as I know few people in Moscow. We agreed that if something went awry with the 'kidnapping' of Malika—if she didn't trust me and decided to run away—then, at the sound of my whistle, that guard would shoot at her, not allowing her to escape!"

"Are you saying you were prepared to kill her? The girl you liked and even intended to marry?!"

"I am an Eastern man—I will not tolerate infidelity or betrayal! She must be mine and mine alone! However, the guard was only supposed to injure her. It turned out, though, that he doesn't shoot very well…"

"And what do you mean by 'infidelity'? She is not even your wife, Nasyrov! Have you forgotten that?… You see—the guard shot

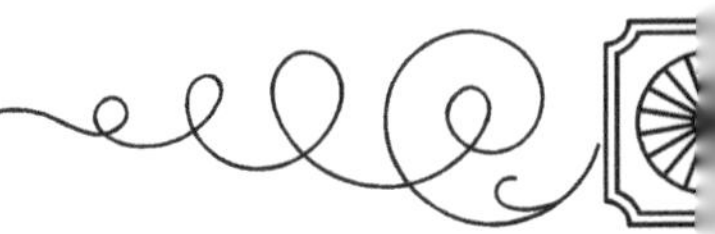

at the girl but ended up hitting her husband!"

"Yes. That's what this husband deserves! He ruined everything for me, the idiot! My plan fell through because of him!"

"It appears he didn't ruin anything but rather saved his wife from you! In effect, he came to that house for her rescue. And who knows: if he hadn't been standing there, with his back to the fence, would this Malika still be alive? He injured himself because he shielded her with his own body!"

* * *

Bahadir was taken in a critical condition to the nearest hospital, with Malika accompanying him. She wept with sorrow and despair—she had only just seen her husband after a long separation, and immediately such a thing had occurred…

What if he doesn't survive?! she thought in panic.

However, the doctors, fighting for the young man's life, managed to stabilise him.

"Miss, do not worry," said one of the doctors who had operated on Bahadir, "there is hope for your husband's recovery. Don't lose heart—everything will be all right!"

Tears welled up in Malika's eyes.

"Thank you very much, doctor! May I see him?"

"Yes, but only for a little while—so that he isn't overly exhausted. But I promise you, he will live!"

* * *

Two weeks later, a plane carrying Malika and Bahadir landed in Tashkent. Bahadir was still not fully recovered; the place of his injury still hurt, but he was already on the mend.

The young married couple was greeted by all their relatives.

"Bahadir, my son!" exclaimed Mukhabbat as she embraced him. "How could this be… Amin told us what happened to you, and your father and I thought we were going to die—the pain in our hearts nearly tore us apart… Of course, it's good that you saved your wife, but I scold you for having put yourself in such danger…"

"My brother, it was your wife who told me everything over the phone," Amin revealed.

"I'm to blame," Malika bowed her head. "Please forgive me, mother Mukhabbat. And everyone—please, forgive me! I only wanted what was best, I wanted to help my husband. But this is how it turned out… I will never again leave my native city, from my own kin and loved ones, for long!"

"But think—how many people in the world have heard your beautiful voice!" said Abdulla Rustamovich. "My dear daughter, we were at fault before you, and you must forgive us."

"And your jewel, darling, is waiting for you in the family home," said Sitora to her. "And your grandmother, Firuz-begim, is waiting for you very much."

"Malika herself is the main adornment for all of us!" declared Said Yakhaevich proudly.

When they all boarded the company minibus of the Fattakhovs, Bahadir said:

"Parents, brother, you know what I've realised thanks to these trials? That no matter what happens in life, no matter what hardships we endure, the most important thing is to believe in those you love. And to know that happiness is when the people dear to you love you and always, wherever you may be, await your return with their hearts and souls with you!.."

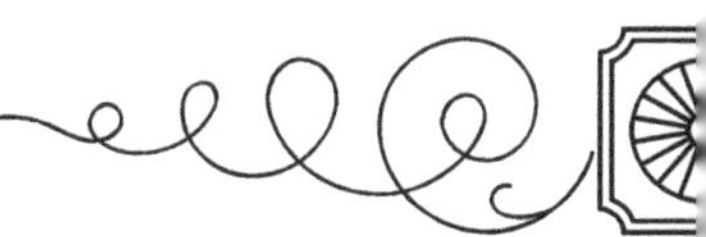

EPILOGUE

Tashkent, 2016

Both Murad Nematullaevich and Mukhitdin Nasyrov were incarcerated—but in different prisons and for different crimes. Testimonies implicating their former "boss" were also given by two of his ex-assistants, Gosha and Roma, who were interrogated by the prosecutor's office; these men were not involved in any of the elder Nasyrov's criminal activities, but merely assisted him in business and everyday matters. Now, both the oligarch father and his son had plenty of time to reflect on their past, present, and future—to analyse everything and, perhaps someday, to repent for their crimes, if only before God.

The former police captain Ravshan Umarov contracted tuberculosis in prison, and the doctors gave him two years to live…

Veniamin Arkadyevich, whose guilt in organising casinos was only slightly less than that of Murad Nasyrov, was also serving his sentence in a penitentiary.

Rudik did not perish in the Alpine mountains, as Bahadir had thought. He miraculously survived. Yet indeed, his car was caught beneath the lower part of an avalanche and overturned by its tremendous force. He was rescued by Italian climbers who were training nearby; however, Rudik suffered a fractured spine, and he remained disabled for life, no longer able to leave Italy—he became impoverished and unwanted by everyone.

Galina repented before Malika for all the harm she had done her. After Mukhitdin had nearly sold her abroad as a slave in place of Malika, she rejected him for life and decided that the kind "simpleton" Roma, who had caught her eye during their conversation in a café, was much more suitable for her. She sought him out herself. And Roma, too, fell for this energetic young woman.

Gosha made a formal proposal to Larisa. Malika and Bahadir helped finance Gosha's latest operation at a high-class burn center in Russia. Gosha and Larisa married and were happy.

Little Samira, despite her very tender age, had apparently not forgotten her adoptive mother, Rano. As soon as Samira learned her first words, she immediately began calling mama. Mukhabbat's heart ached with pain. Together with her grandfather, they explained to the granddaughter that her mother had gone abroad for treatment in a faraway country. Seeing the sorrow in their elderly parents, Bahadir and Malika decided… to take this sweet child in and completed all the necessary paperwork for her adoption! The guardianship authorities readily handed the little one over to them as the closest relatives and as a young couple who could be completely trusted. Both Malika and Bahadir came to love Samira as if she were their own daughter. And six months later, Malika… herself became pregnant!

Her career as a singer continued—but not in Russia, rather in Uzbekistan. She was also occasionally invited to India to record songs by Alisha Chinai. Only now, Malika traveled there and to other countries not alone, but with her daughter and, moreover, with her new producer, Bahadir Fattakhov. Bahadir became a successful head of his own enterprise, Bakh-Atir, and an efficient manager for his wife, the talented performer Malika Mumtazova.

Bahadir realised that the Great Mughal Shah Jahan called for

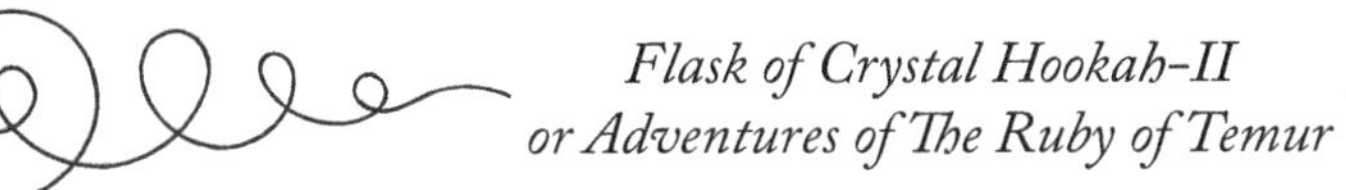

the "Adornment of the Palace" not the expensive Temur Ruby—which, in fact, adorned his Padishah's throne—but his beloved wife Arjumand Begum, or, as he also called her, Mumtaz Mahal! And Bahadir never for a moment doubted that Malika was the true adornment of the "palace" of his heart! Their relationship became completely harmonious—a real and everlasting "honeymoon." Bahadir turned out to be a loving, caring, and attentive husband.

After all these events, the relationship between the two brothers, Bahadir and Amin, was greatly strengthened…

Amin and Dilshoda married for deep mutual love. The wedding was magnificent; all the relatives gathered, and even Amin's paternal aunts from Jahangir's side attended. Soon, Dilshoda became pregnant. Amin and Dilshoda created a harmonious and very happy family.

Said Yakhaevich—we will say a little more about him later…

And as for his wife Sitora, she continued the work of her life with great success—tailoring dresses made of national fabrics. Her practical and beautiful prêt-à-porter outfits became even more popular. Bhodjwani specially organised exhibitions and clothing sales across India in the "ikat" style for her. Her garments began to be ordered by large retail chains in various countries around the world. In addition, Sitora and Bhodjwani jointly created a new line of clothing for women and children, which they symbolically named "Taj Mahal Couture."

Abdulla Rustamovich sold his collection of expensive antiques and gave the proceeds to his son Bahadir for developing the production of his enterprise. And Bahadir, together with Amin and Jean Marchal, began releasing a new line of perfumes—the first fragrance was named "Temur Ruby."

Jean loved Uzbekistan so much that he asked his wife, who

worked in the main office of Air France in Paris, to organize charter flights to the historical cities of our country. And in France, the Marchal and Fattakhov families together launched another business—a chain of boutiques called "Uz Treasures," where, instead of counters, treasure chests filled with unique items crafted by modern, talented Uzbek artisans—the genuine treasures of the ancient culture of the East—stood proudly…

***

The necklace that had been made for Firuz-begim and delivered to her through the Kuwaiti Sheikh from the daughter of the Sheikh of the Arab Emirates, Fatima Al-Nahayyan, Malika decided to give to her father, Said Yakhaevich.

"But how can that be, daughter?" Said Mumtazov shook his head. "After all, this is a gift for you—from Firuz-begim and from our entire family."

"No, Papa, I have made up my mind firmly: it will serve much better for good deeds and for many people rather than for me alone!" Malika replied. "I earnestly beg you, please, sell it to jewelers—and use the proceeds to build, even if only a small but multi-specialty clinic where the poor, the elderly, and the disabled can receive free treatment."

This idea struck a chord with Said Yakhaevich, and he practically immediately set about its step-by-step implementation…

But what became of the very chief, genuine Temur Ruby and the oldest necklace, which belonged to the Sheikh of Kuwait? What is the fate of this astonishing ornament?...

Both Singh Bhodjwani and Misha Leonidov, each on their own, never ceased their attempts to locate and buy back this necklace

with the genuine precious Temur Ruby of Amir Temur! Because… one day a rumor spread around the world that the Sheikh of Kuwait Al-Sabah had sold it to someone! But to whom exactly—that remained unknown. According to one version, he returned it to the Queen of Great Britain, who had once possessed the Temur Ruby; according to another version, he offered it for sale to a wealthy Indian raja, a descendant of the Baburids; and according to a third, it ended up in the hands of some "new Uzbeks" from Tashkent.

The charitable and selfless Bhodjwani had already decided to spend the money he had not on buying treasures that would satisfy only his personal whims as a connoisseur, but rather on developing his modeling business and on charitable causes.

But the greedy and vain Misha Leonidov, on the contrary, had only just come into his element, and the search for worldly treasures had become his irresistible passion. He even hired specially trained people who thoroughly investigated the matter for him and diligently searched for any trace of the coveted necklace with the Temur Ruby that had mysteriously disappeared somewhere.

This marvelous necklace still lingers in people's fantasies to this day, as if it divides them into the wicked and the good, the greedy and the generous, the foolish and the wise…

* * *

More and more music videos featuring the beautiful songs of Malika Mumtazova are being broadcast on television—she sings against the backdrop of ancient monuments of Uzbekistan and in front of the great Taj Mahal in Agra. Malika sings not only for all the people of the Earth but, above all, for her faithful husband, Bahadir, who loves her endlessly and is loved by her without measure.

In these videos and in the sacred dances, as if like mythical fairies, young women whirl about, dressed in outfits of the "Taj Mahal" brand—the collection by Sitora and Bhodjwani, dedicated to the love of Shah Jahan and Arjumand Begum, figures both so distant and yet so close to our hearts…

And from the Crystal Hookah drifts a light wisp of fragrant incense smoke, while Firuz-begim peacefully dozes, enraptured by the scent of herbs and by the aroma of the new perfume "Temur Ruby" that she has already grown to love.

Nothing awakens memories quite like a scent…

And she dreams of a magnificent palace of white marble. At its entrance, in an antique pavilion, Shah Jahan and Arjumand Begum sit in light garments. They hold hands, their eyes turned toward the heavens… and it seems that the beautiful encounter of the two lovers will be eternal…

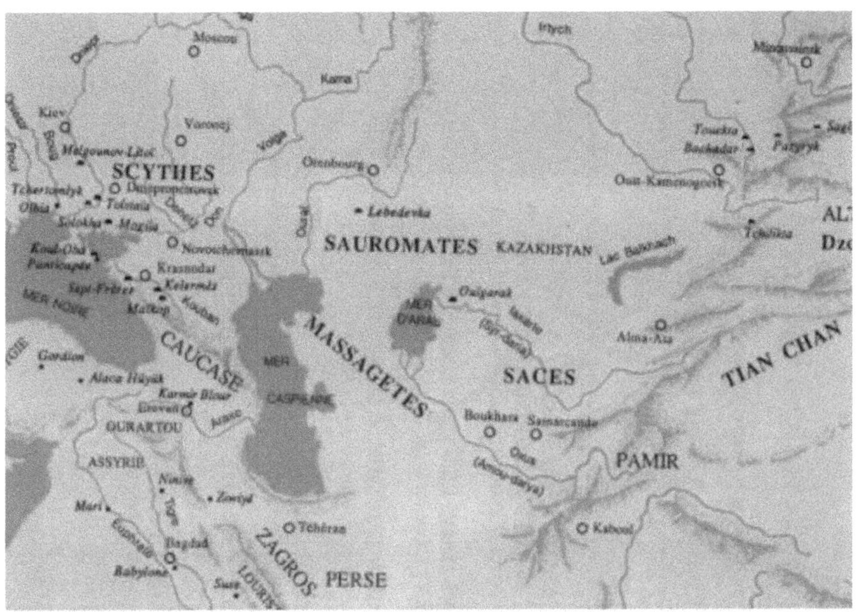
Irtych
Moscou
Kama
Kiev
Voronej
Tosckto
Bochadar
Patzryk
Malgounov-Litsi
Orenbourg
Oust-Kamenogorsk
SCYTHES
Dniepropétrovsk
Tcherianlyk
Tiktaia
Lebedevka
Tchilixa
ALT
Olbia
Solokha
Magila
SAUROMATES
KAZAKHSTAN
D3
Novotcherkassk
Knul-Oba
Panticapée
Krasnodar
MER
Ouigarak
Lac Balkhach
Kelermès
D'ARAL
Sept-Frères
Kichtan
Alma-Ata
MER NOIRE
Maikop
MASSAGETES
SACES
TIAN CHAN
Gordion
MER
Alaca Hüyük
CASPIENNE
Karmir Blour
Boukhara
Samarcande
Erevan
Araxe
OURARTOU
Oxus
ASSYRIE
(Amou-darya)
PAMIR
Ninive
Mari
Ziwiyé
Euphrate
Tigre
Tchéran
Kaboul
Bagdad
Babylone
ZAGROS
Suse
LOURIS
PERSE

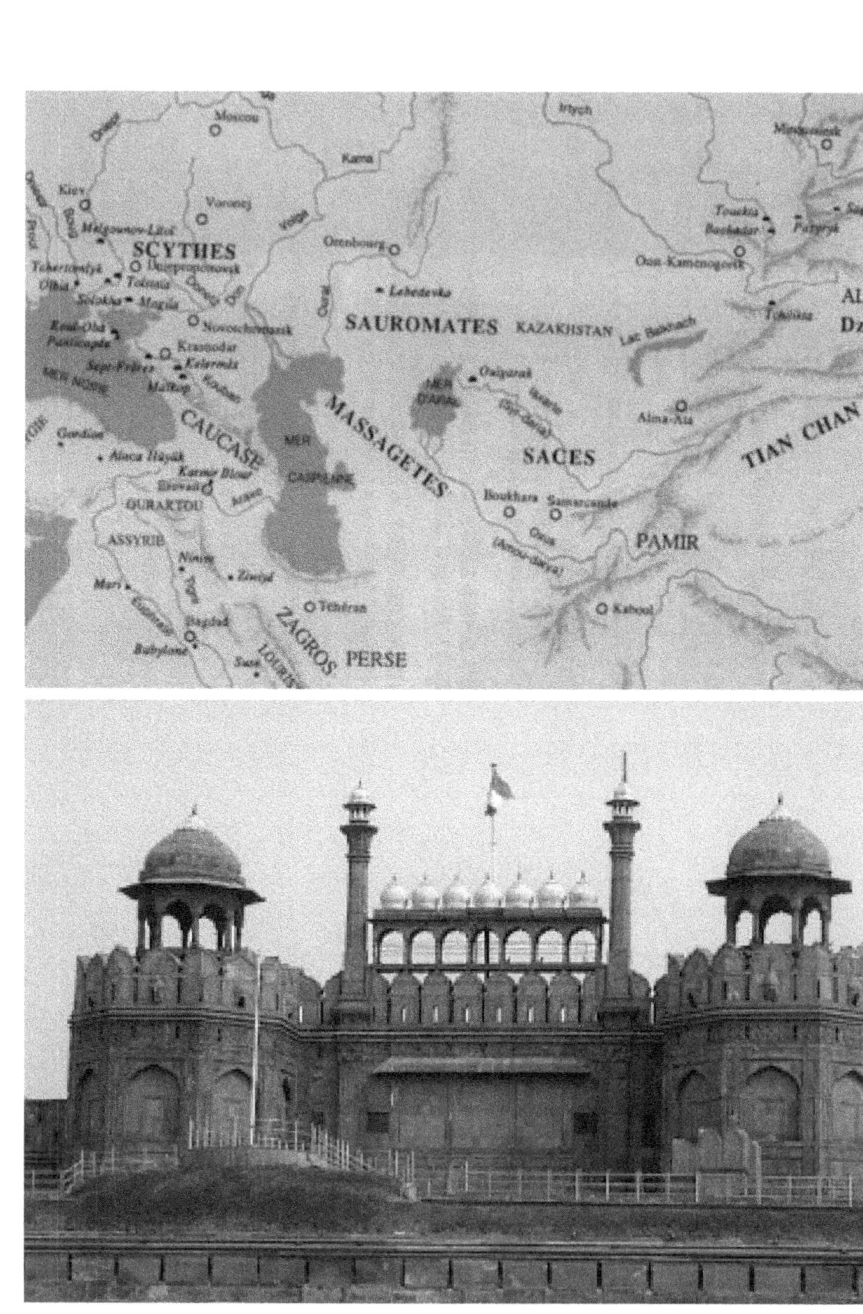

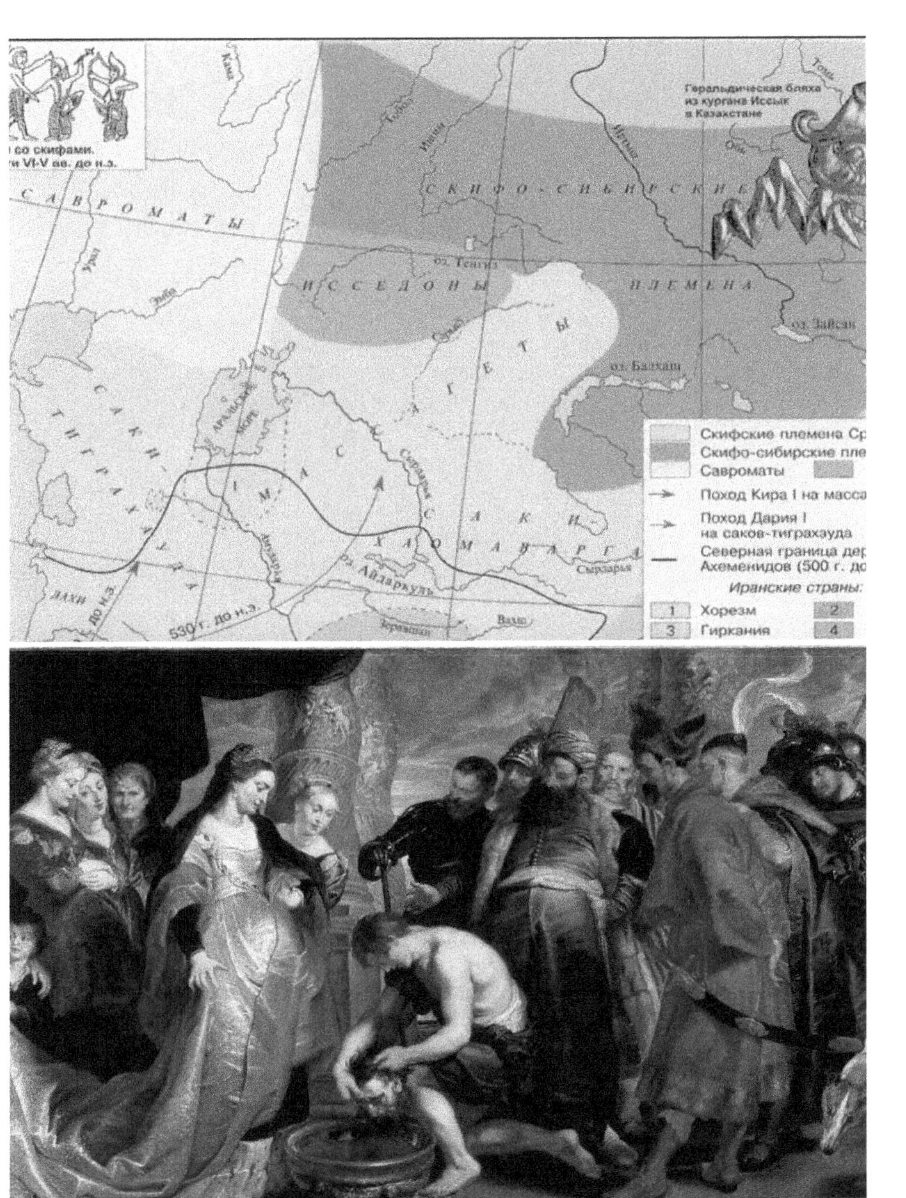
со скифами.
VI-V вв. до н.э.
Геральдическая бляха
из кургана Иссык
в Казахстане
САВРОМАТЫ
СКИФО-СИБИРСКИЕ
ИССЕДОНЫ
ПЛЕМЕНА
оз. Тенгиз
оз. Зайсан
оз. Балхаш
МАССАГЕТЫ
САКИ-ТИГРАХАУДА
САКИ
ХАОМАВАРГА
Айдаркуль
ДАХИ
530 г. до н.э.
Зеравшан
Балх
Сырдарья
Скифские племена Ср
Скифо-сибирские пле
Савроматы
Поход Кира I на масса
Поход Дария I
на саков-тиграхауда
Северная граница дер
Ахеменидов (500 г. до
Иранские страны:
1 Хорезм   2
3 Гиркания   4

Prince Yakub Habeebuddin Tucy is descendent of Ancient Moghuls, former rulers of the Country. He is Court Certified GPA Holder and legal descendant of Emperor Shah Jehan and Emperor Bahadur Shah Zaffar, the last ruler of India.

He has been declared the descendent of Royal Moghul Emperors vide Court Decree in Original Suit No. 5973 issued Hon'ble Civil Judge of City Civil Court, Hyderabad. He is a renowned philanthropist.

- He is president of Moghul Emperor Family Society Registration No. 9265 of 2000.
- Uzbekistan Government has recognised him as the descendent of Great Moghul Babur & Shah Jehan
- Founder of several companies including
- Moghul Emperor Logistics Private Limited
- Moghul Emperor Softec Private Limited
- He has been appointed Mutawalli of several Waqf Properties as the current head of Moghul dynasty

He is lighthouse of religious tolerance as the descendent of last emperor of the country, Bahadur Shah Zaffar, who is also known for his contribution to the 1857 revolt. Prince Tucy understands his social obligation to the people of the country.

His Highness Prince Tucy is torch bearer of great Moghul dynasty and as the descendent of former rulers of the country he has devoted his life to serving the country and its people.

He has been recognised as the descendent of Mirza Babur by the Uzebekistan Government which gave him due recognition and respect after DNA testing. Urbekistan government has invited him to attend the URS ceremony of founder of Moghul Dynasty Mirza Babur with full protocol due to the descendent of Great Moghul.

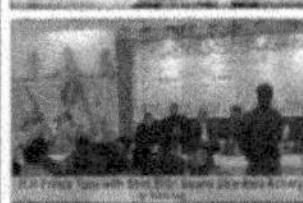

Kohi Nur
Diamond
Kohi Nur
Diamond
FOR WOMAN
Kohi Nur
Diamond
FOR MAN
begin
Treasure Collection
made in France

Rubi of
Timur
FOR MAN
Rubi of
Timur
FOR WOMAN
begin
begin
begin
Treasure Collection

Эмир Бухарский Саид Ахадхан
(1885-1910)
-отец Саид Алимхана

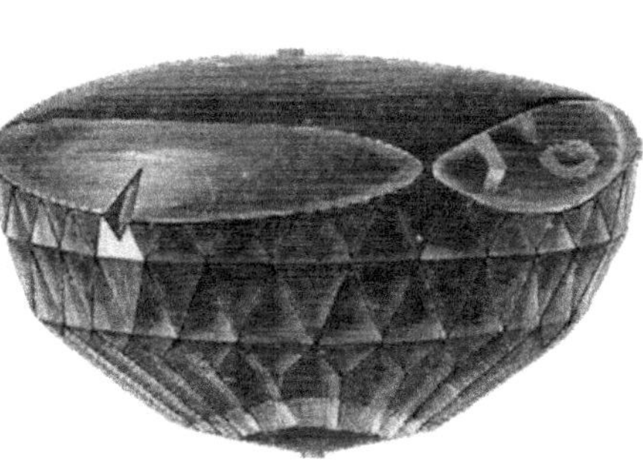